Dear Reader

What could be better to help laze away those long
summer days than our summer reading omnibus
featuring four exciting stories - all set in the beautiful
British countryside? The Yorkshire moors, Scotland,
the Isle of Wight and Cornwall are the glorious
backgrounds to these four wonderfully romantic tales.
Let us know what you think of them, and of stories set
in the UK in general. Would you like more of them,
or do you prefer more exotic climates? Do tell.

The Editor

Romantic Reading
For Long
SUMMER DAYS

MILLS & BOON LIMITED
ETON HOUSE, 18-24 PARADISE ROAD
RICHMOND, SURREY TW9 1SR

First published in Great Britain in 1992 by Mills & Boon Limited

ISBN 0 263 77521 6

Set in Times 10 on 12 pt. 06-9208

Made and Printed in Great Britain

CONTENTS:

Feelings of Love

Gold Ring of Revenge

Guilty of Love

Dark Forces

Anne Beaumont was a reporter, feature writer, agony aunt, woman's page editor, fiction editor and short story writer before realising she actually wanted to write novels. Since then, she's written several for Mills & Boon. One of them, a historical romance written as Rosina Pyatt, was short-listed for the Romantic Novel of the Year Award. She develops her plots while walking her dog along the beaches of the Isle of Wight. Of her three children, two are writers and one a graphic designer.

FEELINGS OF LOVE

BY
ANNE BEAUMONT

MILLS & BOON LIMITED
ETON HOUSE, 18-24 PARADISE ROAD
RICHMOND, SURREY TW9 1SR

First published in Great Britain in 1992
by Mills & Boon Limited

© Anne Beaumont 1992

Australian copyright 1992
Philippine copyright 1992
This edition 1992

ISBN 0 263 77519 4

Set in Times Roman 10 on 12 pt.
06-9208-53897 C

Made and Printed in Great Britain

CHAPTER ONE

FELICE LAWSON snuggled deeper into her pillows, the phone held more or less against her ear, her eyes refusing to open. Huskily she grumbled, 'Jack, at seven o'clock on a Sunday morning my sense of humour's a bit thin. This is a joke, isn't it?'

She knew it was a useless protest, that it wasn't any joke. Jack Carter didn't have a sense of humour. He did have a bit of a conscience, though, because he apologised, 'Sorry, Felice. I wouldn't call you out like this if it wasn't urgent. Dave was on his way to make the pickup when his clutch went, and the job is in your neck of the woods.'

'Nothing is in my neck of the woods. You're the one who's always moaning that I live at the back of beyond,' she pointed out, but she knew she was only stalling for time—time to get her eyes open and her head up off the pillow. She needed the extra money she earned as a weekend taxi driver.

Jack knew that, but he also knew she hadn't finished ferrying home the last of the Saturday night disco revellers until just over four hours ago.

'This customer is bound for Woodlands Hall, and that's practically on your doorstep. You can't miss it, it's the only thing that is,' Jack came back at her, sarcasm filtering through his wheedling tone.

Woodlands Hall! Felice sat up, her curiosity getting the better of her sleepiness. 'There must be a mistake,' she replied. 'The Hall's empty. It's been locked up for

5

months. It looks like something out of an Agatha Christie novel, all creepy and shuttered and overgrown. Nobody in their right mind would want to go there, specially first thing on a Sunday morning. I reckon somebody's playing a practical joke on you, Jack.'

That was all right with her, but not when the joke stretched to her losing sleep. She snuggled down again and yawned. It wasn't unknown for somebody to get a kick out of sending taxis out on hoax calls. 'Have you upset anybody lately?' she went on, her voice getting huskier as sleep fought to reclaim her.

'No, I haven't,' Jack replied, incensed, 'and this is a genuine booking. It was phoned through from London yesterday. I'd cover for Dave myself but I'm on the other side of the island and I can't get there in time.'

'Where's "there"?' Felice asked, sighing fatalistically as she sat up again. Even if it was a hoax, she would have to turn out. It was a nuisance, but it was no use fighting it any longer. Jack definitely had a bee in his bonnet about this one.

'Woodlands Airfield, not even ten minutes from you. A chap called Tobias Hunter is flying himself in and——'

'Who?' Felice exclaimed, the name working on her like a charm. She flung aside the continental quilt and swung her long legs out of bed.

'Tobias Hunter,' Jack repeated, sounding perplexed. 'He's due in——' there was a pause as he consulted his watch '—fifteen minutes. It would have been twenty if you hadn't argued so much. If he wants to play spooks at the Hall that's up to him. Just pick him up from the airfield and get him there.'

'I'm on my way.' Felice slammed down the receiver and began rushing around like a soul possessed. For a big girl, she was surprisingly swift and graceful, even when propelled by excitement.

So the mystery man had surfaced at last! Nearly six months of nail-biting anxiety waiting to learn whether he even existed, and he had to pick dawn on a freezing February morning to prove that he did.

Wide awake now, she forgave him. She had every reason to. Never before had she been so anxious to meet a man, and providence in the guise of a broken clutch had given her the perfect opportunity. What was more, she'd have him all to herself. She wouldn't waste a minute of it.

In record time Felice was in her car and zooming along the winding road that cut through the beech wood as fast as the frosty surface would permit. She glanced at the overgrown driveway to the Hall as she passed it, noting that the ornate iron gates were still firmly padlocked. They'd been that way ever since old Joshua Hunter had died, an embittered eccentric to the last.

She wondered whether this unknown Tobias Hunter was anything like him. Surely not! Old Josh had to be a one-off! In fact, nobody had known he'd had any relatives until he'd died without leaving a will and a search for an heir had been instigated.

Record of a brother, long since dead, had been discovered, then of a nephew, also dead. The last Felice had heard, the search had switched to Canada to discover whether a great-nephew, Tobias, was still alive.

Apparently he was, and very much so if he was hearty enough to fly himself in on a morning like this, Felice mused, as the car dipped into the gentle slope of the valley where the airfield was sited.

It was on Hunter land, although it was leased out to an aviation company, but the fact that it existed might

encourage the last of the Hunters to stay. It would be
nice for a man who could fly to have an airstrip in his
own back yard.

It was very much in Felice's interests that Tobias
Hunter settle on the island. The last thing she wanted
was for him to take one look at his inheritance then sell
up and go away. If that was what he intended, she would
do her very best to change his mind, even if she hated
him on sight.

Reason told her, though, that he couldn't possibly be
as crusty to deal with as Old Josh. Nobody could.

She craned her head around and listened for the sound
of a plane as she approached the airfield, but there was
nothing. Damn, he must be down already. If he was un-
fortunate enough to have inherited any of Old Josh's
genes he wouldn't appreciate being kept waiting for his
taxi. She'd so much wanted to make a good impression,
too!

Felice wished she'd got out of bed as soon as Jack
had phoned instead of giving him such a hard time, but
how was she to know the lost heir was on his way to
look over Woodlands? She didn't have a crystal ball,
even if her eyes had been open enough to look into one.

She drove on to the airfield, stopped by the small
hangar and studied three little planes parked neatly away
from the landing strip. There was enough frost on them
to show they'd been there all night.

There was no sign of a new arrival, no sign of any
life at all. Normally she wouldn't expect any. For one
thing it was a Sunday, and for another not much com-
mercial use was made of the airfield until the holiday-
makers' joy flights started in the summer season.

Felice looked at her watch. It was twenty minutes since
she'd taken Jack's call. She wondered again if this was

a hoax, and yet the name Tobias Hunter was authentic enough. It had certainly got her here in double-quick time.

She got out of the car, closed the door and leaned against it, looking up at the sky. She was a vibrant, glowing figure in the grey, winter-bare landscape. She seemed to have the knack of storing summer and always carrying a breath of it with her, no matter what the season.

Her hastily scrubbed face was rosy and her thick hair, scuffed back into a ponytail, was the colour of corn bleached under a blazing sun. Her eyes were the blue of an unclouded August sky, and they were made all the more brilliant by the long dark lashes fringing them. Her teeth were white and gleaming, and her complexion was never pasty. Summer or winter, she was always bonny.

The burden Felice had to bear, as far as she was concerned anyway, was her size. She stood five feet ten inches in her flat-heeled knee-length boots and, although her waist was neat, her voluptuous curves definitely flowed on the generous side.

Yearning, in those rare moments when she had the time to yearn, to be a willowy beauty like Janetta, her younger sister, or Serena, her top-model cousin, she had to settle for being a sturdy Amazon. It was the joker in an otherwise perfect pack.

Men were fascinated by Janetta and Serena, content to worship them from afar if they couldn't get any closer. Felice they grappled, treating her as if she were some kind of all-in wrestler who might get the better of them if they handled her with care.

At twenty-six, Felice was used to it. That didn't make it any better, but she'd learned to be philosophical. She'd long since stopped looking for a man who'd place her on a pedestal alongside her female relations, and she supposed it was just as well.

For a start, it would have to be a pretty solid pedestal, and she'd probably be bored to tears up there, anyway. As she looked so capable, everybody always assumed that she was, and from being a young child she'd done all her own lifting and carrying, worrying and managing. No wonder she'd grown up on the bossy side.

It was too late in the day to learn the tricks Janetta and Serena had been born knowing. Anyway, the sad fact was that neither nature nor fate had fashioned her into a coquette. She'd simply never had the time or chance to practise.

And she'd sort of got used to men treating her, after the inevitable wrestling match, more like one of the boys than a prospective bride.

She didn't suppose this Tobias Hunter would be any different, either. If she fluttered her long eyelashes at him, he'd probably ask if she had something in her eye.

Oh, well, Felice thought, ever practical, at least it was easier to deal with men once they understood there wasn't going to be any sex involved. Besides, this Tobias Hunter might be married. She found herself hoping that he was.

The Isle of Wight, separated eons ago from mainland England by a thin strip of water, was a perfect place to bring up children, especially in a spot as rural and beautiful as Woodlands Hall.

Yes, it could definitely help if there were little Hunters running around.

Felice, her curvy thighs encased in faded blue jeans and her page-two bosom hidden under a fur-lined leather jacket, turned up her collar as the frost-edged wind began to chill her face. She thrust her hands deep into her pockets then cocked her head as the faint drone of an engine gently overlaid the early morning silence.

She shivered, but it was nothing to do with the cold. It was pure excitement. So much depended on what sort of a man Tobias Hunter turned out to be. She pictured him as a younger version of Old Josh, with steely grey eyes, a hooked nose and shoulders as wide as he was high.

In a word, formidable.

Just as well she wasn't easily intimidated, Felice reflected ruefully, as the sound of an engine solidified into a plane circling over the sea to come in. Sometimes it was useful to be big enough to intimidate men.

Felice watched critically as the light plane, buffeted by the gusty wind, lost height and lined up for the runway. In these weather conditions a lesser man would have settled for the train and ferry, and she felt a gleam of admiration for the unknown Tobias.

It seemed he was the type who, having made up his mind about something, wasn't easily put off. If she'd been younger and not set so rigidly in the practical mould nature had made for her, she might have thought he was a man after her own heart.

It was a good thing she was philosophical instead of romantic, she mused, otherwise she might be feeling wistful. A man after her own heart indeed! As if she didn't know that all they were ever after was her body.

Did she feel wistful, anyway? Felice sighed and tried to convince herself she didn't.

She found herself holding her breath as the little plane swooped over the trees, seeming to falter as it fought the wind. She could imagine the tussle that was going on at the controls to keep it on course. It cleared the trees and the high hedge enclosing the runway then flopped down like a tired bird that had flown too long.

Felice sighed with relief as the plane turned and taxied to the only windbreak the airfield offered, the lee of the hangar where the other planes were parked. The engine cut, there was a pause, and then she straightened up as a man emerged.

Her future, and that of her family, was riding on what sort of a man Tobias Hunter proved to be. Surprise was her first reaction. This man was big. He had the height to balance the shoulder-width she expected of a Hunter, having only Old Josh to go on.

He didn't hesitate or waste time looking around him but came straight towards her, and she got a distinct impression of determination, of a purpose that wasn't easily thwarted.

Felice felt a swift surge of illicit excitement and suppressed it just as swiftly. She didn't want him to be so positively male—not if it made her react in such a positively female way! She hadn't allowed for that, and as she studied him more closely her eyes widened. There were other things about him she hadn't allowed for, either.

He's a good six inches taller than me, she thought, and it took her a few moments to come to terms with that because she'd towered over Old Josh. This Hunter, it seemed, had broken the mould. His shoulders were broad, all right, but he looked perfectly proportioned. His hips were slim and he moved lithely, his long legs cutting the distance between them in no time at all.

He was dressed pretty much as she was, in jeans and a fur-lined leather jacket, and the only thing that was out of place in this rural setting was the leather briefcase that swung from his left hand. His other hand was pushing back a lock of unruly black hair that the wind was tumbling about his forehead.

Somewhere on the other side of thirty, she guessed. An interesting age...

Felice had just a few seconds more to concentrate on his face, and she made full use of them. Not a handsome man, she thought, as she took in his craggy features, then immediately wondered if that impression was fair. With a strong nose, chiselled cheekbones and chin, firm lips and a scar or two, his was definitely a man's face. It had its own power to attract—or would have done, she corrected herself hastily, if she'd been a romantic.

Besides, only seconds ago she'd realised it wouldn't do for sexual overtones to clutter up her relationship with Tobias Hunter. And, since she'd already managed to survive for twenty-six years without allowing sex to side-track her from what was really important, she wasn't about to fall apart now.

Silently applauding her own good sense, Felice told herself that if she'd felt a momentary weakness it was only because this man was so different from what she'd expected. After all, she was an assertive, capable woman. It was the helpless ones who were vulnerable to first impressions. If anybody was going to be overpowered here, it was likely to be Tobias Hunter.

Like it or not, it was the effect she had on men, and she couldn't see this encounter on a freezing February morning making any difference.

Did she feel a twinge of regret about that?

No, Felice told herself sternly, and forced herself to think about the wife and children she wanted to move into Woodlands Hall. This man couldn't possibly be a bachelor—not looking the way he did and sending out sexual signals that even she could pick up. When her mind was on other things, too! Or supposed to be.

Her moment of weakness past, and very much herself again, Felice seized the initiative as a matter of course. Tobias Hunter had stopped just one pace away and she held out her hand, saying, 'Felice Lawson.'

All right, so taxi drivers didn't usually introduce themselves, but she wasn't the usual sort of taxi driver and it never occurred to her to meet anybody on less than an equal footing, even Tobias Hunter. They were going to be neighbours.

If all went well...

To give him his due, he looked more amused than affronted. He took her hand, and said, 'Tobias Hunter. I wasn't expecting a female driver.'

Felice would have preferred 'lady' to 'female' but she smiled, and she had a smile that wasn't easily forgotten. It started in her eyes, lifted her lips and brought an added glow to her face. 'Most people don't, but you can relax. I guarantee not to wrap you around a tree,' she replied easily, used to men making a thing out of her driving a taxi.

'What else do you guarantee?' he asked, a pleasant hint of a drawl in his deep voice.

She liked his voice but was startled by his question. This wasn't the usual reply she got to her working patter—and he was still holding her hand. His grip was firm and strong. His warmth transmitted itself to her gloveless fingers and, she thought a trifle breathlessly, something of his strength was transmitted as well. It was a nice feeling.

She realised then that, whatever effect she was having on him, she wasn't overpowering him. Respect dawned.

She didn't quite know where they were going from here, but respect was a pretty good place to start.

'You're not afraid of me,' she said impulsively. 'Most men are. They take one look at me and feel their manhood threatened.'

'My manhood's more secure than that,' he replied, answering her smile with a knockout of his own, 'and I'm still waiting for an answer to my question.'

Felice chuckled. It was a novelty to meet a man who wasn't easily side-tracked. She drew her fingers out of his but the warmth remained. She knew why. She liked him, and the feeling that she'd met a friend was spreading the warmth pleasantly through her entire body. It was something separate from sexual attraction, something she valued.

'Do I have to guarantee anything else? Most men, when confronted with a lady driver, are happy to settle for a safe arrival.'

'You'll have to stop confusing me with other men,' he replied, his eyes teasing hers. They were grey, but not steely like Old Josh's. They were darker, warmer, more intimate...

Felice felt breathless again, and gave herself another scold to scotch the wild idea that he was flirting with her. This man was a Canadian. Naturally he'd be less formal than the Englishmen she was used to, and consequently more friendly. She could scarcely pick nits about that. After all, she'd given him the lead.

She'd wanted Tobias Hunter to be a friend. It had just happened a lot sooner than she'd expected, that's all. She should count that a plus and stop making these unnecessary emotional waves.

She was congratulating herself on getting her head together when she noticed he was watching the play of emotions across her face with a slight smile on his lips. She had the awful feeling he'd been reading her mind, and very nearly blushed.

'Can I take it you won't confuse me with anybody else again?' he asked, his voice strangely challenging.

Felice almost felt cross. Tobias Hunter was seizing the initiative at every turn, and just as shamelessly as she normally seized it herself. It was another novel feeling, having the tables turned on her, but it didn't do her respect for him any harm. She gave him a thoughtful look, and replied, 'I think I'm getting your measure now.'

'Good. I think I'm getting yours.'

What am I supposed to make of that? Felice wondered. Then she told herself she was being ridiculously sensitive, and she laughed.

'I like that,' he said.

'What?'

'The way you laugh.'

Damn, he'd done it again. Knocked her sideways by saying the unexpected. She recovered quickly and quipped, 'It beats crying.'

It was his turn to laugh, and she liked the way he laughed, too. She realised she was beginning to enjoy herself, perhaps because she'd always enjoyed a challenge—and Tobias was definitely a challenge. Again she felt a swift rush of warmth towards him. It was so long since she'd met anybody to stimulate her, to laugh with. It was almost as if he were a kindred soul.

Her delight was mirrored in her eyes as she said, 'I'm glad you're amused, because I doubt if you will be when you get to the Hall. It's been shut up since Old Josh died. I hope somebody warned you about that.'

'I thought I'd been warned about all the hazards of my inheritance but——' his eyes swept deliberately from her golden head to her size nine boots '—I think the most obvious hazard was missed out. Nobody said anything about Amazonian blondes.'

Felice's eyes sparkled with a mixture of indignation and amusement. 'Thanks very much! I'm not part of the Hunter inheritance.'

'I didn't expect everything to be perfect,' he replied smoothly.

'You're not likely to be disappointed, then,' she retorted, determined he wasn't going to fluster her again.

Tobias just smiled and opened the car door for her, a courtesy she didn't expect, since he was the customer. She was touched, though, and so she had to joke, 'Are you sure you wouldn't like to drive as well?'

'Don't you trust your driving?'

'Of course I do!' she exclaimed.

'Then so will I.'

Felice stared after him as he closed her door and walked around the car, wondering if she really had his measure, after all. He attacked—then disarmed—with a very potent blend of challenge and charm. No wonder she was having such a hard time discovering whether she was on her head or her heels.

More to the point, he was earning all the Brownie points and she had to win some back. It wasn't at all like her to be so dozy. She leaned across and opened the other front door. 'Why don't you sit beside me?' she suggested quickly. 'We're very friendly down here.'

'I've noticed,' he murmured as he got in beside her, and immediately her roomy saloon seemed to shrink. He was a big man, all right.

Felice gave him a sidelong look as she started the engine. She was trying to judge whether their friendship had developed enough for her to presume on it. Her blue eyes met his grey, and it was hers that broke the contact. Better wait a while, she decided, and smothered a sigh as she swung the car out on to the road. Patience wasn't her strong point.

'Say it,' he prompted.

'What?'

'Whatever you nearly bit your tongue off not to say.'

She was startled into taking a bend too fast, fought to hold the car steady as the wheels skidded on the frosty surface, and muttered under her breath as she regained control.

'You can say that, too, if you like,' he offered.

Felice began to laugh again. There were certain things she wanted from this man, very important things, but she was having trouble concentrating on them. Tobias kept turning the tables on her, beguiling her into behaving as though this were some kind of outing. Somehow he made her feel frivolous, light-headed—and feminine.

It was the feminine bit that worried her the most.

'Mr Hunter——' she began, ignoring the road that led to the Hall and nosing the car into a high-hedged lane that led upwards to the cliffs.

'Tobias,' he interrupted.

Felice nodded in unconscious agreement. Of course it was Tobias. From the word go there'd been no formality between them, so it would be ridiculous to start now. 'Tobias,' she began again, and stopped.

'Yes?'

'I like you,' she said, and then really could have bitten off her tongue. Curse her impulsiveness! That wasn't what she'd meant to say at all...

CHAPTER TWO

WHAT an idiot he must think her, and what an idiot she felt! How could she have blurted out anything so inane? He must think she was chatting him up and she wasn't! At least, not in the you-man-me-woman sense. All right, so he'd had a certain physical impact on her, but she was over that now. They were friends, and that was the most important thing.

Felice thought of the wife that must be somewhere in the background, and the little Hunters, and almost died of embarrassment. She said quickly, 'I didn't mean that the way it sounded.'

'Don't disappoint me now,' he replied. 'I was just about to say I like you, too.'

Felice felt relief whoosh through her and said eagerly, 'You mean in a friendly sort of way?' She didn't wait for an answer but rushed on, 'That's what I meant, too. I'm just so pleased you're nothing like your great-uncle that my enthusiasm ran away with me.'

'That's shot me down in flames,' Tobias replied.

The last of Felice's embarrassment vanished and she chuckled. 'Who are you kidding? It would take more than me to shoot you down. When we went into a skid back there you didn't turn a hair. You didn't even remind me I'd guaranteed not to wrap you around a tree. Most men would have...when they'd stopped screaming!'

'But we've already agreed I'm not like most men,' he pointed out.

No, you're not, she silently agreed. Like Old Josh, you're a one-off, but in a much more attractive way. She was wondering how to put that into words without sounding flirty when he said, 'Do you know your meter isn't running?'

'Yes, I know,' she replied, grateful for the change of subject. 'This part of the ride is a diversion. My idea, so there's no charge.' She bit her lip as she wondered how he would take that. A new friendship was a fragile thing. She could be guilty of pushing it too far.

'Am I being kidnapped?'

Felice shot him an apologetic look. 'Do you mind? I promise it's only temporary.'

'Somebody should have warned me that life on the Isle of Wight was this exciting. I'd have brought my tranquillisers.'

He looked so relaxed that Felice had to fight down a bubble of laughter before she could reply, 'Life here is one long tranquilliser...more peaceful than exciting. Do you have any children?'

'Not that I know of.' Tobias glanced at her profile with a puzzled frown creasing his forehead.

'Damn,' Felice breathed. 'I was depending on your having children. Next you'll be telling me you're not even married.'

'I'm not.' He swivelled his big bulk in his seat to study her more closely. 'Should I be?'

'Yes! The island has a lot to offer a married man with children. I'm not so sure about a bachelor. You might be bored stiff and then you won't want to stay.'

'Do you want me to stay?'

'Gosh, yes!' she exclaimed, sounding more sixteen than twenty-six.

'I'm flattered.'

'You might not be when you know the reason,' she confessed.

There was a pause while Tobias assimilated this, then he suggested, 'Why don't you sock it to me straight? A few minutes with you has made me as shock-proof as I'm ever going to be.'

They'd reached the top of the cliffs. Ahead of them were the wind-frothed waves of the grey, wintry sea. Not exactly a sight to encourage a stranger that the island was a good place to live. Felice turned the car so that they faced the valley, heaved on the handbrake, and repeated in dismay, 'Shock-proof? I'm not that bad, am I?'

'I wasn't thinking of bad, just different,' Tobias replied, and his voice sounded vibrant in the silence that enveloped them as she cut the engine.

Felice grimaced. 'You mean I'm not the sort of woman you meet every day of the week?'

He smiled. 'I should think once in a lifetime would be enough.'

'My turn to be shot down in flames,' Felice sighed, more resigned than surprised. She knew she had her faults.

'I meant that as a compliment.'

She didn't belive him for a minute but she appreciated his tact so much that she said impulsively, 'Tobias, you're too nice for your own good. It's only fair to warn you that I'm a bossy, managing sort of woman. When I want something, I don't take prisoners. If you don't watch out, I'll take merciless advantage of you. I won't be able to help myself. It's the way I am.'

'If it's my body you're after, you'd better let me arrange the time and place,' he drawled. 'The spirit's willing but the car's inadequate. We're both too big.'

Felice was so taken aback she was struck dumb, then she began to giggle helplessly, innocently unaware of how attractive he found the sound. 'That wasn't why I kidnapped you,' she managed at last, gesturing to the valley spread out below them. 'I just wanted to show you Woodlands.'

'Is that all?' Tobias sounded disappointed. 'I saw it from the air.'

'Phooey!' she scoffed. 'You can't get the atmosphere of the valley from up there.'

'Do I need to?'

'Of course you do! It would be a crime if you came here, looked at the Hall and went away again without getting the feel of the estate. You might put it straight on the market without realising what a gem it is, and that would be a tragedy!'

'A tragedy for whom?' he asked.

'Me,' Felice admitted, making the mistake of looking him squarely in the eyes and finding she couldn't lie. She added hastily, 'But it could be for you, too. Just look down there—really look.'

'I'm looking,' Tobias said, sounding bored. 'What am I supposed to be seeing?'

'You are seeing Woodlands in winter,' she scolded, as though she were a schoolmarm with a particularly dim pupil to instruct. 'That's at its worst, but it's still quite a place. It's zoned as an area of outstanding beauty, you know.'

Carried away by her own enthusiasm, she made a sweeping gesture with her hand that encompassed the entire valley. 'There's everything you could possibly wish for here. Woods, marshes, pastures, arable fields, streams, beaches and cliffs. Heck,' she added, 'it's even got its own neat little airstrip without ruining the view.

In spring, it's breathtaking. In summer, it's a little paradise. In autumn——'

'Where's the Hall?' Tobias interrupted.

Felice frowned at him, unwilling to talk about the house yet. Deciding she had no choice, she pointed reluctantly to her right. 'See that wood? It's on a rise so it hides the Hall from here. The Hall was built on the far side, to take advantage of a particularly fine view of the sea across the meadows. Now as I was saying, in autumn the valley is——'

'All right, I'm sold on the view,' he interrupted again. 'What's wrong with the Hall?'

Felice, realising again that for all his friendliness Tobias wasn't an easy man to side-track, decided to call a halt to the sightseeing. She needed to play for time while she figured out the most tactful way to answer his question.

She started up the engine and drove back down into the valley. When they rejoined the meandering lane that passed for the main road, she switched the meter on again and temporised, 'Why do you suppose there's something wrong with the Hall?'

'Because you showed me the view first. That suggests the view's a winner and the Hall's a loser... unless, of course, you kidnap all your customers for the sheer hell of taking them on the scenic route.'

'You weren't born yesterday, were you?' she asked, more under her breath than anything, but he heard.

'Just as well we've got that one sorted out.'

Felice glanced quickly at him. Was there a warning note in his voice? Or was she imagining things? She felt a twinge of unease but she was too far into this to draw back now, so she shrugged and went on as breezily as she could, 'Don't run away with the idea that there's anything wrong with the Hall. There isn't. It's just a bit—different.'

'Like you?' he suggested.

'Hardly!' she retorted. 'The Hall's mock gothic. Most of it, anyway.'

'Don't you mean it's a folly?'

'Somebody's got to you before I have,' Felice exclaimed indignantly. 'You might have said.'

'I've done my homework, if that's what you mean, but I'd rather have your opinion. It's got to be more refreshing than the piles of documents I've waded through. You don't mind if I find you—refreshing?'

'N-no,' Felice stuttered. There was no warning in his voice now, quite the reverse. He'd spoken with a warmth, almost an intimacy, that made her feel strangely light-headed. She put it down to missing breakfast, and forced herself to concentrate on essentials.

'About the Hall,' she began again. 'I admit it's been called a folly, but only because it's one of those places you either love or hate. It all depends on how much imagination you have.'

'Are you sure you don't mean taste?' Tobias asked. 'I've read a comprehensive description of the place.'

'Oh, all right then, taste,' Felice agreed, ready to concede a point in the hope that he wasn't noticing how slowly she was driving. She was still playing for time. She had so much to discuss with him but nothing was working out as she'd planned.

Tobias Hunter seemed so relaxed and obliging, but it was beginning to dawn on her that he, not she, was manipulating the situation she'd created. What was he then—a sleeping tiger? She shuddered deliciously as a thrill swept over her, raising goose-pimples on flesh that was far from cold.

Again she called herself to order, worried that she could blow this heaven-sent opportunity to come to a firm agreement with him if she fell into the sex trap. That wasn't what she wanted at all, and yet she almost felt as though he were luring her into it.

She couldn't be sure, because he was far too subtle. Never having come across his particular brand of charm and challenge before, she wasn't certain about anything.

Sometimes, though, she got the distinct feeling he was playing with her. Did tigers play before they pounced?

Again Felice shuddered, but then she remembered that other feeling she'd had about him, the feeling that she'd found a friend. It helped her to dismiss a sudden premonition that everything between her and Tobias wasn't as straightforward as it seemed. Or, rather, that he wasn't as straightforward as he appeared to be.

Convincing herself that her imagination was working overtime, she relaxed, relinquishing his challenge so that she could enjoy his charm.

'What about your taste?' he asked.

Taste? she thought, confused. Then she fell in. 'Oh, you mean the Hall! In that respect, I don't think I have any, because I adore the place. When I was a child I used to wish I lived there instead of on its doorstep, so to speak. That's why I was hoping you'd be married with children. They would have loved the Hall for its own sake, and to blazes with the purists.'

Slowly as she was driving, they had to arrive some time. As she braked reluctantly in front of the massive iron gates barring the driveway, she asked, 'Are you a purist?'

'Ask me after I've seen the Hall,' Tobias snapped, his mood changing so suddenly that she was taken aback. Before she could adjust, he went on, 'What are we waiting here for? I've admired the view; can I skip admiring the gates?'

Felice, normally the most easygoing of people, surprised herself by snapping back, 'Certainly, just as soon as you produce the key to open the padlock. I drive a taxi. I'm not a locksmith.'

Instead of reaching in his pockets or his briefcase, or wherever he had the keys, Tobias put a hand under her chin and turned her face towards his. 'You're mad at me,' he said, looking deeply into her eyes.

If there was one thing Felice couldn't stand, it was being pawed by her customers, but this was different. Tobias's voice was soft, his strong fingers gentle, and his expression was...was...tender? It was another mercurial change of mood she couldn't adjust to.

'You were mad at me first,' she grumbled, 'and I've no idea why.'

'Stop wishing I was married and I'll stop getting mad,' he told her.

Felice wanted to ask him why, but he released her chin to open his briefcase, and the moment was lost. He brought out two ornate keys, each big enough to have opened the Tower of London.

They said together, 'They're never going to fit that padlock.'

They looked at each other and smiled, and the tension that had flared so unexpectedly between them vanished as though it had never been. Felice felt warm and happy again. She switched off the meter and said, 'Over the wall it is, then. I know a place.'

'Somehow that doesn't surprise me.' Tobias switched on the meter again. 'If I want your company, which I do, I'll pay for it.'

Felice shook her head and switched the meter back off. 'The business part of the ride is over. As a friend, I'm not for hire.'

Tobias looked at her long and hard, then nodded. 'Fair enough,' he said, 'so long as you don't lose your job over it.'

'I'm self-employed,' she replied, getting out of the car and going round to open his door, but he was out before she got there. 'I'm not really supposed to be working this morning, because I was on the disco run last night.'

He stood looking down at her, an experience she quite enjoyed—for novelty's sake, she supposed—and then he asked, 'The disco run?'

'That's what I call it,' she replied, waiting for him to fall in beside her, then beginning to walk along the grass verge that edged the high stone wall guarding the privacy of Woodlands Hall. 'Saturday night revellers need transport home because of the drink-driving laws. It's a busy time for taxi drivers.'

'What time did you get to bed last night?'

'You mean this morning! Somewhere around two. I'm not normally on call again until ten, but the driver who was supposed to collect you had a breakdown. A lucky stroke for me.'

Tobias frowned. 'Do you need the work that badly?'

She laughed up at him. 'This particular job is more than work. As soon as I heard who'd made the booking I was out of bed in a flash. I've been breaking my neck to meet you.'

'Why?'

'You're my landlord.'

'Am I indeed?' he murmured, giving her an assessing look she couldn't make head or tail of. 'Is that why you're so friendly?'

'No, but it might have been. You made it easy by being nice.'

'I get the distinct impression you're buttering me up for something,' he replied cautiously.

'What a suspicious mind you've got!'

'Put it down to experience,' he retorted. 'I gather you live somewhere on the estate?'

'Yes, just down the road at Woodlands Cottage, and I want to go on living there. That's why it's so important to me that you move into the Hall. If you sell the estate I'll be chucked out. I'm already under notice to quit. The solicitors served that on me before they knew there was an heir. If the estate is broken up, the cottage will be worth more without a tenant.'

'I knew you had to have some kind of ulterior motive,' he said, and he didn't look happy about it.

'I could have played coy, but I reckon we understand each other well enough by now for plain speaking. It saves a lot of time.' A qualm struck her and she added, 'I am right in judging you as a man who prefers frankness, aren't I?'

'Yes.'

His answer was a bit brief but it was the right one. Felice sighed with relief. The worst was over, but the negotiating would have to wait because they'd reached a place where the grass on the verge gave way to a tree and an outcrop of bushes.

She pushed her way through the bushes and held them apart for Tobias to follow. 'This is it,' she said. 'We climb the tree and step off on to the wall. We have to jump down the other side, but that's no big deal.'

'Do you want a lift up?' he asked.

'Heavens, no!' she exclaimed, nimbly climbing from branch to branch with the ease of long experience. 'I've been doing this since I was a child. Just follow me and you won't even get your boots scuffed. Well, not much, anyway.'

Tobias looked up at her rounded bottom and long legs encased provocatively in tight jeans, then looked away and counted to ten. The minx, he thought. She had to know what she was doing to him! He counted another ten and began to follow.

It was only when Felice stepped on to the wall that she realised what an opportunity she'd missed. Drat! If she'd been a strictly feminine female she'd have played helpless and let him help her. It might have helped her cause. Men always went soppy when they had a helpless woman on their hands, and she could do with all the help she could get in persuading Tobias to do what she wanted.

Her second thoughts had come much too late, though. He was already on the wall beside her. They both sat down and looked at the drop. 'The safest way is to turn, hold on to the wall, ease your body down and then let go,' she instructed. 'It's not much of a drop then, not for people as tall as you and I are.'

Tobias looked at her in irritation. 'I said I appreciated frankness, not stating the obvious.'

'Sorry,' she apologised. 'That's the bossy part of me showing again. I was always that way inclined but I suppose bringing up the children made me worse.'

'What children?' he demanded.

'Janetta, Garth and Gavin. My sister and twin brothers. I've been their guardian since my parents died.'

'When was that?'

'Eight years ago—long enough for me to get set in my managing ways,' she replied in wry self-mockery. 'The twins were only eight at the time, and Janetta ten—much too young to fight back.'

'Are they fighting back now?'

'Not that I've noticed; not yet, anyway.'

'Well, I fight back,' Tobias growled.

Felice only laughed. 'That I have noticed. At the risk of sounding bossy again, I think we should get off this wall. We're melting the frost and it's getting wet. Better throw down your briefcase first, then——'

'Stop telling me what to do!' he snapped.

'Sorry.' She reached out and touched his cheek in an instinctive effort to pacify him. 'I really am.' She saw the irritation fade from his face, couldn't figure out the expression that replaced it, and didn't hang around to find out. Any moment the wetness of the wall would seep through her jeans. She turned and dropped lightly into a mulch of decaying leaves.

Tobias, still feeling the sensuous touch of her fingers on his cheek, again counted to ten, then threw down his briefcase and dropped beside her. Felice was stooping to pick up his briefcase but he got to it first and growled, 'Stop doing things for me, too.'

'Sorry,' she said again. 'Because I'm big, people usually expect me to——'

'I don't,' he butted in, 'and I'm bigger.'

Felice felt light-headed again, and fluttery with it. This must be the way dainty women felt when men wouldn't let them do the smallest thing. What had she been missing all these years? Whatever it was, she'd finally met a man big and powerful enough to redress the balance...

Horrified at the way her thoughts were turning, she began to march over the leaves and through the trees towards the driveway in a way that would have done credit to a guardsman, unable to come to terms with how feminine and fragile Tobias made her feel. It was so novel, she was afraid of making a fool of herself.

Tobias marched beside her and, because she was peculiarly sensitive to him, she guessed he was still annoyed. Yet why should he be? He'd said himself that his manhood was too secure to feel threatened by the likes of her.

Abandoning imponderables, she said candidly, 'If I make a real effort to stop bossing you about, do you think you could bury the hatchet somewhere other than my head?'

They'd reached the driveway and the going was easier, but Tobias stopped and looked down at her. 'Right now your head seems the proper place for it.'

Felice gave way to another impulse, saying with a teasing laugh, 'You never say what I expect you to. I find that very refreshing. You don't mind if I find you refreshing?' She grinned cheekily at him, and they both knew she was mocking him with his own words.

'Where's that hatchet?' he asked, but she could see the amusement in his grey eyes.

'Still in my head, apparently,' she returned, laughing outright. She slipped her arm through his in the friendly way that was so much a part of her and began to draw him on towards the house. 'Now we're friends again, can we talk about my cottage?'

'Don't you mean mine?'

'You're not going to be disagreeable, are you?' she murmured, glancing up at him from under her long eyelashes. Obsessed with sorting out her tenancy, she didn't give a thought to how seductive she looked, but Tobias did.

After a long pause, he replied, 'Just stating facts. You should try it some time.'

'All right,' Felice agreed equably, 'facts you can have, although it's a tricky situation. In a sense you're my landlord, and in a sense you're not, you see.'

'No, I don't see,' Tobias told her, wondering how her eyelashes could look so long and lustrous without a trace of mascara on them. 'You'd better spell it out for me.'

Felice took her last fence at a rush. 'I don't pay any rent.'

'You mean you're a squatter?'

'Yes,' she agreed. 'Dreadful, isn't it? I've got the rent banked, all eight years of it, but Old Josh would never take it. I wish he had, because it means I haven't any rights of tenancy at all. Unless you keep the estate and put the tenancy on a regular footing, I have to get out, and I can't afford to.'

'Shouldn't you be ankle-deep in snow and playing a violin?' he asked caustically. 'That's the right background for a fair maiden pleading with the wicked landlord, isn't it?'

Felice gurgled with laughter. 'Fancy me missing a trick or two like that!'

'I don't think you've missed many others,' he answered bluntly.

Her smile faded and she frowned at him. 'You're serious, aren't you?'

'Aren't you?'

'Well, yes, but though I'd love to stay on in the cottage, I only strictly need it for another two years. That's not too much to ask, is it?'

'What's so special about two years?' Tobias asked, watching her closely.

'That's when my brothers leave school and go to university. Janetta's due to go this autumn, so she's nearly off my hands. If only your great-uncle had hung in there for a couple more years, everything would have been fine.'

Felice's big blue eyes, full of appeal, held his as she bit her lip and continued, 'It was very awkward for me, Old Josh dropping dead like that.'

'I don't suppose he was too keen about it, either.'

Felice gasped, then giggled. When she could, she apologised, 'Sorry, I didn't mean that quite the way it sounded. I must have seemed very selfish.'

'We all have our own corner to fight for.'

'I suppose we do.' She thought for a moment, then went on innocently, 'You must be wondering why your great-uncle wouldn't take my rent.'

'Surprise me,' Tobias suggested cynically.

CHAPTER THREE

SURPRISE him? It was Felice who was surprised. Whatever could Tobias mean, and why did he sound so—so hostile all of a sudden? Had she missed something somewhere? She blinked at him, baffled.

Deciding her senses must be picking up vibes that really weren't there, she shook her head in bewilderment and said, 'I don't know about surprise, although I suppose it is an unusual story. My father was the official tenant of the cottage, but when he and my mother were lost at sea——'

She paused involuntarily. Eight years ago, yet still the tragedy had the power to hurt. She didn't like talking about it, even to a man she felt drawn to like Tobias. But she had to. It was the only way to make him understand the tangled situation she was in.

Felice pulled herself together and went on resolutely, 'My parents were a mad, impulsive pair. That's what made them so lovable. My younger sister Janetta's very much like them, in personality and talent. Anyway, they were seascape painters and——'

'Not very successful ones, I gather, if they couldn't even afford their own home,' Tobias broke in.

For a moment Felice was piqued. Then she supposed he was entitled to make that sort of comment since money was something they'd have to discuss soon. 'They did all right,' she replied quietly. 'They just weren't hung up on possessions. They preferred to spend their money

34

on education rather than a house, and educating four children privately doesn't come cheap.'

'But renting Woodlands Cottage did?'

'Yes, but it's an ancient cottage, much older than the Hall. In fact, it was the original farmhouse for this land before the Hall was built. Anything that old needs caring tenants. Besides, Old Josh was always eccentric, even before he got so odd towards the end. He hated strangers around him and the cottage had been empty for years. It was falling apart when my parents discovered it. For some reason, he took to them and let them rent it.'

Probably because of Mother, Felice thought privately. She'd had the ability to charm the birds out of the trees— an ability she herself could do with right now. Tobias wasn't making this as easy as she'd hoped.

'And then?' he prompted.

'Then,' Felice replied, unaware of the dreamy, reminiscent smile touching her lips, 'the dust flew. Literally. As I said, the cottage was in a bad way and needed taking apart and putting together again. My earliest memories are of us living more or less like gypsies while one room after another was renovated.'

'At my great-uncle's expense?' Tobias asked pointedly.

'Heavens, no! My parents paid, and were happy to do so because it was such a lovely place to bring up a family. I wasn't much more than a tot at the time but my parents always intended to have more children. Janetta and the twins were longer coming than they'd expected, that's all.'

Felice looked up at Tobias anxiously, afraid he was getting bored. The driveway to the Hall was pretentiously long, and they were walking slowly, but she'd wanted to get the business of the cottage sorted out before they got to the final bend.

She'd never intended to tell him her entire family history, but one thing had led to another, as it always seemed to with Tobias.

She didn't think he looked impatient. In fact, she couldn't read his expression at all. She took that as a good sign and rushed on, 'Anyway, when I was away at college studying horticulture, my parents took out their sailing dingy. It was a gusty October afternoon and bad weather was forecast. They trusted to luck, as they so often did, but their luck ran out. The storm struck sooner than expected. Nobody really knows what happened, but their bodies were washed up two days later.'

A sigh she couldn't repress escaped her. 'The only comfort is that they were together when it happened. That's the way they would have wanted it.'

She was glad Tobias didn't say anything trite, but stuck to practicalities. 'So you dropped out of college and you took over the family?' he asked.

Felice nodded, grateful for his understanding. 'Yes— and that's when I tried to take over the tenancy of the cottage. The problem was, Old Josh refused to see me. Of course, he was virtually a recluse by then.'

'I'd heard he was a bit odd,' Tobias agreed.

'He was frozen in time, and everybody else had to be, too,' Felice elaborated bluntly. 'He wouldn't have anything to do with change at all. When somebody quit his staff, he wouldn't hire a replacement. That's why the estate got so run down. The funny thing was——'

She broke off, wondering if she was being a bit too blunt. After all, she was speaking of one of Tobias's relatives.

'Don't stop there. Tell me what was funny,' Tobias said, and she thought she must have imagined the scep-

tical note in his voice, because she couldn't see any reason
for it.

'Well, although he wouldn't see me so I could legally
take over the tenancy, he didn't do anything to evict me
and the children,' she continued. 'He just acted as though
we weren't there. I think that must have been his way
of preserving the status quo. Naturally, we stayed on in
the cottage.'

'Naturally,' Tobias mimicked.

Felice, not looking for double meanings, accepted his
comment at face value and concluded thankfully, 'So
now you know why your great-uncle's death left us in
such a pickle. The cottage is still home to the younger
children during school vacations.'

Tobias's dark eyebrows drew together. 'You mean all
three are at boarding-school? That must cost a packet.'

'It does,' Felice admitted freely, 'but I'm just carrying
out my parents' wishes. They wanted the younger
children to have the same educational advantages that I
had.'

'Did they leave enough money for that?'

'They left some, but not enough.'

'Then paying no rent must have been a godsend to
you,' he drawled laconically.

'The rent is banked,' Felice repeated, a tiny frown
creasing her own brow as she went on the defensive. 'It's
not my fault if Old Josh wouldn't take it. It's yours any
time you want it.'

'Have you increased the amount to allow for
inflation?'

'Well, no, but you're welcome to the interest it's made.
It was never my intention to take advantage of your great-
uncle's oddness.'

'Very high-minded of you,' Tobias observed cynically.

To his surprise, Felice chuckled. 'More desperate-minded, actually. Nobody can predict what eccentrics will do, and it was always possible Old Josh would suddenly demand the rent. I didn't want to be caught on the hop. It was the same sense of self-preservation that made me want to talk to you before you came to a decision about the estate.'

There was a lengthy silence, then Tobias demanded, 'What exactly do you want from me?'

Felice turned wondering eyes up at him again. Surely she'd imagined that suddenly harsh note in his voice? What the devil could he think she wanted apart from a lease for the cottage? 'I've already told you. A legal tenancy for two years.'

'What's wrong with indefinitely?' he asked, watching her closely.

Felice's hopes soared and she responded eagerly, 'Indefinitely would be lovely, of course!'

'I thought it might be.'

Again, she thought she must have imagined the underlying sarcasm in his reply, and again she dismissed it because she was so overjoyed that he had raised the prospect of her staying on in the cottage for as long as she wanted. Oh, how marvellous that would be! It had been her home ever since she could remember, and she didn't want to move.

She simply couldn't imagine any place nicer to live than on the unspoiled Woodlands Estate. Such places were vanishing so fast she almost felt like a dinosaur, doomed to extinction when its natural environment vanished. Involuntarily, she shivered.

With her arm through his, Tobias felt the tremor. 'What's the matter?' he asked.

Felice very nearly told him, then erred on the side of caution. He might think her some kind of nut, and she didn't want him getting the idea everybody in the valley was as weird as Old Josh had been. That wouldn't exactly encourage him to make his home here!

'I asked what was the matter?' he repeated, looking down at her intently.

'I—er—was just thinking how funny it is the way things work out. If only Old Josh had lived for a couple more years, I wouldn't have had to burden you with my problems. It's not very fair on you, is it?'

No need to say any more, she thought. If Tobias didn't know where she was coming from by now, he never would. Besides, she didn't visualise any problem there. Hadn't she sensed from the start that they were on the same wavelength?

At that moment, her foot caught in a bramble that had strayed over the drive and rooted itself among the weeds. It held firm and she tripped. Her arm was still through Tobias's and she clutched at him as she began to fall. Instinctively, he reached out to save her.

Suddenly she was in his arms.

It was entirely by accident but it gave her a taste of his strength. First she'd lost her footing, and now she lost her head. She simply couldn't help herself. There was something in his powerful hold that taught her what it was like to feel utterly defenceless and yet completely secure at one and the same time.

It was a feeling she'd never experienced before, and it was heady stuff. Her breath caught in her throat, her cheeks flushed and her wondering eyes stared unguardedly into his. Suddenly she knew that she wanted him to kiss her, wanted—needed!—to feel his firm lips

against her soft ones. Blissfully, she also knew it was
what he wanted, too.

She read his need in the darkening of his eyes, felt it
in the tightening of his arms around her. Responsively,
she clung to him, feeling her soft body crush deliciously
against the hard length of his. Her eyes closed in willing
and unthinking surrender.

Tobias looked at the long sweep of dark eyelashes
shadowing her flushed cheeks, the wayward tendrils of
hair escaping from her plait to gleam like gold against
her perfect complexion, and bent his head to claim her
waiting lips.

Then he hesitated. His lips had actually brushed hers,
awakening wild and wayward promises of satisfaction
to come, when he changed his mind and thrust her away
from him.

Felice, totally unprepared, couldn't adjust quickly
enough. Dazed and disbelieving, she stumbled and
almost fell. She could still feel the strength of his arms
around her, the imprint of his powerful thighs against
hers, the tantalisingly feather-light touch of his lips. Most
of all, she could still feel his desire—a desire he had killed
with cold and callous deliberation.

Why?

One moment she'd been hovering on the brink of
paradise, the next she was out in the cold. It was too
much to come to terms with. She simply didn't know
what had happened, what had gone wrong. There were
no words she could say, none she could even think of.
She could only raise large, bewildered eyes to Tobias,
mutely questioning.

It was then she saw that the heat had gone from his.
Not even the warmth of friendship remained. She was
looking at a cold-eyed stranger—a stranger Tobias had

never been, not even at the very beginning when they had shaken hands and introduced themselves. It was as though they'd already known each other then, had always known each other.

Now, when she'd thought deepening attraction had forged them into so much more than friends, they were strangers. It was crazy. But it was happening. Had happened.

She felt exposed, shamed, naked.

Slowly and painfully, she began to recover. She'd been rejected. Whatever else she couldn't understand, she could understand that. She had been thrust away like so much unwanted baggage. Her pride flickered like a flame, ousting desire, wrapping its protective cover about her, finding reasons for her behaviour—behaviour that had previously seemed so natural, and now seemed inexplicably fast.

She summoned up a parody of a smile and said, 'Sorry, I tripped. There was a root...'

That didn't explain why she'd clung to him, of course, or why she'd melted against him and waited to be kissed, but he'd encouraged her! She'd never have behaved like that otherwise. Still, whatever had made him change his mind and thrust her away, she expected him to help her over her embarrassment. Out of humanity, if nothing else. She was wrong.

'I don't see any root,' Tobias said.

They both looked down. There were plenty of weeds, but the root that had ensnared her boot was hidden among them. Felice wasn't going to get down on her hands and knees to search for it. She'd already demeaned herself enough, and reaction was setting in with a vengeance.

'It's there,' she replied shortly. 'I don't make a habit of throwing myself into men's arms.'

'I'm glad to hear it, especially when I'm around. I prefer to take the initiative. In fact, I insist on it. The sooner you learn that, the better we'll get on.'

'I don't know what you mean,' she exclaimed, even more bewildered than before.

'Then I'll spell it out for you so you don't make the same mistake again. It never pays to overplay your hand with me. You started off all right, but you've been coming on to me stronger and stronger, and I don't like being pressured—sexually or otherwise. Try for a bit of subtlety to keep the illusion alive a little longer.'

'Wh-what illusion?' she stuttered, not really believing she was hearing all this.

'That you're a nice, sweet country kid who doesn't want anything from me. All right, so we both know that you do, but the illusion was nice while it lasted. It's a pity you had to blow it with too much body language. It made you into just another ''gimme'' girl and, frankly, I've got those queuing up for me. If you want to keep your entertainment value, try to keep the novelty appeal you had back there at the beginning.'

Felice's soft lips parted in indignation. 'Why, you—you arrogant——' She couldn't go on. What he'd said was so preposterous that words failed her. When she recovered the power of speech, she stuttered, 'How dare you suggest I was—was—throwing myself at you? I'd never——!' It was no use. As her indignation deepened into outrage, words failed her again.

Tobias's dark eyebrows lifted sceptically. 'You mean I imagined that coy little kidnap, that provocative waggling of your butt in my face as you climbed the tree, that clinging on to my arm, that hurling yourself in my arms? Oh, come on, Felice! We both know I'm quite a catch, and that isn't vanity, it's stating a fact.'

'If you imagine I'm trying to catch you——!'

'One way or the other,' he broke in wearily. 'Your problem is that your tactics are strictly amateurish compared with some of the tricks women have played on me through the years. My problem is that I'm too experienced not to recognise the syndrome, and I'm bored out of my mind by it.'

'There wasn't any syndrome,' she denied hotly. 'I—I wasn't trying to flirt with you.'

'You mean it never crossed your mind that as a woman you might get more out of me if you used your body than if you stayed strictly impersonal?' he demanded.

Felice opened her mouth to deny any such thing, then closed it again. She couldn't deny it! Not when she remembered how she'd wished she'd played helpless when she'd climbed that tree—because it might have helped her to win Tobias round to her way of seeing things about the lease.

It had been innocent enough, but, interpreted his way, it took on a whole new meaning—but only to a man with an overbearing ego! But it wasn't fair. She was nothing like the women he described. Nothing!

All the same, as the silence lengthened between them, hot shame spread its tell-tale story across her cheeks. She could only mumble helplessly, 'It wasn't like that.'

'It never is,' he replied cynically.

Felice fumed. First he'd rejected her, then he'd humiliated her, and now he was mocking her. Her so-called friend. How dared he! She wanted desperately to hold on to her anger but the hurt she felt almost destroyed her by whimpering, How *could* he?

Tears stung her eyes. She felt so betrayed, and there was never any defence against betrayal. The only help she had was a fierce determination to never, ever, expose herself to being so humiliated again. Whatever happened, there wouldn't be any more unguarded moments with Tobias Hunter!

It was that determination that steeled her to turn away from him. It was a rejection of her own, and she hoped he knew it. Her head held high, she walked on.

Later on she would figure out why war and not love had been declared between them. For the moment, it was enough for her to know that it was war...

They turned the final bend in the driveway and there, spread out in all its conflicting glory, was Woodlands Hall. 'Good God!' Tobias exclaimed, stopping dead in his tracks. 'Is this for real?'

It was a bit much to take in all at once, Felice supposed. If they'd still been friends, she would have smiled at his shock and set about cajoling him into seeing the Hall as she did—as a place of enchantment.

But hostility still crackled between them and she concentrated instead on how strange it was to be standing here in the open, with no fear of being shouted at and chased away.

Always before, when she'd been growing up and the mystery of the forbidden Hall had drawn her like a magnet, she'd had to skulk in the bushes to see it—a trespasser.

Strangely, she felt as though this big man standing beside her was the trespasser now, and she was the one who belonged. Probably because she loved the place. Time hadn't altered that in any way. The Hall still in-

trigued and enchanted her, just as Tobias had such a few
short heartbeats ago...

She felt a strange, sad tug of loss. The feeling she'd
met a kindred soul had been so marvellous while it had
lasted! A sigh welled up within her but she forced it
down. If Tobias's opinion of himself was so great he
actually believed she'd deliberately thrown herself at him,
then he really wasn't worth bothering about.

He and his ego could have a beautiful relationship,
and heaven help any poor woman who tried to come
between them. It certainly wouldn't be her. From here
on in, her sole interest in Tobias Hunter was wangling
a lease out of him for the cottage.

She wished, she really wished, she could say stuff the
cottage, and leave him here in this neglected wilderness,
but she had to be practical. Not for the first time, what
she wanted to do had to come second to the needs of
her family.

She simply had to hang on to the cottage! That was
much more important than her bruised feelings. Finding
another unfurnished house large enough, and at a rent
she could afford, was virtually impossible. She'd already
tried when she'd first been given notice to quit. People
simply didn't want tenants with teenagers, dogs and cats,
and she was encumbered with them all.

No, not encumbered, she corrected herself hastily.
She'd opted to take over the family. Even if a relative
had offered to take on the younger children, she wouldn't
have let them. They were a *family*. Anyway, she'd never
had any regrets, and Tobias wasn't going to make her
start feeling sorry for herself at this late stage.

It might have been eight years of hard graft, but it
had been fun, too, and she'd never been bored. She'd
thrived on the challenges, and Tobias Hunter was just

another challenge. If she had to crawl around him to preserve the family home for a little while longer, then, all right, she'd do it.

Felice was trying to figure out how she could crawl and still preserve some tatters of her already badly mauled dignity when Tobias found his voice again. 'What the hell is it supposed to be?' he asked scathingly, 'I've never seen such a bastardisation of incompatible styles.'

That wasn't what Felice wanted to hear, mostly because it was true. Somehow she had to soften his contempt so that he could come to appreciate the glory as well as the folly of his inheritance. 'Bastardisation,' she repeated, purely to give herself time to think. 'I think you've just made that word up.'

He shot her a baleful look. 'Whoever built this place made it up.'

'You'll feel differently about it when you know its history.'

'I don't need to know its history,' he scowled.

'Of course you do! You own it.' Felice began to walk forward again, glad to have something to talk about that was as far removed from the abortive kiss as it was possible to be. She heard rather than saw Tobias striding to catch up with her.

He said between set teeth, 'Haven't you learned yet that it doesn't pay to be bossy with me?'

'If you expect me to change the habits of a lifetime just to please you, then you expect too much.'

'I don't expect anything from you,' he replied crushingly. 'You're the one who expects something from me.'

He had her there. Felice seethed, then she said hotly, 'All I expect from you at the moment is to listen to a little of the Hall's history. It might help you to understand something for once, instead of the snarling and scoffing you're so good at.'

Not giving him chance to think of another crushing reply, she rushed on, 'Woodlands Hall was built at the end of the eighteenth century by a merchant who'd made his fortune in India. That explains the cupola over the central building, the shape of the windows and the minarets at each corner.'

Tobias butted in sarcastically, 'What explains the two wings? They look like a pair of cut-down castles stuck on to a miniature Taj Mahal.'

'I'm getting to those,' Felice replied, switching to a soothing tone that rattled him more than being snapped at. She studied the squat, crenellated towers that guarded the equally squat wings, and continued, 'They're supposed to look like castles. There was a gothic revival going on when the Hall was built. Our merchant, though, obviously wanted a bit of India as well as a bit of old England, so he built both.'

'Our merchant,' Tobias repeated mockingly, 'had more money than sense.'

Felice scowled at him. 'I like to think he had a dream, and he built that dream regardless of what anybody thought or said. I find that very touching.'

'I find it nauseating. An Indian temple slapped between two sawn-off castles! Good Lord, you'd have to be eccentric to live here. I was prepared for a folly, but this is a monstrosity.'

'It's not a monstrosity!' Felice exclaimed passionately. 'I'm not the least bit eccentric and I'd love to live here.'

Tobias swung round and faced her. All the power of his big body seemed to blaze through his grey eyes as he stared searchingly at her. 'So that's it, is it?' he breathed. 'Your real ulterior motive at last.'

Felice didn't know what he was talking about but she hated the way his eyes were dissecting her. To think she'd once believed them warm, friendly, intimate. Now they were...insulting!

'Anybody with a grain of imagination would love to live in the Hall,' she defended, unsure where his attack was coming from but fighting back, anyway. 'Try it. You might find it grows on you.'

'Like a carbuncle?' he suggested.

His comment was so unexpected that she laughed. She really didn't want to, but she couldn't help herself. She thought his eyes softened momentarily, but she wasn't going to be deceived that way again. She quelled any answering softness and protested, 'That's not fair. The Hall might not be balanced and beautiful like a true architectural gem but——'

She was interrupted by his sudden shout of mocking laughter. She lifted her chin at him and continued doggedly, '—But it's a different kind of gem. It's a place where imagination runs riot, where things that shouldn't be possible have been made possible. It's—it's pure magic. You just have to give the magic time to work...'

Tobias was looking at her in a very different way now. She found her breath catching in her throat, then realised he was only mocking her when he said, 'Maybe I should hire you as my agent when I sell the place. I'm sure you'd do a good job on any passing sucker.'

Felice clenched her hands, her palms itching to slap his face, but he was turning away from her, getting out the two ornate keys. She was even irritated when he chose the right key to fit the lock of the massive front door.

Everything always seemed to go so right for him, and so wrong for her. Still, there was such a thing as a law of averages. He had to come unstuck some time. She found herself burning with a new sort of desire—to be around to see it!

CHAPTER FOUR

ALL the antagonism Tobias aroused within her was driven from Felice's head as the door swung open and they walked inside.

She stared around in disbelief. The Indian part of the building was entirely an entrance hall, tiled from floor to dome in blue and gold. There were a few pieces of Indian furniture scattered about, but mostly there was just an incredible feeling of space, tranquillity and beauty.

Delicately arched windows let in shafts of grey, and Felice could only imagine how magnificent it was when the sun was shining. 'Heavens,' she whispered, awed, her eyes widening into stars of wonder, 'if this is eccentric, then I'm all for eccentricity.'

Tobias didn't answer immediately, then he admitted, 'The inside beats the outside, but it hardly suits the climate, does it? It's like a fridge in here.'

'Imagine it on a sunny day,' she replied, although practical considerations were the last thing on her mind.

She didn't see his critical appraisal switch from the splendour surrounding them to her rapt face. His eyebrows drew together. 'Haven't you been in here before?'

'Never.' She was so bewitched by all she was seeing that she momentarily forgot he was her least favourite person and slipped back into her old confiding ways.

'I had to trespass just to see the outside,' she explained. 'You know how impressionable children are. I'd only ever seen Old Josh from a distance but I'd heard about him, and he was like something out of a fairy story to me—an ogre. I felt I was taking my life into my hands just creeping around the grounds. I never had the courage to go as far as the windows in case I was caught and gobbled up.'

'I think even my great-uncle would have found you a bit of a mouthful,' Tobias murmured, as though he'd also forgotten the animosity between them.

Felice smiled. 'Oh, I wasn't quite so big then.'

'I wouldn't call you big. I'd say you were just r——' He broke off suddenly and frowned, as though he'd already said too much.

She found herself listening hopefully for him to continue. When he didn't, she swallowed the disappointment she shouldn't be feeling and concluded, 'When I grew up, of course, it would have been too embarrassing to be caught trespassing, so I never risked a peek inside the Hall then, either.'

'You're not trying to kid me you'd let embarrassment stop you doing anything you wanted to do, are you?' he asked sceptically.

Gosh, he really did think she was brazen, and probably depraved with it! What sort of women was he used to, for heaven's sake?

But her intrinsic honesty made her admit, 'There was another factor after my parents died. I thought if Old Josh caught sight of me he might remember about the cottage and chuck me out in a fit of rage. I'm probably doing him an injustice, and he wasn't really that awful, but I wasn't in any position to take risks.'

'You still aren't,' Tobias reminded her.

'You enjoy turning the screw, don't you? What is it with you—another notch, another laugh?'

'I don't get my kicks that way,' he denied. 'I just find it impossible to believe you fell in love with this place without setting foot inside. It doesn't make sense.'

Stung, she retorted, 'Don't you ever do or feel anything that other people don't understand?'

'No. I make sure everybody knows exactly where I'm at. It saves a lot of time, trouble and misunderstanding.'

'How boring,' she replied snootily.

It was Tobias's turn to be stung, and he snapped, 'Tell me exactly when I've bored you?'

'You just have.'

The temporary truce was definitely over. Tobias stared down at her, hostility flaring in his grey eyes. 'If you were a man, I'd say you had a lot of balls, and you were about to get them chopped off.'

Now they were really getting down to the nitty-gritty, she thought, determined not to be outraged, since that was clearly what he wanted. She took a deep breath and met his eyes squarely. 'But since I'm a woman . . . ?'

'I'll make allowances and say you have a lot of nerve.'

'Don't spare my feelings now,' she scoffed. 'I might never recover from the shock.'

His expression changed. She wasn't sure whether it was for the better and had further doubts when he continued, 'You've definitely got a certain entertainment value, Felice, but it would be a mistake to trade on it too much. Now let's look over the rest of this morgue.'

He began walking across the entrance hall to a door on the right, his footsteps echoing confidently in the silence. Spooks obviously didn't bother him, Felice thought as she caught up with him, but it wasn't very heartening to know that she didn't bother him much, either.

Drat the man, and he'd come so close to being her darling man, too! Oh, well, she'd have to write it all off to experience—if she survived. Now why did I think that? she wondered, and shivered.

'The cold getting to you?' he asked, glancing down at her.

'Yes.'

It was a fib and Tobias seemed to know it. He paused before leading her into one of the castle wings and said, 'I think you're scared there might be an ogre behind this door.'

'He couldn't be worse than the one I came in with.'

She was startled when Tobias smiled. She wished— oh, how she wished!—he didn't look so darned attractive when he smiled. 'One up to you,' he admitted, opening the door. 'I look forward to levelling up the score.'

Another shiver ran through Felice, although not for the world would she have admitted how much it stimulated and excited her. Again he saw it, but this time his smile wasn't so attractive. 'Precisely,' he almost purred. 'Now you don't know where or when I'm going to pounce, do you?'

Make what you like of that, Felice thought disgruntledly, as he strode away from her. Against her will, she found herself following him. If nothing else, he had a magnetism that she hadn't yet learned to resist.

They were in another hall. It was much smaller but the medieval theme came as a bit of a shock after the Indian splendour they'd just left.

Sightless suits of armour guarded the bottom of a solid oak staircase leading to a minstrels' gallery and the upper storey. 'As Alice said, it gets "curiouser and curiouser",' Tobias quoted, looking at the choice of doors leading from the intricately carved and heavily panelled walls.

'It gets more and more exciting,' Felice contradicted, her eyes sparkling. She thought of how many years she'd been itching to see inside this extravagant building, and how awful it would have been if she'd been disappointed. As it was, the revelation of each opening door was better than a birthday treat.

After that, apart from a few hurried comments, she didn't get much time to say anything as Tobias marched her through sitting-rooms, bedrooms, kitchens, utility-rooms, up and down towers, then back through the Indian hall to the other wing, which seemed strictly for guests.

Most of the furniture was shrouded in dust sheets—very spooky, but understandable enough. Old Josh had never been known to allow anybody over his doorstep, let alone entertain. Felice, longing to peek under the sheets, could have screamed with frustration as Tobias kept striding on as though he was trying to beat a stopwatch.

What drove the man? she wondered. Why come here at all if he wasn't really interested?

Worse, she knew the magic of this magnificent oddity that was Woodlands Hall hadn't touched him at all. Her own mind was full of kaleidoscopic impressions of grandeur, but she knew instinctively that his was as un-impressed as if he had no eyes to see, no senses to be touched by inspired folly and unashamed extravagance.

Strange, considering what enemies they'd turned out to be, that she should be so tuned in to reactions he hadn't even bothered to express.

Strange and frightening.

There was a long, low oak chest in the upstairs passage, warped and darkened with age. Felice sat down on it, determined to halt the hurricane that was Tobias Hunter. He might be egotistically overbearing, but he could scarcely keep on going and leave her here.

Or could he?

Felice found that not quite knowing what he would do added a delicious spice to her determination to make him appreciate fully what he would be losing if he swapped a unique place like Woodlands Hall for monetary gain.

Tobias, missing the sound of her footsteps behind him, swung round. 'Feet given out?' he asked.

'No.'

'Come on, then,' he said impatiently.

'No,' she repeated.

Tobias came back to her. 'What do you mean, no?'

'I want you to slow down, really consider what you've inherited here. You're refusing to see the Hall as anything but a folly, and that's blinding you to all the good things about it. Just stop looking it over with a closed mind. A closed mind is a dead mind!'

'I'll take a closed mind over a demented one any day.'

Looming over her as he was, she felt the power of him, but there was a certain wayward thrill in defying him. 'You just don't know how lucky you are,' she told him. 'Some people would do anything for a place like this.'

'We'll go into that later,' he baffled her by replying. 'In the meantime, let's move on before we're fossilised like the rest of this place.'

Felice found herself following him, her head in a whirl. Go into *what* later? No answer presented itself as she was whisked in and out of rooms again, and up and down more towers. Except, perhaps, that he was as odd as his great-uncle, but somehow she didn't think so.

The problem was she didn't know what to think. About anything at all. Her irritation was growing, though. To keep up with him, she had to hurry past so many things she would have loved to stop and examine in detail.

Had it been her inheritance, she could have spent a week in each wing alone, and still felt she'd missed a lot. Her curiosity was being teased, not satisfied. The thought came unbidden—and unappreciated—that Tobias was having the same effect on her, too.

She looked at his tall, burly form ahead of her and realised that here she was, going through a deserted mansion with a man she actually knew precious little about. All she was certain of was that lately she'd been over-exposed to his challenge and starved of his charm.

She found herself pining for his charm. She was missing that certain softness in his voice that weakened and bewitched her... the humour that made her feel he was a kindred soul... the smile that made his rugged face so heart-tuggingly handsome...

Well, all that had gone out of the window fast enough, she thought, pulling a face at her own gullibility. He was a Jekyll and Hyde. The charming man had vanished somewhere and she was left with a growling monster. She was wrong to hope for another transformation. She'd never be sure how long it would last. And yet... and yet... she did hope.

'What are you thinking?' Tobias asked suddenly.

'You wouldn't want to know.'

'That bad, is it?'

She bit her lip as his mouth curved into the smile she had been yearning to see—and didn't trust any more.

Her nerves still reacted to it, though, sending exciting messages over her susceptible body.

Felice, unsure whether she was about to be hit with charm or challenge, and not quite ready for either, looked away from him, and saw to her dismay that they were in a bedroom. The four carved posts of an ornate Jacobean bed rose solidly above a dust sheet lying over the mattress and covers.

With a sudden movement Tobias pulled the dust sheet away, exposing a faded patchwork quilt. 'Now you can sit down,' he said. 'I'm ready to listen to you.'

It was what Felice wanted, but this wasn't the setting she'd have chosen. She looked doubtfully from the bed to Tobias and hesitated.

'Don't tell me you're afraid?' he asked softly.

She was, but it was a fear of disillusion more than anything else. She hadn't known until this moment that she had any illusions left about Tobias, and it was disconcerting to find that she had. What was even more disconcerting was that she wanted to keep them.

For some crazy reason, the way he'd behaved up until now didn't matter as much as he was about to behave. She wanted to give him a second chance—and she wanted him to give her a second chance, too. The realisation stunned her.

Maybe it's the Hall, she thought frantically. Maybe there really is a kind of magic here that's temporarily bewitched me. Maybe when I get outside I'll be all right again.

Suddenly saw herself as he did, with her tongue moistening her dry lips, and realised he might well mistake it for a sexual signal. Confusion made her stutter, 'W-why should I be frightened?'

'You tell me,' he invited, sitting down on the bed and patting the place beside him. 'Come here and tell me.'

Felice hesitated, unsure of herself, unsure of him, unsure of everything.

'Now,' he added. It was a command, but he softened it by holding out his hand to her.

Felice couldn't find the strength or the will to resist his outstretched hand, and slowly she walked towards him and put her hand in his. It was an act of faith, but she had no idea whether she would be betrayed or not.

She felt his strong clasp, and then he was easing her down to sit beside him. His gentleness surprised her. It disarmed her, too, because she knew he was giving her the opportunity to pull away if she wanted to.

She knew she should have, but she felt strangely helpless. She'd known him such a little while, and yet she felt bound to him by ties she couldn't see and couldn't begin to understand.

'I'm going to kiss you,' he said. 'You know that, don't you?'

She nodded. Every fibre of her being had been aware of his intention from the moment he'd ordered her to come to him.

'Yet still you came to me,' he said softly.

'Yes.' Her voice was a sigh, a surrender, an acceptance of facts. Friends...enemies...whatever they were, she was incapable of resisting the magnetism that drew her to him. It was so strong, it was almost tangible.

He took her face between his big hands and studied her carefully. She thought she felt his strong fingers tremble slightly, but decided she must have imagined it as he bent his head to cover her lips with his. Surely she was the only one who was trembling! Not with fear—

never with fear!—but with anticipation so exquisite that it took her breath away.

His kiss was gentle, feather-light, deliciously exploratory, and it awoke such a blaze of response within Felice that her hands went involuntarily to his face.

She held him just as he was holding her, and as he raised his head to look at her again, she pulled his mouth down to hers and kissed him back with all the soul that was in her. Her eyes closed. She almost wanted to weep, so pure and so deep was the emotion flowing between them.

It was incredible but somehow, somewhere, Tobias had become the most important person in her life. She'd have scoffed if anybody had told her such a thing could happen so quickly, but as their lips separated she smiled mistily at her own naïveté. Feeling like this didn't take *time*, it only took the right two people.

Tobias's lips had taught her that.

'What are you smiling about?' he asked, a frown cleaving a line between his eyebrows.

'Nothing,' she breathed, too shy to confess her feelings until he did first.

His frown deepened and she knew she'd said or done something wrong, but she didn't know what. Her bewilderment deepened when he said harshly, 'Well, don't smile too soon, Felice. Before I commit myself, I want a taste of what I'm getting into.'

As Felice's soft lips parted in surprise, he crushed them savagely beneath his own, his hands moving over her body as though he owned it. His change of mood was so sudden that she was too surprised to even struggle.

The exquisite feeling that had almost reduced her to tears by its sweetness just moments ago was swamped by a tide of passion he was forcefully arousing in her.

Even while she melted physically, mentally she froze, almost choking on the shock and disillusion of his abrupt change of mood.

This callous assault on her senses had nothing to do with caring. It was just an exercise in mastery, and it revolted her. 'Tobias please,' she begged, struggling to free herself. 'Please don't be such a brute! Let me go!'

'You don't mean that,' he mocked, tightening his grip on her and unbuttoning her coat. His hand slid under her jumper and his touch on her bare warm flesh made her gasp. Her nipples tautened, betraying her unwilling arousal, and relaying such excitement to the pit of her stomach that she couldn't stop herself from squirming ecstatically in his arms.

'Now call me a brute,' he murmured triumphantly, and crushed her lips again in a way that made any answer, defiant or submissive, impossible.

Brute, she whimpered silently. Brute...brute...brute...

She loathed what he was doing to her, loathed even more her pagan response, and yet when he pushed her back on the bed and bent his dark head to tantalise her nipples with his tongue, it took all her will power to force herself to go cold in his arms.

But she had to! She wanted so much more than his body. She wanted his love and respect. Anything less wasn't enough for her proud spirit. She wanted it all or nothing...and she knew now that nothing was what it was going to be.

Tobias had no real feeling for her—only the physical desire that made her feel cheap and tarnished. Revulsion at how nearly she'd become those two loathsome things made her drop her arms limply by her sides as she waited for his reaction.

Tobias raised his head from her breast and looked at her. It was a long, hard look but she met it unflinchingly. She guessed he must be wondering what part of her had been strong enough to resist him. She hoped, now his passionate grey eyes were cooling to stony flint, that he'd realise it was her integrity.

It became painfully obvious he realised no such thing when he said harshly, 'I detest women who turn it on and off like a tap, Felice.'

She was too upset to answer. She pulled down her sweater, closed her coat and rolled away from him. It was impossible to fight a man like Tobias on all the levels she'd fought him without feeling as though she'd been put through a wringer.

She stumbled to her feet while she still had the strength to do so. Her mind was numb, her legs weak. She felt as if Tobias had drawn the very life force out of her.

She staggered away from him, not towards the door and freedom, but to a high-backed Jacobean settle that wasn't shrouded with a sheet. She sat on the hard wooden seat, oblivious of the dust, trying to control her ragged breathing as she tidied her clothes and buttoned up her jacket.

Tobias, too, stood up. She watched with sad eyes while he walked towards the window and stood with his back towards her. The atmosphere between them was so tense that it almost choked her.

She knew she was being a fool, resting here like a wounded animal when she should be making a run for it, but she felt as much his captive as she had ever been. There was something in the very essence of the man that made her want to stay close to him, however much he disillusioned her.

Despairingly, she found herself accepting a very unpalatable truth—that Tobias would have to behave a great deal worse than he already had to drive her away from him.

And yet what worse could there be?

CHAPTER FIVE

TOBIAS turned from the window, his eyes seeking hers with the intensity that was so peculiarly his own. 'You were right,' he said abruptly. 'I was a brute. I'm sorry, I never meant to be.'

'I know,' she whispered, and was surprised to discover that she did.

'Thank you for that, anyway. I don't like myself too much at the moment.'

Felice's lips curved in a parody of her normally brilliant smile as she admitted ruefully, 'I don't like myself too much, either. I can only put it down to body chemicals—ours must be too volatile to mix comfortably.'

'That's one way of putting it,' he muttered, looking unconvinced.

'What other way is there?' she asked. 'The plain fact is we went too far too fast, and I shouldn't think that's normal for either of us. Something had to go wrong.'

'Don't you know what?' he asked, looking thunderstruck.

'No,' she sighed, remembering wistfully how she'd thought his fingers had trembled when he'd cupped her face in his hands, beguiling her into believing for a precious fraction of time that his emotions had been as deep and true as her own.

Tobias came away from the window and sat moodily on the edge of the bed, directly opposite her. 'You made me lose my temper. You shouldn't have smiled like that.'

Felice shook her head, mystified. 'How did I smile?'

'Like the cat that's swallowed the cream. That smile said it all.'

'Said what?' she asked, more mystified than ever.

'That you thought I was as easy a target as my great-uncle. All those years of not paying any rent! Did you really expect me to believe it was because he chose to ignore the fact that you were living in the cottage?'

Felice had been expecting some kind of attack—but not from this angle. Stung by its unfairness, she exclaimed, 'It's the truth! I'm not responsible for the way Old Josh was.'

'You're responsible for taking advantage of his senility,' Tobias tossed back at her, 'and ever since we've met you've been working on the best way of taking advantage of me, too. Exactly when did you decide that flat on your back was the most appropriate?'

'How dare you?' she gasped. 'If I were that sort of a woman, I wouldn't have stopped just now, would I?'

'Of course you would. Stupidity isn't one of your faults, and you'd have to be stupid to go all the way without first making sure you'd get what you wanted from me.'

Felice jumped to her feet, her eyes blazing with fury. 'You've got me all wrong. Old Josh was eccentric, not senile, and I've already told you it was never my intention to take advantage of him. He created the situation I'm in over the cottage, not me. And as for you——'

She broke off, biting her lip.

'Go on,' Tobias encouraged her with a sardonic smile. 'Next you should be denying that you intended to take advantage of me.'

Felice's face flamed. 'I can't, and you know it.'

'Yes, I know it.'

Momentarily, she thought Tobias sounded as disappointed and disillusioned as she was herself, but she decided that must be something else she was imagining. 'At least I was honest,' she defended herself. 'I made it plain I wanted a lease for the cottage, but I hoped to talk you into it. *Talk*, Tobias,' she stressed. 'I'd never have used my body to get it.'

'I'm sure you wouldn't,' he agreed softly. 'Your magnificent body is worth far more than that. The cottage was only a gambit. It's the Hall you're really after. You soon made that obvious enough.'

Felice gasped, 'You're mad! Mad in a way Old Josh never was!'

'On the contrary, I'm depressingly sane. Give me credit for knowing when a woman's making a dead set at me, particularly when she's already been warned against it. Heaven knows I wanted to believe you were different. I even gave you a last chance to prove that you were when I kissed you, but you muffed it. That smile of yours was just that little bit too triumphant. No man likes to be used too blatantly, least of all me.'

Felice breathed wonderingly, 'What makes you think you're so marvellous that women want to throw themselves at you?'

'Oh, not at me,' he answered drily. 'At what I can give them.'

'And that's what you think I've done?' she went on, flabbergasted. 'Let me get this straight. You think all women are gold-diggers, is that it? Including me?'

Tobias got up and went back to the window, leaning his elbows on the deep embrasure as he stared moodily over the frost-covered meadows to the sea. 'I don't go in for name-calling, Felice. It's outdated and it isn't necessary, anyway. Let's just say women have a way of letting me know if they're available. After that, it's just a matter of agreeing terms.'

Rigid with outrage, she demanded, 'And you think my terms are the Hall?'

'You're the one who advocated plain speaking on the grounds that it saves a lot of time,' he reminded her. 'I don't know why you're in such a huff because I've taken you at your word. Nor do I know why you threw out all those sexual signals if you didn't expect me to call your bluff. I thought that was what you wanted.'

'Wh-what *I* wanted!' she stammered, disbelieving. 'I don't believe I'm hearing this! I loathe being treated as just a body. It's not my fault if I'm built in a way that puts only one thought in men's minds.'

'It's not a fault, it's a delight,' Tobias contradicted, turning to face her and hunching his powerful shoulders against the wall, 'but you can't have it all ways. If you want to be wooed leisurely with chocolates and flowers you shouldn't have come on to me so strongly.'

'I didn't!' she exclaimed, her voice almost snapping with exasperation. 'I was just being friendly.'

'If you want to avoid similar mistakes in the future, try to be less friendly and more exclusive,' he advised her smoothly.

Felice gasped again, then realised she couldn't explain why she'd been particularly friendly to him—without confessing how deeply she'd been attracted to him! She'd rather be misunderstood than do that!

She seethed with impotent fury, but she was wounded, too. Tobias's cynicism had cut her deeply, partly because of the injustice of it, but mostly because it ridiculed everything that had made her warm to him in the first place.

'Then here's where I start being more exclusive,' she said between gritted teeth, turning pointedly away from him and stalking out of the room. Once in the panelled passage she kept on going, down the beautiful staircase, out of the castle wing and into the splendid Indian hall.

She could hear his footsteps behind her, echoing positively around the old building, and closing on her fast. The temptation to run from him was almost overpowering, but she kept her head high, her back straight, and her strides steady. Contempt was what he deserved, and contempt was what he would get.

At last she reached the front door and gratefully she stretched for the handle. She needed desperately to escape this fantasy world and get outside into reality, where crazy, unbelievable things didn't happen. Then, perhaps, she would be able to shut down the turbulent emotions Tobias had unleashed in her.

But how dared he think such awful things about her? How dared he? All right, so she'd been unguarded, but only because her instincts told her she didn't have to be on her guard with Tobias.

So much for instincts!

Swaying between rage, hurt and a desolating feeling of betrayal, she froze when Tobias's arm reached past her. His strong hand closed over hers, trapping it on the handle, preventing her escape into the outside world.

She couldn't bring herself to swing round to face him, so she remained rigidly as she was. Tobias put his other arm around her waist and pulled her back against him. Unwillingly, Felice experienced once more the shock and delight of feeling her body pressed against his.

The dubious pleasure turned swiftly to indignation when he bent his head and kissed her ear as a lover might. 'Felice,' he murmured, his breath tantalising her ear and all her senses, 'I never meant to offend you by being too frank, but I was only following your lead, remember?'

Felice chose not to remember anything, nor to say anything, either. She was too busy trying to suppress the excitement that the closeness of his body communicated to hers. She thought despairingly that this instant arousal of her senses was another kind of betrayal, melting her anger as it did, beguiling her brain...

Oh, grief, what was happening to her? What *had* happened to her ever since she'd set eyes on Tobias Hunter? It couldn't be love, because love needed certain things to grow, things he knew nothing about.

What did that leave? Lust, she thought, then all her thoughts splintered into confusion as Tobias drew her closer still and continued, 'A situation like this won't go away by our ignoring it. We have to resolve it in a way that will be acceptable to both of us. It's the only sensible thing to do.'

'I don't know what you mean,' she retorted frigidly.

'Yes, you do,' he challenged. 'Something happened between us when we met, something so positive there was an almost audible click. We might be mad at each other right now, and the chances are we'll be mad at each other again, but there's no running away from a feeling this powerful. There won't be any peace for either of us until we're together.'

Felice shivered because every word he said rang with truth, but it was an unacceptable truth—unacceptable to her, anyway. She wasn't like him. She couldn't settle for the best deal she could get, not when it was so much less than she needed to make her happy.

Respect, love, trust. Those were the things she needed, however much her wilful body might betray her.

Tobias's warm breath on her ear again tormented her senses as he went on softly, 'We're both realists, so let's talk about it.'

It was at that moment Felice discovered she wasn't a realist at all. She was a romantic—a hopeless romantic. Her busy life, her practical outlook, her managing ways... all had been a massive cover-up for the emptiness within her, an emptiness she'd been unaware of until Tobias had exposed it.

The irony was that, having exposed it, he could only offer her realism, and not the romance she craved.

Something seemed to wither within her, and it took all her courage to turn within his encircling arm to face him. 'This talk—it would be about an affair, wouldn't it?' she asked with difficulty. 'That's what you mean when you keep talking about terms?'

'Of course.' He seemed surprised she should have doubted it. 'We want each other, and you also want the Hall. You can have it in return for being my mistress for as long as it amuses us both. That will be your only claim on me when we part, but naturally I'll have a legal agreement drawn up to protect both our interests.'

Good heavens, Felice thought, the last of her illusions dying. He sounded so businesslike he might have been negotiating for a car or a yacht—or anything that might have taken his fancy. Didn't he realise she was flesh and blood, with all that that entailed?

Feelings, for a start...

'You don't believe in wasting time, do you?' she managed, when she came out of shock.

'You're not exactly a slowcoach yourself.'

Had she seemed that way? Had she really? It didn't seem possible—any more possible than this 'deal' he was setting up. She shook her head in disbelief and whispered, 'I can't believe you're serious.'

'What's the matter? I've got your terms right, haven't I?'

'You haven't got anything right,' she told him sadly. 'About me—about anything. If you had, you'd know that, even to contemplate what you're suggesting, I'd want so much more than the Hall.'

His eyebrows rose. 'Ravishing as you are, you can hardly suppose you're worth the entire estate! I'm generous, Felice, but I stop short of being foolhardy.'

Damn the man, he'd wilfully misunderstood her again! She couldn't explain, either, not without letting him know that feelings came first, second and last with her. And what a humiliating waste of time that would be, when the only feeling he understood was lust!

Outrage kept her silent, but he misinterpreted that, too. 'My God,' he breathed, 'you're holding out for marriage.'

'No!' Felice denied hotly, her cheeks burning with embarrassment, but Tobias was releasing her and beginning to laugh. Rich, genuine laughter that echoed around the domed hall and returned to mock her.

'Stop it!' she said fiercely. 'Stop it!'

'I'm trying,' he said, smiling at her with a candour that would have tugged at her heart-strings if only she hadn't been the victim of his amusement. 'You should have done your research on me a bit more thoroughly, Felice. Then you'd have known why I always take mistresses, and never wives. Mistresses are more amusing, and a great deal less expensive in the long run.'

Once more his cynicism appalled her, and she scoffed, 'Love on the cheap!'

His amusement faded and he asked scornfully, 'Who said anything about love? I wouldn't call my offer of the Hall exactly cheap, either.'

'Everything about you is cheap,' she retorted. 'Cheap because you see everything in terms of money!'

'I'd have to be blind not to see you put too high a price on yourself,' he snapped back.

Felice gave up. They were arguing from different standpoints and getting farther and farther apart all the time. He believed what he wanted to believe, and that was it! Nothing she said was going to change him.

She drew herself up to her full height and replied disdainfully, 'I'm only for hire as a taxi driver, Mr Hunter. If you're no longer interested in that, I'll be on my way.'

She didn't wait for an answer, but wrenched open the door and left him. She stormed down the drive a lot faster than she'd walked up it, her mind a shifting kaleidoscope of impressions that wouldn't settle into in one clear picture or one uncomplicated emotion. It was all a hopeless jumble. Tobias, if nothing else, had certainly screwed up her head. Or was it her heart?

Oh, hell!

Exasperated, she left the driveway and detoured through the trees to get over the high wall, trying to convince herself that Tobias had somehow got mixed up with her lifelong fascination for the Hall. Once she got them separated in her mind, she'd be all right again.

She breathed a bit more easily when she dropped on to the grass verge outside the wall, but she almost stopped breathing altogether when she reached her car and found Tobias already sitting in it.

He must have climbed over the gate, but then he wouldn't have to worry about doing any damage, would he? He owned the place, although from his attitude he might also have owned the whole of the world and everyone in it.

But now me, she vowed. Never me.

She toyed with the idea of ordering him out, but it was an order she'd never be able to enforce if he resisted. Besides, the quickest way of getting rid of him was by taking him wherever he wanted to go. She climbed into the driver's seat and asked formally, 'Where to?'

'The airstrip. I have a lunch date in London.'

She was startled. A lunch date? That meant he'd only set aside the smallest possible time to look over his inheritance, so he'd never really been interested in it at all. Whatever had happened—or might have happened—between them, in the long run she'd always been wasting her time. He was as impervious to the magic of Woodlands as he was to the magic of love.

She was so rattled to find herself again thinking of love and Tobias at one and the same time that she crashed the gears twice as she turned the car. Damn! What was it about him that made all her normal skills desert her?

When the car was finally facing the right way, she put her foot down hard on the accelerator and speeded back to the airfield. They were almost there before she realised her clumsiness was due to her still being extraordinarily sensitive to his presence.

An annoyed frown settled on her normally sunny face and Tobias, turning in his seat to watch her, said, 'You're sulking. I hate women who sulk.'

'That suits me,' she retorted stonily.

'You know what your problem is, Felice? You enjoy cutting off your nose to spite your face.'

'I won't bother telling you what your problem is. It would take all day,' she snapped back, and drove through the gates of the airfield fuming.

When she stopped, Tobias looked at the meter and wasted no time in paying her or getting out of the car. 'Definitely sulking,' he reaffirmed. Then he slammed the car door on her and walked purposefully towards his aircraft.

Felice watched him for a few moments, her irritation fading into a poignancy that almost made her want to weep as she remembered how very differently she'd felt when Tobias had walked towards her earlier that morning. Everything had seemed possible then, and now nothing was.

She felt a different girl from the one who'd driven out so confidently to meet him, but she blamed herself for that. Hadn't she suspected he was a sleeping tiger long before she'd actually been mauled?

Reaction to her fancifulness set in, and her lips curved in wry self-mockery. All that had really happened, she scolded herself, was that she'd fallen foul of a predatory male who happened to think he was God's gift to women, and for once she hadn't been able to cope.

Well, there was no need to make a major drama out of it. Everybody came unstuck sometimes, and this...sadness that was making her feel so low right now would soon pass.

Her eyes were bleak, though, and her soft lips drooped wistfully as she did a U-turn and drove back on to the road. She didn't look back when the peace of the Sunday-drowsy valley was shattered by the sound of a plane revving to life.

She didn't want to watch Tobias fly out of her life as abruptly as he'd flown into it. For some peculiar reason, she wasn't half as glad about it as she should have been.

As the days passed, Felice waited to bounce back to her normal ebullient self. Somehow, though, she never quite managed to bounce through the cloud of gloom that was hanging over her.

It began to dawn on her that the joy she usually brought to her everyday living was gone, stolen by an impossible man who outraged everything that was straight and true and decent about her. Unfortunately, that didn't stop her pining for him.

He dominated her thoughts and dreams, reminding her forcibly of his assertion that there wouldn't be any peace for either of them until they were together.

Every time she remembered it, she ground her teeth with rage, and in her stronger moments she even managed to convince herself she wasn't pining at all— but merely waiting for Tobias to enforce the eviction order. By trying so hard to charm a legal tenancy out of him, she was sure she'd achieved the very opposite.

So, all in all, she faced each day without enthusiasm, getting through her work with a forced cheerfulness that fooled everybody except herself. But since everybody was used to her being cheerful, they didn't take much fooling.

When she'd dropped out of college, she'd set herself up as a landscape gardener, and, after a precarious start, her business had expanded gradually by word-of-mouth recommendation.

Now she tended large gardens as well as small, and her white van emblazoned with the legend 'Lawson Gardening Services' was familiar in the nearby village of Bixley, and in several other villages as well.

During spring and summer when she was rushed off her feet she hired extra workers, but February was the last of the winter 'dead' months and she could cope easily alone. Too easily sometimes, which was why she worked weekends as a taxi driver to keep her income up.

On the Wednesday after her traumatic meeting with Tobias, she stopped off at the newsagents in Bixley to get the local weekly paper before driving on to the cottage for lunch. The sooner she started house-hunting again, the better. It wasn't a cheerful prospect, and her spirits were at an all-time low as she parked beside the cottage and let her two black and white collies out of the back of the van.

She always took the dogs with her on her gardening jobs. They were well trained and her customers saved titbits for them. Sometimes she felt more of a mobile bone disposal unit than a gardener.

Out of the blue, she found herself wondering whether Tobias liked dogs . . .

Why, oh, why did everything she did or even thought have to return to him? Grimacing, she took the dogs into the kitchen at the back of the house and made some cheese on toast. While she ate it, she scanned the short column of rented accommodation in the paper, and found her pessimism well-founded. Plenty of furnished accommodation, particularly short-term winter lets, but nothing remotely suitable for her.

Felice looked at her watch and decided to put her feet up for half an hour before she set out on her next job. She went into the passage and saw that some letters had been delivered after she'd left that morning.

She picked them up and wandered into the sitting-room, switching on the gas fire and shifting a cat so she could sink into her favourite armchair. The cat promptly jumped on to her lap and she stroked it absently as she sifted through the mail. It was all junk, except for one white envelope embossed with the name of a London firm of solicitors.

She really didn't want to open that letter, so certain was she that the axe hanging over her head since Old Josh had died was about to fall, the last supporting thread cut by Tobias. She chewed her lip in dismay and looked around her.

Every room in the cottage was crammed with the sentimental clutter of her family's lifetime... books, photographs, paintings, ornaments, knick-knacks and goodness knew what else. The attics were crammed with hockey sticks, tennis rackets, toys and all sorts of oddments that were too precious to some member of the family to be thrown away.

Tobias knew nothing of this, hadn't wanted to know. In fairness, there was no reason for him to care anyway, except that if their positions had been reversed she'd have cared.

Tobias, though, had made it crystal clear he cared for nobody but himself. It was the difference between them, and, the more she considered it, the more insuperable the difference became.

Felice turned the letter over and over in her hands, then finally plucked up the courage to rip it open. Sure enough, a frightening-looking legal document fell into her lap. She unfolded it, scanned it quickly, then stared unseeing into space.

She couldn't believe it. It was a two-year lease for the cottage and the authorising signature at the bottom was Tobias's own.

Her fingers shook slightly as she traced his name, willing the bold strokes to tell her why he'd done this. He'd wanted her. She'd refused him. He wasn't magnanimous in defeat. So why?

CHAPTER SIX

THE sudden shrill of the telephone interrupted Felice's thoughts, and it wasn't an interruption she appreciated. She had some hard thinking to do. Really hard thinking.

'Felice?' an exasperated voice asked. 'At last! I've been trying to get you all morning. It's Charles,' the caller added belatedly.

Felice's eyebrows went up as she wondered, What now? Charles Martin had recently taken over his father's estate agency in Bixley and she couldn't imagine what he was exasperated about. She was about to enquire when he went on, 'Felice, are you there?'

'No, this is just my wraith,' she replied, feeling exasperated herself. Charles was a few years older than herself but they'd more or less grown up together, so there was no need to stand on ceremony with him. 'What bee's buzzing around in your bonnet? It isn't like you to lose your cool.'

'You won't be so cool yourself when you hear my news. Tobias Hunter has turned up—Old Josh's great-nephew!'

'Turned up where?' Felice asked, her nervous system going into overdrive at the very thought of Tobias being in her vicinity.

'I don't mean literally, although I gather he's been down to Woodlands to give it the once over.'

'I know,' Felice replied, her alarm vanishing. 'He made a quick inspection on Sunday. I drove him from the airstrip to the Hall.'

'You might have told me,' Charles grumbled. 'What sort of a man is he?'

'Oh, the usual, as far as I could tell,' Felice replied airily. 'You know, two arms, two legs and a head.' She wasn't about to go into raptures over exactly how excitingly Tobias's anatomy was put together.

'Is he anything like Old Josh?'

'Don't ask me, I was only the taxi driver,' she hedged. 'What's it to do with you, anyway? You're not professionally involved with the Hall, are you?'

'From this morning, yes. Mr Hunter's solicitors have appointed me his local agent.'

Then Tobias was selling. Felice didn't understand the disappointment surging through her. It wasn't exactly a surprise. She tried to stay chirpy as she replied, 'Congratulations, but what's it to do with me?'

'Everything, my girl,' Charles replied importantly. 'That's why I need to talk to you. Can you drop by the office this afternoon?'

Felice was puzzled but was too wary to show it. 'We're talking now,' she pointed out.

'Yes, but I hardly ever see you these days, and this is definitely worth a face-to-face. Until this afternoon, then.' He hung up before she could argue.

Felice replaced the phone thoughtfully. It wasn't like Charles to be cryptic or assertive, not with her, anyway. She dated him occasionally, but, although he was good-looking in his way, she'd never been really attracted to him.

A pity she couldn't say the same about Tobias!

Sighing, she whizzed around getting ready to go out again. Charles had dangled just the right carrot to get her into his office without any loss of time. She desperately needed to know what Tobias was up to. It might shed some light on why he'd so unexpectedly granted her the lease.

She'd have to be cautious, though. Charles was a name-dropper and a gossip, loving to give the impression he was on the inside of everything that went on in the neighbourhood. If he got an inkling that anything unusual had occurred between her and Tobias, it would be all round the village by morning.

That wouldn't bother Tobias, of course. For one thing he was too arrogant to care, and for another he wouldn't be around even to hear it. But she would, and it would bother her. She had to live here.

Sitting in Charles's office fifteen minutes later, she was discovering how difficult it was for an outgoing person like herself to be secretive without that causing comment in itself. 'Oh, come on, Felice,' Charles was saying sceptically, 'I'm sure you know more about Mr Hunter than you're letting on. He must have made some sort of impression on you.'

Felice's harassed mind whirled with impressions. The strength of Tobias's arms, the fire of his lips, the fury of his anger, the short-lived belief they were two of a kind and therefore made for each other...

But all these impressions were female and emotional, and for Charles's benefit she had to try to see Tobias as another man would. Not the easiest task in the world.

'He seems used to getting his own way.' That seemed a safe enough thing to say, but Charles looked so dissatisfied that she enlarged, 'Inheriting Woodlands didn't appear to mean much to him, so he can't be hard up for a penny or two.'

'Hard up for a penny or two?' Charles echoed in amazement. 'Haven't you made the connection?'

'What connection?' she asked blankly.

'He's the publishing tycoon. The T.B. Hunter of T.B. Hunter Consolidated Press! His media empire covers everything from newspapers and magazines to TV stations. Compared to all that, the Woodlands Estate is no more than a flea on an elephant's back.'

'It's the sort of flea I wouldn't mind scratching.' Felice tried to speak whimsically but her voice was hollow. With all that wealth and power, no wonder Tobias was used to women throwing themselves at him. His cynicism didn't stem from vanity, then, but from experience, as he'd maintained—but she still couldn't forgive him for lumping her in with all the rest of the women who pestered him.

He should have *known* she was different. She wasn't clear how, but he should have known, anyway!

'What are you looking so thoughtful about?' Charles asked suspiciously.

'Me? Oh, I—er—was just wondering what the "B" in T.B. Hunter stands for,' she improvised.

'Bertram. I've been doing a bit of research on him since I found out exactly who he is,' Charles explained. 'It was his father's name.'

A reminiscent smile she couldn't quite control curved Felice's lips. 'Tobias doesn't look like a Bertie. Anything but.'

'Why should you say that? Did anything happen between you two?' Charles asked, a speculative gleam lighting his greenish eyes.

Felice narrowly avoided blushing the colour of his red hair. 'Heavens, no,' she denied swiftly. 'It's just that Bertie doesn't seem the right sort of name for a Press baron. I mean, they're not exactly pussycats, are they?'

'Felice, you should be more respectful towards T.B. Hunter,' Charles chided her pompously. 'He's an extremely powerful man.'

In more ways than you know, she thought, but Charles was going on, 'His main base is in Canada but he has homes in other parts of the world, including London. It's our good fortune that he intends to use the Hall for weekends when he's in the UK.'

'Use it?' Felice exclaimed, completely taken by surprise. 'You mean he isn't selling?'

'No, and that's good for the village. A man with his resources will provide a lot of local employment—certainly more than Old Josh ever did, with his weird reclusive ways. Frankly, I thought the Hall would go the same road as of a lot of other big houses and be carved up into flats.'

Felice, astutely cutting through Charles's pomposity, knew that what he was really pleased about was getting a slice of the action. She kept her peace, though, because the implications of Tobias living at Woodlands was hitting her, blowing every other consideration from her mind.

Could it be Tobias's businesslike brain had slapped her in some mental file labelled 'unfinished business', and this was his way of keeping her close until he got the result he wanted? After all, there'd been enough conviction in his voice when he'd said there wouldn't be any peace for either of them until they were together.

Did he still, in spite of everything, feel that way?

A tiny shiver touched Felice's spine, and she winced with shame because it wasn't entirely unpleasurable. Then her eyes widened with amazement as Charles asked, 'How do you feel about working for Mr Hunter?'

'*Me*? You mean he needs a permanent chauffeur?'

'No,' Charles replied with a touch of impatience. 'Mr Hunter wants the gardens at the Hall redesigned and put in order.'

'But I didn't tell him I'm a landscape gardener. How could he possibly know?'

'He doesn't,' Charles replied, even more impatiently. 'What's the matter with you today? It's entirely up to me whom I hire on his behalf.'

'Oh, I see! He doesn't know you're hiring me, then?' She could relax. This obviously wasn't a dastardly plot on Tobias's part to get her in his clutches.

'Is there any reason why he should?' Charles demanded.

'No,' she replied lamely.

'Then what are you making all the fuss about?'

'I'm not. It just that he might—er—find it a bit odd that I have two jobs, that's all,' she improvised.

'Really, Felice, if this is your way of saying the job's too big for you, just come right out with it. I thought you'd be glad of a lucrative contract at this time of year.'

He was right. Normally she'd have jumped at the chance of such a big job, and working on the gardens of her beloved Woodlands would have had the added attraction of being a labour of love! But——

'Where is Tobias now?' she asked.

'Tobias?' Charles stared at her. 'Are you on first-name terms?'

Felice could have bitten off her tongue. 'He's a Canadian, not at all formal,' she waffled. 'Mind you, having a lady taxi driver probably took him by surprise and lowered his reserve. It—er—often happens with male passengers.'

'You made it sound as though you were friends,' Charles accused.

'No, we're definitely not that,' she replied, this time with enough conviction to lull his suspicions. 'Do you know where he is at the moment?'

'I understand he's returned to Canada for a month. He wants the gardens sorted out while he's away. Can you round up enough casual labour to get the work done in that time, plus keep up with your normal commitments?'

'Yes.'

'Then you'll do it?'

Felice hesitated only fractionally. Then once more she said, 'Yes.' After all, with Tobias safely out of the way, there wasn't a single reason why she should refuse. The decision made, she stood up. 'Thanks, Charles, for putting the work my way.'

He smiled at her. 'Thank me properly by letting me take you to the country-club dance at the end of the month.'

'Mine will be a family party. The twins and Janetta will be home for half-term, so unless you fancy ferrying all of us . . . ?'

'It's not what I wanted, but, if that's the only way I can get you, all right,' he grumbled.

Felice gave him her first real smile of the day. 'That's what I like about you, Charles,' she murmured. 'You're always so gracious.' Then she whisked herself out of his office before he had time to think of a suitable reply.

She only had one gardening job that afternoon, and normally she'd have used her spare time to catch up on her shopping and domestic chores. But this was no longer a normal afternoon.

At half-past two she was pacing the grounds of Woodlands Hall, her collies at her heels as she made copious notes of work that needed doing. Later on she could sort them into the right sort of order to get the job done smoothly and quickly.

She started in the walled kitchen garden. It was pitifully neglected, and she decided to restore it herself. She imagined it as it should be, with neat rows of vegetables and fruit to keep the kitchen supplied, and aromatic with the scent of fresh herbs during the growing season.

Her imagination went one further and supplied little children running along the paved paths, playing and laughing, and hopefully having fun without doing too much damage. She could even see their faces, and blinked hard as she realised they all looked like Tobias.

The impression was vivid enough to drive her out of one of the wooden gates set in the rose-coloured brick walls and on to a tour of the formal flowerbeds. There weren't many of them.

Most of the extensive grounds were kept in their natural grass and wooded state, needing little care apart from clearing away seasonal decay. Several severe gales had hit the island over the past weeks, though, and Woodlands had had its share of damage.

As time passed and Felice continued pacing the grounds, her notes growing ever longer, she found that few trees were actually down, although lots of branches had been ripped away or were hanging dangerously from otherwise healthy trees. She would have to sub-contract that sort of work to a tree specialist, and a plentiful supply of logs for the house would be a result of it.

Once more her imagination threw out an unwelcome picture—of Tobias and his mistress of the moment sitting by one of the Hall's many fireplaces, the logs glowing brightly, the rugs at their feet ideal for making love...

She was seared with an envy so sharp that she actually gasped, then she looked around self-consciously to see if anybody had heard her, but of course she was alone. Even the dogs had run off, rabbit-hunting among the wildly overgrown blackberry bushes down by the river.

They would find her again soon enough. The early February dusk was already falling and they would be wanting their supper. So should she, but somehow she'd lost much of her appetite since Sunday, and she wasn't quite finished yet.

She still had to inspect the magnolias planted around a summerhouse designed like a miniature Grecian temple. It was sited on top of a gentle hill so that anybody sitting there could enjoy a panoramic view over the gardens and meadows to the sea.

There was barely enough light left, and she'd have to get a move on or it would be pitch black before she got home. Yet she felt no inclination to hurry. Home was no longer a welcoming place where she could relax after a busy day, appreciating her solitude. Home now seemed loveless, barren.

Like herself without Tobias.

Exasperated, she thrust her notebook and pen in her pocket and tried to think more positively, but it was no use. Her melancholy deepened with the dusk as she approached the classical columns and portico of the little temple, gleaming ghostly white in the greying landscape.

The trees behind it were rapidly darkening into a shapeless mass against the sky. Felice knew she'd run out of time, and that the magnolias would have to be inspected another day. Still she walked on to the temple, though, drawn by a force more powerful than reason.

Perhaps she would find some kind of peace there that would drive away her depression. She wasn't a melancholic person, never had been, and she didn't know how to cope with a mood like this one. It was as though she was reaching out for something, and was desolate to the point of heartbreak because what she sought was beyond her reach.

'Felice.'

The drawling voice that so delighted and dismayed her came from nowhere, a sigh on the evening breeze, and she stopped, poised for flight, looking this way and that. Her heart was beating so rapidly that she could scarcely breathe, but when nothing moved she decided the sheer intensity of her yearning had played a diabolical trick on her.

She must be so wilfully and wretchedly obsessed with Tobias that her imagination had again conjured him up for her. It was eerie, and she joked to herself that any more of this kind of nonsense and men in white coats would be coming for her with a strait-jacket!

'Trespassing again?' that well-remembered deep and sensual voice asked.

It was Tobias! He was no trick of her fevered imagination. He was really here…somewhere. But where? Then she saw him materialising out of the shadows at the back of the temple. She couldn't quite suppress a gasp as she was seared with the pain, the pleasure, and the uncertainty of once more being close to him.

'I asked if you were trespassing again,' he repeated.

'Caught bang to rights,' she replied, determinedly making light of it although her heart was hammering so hard that she thought her ribcage would burst.

But her mind was racing to catch up with the situation, and all the messages it flung out were cautious. Tobias had no idea she was here legitimately to assess the state of the gardens, and she had no intention of telling him.

If she couldn't work on them anonymously, then she wouldn't work on them at all. Otherwise Tobias might think she was deliberately throwing herself his way again, perhaps hoping for a better offer than he'd made her last time.

The only better offer, of course, was marriage. The remembered humiliation of when he'd wrongly jumped to that conclusion himself made her cheeks burn so fiercely that she was profoundly grateful for the masking twilight. Much, much better to let him go on thinking she was trespassing.

She cleared her throat and the little sound was magnified by the intense silence of descending night, signalling to him a nervousness she was trying desperately to hide. Gosh, now she'd have to say something, however inane, just to appear natural. 'I thought you were in Canada,' she managed at last.

'How did you hear that?'

'Oh, native tom-toms,' she replied carelessly.

Tobias was leaning against one of the classical columns supporting the little temple's portico, his arms folded, as relaxed as she was tense. 'The tom-toms got the timing wrong,' he said. 'I don't fly to Canada until tomorrow, but, to get back to the point, how are trespassers punished in these parts, Felice?'

She felt the sensitive hairs at the nape of her neck rise but she replied with a good assumption of unconcern, 'Usually they're let off with a few harsh words and a caution, something you're good at if my memory serves me rightly.'

'There's nothing wrong with your memory, but is it punishment enough for a girl who never learns?'

Tobias eased himself away from the pillar and came deliberately towards her. Felice quivered with a thrill that wasn't quite alarm. Well, yes, alarm, but it was heavily laced with something else. Anticipation. She was waiting, the very stillness of the evening was waiting, for what he would do next.

She lifted her chin defiantly and stood her ground. After all, whatever Tobias took it into his mind to do, she'd already discovered there was a point beyond which he wouldn't go.

Wasn't there? Her confidence ebbed but she couldn't—wouldn't!—back down now. She was much too proud.

'You know, Felice,' Tobias murmured, 'you really shouldn't raise your chin at me like that. Given the sort of man I am, it makes only one punishment possible.'

His big hands grasped her shoulders and she felt the shock and delight of being pulled roughly against his hard body. Her gasp was smothered by his lips coming down on hers with ruthless intent. He wilfully, deliberately, kissed her into panting submission, and then he let her go.

'How would you rate that, Felice?' he asked mockingly. 'Punishment or reward?'

'You—you——' she gasped ineffectually, drawing the back of her hand over her lips as though to wipe away the taste and temptation of him for ever.

'Take it as a lesson never to trespass unprotected on my land after dark. I could have been any man, and you'd have been just as helpless.'

'Any man would have been preferable to you,' she flung at him, 'and this land was perfectly safe until you came here. Besides, I'm not unprotected! I have my dogs with me!'

'I don't see any dogs.'

'They're down by the river chasing rabbits. They'd be here in a flash if I whistled them.'

'Then why didn't you whistle them?'

Felice saw too late the trap she'd fallen into. She could scarcely confess that, mesmerised by his powerful effect on her as usual, she'd forgotten all about the dogs. A very Freudian oversight.

Tobias came to the same conclusion. 'You didn't want to be protected,' he breathed, and swept her back into his arms. His lips sought and claimed hers with a triumph she couldn't deny, and yet she was more frightened than she had ever been before.

This wasn't brutality. It was an act of possession. Tobias was confident now that she was his for the taking. And she wasn't. She wasn't!

She was powerless against his strength so she had to find some other way to fight free, and yet it was so very difficult to think of anything with her mind and senses reeling under the onslaught of his passion.

Her passion.

Oh, grief!

It was at that moment Tobias raised his head to look at her, giving her vital moments to recover some shreds of self-possession. She couldn't bear him to think she was won so cheaply and easily, and so she said, 'If I'm supposed to be showing suitable gratitude for the lease on the cottage, I'd rather you raised the rent.'

She had, it seemed, hit on just the right thing to stop Tobias dead in his tracks. He flung her away from him and ground out, 'You bitch! I didn't issue that lease to put you under obligation to me.'

'Then why did you?' she cried. 'And why are you coming to live here if you hate the place? It doesn't make sense—unless you can't bear the thought of a woman rejecting you, so you have to keep on trying!'

There, she'd said it, put into words the doubts and distrust that had bedevilled her since she'd opened his solicitor's letter and the lease had fallen into her lap.

Tobias said pithily, 'I made a point of reading the inspection report on the cottage made by my great-uncle's executors after his death. It confirmed what you'd told me, that the cottage had been restored to the highest possible order, and kept in that condition. Since there was no record in my great-uncle's accounts that he'd borne the cost, I decided you deserved the lease.'

'Oh,' Felice said, feeling a little foolish.

'Yes, "oh",' he mimicked angrily, 'and, as for my decision to keep the Hall, you can blame yourself for that.'

'Me?' she asked uncomprehendingly.

'Yes, you. I'm thirty-six years old and it's time I was thinking about the next generation. Woodlands Hall might not be to my taste, but you were right about its being a great place to raise children. I'm keeping it for that purpose.'

'*Purpose*?' she echoed. 'But—but—children aren't a *purpose*! They're a result of love.'

'They are, or should be, a result of a contract between two people who are attracted to each other, and it doesn't have to be a marriage contract. A business one can give children the same protection. In fact, it can give them even more, since it can't be nullified as easily as a marriage contract can.'

'A marriage isn't a contract,' Felice gasped, horrified. 'It's an exchange of sacred vows between two people in love.'

Tobias laughed sceptically. 'When did you last read the divorce statistics? I'm one of them, and I don't intend to ever be one again.'

So he'd been married, and unhappily by the sound of things. It explained a lot—but not enough! Felice said forthrightly, 'Whatever's happened to you in the past, you can't let it embitter your future. Not if you intend to have children! It wouldn't be fair. It wouldn't even be *decent*!'

'It's realistic, which is more to the point, and if only you could overcome your woolly-headed notions of marriage you'd admit it.'

'Woolly-headed?' she objected fiercely. 'I'm not woolly-headed!'

'Yes, you are. Face facts, Felice. You are as attracted to me as I am to you and——'

'No!' she broke in hotly. 'No!'

'Yes,' he continued inexorably. 'Every time we touch proves that beyond any denial. It's biological, and I can only suppose it's because we met at a time when we both have different needs to be expressed. Mine is for children, and yours is for the Hall. It makes sense to merge those needs into a mutually beneficial relationship that will result in children for me and the Hall for you. All nice and neat and legally tied up so that there are no nasty shocks for either of us at the end of it.'

'No,' Felice whispered, aghast. 'No!'

'You'd say yes fast enough if I deceived you with a lot of piffling love-talk,' he retorted. 'I'm doing you the honour of being honest with you, offering you a steady relationship without the drawbacks of deception and disillusion. We will both know precisely where we stand with each other at all times and, believe me, in the long run that beats anything as transitory as so-called love.'

Felice knew he was cynical, but she couldn't believe he was as coldly calculating as this. Revulsion made her cry, 'That isn't an honour. It's disgusting!'

'Still holding out for marriage, Felice?' he mocked. 'Well, I'm afraid you're overrating your power over me again. I'm interested, but I could just as soon get interested in somebody else. Somebody who will have and raise my children on my terms.'

'Then go and find her! I'll admit I love the Hall, but not enough to take you along with it! And that should prove to you that if anybody's overrating their power here, it's you.'

'I gave you credit for being a sensible woman, Felice, but you're really rather stupid,' he retorted harshly. 'Haven't you learned yet not to cut off your nose to spite your face?'

'My nose, my face,' she retorted angrily. She was doubly angry to find how childish she sounded even to her own ears, and that goaded her to add, 'I'll never be your mistress, Tobias Hunter. Attracted to you, huh! I don't even like you!'

There was another silence, and somehow Tobias always seemed even more dangerous when he was silent than when he was saying something. Her nerves cringed as he warned ominously, 'The temptation to prove you a liar is almost irresistible, Felice, so you've never needed protection quite as much as you do at this moment. You'd better whistle for your dogs.'

Felice didn't argue. She whistled.

CHAPTER SEVEN

THE dogs came hurtling out of the darkness and flung themselves joyfully at Felice as though they hadn't seen her for a week. She made a fuss of them, then called them to order. They sat obediently, tongues lolling, the white fur on their faces and ruffs distinctive in the darkness, showing their collie breed.

'So that's your protection,' Tobias said, looking them over. 'They're not exactly slavering Rottweilers, are they?'

'They'd give anybody a hard time, if necessary,' she replied crossly, thinking that Tobias was very shrewd. There was no hint of aggression in his voice now, nothing to make the dogs react with hostility to him.

In fact, when he clicked his fingers they went willingly to him, and fussed around him as though he were a lifelong friend. The traitors, she thought, but she wasn't surprised. She wasn't proof against Tobias's charm herself, in those rare moments when he chose to warm her with it.

Only remembered moments now, she thought wistfully, almost envious of the dogs as Tobias's strong hands alternately ruffled and smoothed their silky coats. She said involuntarily, 'You can't be all bad, not if the dogs like you.'

He straightened up, and, although it was too dark to read his expression, she thought he sounded regretful as he said, 'Unfortunately, you seem to have an uncanny ability to bring out the worst in me. When I'm with you,

93

I find myself saying and doing things I never intended to.'

Felice's pulses leapt with hope as she sensed he was coming as close to lowering his guard as it was possible for him to. It was on the tip of her tongue to confess, That's the way you affect me, too, when he went on, 'If only you could face up to facts, I reckon we'd have a lot going for us.'

'Everything's what you reckon, isn't it?' she replied sadly, feeling that the moment to re-establish rapport with him had come and gone before she could do anything about it. 'What I reckon doesn't count.'

'It might, if you cared to persuade me.'

His voice was soft, encouraging. Felice's wayward heart began to thump in a painfully erratic way, but she'd lost the courage to lower her own guard. Once more she was afraid of weakening, and exposing herself to his scorn, so she retorted spiritedly, 'Me, persuade you? If ever I'm that hard up, I'll let you know.'

The moment she said it, she regretted it, but it was too late. Tobias snapped, 'That does it! I've finished with wasting my time on you. Don't trip over any more mythical roots on your way off my land——'

'It wasn't a mythical root!' she broke in furiously. 'It was real.'

'—because I won't be there to catch you,' he continued inexorably. 'In fact, I hope you break your damned neck!'

With that, he sheered off into the darkness, leaving her alone. That round to me, she thought, but she felt too forlorn to enjoy her triumph. The dogs were hesitating, looking from Tobias's retreating form to her, as if asking for guidance.

'We've been dumped,' she told them, saying it aloud in a masochistic need to hurt herself so that she could forget how much she was already hurting. 'It's what I wanted and what I've got. And I feel so happy about it that if I'm very, very lucky I *will* break my damned neck!'

A sketchy night's sleep brought little solace but a lot of resolution. As soon as her bank opened on Thursday morning, Felice converted the eight years' saved rent into a cheque made out to T.B. Hunter, enclosed it with a brief note of thanks for the lease, and sent it off to Tobias's solicitors.

There! That should prove to him that she wasn't, and never had been, a gold-digger. She didn't look too closely into why she needed to prove anything to him when he was determined to think the worst of her, anyway. She just accepted that she needed to.

It took all her resolution not to send his lease back to him, too. But, for all Tobias believed she couldn't face up to facts, she knew it would be an unforgivable piece of self-indulgence to fling away the family home while her brothers and sister were still dependent on her.

And money was the reason she decided to go ahead with restoring the gardens at Woodlands. She'd faced a few financial crises over the years, and, although she'd managed to survive them, she'd always had the security of knowing she could draw on the rent if the worst came to the worst.

Now she had no such security, and the Woodlands contract would give her a little nest egg if another cash crisis occurred. All right, so Tobias would be paying her, but it would be money honestly earned.

The nitty-gritty was that she had to go on being what she'd learned to be so well—practical—however much it bruised her spirit and wounded her pride. And, if that wasn't facing up to unpleasant facts, what was?

With teeth clenched and a determined smile pinned to her face, she spent the rest of the week reorganising and delegating her regular work, and recruiting a small army to work at Woodlands, so that first thing Monday morning the work was able to begin.

At first Felice, in spite of all her resolution, couldn't help feeling nervous. Tobias was so unpredictable that she kept expecting him to step out from behind every tree. Eventually she settled down, reminding herself she had his own word for it that he was in Canada.

Besides, if he did return unexpectedly, the worst he could do was run her off his land. She stood in no danger of being assaulted, because she'd succeeded so well in killing off whatever desire he'd had for her.

The tragedy was that she hadn't managed to do the same efficient job on herself.

Tobias, unfortunately, was very much still with her. If not in body, then in mind and spirit. She didn't want to think about her heart. It was numb, and as the days passed the fact that her integrity was still intact became less and less of a consolation.

There was relief of a sort on the following Saturday with the arrival home for half-term of Janetta, fully eighteen years old now and almost a carbon-copy of Felice, except that she hadn't grown as tall and curvaceous.

She shared Felice's affinity for the land and didn't mind hard work, so as soon as she'd unpacked she joined Felice in the kitchen garden at Woodlands.

'It's weird being here legitimately,' she confided to Felice as they dug out rows of cabbages that had gone to seed. 'I keep expecting to have to make a run for it.'

'I know the feeling,' Felice sympathised. 'Being a trespasser's a lot more fun, but it's still a thrill for me to be working on these gardens.'

Janetta tossed a cabbage on to the heap in a wheelbarrow and said, 'You've always had a special love for Woodlands, haven't you? What's the new owner like? Did you tell me his name?'

'Er—no. It's Tobias. Tobias Hunter.' Felice was glad that exertion had already flushed her cheeks. It was terrible to react like a flustered teenager at the mere mention of his name. It was even more terrible to be less than honest with her sister, but she preferred to lick her wounds in private.

'Tell me about him,' Janetta invited.

'I don't know much, except that he's Canadian, a Press baron, and intends to live here for some part of the year. He's in Canada at the moment and he wants the gardens sorted out by the time he returns. That's in about three weeks.'

Felice had no intention of revealing Tobias's reason for keeping Woodlands, far less the part he'd wanted her to play in it—when he'd still wanted her. She winced as a pang of regret shot through her, and then was angry with herself for feeling any regret at all. Tobias simply wasn't worth it. Why, oh, why did she keep having to tell herself that?

'The twins will pitch in as well,' Janetta replied. 'When are they due home?'

'Next Friday. Their rugby tour overlapped the end of term, and they're spending a few days with Nick Holt—you remember the boy who came to us for Christmas because his parents were abroad?'

'Will I ever forget?' Janetta quipped, grinning. 'Sixteen years old and he fell in love with me! I'd forgotten how intense puppy love could be.'

'You poor old lady!' Felice exclaimed, throwing a muddy cabbage at her. 'You're still at the puppy-love stage yourself.'

'I'm not at any stage,' Janetta retorted, tossing the cabbage back. 'I've got college to get through and a career to launch before I'll have any time for that sort of distraction.'

'Very high-minded of you,' Felice smiled, ending the game by dropping the battered cabbage in the wheelbarrow. Janetta obviously had no idea how much of a 'distraction' love could be. Not that she had much herself. What she felt for Tobias couldn't possibly be love...

She was relieved when Janetta changed the subject by asking, 'Seen anything of our least-favourite cousin lately?'

Felice had no trouble identifying Serena, and as she loosened more cabbages in the soil she replied, 'No, she hasn't been down for ages. She phones occasionally, though, when she gets a particularly good job. One that gets her in the fashion mags or takes her overseas. Or both.'

'Envious?' Janetta asked thoughtfully.

'No,' Felice replied, laughing genuinely for the first time that week. 'I'm a country bumpkin and probably always will be. Her life is my idea of hell, and just as well. I'm built more like a Las Vegas showgirl than a catwalk model. Why do you ask?'

Janetta pushed a tendril of hair away from her face, her gloved hand leaving a muddy smear across her cheek.

'It worries me, sometimes, your slaving away down here to get me and the boys through school.'

'There's no slaving about it,' Felice replied quickly. 'I like my work.'

'I know you do, but you should be married with your own family by now. You're the type.'

'Is that what you think? Well, the minute I meet Mr Wonderful I'll drop you all like so many hot bricks,' Felice promised lightly as she dug out the last of the cabbages. 'The trouble is, Mr Wonderfuls never seem to find their way here.'

Until Tobias had come to Woodlands...

The thought came unwanted, unbidden, and Felice chased it away by reminding herself she'd only *thought* Tobias was wonderful in those first moments of meeting—before he'd had a chance to prove he was the very opposite.

'I suppose you're right,' Janetta agreed. 'It would do you good to get off the island for a while. Are you going to return to university when we're off your hands?'

That had always been Felice's plan, but now she wasn't so sure. Somehow, nothing in the future held much appeal since she'd met Tobias. 'I haven't really thought about it,' she replied, ending the conversation by wheeling the barrow away to the compost heap.

When she returned, Janetta had her hands on her back and was stretching. 'My muscles are screaming for mercy. I must be out of practice with this sort of work.'

'I should have eased you in gently,' Felice apologised contritely. 'Would you rather go back home and get a meal ready? Say for six o'clock? That would be a big help.'

'It would be a bigger help to me,' Janetta replied with a rueful grin. 'What shall I cook?'

'Surprise me.' Felice wasn't going to admit that lately she'd gone off her food, or Janetta would be asking questions it would be extremely difficult to answer.

All in all, Felice had lots to ponder on as Janetta left and she carried on working. The casual hands she'd hired were all hard workers, so the work was well on schedule. Seeing the gardens lose their neglected air and become well-tended, almost loved, was about the only pleasure still left to her.

She always felt dissatisfied, peace and contentment a thing of the past, and she constantly had to check herself to stop her unaccustomed misery from showing. She knew very well what the cause was, but the cure was still one she couldn't contemplate.

No, she told herself grimly, she just had to get on with it until time got her over it. The 'it' being her yearning for Tobias, of course.

Thursday brought a shock in the form of a letter from his solicitors. Pinned to it was the rent cheque. In dry legal terms she was informed that it was being returned because the estate of Joshua Hunter, deceased, had been wound up and closed. Furthermore, his executors took the view that Mr Hunter had regarded her as a caretaker rather than a tenant, so no monies had ever been due.

The letter was signed this time by the senior partner in the firm, and seemed to have nothing whatsoever to do with Tobias. So her determination to prove to him that she wasn't a gold-digger had been a waste of time, and that quite robbed her of her relief at having some financial security again.

Why was it that, whatever she did, Tobias always seemed to triumph?

She was still brooding about it that afternoon when she had to drive into Bixley to tend the garden of a lonely pensioner who wouldn't accept a substitute for her—mostly, Felice suspected, because she always lingered for a cup of tea and a chat, however busy she was.

Afterwards, she stopped off at the cottage before returning to Woodlands. She'd promised to put a casserole Janetta had prepared into the oven. She was just closing the oven door when Janetta burst into the kitchen and accused, 'You sneaky thing!'

'Me? Why?' Felice asked, startled.

'The dogs and I were in the greenhouse at Woodlands when I was grabbed from behind, spun round and jolly nearly kissed. And by the most gorgeous man! At least, I think that was what he meant to do,' Janetta exclaimed, her eyes sparkling with mischief rather than outrage. 'Then I was dropped like a hot coal and told, "Sorry, I thought you were your sister".'

'*Tobias* . . .' Felice breathed, her heart lurching drunkenly between joy and despair.

'Yes, *Tobias*!' Janetta repeated wickedly. 'Honestly, I could wring your neck. Here's me fretting about you wasting away while you get us through school, and all the time you've got a hunky caveman tucked away. I tell you, I was absolutely gob-smacked!'

'If you picked up that expression at school, you can leave it there,' Felice snapped, her nerves too strung-out to cope with Janetta's amusement. 'I haven't got a hunky caveman.'

'Tell that to Tobias,' Janetta scoffed. 'He's waiting for you right now. Phew! I almost wished I was you.'

'Stay away from Tobias. He's—he's——' Words failed Felice. She couldn't tell Janetta exactly what Tobias was without giving away the whole story. She could only look into her laughing eyes and finish lamely, 'He's best avoided. He seems to think women are toys, there to be played with when it suits him.'

'He seemed serious enough to me. He looked sort of *robbed* when he realised I wasn't you. He must have been fooled by that old leather coat I borrowed from you, and because my hair's in a pigtail, the way you wear yours when you're working. What's more, the dogs didn't go for him, so they couldn't have been as surprised as I was.'

'They like him,' Felice admitted, her mind refusing to work fast enough to fib her way out of this predicament.

'They're not the only ones, are they?' Janetta challenged. 'Oh, come on, now! You surely don't expect me to believe he'd grab you like that if you didn't want him to. If that were true, you'd never go near the place.'

'I told you, I thought he was in Canada,' Felice replied weakly. 'We—I—well, there was a bit of a situation between us but it's finished now. I thought it would be safe to work on the gardens while he was away. You know how I love the place, and the money will be useful.'

'And that's all there is to it?' Janetta questioned, watching her closely. 'I don't mean to be a pain, but Tobias definitely acted as though he had some kind of claim on you.'

'Well, he hasn't.'

'You mean he's fallen for you and you haven't fallen for him?'

'No, I don't mean that.'

'What do you mean, then?' Janetta wasn't laughing now, and, when Felice failed to answer, she mused, 'You haven't been your usual self since I got home. Gosh, don't tell me you've fallen for him and he only fancies you.'

'I haven't fallen for him,' Felice denied vehemently.
'I might have if—if——'

'Yes?' Janetta urged.

'Oh, can't you be a really nice sister and stop asking
awkward questions?'

'No!' Janetta wailed. 'I refuse to be treated like some
cloistered kid who needs to be protected from real life.'

'Oh, do you?' Felice snapped, her temper fraying as
badly as her nerves. 'When it comes to Tobias Hunter,
I'm the one who needs to be protected. Or I was!'

Janetta's resentment vanished. The sparkle came back
into her eyes and she breathed, 'Who'd have thought
life on the island could be this exciting?'

Felice's voice almost broke. 'It isn't a joke, Janetta.'

'Heavens, no, it's the most romantic thing I've ever
heard. And to think he's waiting for you right now.
Doesn't it just make your toes curl?'

'No, it doesn't.'

'It will when I tell you the rest of it,' Janetta predicted.

'What?' Felice asked apprehensively.

'Tobias said that if you don't go to him he'll come
looking for you.'

'If he thinks I'm going to go running to him he's got
another think coming,' Felice exclaimed indignantly.
'He's obviously too used to people jumping whenever
he cares to crack the whip. Me, I'd rather hang about
and have some coffee.'

'Good thinking,' Janetta approved. 'Sometimes it pays
to be different. What if he comes after you, though?
What do you reckon he'll do?'

Felice, setting about making the coffee, shrugged to
avoid answering. Not for anything was she going to
confess that that particular question was quietly
shredding her nerves to ribbons and making the cups

rattle. From what she knew of Tobias, he was capable of doing anything.

Janetta was watching her like a hawk, but it wasn't until her sister sat at the kitchen table to drink her coffee that she pleaded again, 'Please, please, tell me what has been going on between you two.'

Felice sighed, 'I suppose I shall have to.' She was too keyed up to sit herself, and so she leaned against a kitchen counter and gave a carefully censored version of the situation between herself and Tobias.

The trouble was that her romantically minded sister was more than capable of filling in the gaps, and colouring with purple passion situations Felice imagined she'd made sound fairly innocuous.

Janetta also managed to wangle further information by asking questions that were very hard to dodge. One that almost floored Felice was, 'What was the last thing he said to you?'

Felice had a searing picture of Tobias in the dusk at Woodlands. She felt scorched again by his arrogant fury, and felt once more the crumpling of her heart as she'd recklessly defied him. She forced some coffee down her reluctant throat and admitted, 'He said he hoped I'd break my damned neck.'

'Wow!' Janetta exclaimed, as though that were the most romantic sentiment expressed since Romeo courted Juliet. 'You really have got under his skin!'

'No, I've got between him and his ego.' Felice was finding it very hard not to watch the kitchen clock. As the minutes ticked by, her bravado was wearing thin. She really didn't want Tobias to come after her. Even less did she want him thinking she was shirking an inevitable confrontation out of cowardice.

'He didn't strike me as an ego-freak,' Janetta replied thoughtfully.

'You don't know the man.'

'I do, sort of. We talked, you know, once we'd sorted out his mistaking me for you.'

'What about?' Felice demanded.

'You, the family, that sort of thing. He was surprised to find out you were a landscape gardener, and even more surprised to learn you were *his* gardener.'

'I can imagine,' Felice said wryly. 'That's why he wants to see me—to give me the sack. Well, there's no point in putting off the evil moment any longer. It's not as though I want to work at Woodlands if he's going to be there.'

'Are you sure about that?' Janetta asked, wrinkling her lovely nose doubtfully.

'Yes, I'm sure. Just promise me you won't mention a word about it to anyone. I'd hate anybody else getting the wrong idea.'

'Mum's the word,' Janetta agreed, although she looked disappointed.

Felice had to be satisfied with that, and as she drove the van to Woodlands with Janetta still chattering beside her she listened with only half an ear. All her thoughts, all her nervous energy, were wrapped up in seeing Tobias again.

In a curious way she felt they'd never really been apart, and that everything that had happened to her without him had simply been a distraction, a diversion from the main stream of her life. Such thoughts didn't do her confidence any good.

She dropped Janetta and the dogs off by the greenhouse where her sister had met Tobias, parked the van and walked through lightly falling rain to the back door

of the house. It was open but there was no sign of its
new master.

Felice called. Nobody answered. She took off her
muddy wellingtons and padded into the huge kitchen in
her thick woollen socks. She walked along the service
passage until she reached the main one with its ornately
carved doors. She stopped again. Tobias was close. She
could sense him.

She was so tense it was hard to keep her voice from
quivering as she called again, 'Hello? Is anyone home?'

'Hello, Felice.'

Tobias spoke softly. The tiger was purring, then, its
claws still sheathed, but as she turned with a painfully
pounding heart she warned herself not to be deceived.

'Hello, Tobias.' Her own voice was soft, too soft, but
it was the sight of him that weakened her defences. Here,
in tall, broad and vibrant life was the phantom of her
night and daytime dreams. Her hungry gaze rested on
his shock of dark hair, his dark grey eyes and his firm
lips . . . those lips that could tease so cruelly or satisfy so
blissfully.

He was dressed casually enough in light blue jeans
and a round-necked sweater that revealed the strong
column of his throat, but his very aura spoke of wealth
and power. Suddenly Felice was conscious of what a
sorry picture she must look with her windswept plaited
hair, and her rough working clothes.

She became acutely conscious of her bootless feet as
his gaze roamed slowly over her face and body and came
to rest questioningly on her unglamorous woollen socks.
She said in a surly voice, 'I left my wellingtons at the
back door. They were dirty.'

'The back door . . .' he repeated. 'So that's why I didn't
hear you arrive. Why didn't you use the front?'

'The back door seemed more appropriate. It's the tradesman's entrance, after all.'

Deliberately she brought their new relationship into focus. It was a desperate, self-torturing attempt to get this confrontation over and done with.

It might not be what she really wanted, but now that she'd seen him again and all the emotions that had bedevilled her during his absence struck with renewed force she knew they could no longer go on as they were. It would surely be better to make the break between them final and irrevocable.

Wouldn't it?

CHAPTER EIGHT

Now he could fire her, Felice thought, wishing her heart wouldn't pound so painfully. She'd made it easy for him. Any moment the axe would fall. Then she could go away and lick her wounds in private, and hope that some time over the next fifty years or so they would heal.

But Tobias didn't take the opening she offered. Instead, he stood back and held wide the door he'd come out of. It was a silent invitation for her to enter. Felice tried to remember what room it was but she couldn't be sure.

Not a bedroom, anyway, not here on the ground floor, but she was reluctant to be closed in anywhere with Tobias. However large a room might be, there was something about him that seemed to shrink all available space to just the two of them.

And he was being much too quiet, much too restrained. She said uneasily, 'I prefer to talk right here, thank you.'

'Frightened of me, Felice? I thought you were too spirited for that.'

'Of course I'm not frightened of you!' Her denial came from pride, and her pride was always fierce. 'I'm wary of you, and you can hardly blame me for that.'

'I don't, but everything is different now. My female employees never have anything to fear from me.'

'I'm not going to be your employee for long, am I? In fact, you don't have to fire me. I quit.'

'Why?'

108

Felice was astonished. 'You can't want me working for you!'

'On the contrary, I have a proposition to put to you that will have you working for me in a much closer capacity.' He saw the alarm flash in her eyes and added, 'A business proposition, so stop being foolish and come in.'

Felice was annoyed to find herself obeying, but she was so baffled and intrigued by this new, restrained Tobias that she couldn't do anything else. One way or another, he knew how to keep her guessing.

And hoping, an inner voice sighed...

She ignored it and glanced swiftly round at the book-lined shelves and heavy leather armchairs. She was in the library, a warm library, so the heating had obviously been switched on. She supposed it was as neutral a ground as she could hope for. There was still something very defensive about the way she stood in the middle of the room, though, until she realised Tobias wasn't going to sit down unless she did.

Her strung-out nerves soon told her it wasn't a good idea for her and Tobias to be standing within arm's reach of each other, so she dropped quickly into the nearest armchair.

He reached out and touched her hair. 'You're wet,' he said. 'You should take better care of yourself.'

'Just a little rain. I'll soon dry,' she replied, unable to accept his concern and pulling away from him.

He looked at her for long, thoughtful moments, then shrugged and sat opposite her. His eyes had a brooding quality and almost seemed to devour her. Sitting passively under his scrutiny wasn't easy, far from it, and she couldn't help jumping when he said suddenly, 'I want you to be my housekeeper.'

Felice couldn't have been more surprised if he'd slapped her round the face. 'B-but I'm a landscape gardener,' she stuttered. 'I loathe housework.'

Tobias did something treacherous, then. He leaned across the open space between them and gathered her restless hands in his calm, strong ones. He studied her open palms and murmured, 'Smooth, just as I remember them. You must wear gloves when you're working.'

'Of course I do.' She snatched her hands away, but his touch had already sent sensuous messages tingling throughout her body. It was terrible how the slightest physical contact between them not only awoke her senses but had them sitting up and begging for more.

'You can still supervise the work in the grounds, and I certainly don't expect you to skivvy in the house. In fact, I forbid it,' Tobias told her levelly. 'You can hire all the staff you need to attend to that. The cost isn't important but the objective is.'

'What objective?' Felice asked faintly.

'I want the house fit for a lady to live in, and I want that objective gained in the least possible time.'

'I didn't know you knew any ladies,' she said. She couldn't quite believe her own rudeness, but the penny had dropped with a clang that outraged her. Tobias, the man she might have loved, was asking her—*her*!—to prepare the house she loved for the mistress he intended to install in it.

It was diabolical. The perfect revenge on her for refusing to be his mistress herself! Yet surely even Tobias couldn't be that diabolical! Desperate to believe she'd misunderstood the situation, she asked, 'Why me? Why not an experienced housekeeper?'

'An experienced housekeeper would only see that everything was scrubbed and polished and properly maintained. In other words, Woodlands would be turned from a cheerless mausoleum into an equally cheerless showplace. I want Woodlands to be a *home*, and that's why I need you. You love the place. You could breathe some of that love into it, make it come alive.'

Tobias sounded so sincere, and was so much in tune with her own feelings, that she was actually moved. Then she remembered how skilful he was at manipulating her emotions, and she retorted indignantly, 'You must be mad! I'm not going to work here to be mauled whenever the fancy takes you.'

'Mauled?' he repeated quickly. 'Was that the way it seemed to you?'

Felice bit her lip and looked down at her hands, twisting and turning nervously in her lap.

Tobias followed her gaze and said, 'Relax, Felice. You're completely safe. I've already made it clear I never—maul my employees.'

'You were ready to maul my sister when you thought she was me!'

'I'd no idea you were working for me then, and what happened between Janetta and me was a regrettable mistake which we've sorted out with no hard feelings on either side. By the way, I must congratulate you on the way you've brought her up. She's a fine girl. You should be proud of her.'

Felice looked at him suspiciously, and accused, 'You're trying to side-track me. Whatever you sorted out afterwards, you were still ready to...to...'

'To what?' he prompted when words failed her. When she didn't answer, he went on, 'I was just pleased to see you—what I thought was you. I don't know what's surprising about that. Surely it makes sense, since anything deeper is out of the question, for you and I to be friends?'

'Why?' Felice asked, and she sounded so breathless that she wondered whether, within her, her heart was twisting as nervously as the hands she was trying desperately to still.

'Because I need you.'

Her heart turned over altogether, but mercifully she didn't have to reply because Tobias continued, 'I've been doing some serious thinking about Woodlands while I've been away. The reason I came back earlier than intended was to put my proposition to you. You could have knocked me down with a feather when Janetta told me you were already working in the gardens.'

'That's because I thought the job would be finished before you returned,' she answered, surly.

'I realise that, but, since you're available, taking on the house as well shouldn't cause you any problems.'

'What's causing me the biggest problem right now is that I'm still not convinced it has to be me!'

Tobias stood up. Involuntarily she drew back in her armchair but he walked straight past her. She watched him stop by one of the long windows overlooking the lawn that stretched up to the Grecian temple where last they'd met—and clashed.

She eyed his back and the broad set of his shoulders resentfully. It was soul-destroying, knowing all she did about him and yet still wanting to go over to him, put her arms around him and lean her weary head against his strong shoulders. She could almost feel the contact of her body against his, so powerful was her need, so hard the struggle to resist it.

Fearfully, she finally faced up to the truth that had been causing her so much misery—that if she hadn't fallen helplessly in love with him at first sight then she'd been such a short step away ever since that she couldn't tell the difference.

And she couldn't love him! The man she loved must be prepared to commit himself as fully to her as she did to him, and Tobias couldn't—*wouldn't!*—do that.

'Why you?' Tobias echoed at last. 'The answer is that it could only be you. The proof is out there in the gardens. You've only been working on them for a couple of weeks and already they look—loved. Can you give me the name of another contractor who would give them the same amount of care—as opposed to simply doing a professional job?'

Felice couldn't. That was the trouble with love, she thought resentfully; it showed. She was only surprised that Tobias was sensitive enough to recognise it.

'I thought not,' he said, as the silence between them lengthened. He turned to face her and continued, 'That's why I want you to take on the house as well. I won't be here to supervise much of the time, so I must have complete trust in whoever takes on the job. Feeling the way you do about Woodlands, you're not likely to make any mistakes.'

He wouldn't be here... did that quiver in her heart mean she was glad or sorry? She was so confused that she couldn't tell. She was also beginning to feel pressured, cornered, but in a very subtle way.

Somehow, Tobias was managing to make it sound so reasonable, so right, for her to take on the house—when in her mind she knew nothing could be more unreasonable, or more wrong.

Fighting for time to untangle her emotions, she said, 'Basically the house just needs a thorough spring clean and a few feminine touches, so what mistakes could a professional housekeeper make?'

Tobias returned to the chair opposite hers but this time he sat casually on the arm and leaned towards her. She felt threatened, but deliciously so, as the excitement caused by his closeness pulsed through her body.

She wondered if Tobias knew how she felt, and moving closer was a deliberate ploy to fluster her and affect her judgement. It was more than possible, considering how good he was at playing on her emotions. Look how he was using her love for Woodlands to get her to do what he wanted.

She must resist, be strong, no matter what he said!

But, loving Woodlands as she did, what Tobias said next couldn't fail to get through to her. 'When we first viewed the house together, you said how wonderful it was that some of the rooms are still hung with wallpaper dating back to when the house was built,' he recalled. 'Somebody with an unknowledgeable or unsympathetic eye might decide the paper should be stripped and replaced with something modern.'

'No, that would be vandalism!' Felice cried vehemently. 'That wallpaper is priceless, irreplaceable.'

'Then there are all those oak dressers you admired in the kitchen,' he went on thoughtfully. 'What if they were ripped out to make way for modern equipment?'

'Don't!' Felice's summer-sky eyes darkened with horror. 'There's room enough for improvements without any drastic measures like that. You mustn't let it happen, Tobias.'

'It won't with you in charge, will it?' he pointed out.

Felice felt trapped, and more so as he went on smoothly, 'You will have complete responsibility and, as it's only a temporary position, I'm sure you'll find it

more of a challenge than a burden. You don't strike me
as a girl to resist a challenge, so shall we consider the
matter settled and shake on it?'

He held out his hand. Too late she saw the trap he
had steered her into was sprung, and she protested helplessly, 'But I've no intention of working for you!'

'Don't look on it as working for me, look on it as
working for Woodlands,' he reassured her.

She would still have resisted, but Tobias smiled at her
in that friendly way that had first entranced her, and
somehow her hand just found its way into his.

Once more her body was betraying her brain, and once
more she inwardly crumbled at his touch. How safe she
felt with her hand in his like this, when she was actually
about as safe as she would be in a tiger's den. Which,
come to think of it, was exactly where she was.

It was her own fault, of course. She'd seen the trap
and yet still allowed herself to be beguiled into walking
straight into it. For all she knew, Tobias might be getting
a perverse kick out of ensnaring her so neatly, and
looking forward to her chagrin when she had to hand
over the restored house to his mistress.

What an idiot she was to get involved and yet... and
yet... when had she really had any choice? Love—no
less powerful for being unacknowledged—had dictated
all her actions since she'd met Tobias. And love, as she
was discovering now, was so much more persuasive than
common sense.

She was, as usual, both glad and sorry when he released her hand, and she sounded surly again as she
grumbled, 'What I don't understand is why you're suddenly so pernickety about what happens to Woodlands.
I thought you hated the place. You were scathing enough
when you called it a folly.'

'True, but I didn't know then that a folly could have its delightful aspects.'

Felice looked at him uncertainly. He sounded so ambiguous that for a moment she thought he was referring to her, not to the house. Then she supposed her imagination must be working overtime again. Needing clarification, though, she asked, 'You mean from the point of view of raising children?'

'That as well,' he replied cryptically. 'We mustn't forget the children, must we?'

She was none the wiser but again he smiled, and again her foolish heart lurched. Annoyed with herself, she snapped, 'I don't know who you think you're kidding, but it isn't me. You don't care tuppence about Woodlands. I do, and that's the only reason I'm taking on the job.'

'What do I care about, then, Felice?' he asked softly.

'I don't think you care very much about anything. All you're bothered about is whether the woman you bring here to have your children will take one look at all the neglect and head straight back to the city.'

'No, she won't do that,' he replied confidently. 'When she comes here, everything will be as perfect for her as if she'd organised it herself. It's the very least she deserves.'

Oh, God, he actually had somebody lined up already! There was no mistaking his warmth as he spoke of her. Felice was particularly sensitive to it because she felt so chilled herself. There was even ice crackling her voice as she asked, 'I suppose you expect me to say she's a lucky woman?'

'I never know what to expect from you, Felice, and that's why I'm sure our working relationship will be a very interesting one.'

'You said you wouldn't be here!' she cried.

'I won't be most of the time, but I should manage the odd day or the occasional weekend. There's no reason why that should bother you, is there?'

'No,' she agreed hollowly, since she could hardly do anything else. What was even more soul-destroying was that she knew, from here on in, she would be living for that odd day or occasional weekend...

When Janetta heard the news she exclaimed, 'Golly, Felice! I'm beginning to think you love the man if you've agreed to be his housekeeper! It's not exactly a job that's up your street, is it?'

'It's only a temporary position, and I'm only doing it so that Woodlands isn't spoiled by somebody with no feeling for the place. Besides, Tobias will hardly ever be there,' Felice replied defensively.

'I reckon he's got a nerve expecting you to prepare a nest for his mistress! I'd have told him what he could do with his job!'

Felice just smiled, shook her head, and refused to be drawn on the subject any further. She had so many other things to think about, not least the planning of the best way to set about restoring Woodlands.

After the initial briefing from Tobias, he'd become annoyingly vague. She was to chuck out what she thought was rubbish, install any modern equipment she thought necessary—in fact, do as she pleased so long as she didn't bother him with what he called tiresome trivia.

If she hadn't been so desperately worried about falling deeper in love with him, she would have been in her element, for what he'd actually given her along with a bunch of keys was permission to ransack Woodlands

from the attics to the cellars—something she'd been
wanting to do all her life.

By the time she was finished, she'd know all the
house's secrets…although, of course, she'd still be none
the wiser about what went on in the heart of the man
who owned all this dusty and neglected spendour.

Perhaps it was just as well that she was too busy to
brood too much. Early the next morning she left the
dogs with the still-sleeping Janetta and arrived at
Woodlands to make a detailed survey of the house to
decide exactly what needed to be done, and in what
order.

Once she'd sorted that out, she'd know how many staff
to hire. She'd noticed yesterday that the heating had been
switched on, and she was grateful for it as she left her
coat in the kitchen of the home wing and made her way
up the magnificent staircase to the second floor.

She'd decided to start on a high—with the bedrooms
in the home wing. They'd struck her as needing the least
attention when Tobias had whirled her through the house
on his initial inspection. Later she would get down to
the nitty-gritty of the domestic and the living-rooms.

She went logically from bedroom to bedroom, inspecting wallpaper, paintwork, carpets, curtains, furniture, prints, paintings and ornaments. The scrawlings
in the notebook she carried with her lengthened with
every room, and she smiled ruefully as it became increasingly obvious that Tobias had no idea of the scale
of the job he had thrust upon her.

In his usual autocratic way, he'd said he'd wanted the
house put to rights in the least possible time. What,
exactly, did he regard as the least possible time? By the
time Felice walked into the master bedroom, she'd come
to the conclusion that a year would be pushing it!

Her mind was so full of domestic details that she walked up to the huge four-poster with its scarlet hangings and quilts before she realised that the bed-clothes were rumpled. She stopped dead and stared in amazement.

This, obviously, had been Old Josh's room, but what was equally obvious was that Tobias was using it now.

She hadn't bargained on that. He hadn't asked her to engage any staff for his own comfort, so she'd assumed he'd only been making one of his lightning day trips. If he'd intended staying overnight on the island, he could have booked into any one of the dozens of comfortable hotels the island abounded with.

Why should a multi-millionaire used to every possible comfort choose to sleep in a house that had been un-inhabited for so long? It didn't make sense, but flung across the rumpled bedclothes were a pair of black pyjamas, and who could they belong to if not to Tobias?

Feeling as much of a trespasser as when she used to hide in the grounds, Felice tiptoed across the thick carpet and picked up the pyjama jacket. It was as seductive to her touch as the man himself. Pure silk, with the collar and cuffs ribbed with gold and a flamboyant 'T' em-broidered in gold thread on the pocket. She fingered the 'T' lovingly and was fighting off the urge to bury her face in the sensuous silk when a sound made her spin round.

Tobias, naked except for a white towel wrapped casually around his muscular hips, was silently sur-veying her from an arched doorway. Dear heaven, she'd forgotten the master bedroom had a lavish en suite bathroom! She'd forgotten everything in the need to touch the silken pyjama jacket that now slipped from her nerveless fingers to the floor.

Her wide, defenceless eyes registered that his hair was damp as though he'd just showered, and that his bare chest was glistening with moisture. She was conscious of an ache in the pit of her stomach, an ache that was so severe it was almost a pain.

Tobias looked exactly what he was—a virile, rampant male—and a primitive urge to mate with him parted Felice's soft lips and turned her knees to jelly.

Her hungry eyes roamed over his firm hard body and fixed on the black hair matting his chest. Involuntarily, she followed the dark, tapering line of hair until it disappeared below the fleecy towelling, and she was conscious of the most shameful disappointment that she couldn't see any more.

Too late she realised how blatantly and uninhibitedly her natural instincts were swamping and betraying her, and a slow, fierce blush fired her cheeks and body.

Total panic overcame her as she tried to claw her way back from pure, primitive instincts to conditioned, decently civilised behaviour. The transition was too swift, too contradictory for her to manage with any semblance of composure.

Tobias might be next to naked but she knew the one who was truly exposed here was herself, and she babbled with embarrassment, 'I b-beg your pardon. I wouldn't have b-barged in like this if I'd known y-you were here. I'd n-no idea you'd spent the night here.'

'Felice...' he breathed, as though he hadn't heard a word she'd said. 'My magnificent Felice...'

CHAPTER NINE

FELICE watched helplessly as Tobias's lithe strides cut to nothing the distance between them. How could he have called her magnificent? He was the magnificent one!

Then every thought was blotted out by the primitive call of his bare matted chest and the naked intent she read on his rugged face. *All man*, something deep within her whispered triumphantly. *My man.*

He was right before her, the musky male scent of him filling her nostrils, sensuously overlaying the clean smell of soap on his skin, the spicy tang of his aftershave. Her notebook fell from her nerveless fingers to join his pyjama jacket on the floor.

Then Tobias swore savagely and fluently, and sheered away from her.

'For a moment I forgot you were my housekeeper,' he muttered, picking up a dressing-gown flung carelessly over an armchair. 'Sorry, it won't happen again.'

He shrugged himself into the gown, tied the belt around his waist and turned to face her. 'Sorry about the language, too, but at least I've proved you're safe with me. I hope that means you'll keep the job.'

The job. Yes, of course! Preparing his house to receive his mistress, the one he'd selected to bear his children. How could she possibly have forgotten a thing like that? After all, he no longer really wanted her, Felice Lawson. She'd just happened to be there and, given the right opportunity, a tiger was hardly likely to turn into a pussycat overnight.

'If you'll leave a note downstairs when you're staying over, I won't barge in on you again like this. Now, if you'll excuse me, I'll be getting on,' she replied primly, stooping to pick up her fallen notebook.

As she straightened, Tobias touched her arm. 'There are still some things to be sorted out between us. Give me five minutes and we'll have breakfast together. A working breakfast.'

'Breakfast?' she repeated in dismay, and flinching as his touch seemed to burn through the wool of the long-sleeved blue dress she'd chosen as suitable for her new housekeeping role. 'There isn't a scrap of food in the house. Besides, I've already had breakfast.'

'In that case, we'll go to a hotel, and you can have coffee while I eat.'

'No, we won't!' she exclaimed in alarm. 'If I'm seen breakfasting with you it will be all over the neighbourhood by noon, and nobody's going to believe I'm just your housekeeper then.'

Tobias stared at her with an arrested expression on his face. 'Would that bother you?'

'Of course it would!'

'You're adorable when you're quaint,' he murmured. 'You make me feel I've strayed on to another planet. But I'm still starving, so where can we go that's private enough for us to talk and eat without your neighbours putting two and two together and getting their sums wrong?'

'You'd better come to the cottage,' she replied reluctantly, unable to come to terms with Tobias thinking her either adorable or quaint, and not sure whether it was a compliment, anyway. The adorable bit sounded all right but, given the kind of man Tobias was, the quaint bit could well be the kiss of death.

'I don't want to put you out, but the offer sounds good if you can cope.'

'I can cope,' she assured him. 'The twins haven't arrived home for half-term yet to devastate the larder, so I can guarantee something to sustain you. Er—how long do you need sustaining for?'

'Until I get to London. I'm flying back right after breakfast.'

Felice felt a pang at his leaving again so soon, but it was a pang she'd have to learn to live with. Looking at it coolly, calmly and sensibly, the more he was away, the better chance she'd have of recovering from stupidly imagining herself in love with him.

Unfortunately, it was very difficult to be cool, calm and sensible where Tobias was concerned, and she was far from recovering fifteen minutes later when he was sitting at the big, scrubbed table in the cottage's kitchen, and she was grilling bacon, tomatoes, mushrooms and sausages, and poaching eggs.

No, she was further away from recovery than ever. In fact, she felt almost—complete. Almost ridiculously happy.

She wasn't the least bit flustered by him watching her cook, either. Somehow, with Tobias in a mellow mood and the dogs curled up asleep at his feet, it all seemed so cosy and natural. It was only too easy to forget the antagonism that had caused so much bitterness and misunderstanding between them.

Well, not quite forget, perhaps, but to push it so far back in her mind that she was able to indulge in a little daydream that Tobias wasn't a rich, important man, and she wasn't his unimportant housekeeper, but that they were just man and woman.

Man and wife...

The daydream went too far at that point, and she came back to reality with a jolt. So good had been the dream, though, and so evocative the pictures it had conjured up, that she had to mock it by asking lightly, 'What heading does this come under in your scheme of things? Slumming?'

'If this was slumming, everybody would be fighting for a slice of it,' he answered comfortably. He looked around the cosy room with its ancient beamed ceiling, flagstoned floor and well-worn armchairs by the open fire, and added, 'You have a great capacity for home-making, Felice. I know you'll do as good a job on Woodlands.'

That, she thought with a sigh as she heaped food on to a warmed plate, was as good an illustration as any that he no longer saw her as a temptress. Well, that shouldn't upset her, should it? Her biggest grudge against him was that he'd only ever seen her as a body. She should be glad, not resentful, that he was becoming aware she had other possibilities. She couldn't have it all ways.

And yet...and yet...she wished that she could.

Why, she wondered, did he have this disturbing capacity for making her so dissatisfied? Every time she gained an inch with him in one direction, she felt she lost two in another!

That dissatisfaction, her treacherous inner voice whispered, is love. The unrequited kind. The kind that hurts the most...

'Blue suits you,' Tobias said unexpectedly. 'A frock suits you. I've never seen you in one before.'

'Thank you,' she replied, flushing slightly, and covering her confusion by serving his breakfast. 'I don't get much chance to wear frocks. Jeans are a part of my way of life.'

'Then it's a good thing you're changing your way of life.'

'Only temporarily,' she pointed out quickly.

Tobias neither agreed nor disagreed, but began to eat his breakfast. When he spoke again it was to say, 'This is delicious.'

'I'm all right with the basics but I'm not a dedicated cook,' she confessed, putting toast and a tea-tray on the table, and sitting opposite him. 'A little domesticity goes a long way with me, particularly when it comes to housework. Once I've got a house the way I want it, I'm only too happy to dump the chores on somebody else if I can.'

'That's what you'll be doing at Woodlands.'

'That's one of the reasons I took the job. I don't know why, but I've always preferred to work on the land. I was studying horticulture before I had to give up college. Maybe I should have been born a boy.'

'What a waste that would have been,' Tobias murmured.

There was another little silence between them as Felice wondered how to answer him. Then, to quieten her fluttering pulses, she decided the safest course was not to answer at all. Instead, she poured the tea, and it was only as she was handing his cup to him that she realised she hadn't asked him if he liked tea.

'Drat,' she said. 'Would you prefer coffee?'

'Tea's fine,' he replied easily. 'When in Rome...'

'You drink tea and chew a straw,' she interpreted wryly.

'I prefer to chew toast, thanks all the same,' Tobias said, biting into a slice. 'It's tastier.'

Felice giggled and, to her delight, Tobias smiled at her in the friendly, uncomplicated way that had so enchanted her when they'd first met. Warmth spread through her, bringing with it self-consciousness, and she reminded him a little shyly, 'You said there were still some things to be sorted out between us.'

'We're already sorting them out.'

'Are we?' she asked dubiously.

'Sure we are. What we really needed was to get to know each other better so we can develop a working relationship we can both trust. I reckon we're doing all right, don't you?'

'If you put it that way, yes, I suppose so,' she admitted slowly.

'Good, then I've gained the main objective of this trip.'

Felice frowned a little over that, and reached absently for a piece of toast. She nibbled it as she asked, 'Does everything have to have an objective with you?'

'Doesn't it with you?'

'I don't know. I've never really thought about it, but then I'm not obsessed with business.'

'Neither am I all of the time. I make decisions and then I delegate. That's what my staff is for, to give me time for a private life.'

'Time for Woodlands,' she mused, finishing her toast. 'Time for folly.'

'I wouldn't call it that, not any more. Whatever Woodlands is, I'm serious about it now.'

Yes, Felice thought, you certainly are. There was nothing more serious than planning a background for a relationship permanent enough to have children. She asked quietly, knowing that his answer might hurt, 'Am I right in thinking you've chosen the woman who'll—who'll——?'

'Share my life and bear my children?' Tobias finished for her. 'Yes, I've chosen her.'

His answer did hurt. Too much. It was a moment before she could catch her breath enough to say, 'It seems strange to me that you're not consulting her about the restoration of the Hall.'

'I'll worry about her. You worry about Woodlands,' he replied forcefully enough to discourage further questions. Then he asked one of his own, 'Where's your sister?'

Felice's mind was reluctant to leave the unknown woman willing to accept the terms which she'd found so objectionable, and she answered absently, 'Janetta's sleeping in. She had a date last night with Tom, a local farmer's son.'

'Do you ever take time off?'

'Not a lot,' she admitted. 'Driving a taxi at weekends rather restricts my social life.'

'Driving a taxi is something you won't have to do while you're working for me. In fact, I forbid it.'

'Oh, do you?' she exclaimed, her blue eyes sparkling with indignation. 'On what grounds?'

'On the grounds that I want all your energy devoted to Woodlands; and that you'll be so well paid you won't need to knock yourself out for some extra income.'

Far from being mollified, Felice retorted, 'You can't dictate what I should or shouldn't do for twenty-four hours a day.'

They were glaring at each other, teetering on the brink of another quarrel, then Tobias said unexpectedly, 'You're right. I shouldn't dictate to you. What if I make it a request? It would bother me if I thought you were working yourself into the ground.'

'You don't have to worry about me. I'm as tough as they come,' she replied, unable to accept that Tobias actually sounded worried about her. If she started believing that, next she'd be believing he actually cared about her! And he didn't. All he cared about was getting Woodlands fit for his mistress to live in.

'You don't seem so tough to me,' Tobias said softly, and she was almost beguiled into believing there was a caress in his voice. Clearly a case of wishful thinking!

She still felt jumpy and confused, though, and capitulating seemed to be the quickest way of getting herself back on even keel. 'All right,' she conceded. 'A request, I can live with. I just won't be forced.'

'As I well know,' he murmured, and he smiled at her in a way that made her feel more confused than ever. There was a quality in his smile that made her remember again the good moments they'd shared, before the bad moments had spoilt everything. It was like glimpsing a dream that should have died, but had somehow taken on a life of its own.

Before she had time to get her guard up again, Tobias extended his hand across the table and said, 'We're learning to give and take, Felice, and that's what friendship is all about. Shall we shake on being friends?'

She was so astounded that her hand found its way into his before she'd had time to think about it. His strong, warm clasp reminded her of how vulnerable she was, and she reacted defensively, grumbling, 'I wish I could be sure who's doing the giving and who's doing the taking.'

'We both are,' he replied confidently, 'and there's no reason why we shouldn't both be happy with that. For the moment, anyway.'

For the moment? What did he mean by that? Felice
had no time to find out, because he was rising from the
table and saying, 'Thank you for breakfast. Can I ask
one more favour? I need a lift to the airstrip. I'm having
a couple of cars sent down so I won't have to bother
you again in future. Oh, yes, and a lot of electronic
equipment will be on its way to Woodlands in a few days'
time so that I can keep in touch with my various offices
while I'm down here. Pick out a suitable room for an
office and the men who deliver it will do the rest.'

He was all business now, and Felice had to gather her
scattered wits in a hurry to suggest, 'The library...?'

Tobias thought for a moment, then shook his head.
'No, the library should be a family-room. Apart from
that, I'll leave the choice to you.'

It seemed to Felice as she drove Tobias to the airstrip
that he was leaving an awful lot to her, and that the
woman he eventually brought to Woodlands might be
understandably resentful, to put it mildly. Still, that was
his problem. She, heaven help her, had enough of her
own...

Vivid recollections of the good moments she'd shared
with Tobias continued to haunt Felice over the following
days as she threw herself body and soul into bringing
Woodlands back to life. Moments like the warmth of
their clasped hands, the illicit pleasure of her body
pressed against his, the smiles when things were going
well between them, the reconciliations after they couldn't
have gone worse...

All in all, as she frequently reminded herself, it was
just as well she was so busy. Under her capable direction, the cleaners and handymen she'd hired were

turning Woodlands upside down and putting it back together as good as new.

Apart from the routine work, she called in specialists to shampoo carpets, clean paintings, check the electrical wiring, the central heating and the plumbing; and agonised herself over the choice of new equipment to harmonise with the character of the kitchens and utility rooms.

It was a big responsibility, but a still bigger delight to spend lavishly without having to spare a thought for the cost. After so many years of careful budgeting at the cottage, it was as if every day was Christmas at the Hall.

Sometimes she even forgot she was buying for another woman's benefit, and would find herself behaving as though Woodlands was indeed her own. Then she'd pull herself up sharply, give herself a good talking to, and try to kid herself that such lapses wouldn't happen again.

They always did, but somehow her lapses were all wrapped up in these frantically busy days being both the saddest and happiest of her life. Beguiled by the atmosphere of the house she loved so much, it was easier—kinder!—to lose touch with reality than anticipate having to hand it over to its new mistress.

At least when that moment came, she'd have the consolation of knowing that nobody could have made a better job of restoring the Hall than she had. Love, as she had learned the hard way and Tobias had so surprisingly noticed, definitely showed.

By the end of her first week as housekeeper, a kind of organised chaos characterised the home wing of Woodlands, but a few rooms had received such concentrated attention that they were ready for immediate occupancy.

Tobias would be a lot more comfortable the next time he made one of his lightning visits. In addition, a Range Rover and a silver Jaguar were waiting for him in the gothic coach house that had served Old Josh as a garage. Felice was waiting for him, too, every minute of every day, but that was something else she didn't care to dwell on too much.

He'd given her his personal phone number when they'd parted at the airstrip, telling her she could reach him wherever he happened to be if she needed him. Well, she *had* needed him many, many times, but she'd never actually contacted him.

She'd always decided sorrowfully that decisions important enough to her to be shared would probably only be regarded as trivia by him, and he'd made it only too plain that he didn't want to be bothered with that.

What she really wanted, she knew, was his approval, but that was another need that didn't bear looking into too closely. Instead, she discussed any knotty problems that arose with Janetta, and roped in her brothers, too, as they were now home.

Garth and Gavin had brought with them all the exuberant gaiety of sixteen-year-olds, plus empty stomachs, piles of dirty washing and endless anecdotes about the matches they'd played on their rugby tour. What they hadn't brought with them was the glow that usually filled Felice when the Lawson family was complete. This time there was still an empty place in her heart.

Tobias's, of course, except that he wasn't family and scarcely even a friend, no matter what he said. Besotted as she was with him, she could still see that his change of attitude towards her had happened only because he'd realised how useful she could be to him.

But that, and all other considerations, fled from her mind when she looked out of the leaded library windows late on Friday afternoon and saw Tobias step from a taxi.

A happiness she couldn't suppress surged through her as she left the bowl of flowers she was arranging on a side-table and stepped closer to the window. As if aware of the intensity of her gaze, Tobias glanced her way and saw her.

He smiled and waved. She smiled and waved back, and she very nearly topped that by rushing out to meet him. Fortunately, caution filtered through the euphoria of seeing him again, reminding her that he'd scarcely expect his housekeeper to throw herself in his arms!

Oh, but it was so *good* to see him again, and nothing that had happened between them in the past or might happen in the future could alter that...

Felice tried to be sedate as she returned to arranging the flowers, yet she couldn't stop her fingers from trembling, nor her eyes from watching Tobias pay off the taxi and walk towards the entrance to the Hall until he was lost from her view.

He was home! Now she felt complete! Deep down she knew her happiness was only an illusion, as it always was where Tobias was concerned, but that didn't stop her heart thumping out its wild song of joy.

Nor did it stop her spine contracting as he entered the library a few moments later. She didn't hear him come in so much as sense him, and she forced herself to remain with her back to the door as though unaware of his presence.

'Felice.'

The quiet, almost joyful way he had of saying her name sometimes nearly destroyed her self-control. She made herself turn slowly to face him, as though her eyes weren't starved of the sight of him, her heart not hungry for his beloved presence.

Beloved? Where had that word come from? Her subconscious, obviously. She would have to have severe words with her subconscious...

'Hello, Tobias,' she said with a lightness that belied the crazy hammering of her heart. 'Welcome back to chaos, but we're almost at the stage where we're beginning to win.'

'From the appearance of this room, it looks as though it was no contest,' he said, gazing around him appreciatively. He came right over to her, took a daffodil from her hand and twirled it absently between his fingers as his eyes held hers.

Felice retrieved the daffodil and thrust it into the sponge at the bottom of the bowl that was holding her flower arrangement in place. 'Don't be deceived by this room,' she replied, with the same determined lightness. 'It's one of a very few that are so far fit to live in. If I'd known you were coming home, though, I'd have lighted the fire to make it extra welcoming.'

'You said home,' he replied slowly.

Felice flushed slightly, and kept her eyes on the last daffodil to be added to the bowl. 'Sometimes I forget you have so many that this one's hardly special.'

'I wouldn't say that,' he replied, more slowly still. 'I've got a lot of places to live, but I've never stayed in any of them long enough to think of them as home. It comes as a bit of a shock to realise I'll soon have a real one at last.'

She caught her breath, then whispered, 'Poor Tobias. You've got so much, and yet most people with next to nothing have a real home to go back to. Nothing as grand as the Hall, of course, but home is always home. Special.'

'Good God, you're sorry for me!' he exclaimed, looking thunderstruck.'

'Well, I won't be for much longer, will I?' she soothed. 'Woodlands will soon be as much of a home as you or anybody else could wish for.'

'Including you?' he questioned sharply.

'Including me,' she replied with a sigh she couldn't quite suppress.

'Then it's not "poor Tobias" but "lucky Tobias", isn't it?' he replied obscurely. Before a puzzled frown had time to draw Felice's eyebrows together, he took her arm and continued with a smile, 'I want to see how the rest of my *home* is coming along. Show me the other rooms you've made habitable.'

His clasp on her arm was light, but Felice was nervously conscious of his strong fingers as she led him out of the library, along the hall and into the sunny parlour she'd chosen as his office. Its long windows overlooked the gardens and, beyond, the meadows and the sea. It was just the room she would have chosen for herself if she'd had to be shut in with computers, telephones and fax machines.

Tobias's eyes roamed over the equipment, lingered on the potted ivy and other plants she'd spent so much time choosing for the maximum softening effect, and then looked at the view outside the windows. 'Do you always try to bring the garden into the house?' he asked.

'Yes,' she replied unequivocally. 'If you don't like it, you need another housekeeper. It's a case of love me, love my flowers.'

'I'll remember that,' he promised.

Felice flushed. 'I didn't mean that the way it sounded! I just meant—meant—oh, you know what I meant!' To get herself out of her flounderings, she pointedly changed the subject. 'Are you happy with your office?'

'Very. What's next?'

He seemed to have forgotten he was still holding her arm, so, rather than make a fuss by pulling away, she decided the best thing she could do was appear to forget as well. 'Your bedroom,' she replied. 'I've concentrated on the rooms you're most likely to use when you're down here.'

'What a good housekeeper I've found for myself,' he murmured, as they went along the passage and up the gracious oak staircase to the next storey.

Felice thought it wisest not to reply, but she couldn't quell a glow of satisfaction as he inspected the rejuvenated master bedroom. Everything in the room had either been dry-cleaned, shampooed or polished, so that it was bright and gleaming, with every sign of neglect banished. The final touch was the living, crimson blaze provided by bowls of freshly picked tulips.

Tobias looked at the flowers and said, 'How could you have expected me, when I didn't know I was coming back myself until a few hours ago?'

'I thought a good housekeeper should anticipate,' she answered primly.

Tobias looked closely at her and asked sympathetically, 'Is it very hard to be a good housekeeper?'

'Sometimes,' she admitted, caught off guard.

'I thought it might be.' He let go of her arm and raised his hand to lightly brush the back of his fingers across her cheek.

Felice would have been less dismayed if he'd seized her in his arms and tried to ravish her, because that would have been the Tobias she knew. But this light touch across her cheeks was tender, almost loving, and that was when he was at his most dangerous—because then he was the Tobias that she wanted.

'I haven't been too kind to you, have I?' he asked softly. 'You must think me the most selfish brute alive.'

She should have agreed with him, but something within her had never quite accepted that view of him, and she heard herself denying, 'No, I wouldn't say that.'

'Then what would you say?' he asked, and his eyes were so searching that Felice had the heart-stopping feeling he was deliberately pushing their relationship one step further.

But one step further than what?

CHAPTER TEN

'I'D SAY that—that—sometimes you rush too fast to-wards —towards whatever objective you—you happen to have in mind,' Felice stuttered, her words not coming easily because she'd never considered this side of Tobias before and she was unsure of her ground. 'That might be a good thing in business, but—but in private life it might seem selfish, when it isn't really.'

'You make me wonder what I've ever done to make you so kind to me,' he answered, with a self-deprecating grimace.

'I'm not kind, I just happen to believe that everybody deserves a fair crack of the whip,' she replied, embarrassed. She was also uneasy because they seemed to be drawing closer together. Afraid of reading more into it than was actually there, she continued, 'I'll leave you to get settled now. The kitchen's stocked with basics like coffee and tea, so if you want anything just use the intercom.'

She tried to leave before he could reply, but he detained her with a light touch on her arm. 'Why don't we go out to dinner tonight?' he suggested. 'My way of saying thanks for all you've achieved at Woodlands so far.'

Felice was caught on the hop. She wanted to go out with him more than anything in the world, but she couldn't forget the mystery woman waiting to come to Woodlands, nor could her pride tolerate his motive for asking her. 'No thanks necessary,' she replied stiffly. 'You're paying me well for what I'm doing, remember?'

He looked at her long and hard, then said, 'All right, let's forget the thanks and dine together anyway. Just for the hell of it.'

'What do you mean, just for the hell of it?' she asked suspiciously.

Tobias hesitated, then answered slowly. 'I could do with some company.'

Any company, Felice thought mutinously, and that just wasn't good enough. No way was she going to be a substitute for his mistress! She lifted her head proudly and lied, 'I'm sorry, I already have a date.'

'Tomorrow night, then?'

What was it with him? Did his own pride make him incapable of accepting a refusal? Yes, that must be it, she decided, and shook her head. 'Sorry, I'm busy then as well.'

His eyes darkened and Felice left the room hurriedly, anxious to avoid a quarrel. She spent what was left of the afternoon keeping well out of his way. He seemed to have got the message, though, because he didn't seek her out.

She couldn't help being a little peeved about that, although it bore out what she'd suspected—that he'd asked her out because she was the only woman he knew on the island.

Still, being under the same roof as Tobias and knowing they might come face-to-face at any moment drained what few emotional reserves she had left. She felt like a wrung-out rag when she returned to the cottage that evening.

The twins, like Janetta, were helping out in the gardens of Woodlands, and the early dusk meant they'd finished work and arrived home before her. Garth and Gavin were upstairs but Janetta was in the kitchen preparing a mixed grill.

She turned an eager face towards Felice and asked, 'Is it right what I heard? That the lord and master is back?'

'Whose lord and master?' Felice scowled, slumping into an armchair by the fire and closing her eyes wearily. It was an emotional weariness she was suffering from, and somehow that seemed worse than the physical kind.

Sighing, she went on, 'If you mean Tobias, yes, he's back, but he's not my lord and master. I just happen to work for him, no more and no less than that.'

'You two have been quarrelling again!' Janetta accused.

'We haven't. We no longer have the kind of relationship that leads to quarrels.'

'You mean you don't fancy him any more?'

'I——' Felice broke off, her heart stopping as she heard a car with a powerful engine turn into the driveway.

'That's not him, is it?' Janetta exclaimed, reading her mind and running to the kitchen window to peer out into the darkness. 'Oh, my God,' she went on in an entirely different tone, 'it's a BMW. That means Serena! What ill wind's blown our darling cousin here?'

Felice, feeling that her powers of endurance had already been tested enough for one day, entirely agreed with her, but she still felt compelled to scold, 'Oh, do hush, Janetta. Serena might be a bit of a trial but she's still family.'

'A bit of a trial?' Janetta echoed sceptically. 'She's a monumental pain in the——'

'Hush!' Felice hissed again, and much more fiercely, as Serena sauntered into the kitchen like visiting royalty.

Her doll-like face was beautifully made-up, not a wisp of her gleaming fair hair was out of place, and not even the rigours of the mainland motorways and the island car ferry had dimmed her stunning beauty.

She was zipped into a white couture jumpsuit and she had a white leather make-up case looped over one arm. Over the other arm she carried a pile of plastic-wrapped outfits. She dumped these burdens on the kitchen table and exclaimed, 'Darlings, how lovely it is to see you again.'

'If we believe that, we'll believe anything,' Janetta retorted frankly.

Serena laughed, and confessed, 'Oh, all right, then, perhaps I have an ulterior motive...'

'A motive called Tobias Hunter? Janetta guessed shrewdly. 'How did you hear about him?'

'When a Press baron lands in your back yard, you can't expect to keep him to yourself, lovey. Not with newspapers being what they are. I read about his little windfall, and thought a long-delayed visit to my dear cousins might be amusing. Er—my sources of information are correct in advising me he's down for the weekend?'

'Yes, but he's not likely to be interested in you. He's much more interested in Felice,' Janetta retorted with a misplaced loyalty that made her sister groan inwardly. 'She's his housekeeper.'

Serena's blue eyes widened and swivelled to Felice. 'So you've finally got fed up with sloshing about in mud and manure, have you, darling? Or are you being rather clever?'

'I'm supervising the restoration of Woodlands, if you call that clever. It's only a temporary position, but it's useful until my gardening work picks up again in the spring,' Felice replied with a lightness she was far from feeling.

'So that's the way it is,' Serena mused. 'Well, the fact that you've got your feet firmly over the doorstep at Woodlands might come in handy. Tobias could be so useful to my career, considering he's got a finger in every sort of media pie. Tell me, what manner of beast is he?'

'Why does he have to be a beast?' Janetta interjected indignantly.

'It's in the nature of man, lovey, especially the rich ones.' Serena turned to Felice again and asked, 'Or is Tobias different? He doesn't run with the rat-pack and guards his privacy so fiercely that I've never met him. What do you make of him?'

'I don't believe in pre-formed opinions,' Felice told her quietly. 'It's much fairer to make your own.'

'Do I detect an atmosphere?' Serena purred. 'Poor darling, hasn't the big man taken any notice of you? That's hardly surprising, considering what a dyed-in-the-tweed country bumpkin you are. Heaven knows I've offered to take you in hand enough times, but you've never prised yourself out of the mud long enough to come up to London.'

'There was never enough time or money,' Felice was goaded into replying.

Serena studied her more closely. 'You know, you're looking and sounding a trifle peaky, darling. Is all this slavery getting to you at last? I warned you the day would come when you'd regret taking on the youngsters. Talk about a thankless task! Kids just don't appreciate martyrs, do they?'

'I don't regret anything, and I'm not a martyr,' Felice snapped, 'so take your claws out of me. I've had a long, hard day and any blood that's drawn is likely to be yours.'

Serena's eyebrows rose. 'My, you are touchy today!' Her eyes rolled expressively towards the ceiling as a thump sounded upstairs and she went on, 'Don't tell me your baby brothers are home, bless their little cotton socks. Now I can understand your nervous state. There's nothing more trying than a family gathering, is there?'

'We were doing all right until you came,' Janetta grumbled.

Felice frowned at her, then told Serena, 'Yes, the twins are home. They're also over six feet tall, with appetites to match, and you could stuff pillows into their little cotton socks. They're sixteen now, you know.'

'Sixteen!' Serena flew over to a wall mirror and studied her reflection. What she saw seemed to reassure her because she relaxed and cooed, 'Well, that's hardly surprising, I suppose. I wasn't much more than a baby when they were born, after all.'

'A baby?' Janetta marvelled. 'I was the baby, and I'm ten years younger than you. Even Felice is younger than you.'

Felice couldn't help smiling, but Serena scowled and gathered up her outfits. Moments later she recaptured her customary sweetness, however, and said, 'I think I'll eat out. I wouldn't want to get in the way of the lions' feeding time, and I really should pay a call at Woodlands. I wouldn't want Tobias to think we're not neighbourly down here. Same old guest room, is it, darlings?'

She drifted out of the room and Janetta said sourly, 'If somebody could package her, she'd sell better than saccharin. Felice, if you want Tobias, fight for him. Once Serena's got her claws into him——'

'Serena is wasting her time,' Felice replied quietly. 'Tobias already has a mistress to install at Woodlands as soon as it's ready.'

'Oh, you poor thing! I know you're still nutty about him. I just know it!'

A strained smile touched Felice's lips momentarily, lighting her face before extinguishing as though the effort had been too much. 'Then keep it to yourself, there's a honey,' she begged. 'Or should I say "lovey"?'

'Don't you dare! I want to beat Serena's head in every time she calls me that!'

'I know, but she won't stay long,' Felice comforted her. 'Tobias has a very forceful way of dealing with women on the make.'

But Serena dined out with Tobias that evening, and Saturday as well. Felice, feeling she had to back up her lies to him about having dates, went out with Charles. Since all Charles wanted to do was talk about Tobias and hope he'd have further business commissions from him, though, neither evening was very successful.

The days were hazardous enough, as well, since Serena couldn't resist gloating about her conquest of Tobias, and Janetta's eyes were full of unspoken sympathy whenever they dwelt on her suffering sister.

When Serena left for London on Sunday afternoon because she had a modelling assignment the next day, she said to Felice and Janetta, 'I'm working on Friday so I won't be back until Saturday, darlings. It's the country club's annual charity bunfight, isn't it? I've dropped a word in Tobias's ear about it so I expect he'll escort me. Anything special you'd like me to bring down when I come?'

'Just your own sweet self,' Janetta mocked. Then she horrified Felice by adding with youthful and devastating frankness, 'Are you sleeping with Tobias?'

'Don't be silly, lovey,' Serena replied, amused. 'I want something from the man, and I'd be silly to sleep with him before I get it.'

Felice went quite cold. That was the syndrome Tobias recognised and hated—and yet he was tolerating it from Serena. Why? Because he'd fallen victim to her incredible beauty? She felt a pain that was unlike any other pain she'd ever experienced. It wasn't jealousy. It was even worse. It was despair.

She just wanted Serena to go, and could have screamed when Janetta delayed the moment by persisting, 'What exactly do you want from Tobias? To marry him?'

'What a tempting thought, but I don't believe in beating my head against a rock.' Serena replied laughingly. 'Tobias isn't the marrying kind. I'm not sure I am, either. Not yet, anyway. No, I want to get into TV commercials, and he can fix it for me.'

Felice said hesitantly, 'Can't you fix it for yourself?'

'I've had auditions, darling, but I've been told I'm too beautiful for the average woman in the street to identify with, and identifying is all the rage at the moment. Tobias, though, is powerful enough to kick that little stumbling-block aside.'

She smiled and went out to her car, leaving a trail of perfume behind her. Both sisters waited until they heard her car start up and drive away, then Janetta burst out, 'You could give her a run for her money if you wanted to, Felice. You're every bit as lovely as she is.'

'Don't you mean there's so much more of me than there is of her?' Felice mocked wryly.

'So you're not as thin as a rake and you're too tall for most men. So what? You're a real woman and your height doesn't matter with Tobias because he's tall himself.'

'What matters,' Felice pointed out sadly, 'is what Serena just said. The man's only interested in mistresses and I'm only interested in being a wife. And I won't share him, either, which is what it would boil down to, considering the way he is.'

'You could make him love you!'

'No, I couldn't. Love is either freely given, or it isn't given at all. You'll realise that when you're older.' She turned away as the twins came boisterously into the sitting-room, the dogs leaping about them, and there wasn't a trace of sadness in her voice as she asked, 'Where are you two off to?'

'Walking the dogs,' Gavin replied. 'Care to come?'

'No, thanks. I'm going to give Janetta a break from the kitchen and cook the dinner myself. I suppose I can depend on you to get back by six? It will be pitch black then.'

'Sure thing,' Janetta replied for the boys. 'I feel like a walk so I'll go with them. You won't catch me being late when there's a roast in the offing.'

Felice, left to her cooking and her thoughts, spent a thoroughly miserable afternoon. The swift way Serena had been able to ingratiate herself with Tobias showed just how transitory and unreliable his emotions were. Not her sort of man at all! But, oh, she did love him so!

There was no use pretending any longer that she didn't, and she despaired of ever finding anything that would break the steadfast grip Tobias had on her heart. Disillusion alone couldn't do it, or she'd have been cured weeks ago.

The meal was just about ready to serve up, and she was making the gravy when she heard a car stop in the driveway. For a moment she thought it was Charles calling on the off chance that she'd go out with him again, but then there was a commotion of laughter and barking and the door burst open.

In tumbled the dogs, the twins, Janetta—and Tobias. Felice froze. Then, only one logical reason for his visit occurring to her, she said to him, 'Serena's left, I'm afraid.'

'Oh, he knows that!' Garth told her carelessly. 'Felice, the most marvellous thing! We found this old kite in one of the attics at the Hall and Tobias let us fly it. It was cracking fun.'

'Yes, and there are some super fishing rods, too, and he's said we can try them out!' Gavin exclaimed. 'You can't imagine the stuff that's stored away up there!'

'What I can't imagine is what you were doing in the attics in the first place,' Felice replied. She switched her attention back to Tobias and added awkwardly, 'I hope they haven't been making nuisances of themselves.'

'No, we haven't,' Janetta chipped in indignantly. 'We weren't even trespassing. We just happened to be walking the dogs when we met Tobias and he invited us in.'

'Yes, and he flew the kite as well,' Gavin elaborated. 'What's more, he's coming fishing with us next weekend, which is our last one before we go back to school. He's letting us fish the river at Woodlands, too, which we've never done before! We thought the least we could do was invite him home for dinner. It's bound to be better than a hotel meal.'

Felice, unable to picture Tobias flying a kite with her boisterous family, far less going fishing with them, looked helplessly at Tobias. He said quietly, 'If it's convenient . . . ?'

'Of course it's convenient,' Janetta affirmed, taking the greatest care to avoid Felice's accusing eyes. 'My sister doesn't cook often, but when she does there's enough for an army.'

Tobias was still looking questioningly at Felice, and she heard herself saying politely, 'Naturally you're welcome, although it's just a family sort of meal.'

'Sounds like the best kind,' Tobias replied, smiling in the way that always made her go weak at the knees. 'Do you need any help?'

'I'll help as soon as I've washed and changed. You lot get out of the way,' Janetta replied, driving Tobias and the twins before her from the kitchen as unceremoniously as if he were just another brother.

Felice found herself alone, staring bemusedly at the gravy. She was still staring at it when it boiled up and over the edges of the saucepan. That brought her out of her trance. She removed the pan from the heat and went over to the wall mirror to stare at herself.

Her face was flushed from cooking, her hair was caught up in a pony-tail, and there was a starry look in her eyes that frightened her. Fiercely she reminded herself of his mistress, of Serena, and of goodness knew how many other women he was probably stringing along.

That took the stars out of her eyes but she still felt she was living at a higher, more vital level—the way she always did when Tobias was close.

The beef was on the carving platter and she was just about to transfer the vegetables to heated dishes when Janetta came back, having hurriedly washed and changed into a pink wool frock. She lifted a pinafore from a hook behind the kitchen door, and said as she threw it on, 'I'll finish that. You whizz off and change. Let your hair down, too. Now's your chance to outshine Serena!'

'You must be mad! I couldn't outshine Serena in a million years.'

'You can do it in seconds. She's only a clothes horse. Just remember what I told you earlier—you're a real woman.'

Felice stared at her in horror. 'You plotted all this! Oh, how could you? I could die of embarrassment! Don't you realise this must be the last place Tobias wants to be? You must have invited him here in a way that he couldn't refuse. I know you did!'

'No such thing,' Janetta retorted blithely, pushing her towards the door. 'I just mentioned we had to be going because you were cooking a roast, he said that sounded great, so I said come and join us, and he did. What's the big deal?'

'You're meddling, that's the big deal. You're doing me no favours, Janetta, honestly you're not.'

'Phooey! It's Tobias who's getting the favours. He might be a multi-millionaire but he's *starved* of all the things we take for granted—family, fun, home-cooking...'

'Since when have you become an expert on Tobias Hunter?' Felice exclaimed.

'Since you started making such a botch of it. Look, I just want Tobias to see you as you really are, then I'll never meddle again,' Janetta promised.

'Can't you get it through your thick head that I've no intention of joining his harem? I could have done that weeks ago if I'd wanted, and without any help from you.'

Gavin came into the kitchen, asking, 'What's the hold-up? I'm starving.'

'So are we all,' Janetta told him, greeting his appearance with relief. 'Don't worry, I'm serving up now and we'll eat as soon as Felice gets changed.'

Felice had no choice then but to run upstairs and search for a frock that was dressy without being too dressy. She hurriedly settled on a frock of fine cream wool, draped from the shoulders to the hips where it was loosely belted before it fell in fluid pleats to just below her calves.

It made her look incredibly elegant, but it also made her feel incredibly tall, and she was frowning at herself as she brushed her hair. She let it fall loosely to her shoulders, added a quick touch of pink to her lips and blue to her eyelids, and hurried downstairs.

When she went into the sitting-room Tobias stood up, and she didn't feel so incredibly tall, after all, but just about right. 'You look like a Greek goddess,' he said, and he sounded so sincere that Felice caught her breath.

Garth glanced at them and asked innocently, 'Aren't Greek goddesses dead, and armless with it?'

Felice chuckled, Tobias laughed, and suddenly everything was all right. They just seemed a family again, with no awkward guest, not that anybody had ever felt awkward about Tobias except herself. But she was over that now, and when they went into the dining-room and began to eat she felt as relaxed and happy as when she'd first met him.

It didn't seem the time to think about conflict and antagonism, and so she didn't. Instead, she indulged in one of her daydreams of how wonderful it would be if they could always be like this, and the dream lasted until long after the meal was over and they sat chatting in the sitting-room. Reality didn't creep back until Tobias stood up reluctantly to leave, explaining that he had to return to the mainland that night.

'Felice will see you to the door,' Janetta said, and instantly Felice was embarrassed again, and no dream, however delightful, was proof against embarrassment. As his hostess, politeness dictated that she see him to the door. How could Janetta have been so crassly obvious, especially after promising not to meddle any more? And why were the boys grinning like that?

Much as she loved her sister and brothers, she could have boxed their ears, and she hoped Tobias wasn't as embarrassed as she was as she also rose to her feet. It was difficult to walk with her usual grace as he followed her out, so conscious was she of him behind her.

In the confines of the passage, she felt even worse. Tobias was so close that the full force of his magnetism hit her, and she had to stiffen every muscle not to sway helplessly towards him. Hating her weakness, she hurried on to the front door.

Tobias didn't seem in any hurry himself, and when he caught up with her, he said with leisurely politeness, 'Thank you for a lovely meal and a delightful evening.'

'You're welcome any time,' she responded, studiously polite herself as she reached nervously for the door handle.

Tobias's lips twisted wryly. 'Give me an open invitation like that and I might make a pest of myself. That's something I'm very good at, isn't it?'

Felice swallowed hard. 'I wouldn't say that.'

'Then maybe I'm making progress,' he replied obscurely. 'Felice...'

There was a special deepness, a special softness, in his voice that flustered her. She jerked the door open and shivered violently as a blast of icy air cut through the fine wool of her frock. Tobias's attitude changed, and he frowned. 'Don't stand here catching cold. I'll see you next weekend.'

'There'll be more improvements at Woodlands by then,' she promised, striving hard for normality.

'To hell with Woodlands,' he growled, and went out into the night.

CHAPTER ELEVEN

OVER the next few days Felice was grateful that the restoration of the Hall and its gardens took all her time and energy because, whether she was waking or sleeping, Tobias was always with her. No matter how much of a womaniser he had proved himself to be, or how much she cursed herself for being such a weak and lovelorn fool, he'd become an integral part of her.

Her motivation for living, in fact. That was something she had to come to terms with...as soon as she figured out how.

Busy as the days were, though, gossip filtered through to her. The neighbourhood was buzzing with tales of a romance between Tobias and Serena because they'd been seen out together for two nights in a row.

Hearing his name constantly coupled with her cousin's depressed her unbearably. It also reinforced her conviction that, although Tobias complained about women always wanting something from him, he wasn't slow to capitalise when those women happened to take his fancy.

As she once had.

Yet in spite of all this, she couldn't stop herself living for Friday when he would return.

So hungry was she for just the sight of him that when Friday finally dawned, she was at the Hall even earlier than usual, plundering daffodils from the garden to make fresh flower arrangements for the library, and lighting the log fire in the ancient fireplace.

Then she turned her attention to his bedroom, carrying up more vases of flowers, switching up the central heating and checking that her orders for clean bed linen and towels had been properly carried out.

By nine o'clock that morning everything was ready for him, and by half-past four that afternoon he still hadn't arrived. Soon the daily workers would be leaving and unless she waited on he would be returning to an empty house. She didn't want him to do that, even if it would be his own fault for not telling her exactly what his plans were.

As the best part of another hour dragged by, Felice began to wonder if Tobias had decided not to return until Saturday, because Serena wouldn't be back on the island until then.

So much for all the welcoming touches she'd arranged for him! Well, there was no reason for her to be piqued. Tobias wasn't exactly answerable to his housekeeper for his actions, was he? And there was absolutely no reason why she should think she meant more to him than that, just because he meant so much more to her than an employer!

Her staff was checking out in ones and twos when Tobias finally came striding into the Hall, delighting her eyes and senses—and making nonsense of her secret hope that when she saw him again she would be 'cured'.

Just one glimpse of his burly form, his rugged face and dawning smile, and her heartbeat accelerated so much that she knew she was as far from being 'cured' as she had ever been. 'You're late,' she said accusingly, before she could stop herself.

'Have I been missed?' he asked, looking at her intently.

Felice turned away to hide a self-conscious blush. 'I just meant that you're usually home before now.'

'All I like about that is the word "home",' he replied, his grey eyes more intent than ever. 'Haven't I been missed even a little bit?'

Felice thought he was being deliberately provocative. 'You're not exactly living here, so it would be difficult for you to be missed,' she told him repressively. 'We all normally leave around now and I thought you might find returning to an empty house a bit depressing, that's all.'

'You're right, and I'm glad you took pity on me and stayed. What would I do without you, Felice?'

His voice had taken on a caressing note and she looked at him indignantly. Damn the man, he just couldn't stop flirting, even though he knew she wasn't interested in that sort of thing. She'd made it plain enough for long enough!

Her indignation was reflected in her voice as she replied, 'I didn't take pity on you. I was just trying to do my job.'

'And you're doing it magnificently,' he soothed her, then had all her senses running riot again by taking her arm and propelling her into the library. It wasn't fair what his touch could do to her, she thought mutinously. It just wasn't fair!

Nor was it fair the way Tobias kept hold of her arm when they were in the library. He looked around and said appreciatively, 'This room is getting cosier and cosier. How is the rest of the house coming along?'

Felice didn't want to make an undignified fuss by shrugging herself free of his grip, so she said with a primness she was far from feeling, 'All the bedrooms and sitting-rooms in this wing are ready for use, so there's nothing to stop you bringing guests with you if you want.'

'I don't want,' he replied bluntly. 'Not immediately, anyway.'

'Don't you think your mistress might be interested in what is being done here? I know I would if——' She broke off as she realised where her impetuosity had led her.

'If you were my mistress?' Tobias finished for her. 'But you've no intention of being my mistress, have you? Or the mother of my children?'

'No, I haven't,' she retorted, beginning to think he was deliberately playing with her, and haunted once more by the notion that he'd made her housekeeper at Woodlands just to punish her. Oh, how could he? Didn't he realise that loving him the way she did was punishment enough?

No, of course he didn't, because he didn't know she loved him, and he must never find out. She managed to free herself from his grip on her arm by walking over to the fireplace, where she bent down to add another log to the fire. 'Anyway,' she continued, 'the point I wanted to make is that if you do want to entertain guests for the weekend, I can always hire a cook and some domestic workers to make you comfortable.'

'I won't want that sort of staff until I move in properly,' Tobias replied decisively.

'What about your own comfort, then?' she persisted, wishing she could stop worrying about him—even if she couldn't stop loving him. The trouble was, the two seemed inextricably bound together.

'For the moment I can fend for myself.'

'But you can't be used to that!' she objected violently.

'I'm not, so it has a certain novelty appeal. A kind of entertainment value. Do you remember when I said you had entertainment value, Felice?'

Of course she remembered! It was on the very first day they'd met, and the only reason he could have for reminding her of it was to provoke her. So she'd been right, then, in thinking he was getting a kick out of playing havoc with her emotions.

What was more, he'd moved so close that he was standing right over her and instinctively she knew he was waiting for her to raise her eyes to meet his. It was the last thing she wanted to do, and so she kept her head bent towards the fire, hoping he'd think she was more interested in watching the flames lick hungrily around the newly added log than in looking at him.

As she watched, two woodlice that had been nesting in the log ran along the top of it, close to the licking flames. Swiftly she scooped them into her hand. Then she rose to her feet and, carefully side-stepping Tobias, went over to open a window and throw them out into the garden.

As she closed the window again, Tobias said disbelievingly. 'You'd risk burning yourself to save a couple of insects most people would regard as pests?'

'Everything has its place in the scheme of things,' she replied, surprised he should see anything remarkable in her action. 'Why shouldn't I save them? They haven't done me any harm.'

He stared at her. Then he said, his voice deepening so that his Canadian drawl seemed to throb on the air. 'Have I done you any harm, Felice? I think I have, and I can't tell you how sorry I am.'

She felt her heart constrict because he sounded so sincere, then all her defensive mechanisms came into play. She couldn't soften towards Tobias for fear he'd take merciless advantage and start talking about horrible things like terms all over again.

'Do you believe I'm sorry?' he insisted, the same soul-destroying throb in his voice.

Felice forced herself to shrug and reply lightly, 'Oh, I don't bother about anything that's over and done with. I'm strictly a today and tomorrow person. I imagine that answers your last question, too, the one about me remembering you once said I had entertainment value.'

Tobias was quiet for a moment, then he asked, 'Would it help if I said that you still do?'

Again Felice's heart constricted, and again she didn't dare let herself believe what her senses were telling her. How could she, when he had Serena on a string and an unknown mistress lurking somewhere?

All the same, it hurt her a lot more than it hurt him to scoff, 'If you're interested in entertainment value, I'd say it was time to bring on the dancing girls, and that lets me out. It's time I was going home, anyway. I'm late as it is.'

Tobias's voice and attitude changed, and he sounded quite cold as he said. 'By that I gather you're busy again this evening?'

'Very.'

'So busy that you couldn't get un-busy if I asked you to dine with me?'

This time Felice's heart not only constricted, it lurched. Oh, how wonderful it would be to stop fighting him and succumb to what he wanted—what she wanted, even if it wasn't *all* she wanted. She hesitated, momentarily allowing delicious tendrils of temptation to wrap themselves around her pride and silence its objections.

Tobias sensed her weakness and put a strong hand under her chin, forcing her face up to his. 'I think you want to dine with me,' he said. 'I think you just don't know how to admit it.'

Oh, if only he'd allowed her to come to that conclusion herself, instead of driving her too hard and too fast, so that all her pride came surging back to defend her against what she could only see as his arrogance!

'I'm afraid I want to dine with somebody else more,' she blurted out, and was rewarded by him releasing her chin as though he'd been stung—if that could be counted as a reward, she thought miserably.

Tobias turned away from her. 'Then I won't detain you any longer,' he said icily. 'Goodnight, Felice.'

'Goodnight,' she replied, struggling to keep her utter wretchedness to herself.

She succeeded, but wretched was how she remained for the rest of the evening. It was a wretchedness that increased when Serena came swanning in burdened with more outfits than she could possibly wear for one weekend.

'Greetings, darlings,' she cried gaily, bursting into the sitting-room just as the Lawsons were settling down to watch television after dinner. 'My assignment went so well I was able to get away sooner than I expected. Oh, don't move any of you, I'm off again as soon as I've changed. I phoned Tobias while I was waiting for the car ferry at Portsmouth, and he's taking me out to dinner. Must rush, as it seems the beast is starving, and far be from me to keep a starving beast waiting.'

She hurried upstairs, leaving a trail of laughter and perfume behind her. Janetta glowered after her and grumbled, 'I wish she wouldn't call Tobias a beast. Not even you call him that, Felice, and you've got reason if anybody——'

'Oh, hush,' Felice pleaded. 'Serena talks for effect. She doesn't mean half of what she says.'

'Just as well,' Gavin chipped in. 'Tobias is a good bloke. Far too good for her.'

'You can say that again,' Garth agreed. 'Felice, why don't you——?'

'Why don't we change the subject and watch some television?' Felice interrupted desperately. 'I know you all mean well, but please let me lead my own life. I've done my best to let you lead yours.'

That was so true that her sister and brothers were silenced, although Felice was so conscious of their fierce loyalty and furious sympathy that she was driven to bed far earlier than she normally went.

It was a mistake. She lay there tossing and turning hour after endless hour, trying hard not to think of Serena pouring all that saccharine sweetness over Tobias, and being beautiful enough to get away with it.

The fact that Tobias had asked her out first didn't help one bit. It only emphasised what an opportunist he was, she thought wearily, trying to forget how breathtakingly lovely and femininely frail Serena had looked in a pink chiffon gown that was really far too dressy for a dinner date, except that she had the confidence to carry it off.

Felice wondered if she could depend on Tobias being astute enough to realise that Serena was about as frail as the Rock of Gibraltar. Not that it was really any of her business, yet she snapped upright in bed ages later when she heard the front door close and a murmur of voices. One was so deep that it had to be Tobias's.

She looked at the luminous hands of the alarm clock beside her bed and saw that it was just after midnight. She'd heard the twins and Janetta go to bed some half an hour ago, so Serena and Tobias were all alone down there, alone to get to know each other better, and in her home, too!

Felice groaned and pulled the duvet up over her head. She stayed that way until she heard the front door open and close again, to be followed shortly by the sound of a car starting up. She lowered the duvet and looked at the clock again.

Tobias had only stayed fifteen minutes. Was there any hope for her in that, or was Serena still playing an extremely cagey game? Probably, Felice decided with the wretchedness that still had her in its grip.

Not loving Tobias, Serena would be able to manage him much better than she herself could. Love played such games with her senses that her normal judgement and common sense never got a look in. The best she seemed to manage was to stumble erratically from one mistake to another.

Felice groaned again, and once more tried to sleep. Eventually she succeeded but her rest was patchy, long periods of wakefulness interspersed with periods of oblivion that would have been bliss if only they hadn't been so brief.

Eventually she decided that trying to sleep was more exhausting than not sleeping at all. She got up as soon as it was light and moved like a ghost through the still-quiet cottage. The last thing she wanted was to awaken any member of her family. She just didn't feel strong enough to face anybody yet, particularly Serena.

Shortly before eight, muffled up against the bitter cold but still shivering as she went outside, she piled the dogs into the van and drove cautiously down the frost-covered driveway. Ever since she'd started work at Woodlands, she'd used her Saturdays to honour her gardening contracts with those of her customers who didn't want anybody else working for them. She was on her way to one of them now.

As she nosed the van out on to the road, telling herself that a hard bout of physical work might just make her feel better, she had to slam on the brakes as a Range Rover roared by heading for Bixley. The driver's head turned and grey eyes bored fleetingly into hers.

Tobias!

Felice wanted to go to Bixley, too, and there was absolutely no reason why she should panic, yet instinctively she slewed round the steering-wheel and accelerated in the other direction.

She was furious with her impetuous, schoolgirlish reaction, but there was nothing she could do about it now. As if that wasn't bad enough, just that brief glimpse of Tobias had started the adrenalin pumping through her veins, bringing her to pulsing, vital life again.

It was only when her pulse-rate began to slow down that she asked herself exactly what she was so excited about—the prospect of more emotional punishment?

She frowned and tried to concentrate on the frosty, slippery road. It was all right for Tobias to zoom along like that, he had a four-wheel drive. She hadn't, and she also needed to turn back towards Bixley or face a detour of several miles.

The driveway to Woodlands was the first opportunity the narrow road offered, and once she'd circled she drove slowly, not that there was any chance of catching up with Tobias the way he'd been shifting. She'd just passed her home when she was dumbfounded to see Tobias coming back the other way. He shot past her, slammed on the brakes and used the cottage driveway to turn again so that he was behind her.

She couldn't imagine what he wanted with her but she wasn't hanging around to find out. It was Serena he should be chasing now, not herself. Her foot came down hard on the accelerator and she slithered into a bend, managed to straighten and skidded into the next.

She and the dogs sitting up beside her were riding the swaying old van like a bucking bronco while the gardening equipment in the back rattled and crashed about.

It was a mad bid to escape, but it seemed doomed to failure as Tobias closed up behind her. Felice had one thing in her favour, though. She knew every curve, pothole and bump in the tortuous old road, and that knowledge enabled her to stay ahead of him—just.

She also knew all the by-ways and back roads when they roared into Bixley, so that Tobias overshot when she turned off the main road. She soon heard him behind her again but kept turning through the network of lanes until she'd shaken him off long enough to zoom into the driveway she wanted, around to the side of the house and stop out of sight of the road. She switched off the engine and waited. She wasn't cold any longer, she was sweating.

She heard the Range Rover go by, return and then go by again. Tobias knew roughly what area she was in, then. He was searching for her, but he could scarcely trespass into the driveways of all the big old houses along this road. At least, she hoped he wouldn't.

For a few minutes she heard nothing but the frantic beating of her heart, then slowly she relaxed. She'd shaken him off. She still couldn't explain to herself what had made her flee from him any more than she could puzzle out why he'd pursued her so doggedly.

What could he possibly want with her that was so urgent he was prepared to turn the quiet roads of Bixley into some kind of grand prix circuit?

That question was to plague Felice so persistently that she got through her work without ever being aware of

doing it. It was still on her mind hours later when she
parked the van in the high street to get some fresh bread,
newspapers and other odds and ends of shopping. The
larder needed constant re-stocking when her brothers
were home.

But *what* had Tobias wanted with her?

She was staring in the bakery window, seeing nothing
while she tried to fathom out the unfathomable, when
an arm came around her waist and squeezed her. She
almost jumped out of her skin, then gasped, 'Charles!
You nearly frightened me to death!'

'I can't think why,' Charles replied, a little peeved.
'I'm not exactly Dracula.'

No, but you're not exactly Tobias, either, she thought
wistfully. For a moment there she'd thought—— Oh,
hell! She was going off her head, she really was. As if
Tobias would try to cuddle her in the high street!

'What do you want?' she asked Charles, not meaning
to sound quite as ungracious as she did.

'The first dance this evening, the last, and all the
dances in between,' Charles replied promptly.

Felice looked at him blankly, then remembered that
it was the country club's annual charity ball that night.
Tobias had driven all thought of it from her mind. She
thought about it now and decided that, although Charles
was all right, she didn't fancy being monopolised by him
all evening. 'Leave yourself some time for propping up
the bar,' she countered lightly. 'You men always seem
to find dancing thirsty work.'

'Promise me the last dance, then, and a few in between, and I'll offer a fabulous sum for you at auction.'

'That reckless offer could very well cost you a fiver,'
she joked, trying to loosen up, be more like her old self.
Each year girls were 'auctioned' for the supper dance

and the proceeds went to charity. Whoever 'bought' them had the right to the dance and to take them in to supper afterwards.

'Cheap at twice the price,' Charles murmured, giving her waist another squeeze.

Felice was just about to extricate herself from his grip when for some reason her head turned. Standing across the road staring angrily at her from under lowered brows was Tobias. She felt her colour rising as though she'd been caught out in some infamous act, which was ridiculous, because Tobias had no claim on her.

Now, she thought in a flurry of panic, she was about to find out why he'd pursued her so doggedly earlier, but Tobias just swung on his heel and walked away. She was relieved and disappointed, and as if those two emotions weren't conflicting enough she was also more baffled than ever. What had been so urgent earlier that morning that wasn't even worth crossing the street for now?

It was something else to puzzle over while she managed to get rid of Charles, finish her shopping and drive back home.

Janetta was sitting at the kitchen table reading a book. She was wrapped in a bathrobe, her hair a network of huge pink rollers, and only her eyes moved as a mud pack dried to a deathly pallor on her face. 'I'm going to knock Tom dead tonight,' she breathed, trying to speak without moving her facial muscles.

'What's special about Tom?' Felice asked, unaware her sister had any particular interest in the local farmer's son, pleasant though he was.

Janetta stifled a giggle for fear of cracking her face pack, and confessed, 'He's my best bet for bidding a high price for me at the auction.'

'He'd pay double not to dance with you if he could see you now.'

Janetta laughed and her face pack splintered into a thousand pieces. 'Now look what you've made me do,' she wailed.

'With your complexion, you don't need it,' Felice replied, cramming two fresh loaves into one inadequate breadbin.

'Perhaps not, but it's fun to make a special effort. I'm going to borrow Serena's pink chiffon. She'll never wear the same gown twice in a row, will she?'

Felice shook her head. 'I suppose she's still in bed?'

'Where else? She loves her beauty sleep and she didn't get in until midnight.' Janetta paused then continued hesitantly, 'Tobias came in with her. I heard his voice, but he didn't stop long.'

'I know.'

'Felice, I wish you'd——' Janetta began passionately, then broke off and cocked her head as sounds of movement came from the bedroom above. When she spoke again it was in an entirely different tone. 'It sounds as though her ladyship is about to join us.'

'I wish you wouldn't speak about Serena like that.'

'It doesn't bother her. In fact, I think she takes it as her due. Vanity has its own armour, you know, so she must have a hide like a rhinoceros.'

'Well, I always say, if you've got it, use it,' Serena said in amusement as she drifted into the kitchen tying the sash of a black silk dressing-gown around her willowy waist. 'Is that tea you're making, Felice? No sugar for me, darling, and thank you for sending out the boys. I do like to wake up gently on a Saturday morning.'

'I haven't sent them anywhere. I've just got back from work.'

'They're over at Woodlands,' Janetta butted in. 'Tobias said they could use his river to try out some fishing rods they found in an attic.'

'I suppose Tobias is being kind to them because they're my cousins,' Serena smiled, settling herself at the kitchen table in a flutter of silk, and repulsing the cat that tried to jump on to her lap. 'And he's being kind to me, too. I told him having noisy teenagers around the place isn't exactly restful.'

'It's not exactly restful having you here, either,' Janetta retorted. 'Is Tobias taking you to the dance tonight?'

Serena inspected her perfect fingernails for possible flaws before replying, 'No, he has some kind of business to attend to this evening.'

'On a Saturday night?' Janetta asked disbelievingly.

'Men don't get to be multi-millionaires by working regular hours,' Serena replied patronisingly. 'He said he'll look in later if he can. Which means he will.'

'Then you certainly won't be wearing the pink chiffon because he's already seen it. Can I borrow it?'

'If you don't mind Tobias knowing it's mine.'

'Oh, I'm not bothered about that.' Janetta smiled brilliantly and wrecked what was left of her face pack. 'That does it, I'll wash this lot off, then I think I'll take the dogs for a walk. I know you've just brought them back, Felice, but I could do with the exercise.'

'What a restless lot you are,' Serena grumbled, as Janetta left the kitchen and ran noisily up the stairs. 'I suppose it will be bedlam here tonight when we're all preparing for the dance. How are you getting there, by the way?'

'Charles is taking us. I expect he'll drive his estate so they'll be room for you as well, if you like.'

'Thanks, but I'd rather take myself than be a crushed sixth. I could phone an old boyfriend, of course, but then I'll have the hassle of ditching him when Tobias arrives. No, I'll definitely be best off on my own.'

'What if Tobias doesn't go?' Felice asked quietly.

'He will,' Serena replied with a confidence that twisted like a knife in Felice's aching heart.

She wasn't looking forward to the dance at all, but, when they were all dressed and ready that evening, she was conscious of a certain pride as she checked over her brothers and sister.

Garth and Gavin looked youthfully handsome in their dark suits and immaculate white shirts, their ties knotted neatly for once by her skilful fingers. Janetta was a vision in the floating pink chiffon, with her fair hair a riot of curls and her make-up so light that she looked angelically lovely.

Felice herself, swishing the billowing skirt of her blue silk gown into place, felt unaccustomedly feminine. The gown might not be new, but its scooped neckline revealed the swell of her breasts, and the fitted bodice flattered her neat waist. Blue eyeshadow and dark mascara emphasised her brilliant eyes, pink lipstick glossed her full lips and her fair hair fell luxuriantly to her shoulders.

She tried very hard to convince herself that she hadn't chosen the gown against a newer one because Tobias had once said blue suited her...

She glanced at Serena, exquisite in a figure-hugging black crêpe gown, with real diamonds gleaming at her ears and her fair hair secured elegantly above her graceful neck with diamond clips. Her make-up was vividly and professionally applied. She was so secure in her conviction that she was unmatchable that she didn't mind

Janetta looking stunning in the pink chiffon she'd lost interest in herself.

'There's a car,' Janetta said excitedly, as they all waited in the sitting-room, the girls drinking sherry and the boys settling for Coke.

'For heaven's sake don't peek through the curtains like that. It's only Charles,' Serena scolded, although she posed automatically as Gavin went to let him in.

Charles, immaculate in a dinner suit, looked admiringly at the three girls when he came in and exclaimed, 'Talk about being spoilt for choice. I didn't know you were coming with us as well, Serena, but we can make room.'

'Thanks, but I prefer to drive myself,' she replied, picking up her black crêpe evening bag and scarlet wrap, and using her model's walk to lead the way out of the room.

'She's a hard act to follow but we're no slouches ourselves,' Janetta whispered irrepressibly to Felice as they followed her out.

'For heaven's sake don't let Charles know Tobias might be attending or he won't talk about anything else all night,' Felice whispered back desperately. 'Charles is so ambitious his night will be ruined if Tobias doesn't turn up.'

And mine will be if he does, she added silently to herself, not knowing how she would be able to endure seeing Serena in Tobias's arms. It was a spectre that failed to materialise during the first couple of hours of the dance, when her undeniable popularity provided her with so many partners that she had no time to stand around brooding.

Brood she did, though, whoever's arms she happened to be in. The clubhouse was full to bursting, she knew just about everybody, and yet still she couldn't relax and enjoy herself as much as she usually did. All the time she kept wondering, waiting, and dreading that Tobias would put in an appearance. Her eyes kept straying to the door, and then to Serena, who was also watching for him.

She must be getting impatient, Felice thought. The evening was wearing away. It would be a blow to Serena's self-esteem if Tobias failed to appear—and a blow to her own heart if he did. She sighed, and the sound came from so deep within her that it almost hurt. Well, why not? Ever since she'd tumbled headlong in love with him she hadn't had a comfortable minute.

She was dancing with Charles at the time and he said indignantly, 'What was that sigh for?'

Felice felt so guilty because he was being particularly attentive tonight that she raised her hand to touch his cheek in a light gesture of apology. 'Sorry, my mind was wandering,' she confessed.

'That's not very flattering,' he complained, catching her hand and planting a cheeky kiss on her fingers.

At that moment the music ended, and a force Felice couldn't resist drew her eyes once more to the door. This time she knew he would be there, and he was.

Tobias.

He stood just inside the entrance, darkly handsome in a dinner suit and gleaming white shirt, his unruly hair tumbling across his forehead in such a heart-tuggingly familiar way that Felice's fingers itched to brush it back. The sudden pounding of her heart was familiar, too, and so was the stormy look in his dark eyes as he looked directly at her.

She frowned, bewildered, as he was always bewildering her. What was it to him if Charles's lips were still lingering on her fingers? She was thankful, though, when Charles lowered her hand and whirled her away as another dance began, so that Tobias was lost to her sight.

That was the last dance before the auction. Everybody drifted to their tables around the dance-floor and Charles escorted her to the Lawson table. They were the last to be seated, and Felice's heart fluttered like a wild thing when she saw that the chair next to Serena's was empty.

Her eyes went questioningly to Serena, who smiled and said, 'Tobias has arrived. He was cornered by some club officials in the bar but he'll join us any moment.'

'Tobias?' Charles exclaimed. 'You don't mean Tobias Hunter?'

'Who else?' Serena asked sweetly, and transferred her attention to the stage as a roll of drums brought all conversation to a halt.

The club chairman adjusted the microphone, then said into it, 'As you all know, this dance is the first of many functions we hold each year to raise money for charity. Our particular project this year is a recreation centre for handicapped children. We've set our sights on donating twenty thousand pounds—yes, I know that's a lot of money but, with fêtes, jumble sales and sponsored walks to come, I'm sure we can manage it. The profits from this function will start the ball rolling, boosted of course by the proceeds from our popular supper dance auction. So if all you gentlemen will get your cheque books ready, I'd like the ladies who have sportingly agreed to participate to stand up for a round of applause, please.'

Felice stood up with Janetta, Serena, and several other girls. They all gave a general wave round the ballroom and sat down again. In a friendly atmosphere like this there was no embarrassment because there was always somebody to bid, even for the plainest girls.

At least, there never had been any embarrassment before, but Felice was always self-conscious when Tobias was near. She was also acutely aware that Serena was looking round for him, and was hard put not to look for him herself.

'Thank you, ladies,' the club chairman went on. 'We'll proceed in alphabetical order as usual.' He called out a girl's name and the bidding began. The average sum reached was around twenty pounds but when Janetta's turn came the bidding was fiercer and Tom finally secured her for fifty pounds.

Felice whispered her congratulations but Janetta laughingly murmured, 'It's the pink chiffon. I wonder if I can coax Serena into making it a permanent loan?'

They both looked across the table at Serena, but she was looking over her shoulder towards the bar. Felice could have said what she was thinking for her: *Where is Tobias?* But then Felice's own name was called out and she pinned a smile on her face and tried to look like a good sport.

'What am I bid for this lovely and popular lady?' the chairman asked.

From the entrance to the bar, a deep Canadian voice drawled, 'Twenty thousand pounds.'

CHAPTER TWELVE

THERE was a stunned silence, then everybody's heads turned in disbelief towards Tobias. He was leaning non-chalantly against the door-frame of the bar, a drink in his hand, completely unruffled by the sensation he had caused.

Twenty thousand pounds! Felice just couldn't absorb the shock. The colour drained from her face and she was robbed of all power to move, speak or even think.

Her first wild reaction was that he was joking, and yet she knew he wasn't. His compelling eyes were riveted on her, making love to her, blatantly claiming her, as though she were the only person in the crowded ballroom who mattered. Or the only person there at all.

Felice was devastated. All right, so twenty thousand pounds might mean as little to him as fifty pounds meant to other people, but she'd never live down the sensation he'd caused. Never!

How could he single her out like this? How could he make her such a target for gossip? Now everybody would be whispering about her, conjecturing, and coming to the conclusion that she was so much more to him than his housekeeper.

Was this his way of punishing her for refusing to be his mistress, or was he manoeuvring her into a position where she might as well be, since after tonight everybody would think that she was, anyway? Whatever, Tobias was getting his precious entertainment value out of her now, and she hated him for it. Hated him!

The stunned silence still held and her eyes were still locked on to his as colour flooded back to her ashen cheeks with a vengeance. She blushed a fiery, guilty red, and it wasn't fair. She wasn't guilty of anything. She wasn't!

Serena, sitting like marble on the opposite side of the table, was the first to come out of shock. She said bitterly and distinctly, 'You devious bitch!'

Felice swallowed but no words came. Suddenly pandemonium broke loose as everybody started speaking at once. The babble increased until the club chairman used the microphone to call for order. As the noise died down, he said, 'That most amazingly generous offer meets our charity target in one go. I don't anticipate it will be surpassed, so the supper dance with Felice goes to our newest member, Mr Tobias Hunter.'

Charles, sitting stunned beside her, came to his senses enough to gasp, 'What's going on between you two?'

Felice scarcely heard him. She was watching Tobias walking purposefully towards her, threading his way around the tables, coming inexorably closer and closer. Her nerve broke and she got up and fled, causing an even bigger sensation than his incredible bid.

Dimly she was aware that the twins, Tom and Charles were rising, too, but she heard Janetta order sharply, 'Leave them alone! It's a lovers' tiff, that's all.'

She'd spoken loud enough for half the hall to hear and Felice thought, 'That's all?' With Tobias changing direction to come after her, what did it need to be really something?

She fled out of the hall and into the car park. Only then did it occur to her that she hadn't brought her own car. The clubhouse was out in the country and she couldn't get away without transport. She would have to go in again and phone for a taxi.

She turned, but there was Tobias so close behind that she turned again, lifted her full skirts and ran in the opposite direction. She didn't get far before Tobias caught up with her and snatched her up in his arms.

She struggled and kicked but his arms only tightened as he carried her to his Jaguar and dumped her unceremoniously inside. 'Stay there or I'll strip off that gown so you can't run away,' he threatened.

'You wouldn't dare!' she panted.

'You know I would. I've bought your company for the supper dance—shall we say an hour of your precious time? I mean to have every minute of it, so you can make it easy on yourself or you can make it hard. Which is it to be?'

'I hate you,' Felice said. 'You've ruined my life. You've made everybody talk about me. Even Serena called me a devious bitch.'

'She's the devious bitch,' he said shortly, pushing the billowing folds of her skirt inside the car door and slamming it shut. Then he was beside her, overwhelming her as he always did by the force and power of his presence.

She shrank back into her seat as he leaned over to pull her seat belt across her and snap it into place. His purposeful hands brushed her breasts and she quivered with far more than anger, hating both herself and him for her reaction.

Her mind was having trouble keeping up with the physical sensations that flooded her, partly because she was still coming to terms with being manhandled as easily as if she had as little substance as a rag doll.

She wasn't used to being defenceless, and yet that was exactly how she felt when the powerful engine roared to life and the headlights snapped on. Almost mesmerised, she watched them probe ahead as Tobias drove out of the car park and gunned the car expertly along the narrow lanes.

For several minutes Felice fought to maintain a dignified silence while Tobias drove on through the night. Finally her overwrought emotions got the better of her and she burst out, 'Twenty thousand pounds! How *could* you? I have to live here, you know. I can't go swanning off to Canada when things get tough. Now everybody will think I'm a whore.'

'If you were a whore you wouldn't be here now, and neither would I. It wouldn't be necessary,' he replied grimly.

'What am I supposed to make of that?' she demanded.

'You're supposed to stop being silly. Nobody will think any the worse of you, and if they do, it's their problem. The next time they see you again you will be my wife.'

Felice failed to see the joke and said bitterly, 'I'll give you ten out of ten for a sense of humour.'

'I was never more serious in my life.'

'Then you must be crazy.'

'Yes,' Tobias agreed calmly. 'Crazy about you.'

Felice couldn't accept that and she cried, 'Crazy to get me to bed with you, perhaps.'

'That, too,' he agreed.

'What do you mean, "That, too"? That's all it is. All it's ever been with you. This is all spite because I wouldn't become one of your mistresses. You're so used to winning you simply can't bear to lose!'

'I certainly couldn't bear to lose you.'

It was driving her mad, the way he kept agreeing with her, and yet not agreeing with her, and she exploded, 'You mean your ego couldn't bear to lose! And because of that, you've deliberately humiliated me, made everybody think—think——'

Words failed her, and Tobias broke in savagely, 'If anybody is going to be humiliated tonight, it's going to be me. That's my problem, and to hell with everybody else, including Serena. Just get it through that lovely head of yours that I'm the only one you have to worry about tonight.'

Lovely head…? Having made her the subject of every spiteful tongue in the district, manhandled and kidnapped her, was he now trying to *charm* her into bed? Well, he'd left it a bit late! Felice opened her mouth to tell him so, when the car slowed and she demanded in alarm, 'Why are we stopping?'

'We're home. Our home—Woodlands. Or it will be as soon as we're married.'

'It's not my home,' she snapped, unable to believe that even Tobias would stoop to such deception to get his own way. 'Even if you were serious, I'd never marry you.'

'I warned you once before not to say "never" to me,' he reminded her calmly as he released her seatbelt, 'but I'm willing to let that pass for the moment. I'm sorry I've had to be so rough with you, but you gave me little choice. It was the only way I could get your attention for more than five minutes at a time. I'll explain everything when we're inside.'

'No!' she exclaimed, distrusting him.

'Yes,' he contradicted. 'You can tell me all your reasons why you're not going to marry me, then I'll tell you my reasons why you are.' He looked at the clock on the dashboard and added, 'I still have forty-five minutes of your time. Of course, if you prefer to stay here...'

He leaned towards her and Felice got hastily out of the car. The joke, when he finally sprung it, was bound to catch her unawares, and she didn't want to be within arm's reach of him at the time. Shivering in the cold night air and shaking out the crushed folds of her gown, she followed him into the Hall and through to the library.

He indicated an armchair by the fire. She sat down reluctantly, watching him like a hawk as he added logs to the glowing embers of the fire. He studied the logs as the embers kindled to flame, then turned to her with a crooked smile that tugged at her heart-strings.

'No woodlice for you to save tonight, Felice,' he said softly. 'Only me—from my loneliness. Will that loving heart of yours stretch to take me on as well?'

'Stop it! Stop playing with me,' she flared, jumping out of the armchair and prowling restlessly around the room. 'You've had your fun. Let me go home now.'

'You are home,' he told her. 'Sometimes I'll have to take you away from it because I want you with me wherever I go, but I'll bring you back often enough to keep you happy. I promise——'

'Stop it!' Felice cried again, her hands clenching into fists at what she saw as his merciless determination to play out to the bitter end the game he was making of her. 'Just stop it.'

'But I can't,' he replied, his voice deepening in the way that had bewitched and bewildered her over the past traumatic weeks. 'Tonight has always been inevitable, Felice. We've both fought against it for different reasons, but we've both been wasting our time. I've known it for a long time now. Haven't you?'

'No!' she exclaimed, incensed. 'All I know is that I've been preparing this house for your mistress, the one you picked out to have your children. Have you forgotten about her?'

'Not for a moment,' Tobias replied, coming towards her. 'She haunts me day and night, wrecking my sleep, driving me to distraction. Housekeeper, mistress, wife—they've always been one person in my mind. You, Felice.'

'I don't believe you,' she whispered, her voice almost breaking on a sob.

'It's the truth,' Tobias told her, coming closer still. 'You love Woodlands so much—how could I possibly let anybody else loose on it? You've been preparing this house for yourself, my darling. I haven't been able to tell you until now because you had too many things against me.'

Felice's heart began to pound, but she was still frightened to trust the message it was pulsing to every taut nerve in her body. 'What was Serena, then?' she asked desperately. 'A convenient diversion?'

'Serena was a mistake, and you can blame yourself for that. All I've had of your company were whatever crumbs you cared to throw my way while you were working for me. It wasn't enough and it will never be enough. You chose to spend your spare time with somebody else, and I refuse to be responsible for the things I do when I'm out of my mind with jealousy. Stop making me jealous, and there won't be any more Serenas in my life. I won't need them.'

Felice caught her breath, and as she felt a betraying surge of tears, she blinked furiously and begged, 'Stop playing with me, Tobias. You've had your fun...your revenge. Let me go. Please...'

'That's the one thing I can't do, my darling. I love you far too much.'

Felice's white teeth bit hard into her full lower lip, and she protested, 'If you loved me, if you knew even *any* small thing about love, you wouldn't have made that dreadful bid for me at the auction.'

Tobias was so close by now he towered over her. He took her trembling hands in his, sapping what little resistance to him she had left. His voice throbbed as he breathed, 'That wasn't a bid, it was a declaration of love. Everybody knew it except you, my woolly-headed little darling.'

'D-don't call me that,' Felice stuttered, starting to panic now that she had no fury left to sustain her. 'I'm not your darling!'

'Yes, you are.'

'Don't!' she insisted, adding foolishly, 'I'm certainly not little, anyway.'

'No, my darling, you are the most stunning of the lovely Lawson girls. The pick of the batch. Not only stunning but kind, caring and loving. How many girls would throw away their own ambitions to raise their younger brothers and sister, and make such a fine job of it? Just the sort of job I know you'll do on our children.'

'Stop it!' Felice begged desperately. 'If you've been listening to Janetta and the boys, they're biased and——'

'I've been listening to my own heart,' he broke in. 'If I'd listened to it in the first place none of this would have happened. Unfortunately, your kind of integrity, love and loyalty is too rare for a man like me to believe in right away. Can you forgive me for my doubts, Felice? Doubts I learned from others but punished you for?'

'I can't believe you're saying all this,' she whispered, her heart breaking with love for this humble man who was so different from the stormy Tobias who'd made her life both heaven and hell. He sounded as though he had a heart that could feel love and pain in the same way hers could.

'I'm saying it, and I'll keep on saying it until you believe me.'

'Oh, don't,' she begged again.

'What do you mean—don't?' Tobias asked, his patience wearing thin and his dark eyebrows snapping together in the way she knew so well.

'I mean you don't have to explain anything to me. Not if——' She wanted to say 'not if you truly love me' but the words wouldn't come. She still felt too insecure, too shy.

'I do have to explain otherwise you'll never understand why I was so suspicious of you.' Tobias lifted her hands to his lips and kissed them lingeringly before he continued, 'Twelve years ago I married a woman who didn't want me, but the things I could give her. A gold-digger, in fact, although I couldn't see it at the time. When I did, it cost me a lot of wrangling, a lot of bitterness and a fortune to get rid of her.'

He smiled, but it was a smile made painful by bitter self-mockery. 'I thought that in the long run the experience was worth it because it made me too smart ever to be caught a second time. I vowed I'd never again confuse wanting a woman with loving her, and I didn't. Whenever I fancied a woman after that, I paid first and walked away a free man before disillusion could set in. It worked like a charm until I met you, Felice.'

He took her face gently between his strong hands, staring intently into her eyes. 'I fell for you within

minutes of meeting you, but I was too cynical to believe
it was love. By the time I realised you were as loving as
you were lovely, as genuine as you were loyal, it was too
late. I'd spoilt it all.'

He sighed and kissed her hair gently, then pulled her
against him and cradled her head into his shoulder. Felice
felt the warmth and strength of his hard body. It no
longer seemed a threat but a power she could depend
upon. She knew she was being overwhelmed again,
trapped, and yet it was in such a delicious way...

After a moment, Tobias continued, 'Deep inside I
always knew you were really as wonderful as you appeared to be—but I needed to doubt. To protect myself,
I punished you. I drove you away from me, and you
kept on running, no matter how hard I chased.'

He turned her face up to his and pleaded, 'Don't run
any more, my darling. I've been going out of my mind
with jealousy and despair.'

'You?' she whispered wonderingly.

'Yes, me. That red-headed fellow who was drooling
all over you in the village this morning and at the dance
this evening will never know how close he came to being
flattened.'

'He's just a friend, Tobias.'

'That's more than I am, isn't it?' he asked bitterly.

Felice saw all the anguish she'd been suffering herself
reflected in his face. Her heart lurched, and she asked
with difficulty, 'If—if you felt like this about me, why
did you date Serena?'

'Because you wouldn't come out with me. Because I
was out of my mind with jealousy. Because—oh, my
God, Felice, don't you realise I haven't said or done a
rational thing since I first met you?'

That struck a chord Felice couldn't doubt, so aptly did it describe the way she'd been feeling and behaving herself, and yet there were still things she needed to know. 'It didn't seem too rational the way you chased me in your car this morning,' she admitted. 'I still don't know why you did.'

'I'd reached the end of my tether. I was going to risk telling you that I loved you.'

'Risk?' she echoed, bewildered.

'Yes, risk. I'd made you despise me so much that I only had your love for Woodlands to work on to keep you close to me. I hoped that in time you'd forgive me for all the mistakes I'd made and give me a second chance. But all you were interested in was the house, never me. You didn't give me any opportunity to get closer to you, and I couldn't show how I really felt about you. With my track record, you'd have thought I was only trying to get you into bed with me, and I was frightened you'd take off for good.'

The thought of Tobias being frightened was something Felice was still trying to get to grips with when he said, 'I gambled everything on tonight, and I still don't know whether I've won or lost.'

Felice stirred in his arms, and raised her head from his shoulder to look up into his eyes. 'What if you've lost?' she asked.

Tobias's face hardened. 'Then I'll try something else, and keep on trying until you give up. One thing you'd better understand, and understand right now, is that *I'm* never going to give up.'

That sounded more like the Tobias she knew—and loved to the point of madness. But she still had enough spirit left to object, 'That sounds more like an ultimatum than a proposal of marriage.'

'It's the way I feel,' he growled.

'Because you think I'm suitable for bearing your children?'

Tobias grasped her shoulders and shook her none too gently. 'I no longer care if we don't have any. I *love* you, can't you understand that? I can't even *look* at another woman.'

A brief flare of jealousy made Felice grumble, 'Serena would have something to say about that.'

'I never looked at Serena, not in the way I look at you. I endured her company because I couldn't have yours. You can blame yourself for that.'

'Somehow I knew it would come round to being all my fault,' Felice murmured. 'I suppose if our marriage doesn't work, that will be my fault as well.'

Tobias realised what she'd said before she did herself. His arms tightened around her and he buried his face in her hair. 'Then you will marry me? Oh, my love, you'll never regret it, and our marriage will work. The way I love you, it can't fail.' He lifted his head to gaze at her, and added, 'So long as you love me, too. Tell me that you do, my darling.'

The uncertainty in his eyes went straight to Felice's heart, banishing the last of her doubts. 'I love you,' she admitted at last, and sighed as though a burden had fallen from her. 'So very, very much.'

She heard Tobias sigh as well, and knew he was feeling the same kind of release that had freed her of the unhappiness of the past few weeks. His lips closed on hers, claiming all the love she'd withheld so stubbornly from him, and giving in return all the love that he was capable of.

It was more than enough. So profound was the emotion flowing between them that the world receded until only they had any reality.

When Tobias raised his head again, it was only by a fraction so that he could murmur against her lips, 'We'll fly to London tomorrow and be married by special licence as soon as we can. We can have a proper wedding here later if you like, but I must and will make you my wife as soon as possible.'

Felice drew away from him a fraction more to ask teasingly, 'So I don't get any time to change my mind?'

'No, you don't,' he replied, passion roughening his voice. 'No time at all. You have to trust yourself to me. I know we've fought, but I'll spend the rest of my life making up for it.'

'Oh, Tobias,' she sighed, winding her arms around his neck and brushing her lips against his provocatively, 'I wouldn't have missed a moment of it, beast that you are.'

'Tame me,' he breathed, and kissed her.

'Tame me,' she responded, and kissed him back.

But the bonding of their lips inflamed them both. It fired all the passion that had been simmering beneath the surface since their eyes first met, their hands first touched and they first learned the danger of being in each other's arms.

Tobias groaned, thrust her away from him, and said between clenched teeth, 'I'm not quite—civilised right now. You'd better take yourself off to one of the bedrooms, right this moment, while you still can. I don't want you thinking I've brought you here just to seduce you.'

Felice stretched out a hand to touch his stormy face with loving fingers. She sighed, thinking that a nice girl would flee this very instant. But she stayed and asked tremulously, 'What if I want to be seduced?'

'For God's sake, don't torment me now, Felice! I'm trying to do things right for once in my life.'

'So am I,' she responded, 'and I can't see how you and I staying together, feeling the way we do about each other, can possibly be wrong.'

Once more she was given no chance to reconsider. Tobias swept her up in his arms and strode with her to the couch by the fire, sitting down with her still in his arms. She coiled her arms around his neck and drew his dark head down to hers, scattering kisses all over his face, and receiving his in return.

She felt his hand slide from her neck to her shoulder, and gasped as it slid under the silk of her ballgown to cup her breast. Her nipple tautened, demanding his attention, and she gasped as his probing fingers found and grasped it.

Sensations so sweet suffused Felice's entire body that she could scarcely breathe for a moment. She went limp in his arms, her head falling back so that he could press burning kisses along the supple line of her throat.

She didn't feel him unzip the back of her bodice, but she felt the soft silk slip from her shoulders, exposing both her breasts to him. He bent his head and kissed them lingeringly in turn, his lips fastening against first one nipple and then the other.

'My lovely Felice,' he murmured. 'My magnificent darling.'

For the first time in her life she felt not too much of a woman, but just enough, and a surge of passion banished her weakness and gave her a power of her own.

She unbuttoned his dinner-jacket and then his shirt, and threw them aside as he shrugged out of them. They were both bare to the waist now, and flesh called to flesh, so that he once more clasped her against him.

They both gasped as her soft breasts were clamped against the hard hairiness of his chest, neither moving for long moments until their lips instinctively bonded again. Still kissing her, Tobias lifted her up and laid her gently on the fur rug in front of the log fire.

Vaguely Felice remembered how jealous she'd been when she'd thought of Tobias claiming a woman right here, and in this passionate way. She'd always wanted to be that woman and, even now, she could scarcely believe that she was.

It was almost dreamlike, but then Tobias began to take off the rest of her clothes, kissing every inch of newly exposed flesh, and her responses became earthy, primitive, very much of this world.

His own clothes became a hindrance and she stripped them off him, her hands running possessively over the lean length of him, glorying in his strength and the latent power she detected under his rippling muscles.

'I love you,' he murmured, kissing his way from her breasts to her midriff, then his tongue reaching and exploring her navel. As he continued his downward quest, he demanded roughly, 'Say you love me, too. Say it, Felice.'

'I love you,' she whispered, her hands exploring the taut muscles of his shoulders and back. 'You'll never know how much.'

'I need to know now,' he gasped, kissing her silken thighs as he parted them.

'I love you,' she repeated, and then her body arched in an explosion of sensation as he discovered and explored the secret parts of her. 'Tobias,' she added brokenly. 'Tobias, for heaven's sake...'

But he had reached the limit of his own endurance and he thrust into her, uniting them in the flames of passion that had been threatening to consume them for so long. Felice, responding to his frantic demands for satisfaction and matching it with demands of her own, knew that her senses hadn't played her false. This was the ultimate consummation, the ultimate act of a love that both had craved but resisted for so long.

When Tobias collapsed against her with a great cry, she cradled him to her, keeping him safe until strength and reason returned to both of them. This was her moment, she thought, her eyes misty with tears. He was totally hers now. And she was totally his.

She felt complete, sated, no tiny corner of her questioning or unloved. When Tobias finally moved away and cradled her, in his turn, in his arms, she lay against him, the happiest woman in the world.

When he spoke at last, it was to ask, 'Are you warm enough?'

'Mmm...' she replied dreamily.

He still reached up, snatched a rug from the couch and spread it over them before he lay down again. 'No regrets?' he asked anxiously, flooding her again with the need to soothe and reassure him.

'What regrets should I have?' she teased. 'You're not going to spank me on the bottom and send me back to the servants' quarters, are you?'

Tobias laughed and hugged her. 'You sound like yourself again. The lovely, laughing girl who met me from the plane when I first came to Woodlands... the girl I was so harsh with... the girl I've been pining for ever since. I was so afraid I'd killed off all that was best in you.'

Felice pressed her face into his shoulder and murmured, 'You got what you wanted in the end, though, didn't you? I've ended up what I was determined not to be—your mistress.'

Tobias tangled his hand in her hair and pulled her face away from his shoulder so that she had to meet his eyes. 'Don't say that,' he growled. 'We'll be married in a few days.'

Felice smiled at him. 'It's not so important any more. Now that I know I'm loved, the ring doesn't seem to matter.'

'It matters to me,' Tobias responded fiercely, his hand tightening in her hair. 'I won't rest until you're tied to me so tightly you'll never get free.'

'I thought that was your own particular nightmare—never getting free, I mean.'

Tobias began to kiss the strands of her hair that were twined like silk between his fingers. 'That was before I knew what it was like to love a woman I had no claim on at all. It was hell. Why do you think I couldn't stay away from Woodlands? Why do you think I found a way to tie you to Woodlands? Why do you think I stopped you working as a taxi driver?'

'Tell me,' she invited, entranced by this lover-like side of Tobias that had been hidden from her for so long.

'To keep you close, to keep you safe, until I could claim you for my own. But you kept wriggling free. This time you won't, though,' he vowed, releasing her hair and pushing her head back to the safety of his shoulder.

Felice kissed his salty skin and confessed, 'I've loved you since day one, but I wouldn't admit it even to myself. I'm still not sure why you didn't fall for Serena—or even Janetta. They're both so much lovelier than I am.'

'In a standard sort of way, perhaps, but I've never been interested in what was standard. I'm a high-flyer, Felice, and nothing less than exceptional satisfies me. You, my magnificent darling.'

She felt her eyes moisten with tears again, and said huskily, 'I'm beginning to think you really do love me.'

'Beginning to think...?' he questioned, almost speechlessly. 'Do you think I'd be prepared to live in this mausoleum of a house if it wasn't for love of you?'

'It isn't a mausoleum,' Felice objected, her head snapping up indignantly. 'It's a beautiful house.'

'It's a folly,' he replied in a voice that brooked no argument. Then his voice softened and he continued, 'Maybe we should crack open a bottle of champagne and drink to folly. Is there any champagne in the house?'

'No,' Felice admitted forlornly, 'and I thought I was a pretty good housekeeper, too. I'll just have to try to be a better mistress.'

'A better *wife*,' Tobias corrected her severely. 'Well, if we can't drink to folly, what shall we do?'

'We could always make love,' she offered hopefully.

'Truly a girl after my own heart,' he breathed, and folded her into his arms again.

Lilian Peake grew up in Essex. Her first job was working for a writer of mystery stories. Subsequently, she became a journalist on a provincial newspaper, then moved to a trade magazine and reported on fashion. Later she took on an advice column on a woman's magazine. She began writing romances because she loves happy endings! She lives near Oxford, England, with her husband, a retired college principal. They have two sons and a daughter. Her hobbies are walking, reading and listening to classical music.

GOLD RING
OF REVENGE

BY
LILIAN PEAKE

MILLS & BOON LIMITED
ETON HOUSE, 18-24 PARADISE ROAD
RICHMOND, SURREY TW9 1SR

*First published in Great Britain in 1992
by Mills & Boon Limited*

© Lilian Peake 1992

*Australian copyright 1992
Philippine copyright 1992
This edition 1992*

ISBN 0 263 77517 8

*Set in Times Roman 10 on 11 pt.
06-9208-60846 C*

Made and printed in Great Britain

CHAPTER ONE

PUTTING down her suitcases, Rhea massaged her aching arms. Then, shifting her bulging shoulder-pack into a more secure position, she retrieved the cases and continued walking.

Anger had kept her going through all the hours that she had been travelling, and it was that same anger that spurred her on now, overriding the tiredness that seemed to increase with every step. In her suitcases she carried all the worldly possessions that fate, in the form of the law, financial establishments and other people's trickery, had allowed her to keep.

Now she was on her way to find someone, a man who, she had been told on reliable authority, cared nothing for others, and women in particular; who was harder in nature than granite and who took life as it came, using it to the full and, when he had drained dry that particular experience—for 'experience', she had been advised, read 'woman'—putting it, and her, out of his mind and his life, moving on to the next . . . and the next.

She wished she knew where to look for him. He lived, she had been vaguely told, here in this village in the Yorkshire Dales. Its name was Cuttingbeck, but there was no one around from whom she could ask directions. Not a soul walked along the dusty road, nor stood in any doorway in the fitful sunshine.

As she walked, her feet dragging now with tiredness, a sound impinged on her ears. It rang like iron striking iron, hammering and pounding, then stopping with a clatter. Skylarks sang in brilliant chorus overhead and from behind a gate in a flower-filled cottage garden a dog barked fiercely.

The rhythmic hammering started again and, city-influenced though her hearing was, it could still interpret the meaning of those sounds. They told her that, somewhere nearby, there just had to be a forge, a blacksmith's, maybe, with someone working there from whom she could ask the way.

Optimism being an essential part of her character, she felt her heart lift at the prospect of an end to her journey—a long train-ride northwards from the environs of London. After which, having missed the bus with, apparently, a wait of three hours until the next one, she had had no real alternative but to start out on the three-mile walk which, she had been informed by a station attendant dubiously eyeing her baggage, stretched between that station and the village of Cuttingbeck.

Now and then she had rested, even climbing over a padlocked farm gate and falling asleep with utter weariness in the breezy sunshine in the corner of a field. After a series of sleepless nights, not to mention weeks of hassle and worry and emotional devastation, fatigue had finally caught up with her.

Unfortunately, as she had climbed back to the road, the old and rickety iron gate had rocked beneath her and her foot, having found a precarious perch on a bar, slipped and twisted awkwardly as it hit the ground. She had dropped to join it, rocking to and fro with the pain, then, biting her lower lip, rested back on a suitcase, hugging her throbbing foot.

Pausing now, putting her weight on her undamaged leg, Rhea tried to locate the place from which the hammering, which had stopped again, had come. To her relief it was resumed, and she traced it to the ancient stone-built barn which stood only a few yards distant. So the man—it had to be a man, because, she reasoned, surely no woman possessed such strength as the person working inside that building appeared to have—had not gone away.

Hovering in the open doorway, she saw the man pause as he leaned over the anvil, hammer held aloft, postponing the strike as if he had become conscious of the presence of another human being—had she perhaps cut off some of his light?—but unwilling to shift his eye from where it was pinpointed, and turn to investigate.

She hadn't said a word, had scarcely breathed, but the strike was abandoned and the hammer lowered. The man looked over his shoulder, registered her presence and turned fully to face her.

It was a moment which, to Rhea, seemed to be frozen in time. She would never forget her first sight of him. He was tall, with thick black hair, and stripped to the waist, his torso highlighted and outlined by the fire burning in the wide, blackened grate behind him. He was lean, yet muscled, his waistband sitting low over hips that boasted not even a pinch of spare flesh.

'Yes?' The hammer found a clattering place on a wooden table, the coke fire spitting as if irritated by the workman's straying attention.

Rhea tried to speak but found her lips were dry. Moving her tongue across them, she cleared her throat. 'I'm sorry to have interrupted you, but——'

He reached for a black T-shirt, pulling it on, then strolled towards her, hands in the pockets of his work-grimed trousers. It was then that she felt the full force of his eyes. They were a steely grey, piercing and telling of a formidable intellect, revealing an interest that was disinterested yet coldly sensual, but whose message held no gladness. Will you tell me what you want, it said, then go.

Near as she was now, Rhea became aware of how his neck and arms gleamed with a moisture imparted by the heat from the flicking flames, combined with the sheer physical effort the man had been expending. His upper lip held a sheen which clung to the dark roughness of a jaw that seemed not to have felt the scrape of a razor for a good many hours.

His eyes lowered to the suitcases she had dropped to the ground, taking in her shoulder-bag and her untidy brown hair, noting her general dishevelment. She held his gaze and, despite the extraordinary havoc it was causing inside her, tried to read his reaction, but found only an uninformative blankness.

'I'm sorry to interrupt you,' she said again, 'but I'm new to the area,' a self-evident statement which, she supposed, merited the faintly satirical flick of his brow, 'and I'm looking for someone. There was no one else around to ask, so I took a chance and came over here.' Do I have to babble so? she reproached herself, but the man's whole demeanour seemed to have reduced to rubble her powers of verbal self-censorship. 'His name is Leo Dower, and I'm told he lives in Cuttingbeck. I wondered if you'd heard of him?'

The faintest pause, then, 'I've heard.'

Despite her injured ankle, which had begun to ache alarmingly, a smile of sheer relief lit her face. 'So maybe you could direct me to his house?' He let the question hang in the air and she wondered if it was his way of saying no. 'I—I desperately need to talk to him——'

'Business or——' his eyes did a quick raking job and Rhea's reflexes quivered with a cocktail-mix of both excitement and anger '—pleasure?'

She could not stop the hectic flush. Male this man certainly was, but, instead of his innuendo annoying her as it should, to her consternation it made her heart beat faster.

'Certainly not the latter,' she returned indignantly, 'but,' her shoulders lifted, 'I suppose it could be categorised as business. His br——' Just in time, she stopped herself. She had no intention of giving away any more than necessary to this arrogant, not to say abrasive stranger.

His eyes flicked with a faint disparagement to her cases. 'You look as if you've come to stay for a year. Is this man expecting you?' His voice was even and cultured, bearing no overtones of a regional accent.

'Well, no, but... Anyway, I've got no intention of dumping myself on him uninvited. In all the circumstances, I'm sure he'd find me very unwelcome. I thought I might book a room at the local pub. Or find somewhere that does bed and breakfast.'

A piece of coke rearranged itself meaningfully, then hissed and flared. It seemed to be calling the man back to his work.

'OK.' He appeared to relent, approaching the doorway, brushing past Rhea, whose skin through her cotton jacket prickled alarmingly as his bare arm made fleeting contact with hers.

He lifted that arm and pointed. It was, Rhea noted in passing, liberally sprinkled with a layer of dark hair. 'See that rough track along the street, branching off to the left? It goes down to the river. Cross by the stone bridge—you see it?—and his cottage is just off to the left. You can't miss it.' He turned back to her. 'He won't be there, but don't let that worry you. Just open the door and walk in.' His smile mocked her worried frown. 'It's the custom in these parts.'

'He won't mind?'

'Believe me, he's not the kind of guy to worry one way or the other.' His gaze moved to her hair and, with a curiously familiar movement that unnerved her, his hand reached out, his fingers plucking at the deep brown strands and making a capture. He held it up. 'Grass? How come?'

There was no need for her to explain, but she did. 'When you feel you can't take another step without a rest,' she told him, reluctant to confide any weakness to a man with such obvious strength, both of body and mind, 'you find somewhere, anywhere, to do what your brain, and your body, tell you. I saw an empty field. My feet and legs took over from there.'

Plainly comprehending, he moved his mouth in the semblance of a smile. Thanking him for his directions, Rhea picked up her cases.

He was pulling off his T-shirt even before she moved away, seemingly anxious to return to his work. She felt that he watched her as she followed his directions, her tired legs dragging as she forced her painful foot to take its share of her weight, not to mention the burden of her cases, resisting the urge to turn round to check whether her suspicion was correct.

A silver birch, moving gracefully in full summer green, lifted itself high by the bank of the boulder-strewn river which passed within a forceful stone's throw of the cottage.

The road went on its winding way up the hill that led across the bare moorland, but, obeying instructions, Rhea descended from the bridge, leaving the road by an uneven track which led down to a lawn whose boundary was the stone-strewn path bordering the river.

Pausing, she looked at the cottage—more of a rambling two-storeyed house, really—with its slate-covered roof, its stone-silled windows tall and wide, a trellised archway interwoven with wild roses embellishing the main entrance door.

'Just open the door and walk in,' he'd said, so she did just that, but knocking first, in case the owner had returned without the stranger's knowledge.

Silence greeted Rhea's tentative, 'Mr Dower, are you home?' To make quite sure, she repeated the question, louder this time, but again there was no reply. The cases thumped from her stiffened fingers, her shoulder-pack hitting the carpet beside them, her undamaged leg again taking the strain.

The owner of the cottage, judging by its furnishings, well used but of good quality, was most decidedly not poverty-stricken, but this she already knew. Something inside her responded appreciatively to the countrified fabrics covering the sofa and easy-chairs, the theme followed through in the curtains, all but one of which remained pulled across from the night before.

With a sense of daring, Rhea limped round a low wooden table, a rack from which magazines spilled, and a couple of footstools piled high with books, and pushed wide the curtains covering the remaining window. The late afternoon sunlight flooded in, filling the room and dazzling her tired vision, making her acutely aware of her own fatigue.

Looking around, the feeling still strong of having trespassed, she sank on to a sofa, glad most of all to be able to rest her throbbing ankle. Only now did she allow herself to lift her trouser leg and inspect the damage, aghast at what she found. Her ankle had swollen, her foot, likewise, having become puffy and increasingly difficult to move within her shoe.

Rhea knew she should bathe it, bandage it even, but felt she had no right to do even that in a stranger's house. When she had found somewhere to stay, she told herself reassuringly, she would try and repair the damage with some plaster from the small first-aid kit she carried with her.

The tranquillity that came with the peace and quiet all around her was to her troubled senses like a stroking, soothing hand, although, closing her eyes, she could not prevent her thoughts from turning in on themselves.

The past returned like a slow-motion playback, but not in colour. It was all in black and white, with the brightness turned down and the contrast badly adjusted, the pictures that followed each other in relentless procession comfortless and bleak.

'What use are you to me now?' a man's voice said. 'Why should I hang around now there's nothing in it for me? What have you got to offer except what all women have got? And most of them know what to do with it a darn sight better than you.'

'But right from the start,' she whispered back, horrified and totally unbelieving, 'you said you loved me.'

'Of course I said that. What man wouldn't, to a girl with all that lovely money behind her? Devoted parents, her rich daddy doting on her, naming her his heiress. Some heiress!' He seized her shoulders, half shaking her. 'And to think I held off all that time, because "Mummy and Daddy" were so strait-laced and old-fashioned that they might ban me from their sight, not to mention their daughter's life. So I reminded myself every time I got within smooching distance and nearly overstepped the mark that Rhea Hirst's future fortune was worth holding off for.'

'Why, you——!' She tore away and lifted her hand, stinging his cheek. In his fury, his lips had almost disappeared, but she hid her fear and stood her ground. 'Get out,' she spat, 'out of this house and out of my life. I never want to see you again!'

'That's OK with me, pal,' he answered, and ran outside, getting into her car, firing the engine with the keys with which she had entrusted him. 'If you want this great bit of engineering back,' his hand came through the opened window and stroked the car's bodywork, 'contact me through my solicitor. Except that he won't tell.'

The engine roared under the pressure of his foot. 'If you want payment for this car,' he shouted, 'my brother will oblige. He's rolling in it.' He reached into a pocket and threw an envelope through the window. 'There's his address. But give him warning that you're coming, won't you? Otherwise you might walk into an embarrassing situation. He just *loves* the opposite sex. But I've told

you that before, haven't I? 'Bye, Rhea. Thanks for all
the happy memories we never had!'

Tearing off her engagement ring, she ran across and
hurled it into the car through the open window, then
watched helplessly as her own car—it had become hers
when her father had died, being all that she had managed
to salvage from the wreck of her life—became a mere
speck in the distance.

She awoke to sounds that seemed to be muted so as not
to awaken, a disturbance of air cooling her and making
her aware of the dampness on her cheeks. With the back
of her hand she tried to brush it away, but her eyes
seemed to be intent on supplying yet more.

A shuddering sob came from her depths as she awoke
fully and the figure of a man floated into her still misty
vision. He was staring down at her with neither condemnation nor welcome, nor even with surprise... Of
course he wasn't surprised to see her, she told herself
sharply. This was the man, wasn't it, who had directed
her to this cottage? But, judging by the taut line of his
mouth, he seemed more foe than friend. Swinging her
legs to the floor, she sat upright.

'Are you Leo Dower?' she demanded.

'I'm Leo Dower.'

'Why,' she challenged, 'when I spoke to you in the
forge, didn't you tell me who you were? Why did you
pretend to be someone else?'

His smile held no mirth. 'I didn't want you to turn
and run. There are too many questions needing answers,
Miss Hirst. Like, where's my brother Jerome?'

'You know who I am?' Unsteadily she got to her feet,
surreptitiously favouring her uninjured foot. His hand
reached out, the back of it succeeding in reducing the
dampness on her cheeks where hers had failed.

'Nursing a secret sorrow?' he queried, with more
cynicism than sympathy.

She shrank from the contact, slight though it had been, but the smooth skin of her cheeks seemed to have a mind of its own. It retained the faint impact of his touch as if it had actually liked it.

'I know. Jerome sent me an assortment of photos, of you, of himself with his arm round you. An engagement portrait such as loving, if a mite old-fashioned parents demand.'

His hair was damp, which indicated that he had showered while she had slept. He pushed his hands into the waistband of the dark trousers into which he had changed. His potent cleanliness made her even more conscious of her dust-laden self, and she found herself longing for a bath, for a change of clothes, for a mirror. Then she'd be able to tidy her long hair and apply a little make-up and show this sardonic individual that she had more feminine attractions than at that moment he seemed to consider she possessed.

'So where's Jerome?' he pursued.

'I wish I knew, Mr Dower,' she snapped. 'He owes me—oh, yes, he owes me. If I ever come across him again, I'll make him pay—oh!'

A cry escaped her and she fell forward, her face crumpling with pain. He caught her, holding her away from him by her arms. Rhea cursed herself for her stupidity. Forgetfully she had put some weight on to her injured foot, and the agony was such that she felt she could hardly bear it.

All the same, with her head rigidly high, she braced her shoulders to pull from his hold, refusing to display any kind of weakness in front of this macho, sardonic creature. But through sheer force of habit she used the damaged foot yet again and, with an anguished gasp, fell against him. This time he permitted the contact, tolerating her arms as they clamped for support around his waist.

Her head drooped this time, her cheek of its own accord finding a resting place against his chest, the drumming of his heart beneath her ear reminding her of the rhythmic hammering she had heard as she had approached the forge.

An image of his torso, moist and tough and muscled as it had been when she had first set eyes on him, flashed before her eyes, and a strange excitement coursed through her, a feeling she suppressed as fast as it had arisen.

'OK,' he eased her from him, 'you can switch off the righteous indignation. It takes two to land you in the mess you're in. So he's made you pregnant. When's the child due?'

She jerked away and stared up at him. 'What child?'

'Oh, come on, now, Miss Hirst, there's no need to be coy with me. I know my brother as if he were part of me.' He released her and she forced herself to remember to stand on her good leg. 'You think you're the first young woman in that kind of trouble that he's pointed in my direction?'

Rhea could only stare at him.

'So you're shocked, horrified at what I'm telling you,' he went on, plainly having no intention of sparing her. 'He'd given you a ring, you're thinking, which surely meant he was genuinely in love with you? He put on such an act of devotion you don't believe me?' He shook his head slowly. 'I know his ways. He's a smooth talker, my brother, the kind that women fall for by the dozen.'

'I think,' she answered fiercely, knowing she also had once fallen for that 'smooth talk', 'that you're the most arrogant, unpleasant-minded individual I've ever——'

'Let's be realistic, Miss Hirst.' There was a faint impatience in his tone. 'You think you're the first—er—lady to come running to me for that reason? Then think again.' He held up his hand, his fingers indicating four. 'So far, that is. You want payment for services rendered? OK, as Jerome knows only too well, I'll oblige. All the others went away satisfied with the sum of money I offered them.'

'Oh! You're no different from your brother!' Her hand itched to make stinging contact with his cheek as it had with Jerome's. 'You're both as callous, as un- scrupulous, as uncaring of people's feelings as each other!'

'Uncaring?' He seemed really angry now. Those grey eyes held the flash of steel. 'You call my offer of help an *uncaring* act?'

Rhea took a sharp breath. Maybe he was right, maybe in his own eyes he *was* doing his best to right the wrong he thought his brother had inflicted.

If only she hadn't injured herself, she fretted. If only she could pick up her belongings and walk out.

'You have the effrontery to call me callous,' he was saying, 'when I'm doing the honest thing, uninvolved though I am, and offering you cash as some kind of reparation for the coming total disruption of your life— brought about not by me, but by my brother?'

'Thank you for your kind gesture,' she answered levelly, 'but——' There is no child, she had been about to say, but at that moment her uninjured leg started shaking under the stress of keeping her upright and she sank back on to the sofa, white-faced with pain.

He frowned down at her, and she remembered that he could not know the reason for her distress since the leg of her jeans hid the swollen flesh around her foot and ankle. If she could manage to stave off his intruding questions and remain there for an hour or two until the swelling subsided, she would probably be able to make it to the local inn and in a few days make her way... where?

In the depths of the nightmares that had followed Jerome's departure, when she had felt so utterly alone, the idea had taken root of seeking out this unknown relative, as Jerome had suggested. Somebody in the Dower family owed her, and who better to make that payment than the brother called Leo?

'OK.' Leo's voice was hard. He plainly thought that her show of pain was staged for his benefit. 'Let's quit the melodramatic routine, shall we? Then you can tell me what it is you want.'

She knew now, beyond doubt, what she wanted. It was revenge—revenge for all the unhappiness and misery that his brother had inflicted on her... for the lies, the double dealing, the fraud he had perpetrated and the destitution she now found herself in, but, most of all, for the way he had emptied her life of feeling, of meaning, of love itself...

'Strange that my brother cast *you* adrift,' Leo was saying, arms folded, expression malely appreciative, although overlaid with a measure of contempt. 'Yet not strange. Amber eyes that should melt a man, yet they're cool enough to make him shiver. I wonder why.'

He considered her for a few moments.

'A face the shape of a heart,' he went on, 'but without the warmth that keeps that vital organ beating.' He shook his head. 'How can I believe what I've heard? That this time my little brother had hit the jackpot? He'd got himself engaged, he said, to a girl who had everything. Not only was she sexy, he told me, but she also had a fortune behind her. Provided, of course, he said, that he was nice to her daddy and watched his step by playing the old-fashioned gentleman, in public at least, towards the daughter whom the father, not to mention the mother, worshipped.'

Hearing Jerome's exact sentiments confirmed by this pitiless man, hearing the truth as Jerome had so cruelly spelled it out in the weeks following her parents' deaths, hit Rhea like a hammer blow. She would, she vowed, get even with the Dower family as unscrupulously, as

calculatedly, as its younger son had robbed her, Rhea
Hirst, of all that she had held most dear.

'Except,' Leo Dower went on, his dark gaze raking
her, 'it's plain he didn't keep to his resolve. I could never
in a million years imagine my brother playing the
"gentleman" where his girlfriends...I beg your pardon,'
with sardonic courtesy, 'fiancées... are concerned.'

The telephone rang distantly and Leo, with a brief
'Excuse me', opened a door which, Rhea noted with a
turn of the head, appeared to lead into an inner hall.
Stairs could be glimpsed rising to the upper floor. Her
heart sank. In pain as she was, how could she hope to
make it up that staircase to the bathroom?

'Sonya!' His voice carried clearly, and to Rhea's ears
there was no mistaking the softening of his tone. 'The
gates are coming along fine. Timmy thinks he's cracked
the problem of the mechanism. Tonight? Well, maybe,
maybe not. I'll get back to you on that.'

There was a pause and Rhea could see Leo's fine-
shaped head turn in her direction as he leant against the
wrought-iron rails of the banisters.

'I've got a "problem" of my own right now,' he went
on. Rhea was sure she heard a high-pitched groan. 'Yeah,
another of Jerome's cast-offs has just presented herself
on my doorstep.' He had made no attempt to lower his
voice. 'Strangle my brother?' He laughed, and it was
such a good sound that it sent shivers up and down
Rhea's spine. 'Maybe I will one day. As you and I know,
he does have this compulsion to keep proving his vir-
ility... One more of his little bundles of joy sent my
way and I might just, next time, send the lady back and
force Jerome to face up to his responsibilities and the
consequences of his actions.' He turned away, lowering
his voice at last and conversing about private matters.

How I wish, Rhea fretted, wincing at the pain in her
foot which, instead of receding, was growing by the
minute, I could go right over to that door and slam it

shut. So the macho older version of Jerome Dower was still convinced she was in 'that certain condition'? Let him, she thought, her head resting back, her mind trying to fight the agony her injury was causing, not only to her foot now, but to the rest of her body.

It didn't matter what he thought, because before long she would be on her way again, although heaven knew where. It was obvious that her journey had been in vain. Leo Dower knew no more of Jerome's whereabouts than she did. Which meant that he couldn't retrieve her car from his brother's illegal possession any more than she could. But, she admitted again, all these things had not been the only reason why she had made the trek northward to a man she had never met.

A curious kind of instinct, dredged up from beneath the floor of her subconscious mind, coupled with an overpowering intuition, had instilled in her a conviction that, after the upheaval and the turmoil that life in the past few months had flung at her, the place she was travelling towards, unknown to her though it might be, was a kind of blissful sanctuary, beckoning her on.

CHAPTER TWO

'IF YOU'D like to freshen up,' Leo Dower stood before her, hands in the pockets of his dark trousers, 'the bathroom's up the stairs. Unless you've already found your way there?'

Rhea shook her head. 'Do you,' she asked, her fingers crossed, 'have a cloakroom downstairs?'

He looked faintly puzzled, then shrugged. 'If you'll follow me, I'll show you.'

Gritting her teeth, Rhea made to stand, tentatively putting some weight on her injured ankle. She just managed to suppress a shriek, but a strangled gasp of pain did escape her throat. She knew then that she couldn't make it anywhere, not a single step, under her own steam. What was more, she had to face the appalling fact that it would take more than the couple of hours she had estimated for the swelling, which was now crowding her shoe to bursting point, to go down.

'What the hell——?' He had returned to stand in front of her as she sank on to the sofa again. She unintentionally glanced down, and he followed her gaze. Crouching, he lifted her left foot, the undamaged one, then pushed up the other trouser-leg.

'Please,' she gasped, white-faced, 'just—just don't touch it!'

'For...God's...sake!' He stared at the ankle and Rhea saw with horror the size it had swelled to. 'How far did you count on going with that?' His hands sprang to action, sliding beneath her, easing her body sideways so that her legs were resting on the sofa.

His tone might have been harsh, Rhea reflected abstractedly, but his hands which, as she had witnessed from the door of the forge, possessed the strength to hammer and bend and fashion objects out of iron, were so gentle that she almost wept.

A couple of tears did escape, she could not stop them. She had been tired before, but fatigue plus agony was, as she was discovering, almost too much to bear.

Leo stood abruptly, fingers spread on hips, jaw thrust forward, eyes narrowed. 'When?' he asked. 'Where and how?'

Haltingly, she explained how she had rested in the corner of a field. 'As I climbed back, the gate wobbled under me. It was loose on its hinges and rusty, and my foot lost its hold when the bar I was standing on broke. The gate went over with me. I did rest it back into place in case the sheep got out, but——'

'You mean you carried on walking?'

'I had no alternative, had I? Anyway, it didn't hurt quite so much then.' She turned away. 'I'm sorry—it's not really your concern. Just drive me to the nearest pub or hotel and I'll take it from there.'

'The nearest hospital, more like it,' he countered grimly. His hands slid under her again and he lifted her, making for the inner hall.

'Where——?' she asked, holding her head stiffly upright, then realised with some embarrassment just where he was taking her. He pushed at the cloakroom door with his foot and slid her down. She stood on her uninjured leg, her hand against the wall.

'Call when you're ready,' he threw over his shoulder as he walked away.

Beneath her pallor, her skin was suffused with pink. Tough and hard his exterior might seem, she thought, not to mention the inner man too, but he didn't seem quite as devoid of finer feelings as Jerome had made him out to be.

'Where are you taking me?' she asked a few moments later as he put her into his car, a low-slung, clearly expensive vehicle which stood in the rear yard that gave on to the road.

'The nearest hospital. I rang the local doctor and I'm taking his advice.'

'But, Mr Dower,' she protested, 'there's no need for you to put yourself out like this. I wished myself on you. I'm not even an invited guest.'

'What kind of a guy do you think I am that you assume I can ditch you, my brother's girlfriend, in the condition you're in?'

What condition? she wanted to ask, but decided to let it go. The answer was obvious anyway. Closing her eyes, she felt the pain wash over her.

The second time Rhea walked into Leo Dower's house, she was on crutches. 'There's no need for you to stay,' she had told him as they had waited for attention at the hospital.

He hadn't even deigned to answer, striding about the waiting area, picking up, skimming through and discarding magazines, and staring through the windows as ambulances came and went.

Once or twice he had come to sit beside her, throwing himself into the chair as if it had done him an injury. Rhea had felt she couldn't blame him for resenting the situation into which she had plunged him, but if it hadn't been for his brother, she had reasoned, she wouldn't be there at all, would she?

Now he walked beside her, watching her slow, uncomfortable progress as she gritted her teeth and did her very best to keep her foot, which a cast now embraced from knee almost to toes, from any contact with the ground. It was no easy matter, she discovered, doing even such a simple thing as lowering herself into a chair.

Hands in pockets, Leo looked down at her, and as she raised her head and sought his eyes she felt again the same kind of shock as she had experienced at their first encounter. Try as she might, however, she still could not read his thoughts. But, she told herself, she didn't need to, did she?

Being apparently too polite to express his feelings in words, inwardly he was almost certainly cursing her presence, not to mention her link with his brother. No doubt he was trying to work out a way of ridding himself of her as quickly as he could arrange it.

'Thank you for all you've done,' she said, to put his mind at rest about her immediate intentions. 'Now, if you would be kind enough to give me a drink of water, then take me to the hotel——'

'What hotel?'

'As you can see, I'm able to walk now,' she gestured to the crutches, 'after a fashion. I don't expect it will take me long to learn to manoeuvre myself up and down the stairs. So——'

He stood unmoving, just staring down.

'I can't stay here,' she remonstrated, her voice rising, 'not for the two weeks they said I'd have to keep the plaster on.'

'Do you really believe I'd turn my brother's fiancée out?'

'I'm *not* his fiancée,' she cried, 'nor even his girl-friend. Don't you understand? He's stolen my car, taken things that I really value that I'd packed in it. Not only that, I'll never forgive him for all the other things he's done. He's wrecked my life, he's——'

'OK, OK, he's a miserable swine. That's what the others called him. I've heard it all before.' Leo's broad shoulders lifted and fell. 'If you'll excuse my saying so,' he said coldly, 'if women—and, apparently, you are no exception—are so stupid as to line up to be ill-used and pushed around by types like my brother—who, to me, is so transparently out only for his own ends—that's their fault. What puts my back up is that he always sends them to me to pick up the pieces.'

'You,' Rhea raged, goaded almost beyond endurance by his dismissive manner, 'are just as unfeeling and uncaring as your brother, except that you're even more macho. I *hate* him, do you understand? And because you're so like him in character, I——'

'You hate me too.' Another shrug. 'I can take it. Why don't you recite the usual list of accusations? I'm a cold fish, heartless, made of stone, et cetera. Take it or leave it, that's my way. All the same, you're staying here.' He went through into the inner hall, returning with the water she had asked for.

She drank thankfully and greedily. It was the first liquid that had passed her lips since very early that morning.

'Another?' He took the proffered glass, smiling faintly as she nodded. 'It seems I might have to warn the water authorities to be on the alert in case the reservoirs run dry.' He returned with the filled glass. 'There's a bed made up in the guest room. You can have that. And,' his hand thrust out, covering her mouth as she made to protest, 'you should have told my brother "no", shouldn't you, before he landed you in your present mess?'

Once again she frowned, about to ask, What mess? when once again she realised what he was implying. She stayed silent. Even if she told him, she reasoned, that there was no way he could be right in his assumption about her 'condition', that there had been no true intimacy between her and Jerome because Jerome had had his own selfish, and self-interested reasons, Leo Dower wouldn't have believed her.

Their evening meal over, Leo stood, hands in his pockets, and looked down at her. He had cooked the food, carrying in a low table so that Rhea could eat from it while still seated on the sofa. He had joined her and, having switched on the television, consumed his meal while watching a programme about the history of art.

'I won't apologise for the informality,' he had said, looking a little mockingly at her from across the room, 'but it's my way. Belonging to the moneyed classes as you do——'

Rhea shook her head. 'Did. Past tense.'

His cynical smile dismissed her statement. 'If my easygoing ways go against the grain—your grain, then——' An expressive shrug dismissed any objections she hadn't even thought of making.

Now she said, 'There's no need to look at me as if you'd like to send me down the nearest rubbish chute. If you want to keep your date with your lady friend, please don't let me stop you.'

His eyebrows flicked up and down, then he seemed to make up his mind. Surprising her, he bent to pick up the container of painkillers which the hospital had prescribed, shook out two on to a paper tissue he had pulled from a nearby box and left them on the low table. 'For you, should you need them in my absence,' he said. Then he pocketed the container.

'You can stop looking outraged,' he added, rattling the confiscated tablets. 'It's merely a precautionary measure.'

'But I'm not like that,' she protested. 'In my view, life is for the living. And I'm a fighter. I don't give in to adverse circumstances——'

'I had noticed,' he commented drily.

'And,' she went on, 'no matter how much of a mess my life might be in I'd never take anything that might bring it to a premature end. I assure you, Mr Dower——'

'For God's sake,' he broke in irritably, 'make it Leo. I am, after all, almost your brother-in-law.' She started to protest that he was so wrong, for some strange reason not liking the 'brother' idea one little bit, but he went on unperturbed,

'Maybe you wouldn't take drastic measures—in your normal state, but bearing the scars as you do of my brother's misuse, I'm taking no chances. The others who came here——'

'But I'm not——'

'Not like them? I'm taking no chances.'

I'm not pregnant, she had been going to confess at last, but he had prevented her from doing so. It was her business anyway, she told herself. 'If it makes you happy,' she tossed at him with a long-suffering sigh, leaning back.

He considered her again, and under his intense scrutiny she felt her toes curling and her palms growing moist. There was an electric quality in his eyes, something in them that made her squirm and twist inside, then let the tension snap, reaching out and . . .

'Before you go,' she burst out, wanting to distract his attention from her and to give herself time to bring her wayward reactions back under her reason's calmer control, 'would you mind bringing me a glass of water, in case I need to take the two tablets you've been so *kind* as to allow me to keep?'

He obliged, from the door advising her with a half-smile not to get drunk on it.

Rhea's head sank back and she let the silence of the empty cottage wash over her. Her reaction to Leo Dower both puzzled and worried her, and she wished more than ever that she had been able to walk out of his life as easily as she had walked into it.

Staying right where she was, she knew instinctively, held greater dangers than the world outside could ever offer. Danger to her equilibrium, which she had only just regained after her devastating experiences at the hands of authority and the powers-that-be, and, most of all, one man's unscrupulous behaviour.

Also, danger to her future well-being, not physical, but to her inner peace, which she was still struggling to rediscover, but which so far had eluded her. One thing she knew for certain: the man who had just walked out of the door wouldn't give that peace back to her.

Operating the remote control, she tried to forget her troubles by concentrating on the film. In spite of everything, she found it so gripping that, when it was over, she returned with a shock to reality and pain. The grandfather clock told her from the inner hall that it was eleven o'clock. It also told her that the effect of the two painkilling tablets she had taken some hours before had worn off.

Swallowing the two that Leo had left her, she drank the water, then looked around. No man, she thought with unusual cynicism, would leave the arms of his lady love—and she was convinced that the lady called Sonya to whom he had gone was just that—before the early hours, if indeed the man in question ever left his lady before morning dawned.

Since she was too uncomfortable to stay where she was for the night, she gave the low table a small push to clear a space, then slowly swung first one leg, then the other, to the floor. Having encountered only a little pain, and therefore feeling pleased with herself, she reached for the crutches and levered herself to her feet.

She made straight for the stairs and, gritting her teeth, climbed painfully up them. Now and then she stopped for breath, forcing herself to look neither up, for discouragement, nor down, through fear, making it to the top, feeling beads of moisture on her forehead and clamminess in her hands.

Walking along the landing, by elimination she found the guest room. It was soberly furnished in browns and dark greens, its drapery practical rather than pretty. The bed, as Leo had claimed, had been made up, and she wondered how many overnight visitors he entertained that he found it worth his while to keep the room in a state of readiness.

In the bathroom along the landing she looked with longing at the tub, but in her present state there was no question even of using the shower. Washing herself as thoroughly as she could, she took a towel from a pile which she found on a chair.

By the time she had managed to remove her clothes, rummage about in her cases for a nightdress to wear, pulling it on and shifting herself sideways beneath the bedcover, she had, she discovered, used up every scrap of energy she hadn't even realised she possessed.

Bed was a haven, a paradise of softness, and she sank back, totally exhausted, into its welcoming comfort. But, try as she might, sleep escaped capture. The events of the day built up in her mind, brick on relentless brick, into a wall that had to be scaled before the longed-for state of unconsciousness was achieved that would give her respite from the pain of her injury and rest from the commotion of her thoughts.

There was the rustle of the breeze through leaves and the sound of water flowing, which told Rhea that the guest room overlooked the river, and was therefore at the rear of the cottage. There were other night sounds too, unfamiliar to her suburban-accustomed ear, sounds which were no doubt natural to the countryside, but which caused a *frisson* of fear to run down her spine.

The scrunch of car wheels swerving to a halt on the parking area at the front of the house made her still-alert brain go into overdrive. Despite the fact that her reason told her that, since midnight had just struck on the clock downstairs, it was probably Leo returning, her imagination, in conspiracy with her almost helpless state, made her fingers grasp the bedcover in a trembling hold.

As swift footsteps took the stairs, she forced herself to face the truth—that it hadn't really been the fear of an unknown stranger intruding with ill intent, but the imminent reappearance on her particular scene of her host, Leo Dower. In her tired and defenceless state, she felt unequal to him in every way.

'Miss Hirst,' he shouted, 'where the hell——? Rhea——?'

All she could do was to stare as Leo Dower strode into the room. 'It's you,' she managed hoarsely, her mouth dry with the fear that hadn't completely left her.

'Of course it's me,' he threw back, hands on hips. 'Who else could it be? Or did you hope it was Jerome returned to hug you to his penitent bosom?'

Rhea stared back at him, resenting his vigour, which had not diminished in spite of the late hour, the muscularity of his build which, because of his height, he carried so easily, the powerful life flowing through him which, unless she built impregnable sea defences around the turbulent femininity within her, might break out and surge towards her, swamping her totally.

'Tell me something,' he said conversationally, folding his arms, but Rhea was sure that underneath his smooth manner there was more than a spark of irritation, 'how did you get yourself into this bed?'

'Well,' she returned, aware that she was being provocative, 'no knight on a white charger came to my rescue and carried me here. I proceeded upward in the usual way. I trod one stair at a time——'

'Don't try and be clever, Rhea. Suppose you'd missed your step, or fallen?'

'Don't worry; because I as good as wished myself on you, I wouldn't have sued,' she retorted, wishing he would go. With her barriers down and fatigue clamouring to be indulged, as each second passed he seemed to her to take on the substance of a great rock to which she might cling in the aftermath of the storms which had so recently battered to pieces her life as she had known it.

His lips thinned at her provocative reply, but he stayed
silent. Then it occurred to her just why he was so concerned about her well-being. She gave a mental shrug.
If he chose to classify her with those others he kept referring to—his brother's 'cast-offs', he had scathingly
called them—then that was his prerogative.

Anyway, she decided, now was not the time to let the
truth come pouring out. The story was a long one, with
many twists and turns, and, anyway, it seemed that he
couldn't bear to hear one word spoken against his beloved brother. And she had, she reflected, so much to
hold against Jerome Dower that it would fill a book.

It was late too, and she could hardly keep her eyes
open. The painkilling tablets seemed finally to be taking
effect and sleep beckoned at last.

'If you really want to know,' she murmured drowsily,
shutting him out, 'it was sheer will-power that got me
up here. I told you,' her eyes fluttered open, but she
could not see his expression because he had switched off
the light, 'I'm a fighter. If I weren't, Mr Dower,' her
voice was a tired whisper, 'I can assure you, I wouldn't
be here now. I mean, in your house, with all I've got
left in the world scattered around your guest room...'

Rhea knew he was puzzled by the tone of her voice.
'What happened to the alleged fortune?'

'"Alleged" is right, Mr Dower...'

Through the mists of the sleep that was claiming her,
she heard him go.

She heard herself crying out, felt a hard hand shaking
her, not roughly, but sufficiently to bring her out of the
nightmare.

Her head was throbbing along with her heart and her
injury. She was enfolded in arms that were tenderly
strong, offering a haven from the terrible dream she had
fought to get out of. She found herself succumbing to
the seductive comfort of those arms, letting them take

over her problems, solving them and offering the security and love she had so recently lost.

In unbuttoned shirt and trousers which he seemed to have hastily pulled on, Leo sat sideways on the bed. His face was so near that, despite the half-light, Rhea could see the ruggedness of his eyebrows, the way his nostrils flared, the thick sensuality of his lips... And as if that weren't enough, there was the fine mat of chest hair, the muscular fitness of his torso...

'What are you doing?' he growled. 'Fantasising that I'm Jerome and willing me to kiss you as he must have done many times? So why not oblige a lady by acting out her fantasy, hm?'

His broad shoulders had shrugged as he had spoken, and Rhea could detect in their action the character of the man as his brother had described it. Harder than granite, Jerome had said, taking women and leaving them, taking life as it came, with not an atom of sentiment inside him.

All this time he had been lowering his mouth towards hers. Her head had had plenty of time to turn itself away, her mouth to take avoiding action, her body to stiffen, but none of those things happened. Instead, her hypnotised eyes watched his lips approach, her brain recognising the consequences, but giving out no frantic signals to avoid them at all costs.

He had slipped his arms under her shoulders and they half lifted her the rest of the way, his lips touching lightly all over hers, then, without warning, pressing down and taking them over, prising open an entry and making free with all the welcome they found there and which for the life of her she had not been able to withhold.

Panic made her heartbeats thunder in her chest. This man, she told herself, shouldn't be doing this, he had no right—and, for the sake of her self-respect, she had no right to let him.

'What a foolish little brother I've got,' he commented, his voice dry, as he held her away and looked her over quizzically, 'to walk out on everything that *you* would be able to offer a man.'

So it had been a game to him, the kiss that had transported her to something very like the foothills of heavenly heights? It started then to register on Rhea's dazed brain that the owner of the arms that held her, that mouth which had relentlessly demolished her barriers and brought her dulled and deadened senses back to leaping life, was Jerome's brother, and as such as much her enemy as Jerome had become.

She began to struggle, attempting to extricate herself from his hold.

'Let me go,' she got out, panting with a residual excitement so pleasurable that it frightened her. 'I don't want any other member of the Dower family to touch me ever again!'

Another shrug—the action was becoming familiar— and Leo complied at once, letting her sink back on to the pillows. He pocketed his hands and stood tall and aloof and indifferent in the semi-darkness. She told herself agitatedly that, as he had disengaged from her, her body had *not* felt deprived and disappointed.

'You were screaming with fear,' he said tonelessly. 'You were crying out for your parents. You loved them, you said, and why did it have to happen?' His voice was so unemotional that it helped to banish the tears that would otherwise have started all over again. 'Where are they now?'

'My parents? They died,' she answered dully, 'in a plane crash.' She took a dragging breath. 'Their own plane—a small one. My father was at the controls. They were on their way to the South of France for a holiday, just the two of them. They never got there.'

He stayed silent, looking down at her, expression inscrutable.

'It's a recurring nightmare that I have,' she went on slowly. 'I dream I'm with them . . .' She turned her head away.

After a long silence, Leo said, 'And Jerome—afterwards, he left you? Despite the fact that you were bereaved, that you were carrying his——'

'He left me,' she broke in quickly, wishing he wouldn't keep referring to something that just was not true. 'He left me,' she repeated, 'taking my car and all the things I had packed in it. Which is why I came to you—to find him and get my property back. But it seems I was wasting my time, because you don't know his whereabouts either. So,' she sighed, longing to sleep now, 'as soon as I'm able to leave your house, I'll be on my way.'

'To—where?'

'Who knows? If I knew, Mr Dower, I'd tell you.'

Between his teeth he said, 'Leo.' There was a rattle of pills and he took her hand, apparently with the intention of placing two tablets on her palm. The sight of the diamonds sparkling in the half-light stopped him. 'Jerome's ring?' he asked sharply.

'No. I threw that back at him—literally.' His expression seemed to change and she guessed he was smiling. 'This belonged to my mother. She had a lot of jewellery—my father showered her with it. They were so in love.' Her voice wavered and she cleared her throat. 'Most of it went to pay off debts, but I managed to salvage some pieces. Some of it,' her voice cracked, 'was in the car that Jerome took.'

Leo swore under his breath. All this time he had not relinquished his hold on her hand. In spite of herself, and her statement that she wanted no more contact with anyone named Dower, Rhea found the gesture, impersonal though it was, strangely comforting. In all the unhappy weeks that had followed the loss of her parents, there had been no one to offer her sympathy and understanding. Advice and guidance and professional assistance in abundance, but no human warmth, nor comfort.

'Is the pain bad?' He indicated her injury.

'Yes,' she whispered. 'The bedcover—it seems so heavy.'

Two tablets dropped on to her palm and he went away, as she had guessed, to fetch water. 'Need help with taking them?'

He did not wait for her answer. Sliding his arm beneath her back, he eased her into a semi-sitting position. One by one she took the tablets and, thanking him, handed back the glass. He lowered her slowly, but something perverse inside her had not wanted the contact to end.

He went away again, returning with a pile of pillows. Pushing aside the bedcover, he placed them each side of her leg, draping the cover over them, easing down her nightdress which, to her embarrassment, had ridden high over her thighs. His quick glance at her flushed face told her nothing.

'That should help to take the weight,' he said. From the door, he added, 'You can stay here for as long as you like. The Dower family you so dislike owes you at least a roof over your head.'

'Please don't let *your* conscience be troubled by my circumstances, Mr——' he made a belligerent movement '—Leo,' she corrected. 'There's no need to take the sins of your sibling on to *your* shoulders.' Powerful and near-irresistible though they are, a wilful voice whispered. Resting your head on those could become habit-forming... He's worth two of Jerome, it persisted tormentingly.

'OK, Rhea,' he strolled indolently back, 'so you don't like the brothers Dower. You bear a grudge and you've declared war.' His glance slanted down to where her middle would be underneath the cover. 'I guess I can't blame you. But cut the sarcasm, will you? Because I could pay you back in the same coin, and lady, if I did, I'd carve you up inside.'

He had changed in a fraction of a second from friendly acquaintance to implacable enemy. Rhea had begun to look to him for a measure of reassurance, for some kind of security, for a helping hand in the wilderness.

Now she realised what a mistake she had made in letting his kindly actions encourage her to allow her feelings to come back to cautious life. She had sworn to hate him because of his relationship to Jerome. And hate him she would go on doing, because otherwise, her insight told her, she could well be hurt, torn apart, all over again.

She gritted her teeth in an effort to harden herself, then with dismay felt tears gather behind her eyes. Try though she did, by closing her eyelids tightly, nothing was able to stop the tears from spilling over.

There was a sound like breath catching, then he was bending over her. 'Look at me, Rhea.' He flicked the tears away with a hard-skinned finger. 'It's been a hell of a day for you, so we'll call a truce, hm?' His finger hooked under her chin and his mouth found hers again. But this time the kiss was like one passing between a concerned parent and a fretful child.

'I'm in the next room if you need me. Goodnight.'

CHAPTER THREE

RHEA woke late, so late that it was almost lunchtime. She lay there for a few moments listening to the country sounds—birdsong, the river's singing coming faintly in through the opened windows, a distant sheep bleating.

Together they combined to tranquillise and soothe, allowing her to forget for a few precious minutes the twin pains of past and present. Then, knowing she could not delay getting up any longer, she moved into action, taking her time, going out to the bathroom, reckoning on Leo's being out at work.

Which, as she discovered on descending the stairs, hanging on for dear life to the banisters with one hand while the other managed to hold the crutches, was right.

A note was propped against the toaster.

> Make free with whatever. For Pete's sake, don't starve yourself or the generation to come.

Her instinct was to crumple the paper because of its false assumption about her condition, but she spared it, reluctantly recognising its caring tone, even if it was tinged with the sarcasm he had promised to use against her should she try to use it first on him.

She was resting on the crutches in the centre of the living-room, wondering what to do with the rest of the day and hating the injury and pain that made her so immobile, when approaching footsteps made her stiffen. Leo had left his work to see how she was managing? More likely, she told herself acidly, to make sure she was not damaging any of his precious property.

'Hi.' A man of around forty stood in the doorway. Of medium height, sandy-haired, he was casually dressed, with a manner to match. He seemed surprised—no, Rhea thought, that was too mild a word. Astonished was more accurate. 'Oh, dear,' he seemed amused, 'what will Sonya say? I'm Nathan Oxley, Leo's friend.'

Rhea nodded, summoning a smile. 'Good morning, Mr Oxley—I'm Rhea Hirst. And the lady called Sonya need not "say" anything. I've no intention of supplanting her, or any other woman, in Leo Dower's affections.'

She hopped painfully towards the settee and with the help of the newcomer, who stepped swiftly across to offer a hand, sank down with some relief.

'You might as well know, since you say you're Leo Dower's friend,' she smiled tiredly up at him, 'that the family Dower tops my hate list.'

'Hey,' Nathan Oxley took her up, seating himself sideways on an upright chair, 'Leo's a great guy. What's he done to deserve such censure from a lady I've never heard him even mention before?'

'It isn't what *he* has done.' Rhea stroked the leg cast for something to do. 'It's what his brother's done...' Too late she realised the interpretation he would put on such a statement, and, from his slightly embarrassed expression, she knew he had.

For heaven's sake, she thought, how many other girls had Jerome sent packing as he'd finally sent her? And *she* had been engaged to him...

'Jerome. Ah.' Nathan's pause spoke volumes. 'But surely,' he frowned at the cast, 'Jerome wasn't also responsible for that?'

She shook her head. 'Unfortunately, this was the result of my own carelessness. Or maybe a farmer's negligence, but I suppose I had no right to climb over his gate, whether it was rickety or not.' She went on to ex-

plain what had happened, feeling more at ease in the
stranger's company than in Leo's.

'So, for more reasons than one,' Nathan said slowly,
'Leo's taken pity on another of Jerome's casualties. Only
this time he's not only had to——'

He hesitated, finding his fingernails unexpectedly
interesting.

'Taken pity.' Rhea noted Nathan's words. She
wouldn't have associated Leo Dower with any form of
sentiment, not even such an easily provoked emotion as
pity. Anyone who mismanages their lives, she could hear
him saying almost as if he were present, as she had
seemed to mismanage hers, deserved what they got.

She took Nathan up. 'Not only had to pay me off—
that's what you were going to say, wasn't it?—but also
had to put me up, or put up with me, whichever you
prefer, for the duration of my immobility?'

He ran his hand lightly over the dark polished wood
of the high chairback. 'You sound like one hell of a sore
and disappointed person. The others, Leo said, didn't
seem to care a damn, just as long as he was prepared to
help them out of their predicament. Every one of them
was intending, they told him, to rid themselves of the
consequences of their actions. All in a day's work for
them, he reckoned. Which, Leo being the kind of man
he is, infuriated him.'

What kind of man? she was going to ask, but her embittered mind suppressed the question. She didn't want
to know anything about Leo Dower as a person. He
meant nothing to her, nor would he ever.

There had been genuine concern in Nathan's voice,
and Rhea felt herself warming to him. Leo's friend he
might be, she thought, but his surname was not Dower,
and that made all the difference.

'I'm more than sore and disappointed, Mr Oxley,
much, much more,' she told him.

'Do you think you could call me Nathan, since it seems you're likely to be here for a while yet?'

'If you like. And I'm Rhea.'

He smiled. 'Rhea. The others,' he continued with his theme, 'were, or so Leo said, hard-bitten bi—— Sorry, *ladies.*'

'Does Leo know you're here?' she asked, partly to change the subject.

He nodded. 'I popped into the forge during a break from my work. He told me that if I paid a visit to his cottage I'd find another surprise package that had been delivered to his doorstep, courtesy of Jerome. Sorry,' as he noted her heightened colour, 'to be going on about that subject. He actually asked if I'd mind making sure you were OK.'

'A caring Dower? I just don't believe it.'

'Yes, well... I can understand your feelings, but including Leo in your low opinion of that family...' Nathan shook his head. 'When you get to know him better——'

'That's something I don't intend to do, Nathan.'

'Pity.' His shoulders lifted and fell. 'He's a great guy, and a superb craftsman.'

'Does he work for his uncle?' she asked, then reproached herself for showing even a passing interest in the man.

'*With* his uncle—a subtle difference. Timmy Dower's a good old-fashioned blacksmith. Leo's alter ego's a businessman.'

'You mean he's taking time off from his real work?'

Nathan nodded. 'He believes that a man's—not to mention a woman's—inner needs are as important as his—or her—material needs. So now and then he says to hell with the pursuit of wealth and position and takes a few months off to refresh his spirit.' Nathan glanced at her. 'Didn't you know any of this? Didn't Jerome tell you?'

'He hardly ever talked about his brother,' Rhea answered slowly, 'except on one occasion when he gave a none-too-tasty character reference.'

Nathan smiled and after a small pause asked, 'Are you in pain?' He nodded towards her foot.

'Yes, but I try not to think about it. I wish I hadn't been so stupid as to cause it to happen. I wouldn't be here now...'

'Hey,' Nathan glanced at the carriage clock on the mantelpiece, 'it's coffee time.'

Rhea made to rise. 'I'll get it——'

'Oh, no, you won't,' Nathan joked, getting to his feet. 'I'd know my way round this place blindfold, so I'll do the honours.'

'What's your line?' Rhea asked as they sipped coffee and nibbled biscuits.

'I'm a potter. You must come and see my place some time. That is, if you could see it—my house, I mean—for the chaos I live and work in.'

Rhea smiled. 'Doesn't your wife complain?'

Nathan studied his hands. 'My wife upped and left. I'm currently partnerless.' Subject closed.

Rhea sensed that he didn't even want her to offer sympathy. 'Pottery,' she said instead, 'the making of it, has always fascinated me——'

'Cosy twosome,' said Leo from the doorway, giving Rhea a fright, but not startling Nathan in the least.

'Talk of the devil,' Nathan said.

'Which you weren't,' Leo remarked, strolling in, hands in pockets, his solid frame encased again in black T-shirt and dark, workworn trousers. 'I heard the conversation from the invitation to visit your place onwards.' He looked inscrutably from Rhea to his friend.

Nathan smiled. 'Want to make something of it, pal?'

'Not if the lady doesn't.' His glance brought the colour rushing to Rhea's cheeks. Not only was his look overtly sensual, but he was insulting her by assuming that because she had been Jerome's girlfriend she was the type to run after any man.

As he moved nearer, Rhea grew annoyed with her heart which insisted on trying to run the two-minute mile. This man, she tried telling it, means nothing to me . . . or you. Understand? But it continued to ignore her sharp reprimand.

'Would you like some coffee, Mr Dower?' she asked, her tone as matter-of-fact as she could make it.

He reached out and fitted his hand threateningly round her neck, tilting her head back. She felt herself shiver alarmingly, trying to suppress the tingle that ran up and down her spine. 'L-e-o, Leo,' he spelt out. His clasp tightened. 'Say it.'

'Leo.' It came from her chokily, her eyes fighting his. It was Nathan's turn then to look from one to the other.

'I've already discovered, Leo,' he remarked, 'that your guest seems to bear an enormous grudge against the Dowers. You must find it refreshing to discover a lady who isn't chucking herself at your feet.'

'Only to be trodden on in the true Dower tradition?' Rhea queried with an over-sweet smile.

'I,' said Nathan, draining his cup and rising, 'had better be making myself scarce. A war seems about to break out between you two, and I'd hate to get caught in the crossfire.' He left, saying he had enjoyed meeting Leo's 'surprise package', and repeated his invitation to Rhea to visit his place some time.

Pouring coffee, Leo turned to Rhea, eyeing her disconcertingly over the rim of his cup. Her disobedient gaze strayed, contemplating the well-formed arm muscles, the layer of dark hair from his wrists upwards, the way the T-shirt moulded to his solid frame.

Then she told her eyes to stop being swept towards the whirlpool, because, if they didn't, she would surely drown there. Couldn't they, she asked them, see the word 'Danger' flung across the dark vortex that was his physique, his ambience, his entire personality, drawing her ever closer?

'You were getting on well with Nathan Oxley.'

His voice was edged and her eyes sparked defiantly.

'Better than with you, you mean? *He* seems a very easy person to get on with.'

He ignored her provocative emphasis. 'Added to which, of course, you don't possess this grudge against him that you've got against the name Dower?'

'The *two brothers* named Dower,' she threw back, the rancour in her own voice surprising even herself. 'Jerome and——' Some strange restraint held her back from completing the sentence.

'Leo?' He seemed unduly annoyed. He crossed to stand in front of her. 'What the hell have I ever done to you?'

'Just—just being Jerome's brother is enough.'

'How can an apparently well-balanced woman get so prejudiced?'

'He told me things about you, like...' Dared she? 'You were——' Once again something made her hesitate.

'I was——?' His eyebrows arched, his lips twisted. 'Go on.'

'You cared nothing for others, particularly women. You took life as it came, kind of shrugging it off. You were as hard as granite and used every experience— women, Jerome said he meant—to the full, then put it— them—behind you and moved on to the next, and the next...'

'Wow!' It was a long-drawn-out, sarcastic sound. He drained his cup and clattered it down, anger in the gesture, but there was only a silky rebuke in his voice as he commented, 'Has he given me a glowing testimonial! A truly brotherly one. Have I so far, in your opinion, lived up to my callous reputation?'

No, a voice whispered. Rhea looked down, moving her injured leg, then wishing she hadn't. 'I—I don't know

you well enough yet, do I, to answer that question? And,'
she challenged him, 'I don't intend to hang around here
long enough to find out.'

He found a footstool, lifting her leg on to it, pushing
another cushion behind her back for better support.
Startled, she stared up at him.

'Uncaring, eh? Self-orientated? Others can go to hell,'
he stood in front of her again, hands on hips, 'when
I've finished with them?'

She frowned up at him. '*I* didn't say that. It was your
brother.'

'Nevertheless, you believe it.'

She looked away. 'Thank you for your thought-
fulness. But please, don't go overboard in trying to please
me just to prove that your brother's opinion of you is
wrong.'

'I could,' his eyes narrowed dangerously, 'take exception to your colossal impudence.'

'OK, so throw me out. I'll manage to cope. I've had
problems to overcome in the recent past that were much
more difficult than merely having to incorporate a leg
in a cast into my daily life.' Her voice rang with defiance, her eyes carrying on the fight.

Leo considered her, his expression unreadable, appearing in the end to let her challenge go.

'So,' he said slowly, 'no acquittal for the Dowers? No
reassessment of your prejudiced judgement of them?'

'No. But there's no *prejudice* involved, only brutal
facts to back it up. And please don't try and plead your
brother's cause. You don't know what he... You just
don't know.'

'Rhea, look at me.' She forcibly suppressed the shiver
that took hold at the piercing gaze that met hers. 'Did
he force you to lose the child?'

It actually seemed to matter to him! 'Of course not,'
she returned, 'how could he, when there was no——?'
Child, she had been about to say, when he broke in,

'Of course,' with an inexplicable bitterness, 'no force was necessary because there was never any need, with big brother Leo's bank balance always there to come to his—and his assorted girlfriends'—rescue.'

The rear entrance door opened and a short, grey-haired man in an overall and tweed cap stepped in, nodding and smiling with great affability. He removed the cap, stuffing it into a pocket.

Didn't he know, Rhea pondered, wondering at his warmth and apparent acceptance of her, who she was? Hadn't he heard about the low status that had been conferred on her by Leo Dower as merely one of his brother's throw-away women?

'Rhea Hirst, Timmy, my uncle,' said Leo, his careless sweeping gesture concluding the casual introduction, 'my father's brother. Beware of the lady, Timmy. She snarls and bites anyone with the name Dower.'

'No, I don't,' Rhea exclaimed, taking an instant liking to the newcomer. 'Not everyone.'

There was, she noticed, a family likeness, a faint look of Jerome about him; a trace of Leo too, although the older man's face was creased with sympathy lines, which meant that the comparison ended there. Leo's character contained not an atom of sympathy—hadn't she been warned, and hadn't she seen it for herself? Also, Timmy Dower lacked his elder nephew's hard resolution, the rocklike determination that flared in Leo's eyes. 'I'm very selective,' she added, 'in the people I put on my hate list.'

Timmy chuckled loudly, his pale eyes seeking those of his nephew. 'She's either an impudent baggage, this young lady, Leo, or she's got real guts, to pit herself against you.'

'I think the latter, Mr Dower.' Timmy waved Rhea's formality away. 'Timmy,' she amended. 'Because *they* have been well and truly tried in the last few months.'

She flashed Leo a belligerent look. 'I don't think they were found wanting.'

'It's plain Rhea knows her own worth, lad,' Timmy said, easing his small frame on to the chair Nathan had recently vacated.

'I wasn't meaning to boast, Timmy,' Rhea explained, 'but in the past few months I've really and truly had to come face to face not just with life, but with myself. I had to trust someone, and since there was no one else I could turn to I just had to trust me.'

'Leo's told me about you, lass,' Timmy said soberly. 'About your accident. About you and Jerome...'

That hadn't been what she had meant, but she did not correct him.

'It's shocking, Leo,' Timmy was saying, 'the way Jerome plays around, messing up young women's lives. Crazy,' he scratched his head, 'the way they let him. And to think of the little mites he——'

'Procreates and runs away from, yes,' Leo broke in grimly. 'If I knew where the little s——' he glanced at Rhea, then continued '—beggar was, I'd wring his neck, then I'd give him an ultimatum. Marry the latest mother-to-be of your child, or I'll throw you off my list of charities.'

'For heaven's sake,' Rhea's voice hit a high note, 'I wouldn't want to marry him. I hate him now, *hate him*!'

To her horror, she burst into tears, her shoulders shaking with sobs. She hadn't the slightest idea why it had happened. She had no feelings left for Jerome Dower. The sofa cushion beside her gave and an unfamiliar arm went round her shoulders.

'There, there,' an understanding voice said, 'don't cry like that, lass. I expect you're in pain with your ankle?' She nodded. 'Well, everything'll turn out right, you'll see. Leo will make sure of that. It's too bad, Leo, what Jerome's done.' The shocked voice quavered. 'Isn't there any way of tracing him?'

'I don't want him traced!' Rhea exclaimed through her tears. 'I don't care if I never see him again. All I want is my car and the personal belongings I'd packed in it. Jerome can go to——'

'Uncle, let me...' An exchange was made, a bigger, bulkier figure positioned itself beside her. 'We understand your reaction, Rhea, the resentment you feel at Jerome's treatment after all there's been between you. And you were his fiancée, for God's sake.'

There was a gasp of surprise from the older man. 'You mean he'd even proposed marriage, then went off just like that?'

'He's let me down,' Rhea's voice emerged thickly from between her hands, 'as no one in the whole world has ever let me down before.'

An arm came round her whose potential strength sent urgent messages to her reflexes to give in to her instincts and succumb to the reassurance and security it offered. She was urged sideways, and she didn't resist. Her heated forehead found a hard, broad sanctuary beneath which was a pounding drum similar in noise and rhythm to the hammering that had greeted her as she had walked down the village street the day before.

A wide-spanning hand rubbed up and down her back in a gesture similar to that of a mother—or a father—comforting a child. Her reaction to the comforter's touch was, to her dismay, anything but childish. Her reflexes jumped to life, her skin seemed to shiver and tingle, and her eyes, which had been closed, came open.

Her head eased back and she gazed into the piercing gaze that had brought her limbs and, almost, her heart, to a stop the first time she had met and locked with it.

She searched those eyes, watching as a momentary shaft of sensual light overrode the detached concern. Then it had gone, but it had left her senses reeling. And her heart afraid. She mustn't, she told herself, *she must not* let either herself or her emotions become entangled in the invisible, dangerous net that billowed around this man.

Intuition told her that, if she were ever to be so foolish, there would be no way out, she would be caught for ever, because from a man like this there would be no merciful hand throwing her back into the sea, into the outside world.

His jaw had ridged under her seeking gaze, his arm muscles had tensed and she sensed that for some reason he was angry, and with her too. She separated herself from him and he leaned back, arms folded, expression grim.

'There's not much resemblance, is there,' Timmy broke into the brittle silence, 'between him and his brother? I expect that was what you were looking for, dear.' There was sympathy in his tone. 'The nose, maybe, the eyes——'

'Not the eyes!' The words burst from her, surprising her listeners and even herself with their vehemence. 'Same colour,' Rhea remarked more calmly, 'but——' How could she explain? 'Jerome's aren't so—so forceful, so analytical, so...' Exciting, electrifying, *inviting*... She couldn't say those words aloud, so she lifted her shoulders as if lost for words. 'So cold,' she finished, with a daring glance at Leo.

Timmy laughed. 'She's got you taped, lad,' he commented. 'All fact and no fantasy, all brain and no heart, that's what others say about him.'

But *I* know, Rhea thought, that underneath that stony, impassive exterior, something—a spark, a smouldering ember—exists that, given the right circumstances, could fire a woman's femininity to ardent, eager life. Hadn't others noticed? Surely his women friends had glimpsed what she had sensed... no, *seen*?

But then a man who held himself as aloof from emotion, from any depth of feeling, as it was perfectly obvious Leo Dower did, would surely take his lovers coldly and clinically, no matter how warmly and fervently they might respond to his lovemaking?

'Thanks, Timmy,' Leo said sarcastically, 'for confirming in our guest's mind everything she's been told about me by my dear brother. Got your sandwiches?'

Timmy reached into the pocket of the dusty jacket he had hung over the chair back, pulling out a packet.

'Cheese and pickle,' he informed then. 'They always are. I made them myself, as usual.' He sighed. 'I miss your auntie's clever hand with fillings, Leo. I miss her more than anyone will ever know.' A long pause, then, pulling himself out of his unhappiness, 'Where are the cans of beer, lad?'

Leo disappeared to the kitchen.

'I lost my wife,' Timmy told Rhea, peeling the wrapper from the sandwiches, 'a year ago.' He crumpled the paper. 'We're a close family, the Dowers—what's left of us,' he added, tearing off a chunk of sandwich and chewing it reflectively. 'Leo's mother died when he was ten. His father brought in another woman, name of Andrea, then eventually married her. She and Leo—they never hit it off, and she never seemed to take to Jerome either.'

Rhea listened, half of her not wanting to because there must be no softening of her attitude towards the Dower brothers, the other half so interested that she could hardly wait for Timmy to continue.

'Which meant,' Timmy went on between mouthfuls, 'that Leo turned protective towards his brother and shielded him from the harsh words meted out to them both by their stepmother. Their father, Horrie—Horace, short for——' Rhea nodded '—never seemed to notice, he was so wrapped up in his work. Ran the Dower steel fabrication business.'

Even Rhea had heard of the Dower Corporation and, since the name could hardly be called a particularly common one, could not understand why she had not connected the two brothers with it.

'So Leo and Jerome have always been close,' Timmy concluded. 'You understand, lass?'

Again Rhea nodded. It explained a lot of things. 'Jerome never told me anything about his background,' she remarked.

'He wouldn't, would he? Not to a young lady he never intended——'

'But we were engaged!' Rhea exclaimed.

Timmy shook his head. 'It might have meant a lot to you, Rhea. It didn't mean anything to Jerome, I can tell you that, fond uncle though I am.'

'Does Leo's father still——?'

'Run the Dower Corporation?' He shook his head, dusting the crumbs from his clothes. 'In name, maybe, but he b——' he cleared his throat, glancing sideways at Rhea '—he buzzed off to the Bahamas with his second wife. He leaves it all to Leo now. Who leaves it to his deputy when the urge comes upon him to throw it all aside for a few months and join me in the forge. It's his first love, the forge—isn't it, Leo? Ah, thanks,' as his nephew handed him a beer from the tray he had carried in. 'What about the lady?'

'No alcohol for her. Fruit juice,' said Leo decisively, and gave Rhea a prepared drink. Rhea guessed the reason at once. Let him think whatever he likes, she thought with a mental shrug. In two or three weeks she'd be leaving and he need never know the truth.

While Timmy demolished an apple, Rhea watched as Leo sliced hunks of bread from a long French loaf. He added a chunk of cheese, then quirked an eyebrow and asked, 'Rhea, you like? Yes?'

Shaking pieces of washed lettuce from a dish, he placed them on her plate, adding a whole tomato, then hesitated as he reached with a spoon for a small brown onion. He looked at her, his brows arched in query.

'I—well, I——'

'If you're worried about the residual aroma,' he said, to the accompaniment of Timmy's deep chuckle, 'don't be.'

'Well, if you're having one...' Then she stopped, colouring deeply. She had strayed into forbidden territory, and he took her up with a sardonic smile.

'Rest assured,' he remarked, 'there's no way I'll be kissing you today. Nor you me. OK?'

Rhea nodded, blushing, annoyed at the way her fair skin always let the world know her feelings. And why, she asked her heart desperately, do you have to hammer as fast as a woodpecker at a tree-trunk?

'I've been telling this young lady a thing or two about you,' Timmy announced to his nephew. 'Put her in the picture—that's what they call it nowadays, isn't it? Seeing as how she's going to produce the next generation of Dowers.' The crunch of his apple sounded loud in the difficult silence. 'You and Jerome—inseparable, you were. Which is why Jerome's always running to his brother for help. Isn't that so, Leo?'

'Is it?' Leo answered flatly, bringing an end to his uncle's revelations.

'Is this,' Rhea ventured later over the coffee which Leo had made, 'your usual lunchtime routine? You eat here——?'

Timmy shook his head. 'We go to the Dog and Badger most days, don't we, Leo? Meet our pals there. We came back here today to keep you company—Leo's idea.'

'That was very nice of you both, and I've enjoyed it,' offered Rhea, 'but please don't worry about me in future.'

'Think nothing of it, lass. Would you,' Timmy looked at her doubtfully, 'would you come with us sometimes?'

'To the Dog and Badger? I'd love to.'

'She sounds as though she means it, Leo,' said Timmy, going to wash his hands.

'It's something I never did with Jerome,' she said slowly, as Leo cleared the debris.

'Have a ploughman's lunch or go to a pub?'

'Both. It was always the best restaurants. He never seemed to tire of the formality, the slightly exotic food that some of them serve, the subservient waiters. I tried telling him I'd like to go somewhere else, but——'

'Jerome loves playing the wealthy tycoon,' was Leo's brotherly comment, 'even though his intellectual powers could never raise him up to that standard. Where did you meet him?' Hands in his pockets, he slanted a glance down at her as she reclined lengthways on the sofa, both legs resting.

'At one of those "best" restaurants.' She smiled faintly at the irony. 'At the bar. I was with my parents. We'd gone there for a celebration meal. It was my mother's birthday—her fiftieth.' Rhea paused because it pained her to remember that her mother had seen only one more birthday after that.

'So Jerome got talking?' Leo prompted. 'He usually does.'

'To my father, yes.'

'With his eye on you. And you returned his interest, giving him come-on signals?'

'No, I didn't. I——'

'Oh, come on, Rhea! You must have given him some encouragement. He asked you out, and you went? Which is how it all began, yes? I know by heart Jerome's routine in his pursuit of the opposite sex.'

Timmy returned, pulling on his jacket. 'I'll be off, Leo. See you again, lass.' He smiled in a kindly way. 'I can tell you've got more pain from that foot than you let on about. No hurry, Leo. Take your time.'

'Is it hurting?' asked Leo. 'Why didn't you say?' He produced the bottle of painkillers, but Rhea shook her head.

As the door closed on Timmy, there was a heavy silence. 'There was more to it than that,' she said slowly. 'My father was head of a big company, an up-market clothing chain.'

'Daniel Hirst?' Leo queried with some surprise. 'I've bought their clothes myself in the past. Couldn't discover what happened to the firm.'

'They were bought up,' Rhea answered heavily. 'It was the name the buyers were after. The company itself was hardly worth anything. It was on the verge of collapsing even before my father's death, though I didn't know that at the time.'

'So?' He dropped into an armchair, seeming impatient with her silence.

'Jerome made such an impression on my father at that first meeting that he offered him a job—general manager. Jerome jumped at it.'

'I can imagine,' said his brother drily. 'He told me something about his future father-in-law giving him a plum job.'

Rhea nodded. 'We became engaged very quickly. About two months later, in fact. Then, seeing him—and trusting him—as his future son-in-law, about which Jerome did nothing to discourage his expectations, Dad promoted him.'

'You fell in love with my brother?' Leo's face, like his tone, was expressionless.

'Is it surprising if I did? Good-looking, charming...loving. Told me I meant the world to him. Bought me presents.'

'I can understand your bitterness, Rhea, but women by the dozen have fallen for his wiles. I would have thought,' Leo said reflectively, 'that an intelligent girl like you——'

'Intelligence doesn't come into it,' she returned sharply. 'But you wouldn't know, would you, with your cool and clinical approach to all matters affecting the heart. Heart to you,' she realised she was speaking too fiercely, 'means this,' she touched her chest with her fist, 'something that keeps a human being alive, nothing to do with emotions, feelings...'

'OK, you hate me.' He shrugged and rose. 'I'll relieve you of my obnoxious company. In an emergency, you can always ring me at this number.' He found a telephone pad and scribbled on it, handing it to her. 'It's the forge.' With that, he was gone.

The room, which had seemed so cosy, seemed to ring with the emptiness he had left behind. Rhea told herself firmly to stop being so stupid. She wasn't really missing his vital presence. Because of her incapacity, she had grown dependent on him, on his latent strength, on the reassurance his presence offered.

There couldn't possibly be any other reason. Could there?

CHAPTER FOUR

LATER, Leo rang, startling her. Rhea almost dropped the phone as she picked it up.

'Leo Dower's house.'

'Is it, now? Whadderyouknow!' Rhea visualised Leo's tantalising solidity leaning indolently against some support, his strong mouth curved sardonically. 'Seems I've got myself a real live answering machine.'

'What do you want?' she asked, annoyed because at the sound of his voice her heart had done its usual ballet-dancer's leap.

'Could you feed yourself this evening? I've got a date.'

Why did her heart jolt now like a car doing a crash stop? 'Yes, I could. Thank you for calling.'

His sarcastic laughter rang in her ears long after he had gone. It was a long evening. She took some cold meat from the fridge and made a salad, hopping around and holding on to the modern kitchen units. She wriggled on to a high stool and ate sideways on at the breakfast bar, her leg propped stiffly on the footrest.

Using one of the crutches, she managed to wash the dishes, finding the dishwasher too awkward to cope with in her present state. For an hour or two she watched television, then, aware of a general feeling of discomfort, she decided to attempt a shower.

The nurse at the hospital had said that, if she was careful, this was permissible because the leg cast, being made of a water-repellent material, would stand up to a wetting provided she didn't allow the water to trickle down through the gap at the top.

There was a shower over the bath, with curtains fixed to slide all round the bathtub, which pleased her, just in case Leo arrived back early and came to seek her out. Although there was no way, she was certain, that he would tear himself from the arms of his beloved Sonya until the early hours at least, if then.

Securing her nightclothes under her arms, she hopped painfully with the crutches into the bathroom. Getting into the bath was easier than she had thought. A conveniently placed soapdish became a useful item to hold on to. She had never had a one-footed shower before. It proved quite difficult, but as she reached to turn the shower off she rejoiced in the resulting feeling of cleanliness.

Turning, standing on her good foot, she faced the problem of getting out of the bath. She bent down to rest her hand on the side, intending to seat herself on it, reversing the process of getting in, but she had not reckoned with the slipperiness of the shower gel still clinging to her skin through hurried and insufficient rinsing.

To her horror, she felt her foot slipping slowly along the base of the bath, and, unable to save herself, she landed with a bump that jarred her spine. She tried in vain to get up, looking round helplessly and wishing she had never attempted to have the shower unaided and unsupervised.

Then her reason told her that even if Leo had been there she wouldn't have allowed him into the bathroom to help her, not under any circumstances. Now she would have to make the best of it and stay there, all night if necessary, until help arrived. That it might well come in the form of a hunk of a man with powerful arms and a lashing tongue she hardly dared to contemplate.

Seizing her sponge-bag, which she had placed, together with the towel, within easy reach, she lowered herself until she was lying flat, elbowing the sponge-bag so that it acted as a pillow. She spread the towel over her, wishing as she did so that the sun's warmth had lingered longer. She must, she thought, have drifted off, since she was jerked back to consciousness by the sound of a car half skidding to a stop.

The entrance door was flung open and she started to shiver. There was a pause, the proverbial calm before the storm. Footsteps pounded the stairs, then came the explosion.

'Rhea, where in *hell's name* are you?' In two seconds he was in the bathroom, dragging aside the shower curtains and staring down at her. He had blanched and his breath came in short, angry bursts. 'My God, I thought you'd——'

'Gone? Or,' she suggested, trying a smile but discovering that her mouth was shivering too, 'got so desperate I tried to——?' She shook her head slowly, except that it juddered at the movement. 'I've already told you, I'm not like that. I face my problems—and solve them.'

'So,' colour normal now, hands on hips, his anger having been overtaken by ironic amusement, 'how did you intend solving this little problem?' His eyes were travelling the length of her as though she were an interesting and rare species of *Homo sapiens* that might be reported to be nearest anthropological society. He actually seemed to be enjoying it.

The towel had slipped to one side and, damp though it now was, she grabbed it and tried to cover her vital parts. But she couldn't stop shivering. She was tired and cold, and, in her present plight, the injured foot was showing no mercy, turning on a nagging pain.

Leo left the bathroom and she thought he had walked out on her. Forgetting her promise to herself that she wouldn't even allow him into the room, she cried out,

'Please, Leo, don't leave me like this! I'm c-cold and t-tired and——'

He returned, his smile taunting, in his hands a fresh, dry towel. 'Can't do without the Dowers, can you?' he mocked, looking down at her again and missing nothing of her curves and mounds and other physical attractions. 'Hate them though you do, you've got to admit they have their uses.' He still made no move to remove her from the bathtub. 'She's at my mercy.' The words rumbled around his chest. 'What condition shall I impose for getting her out of her predicament?'

'None, Leo.' She stared up at him, eyes wide, teeth chattering. 'I'm not—I don't—I can't.' I know what he'll think, she told herself frantically, but I don't care.

'OK, message received.' His expression tightened. He seemed angry again. He gave her the towel, which she wrapped around herself as best she could. Then those arms scooped her up and held her against him, the leg imprisoned in plaster protruding at an awkward angle. She gave a great sneeze, her body jarring with it.

It was late, and her rescuer's jaw was dark with stubble shadow. Rhea felt the totally forbidden urge to run the back of her fingers over it. That urge had come from nowhere, and she told it that that was where it must return.

Beside her bed Leo let her down, threading her carefully through his hands. Rhea was thankful that the towel was around her. Nevertheless, the pressure of his palms in over-sensitive places made her skin prickle beneath the shiver that still had her teeth chattering.

Without warning her of their intention, her arms lifted to cling to his solid frame. Her body started shaking again, almost out of control. His enveloping arms pulled her to him, and the warmth of him flooded through her, steadying the trembling that frightened in its intensity. Her head bumped against his shoulder, her fingers grasping upper arms that were rock-hard beneath the cotton shirt he wore.

'S-sorry about this,' she managed, compressing her quivering lips.

He tipped her chin, looking at her keenly. 'What's wrong?'

'C-cold.' Her tired amber eyes stared worriedly up at the face that was becoming alarmingly familiar, and not only because it bore minute traces of Jerome. 'I c-can't stop shivering.'

Lips tight, almost forbidding, he helped her slide her nightdress down her body, his touch, like his glance, coolly impersonal. Then he folded the covers down, turned her so that she sank on to the bed and lifted her legs, easing the covers over her as she reclined against the pillows.

'Five minutes.'

He took three, giving her a cup of hot milk and seating himself, arms folded, on the bed while she drank it. 'How's the injury?' he asked.

'Making itself felt.' Shivers banished at last, she found she could speak without stammering.

'Tablets?' Reluctantly Rhea nodded. Counting out two, he pushed the bottle back into his trouser pocket. 'Just what the doctor ordered.'

'There's no need,' she protested, 'to dole them out. I told you——'

'This Dower is taking no chances where the next generation's concerned.'

She closed her lips over the denial that sprang every time Leo made the false assumption that the 'next generation' of Dowers was on the way. Anyway, if she told him the truth before her mobility returned, he might throw her out, and she needed his help too much at the moment to risk that.

As soon as the plaster was off, as soon as she could walk normally again, she would be gone. She couldn't stay here any longer. Something was happening to her emotions. Every time the man she told herself she hated came into view, they behaved crazily. Every time, even, that she thought about him ... Like the teeth-chattering shock that had been so frightening in the way it seemed to have taken hold of her, so the thought of her emotions getting beyond her control worried her immensely.

When she left this house, that problem would be solved. The Dower family would be left behind, going out of her thoughts and out of her life. Forever.

Gritting her teeth four days later, Rhea made her slow way over the bridge and along the road to the forge. She had seen very little of Leo since he had rescued her from the bath. He had left for work by the time she had struggled down to breakfast. He had not returned for the evening meal, staying out late, she presumed, to get away from her.

Well, she told herself acidly, his dislike of her was heartily reciprocated. He was Jerome's brother, and that was enough to make her hate him for life.

Over the ringing of the anvil and the striking of the hammer came the sound of voices. A woman's laughter mixed in with a man's deeper laughing note, jokes striking sparks, words tossed between friends, meaning nothing to an outsider.

Which was exactly how Rhea felt as, supported by her crutches, she stood at the door gazing into the semi-darkness. The fire cast flickering shadows all around. She was hot and tired with the concentrated, teeth-gritting effort that the walk from Leo's cottage had demanded.

Lounging back against a wooden table, Leo stiffened, a can of beer halfway to his mouth. His female companion was seated, legs drawn up gnome-like, on a battered stool.

'What the hell are you doing here?' Leo asked, lowering the can and straightening. 'You're supposed to be resting with your feet up.'

So he's annoyed with me for spoiling his tête-à-tête with his girlfriend. 'I got bored,' she told him, 'and anyway, I needed the exercise.'

'Sonya,' Leo sketched a brisk introduction, 'Rhea Hirst. Rhea, Sonya Selby.'

'So, Leo,' said the lady, unfolding her legs and inspecting Rhea as if she were of a different species, 'this is the "Jerome cast-off" you were telling me about?' Slowly, encased shoulder to ankle in a fluorescent pink outfit that emphasised the dimness of the interior, Sonya approached. 'What a clever girl you are,' she remarked, eyeing Rhea from top to toe, 'to have outdone your fellow sufferers and discovered a way they never thought of, of getting Leo to accommodate you not just financially but physically.'

In the background, the coke fire spat and crackled like Rhea's anger. 'If you think, Miss—Mrs?—Selby, that I deliberately injured myself so as to play on Mr Dower's sympathies——' She switched her fiery gaze to Leo. 'Is that what you think too? That I fell off that farm gate and broke some bones to force you to take me in?'

Leo took a drink, head slightly back, eyes watchful.

Goaded by his silence, Rhea flung at him, 'No answer, which means that you do.' She made to swing round, but a crutch settled on a stray piece of iron on the floor and started to unbalance her. Leo was there, catching her by the shoulders, steadying her.

She twisted out of his hold, lifting burning eyes to his. She had had her fill of his touch the other evening when he had rescued her from the bath. She couldn't stand what it did to her, the way it played on her senses and lingered in her mind. 'Will you tell me, please, where Nathan Oxley lives?' she asked him.

'Down in the village.' Leo's eyes narrowed. 'Why?'

'To seduce him, that's why!' she retorted.

Sonya's laugh rang out. For a few frightening seconds, a lightning-strike of fury flickered across Leo's eyes.

'You don't really think I meant——?' Rhea choked, then, Yes, he does, she thought, he thinks exactly the same of me as he did of those 'others' they all talk about. Well, let him!

She added more calmly, 'He invited me to call on him any time. I'd like to see his work. Any objections, *Mr Dower*?' She knew she would anger him by using his surname, but she didn't care. Two against one, she thought, looking from one to the other, wasn't fair, but she'd hold her own come what may.

'His place is about half a mile on from here,' Sonya told her, plainly anxious to be rid of the irritating outsider. 'On the left as you enter the village.'

Into two mugs she poured tea from a large pot. Rhea noted that she had not been invited to join them and accepted the snub with a mental shrug, consoling herself with the thought that every day that passed brought her nearer to release from the leg cast and her exit from these two people's lives.

'I'll drive you,' said Leo, going to the door.

'Thanks, but no. As I said, I need the exercise.' With a saccharine-sweet smile, she bade goodbye to his lady friend.

Her instincts, too finely tuned where he was concerned, told her that he stood watching as she moved with painful slowness along the road. When, after a few moments, she paused for breath, she turned, hoping he was still there. At that moment she would have given anything for the lift he had offered, but he had gone.

The morning sun shone warmly as, a short while later, she paused again, wondering if she could make it to Nathan's. A car approached slowly and she stood to one side of the narrow country road.

The vehicle stopped and the driver wound down the window. 'Hi, there, Rhea,' said Nathan. 'Just got a phone call from Leo. "One temporarily disabled lady is on her way to pay you a visit," he said. "For heaven's sake, go and meet her. She's making such slow progress it's painful to watch her."'

'I'm surprised,' Rhea commented, thankfully easing herself with Nathan's help on to the rear seat, 'that I touch any part of Leo Dower's feelings, but I'm sure he resents my presence so much, "pain"—as "in the neck"—would, I suppose, be the one word he'd associate with me!'

'Don't you believe it,' remarked Nathan good humouredly. 'Any unattached male would be glad to have someone as decorative and attractive as you in his house, even for a few weeks.'

'Attractive? Using crutches?'

Nathan's glance moved momentarily to the driving-mirror as Rhea shook her head, then stifled a sigh. 'You just don't know, Nathan. I hope,' she went on, changing the subject, 'you don't mind my taking you up on your invitation to visit you.'

'Delighted,' he said, driving along the village street and turning into a parking area adjoining a grey stone cottage bounded by an equally grey stone wall.

The entrance door led into a living-room which, she noted, was welcomingly, although somewhat shabbily, furnished. Nor could it be called tidy. Was this what Nathan's wife had run from, she wondered, chaos such as this which so often went with creativeness and artistic ability? Or had something deeper and more serious undermined their relationship?

Making sure she was comfortable, Nathan made some tea, generally trying to make her feel at home. She found that surprisingly easy, experiencing none of the awkwardness and restraint that tied her feelings into knots in Leo's house. Here, she felt she was welcome. There, she knew she was not.

Nathan took her into his studio. Tables and shelves were covered with partly finished work. Here again there was a general air of untidiness. To one side stood a stool pulled up to a solid-looking table bearing a potter's wheel, hand tools, pots of varying sizes holding coloured liquids and powdered chemicals and, close by, a pair of clay-caked rubber gloves.

'My kiln,' said Nathan, pointing across the room. He opened its door, revealing the pieces awaiting firing. In a display cabinet were finished products, table-lamps and vases, dishes and ornaments, children's night lamps— hollow earthenware tree-trunks with tiny animals peeping from holes.

'There are different types of pottery,' he explained, 'depending on the clay used and the temperatures at which the articles are fired.'

Rhea nodded. 'Such as earthenware, stoneware, porcelain.'

'You know?'

'Mm.' She pointed to the brilliant colours he had used on some of his work. 'Your designs—they're really attractive,' she commented. 'Do you, like me, get them from nature, or do they come out of your head?'

'They're not my work. My—er—wife added those.' A short pause, then, 'It's over, Rhea, whatever others might say. I've no regrets. Well, very few.' Nathan looked at her. 'You said something just now that puzzled me. About the source of these designs.'

Colouring a little, she played back her own words. *Like me,* she'd said.

'There's an awful lot you're not telling us, isn't there,' he remarked, his interest apparent, 'about Rhea Hirst's abilities?'

They were in the living-room again, Rhea seated on a settee with her injured leg on a footstool. What should she tell him? The truth? She felt she owed it to him since, of the people she had so far met, he had been the most pleasant and friendly.

She opted instead for the partial truth. 'I can embroider and weave.'

'Ah—hobbies.' He smiled, satisfied with his own explanation. 'You've probably read craft books?'

'Yes, I have.' That at least was true.

He drew some volumes from his packed shelves. 'While I brew some more tea, have a look at those. We've got a craft group going in the village. You might like to come along some time.'

Rhea smiled, her eyes still on the colourful pages. 'I certainly would,' she raised her voice to reach him in the kitchen, 'but I won't be around here for much longer. The moment I get rid of this leg cast, I'll be on my way.'

'Where to?' He was placing her tea mug on a handy table. 'Or are you going to tell me it's none of my business?'

'No.' She stared at the book, not really seeing it. 'The honest answer is, I don't know.' She closed the book and saw Nathan's concerned frown. 'I'll land on my feet, Nathan, like a cat's always alleged to do.'

'You're no cat, Rhea.' He removed the book, then lifted her hand, inspecting her nails. 'No claws, like the others Jerome Dower played around with, then chucked aside.'

'Thanks.' She spread her hand against the back of his. 'Your hands are large,' she commented with interest.

'A potter's hands.' He turned his palm to hers. 'You need the width and strength to control and form the clay on the potter's wheel.'

'Sorry to break things up,' said a cynical voice from the doorway, 'but I've come for my guest.'

Embarrassed, Nathan detached his hand from Rhea's and faced his visitor.

Leo's hand lifted to rest against the doorframe, disapproval in every line of him. 'A word of advice, pal. If you don't want an interloper to ruin the romance in your life, you shouldn't leave your door on the catch.'

'Come on, Leo,' Nathan protested, 'you've misinterpreted and you damned well know it. I was merely telling Rhea that——'

'Unlike her predecessors, she was clawless. I heard.' Leo's glance sliced down, hitting Rhea, making her shiver. 'Don't you believe it, Nathan. I guess that, being among new acquaintances, she's been on her best behaviour and the claws have been sheathed. She wouldn't want to be thrown out in her state.'

'Don't you mean "condition"?' Rhea asked oversweetly.

His eyelids drooped. 'Don't provoke me—I can get really unpleasant if pushed too far. Nathan will bear witness to that.'

'Leave me out of it, pal. I've got enough troubles of my own. Tea?'

'No, thanks. When my house guest has finished hers, we'll be on our way.'

It was an order, given with a little too much authority for Rhea's liking. Nevertheless, she drained her mug and lowered her leg to the floor. 'Thanks, Nathan, for our interesting chat and for showing me your work.'

He helped her to her feet and handed her the crutches. 'Don't forget my invitation to the group. Did you know, Leo, that your guest was clever with her hands? Her hobbies are embroidery and weaving, she told me. Isn't that right, Rhea?' It was and it wasn't, but Rhea opted for the non-committal course and nodded. 'I've been trying to persuade her to attend our group.'

She was standing now, crutches in place. 'If only I were more mobile...'

'Then you wouldn't be here.' Leo's expression implied so much more than his words conveyed. You'd have gone joyfully on your way like all the others, it said, with a large cheque to pay into your bank account at my expense.

'I can't wait, Mr Dower, to make my getaway,' she dropped acidly into the sudden silence. 'Thanks again, Nathan, for the tea.' To Leo, she added, 'You're waiting to take me home?'

'Home', she heard herself say, and coloured uncomfortably. The last thing she must do, she told herself, was to look upon this man's cottage as her home.

He had noticed her slip, of course, and the mockery in his eyes only increased her confusion. His car was more comfortable than Nathan's, more roomy and smoother-running.

'If you dare to say,' her voice rose over the taped music, 'so you're not just a pretty face, I'll——'

'Thump me? Try, Rhea, try. I retaliate when provoked—in unexpected ways. As my brother has no doubt told you, where conventional behaviour's concerned, I don't run true to form.'

Classical music filled the conversational silence until he broke it with, 'As the daughter of a wealthy man, I guess, you wouldn't have needed to work? Which meant that your hobbies took up most of your time?'

'I gather,' she answered, tight-lipped, 'that you're saying in a roundabout way that educationally I'm a moron?'

'*No,*' he answered with mocking emphasis. 'No doubt finishing-school rounded off your corners and taught you how to cook, how to draw——'

'How to be *clever with my hands*? Just how patronising can you get, Mr Dower? Anyway, I see no reason to tell you anything about myself. Our acquaintance is going to be so short that my abilities, either mental or manual, can be of no concern to you.'

Something inside her erupted. She craved to break away, to get out, escape from the disturbing, disrupting

aura of the man beside her. The country quietness outside
beckoned and, in itself, offered sanctuary from the destructive force beside her.

'I want to walk,' she got out, her hand on the door
catch. 'I'm not staying in this car a moment longer. Let
me out, please.' He did not stop, so her wilful hand
opened the door.

'For God's sake,' he shouted, stamping on the brake,
'what the hell do you think you're doing?'

'G-getting away—f-from you.' Rhea swung out her
good leg, with her hands lifting out the injured one and
struggling free of the car's confines. The crutches were
on the rear seat, but with one leg out of action she could
only stand there.

After a few moments Leo joined her. 'Don't you dare
try and put me back in the car!' Rhea cried.

'I wouldn't dream of manhandling a *lady* against her
will,' he returned, his emphasis implying that she was
the very opposite. He pulled out the crutches and handed
them to her one by one.

When she was ready to move, he returned to the car
and drove on. He's going to leave me, she thought,
furious with herself for having given in to such a foolish
impulse. How could she have expected any sympathy,
any understanding of her state of mind, from such a
man?

To her astonishment, he stopped. When, slowly and
painfully, she had caught up with the car, he drove on
again, waiting once more, staring ahead, moving a short
distance, then halting a third time. His cottage was in
view, for a normally mobile person within easy reach,
but for her, every step bringing pain with it, a tantalisingly distant goal.

'Please go,' she said through her teeth, determined to
show her independence of him. 'I'm OK. I'll manage.'

With a dismissing lift of the shoulder, Leo complied with her request, driving on and disappearing to park in his back yard.

Weary from her earlier walk and with her laborious efforts now, she continued doggedly on, mauling her lower lip in an effort to stop it trembling. But trembling she was when she reached the cottage, fumbling with the catch and steeling herself to take on the chin his mocking laughter as she entered.

He was not there. The place seemed empty, and she collapsed on to the settee, white-faced and low-spirited, angry both with herself and with him for doing what she had asked.

Lying back, she closed her eyes, only to open them again, having sensed a presence. The trembling hadn't completely receded.

'OK, so crow if you want to,' she challenged. 'I'm tired, I'm exhausted. I'm a fool to have left the car.' Her eyes came to blazing life. 'I don't care, do you hear? I don't care about anything...'

'Not even about Jerome?'

Was that what he thought was upsetting her? That she was still in love with his errant brother?

'Certainly not about *him*!' Which, no doubt in Leo Dower's mind, implied that if it wasn't her unrequited love of Jerome that was the cause it was the 'trouble' that he had supposedly brought on her.

She leaned back, eyes closed, feeling composure return. Yet a battle still raged within her—of wanting to fight this man, yet longing for comfort from those powerful arms. *And not just his arms.*

Her eyes flew open to rest on his mouth, his swept-back black hair, the darkly defined eyebrows, and those eyes, those unsettling, all-seeing eyes, that held secrets she, Rhea Hirst, would never hear...

To her horror, tears sprang, but she dashed them away, wishing her limbs would stop shaking, not just from shock now, but from some deep-down inner knowledge, so new, so frightening that she told herself it must never be allowed to erupt to the surface of her mind.

He was handing her a drink, his face expressionless. The alcohol was potent, but she finished it and handed him the glass as, slowly, calmness returned.

'I'm fine, thank you. You can call off the surveillance of my physical state.'

Even to her own ears it sounded ungrateful, but, she repeated to herself this time, she didn't care, she just didn't care. Did she?

The telephone rang in the living-room one evening as Rhea watched television. Alone, she wondered if she had time to fit the crutches into place and answer it before the caller gave up.

As she hauled herself upright and adjusted the crutches, Leo materialised from nowhere, taking the call. There was a room in the cottage which he kept locked but in which, while at home, he spent a lot of his time. In the few glimpses inside which Rhea had been allowed to snatch, it seemed to be fitted out as an office.

'Leo Dower.' Rhea thought she must have imagined the sharp intake of breath until he clipped, 'Jerome? Where the hell are you? You land me with yet another of your peccadilloes, then make a break for it. It's time you acknowledged your responsibilities and came back into circulation. So come on, brother, give.'

Leo beckoned to Rhea, who made it across to stand beside him.

'I don't want to talk to Jerome,' she whispered hoarsely. 'We've got nothing to say to each other.'

'Just listen,' said Leo, operating a switch on the telephone, at which Jerome's amplified voice came over loud and clear.

'I take it from your statement,' he said, speaking slowly, 'that you had a visit from—er—a lady called Rhea, Rhea Hirst?'

'I did. She's still here.'

'Oh, dear,' with false sympathy. 'You mean you haven't been able to pay her off like you have the others? Now I wonder why?'

His tone implied that he knew the answer.

'You'd agree with my description, would you?' he went on. 'A lady. She's made an impression on you, has she, so you haven't had the heart yet to tell her to go? You'd better cut her loose, brother, pronto. She's bad news.'

There seemed to be the faintest note of urgency in his voice, which his brother appeared to pick up, raising an eyebrow.

'She injured her foot—her ankle,' Leo said. 'She's in plaster, partly disabled. Get it, Jerome? She's here until she's able to walk unaided again. And I've a mind to keep her here until you come and get her, then do your duty by marrying her.'

There was a minor explosion at the other end. '*Marry her*? You must be joking! What do you take me for?'

'Yes, marry her and accept the responsibilities that paternity and fatherhood bestow on a begetter of children.'

Jerome gave a prolonged, choking cough. 'A *w-what*?' he stammered, recovering. 'She told you *that*?' He swore, making Rhea flinch. 'For Pete's sake, I only told her to get some money out of you to pay for the car I—er—bought from her.'

'He *stole* it,' Rhea intervened under her breath, but no one listened.

'So she's used the oldest trick in the book, has she, the cunning little bi——' Jerome checked, then amended '—beggar, to get me to tie the knot.' A pause, then a different, more persuasive tone. 'If you're so keen, Leo, to give the new generation of Dowers the benefit of a father and his—or her, as the case may be—rightful name, why don't you marry her yourself?'

Rhea expelled a furious breath and swung a crutch to move away. Leo's hand came out, grasping her arm, holding it.

'Ask her, Leo, see what she says. You never know your luck, pal.' There was barely suppressed laughter in Jerome's unrepentant voice. 'She's so hard up—did you know that?—she might say yes for the money—your money—in the bank. No doubt she's guessed by now what a wealthy guy you are. Oh, and tell her I'll pack up her things I found in the car and send them on. Bits and pieces of jewellery—junk, of course——'

'They were my mother's!' Rhea hissed furiously.

'And her squares and rectangles of weaving—tapestries was the grand name she gave them—plus something she called "batik". Has she told you, Leo, what an accomplished little *lady* she is? Must ring off—this call's costing me a fortune. Say "hi" to my darling ex-fiancée, will you?'

'Where are you, Jerome?' Leo rapped out.

'Ah, that's a secret. You won't find me walking into the noose that's waiting to strangle me.'

'What noose?'

'Why,' a long-drawn out laugh, 'marriage, of course, and the *fatherhood* you talked about. What else?' There was a click, then silence.

Rhea stifled a gasp. Jerome had played along with his brother's assumption that she was expecting a child, which meant that the idea was now fixed, hard as cement, in Leo's mind! Released at last from Leo's hold, she swung herself back to the settee.

Leo proceeded to walk up and down, hands pocketed, pausing at the windows which, at each end of the room, overlooked the rear and front gardens. He seemed to be fighting a battle, or was it anger? But if anyone has a right to be angry, Rhea thought, I have. It was she who had suffered at Jerome's hands, not Leo.

'Even now you won't condemn him, will you?' Rhea thrust thickly into the silence. 'I'm the one you've branded as no good. I'm just passing through your life, so I don't signify, do I? You're no doubt arguing inside your head that blood's thicker than water. Brother means more than brother's cast-off woman, so you accept his word against hers. Well,' her own head lifted proudly, 'I can take it, all the blame, all the censure. I've taken so much in the past few months; a little more, for a little longer, won't break my spirit.'

He came to stand beside her, and she felt the full impact of him, his power, his magnetism. His very posture seemed to threaten, his legs slightly apart, his strong thighs, his wide hips, lean waist above the waistband. So much masculinity had her senses swimming, but she refused to raise her head and meet his eyes. All the same, she had to. His hand came out and tilted her face, fastening around it so that she had to look him in the eye.

'So there's an idea.' The cynicism mouthed by his twisted lips clashed with the strange bleakness in his hard, handsome face. 'Since my dear brother Jerome refuses to do his duty, will you take me as your husband, Rhea Hirst?'

CHAPTER FIVE

HIDING her moist, bunched fists, Rhea did not, could not, answer. Speech had deserted her, her thoughts becoming scrambled like a secret message.

Her hatred of Jerome became paramount, pushing reason into second place. And since, by all accounts, this man in front of her made it his business constantly to connive with his brother, pacifying and paying off the women the brother had wronged, that hatred spilled over to encompass Leo Dower too.

His consideration in putting himself out to obtain medical attention for her—yes, of course, she was grateful for that, not to mention his offer of a roof until she had recovered from her disability. But such gestures arose only from his sense of duty, from his feeling of obligation to her because of her supposed treatment at his brother's hands. And this proposal of marriage arose from these sentiments too.

'There's no need, Mr Dower,' she said at last, 'to let your conscience drive you to take such a step as to offer marriage to someone you despise, as I know you despise me.'

He looked at her sharply, but, to her curiously intense disappointment, he did not deny her statement. He walked by.

'No doubt,' came from him bitingly, 'in your eyes Leo Dower would be a poor substitute for the man you really want.' He shrugged, walked away, came back. 'Get this, Rhea. No Dower is going to be born outside marriage if I have anything to do with it.'

'You—you mean you're so determined to give the—the new Dower you're so convinced is on its way a name that you'd even be willing to sacrifice your freedom?'

Those broad shoulders lifted and fell. '"My freedom"?' He returned to stand in front of her. 'What a curious expression! In these times, freedom, like a marriage, comes and goes.'

'All right, then, for the sake of your family name, you'd actually *tie* yourself to a woman you don't love and whom you look on with contempt, and always will?'

He stared unreadably into her eyes.

'So,' as if she had not spoken, as if she had actually agreed, 'you will marry me. Then, when the child is born and is registered as a Dower, you'll be free to do as you wish. Go or stay. A divorce would be one way of dealing with the situation. Separation, any other variation,' his shoulder lifted, 'it doesn't matter to me.'

So, Rhea thought, her mind still reeling under the impact of his suggestion—or had it really been an order?—Jerome had been right in one thing, even if he had been wrong in all the others. Leo did take life as it came... and went. Putting any woman out of his mind and moving on to the next and the next...

'I'd give you an allowance,' he was saying, 'sufficient to cover your needs and that of Jerome's——'

'There isn't going to be a child,' the declaration burst through her unguarded lips, 'so will you stop——?'

'You will not take that step,' he rasped, eyes dark as night, 'do you hear? You came to me for help because my brother refused to accept his responsibilities. I am therefore taking full responsibility for you on his behalf.' He walked away.

So he had misunderstood her outburst! Well, her conscience was clear, she had told him the truth and he had chosen to disbelieve it. He returned, his eyes holding hers. Unable to stand his penetrating gaze, Rhea looked elsewhere, but that look still burned through, so she covered her face to shut it out.

A hand touching her hair made her shiver. That hand slid slowly down her cheek, leaving a tingling trail. The pulses in her neck leapt as his fingers crept over her throat. The effect of his touch was so electric that it frightened her.

Hands fastened under her armpits and drew her to her feet. Still she refused to open her eyes. If only her breathing would even out, filling her lungs instead of manifesting itself in short jerks, shaking her.

Arms with the power to forge hard metal into flowing shapes pulled her to him. Lips, firm and cool and totally masculine, claimed hers, and she found her errant self responding, allowing her mouth to be caught and tantalised and played with, then completely possessed. Her arms began to let her down, lifting and clinging as her body swung this way and that as the fancy took the arms which held her.

'That,' he said thickly, as her eyes sprang wide and dismayed at the way her inner sexuality had responded to—worse, actually *collaborated* with—his, 'is all I wanted to know.'

He walked away again, leaving her strangely cold and inwardly trembling, her leg, the one that had supported her, so weak that she feared she would fall if she didn't find her seat again.

'I'd respect the fact that you're expecting Jerome's child,' he said coolly, as if the kiss had never happened, 'which means that it would be a marriage in name only. I'd ask nothing of you, no sacrificial acts of intimacy, or so-called love. You would simply wear my ring until your life after the event settled down and you found yourself able to cope with your changed circumstances. Then I'd release you. No recriminations, no conditions to be fulfilled. At a time convenient to us both, the marriage would end.'

There won't be an 'event'! The words shrieked inside her head. But hadn't she tried just now to tell him the truth, and hadn't he misinterpreted? So her lips stayed sealed on her secret.

'You wouldn't want for anything,' he was saying.

'Not even—even after the divorce?' she broke in with a bitterness that surprised her.

'Not even after that. Nor for the rest of your life.'

Divorce? Her inner self was actually contemplating accepting his proposal? Why not? a voice whispered. Then it came to her like thunder from a clear blue sky— what better way, she thought recklessly, to wreak that revenge she longed to have on the Dower family...a kind of payment to her by them for all the misery and un-happiness that its younger son had brought crashing down on to her head?

She released the breath she didn't even realise she was holding.

'Yes,' she answered, eyes bright, head held high, 'I'll marry you. For all the reasons you said.'

Two days after the cast was removed from Rhea's leg, the wedding took place. During the ceremony the best man, Vince Adley, an old friend of Leo's, took care of the walking stick which Rhea still needed.

Nathan was there, acting as one of the witnesses, Leo's uncle Timmy being the other. To Rhea's immense relief, there was no sign of Sonya.

Rhea's cream-shaded dress was fashioned to follow her shape, and if Leo, in his swiftly appraising glance as she had walked slowly down the stairs, had wondered at her persisting slimness, he had made no comment. Her satin shoes matched the dress, likewise the cream satin ribbon around the navy wide-brimmed hat which framed her face.

Where the wedding breakfast was concerned, had she been a true bride, both loving and loved, she could not have asked for more. At a fashionable hotel in the town, among flowers and bridal decorations, they were served with choice dishes and wines. Champagne, the best, flowed, and, to Rhea's astonishment, Leo had even taken the trouble to order a wedding cake. A miniature loving couple, made of icing, stood amid swirls of sugar flowers.

The handful of guests whom Leo had invited insisted that the bride and groom stood together, knife poised, while cameras snapped and whirred. Rhea did her best to hide her embarrassment, part of her wanting to cry out, Don't bother, please. This is a phoney wedding, we don't love each other at all. But, to her dismay, the other part of her wanted it to be real, to be meaningful and truly loving, followed by a fulfilling, not an empty marriage.

Laughter and warm feelings filled the room, jokes, largely at Leo's expense, flying back and forth as the wedding breakfast progressed. Carrie, Vince Adley's sister, tall and curly-haired, kept smiling at Rhea as if for encouragement, making her acutely aware of her own tension and lack of spontaneity.

Seated beside her, their arms brushing now and then, Leo seemed to have noticed.

'By marrying me,' he whispered, his mouth close to her ear, 'you haven't signed your death warrant, merely taken my name for the sake of things to come. Nothing's permanent, and nothing's changed, except *your* name. Will you play out your role as the happy bride, with or without the blushes, for the next hour or two at least? If it's any help, you look beautiful.'

Rhea turned to him, secretly pleased by his compliment, although she knew it to be false. 'There's really no need to flatter me,' she responded tartly, then caught a look in his eyes that set her pulses leaping. Had he been sincere, after all? Her smile broke through like the sun from behind a blanket of cloud.

'That's better,' he murmured, turning her by the shoulders and placing his cool, wine-tinged lips on hers. From the men there was an ironic cheer, while the women happily applauded.

Now, seated beside a silent and strangely preoccupied Leo, Rhea leaned back tiredly, staring out at the passing scenery. It was the state of her emotions that troubled her most. Even now, just thinking about that careless kiss he had given her simply to please their audience, she found her heart beating faster, the touch and taste of his mouth on hers lingering alarmingly.

'You did well.' His abrupt praise broke into her reverie, startling her.

'You mean you've discovered an unexpected side of me?' she returned, still staring out. 'You're surprised to find that I can role-play? You asked me to, remember?'

He shrugged, accelerating to climb a hill. 'Whatever.' After a pause, 'You rose to the occasion.'

'Thank you,' she responded stiffly, then removed her hat, twisting to place it on the rear seat.

The rice had rained on them, confetti floated down, cries of 'Good luck!' following them. Plainly their guests had managed to fool themselves into believing it was a love match after all.

'My parents,' Rhea found herself explaining, 'loved having people around them, and they entertained a great deal. My mother suffered from indifferent health, so sometimes I took her place. All my education, my home environment, conditioned me into acting the sparkling hostess, no matter how I might feel.'

Eyes on the road, Leo remarked, 'You must tell me some time.'

'There's nothing to tell.' But there was, so much that it would fill volumes.

There would be no honeymoon. She had insisted on this from the start, and Leo had merely shrugged in his usual offhanded way. As they crossed the ancient bridge spanning the river, something deep inside her leapt at the sight of Leo's cottage.

In the few weeks that she had lived there, she was secretly forced to acknowledge that she had grown to love the place. Wasn't it ironic, she asked herself, as Leo parked in his usual place, that she had come to feel a deep affection for this man's home, if not for the man himself? Sensitivity to his presence, acute and disturbing though it was, she told herself firmly, must not be mistaken for anything but irritation.

The country silence came rushing in through the opened windows.

'Rhea?' Steel-grey eyes, resolute and inscrutable as they usually were, rested on her face. He reached out and removed something from the silky tendrils, holding it out. The gesture reminded her of the day they had first met, when he had extracted a piece of grass from her hair.

Now it was a piece of confetti, tiny, heart-shaped, which he placed in the palm of her hand, closing her fingers over it. She looked at it and put it in her purse. She never wanted to lose that minuscule heart; it was a symbol of something which she knew for certain would for ever be beyond her reach, but keep it she would.

Taking her other hand, Leo looked at the ring which a couple of hours earlier he had placed on her wedding finger.

'You may kiss the bride.' The traditional words drifted into her mind. And, in front of the wedding guests, he had done so, sweetly, softly... and totally without passion. All the same, her lips still felt that kiss as if it had only at that moment been placed there.

'Yes?' It seemed that it hadn't been a question since he shook his head. 'I——' She moistened her lips. 'Thank you for what you've done, but——'

Now, a voice shrieked inside her head, tell him the truth... tell him *this minute*. The revenge you planned to have on the Dower family—now you legally wear his ring... this is it, your moment of triumph, of glorious victory. 'But——' It wasn't necessary to marry me, because there's no new Dower on the way... The words stuck fast, almost choking her.

Leo swung open his door and came round to help her out. The moment had passed, the time for confession receding into the background. The relief was so strong that it frightened her. It didn't mean—did it?—that, for some reason she couldn't fathom, she was actually glad to have become this man's wife?

In the living-room he left her and went upstairs, coming down in T-shirt and jeans, his working clothes.

'If you need my help for any reason,' he said, gesturing to the telephone, 'you know where to find me.'

Rhea sank back in the chair, anticlimax swamping her. So this was it—marriage to Leo Dower, a house full of silence? The clamour—for what? conversation, companionship, *love*?—was all in her head. With the aid of her walking stick, she pulled herself up the stairs and slowly divested herself of her wedding outfit.

The hat she replaced carefully in its box, the dress and jacket she slid on to a hanger. Pulling off her shoes, she stared at them, at their shining, *virgin* newness. Drawing a shuddering breath, she drew back her arm and hurled them one by one through the open window.

Hours later she stirred to darkness, her face damp with the tears that had shaken her slender frame until an exhausted sleep had claimed her. Something had disturbed her and, opening her eyes, she saw Leo, frowning down at her. He held up the shoes, one in each hand. 'How come?' he asked with a hint of amusement. 'Did they jump out of their own accord? Maybe they fancied a riverside walk in the dark without their owner?'

She had to smile. 'I was letting off steam.'

'Some steam! Do you blow your top every time you get yourself married?'

'Every time,' another smile, less shaky this time, 'without exception.'

'Was I your imaginary target?'

'Yes,' she answered. And the circumstances, and...everything you don't know about. She became conscious of her partly undressed state, her silk slip having ridden high above her thighs.

Seeming to notice her embarrassment, Leo dropped the shoes and slid his hand beneath her thighs, easing the silky fabric down. Her mouth opened on a gasp, but she masked it with a strangled 'Don't!'

His touch was electric, stinging her violently like a shock from the mains. Never, she vowed, would she let him touch her again. Its effect was so devastating that she did not dare to imagine what it would do to her if she ever...he ever...

'For God's sake, I'm your husband!' He seemed angry, but so was she.

'In name only,' she hit back. 'You'd ask nothing, you promised. If—if you want me to regard you as a man of principle, as you seem to think you are, then keep that promise. It was the basis of this marriage contract we entered into.'

'Then why have you been crying?'

Why? How could she answer when she didn't even know herself? She sat up slowly, to give herself time. 'Because——'

'I'm not Jerome?'

'No, no!' But let him think that, she chided herself; it was as good a reason as any, wasn't it? 'My foot,' she added for good measure.

'It still hurts?'

She nodded, averting her eyes from his overpowering masculinity. Looking at him in the semi-darkness, she felt something begin to stir inside her, some deep, in-

explicable feeling . . . Surely it wasn't a sense of *longing*?
Of course it wasn't. Fatigue, more likely, reaction to the
long day, and all that it had contained, meaningless
though it had been.

'That,' she temporised. 'And—and other things.'

To her relief, yet perversely to her disappointment, he
turned, his measured footsteps carrying him away.

He had breakfasted and gone by the time Rhea made
her way downstairs. She wondered, on this first day of
their marriage, whether he would bring his sandwiches
and his uncle Timmy as he had on her first day there,
but he did not.

''Morning, dear.' Mrs Litton, Leo's twice-weekly help,
let herself in and smilingly surveyed her employer's new
wife. 'Nice wedding, was it, love? I bet you looked fit
to eat in that dress I saw hanging on the door of your
wardrobe!' She inspected Rhea's face. 'Your foot still
troubling you? You look a bit pale.'

Swiftly Rhea turned on a brilliant smile, doing her
best to fit Mrs Litton's idea of a radiant bride. 'You're
right about my foot, but otherwise I'm fine, thanks.'

The lady help, romantically satisfied, went about her
business, getting through her work with extra speed. Did
Mrs Dower mind? Mrs Litton asked, leaving a light lunch
on a tray nearby. 'My daughter and her kiddies are
coming for a couple of days.'

Mrs Dower, startled by being thus addressed, and
wanting to declare that inside she was still Miss Hirst,
said she didn't mind at all.

Late morning the postman delivered a heavy box,
obligingly carrying it into the cottage. 'From foreign
parts,' he commented, pointing to the stamps and the
postmark.

'Foreign' to people living there, Rhea knew, could
sometimes mean from another part of the country, but
this time it had meant exactly that. The box had been

mailed in Singapore, and Rhea guessed at once who had sent it.

> Herewith your rubbish, but you won't get your car back. It's mine now, safely locked away. Don't I deserve it after everything? Tell my brother not to jump to the conclusion that if he drops everything and flies over here he'll find me. I'm en route, and I'm not telling where. Has he married you yet? I guess he has. He's a stickler for doing the right thing. Unlike me, I hear you say. Hope you enjoy the patter of tiny feet. Ha! Happy memories, yes? Jerome.

At the last brash phrase, Rhea almost tore the note into shreds, but restrained herself. Leo had a right to see its contents. She was reaching into the box, surrounded by the items she had already withdrawn, when there came a knock and the turn of the door-handle.

'How's the newly-wed?' asked Nathan, looking with interest at the articles scattered over the floor.

Rhea knew that for Nathan she didn't have to put on the 'blushing bride' act. He, like Leo's other close friends, knew the truth, or what they assumed was the truth.

'Happy now I've got my things back,' she answered, gesturing to the articles all around her. Her mother's jewellery she had carried up to her room and locked away.

Nathan did not ask 'back from whom?' 'Hey, what's all this?' he exclaimed, kneeling beside Rhea and gazing around as if he had found buried treasure. 'Whose handiwork is this? And this?' He picked up pieces of unfinished embroidery, squares of hessian and linen, rough sketches on graph paper, triangles of canvas, lengths of material both plain and dyed.

'Mine,' Rhea told him with a smile. 'Just experiments with designs and colours.'

'A hobby, you said. Craftsman that I am, looking at these I'm not fooled, Rhea. You're a professional.' He spoke almost accusingly, and Rhea laughed.

'Maybe, maybe not. I'm qualified enough to make a living at this kind of work. Even to teach it if I want.'

'You're a dark horse, Rhea. Why?'

She shrugged and shook her head. Nathan knew her well enough not to probe. The door opened yet again, and Rhea's heart nearly leapt sideways as Leo strolled in. Eyes narrowing a fraction, he glanced from one to the other, then at the contents of the box.

Rhea thought he deserved an explanation. 'Jerome sent them back to me. He kept his word.'

'You sound surprised.'

'I have reason to be,' she murmured, picking up a square of fabric.

'No car? Or rather, promise of its return?'

She shook her head, handing him Jerome's note. After scanning it, he threw it aside. 'I get the feeling it's coded.'

Rhea looked up quickly, but he said nothing. This man was, for her peace of mind, too quick on the uptake.

Nathan rose, pointing. 'That girl has been pulling the wool over our eyes.' Rhea's heart leapt again. Had Nathan guessed her secret? It seemed he hadn't. 'All this—this work, it's all hers. Would you believe?'

'OK, Rhea, enlighten us.' Leo's voice was low and compelling, and she found herself saying,

'I'd have told you, but it didn't somehow seem relevant. I've got a degree in art.' She looked directly at Leo.

'You have?' said Nathan, sounding strangled.

'So.' Leo this time. 'Why the mystery?'

Tingles ran down her spine and she wished she could read his expression. As his hand came out to help her up, she jerked in surprise. He did not release her hand, clasping it in a handshake. 'As one craftsman to another, Rhea Hirst, welcome to the club.'

Distantly she heard Nathan say, 'I echo that.'

Leo had called her 'Hirst', but it didn't matter. Her heart nearly danced for joy. For the first time ever, she glimpsed warmth in Leo's eyes, the merest flicker, but to her it was as warming as a fire on a cold day. He released her hand.

'Yes, well,' said Nathan, looking from Leo to her. Was he thinking that, in spite of everything, the man who now called himself her husband had some feeling for her after all?

How wrong he would be, Rhea thought.

'I just called in to say "hi",' Nathan added. 'I'm on my way to the town.' He smiled broadly at Rhea. 'Wait until I tell the group about the accomplished lady we now have in our midst! They'll welcome you with open arms. You—er—' with a quick glance at Leo and making for the door '—you won't let them down, will you? What I mean is, you'll agree to meet them?'

'Of course. I'll be delighted to meet them all.' With a defiant lift of the head, 'With or without Leo's permission.'

'What was that supposed to mean?' asked Leo when Nathan had gone, picking up Jerome's note again.

Rhea's shoulders lifted. 'Nathan seemed to think that now we've gone through a marriage ceremony we operate as a single unit. That we can't bear to be apart, that we tell each other our movements and——'

Leo, reading the note, did not seem to be listening. '"Happy memories,"' he quoted. 'Which means that, whatever you may say about your association with my brother——'

'He was being facetious. There may have been happy times, but my memories of him now and everything to do with him are the very opposite of happy.'

'You really do bear him a grudge for what he did to you, don't you?'

'Who wouldn't?' she retorted. 'He changed the course of my life completely...' Then she realised what he had meant. So we're back to the 'baby' issue, she thought miserably. Some time soon she would have to tell him.

To her relief, Leo changed course.

'What was the make of your car? The one he "borrowed"?'

'One of the very few that might well keep its value while being locked away.'

'A Rolls? You owned a Rolls-Royce?'

'It was my father's, the only thing I managed to salvage from the mess.' Why did she feel she had to defend herself? 'I thought I told you. The entire business toppled. It was failing for some time before he, and my mother, died.'

For the rest of the day, Rhea worked on the items Jerome had returned to her. With Leo's iron and with loving care she pressed the specimens, then labelled them methodically.

Looking up from her work, she realised not only that she was hungry, but also that she was still alone. She made a light supper for herself and, having cleared away, stared out at the darkening moorland.

Pulling on a jacket over her T-shirt, and pushing her feet into walking shoes, she found her stick and went outside. She looked right, left, then right again. Something drew her that way, over the old stone bridge and down the road that led to the village. And the forge.

If he was not there, she would swallow her pride, remind herself that he was a free agent, despite the ceremony they had gone through, and force herself not to be jealous. After all, Sonya Selby had a great deal to offer a man. Why should he leave her arms to return to the woman he had married simply to protect the new member of the Dower family he was so convinced was on its way?

If Leo was there—well, she'd turn back, wouldn't she? Telling herself that at least she knew where he was. The telephone? That, he had said, she could use if she needed him. Which she didn't and, she told herself, never would.

He was there—the ringing strike of hammer on metal told her that in advance. So why were her feet still carrying her on ... and into the semi-darkness?

His back was to her, but he paused, hammer raised, as if sensing, as he had the first time, that she was there. He turned, staring at her just as he had before.

Flickering and uncertain though the interior of the old forge was, the impact on her senses of his height, his muscled breadth, the sheen upon his torso, was even greater than that first time.

As if drawn by an invisible force, Rhea went towards him and stood leaning heavily on her stick. Why had she come? If he asked her, she wouldn't know. All she did know was that she had forcibly to hold herself back from going to him, touching his chest, moving his arm until it encircled her, putting her lips against his ...

Slowly his hand released the hammer, its clatter making her shiver—or was it the look in his eyes? He did not, on this occasion, pull on his T-shirt out of courtesy and politeness.

'You want me?' His tone was clipped, discouraging.

She came to her senses. Of course he did not want her here! 'No. Thank you.' She turned to go.

'Liar.' He moved to cut off her retreat. 'You *want* me. And you want this.'

His arms swung her round, her stick hitting the ground. There was no mercy in the way he roped her body to his, no consideration in the way his mouth descended. There was a world of sensuality in the way his lips crushed hers, his tongue rasping against their tender skin until she submitted and allowed him thrusting access. Without restraint he plundered the secret moistness of her mouth, disregarding her throaty cries, only relenting and softening when her resistance died away and she melted into him.

His head lifted, although his lips remained in tingling contact with hers. 'You wanted that,' he said thickly. 'You wanted a little *romance*, did you, to sweeten your memory of that sham marriage ceremony we shared yesterday?'

'No, I——' She shook her head, only to hear him laugh deep in his throat.

'Don't lie again, lady. I gave you what you came for. Or——' he drawled, drawing away enough to look down at her warm, upturned face '—am I to regard that as just a preliminary to——'

'No! You'd be breaking our agreement, breaking your word.' If he made love to her now, he would guess— what would he guess? What she hadn't allowed even herself to guess, nor even to think about. 'You can keep your lovemaking!' she heard herself cry. She struggled to free herself and he let her go, his expression sardonic. 'For your beautiful girlfriend,' she added, retrieving her stick. 'You think I'm not intelligent enough to have guessed?'

His broad shoulders shrugged off her questions. 'Oh, you're intelligent,' he said sarcastically. 'I've never doubted that.' He turned to replenish the fire.

Rhea found her eyes upon his back, closing them fiercely until she had managed to discipline the feelings the mere sight of his moving unclothed torso aroused.

Desperate to bring the emotional temperature down to normal levels, she moved around the uneven stone floor. Sensitive to the atmosphere of the place, she could almost swear she could hear the whinnying of horses of olden times.

With a professional eye, she studied the metallic shapes that were scattered about the place.

It was the artist in her that asked, 'Are these designs experimental, or part of a whole?'

'Both.' Leo moved to stand beside her, and only with the greatest difficulty did she keep her reactions to him on an intellectual plane.

'I didn't realise there was a place for a forge in modern life.'

'A fair comment, coming from a suburbanite, as you are.' No criticism there, just a simple observation. 'But you're not alone in thinking that by a long way. My uncle Timmy has enough work to keep him going for a long time to come.'

'Which is why you break away from your business responsibilities now and then to help him?'

'Who's been talking? Nathan? Yes, I guessed. I don't just come here to help my uncle. To me, it's a relaxation as well as a hobby. Timmy says it's an obsession with me.' His broad shoulders lifted. 'Whatever, he's glad of my help.' After a moment he added, 'It's the constant challenge, having to fulfil tricky orders, that I can't resist. Not to mention,' with a quizzical lift of the eyebrow, 'as you will no doubt appreciate and understand, the demand on one's creativity, that keeps me tied to it.'

'I understand,' she replied fervently. 'I feel that constant drive myself.'

'I guessed that.'

Rhea revelled in the way he was confiding in her, talking to her as an equal. 'What kind of things do you make?' she asked.

'We repair the kind of objects that people treasure, like much-loved spades, gardening forks; things people value, like old kettles. Obvious items like horseshoes, forged door hinges, window catches for renovation jobs. Once Timmy and I rehabilitated a wind-battered cockerel from an ancient church tower.'

'And creative work? Like those gates I heard you talking about to Miss Selby?'

'Decorative folding iron gates. Larger contracts like that, yes. They're what interest me most.' Leo wandered back to his work. 'It's a traditional coke-fired forge,' he explained. 'Timmy and I decided against changing to a more up-to-date gas-fired model.'

He turned towards the flames, their scarlet heat dancing over his tough arms. Rhea watched him at the anvil, and winced as he handled with nonchalant assurance pieces of red-hot metal he had drawn from the fire. Sparks flew and she held her breath as the incandescent rod kept inching ever closer to his horrifyingly vulnerable skin. Why she should worry in case he got hurt, she didn't know, but worry she did.

She sat on a battered wooden upright chair, her walking stick leaning against her side. Her ears rang with the sound his hammer strikes were making, reverberating around the wide, low-ceilinged building and ricocheting against the stone walls.

His face drew her eyes, the intense concentration in all its angles illumined by the glow of the white-hot metal he was manipulating. His full lips, which only a few minutes ago had been crushed against hers, were compressed by the determination with which he handled and controlled the object he hammered into submission. He leaned forward, the better to produce the shape he required, his wide shoulders curving slightly, his flesh gleaming.

Rhea was certain he had forgotten her presence, but some minutes later, apparently satisfied with the form he had created, he put down his tools and looked up, as if he had been perfectly aware of her the whole time. Taking a towel from a pile, he rubbed at his moisture-laden neck and shoulders, drying his arms and lifting them, revealing the patches of hair, moving the towel downwards to skim over the curling mat on his chest. Discarding the towel, he looked at her, and the words he spoke were to turn her whole world upside down.

'Tell me something.' He moved to stand in front of her, arms folded, his physique daunting, although a flicker of a smile brought a momentary softening to his expression. 'I guess I should have asked before, but typically man-like, as a woman would no doubt say, it slipped my mind. When is Jerome's child due to be born?'

CHAPTER SIX

RHEA'S heart began to pound, her breaths wrenched from her lungs. This, she told herself emphatically, was the moment she had been longing for. This was the moment when she wreaked her revenge on the Dower family, the revenge she had sworn to have from the time Jerome's treachery and fraudulent behaviour had been revealed to her.

It had been a reckless revenge that she had embarked upon, she saw that now. How *could* she have chosen such a way of achieving her ends? But didn't she deserve some reparation for the havoc and pain Jerome had caused in her life? The way he had contributed to her father's financial downfall? And, eventually, to her parents' deaths? If she had chosen this way of evening things up with the Dower family, could she really be blamed?

Leo stood there, towering over her, his expression unreadable in the shadowy semi-darkness, and she realised what a terrible error she had made. Like a lightning flash, her intuition revealed to her the real reason she had agreed to marry this man.

Beyond a shadow of doubt, when she was about to be thrown out of his life for ever, she knew that she had fallen in love with Leo Dower the moment she had set eyes on him ... and that she loved him more than she had ever loved another living being.

Her mouth had grown parched, her throat rough with tension. She answered, 'I'm not expecting Jerome's child.' As he didn't seem to comprehend, she added, slowly and clearly, 'There isn't going to be a baby.'

It was as though he had become carved in stone. A spark leapt from the fire. Even if it had started a blaze Rhea doubted if he would have stirred. Then slowly, gropingly, he picked up his T-shirt, with mechanical movements pulling it over his head. Eyes a steely grey, the look in them frightening in its intensity, he said, 'Are you telling me that you "lost" the child before you came here, then proceeded to pretend you were still carrying it?'

Rhea shook her head. When *would* he understand, accept the truth?

'Jerome didn't make me pregnant——'

His lips tautened into a snarl. 'But someone else did, then you pretended it was Jerome's?'

'No!' she almost shrieked. 'Don't you see? I've never expected a child. I——' It had to be said, and right now. She swallowed hard. She didn't love this man, she hated him, didn't she? So why wasn't she enjoying her revenge, instead of standing there attempting to explain her actions? 'I married you,' she flung at him, 'to get even with the Dower family, because of all the terrible things Jerome did to me, to my life.'

'And you're trying to tell me those "terrible things" were completely unconnected with a pregnancy that my brother caused? Oh, no, that won't wash. I can't believe what you're saying. I've been on the receiving end of too many demands for payment for the expectation and birth of Jerome's unborn but oncoming offspring, careless as he is, and as the women have been that he's chosen to sleep with.'

'I've never expected Jerome's child. You have to believe me!'

He moved nearer, face twisted with anger. 'When I've seen it in writing in the note he sent you? Where he referred to the "patter of tiny feet" to come? To me, that can mean only one thing.'

He had taken Jerome's note seriously! 'He was joking, Leo. He knew the situation——'

'Did he?' His hands on her arms forced her to her feet. 'Did you tell him you'd had an abortion? Isn't *that* the true situation?'

'No, because, I keep telling you, it wasn't true!'

'Yet you came here, accepted my hospitality, would have accepted my money if I'd offered it to you as I offered it to all the others? Then gone on your way if you hadn't hurt yourself and been forced to stay here? Not to mention,' cuttingly, 'accepting my offer to marry you. A novel way, you no doubt thought, of not just taking the very generous hand-out I gave to the others— to you, cocooned by your father's wealth, a tiny amount, no doubt—but, as my wife, gaining limitless access to my bank account? Which meant,' with a sneer, 'that I'd be able to keep you in the comfort to which you'd grown accustomed.'

His fury, all the more powerful for being controlled, was at white heat, more dangerous even than the incandescent metal he drew from the fire. As he spoke, Rhea was sure that sparks flew, hitting her, searing her skin. How, she asked herself again, could she have been so foolish as to choose this man as her means of wreaking revenge?

'My God,' he was saying, 'at least those other women were honest. At least they admitted bluntly that they wanted—would be completely satisfied with—the lump sum Jerome had promised would come their way. Better educated as you were, you were far more cunning, weren't you?' His teeth snapped and he seized her shoulders, then contemptuously threw her from him. He walked a few paces. 'You rid yourself of Jerome's little burden, then came——'

'For the hundredth time, I didn't!' she cried. 'Let me tell you something. Your wonderful brother Jerome is a fraud, a thief, a——' 'Murderer' she almost said.

He swung round. 'Call him names, would you, names that could be actionable, simply because he broke the engagement and stole your car?'

She shook her head, realising how useless it was trying to break down in his mind the high wall he had erected around his brother's integrity. There seemed to be no way open to her of getting him to accept the truth.

Hadn't his uncle Timmy told her their family story, how protective Leo had been since childhood towards his younger brother? So how could she ever expect him to believe anything but good about Jerome?

'I'll pack and leave,' Rhea told him heavily.

'You will?' he rasped. 'You realise that would be admitting your guilt, tacitly agreeing that I'm right in accusing you of having had an abortion prior to coming here? And of accepting my proposal of marriage under false pretences?'

'Would that matter? I wouldn't be here to hear the gossip.' Rhea lifted her shoulders. How bitter her revenge tasted now! 'I just want to get on with my life. And—' she raised her eyes to his '—and allow you to get on with yours.'

Leo moved closer, holding her gaze. 'Exactly why,' he asked curiously, 'did you marry me?'

'Because I——' The truth so nearly burst from her! But even if she had told him she loved him he would have laughed in her face. 'I told you why.' There was a long silence. 'OK, you win,' she conceded falsely. 'I was after your money. And the usefulness to me of your position in life,' she threw in for good measure. 'Plus the benefit of the Dower name.' She had meant to sound cynical, but it came out levelly as if she had honestly meant it.

He nodded as if he had believed every word. How ironic, she thought, that he'd accepted her lies as the truth, yet when she had told him the truth he had regarded it as a lie.

'Where would you go?' he asked.

'On leaving here? Youth hostels, cheap hotels.'

'Not back to Jerome?'

'*Jerome*? Oh, no, thank you. I wouldn't know where to find him, would I?'

Too late she realised that he had probably taken her words to mean that if she had known of Jerome's whereabouts, she would have had no hesitation in joining him.

Hands deep in pockets, he regarded her for a long time. She grew uncomfortable under his scrutiny and stood up, reaching for her stick. His hand came out, taking it from her.

'I've come to a decision,' he declared, tight-lipped. 'You'll remain here as my wife—which you are—for as long as it takes for our marriage, shall we say, to be "given a chance"? Then, despite our "efforts", it can appear to be failing. Then I might—*might*—reconsider the position.'

'But a divorce,' Rhea cried protestingly. 'You promised—— '

'After the birth, I said. But, according to you, there won't be a birth, will there? Which absolves me from that promise.' He moved towards her, making her skin prickle, standing close enough for her to feel his breath on her lips. Part of her wanted to back away, but that recalcitrant other part wanted to close the tiny gap that separated them and...

'You've sold yourself, Rhea Hirst,' he said, his voice low, tone menacing, sending a *frisson* of fear through her nervous system, 'into my keeping. By marrying me, you don't know what a dangerous game you've embarked upon.' In the half-darkness and the ruby glow from the dying fire, he looked devilish and dark and handsome, with a hardness that caused an icy sensation to shiver all down her spine.

'It's—well, it's just a matter of sitting it out,' she said, affecting a careless shrug, 'long enough to convince your friends and neighbours that we're not compatible. You've just said as much. Then I'll pack my things and get out of your life.'

'In *my* time, my dear wife,' the endearment was charged with sarcasm, scraping her nerves, 'in my own time. Not yours.'

He pressed against her and she thought his arms were coming round her, but it was his eyes that stroked her lips, not his mouth, and she forced herself to quell the treacherous uprush of disappointment.

'You've got to let me go,' she heard herself protesting. 'You take life, and women, with equal ease. Jerome told me so, and, from my comparatively small knowledge of you, I've seen that he was right. So why is it so important that you feel you have to convince your acquaintances that you're putting yet another woman out of your life?'

'You believed Jerome, those stories he told you about me? You didn't for one minute think they might simply be brotherly comments?'

They just had to be true! Yet, as she had discovered, Jerome *had* lied to her many times. Any thought that the 'stories' might not be true filled her with dread, a sense of being captured, imprisoned, and that he might never let her go.

'You mean—the women in your life,' she asked, 'they've never come and gone?' Leo stared down at her, still disturbingly close. Since he didn't answer, Rhea assumed that that side of his personal history was, as far as she was concerned, a closed book. 'All the same, you made a promise about this marriage of ours——' she suddenly remembered '—as Jerome said in his note, you're a stickler for doing the right thing——'

'It all depends, doesn't it, what that ''right thing'' might be?'

Unnoticed, his arms had crept round her, holding her loosely. Now they were tightening and his head was lowering slowly, his eyes on her lips, his hand pressing against the back of her head, arm hooked around her slender waist. 'And this,' he murmured, his eyelids drooping, 'is the "right thing" at this moment. Don't you agree?'

Rhea felt the late-evening stubble abrasive against her skin, his wide mouth playing with hers, persuasive and persistent, parting her lips, his tongue invading and withdrawing until her inner mouth almost hungered for the taste of him. Yet she didn't want him kissing her, didn't want her body to succumb as it was doing, loving the touch of his hand on her breast... *how* had it got there?

The telephone broke through her gasp at his stroking fingers' audacity, demanding attention. Eyes pin-points in the fireglow—it was dark outside now—he uttered a curse and turned to silence it, her cotton top sliding down into place as he withdrew his hand.

'Yes?' shot curtly into the phone. 'Hi, Timmy,' barely tolerant, but polite. 'You want something?'

Timmy's voice came over loud and clear in the stillness. 'You still there at the forge, Leo? You OK? I saw the light from the fire from my window and wondered if you'd left and forgotten to put it out.'

'I'm here, Timmy,' long-sufferingly. 'I'm OK.'

'Isn't it time, lad, you...?' A thoughtful pause. 'You alone? Or is Sonya——?'

'My *wife*, Timmy, my *wife* is with me.'

'Ah.' Silence, then, 'Isn't it time she was home and resting? What with her foot still not back to normal and the babby on its way?'

Through teeth that were gritted, his nephew offered, 'There's no baby expected, Timmy, there never was.'

'No—no babby? You can't mean it?' The disappointment in his voice cut Rhea to the heart.

'No child on its way. Rhea's come clean. She's told me the truth at last. All this time she's been lying to me——'

Rhea's hand shot out, taking Leo by surprise and seizing the phone. 'I've never lied, Uncle Timmy,' she cried, 'I tried telling Leo that I wasn't pregnant, but he—he wouldn't believe it.'

'You mean—you don't mean, dear, you—well, *lost* it before you came here?'

'That's what Leo kept thinking I meant. Uncle Timmy,' she declared, 'I only ever came here because Jerome had told me his brother would help me financially, until I found my feet again after... after...' But Timmy wouldn't believe what Jerome had really done, any more than Leo would. To them both, Jerome was the tops, a 'good lad', who could never do wrong.

'That Jerome,' he sighed, 'that other rascal of a nephew of mine,' at Timmy's tone, and listening to Timmy's choice of words Rhea knew she had been right in guessing that Dower would defend Dower, no matter what, 'he's bad to women, that he is.' No censure there, just a touch of indulgent amusement. 'He treats 'em like he gets chewing gum from a slot machine, then throws 'em away. And he had to do it to you, dear.' Rhea could almost see him shaking his head. 'After getting engaged to you, too. Are you *sure*, lass, there's no——'

Leo turned the tables and seized the phone from Rhea's unsuspecting hand. 'You have to accept it, Timmy. She's not pregnant.'

Timmy hadn't finished. 'What about your marriage, Leo? It's hardly begun. Even if your reason for marrying the lass doesn't exist now, you'll surely give your marriage a chance? You aren't going to send her away, are you?'

'Can you think of any good reason why not?' Leo half turned to eye her, apparently amused by her heightened colour, her indignation.

'She's a good lass, Leo, that's why,' came Timmy's unhesitating answer, 'whatever she might or might not have done. She's what you need. Better for you by far than that Sonya. You'll be a fool if you let her go.'

'I'll bear your advice in mind, Timmy,' Leo drawled. 'Thanks for ringing and checking up. Everything here's OK.' Cutting the call, but still speaking into the unreceptive mouthpiece, he added, 'When a woman tells me she's married me merely to use me as a weapon of revenge, she gets everything that's coming to her.' Slowly he replaced the receiver and leaned back, fingers pushed into his waistband, and fixed her with a steely gaze. 'Got that, Miss Hirst?'

'Who's breaking the moral rules now?' Rhea hit back, infuriated by his arrogance, but most of all worried by the implication behind his words. 'You promised you'd ask nothing of me. Now you're as good as threatening to break that promise.'

'That promise was made before you told me the truth. Of course I wouldn't have touched you if you really had been expecting Jerome's child, either before or after. Now you tell me it's not so?' He seemed yet again to be wanting confirmation.

'I repeat, it's not so. I'm not pregnant, never have been.'

His broad shoulders lifted and fell. 'OK.' A long pause, as if he were weighing up the pros and cons. 'So, as my lawful wedded wife, and in view of the outrageous reason you've given for taking up that role, as I said, you take the consequences. No holds barred. Any normal man needs a woman now and then. One day,' his mocking glance raked her slender figure, 'I might want you.' His tone implied 'if I could ever bring myself to touch you'. 'And if I do——' Another shrug. 'You'll be there to gratify my needs,' was, Rhea knew, his unspoken innuendo.

How could she ever have thought she loved this man? A flare of hatred came burning through the emotion she had told herself was love. It had, she argued, been the only way she had been able to face being married to him—fooling herself into believing she loved him.

She saw him once again as a Dower, one of whom had already wrecked her life as she had known it. She refused to allow this Dower to repeat the devastating exercise.

'You,' she exploded, fear mixing with a frightening wanton excitement, 'you're as unscrupulous as your precious brother! The Dower family,' she stepped forward and clicked her fingers in his face, 'I don't give that for them. No one, not even a *Dower* takes me against my will. Not even the man who, for a short time only, calls himself my husband!'

Lips drawn into a thin line, Leo reached out and caught her wrists, jerking them to her sides and pulling her body against his. She gave a choking cry. In stepping forward to balance herself, she had inadvertently used her injured foot.

He seemed to think that it was because his grip around her wrists was inflicting pain, but he did not give an inch, forcing her head back with the pressure of his mouth. Again she took into her the intoxicating taste of him as his merciless kiss ground into her lips, leaving them throbbing and quivering with tension. She sagged against him, her head on his shoulder, finding a fleeting sanctuary in the strength and hard comfort of him.

When he saw in the flickering half-light how white she was, he jeered, 'What's wrong? Don't my kisses please you? Don't they measure up to Jerome's?'

'My foot,' she managed, biting her lip with pain and sinking weakly down on to the stone-flagged floor, her arms extended as her wrists remained in his hold.

Cursing, he lifted her, gathering her into his arms. She tried to tell her head to stay upright, tried to scold

it when it rooted once again for the shoulder it seemed
to have developed a sudden liking for, resting there with
a perverse contentment all the way outside. This man
was her enemy, she lectured the suppliant self over whom
she strangely seemed to have no power.

He lowered her with an aloof kind of care on to the
rear seat and drove her home.

In her room, he looked down at her as she sat on the
bed. 'Will you be able to manage, or do you want my
help?' he asked distantly.

Angry with herself for allowing her body to be fooled
by his momentary softening towards her, Rhea stared
up. 'I wouldn't accept your help if it came with a
fortune,' she declared belligerently.

But she just had, hadn't she? she reminded herself as
he strode from the room. She had been accepting his
help from the day she had arrived on his doorstep. And,
she was forced to acknowledge, she would go on needing
that help for some time to come.

Nathan discovered her ten days later seated on a fallen
tree-trunk near the river bank. With her left hand she
held a drawing-board firmly on her lap, while with her
right she sketched the river scene.

'Hi,' he said. 'I was passing and thought I'd call in.
Mind if I join you? Just carry on.' He sat beside her.
'I'll do my best not to disturb the artistic equilibrium.'

'Be my guest,' she answered with a smile. 'I'm only
too glad to have company.'

He frowned. 'Feeling lonely? What about your
husband? He's around, at the forge every day.'

He's not my husband, she wanted to say. Instead she
answered with a shrug, 'Yes, he's around.' Let Nathan
make what he likes of that, she thought.

Leo had indeed been around. He had filled the cottage,
been within her hearing, her sight, near enough to touch
if she had stretched out her hand. But scarcely a word

had passed between them. Yes, she was feeling lonely, she could have confided to Nathan.

At night, she and Leo had gone their separate ways with a polite 'goodnight'. Rhea usually went up first, using the bathroom quickly to avoid meeting him there. He came up much later, and she had found herself listening to his footsteps, trying to work out his movements, wondering whether this—this was the night when he... But he hadn't. The door of his room had always closed firmly behind him. It was as though they were mere acquaintances, and she had to acknowledge that it was wearing her down, almost to screaming pitch.

She couldn't hide it from herself any more: that she would almost have welcomed that demand on her as his wife which, that evening in the forge, he had hinted that he might make one day. Anything, she thought, to release this pressure that was building inside her, tormenting her; anything—a quarrel, even—to be able to put into words the mounting feeling of resentment, of anger, of—yes, she had to accept, even of frustration. Let him get it over with, she had found herself thinking. I could grit my teeth and allow him nearer to me than I ever allowed Jerome, than I've ever allowed any man...

'That's good,' commented Nathan, looking over her shoulder. 'That's great. Is it a sketch in itself, or——?'

'A design for a batik wall-hanging. The bridge fascinates me—its shape, its brickwork, its enduring strength despite its age.'

'You're filling the scene with birds and plants that I can't see anywhere around. Artistic licence?'

Rhea laughed. 'I'm adding interest and colour. And movement.' She stopped work and looked around. 'What I don't feel it's possible to capture in a picture like this, and I'm not even going to try, is the naturally subdued light of the countryside, the flowing tranquillity.'

'The peace and quiet,' Nathan offered, 'that soothes mixed-up emotions?'

She looked at him curiously. 'You understand?'

He nodded. 'Only too well. I guess,' he took a long breath, 'tell me if I'm wrong or intruding, that you're finding a certain relationship as difficult to cope with as I found my—certain relationship.'

He was, she realised, talking about his separation from his wife. 'You're not wrong, Nathan. Or intruding.'

There was a long, comfortable silence. Rhea resumed her work, adding, erasing, shading in.

'When——' He hesitated, taking a breath, starting again, 'When the—er—event happens, what will you do?'

Rhea did not hesitate to enlighten him. 'There won't be an "event", Nathan.' He made a startled movement. 'It was never a possibility. A misunderstanding—crossed wires. You know?'

'Ah,' as if he understood, although her softly spoken statement hadn't explained a thing. 'Tonight,' he said at last, 'there's an informal meeting of members of the local craft club—coffee and biscuits. We'd be delighted, Rhea, if you'd come along. We usually take whatever small piece we're currently working on, keep ourselves occupied. Vince Adley's place. I'll call for you. Unless you've got other plans?'

Such as going places with my husband, he meant, Rhea filled in. She shook her head. 'Leo spends every evening at the forge—or so he says.'

He got the implication. 'Sonya—she's a bitch.'

Rhea's heart sank. Had she really thought Nathan would set her mind at rest, telling her he knew for certain that there was nothing between Leo and Sonya Selby? But why should she care? If Leo was continuing his liaison with his girlfriend, she reflected, at least that kept him from making demands on her.

Leo had not returned home by the time Nathan called for her. Which meant she had had no opportunity of telling him where she was going.

'Vince Adley and his sister Caroline—you know them?' asked Nathan as they drove away from River Cottage. 'Of course you do,' he remembered, 'they were at your wedding. Vince was Leo's best man. They run this guesthouse, Moorview. They've got a big room they let us use for our craft meetings. This evening we'll just be a small group.'

Moorview was large, with a feeling about it that was as friendly and welcoming as its owners. Vince embraced Rhea as if he had known her all his life, while his sister took her hands, laughingly reminding her brother that Rhea was a married lady.

'Thanks for coming,' said Caroline.

'Thanks for inviting me,' Rhea answered, surprised and a little daunted by the interest and frank curiosity in the other people's faces.

'It's not often,' Vince declared loudly, 'that we get a real live professional in our midst.'

'Vince, you're embarrassing Rhea,' Caroline protested. 'Come and sit with me,' she added. 'And I'm known to my friends as Carrie. Have a coffee, and a biscuit. Go on, be a devil—they're home-made.'

As Rhea chewed appreciatively, a young woman asked from across the room, 'Is it true you've got a degree in art?'

'Applied art, specialising in textiles,' Rhea amended, somewhat startled by the efficiency of the village grapevine.

'I told them, Rhea,' Nathan explained. 'Hope you don't mind.'

'Don't let it put you off,' Rhea answered, laughing. 'I bet I'm no more skilled in my line than all of you are in yours.' She looked around the semi-circle of bright, friendly faces. 'What do you all do?'

'Come on now,' Vince ordered in a joking, military voice, 'confess by numbers. And introduce yourselves while you're about it.'

'I'm Maisie Kelney,' said a middle-aged lady. 'Leatherwork. And this is my daughter Joanie. She helps me.'

'Tommy Scott, clock restorer,' a bespectacled young man seated beside Joanie stated.

'Mildred Smith, and I make corn dollies.'

So the dozen people announced themselves and their crafts. They all held small samples on which they were working. The conversation became general and Nathan, seated on the other side of Rhea, refilled her cup.

Nathan crossed the room to continue his discussion with Tommy Scott and Carrie admired the piece of embroidery Rhea had brought along to work on.

'I'm a knitter, by hand, not machine,' Carrie told her. 'I find it relaxes me after a busy day caring for our guests. Would you . . .?' She hesitated, lowering her voice and colouring a little. 'I'd be delighted to knit anything you want, Rhea, in the way of outfits for the baby. Just make a list and——'

'Carrie!' Rhea had to cut her off. In an inexplicable way it hurt having to enlighten her. 'There's no baby coming. There never was.' Carrie's face fell, as Rhea had known it would. Hadn't even Nathan received the news with barely hidden disappointment? Not to mention Uncle Timmy. 'All the same, I really appreciate your offer.'

Carrie nodded, starting to speak, but changing her mind. The telephone rang on a table behind them, and Vince sprang to answer it, his eyes swinging to Rhea.

'Yes, Leo, your wife's here. Want to speak to her?'

Rhea's heart sank, having just caught the shout and the angry crash of metal on metal. Vince moved the receiver from his ear, his brows arched comically. Then he shook it and listened again, making a face and replacing it in its cradle.

'Oh, dear, one furious husband checking up on his wife's whereabouts. Didn't you tell him, Rhea?'

'Obviously not, Vince, and it's none of your business,' his sister reprimanded.

The evening passed too quickly for Rhea's liking. Not only was she enjoying the company of people who could, in a sense, speak her own language, but she couldn't forget Leo's minuscule, but none the less resounding explosion of anger.

When Nathan, taking her home, invited her in for a coffee first, half of her wanted to accept his invitation. The other, more sensible half, however, made her shake her head. 'I'd better get back,' she said.

'OK, another time,' he answered understandingly.

Leo's explosion on the telephone was nothing compared with his anger as she entered the front door. Furious and formidable, he stood in the doorway of the living-room, his shirt unbuttoned and pulled free as if he hadn't been able to bear its constriction. Since it was necessary to go through the living-room on her way to the kitchen, Rhea had no choice but to draw a deep, steadying breath and face Leo's anger.

CHAPTER SEVEN

REMINDING herself that the best form of defence, or so they said, was attack, Rhea made a pre-emptive strike.

'How could I tell you,' she challenged, her brown eyes flashing, 'when you weren't here?'

Leo thrust a thumb in the direction of the telephone. 'There was that.'

'That's true, and it did actually occur to me to call you, but I told myself you wouldn't care where I went or if I never came back. And don't deny it,' her voice rose accusingly, 'when you know it's true.' His anger seemed to be increasing with her every word, but she overrode a warning voice and plunged on, 'You're never here. When you are, you treat me as if I don't exist.'

Stop! her better judgement urged. You're as good as telling him you care, which you don't, you don't... Useless trying to stop now she had started.

'Day after day,' she went on, 'evening after evening, you take yourself off to the forge. Your uncle Timmy was right when he said you were obsessed with black-smithing. Or is it the most effective way you know of getting away from *me*? Or,' dared she? yes, she dared, 'maybe it's your *lady friend* you're obsessed with. Is it her you go to, not the forge? I bet she welcomes you each evening with open arms, which you go into without a single hesitation, a single qualm——'

One stride and he had seized her by the upper arms.

'Accusing me of adultery, are you?' he snarled, his eyes spitting like the forge fire. 'Because, if so, put it in writing, and I'll sue the hide off you!'

108

'That's right,' she cried wildly, struggling in vain to free her arms from the clamp of his fingers, 'talk like a true Dower! Take people's money away from them, leave them with nothing. Ask your wonderful brother what I'm talking about. As for you and your extra-marital activities——'

He slammed her against him. Jaw thrust forward, he ground out, 'So you'd rather my activities were *intra-marital*? That's OK by me, lady. Lead the way to your bedroom. No, on second thoughts, why waste time making the journey? Over here,' moving her towards the settee, 'will do very nicely. A little farewell get-together, before I leave.'

'Leave?' she asked, closing her eyes to hide her anxiety. 'You're—leaving?'

'Not for good, dear wife,' he rasped, 'although no doubt you're disappointed to hear it. On business, to London. But don't let your hopes rise. I'll be back. And demanding *this*, like any man in his right mind who's been parted from his *beloved*.'

He held her from him far enough for his hands to jerk her cotton top over her head, pull down the straps of her bra and, despite her gasps and protesting cries, fasten his mouth with a relentless, erotic possession over her burgeoning breasts.

Urging her backwards on to the sofa, he came down on top of her, the muscled weight of him robbing her of breath, the touch of his hands and sensual movement of his lips inflaming her and robbing her of any wish to repulse him.

On the contrary, she wanted—she actually wanted—to enfold him in her arms, stroke his hair, arch against him, whisper his name. She heard her own voice murmuring it, felt her own body slowly succumbing...heard the screech of the telephone splintering the tension and cooling the white-hot atmosphere to zero.

Leo's head lifted, and with a curse he broke contact and picked up the telephone, his other hand running through his hair. Rhea pulled on her cotton top and hated herself for her impassioned response to Leo's love-making. Except, she told herself, that 'love' hadn't come into it. She couldn't *love* a man she hated. Could she?

'Yes?' Leo barked into the phone. He listened, frowned and rapped out, 'Where the hell are you now?'

Dismayed, Rhea sank on to the sofa, guessing the identity of the caller. Agitatedly, she picked up and shook the cushion which still bore the imprint of their two heads.

Leo must have activated the voice amplifier, since Jerome's answer came over clearly. 'Now that'd be telling.'

'Cut that out, Jerome. You can't spend the rest of your life wandering the world.' Leo rubbed his chest hair abstractedly. 'What are you running away from?'

'Has she been talking?' There was a trace of anxiety in the question.

'She?' Leo asked coldly.

'My ex-fiancée, now your wife. I heard via the grapevine that you married her. So how are you liking her—er—charms, pal? As much as I did? I taught her a thing or two.'

Jerome burst out laughing, and Rhea clapped her hands over her ears. It's not true, she wanted to cry, but Jerome was talking again.

'I expect you know by now,' he went on as if he were enjoying himself, 'about her non-existent pregnancy. Caught you nicely, didn't she? Or did she own up *before* marriage, but, being the gentleman you are, and—er—because of what she told you, you kept your promise and got spliced to her all the same? One thing I know, you wouldn't have married her for love. Still,' in an amused, throwaway tone, 'you can always divorce her, can't you, when the time's right?'

'Both brothers,' Rhea exclaimed, unable to stay silent any longer, 'tarred with the same brush! Unscrupulous, manipulating——'

'What's she saying? Never mind,' Jerome remarked blandly, 'I guess she's kept quiet about—um—certain things; otherwise you'd be jumping down my throat by now. *Ciao*, brother, *sweet* sister-in-law.'

The call was cut with a clatter. Leo turned, hands in pockets, head slightly lowered. 'What things?' he asked.

I won't be intimidated, Rhea vowed. There's no one in the whole world now who'll stand up for me except myself.

'You're not interested in my past history,' she answered boldly. 'I drifted into your life temporarily, and I'll drift out of it *permanently*. As your brother said, you can divorce me when the time's right.'

'Stop prevaricating and answer my question.'

'How do I know,' her eyes defied him, 'that you aren't in league with him? Look how neatly you both had that business of his women tied up. He played around with them, then he sent them to you to pay them off.'

'So?'

'So how do I know you weren't his partner in crime?'

'What crime?'

Even now she could hardly bring herself to talk about it. 'I'm surprised you don't know. But then he wouldn't have told you, would he? Wanting to keep on the right side of his big brother. You were, after all, the one who got him out of his woman troubles.'

He stood in front of her now, arms folded, legs firmly placed. The rest of him towered. Tall as he was, he made the ceiling seem low. He waited with a false patience, his face unreadable in the subdued glow from the table lamp.

'I——' She looked at him, looked away.

'Take your time. We've got all night.'

All night? How would she sleep after what had taken place between them before the phone rang? Then her mind played over the events of the past, resentment returning. Why should she have a guilty conscience over marrying Leo out of revenge? Especially on the terms he had set out as a basis for their 'marriage'. Surely she had deserved some form of reparation for what Jerome had done to her family, her life.

And telling Leo the truth didn't mean he would believe her. Remember, she told herself, he's a Dower, and the Dowers stick together regardless. Not once during Jerome's calls had Leo got really angry with him. Which surely proved—didn't it?—that he was on his brother's side, always had been and always would be, judging by what Uncle Timmy had told her about their past.

'Why shouldn't I have sought payment for what Jerome did to my life?' The bitter words came tumbling from her of their own accord. 'Why shouldn't I have sought revenge for the way he behaved——?'

'You distinctly told me,' Leo interrupted, frowning, 'that Jerome hadn't made you pregnant.'

'Which was true. It's his fraud I'm talking about, his fraudulent activities.'

'*Fraud*?'

'Yes, *fraud*. And theft.' She leaned forward, rubbing at her ankle, which still pained her, like the events of the past which just wouldn't let her rest. 'If I tell you, will you believe me?'

'Try me.' He joined her on the sofa, reclining, arms extended, head turned her way.

Rhea enlarged the space between them, while Leo watched the action with narrowed eyes.

She rubbed her neck, which had begun to ache with tiredness, pushed a distracted hand through her hair. 'Jerome wangled a high position in the family firm——'

'Daniel Hirst?'

She nodded. '—by becoming engaged to me. Liking Jerome—he had his charms,' she admitted wryly, 'and seeing him as his future son-in-law, my father trusted him implicitly. Jerome abused that trust.'

Rhea stole a glance at Leo, seeing his half-closed eyes and wondered if he was asleep. 'Are you listening?' she thrust into the silence.

'He betrayed that trust, you were saying. How?'

He was, she realised, fully alert, watching her face, her mouth, her every agitated action.

'No doubt you won't believe me, and Jerome would deny it yet again if he heard me.' She sighed, recalling every unhappy detail. 'I'll tell you, all the same. Slowly but surely he bled the firm's finances dry. He not so much pocketed the company's money as moved it in shovelsful, into an account with an overseas bank.'

Leo was listening now. He got to his feet, walked up and down.

'No one,' Rhea went on, eyes closed, seeing the past so clearly it hurt, 'no one ever discovered how much, or where, or how he did it, and he wasn't telling. He denied everything, as his legal adviser told him to do. The money was never recovered.'

Leo stood at the window, staring into the darkness.

'I was left with the private mess, the public debts,' she said. 'Only when everything had been sold that could be sold, the house, the paintings my father had bought, all his investments cashed, his savings swallowed up, was I able to settle those debts.'

'You were left with nothing?'

'Not even anywhere to live. All my worldly goods I carried in the cases and backpack I took with me. They're up there now,' she gestured overhead, 'in the room you've allowed me to occupy.'

Leo broke the long silence. 'Until Jerome came on the scene and started to do as you've just alleged he did——'

There it was again, the doubt, the 'Jerome could do no wrong' attitude of his. *Alleged*, he'd said, not proven, as the judiciary had decided, letting Jerome off; Jerome, who had been so clever, allowed to walk free, able to keep his money, free of all responsibility for the company's demise.

'Until then,' Leo was saying, 'the company, Daniel Hirst, was thriving?'

'No—I did tell you. It started going downhill just before Jerome joined the firm. Which is why my father was so eager to appoint him. His son-in-law-to-be, filling the place of the son he'd never had—he was delighted with my *wonderful* fiancé, he trusted him implicitly. He'd save the firm, my father said, with his new, young ideas.'

He must have heard the bitterness, but he did not comment.

'Even if Jerome had been honest,' Rhea went on, 'it wouldn't have worked. The customers who had patronised Daniel Hirst so faithfully in the past noted the new direction the firm was taking and expressed their annoyance by drifting away. The young people didn't turn up in their droves as my father had hoped, and the slide down became an avalanche.'

'On whose recommendation did your father appoint Jerome?'

'His own. He produced his own CV, forged his own references. A pack of lies, as I found out later, after my parents had died—at least Dad was spared that. Jerome had made up his own qualifications, his "past experience" in management and finance. They were all phoney.'

There was another long silence, giving Rhea time to reflect. Recalling the past and talking about it brought it all back. It had stirred up all the bitterness and rancour she had felt when it was all over and Jerome had walked away, leaving her with nothing but his brother's address and a promise of payment on demand.

'So now do you see,' she challenged, 'why I vowed to get my own back on the Dowers in whatever way I could?'

Leo came to stand in front of her, tall and broad, eyes glacier-cold.

'And that way was handed to you on a plate, wasn't it? By me. OK, you've been through a hard time, I accept that, but what I can't find it in myself to forgive is your ruthless decision to use me as if you had really been expecting Jerome's child. Used me,' he pulled her up to stand in front of him and she quivered inwardly under the lash of his anger, his blazing eyes, 'deviously, as a weapon of revenge, to hit back at Jerome for all the harm he did you.'

'And my family,' she put in swiftly.

'A big debt, wasn't it, to seek reparation for? For which *I* paid. OK, so I'll pay in my own way, by keeping my promise to fund you while you bear my name and live in my house...but also by making *you* pay—for your ultimate freedom from me.'

'But you promised!' she cried, hearing the threat and guessing its meaning.

'That promise,' he released her arms with a jerk that shook her, 'was made null and void when you confessed you weren't pregnant—I've already told you that. From now on, Rhea, as far as our relationship's concerned, *I'll* be the one who calls the tune. Do you understand?'

White now, and reeling inside under the impact of his words, Rhea went slowly to the door. If he ever made love to her, slept with her *no holds barred*, as he had threatened, she would never be able to hide from him her true feelings, her need of him, both physically and mentally. She realised again how reckless she had been in using Leo Dower as her means of revenge.

'Thank you,' she said, turning, 'for giving me a roof over my head, temporary though it is. And for listening to me. And for believing me.'

He made a cut-off movement, but she climbed the stairs, too weary and too dispirited to take any more of his anger that night.

Rhea filled the days of Leo's absence by concentrating on her work. Mrs Litton continued to come twice weekly, and complained that there was hardly anything for her to do.

'You've done it all, Mrs Dower. And you're ever so much easier to tidy up after than your husband.'

Rhea laughed, wondering what Mrs Litton would say if she told her, 'I know hardly anything of my husband's ways. We live separate lives…and it's getting me down.' The thought escaped her control like a wild animal breaking free of its cage.

It isn't, she told herself frantically, it's what I want until we finally part. I'm *not* missing him. I *mustn't* become involved with the man I married, either emotionally or in any other way. What's more, I won't, she decided, switching her attention to her work. I'll carry on keeping him at a distance. I won't even *think* about him.

All the same, he intruded on her thoughts, and even had the temerity to appear in her dreams. Sometimes, rather than let him into her sleeping hours, she would fling out of bed and reach for her work, pieces of which littered her room.

Evenings were the hardest part, when she was tired and fed up with her own company. When Nathan rang a week into Leo's absence, inviting her to join the crafts group at the Dog and Badger, she jumped at the idea.

'I'd like to put a suggestion to you,' he said, but did not elaborate. 'I'll be round in ten minutes.'

'I'd rather walk there, honestly,' Rhea assured him. 'It's a beautiful evening, and I love the exercise.'

With some reluctance she turned her back on the moorland that stretched into the far distance, green and brown and golden in the setting sun, and opened the door of the pub.

Shouts of welcome greeted her from the dimness of the interior, the low wooden beams causing even Rhea to lower her head a little.

' "When the cat's away",' Timmy's joking voice came out of the shadows. 'Hello, lass. Missing your other half?'

'Yes, I am.' The admission came off the top of her head, she told herself firmly, not from her heart. Nathan patted the empty space he had saved and she eased her slender frame into it. Carrie sat at his other side.

Timmy laughed at Rhea's uncensored admission, plainly believing it. He swallowed the contents of his glass and thumped it down on the bar counter where he stood. 'I'll tell him, that I will,' he promised, patting her shoulder as he passed her on the way to the door.

'Please don't,' she pleaded, but her words were lost in the general hubbub.

'Glad you could make it,' remarked Carrie, leaning forward and talking across Nathan.

'Good to see you,' commented Nathan, his eyes appreciating her scarlet cotton sweater and matching trousers. Flattering to my ego, Rhea considered, but perhaps just a little too appreciative for a comfortable friendship. Carrie's bright gaze told of a touch of envy, and maybe a trace of jealousy? Or is it my imagination? Rhea wondered.

Vince, who had been chatting to the girl behind the bar, placed a drink in front of Rhea. 'It's alcoholic. You're not on the wagon, I hope, as well as virtually living in purdah?' was his joking comment as he put the glass in front of her. 'All creative artists such as we are,' everyone pretended to bow, 'need to come out into the world now and then to recharge their imaginative batteries. Tell that husband of yours to open the door of your gilded cage and throw away the key.'

Rhea joined in the laughter, but she knew how mistaken Vince was to think that Leo actually wanted to *keep* her. She had no doubt that the greatest moment of his life would be when she walked out of his cottage for the last time.

'Have you heard,' Carrie asked, capturing Rhea's attention eagerly, 'about the craft show we're putting on next month in the town? We've hired a hall with an entrance on to the main street.'

'We've done it before,' Nathan put in, 'and it's been a roaring success. We charge a small entrance fee, put a notice outside and sit back and wait for the custom.'

'We usually do well, get a lot of interest from the townspeople and tourists alike.'

'Would you like to exhibit?' enquired Vince, getting up to buy more drinks. 'We'd reserve a stall for you.'

Rhea, who had been smiling from one to the other, nodded happily. This camaraderie, this sharing of interests, was something she had never known in the life she had left behind. 'I'd love to,' she answered simply, and watched as Carrie made a note of the date and place, passing the scrap of paper to her.

Nathan reached into a bag at his side. 'This is the other thing I wanted to talk to you about,' he said, producing a couple of items of pottery he had made. 'These are plain and simple, straight from the hand of the potter. But it occurred to me that——'

'You'd like me to add some colour?' asked Rhea, comprehending at once. 'Decorate them, in other words?' The kind of thing your wife used to do? she almost added, but thought better of it. Nathan wouldn't want to discuss his personal affairs in public.

'Or otherwise adorn them, yes. Would you be willing?' he asked eagerly. 'To collaborate, I mean?'

She handled the pottery, admiring its lines, considering Nathan's proposition. 'It would be a new venture for me,' she admitted with a smile, 'but yes, I'd love to

have a go.' She frowned. 'The trouble is, I don't have a
workplace, only the——' She checked herself quickly.
She had been about to say, 'only where I sleep', telling
the world that she and Leo did not share a room!

'Not even a table,' she filled in hurriedly, 'to mess
around on with my batik.' She felt she'd said enough.
Much more and she might be giving away the true state
of affairs between herself and Leo.

'There's a——' Nathan stopped himself too, realising
that they could be overheard by other customers.

'I could clear a table in my workroom for you,'
Mildred Smith offered. 'It's only covered in bits and
pieces for my corn-dolly work.'

'That's very nice of you, Mildred,' Rhea
acknowledged.

'No, no,' Nathan intervened, 'I was going to say that
there's a spare area in my studio that I could let you
have. You've seen it, Rhea. You remember it? You could
make as much mess with your batik or whatever as you
liked. Also, you'd be on the spot if there was any decision to be made, such as colour and so on. There's a
folding bed in the room too, if you ever want to work
too late to go home.' Here Vince whistled loudly and
shook his head in mock disapproval. Nathan caught
Rhea's hand. 'How about it?'

He was so excited that Rhea would have found it difficult to refuse even if she'd wanted to. 'Wonderful! Fine
by me,' she answered, her eyes shining. 'Just as long as
you don't mind my mess.'

'Shake on it, pal.' And they did, Nathan holding her
hand just a little longer than necessary.

'Hi, there,' said Vince to the couple who had just entered. The man, who was tall, dark and business-suited,
ducked to avoid the low beams. 'Your wife's being
seduced by a friend of yours.'

Leo's eyes were cold as they rested on Rhea's flushed
face. She could not hide her pleased surprise at his return,

until she saw the woman at his side. So that was why Sonya had been missing from the village in the last few days! She had been with Leo in London.

Ice, as cold as Leo's appraisal, began to form around her heart. She told herself she should have known that Leo's relationship with his girlfriend was still on the agenda, despite his marriage. After all, it was an empty marriage, which was how she wanted it, she told herself, so why should she feel as if she wanted to cry?

'How did you know where to find Rhea?' asked Carrie, glancing uncomfortably at Nathan's hand which was still linked with Rhea's.

'I met my uncle Timmy, and he told me my wife was here. She was missing me, he said. It seems he was wrong.' Leo's glacial gaze moved from the half-filled glass in front of Rhea to her hand which Nathan, for some reason, refused to release.

Sonya's arm slipped through Leo's. 'My tongue, darling,' she stage-whispered, 'it's dry as a bone!' She nudged him towards the bar counter. He nodded briefly and moved at her bidding.

She can have him, Rhea found herself thinking, he's not mine, nor I his. To hide her agitation, she reached out for Nathan's pottery that still stood on display, running her fingers over it. Her eyes slid of their own accord to the two figures at the bar. Sonya was in conversation with an acquaintance, but, to Rhea's profound shock, Leo was leaning back against the counter, drink to his lips, eyes narrowly and assessingly on her, his wife. She shivered under that implacable, faintly lecherous regard, sure that he was mentally undressing her, layer by layer, until he laid bare not only her naked self, but her most private thoughts, her very soul.

One day, she knew for certain, he would make it his business to break down the invisible barrier between them and, coldly but relentlessly, make her his—hadn't he said as much?—if only to prove his domination over the woman in her. What frightened her most was that, no matter how many times she told herself she hated him, that woman in her wanted his lovemaking with a piercing longing that was slowly but surely eating away at her equilibrium, her very peace of mind. But, she vowed, when that time did come, she would fight him every inch of the way.

CHAPTER EIGHT

'ANOTHER drink, please, darling,' Sonya was saying, and Leo, turning his back on the assembled company, but most of all, Rhea felt, on herself, obliged.

She wasn't consciously intending to leave, but her legs made their own decision, pushing back the chair. Taking leave of her friends, she made for the door.

Nathan, following her example, left with her. 'I'll take you home,' he offered, leading the way to his car.

'Thanks, but I think I'll take a walk. I need...' 'to get away', she had been going to say, but amended it to '...the exercise.'

Nathan looked worried. 'At this time of night?'

Rhea looked at the clear blue sky, splashed across with sunset colours. 'It won't be dark for a while. I'll be OK.'

Still anxious but respecting her wishes, Nathan drove off with a wave.

Alone, Rhea shivered as the cool of the evening penetrated her thin jacket and plain cotton trousers, but the lower temperature did not deter her. She did need to get away, to sort herself out, her thoughts, her feelings.

Soon the straggling line of cottages ended, the road climbing up on to the moors. Rhea loved the sweeping line of them, tracing the gentle slopes as they lifted to meet uneven escarpments rising high and, as daylight faded, menacingly in the near distance.

This was a beauty, a freedom which a town dweller such as she had always been knew nothing about. To live among these for the rest of her life with a man she loved—she would ask for nothing more. Her subconscious mind made a correction...*the* man she loved. No, no, she disputed it, she loved no man, *no man.* How could she, after the man she thought had loved her had treated her and her family so badly?

Leaving even the drystone walls behind, she trod the springy surface of the moors themselves, straying from the road, lost in the past. Deciding to rest, she sank down on to the hard, tussocky ground, leaning back on her hands. Pictures arose, and sounds from the past, superimposing themselves over the intense peace and beauty around her. She lay full length and closed her eyes.

'My dad and my mother!' she had shrieked, throwing open the door of Jerome's office in the heart of London. 'The police came to see me at work. Oh, Jerome, Jerome, my parents, they're——' she could hardly get the words out '—the policewoman told me—they're dead!'

She had rushed to his side as he had sat at his desk, grasping his arm and shaking it. 'For God's sake, Jerome, tell me it's a bad dream, that it isn't true!'

Jerome had risen, looking at her with horror and something very like fear. 'Of course it's not true.' He had glanced at his watch. 'They've reached the South of France by now. Your dad's an experienced pilot, he'd take all the necessary precautions about landing, following all the instructions from ground control. The police have just got the wrong name, that's all.'

He had satisfied himself, but not Rhea. She'd shook her head madly, sick with anguish, bewildered by the attitude of the man she was going to marry. 'They're dead, I tell you!' she'd cried. 'The police wouldn't make that kind of mistake. They gave me a description of his plane and its number, and they're all correct.'

Instead of his arm going round her shoulders, it had reached out to the telephone. A call or two later, during which Rhea had stood trembling at his side, he'd replaced the phone slowly and looked at her with anxious, and strangely wary eyes.

'It's true,' he'd told her. 'They crashed as they approached the Channel. Your dad must have realised something was wrong. He'd made for some woods, obviously hoping to soften the landing, but it didn't.' He'd paused, then in a deadpan voice added, 'I'm sorry to hear it, Rhea. My deepest condolences.'

'Is that all you've got to say? You don't care, do you? Either for me or about them!' she had accused. 'If you did, you'd be holding me, comforting me, telling me you'd see to everything. For heaven's sake, Jerome, you're going to be *my husband*!' she had cried. 'You've told me you love me. I believed you, Jerome, but now I—I'm beginning to wonder...'

'Hush,' he'd soothed, his arm around her now but more brother than lover, 'you're being hysterical. It'll all come right, you'll see.'

She had drawn away from him then, in horror. 'All come right?' she had shrieked. 'When my parents are *dead*? How can you be so unfeeling?' She had stared at him as a terrible thought had occurred. 'You never did what you'd promised to do, did you? You didn't do a single thing about——'

The sound of a car on the moorland road nearby broke into her nightmare thoughts. If I lie still, she thought, wiping away the tears that just wouldn't stop coming, the driver won't see me. But it seemed the driver had, apparently spotting her even in the darkness that had hidden the moors as she had been lying there, leaving only their outline beneath a clear turquoise sky and the rising moon to see by.

Her heart pounded as a tall, unmistakably masculine figure loomed in the semi-darkness, striding, angry, standing over her. It took no more than two seconds for her to recognise him, but her heartbeats speeded up rather than slowed.

He must have contacted Nathan, believing him to have taken her home, discovering from him not only her intention to go for a walk, but the direction she had taken. So what, she thought, if he had come to find her? It meant absolutely nothing. It was in his own interests to find her, wasn't it? A missing wife, lost on the moors at night through his negligence, as others would see it, would sit sorely on his conscience.

'*Sunbathing*?' was his caustic comment as he watched her sit up and shake her long hair to free it of pieces of last year's heather. 'Or should I coin a phrase and call it moonbathing? What the hell are you doing here? Are you so suburban-minded, so ignorant of country ways as to think it's safe to come up on to the moors in the late evening, on foot, alone, without adequate clothing or footwear or a torch?'

'Why should you care?' she challenged, rubbing her damp cheeks with the back of her hand. 'I'm just an encumbrance to you. I married you under false pretences, remember? If I lay here all night and died of exposure, no doubt you'd be glad——'

He reached down and secured her wrist in a grip of iron, pulling her to her feet. 'Don't play with me, lady, don't provoke me, or you might get more than you——'

He saw her wince. 'What's wrong?' Dumbly, she pointed to her foot, and he flashed a torch down. 'For pity's sake, you've hurt it again?' She nodded. Then the torch beam showed him her tear-stained face. 'It hurts that much?' She shook her head. 'So what have you been crying over? Or should I say who? Sorry now you married me and therefore aren't free to pursue your relationship with Nathan Oxley?'

'That's ridiculous! He's OK, he's a nice man, but——'

'So who caused those tears?' Hooded eyes fixed on her face. 'Don't tell me, let me guess. Jerome.'

It was so true that she found herself nodding, realising too late just how he would interpret the admission.

'So,' his lips thinned, 'although he let you down, treated you abominably, you're still missing him, are you, missing his arms, his lovemaking?'

He disregarded her fiercely shaking head. His arms lifted to encircle her waist, wrapping her so tightly to him that she had to struggle for breath. His mouth was so near to hers that she felt its movement as he talked. 'Don't fret, my lovely. I've already taken his place in your life, so I'll take his place in your bed. And,' he moved her slightly to one side, 'what better bed than the moorland we're standing on?'

'Leo, please don't. I know you're only fooling, but——'

'And that's where you're wrong, my heart.' A beautiful endearment, but so cynically spoken. 'I'm deadly serious. We're entirely alone. Few people come up here in the darkness. And even if we're seen, a man and woman lying together, people would jump to the usual con- clusion—in this case, the correct conclusion. So no one will disturb us.'

She tried again. 'Leo, not now, not here. Not *ever*. It would be a meaningless act.' She was frightened now, by the look on his face, the cold intent in his eyes as they gleamed in the moonlight.

He bent her slowly, and, although she stiffened to resist the pressure he was imposing on her much frailer frame, her knees buckled and she found herself lying beneath him. The woman in her leapt with joy to find that this man, at last, was where often in her dreams she had imagined him. But her reason cried, Hold him off, stop him somehow...

Summoning all her strength, she twisted and turned, flailing with her legs, even managing to bite his hand as it held her face still.

'Little bitch,' he hissed, lowering his twisted lips and covering hers with them in a kiss that robbed her of any strength she had left. His mouth, merciless in its intent, worked at hers until they parted, allowing him all the access he was demanding.

Somehow his hand had found its way inside her cotton top, capturing a breast and fastening punishingly over it, then miraculously gentling, moulding, moving across to stroke the other. His change of tactics was almost her undoing, and his mouth absorbed her shuddering breaths, his tongue discovering her inner sweetness, his free hand lifting to caress her throat.

'Did Jerome do this to you?' his lips asked against hers. 'Did he get through your defences, take what he wanted, as he did with all the others? And like them, did you give him all he asked and more? Did you fight him like you're fighting me?'

'Yes—no.' He was giving her a breathing-space, one which her dazed but still rational mind told her to take but which her emotions didn't want. The fight was within herself now, and she was torn in two.

Anger came to her rescue, and provided her with the ammunition with which to return his fire. 'While you were away,' she spat, 'did you do this to Sonya Selby? Did you share a hotel room and make love to her every night?'

Slowly Leo loosened his hold, staring into her moon-washed face, his expression dark and unfathomable. He rolled on to his side, lying back, a hand cushioning his head. If Rhea had expected a denial, she was bitterly disappointed.

'If I did, what of it? Our marriage is barren, that you can't deny. Look at your response to me just now. I married a frigid woman, didn't I, Rhea Hirst?'

'No!' Her denial was like the cry of a wounded animal. 'I'm not that, I'm not!'

'You're *cold*, you're *frigid*,' Jerome had accused, shifting away from her petulantly in the car, on the sofa in the sitting-room while her parents had slept. 'It wouldn't even be any good undressing you and taking you to bed. To function as a man, I like a woman with fire, who spits and scratches, then throws herself at me. My God,' he would get up, stare disgustedly down at her, 'it wouldn't even be any good, would it, softening you up with alcohol? You'd just get drunk and fall into bed—alone. What did I get myself engaged to you for?'

She hadn't known then, but she subsequently and excruciatingly had learned that particular answer. Yet here was another Dower brother making the same accusation, calling her unresponsive and cold...when with all her heart and soul she longed to make love with him, join with him in a true and lasting and *loving* relationship. Yet the very terms of their marriage precluded that. They'd married for expediency, nothing else.

She hadn't really loved Jerome—she'd realised that long before the final split. Puzzled by her own inhibited reactions to the man she called her fiancé, she had wondered if the fault lay with her own personality. She started to compare her relationship with Jerome with the one that existed between her parents.

There had been no mistaking that they had loved each other, from the way they'd caught each other's eye, hugged each other on the spur of the moment, even held hands sometimes while walking. Yet it had taken three cataclysmic events in her life to wake her up to the truth—that she didn't love Jerome, never had, never would. Nor did he love her.

Rhea walked beside Leo to the car parked at the roadside. Her ankle still hurt a little, but she was darned if she was going to tell him.

Preoccupied, he moved slightly ahead, then turned, noticing her plight. 'What's wrong? Old trouble come back?' She nodded, shrugging it off. When she was level with him, he placed a supporting arm around her waist.

'I'm all right, thanks,' was her snapped response, but his hold only tightened.

'Much more and I'll carry you,' he clipped.

At once Rhea tolerated his help. If he picked her up, she wouldn't be able to stop herself clinging to him, wouldn't be able to resist the attraction which his own particular aroma had for her, couldn't stop her cheek from nestling against his shoulder.

What am I going to do, she asked herself as she lay in bed later in the dark silence, about this love for Leo Dower that's taken such firm hold inside me that I know I'll never be able to uproot it and replace it with love for any other man on earth?

Finding no answer, she twisted and turned, unable to rest. Her watch told her that two hours had passed since Leo had left her at the door of his office.

'You're starting work,' she had asked him, 'at this time of night?' Then she realised how 'wifely' the question must have sounded.

'That was my intention,' he answered, leaning against the door-frame, in his eyes the coolly indolent look with which he had regarded her through the semi-darkness and smoky atmosphere of the pub. 'Why, have you got a better idea?'

She knew what he meant and cursed herself for inadvertently providing the encouragement he had plainly detected in her innocent question. But had it truly been innocent? she asked herself as she fled up the stairs. Of course it had, she told herself. In fact, the sooner the door was closed between her and his mocking amusement the better.

Switching on the bedside lamp, she flung out of bed. Standing at the window and staring into the darkness, she forced herself to face the fact that the woman in her, having been awoken from her long sleep in those passionate moments on the moors, was not only refusing stubbornly to return to her slumbers, but was threshing about demanding to be noticed and pandered to—by the man who cared nothing for her, but who had so carelessly and so implacably aroused that femininity, not in love, nor even affection, but in anger and cynical retribution.

She would do some work, she decided—no, better than that, she would assemble and pack everything she would need in order to do her work at Nathan's place. As she piled brushes and cutting tools and pieces of fabric into a suitcase, she heard the creak of a floorboard.

Freezing with a primitive kind of fear, she listened. The door-handle turned and, with agitated hands, she pressed the contents more firmly into the bulging case and lowered the lid. Springing to her feet, hiding the telltale case, she faced the newcomer.

He entered slowly, staring at her with a look that set her pulses racing. She tugged ineffectually at the neckline of her fine lawn nightdress, aware that against the light it was semi-transparent, and reproached herself for not having had the forethought to pull on a robe.

'We have, I think you'll agree,' he said, his eyes carrying out a leisurely reconnaissance of her outlined shape, 'some unfinished business to attend to, you and I.'

In the semi-darkness, he looked overpoweringly handsome. He wore creased denims that hugged his thighs and a navy cotton shirt from the opened neck of which sprang a patch of curling hair which matched in colour the evening's growth of stubble.

All Rhea's instincts were telling her to stay right where she was. Since she couldn't physically escape him—he stood, hands on hips, elbows jutting out, a barrier in themselves across the path to the door—she had no alternative but to keep him at bay with words.

'Unfinished business? I—I don't know what you mean,' she lied. 'I'm sure you finished your *business* activities to your complete satisfaction back there in London with Miss Selby.'

'Are you being deliberately obtuse?' Leo moved slowly towards her. 'Or maybe you're baiting me?'

One step, two... her feet took her backwards, away from him. She awarded them full marks for initiative, but they were out of phase with the rest of her body. The one thing in the world she did not want to do was run away.

'Because if you are, you'll get more than you bargained for. And,' he halted in front of her, 'if you don't stop looking at me as if I were something unpleasant from a waste-disposal site, I'll——'

'I'm not frigid, Leo.' Horrified, she heard the words burst from her. To his ears they must sound like blatant encouragement.

'You aren't? You know that for certain? You and Jerome—— '

'Not Jerome!'

'You've had other men? This is getting interesting,' he responded, deeply sarcastic. 'Is my beautiful wife about to confess the secrets of her romantic past? Or,' his eyes gleamed, 'was it all so mechanical and *un*romantic that it turned you sexually cold?'

'What you're saying is pure invention on your part,' she declared. 'All the same, you—you mustn't make love to me, Leo.'

'*Mustn't*?' His brows drew ominously together. 'What is this? First you try and assure me you're not cold, which is come-on number one. Second, you stand there,' impatient fingers untied the bootlace shoulder-straps and eased the nightdress to waist level, 'telling me, your husband, that I *must not* make love to you, my wife? Did you honestly think,' now his palms caressed her milky-white breasts, and her eyes closed at the overwhelmingly pleasurable sensation he was creating, 'that ours would be a brother-and-sister relationship? Despite my warning that, sooner or later, I'd make you pay for using me as your means of revenge against Jerome?'

Leo didn't wait for an answer. He swept her into his arms and dropped her on to the bed, tearing off his shirt and throwing it aside. Bending over her, he made short work of removing her nightdress, tossing it to join his discarded clothing.

In his eyes as they surveyed her nakedness, search though she might, she could perceive no warmth and certainly nothing at all approaching love, only desire and sensuality, a feeding of his male appetite before swooping on his prey.

'Please,' she protested hoarsely, 'not like this! Not coldly and deliberately, as if I . . . as if I were——' She found she couldn't go on because to her dismay her voice had grown thick with tears.

For a fraction of a second, his eyes closed. He took a deep breath and let it out slowly. Rhea guessed he had put a brake on his own masculine reflexes, and experienced a rush of gratitude for the way he had answered her plea.

Discarding the rest of his clothes, he dropped beside her. He pulled her round until she was lying intimately against him and she felt the full impact of his aroused masculinity. With his forefinger he wiped away the tears that had escaped from beneath her eyelids.

He ran his palms over her tingling skin, wound his legs around hers and lowered his head to suckle and tease at her hardened breasts. Her fingers dug into the muscles of his upper arms and her throat opened on a shuddering gasp.

His head came up and he covered her parted lips with his probing mouth, exploring deeply until her body tensed with a desire that had nothing whatsoever to do with revenge or retribution and everything to do with taking and giving and loving.

His lips moved down, following a tantalising trail around her ears and down her throat, where her breasts caused a fiery diversion. He suckled and nipped alternately until she could hardly breathe for the pleasure he was giving her. On the trail again, his breath created a

heated path down, down to places that throbbed unbearably under the onslaught of his tongue, his hands
joining in the piratical assault on her sexual sensibilities.

His head lifted, only to come up against the restraint
of her hands gripping his hair—anything, she thought,
to help her withstand those alien yet unbelievably
pleasurable sensations he was arousing within her.

His head went down again and he imprisoned her lips
in an erotic, delving kiss. Parting her thighs, he stroked
and coaxed and eased an intimate path into the warm
and pulsating essence of her. She gasped at his forced
intrusion and he took her breath into him, pausing and,
she sensed, restraining his own instincts, giving her time
to accept him.

She felt his muscles tense beneath her curling fingers
and his arousal of her began all over again. Taking his
time now, with subtlety and a tingling excitation of her
feminine responses, he touched and stroked and invaded
the most secret areas of her writhing body, raising her
desire and her passion to fever pitch.

At last her gasps and breathless cries of 'Oh, please,
please,' must have drawn some mercy from him, since
he took pity on her, at the same time giving free rein to
his own driving male needs. Mindlessly and with a cry
of pure delight she followed him every step of the way,
soaring with him at last to a golden summit of wild and
joyful fulfilment.

She awoke to an empty place beside her and the sound
of water running. As she stirred and blinked, easing her
luxuriously contented body and mind into gear, Leo appeared in the doorway, hair wet from the shower, a towel
slung carelessly over his still damp shoulder, and wearing
nothing else at all.

Rhea's heart jolted. Gazing at him, at his fit and virile
body, the blatant masculinity that had swept her to a

kind of earthly paradise only a few hours before, she felt her senses stir all over again.

He strolled to the bedside, pulling back the covering and looking down at her. She grew overwhelmingly conscious of her nakedness and, to his mocking amusement, colour suffused her cheeks as she gazed up at him.

'Now you know,' she remarked, using speech as a way of countering the almost unbearable desire he was arousing in her just by looking at her like that, 'that you were wrong in your accusation that I was frigid. I——'

'Poor Jerome! No wonder he——'

'He what?' she demanded, swinging her legs to the floor and seizing a wrap from a chair. 'The next time he phones, ask him, "Why didn't you take what an engaged man usually——?"'

'I'm asking you.'

'Do all your acts of lovemaking,' she challenged evasively, knowing the answer but not wishing to give it, 'end with your interrogating the woman who's allowed you to share her bed? For instance,' her eyes flashed fire, '"How many men have there been before me?" And, if she's virginal, "Why? Hasn't any man desired you enough to storm your defences?"'

He seized her wrists and forced them behind her. 'Any more insults, lady?' Her wrap fell open and he eased her backwards, his head lowering, his lips making free with her breasts. His arousal of her had started all over again.

His head so intimately near her, his deliberate onslaught on the still-tender flesh, made her want to push him away, but together they had an effect on her so potent that she forgot her vow of vengeance and felt herself longing to kiss the dark hair at his nape and the tanned skin of his neck.

He moved her back on to the bed, pushing her down and putting himself on top of her, and began to make love to her all over again. When the time came for him to repossess her, there was not an atom of resistance left inside her, and again she knew the sheer delight of erotic fulfilment, clinging to him and returning his kisses and glorying in the feel of the essence of him flowing into her.

A clock chiming somewhere in the house roused them, and he rolled from her, lifting her upright with him and kissing her deeply, holding her to him and staring into her radiant face.

Letting her go, he pulled the wrap around her throbbing body and picked up the towel, winding it round his waist. He took to wandering round her room, glancing at her possessions.

Secretly she watched him, his potent masculinity a magnet she was powerless to resist. She had never, until now, believed it possible to love one's enemy, but now she knew. She loved *this* enemy on whom she had sworn revenge for what his brother had done to her, she loved him with a strength that shook her to her very core.

He moved to leave, coming up against the suitcase into which she had been cramming her work. The catches were not fastened and the lid was propped half open.

Her heart nosedived as he stared down, pushing with his bare foot at the fabric spilling out. Slowly he turned, and Rhea saw that all indulgence, all warmth had been wiped away.

Narrowed eyes sliced into her. 'Thinking of leaving? Remember to give me an address for forwarding, won't you?'

Rhea shook her head. 'You've got it wrong, Leo. I'm not leaving. I—I meant to tell you. Nathan's offered me space at his studio where I can make as much mess as I like. I couldn't do that here in your cottage, and anyway you haven't got a room to spare, a room that's—that's suitable.'

Anger forked across his eyes, causing her to falter. 'And,' she went on, 'there's the lighting aspect to consider, not the artificial variety, but daylight...'

He approached with measured steps. 'Did you ask me?'

'For—for permission? Of course not. We're free agents, you said.' She brazened it out. 'That was the condition under which I married you. We agreed to live our separate lives——'

'Ask me,' Leo persisted as if she hadn't spoken, 'if such a room existed in this cottage?'

Where had the wonderful feeling gone, the togetherness, the sense of belonging to this man?

'No. Nathan made the offer, and I couldn't think of any reason why I should refuse.' Attack, her other self was urging, don't defend! 'But, Leo,' she pretended bewilderment, 'you surely aren't *jealous*?' She knew she was goading him by his indrawn lips, but she went recklessly on. 'Of Nathan Oxley? I might as well be jealous of Sonya Selby.' Accusingly, she added, 'I'd have greater reason to be, the way you go around with her, travel with her to your *business* appointments, come back with her and flaunt her as your woman at the local pub in front of all the villagers.' She had to stop, her heart was pounding so. At the look in his eyes, she wanted to turn and run, but pride kept her there.

He stayed silent, but she wished he had shouted, raged at her accusations, telling her she was wrong in her assumption that he and Sonya were lovers.

'J-Jerome was right about you,' she flung at him, irritated beyond words at his silent domination of the conversation, 'you take up with a woman, sleep with her, then, when you're tired of her, ab-abandon her. You two make a good pair, don't you? I'd—I'd begun to trust you, Leo, I don't know why. I thought you possessed a quality that was so much more dependable and trustworthy than your brother, that placed you head and shoulders above Jerome. But I was wrong, wasn't I?'

He did not deign to answer her questions. 'Since we're into character analysis,' his eyes castigated and at the same time raked with a sensual indolence her figure beneath the flimsy wrap, 'two can play at that. Let me rip *yours* to pieces. You lied to me.' He mouthed the accusation slowly and clearly.

'What about? The non-existent pregnancy?' she took him up. 'It was *your* invention, not mine.'

'But you played along with my assumption. You used it, me, as a means of gaining access to my bank account, to the comfort and security I could offer, to a return to the social and financial status that had eluded you since the break-up of your life as you knew it.'

'I——' She was shaking her head when the telephone rang.

'Who?' she heard Leo bark from his room. 'Nathan? Yes?' No friendly greeting ensued, just another bark that summoned her to the phone.

'Hi, Nathan. Collect me and my things? That's nice of you. Give me an hour and I'll be ready when you arrive.'

Replacing the receiver, she turned, defiance in her eyes, but Leo had gone. The cottage seemed to shake with the slamming home of the front door.

It took Rhea no time at all to settle down to her work in Nathan's studio. Carrie, who told her she was often in and out of Nathan's place, helped her unpack, placing her books and illustrated volumes on the shelves that Nathan had allotted to her.

Intrigued, Carrie and Nathan watched her arrange her assortment of equipment, smiling at the double saucepan which, she told them, she used for melting the wax she had bought from a specialist craft shop.

'I could have provided you with cooking facilities,' Nathan declared, puzzled by the appearance of an electric hotplate which Rhea told them was a vital part of her work.

'Thanks,' she said with a smile, 'but I like to keep my mess, like my tools, in one place.'

Carrie inspected the fabrics she had brought, the bundles of cotton, silk and linen. She pored over the batik designs which Rhea had sketched in a notebook.

'Would you make me a skirt some time?' she asked wistfully. 'These designs are all so unusual and attractive.' Rhea promised that she would.

It was easy, Rhea discovered, working with Nathan in the room. As he fashioned his models and shapes, he became so absorbed that it was as though sometimes she was there on her own. That first day, he showed deep interest in her work, listening to her explanations and watching as she worked, invading his kitchen with his permission, waxing the fabrics, then dyeing them to the shade she required.

He took her home and she told him she had felt happier that day than for a long time.

'Can I take you for a meal, Rhea?' he asked with a touch of wistfulness.

She thought of Leo, arriving home to an empty house—after last night, surely he would break his routine of working late at the forge and join her?

She shook her head. 'It's a nice thought, Nathan,' she answered, 'but——'

'Another time? OK.'

'What about Carrie? I'm sure she'd love to be spoilt for once.'

He shook his head. 'This time of the day, she's always busy waiting on her guests.' He drove off with a wave.

Pushing open the door, Rhea stopped in her tracks. Leo was there before her, and her heart leapt at the thought that their closeness last night had meant more to him than just a passing satisfaction of his masculine desires. But a glance across the room changed all that.

His girlfriend lounged on the sofa, a glass in her hand, her relaxed attitude boasting of a familiarity with Leo's cottage that put Rhea firmly in her place as an interloper and temporary resident. Her outfit was a slinky kind of trouser suit, exotic flowers grown large, splashed across a black background.

Then Rhea realised that Leo too was dressed as formally as his guest, which could only mean that they had a dinner date. How could she have thought that last night had meant anything to him, that the day away from her had for him seemed as long as it had for her? Just how foolishly romantic could she get?

If that, Rhea thought defiantly, swallowing her intense disappointment, is how he's playing it, so can I. She nodded briefly at Sonya, who looked somewhat put out at the touch of hauteur in her hostess's manner, said 'Excuse me' to Leo, who stood in front of the phone, and dialled.

Leo, whose hand also held a glass, watched the stabbing action, leaning back against the cabinet that held the telephone.

'Nathan?' Rhea asked, injecting a warmth into her voice that must have brought a smile to Nathan's face. 'That meal you offered me—does the invitation still stand?'

'You bet,' Nathan answered. 'How does the Black Bull strike you? OK, I'll make a booking and call for you. Half seven? Hey, Rhea, I'm sure the sun's rising instead of sinking. Will you have to report first to——?'

'My prison warder? No, Nathan,' with a murderous flash of the eyes at Leo, 'he doesn't consult me about his moves. Why should I consult him?' She disconnected with a crash and flung out of the room.

'Black Bull be darned,' Sonya was saying on an explosion of laughter. 'I could hear *Nathan* pawing the ground in anticipation! What's it like, darling, to have a rival in love?'

'First,' came Leo's rasping reply, 'you have to be in love to have a rival in it.'

His cynical statement was, Rhea thought, her lip quivering, like a well-aimed missile crashing against her back. And if she hadn't been so stupid as to leave the voice amplifier switched on, they wouldn't have heard Nathan's replies.

For Nathan's sake, Rhea smiled and talked animatedly throughout the meal. Since most of their discussion ranged around their crafts, it wasn't difficult to sound enthusiastic. What Nathan did not know was that half the time her mind was on Leo and Sonya. He's *my* husband, she found herself thinking. Yet he had gone off with another woman in front of her very eyes! From her bedroom window she had watched them leave, Sonya's arm clinging to Leo's.

Nathan took her home, returning her thanks with a kiss on the cheek. Rhea hadn't cared if Leo had been standing at the window, but her defiance was pointless. The cottage was empty.

She went to bed, but could not sleep. It's the old, old story, she thought bitterly, rejected wife hoping against hope that the husband she loved would come home to her after all. Why should I take it on the chin? she asked herself, irritable with tiredness and a terrible sense of rejection. Pulling on a gown, she ran upstairs and down, disconnecting all the telephone points. Even if he rang there would be no answer to his calls, and he could put whatever construction on that that he liked. Eventually she slept, dreaming that she lay in Leo's arms and that he whispered over and over again that he loved her.

She awoke to daylight and pouring rain, convinced that Leo had stayed the night with his girlfriend. He certainly hadn't returned home. His room was empty, and she stared at his undisturbed bed, feeling shattered inside.

CHAPTER NINE

THE telephone rang as Rhea reconnected it. It just had to be Leo. Her heart sank when she heard Nathan's voice.

'Like me to come and get you?' he asked. 'This weather——'

'The river level's risen,' she told him, telling herself to accept the fact that Leo had spent the night with his girlfriend. Theirs was that kind of marriage, wasn't it? 'I can see it from the bedroom window. Thanks for the offer of a lift. The answer's yes, please. Ready in half an hour.'

Uncle Timmy was munching lunchtime sandwiches at the Dog and Badger as she preceded Nathan into the bar. Her heart leapt, then dived. Leo wasn't with him. Lifting his tankard, Timmy didn't quite manage to hide his worried look at the sight of her coming in with Nathan so, while Nathan ordered, Rhea made straight for Timmy's table. But nothing, she decided firmly, would make her ask where Leo was. All the same, she couldn't help wondering...

Hanging Nathan's damp jacket, which she had taken from him, around the back of a chair, she divested herself of her own, swinging it across the back of her own chair.

'It's still raining,' she offered as a conversational opening.

Timmy nodded. 'Cats and dogs.' He lapsed into an uncharacteristic silence. He's still annoyed with me, Rhea thought, for spending my lunch-break with Nathan.

'I've been working hard,' she remarked as a way, she hoped, of setting his fears at rest. She smoothed her

141

damp hair, then played with a beer-mat, jumping when Timmy's hand reached out for her own.

'I can see,' he said. 'Looks as if you've painted your hands as well as the canvas, or whatever it is you use.'

Rhea laughed and looked up gratefully as Nathan set a plate of sandwiches and a glass of fruit juice in front of her. 'Those colours are from the dyeing process,' she told Timmy. 'I'm working on a series of batiks for the craft fair.'

'Not long now,' Nathan supplied, tucking into his lunch.

'First you wax the fabric,' Rhea went on, doing likewise, 'then you dye it to the colour you want. Then it's drained and dried, and——'

'A craft fair, you say?' queried Uncle Timmy. 'I think I·heard Leo mention it.'

'Is he contributing?' asked Nathan, pushing away his empty plate. 'That'll be the first time, if he is. Refill, Rhea? Timmy?' He made his way to the bar.

'Leo's back at the forge,' Timmy said. 'Working himself into the ground, he is. After completing those gates, and the celebration last night——'

'What celebration?' Rhea asked tautly.

'Why, the installation of the gates, lass. I thought you'd be there, as his wife, like. But Leo said you—er—well, had another engagement.' He glanced across at Nathan's back. 'Said you stalked out, nose in the air. Said you were an impudent, ungrateful little package, and for two pins he'd either put you across his knee, or——'

'Or divorce me.' Rhea, her face scarlet, shot to her feet, to the astonishment of the other customers.

'My dear lass,' Uncle Timmy extended a soothing hand, but she evaded it, 'you said it, not me, nor Leo.'

'Rhea, wait a minute,' Nathan, returning to the table, tried to reason, 'just calm down.'

Rhea ignored their pleading restraint. 'OK, so let him divorce me. Let him. What's more,' she hauled her jacket on, 'I'm going to tell him so. See you later, Nathan.'

She raced along the road towards the forge, oblivious of the pouring rain and the way her shoes were filling as they splashed in puddles. She didn't care if Sonya was there, she didn't care about anything except telling her husband he could go jump in the river.

Bursting in, she stopped short, her eyes confused by the switch from daylight to semi-darkness. Then they cleared and she saw that he wasn't there. But Sonya was.

'Hi.' She rose from a desk which was tucked away in a corner. 'Oh, it's you, Mrs Dower. If you're looking for your——' obviously the word was anathema to her tongue '—Leo, he's——' her hand waved vaguely '—gone home.'

'So what are you doing here?'

A slow smile spread across Sonya's face at Rhea's show of jealousy, and Rhea wanted to kick herself for handing that piece of juicy knowledge to Leo's girlfriend. 'Wouldn't you like to know?' Sonya drawled, and turned back to the desk, shuffling paper.

So, Rhea perceived, Sonya Selby provided the clerical help that she, his wife, hadn't even known he needed.

It was still pouring as she arrived, panting, at the door of River Cottage. She scoured the downstairs and was in the hall when Leo appeared on the landing, wearing only a towel fixed around his waist. A swift glance took in her panting, shivering body.

'What the hell——?' was his biting question.

She made short work of the stairs and put herself on his level, except that his height, in comparison with hers, always gave him the advantage.

'No, not *hell*, and certainly not *heaven*. If it were, you wouldn't figure in it,' she got out between gasps for breath. 'All I want to say is, if you want to start divorce proceedings, go ahead—I won't stop you. It's time I was on my way, anyhow. Our marriage has lasted quite long enough as far as I'm concerned. Too long, in fact.'

Folding his arms across the whipcord leanness of his midriff, he surveyed her surveying him. For the life of her she couldn't stop her eyes from gazing at his stubborn jawline, his broad shoulders, his expanse of chest. Fascinated, she saw the tiny beads of water from the shower he had clearly just taken, still clinging to his mat of chest hair.

'OK,' a muscle twitched in his cheek, 'so what's this all about?'

'You want a divorce, so it's the end, Leo.' The rain ran uncomfortably down her neck from dripping strands of hair.

'Who said?'

'Uncle Timmy over lunch.' He hadn't, she corrected herself, but he had had time, if he'd wanted to, to contradict her statement before she had rushed out. 'It's Sonya you want in your life, not me. She's at the forge now, working with you, and you want her living with you too. I could see that last night a mile off. You took her out for the evening.'

'A celebration. We finished the gates and they're fixed in place. It was a big order, and the customer gave a party. I'd have taken my wife, but she walked out on me into the arms of another man.'

'You had your girlfriend with you,' she flung back, 'don't try to deny it. So why shouldn't I use the freedom of our marriage arrangement and accept a *man* friend's invitation? What's more, you stayed the night with her. And you didn't even telephone to tell me you wouldn't be home.'

'Oh, yes, I did.' He moved closer, towering over her, his stance intimidating, his bearing, his muscular solidity almost irresistible to Rhea's inflamed senses. 'Three times I tried, but no reply. You were out, at Nathan Oxley's place—all night.'

With the back of her hand Rhea rubbed at the water still coursing down her cheeks. 'I wasn't! I was in bed—here, at home—our...no, *your home*.' Then she remembered how determined she had been to get even with him, and had deliberately unplugged the telephone sockets. Which meant he wouldn't believe her, however much she denied spending the night with Nathan.

'S-so what if I was?' she defied him, not caring that she was making matters worse. 'You—you were well occupied too, making love to——' *Too*, she'd said, which would imply, in Leo's eyes, that she, Rhea, had indeed been with Nathan. She looked up at him, sick at heart, frightened by the look in his eyes.

'Ours—ours would be an open marriage, you said,' again realising too late how much she was incriminating herself, how her words still implied that she had a relationship going with Nathan.

She shivered under his icy regard, then the trembling intensified and she realised how cold she was feeling, how wet she was from her precipitate race up and down the village street. 'No ties, no conditions...'

'No woman,' he rasped, his hands gripping her hips, 'no *man* makes a cuckold of me!'

He propelled her backwards into his bedroom and jerked her against him, divesting her forcibly of her jacket. Then his mouth hit hers, drawing from her a cry of protest which, as he worked at her lips until they parted under his forceful persuasion, turned into a groan of despair mixed with helpless surrender.

Her legs grew weak, her arms crept around his neck and her body sagged against his, the intimate contact telling her how aroused he had become. Her lips throbbed under the stimulus of his kisses, trembling as his mouth gentled slightly, firming again as her resistance crumbled entirely away, her thirsting mouth allowing him all the access he demanded.

Conquest of an unwilling woman, that was all it was, she thought, gasping for the air he was denying her. Slowly but surely, she at last conceded, he *was* conquering her, imposing his will and his domination on her.

When at last he let her go, she crumpled at his feet, a wet and shivering human form that must have touched his compassion, if not his warmth, since he lifted her up and appraised her shaking body.

'OK, strip,' he ordered, waiting, hands on hips, for her to obey him. 'For Pete's sake,' as she hesitated, 'I've seen you naked before.' His dark-browed gaze was filled with reminiscence. Impatient at her slow movements, he unfastened her blouse buttons and made short work of the bra beneath it.

Her arms went across her breasts in spite of his mocking smile at her over-modest action. 'Leave the r-rest,' she stammered, but he was deaf to her plea. They followed the other garments, forming a damp pile on the floor.

Plainly the sight of her inflamed him even more, and he swept her pliant body on to the bed and, tugging away his own meager cover, proceeded to make devastating love to her.

'You can't, you mustn't,' she croaked as his lips savoured her throat, her breasts and beyond, 'not now, not at this time of day.'

'To hell with the time of day,' he returned thickly. 'I can make love to you whenever I please—remember that. And I'm going to make sure you remember this. And this. And this.'

She gasped and cried out at the pleasure he was giving her, the intimacy of his kisses, the places he kept discovering that aroused her almost beyond endurance. At last she pleaded with him to take her, but still he kept her waiting. Relenting at last, he possessed her, and this was so complete that she felt she would die in his arms.

A long time later he rolled off the bed, tugging her into his arms and carrying her into the shower. The water cascaded over them, and again he took her into his arms, only the ring of the telephone preventing him from taking her all over again.

It was a business call, and by the time it was finished Rhea had dried herself and run to her own room to find dry clothes.

He came in to find her combing her hair. Narrowed eyes settled on the mirror's image of her face, flushed and radiant from the aftermath of his lovemaking.

'Why were you here, when Uncle Timmy said you'd be at the forge?' she demanded.

'He must have forgotten I've got an appointment with a potential customer—someone who was at the party last night and admired the Dower craftsmanship. He wants something similar for the entrance to his drive.'

'Are you taking Sonya?'

Leo smiled at the sarcastic undertone. 'Maybe, maybe not.'

'All right,' she turned on him fiercely, crying inside because the joy they had just shared, the beautiful act of *love*, had been to him merely an act of *lust*, 'take her. I don't care one way or the other. It's the old sordid story, isn't it?' she added bitterly. 'I can see it in headlines. Boss's ego boosted by adoration of secretary. Takes her everywhere, even to bed.'

His lips thinned, his hands lifted, curling and uncurling. 'I could do this,' he fitted them round her neck, making her shiver, 'or I could up-end you and give you a hiding you'd never forget.'

Bravely her eyes held his and his hands around her neck softened to a caress, turning her legs to water as desire tugged at her insides.

'For your information,' he said on a calmer note, 'Sonya only helps me with the paperwork as a sideline. She happens to be a designer with an established reputation.' He put a couple of paces between them. 'Eat your heart out, Rhea Dower. You're not the only one with artistic ability.'

Jealousy, even stronger than before, fountained inside her. Sonya, the woman who has everything, she thought sourly. 'I never claimed I was,' she snapped. 'It also shows—doesn't it—that Leo Dower likes his women not only to be attractive, but intelligent. Good for you, Mr Dower!'

He smiled at her sarcasm and watched her go to the door. 'Where now?'

'It's stopped raining, so I'll walk. Back to Nathan's.' She steeled herself for his black gaze, which duly came her way. 'To *work*. And, unlike you, I don't mix *pleasure* with it.'

Early evening, Leo telephoned. Nathan, hands thickly coated with clay, asked Rhea to answer it. She was wrist-deep in dye, so she seized a cloth to hold the instrument.

'Thought I'd find you still there,' her husband's voice drawled, 'but why the long delay?'

'In answering? We were—er—otherwise engaged,' she retorted, deliberately provoking him. 'Couldn't you guess?'

Nathan shook his head. 'Don't do that to him,' he whispered, and Rhea coloured deeply.

'If I thought you were speaking the truth,' Leo spat through teeth that were clearly clenched, 'I'd——'

'Why did you call?' Rhea asked, contrite now, but unable to convey it through her voice.

'To tell you I'd be late home.'

'Thanks, but, knowing that Sonya's with you, I'd be surprised if you came home at all,' Rhea returned, angry again.

'We've been invited to stay to dinner.' His tone showed that he too was angry. 'I'll see you in the morning.'

'Will you?' She ended the call quickly, afraid that he might detect the tears in her voice. After the swift and devastating passion of their middle-of-the-day love-making, their cold, ill-humoured conversation left her feeling shattered. She tried to lose herself in her work, but was glad when Carrie called round, inviting them to a meal at her and Vince's guesthouse.

Rhea spent most of the evening talking to Vince, if only to give Carrie the chance of monopolising Nathan, which she clearly wished to do. Rhea could not understand how oblivious Nathan seemed to be of Carrie's liking for him—more than liking, Rhea was sure.

When Vince offered to give her a lift home, she jumped at it, even though Nathan said he would do the honours. Rhea had seen the pleasure in Carrie's eyes as Vince made the announcement, and trusted that the man responsible for its being there might see it too.

Vince drew away with a wave as soon as Rhea opened the cottage door, although he did not see her hesitate before closing it. Leo was there, but he wasn't alone. How, Rhea wondered, could she have been so stupid as to believe he would be?

His cold stare made her want to sink into the ground, but she was darned if she would give him an explanation of her lateness—it was almost midnight—in front of Sonya Selby. Let him think she had been at Nathan's, let him think Nathan had just dropped her at the door. What's more, she thought, I'm darned if I'll play hostess to his girlfriend!

'I'm tired,' she said with a commendable coolness, 'so will you please excuse me?'

'Oh, Rhea—if I may call you that? Must you go? I was so looking forward to a heart-to-heart about our mutual subject.' Sonya gestured to the seat beside her. As if, Rhea fumed, not moving, *she's* the hostess and *I'm* the guest.

Catching the mockery in Leo's gaze, she had to suppress the urge to hit him.

'I adore your skirt, Rhea,' Sonya was saying. 'I can see we share a love of bright colours. Would you—could you make me one like that? Not an exact copy, of course, but something similar?'

Rhea could not decide whether Sonya was really making an effort to be friendly—what wife could ever be, Rhea found herself wondering, with her husband's *mistress*?—or coveted something she knew perfectly well she couldn't have? Or was Sonya subtly telling her, 'I know darned well your skirt is homemade, and what's more, in case you don't know, it looks it.'

'Thanks for the compliment,' Rhea heard herself say, 'but I'm very busy at the moment making things for the craft fair. I'll bear your request in mind, though. Goodnight, Miss Selby.' With a look that mixed defiance with accusation, she added insinuatingly, 'Goodnight, Leo. Enjoy your night's *rest*.'

The days took on a pattern, with Leo leaving early for his work at the forge, and Rhea staying late at Nathan's. Like her, Nathan was working flat out to make enough pottery to fill his stall.

In between completing her own fabric designs and, with Carrie's help, making them up into skirts and tops, wall-hangings and lampshades, Rhea kept her promise to Nathan and fitted in the decoration of his ornaments, his bowls, jugs and flower vases.

Consequently, each evening on returning home, she was completely exhausted, falling asleep as soon as her head burrowed into the pillow. Once, she could have sworn her door had opened and that someone had entered, but on stirring and sleepily opening her eyes, she found that no one was there.

Another time, in the early morning, birdsong awakened her, and she turned on to her back to listen.

Her arm came up against a human form and she almost cried out in terror, until she discovered what had really awakened her—Leo's arm across her breasts, his demanding hands pulling her towards him. He was, she discovered, naked.

'How...' she croaked '...when...?'

'Did I get into your bed? In the early hours. If a man can't sleep, he does the sensible thing—he goes and finds a woman. In this case, *his* woman. Come on, baby,' he commanded, his tongue busy around her ears, making tingling trails around them, 'I'm making love to you right here, right now.' In no time, her nightdress was disposed of over the side of the bed.

'Leo, no...' Already she was shivering in anticipation of his caresses.

'You know damned well it's "Leo, yes,"' he growled, fitting his mouth over hers and stifling any further attempts on her part to dissuade him. She didn't want to, she discovered; she wanted him with all her heart and soul. She turned into him and lost herself in his overpowering masculinity, knowing his needs now and matching them with her own, feeling her insides alternately curl and unfurl, while her body ached for his intrusion, yet loving the torment with which he promised yet withheld the ultimate joy, rejoicing at last in his complete and utter possession of her.

When she awoke for the second time, she discovered that, yet again, she was alone. It was, she thought hazily, like being made love to by a mystery lover, one who came in the dark hours and took her, then disappeared until the next time and the next...

Then she reproached herself for being a romantic fool, because the man in *her* life needed her, wanted her for only one reason, the satisfaction of his male desires. Which was precisely why he had come to her in the night when, he had said, he had not been able to sleep.

Every morning she hoped to see him at breakfast; every evening she tried to stay awake until he returned. She began to believe that she had dreamt they shared the same house, that maybe he didn't exist except in her thoughts and her dreams!

When she saw him again, it was in the pub one lunchtime. For days she had made up her own sandwiches, eating them as she worked. This particular day, she went with Nathan to the Dog and Badger for sandwiches and a drink.

Leo was at the bar, his back to her, but even so her heart thumped and her muscles contracted with excitement, her body starting to ache for him.

He turned and caught her eyes upon him. As if he had guessed her thoughts, he smiled, and her heart turned over, but it soon righted itself as she detected mockery in his eyes.

'Rhea, lass,' Timmy spoke from a dark corner, 'it's a long time since I saw you. Nathan, bring her across. Leo, get your wife a drink, will you?' he shouted. 'And your old friend Nathan too.'

Leo looked with anything but friendly eyes at the man to whom Timmy had referred, but he obliged his uncle and bought drinks all round, bringing them to the circular table and taking the seat beside his wife, Nathan having tactfully joined Timmy on the high-backed wall seat.

'Busy, then, are you?' commented Timmy, noticing Rhea's paint-stained hands. 'Dyeing again?' he joked.

'Partly, yes,' Rhea replied, over-conscious of her husband's interest even though he was drawing deeply on the contents of his beer glass. 'Mostly, it's paint. I'm decorating some of Nathan's pottery.'

'After biscuit firing, or before?' Leo asked casually, separating his sandwiches and chewing one.

She glanced at him with surprise. She had expected hostility because it was Nathan for whom she was working, not informed interest. 'After,' she answered, looking at him fully for the first time since he had joined them. 'Before glazing takes place.'

He returned her gaze, and she was intoxicatingly aware that their ensuing silent exchange had nothing whatever to do with the subject in hand, and everything to do with intimacy and passion and desire.

'Painting with pigments, that is, metal oxides or underglaze colours...' Her voice trailed into silence, while her heartbeats almost deafened her.

'You're talking,' Nathan commented with a smile, 'like someone who's made pots all her life.'

Rhea moistened her lips, which had become strangely dry, dragging her eyes from Leo's. 'It's only what you've taught me about decorating pottery,' she returned. 'It wasn't part of my degree syllabus.'

'You've been a very apt pupil,' Nathan told her, apparently engrossed in estimating the depth of the froth on his beer.

Leo's expression registered irritation-plus, which must have flowed through him to his feet, since he rose abruptly, nodded unsmilingly to his wife and her companion and pushed in his chair with a clatter. 'Coming, Timmy?'

Timmy nodded, making a rueful face at Rhea, and followed his nephew outside. Nathan let out a sigh. Whether it was one of relief, or an expression of bewilderment at the ways of husbands and wives, bearing in mind his own experience in that respect, Rhea could not tell.

A few days before the craft fair was due to open, Rhea found Leo still at home when she came down for breakfast. He wore a suit and tie and an air of business to come in the big city hung around him.

'How long this time?' she asked, putting her sinking heart firmly back in place and anticipating his announcement of yet another period of absence from home.

A shrug of broad shoulders was followed by a clipped, 'Who knows?'

'It depends,' she heard herself burst out, 'on the whim of Miss Selby, no doubt.'

A quizzical I'm-not-telling eyebrow lifted. 'Who knows?' he repeated with a sardonic smile.

His arm came out and swung her to him, taking her so much by surprise that she had no time to erect her barriers. His hands cupped her face and his brilliant gaze stared into her wide eyes. 'Anyone would think,' he commented drily, 'that you were jealous.'

She tried to struggle free. 'Not on your life,' she retorted. 'Feel free to *take* any woman you want.'

He laughed at the deliberate double meaning, lowered his head, helped himself to a long and devastating kiss and left, picking up his executive case as he went.

The nights were lonely and long, but the work Rhea had to get through before the fair opened kept her hands busy in the daytime, and at night her mind preoccupied in between bouts of restless sleeping.

Two evenings before the opening, she worked without pause, except for a snatched evening meal of soup and fruit and coffee.

Nathan mopped his brow. 'Sorry to mention it, Rhea,' he said, 'but there are half a dozen more jugs ready for decorating.'

Carrie worked at a sewing-machine in another room, putting together skirts and tops which Rhea had designed and processed. She joined the others for the sparse snack, sinking down wearily in the only uncluttered chair in the room.

'I'm glad my knitted offerings are all pressed and packaged,' she sighed, 'ready for Vince to take to the hall. He'll take all these too, Nathan,' indicating his work, 'not to mention your stuff, Rhea. Tommy said he'd help us with our stalls if we wanted.'

'Nice of him,' commented Nathan offhandedly, 'but he'll be too busy setting up his clocks to worry about us.' He smiled at Carrie. 'I'll be your strong man, love, OK?'

Carrie smiled back, and Rhea rejoiced in the way the two of them seemed to share some wonderful secret. She had, in fact, suspected that Carrie might have stayed more than once at Nathan's overnight and had been glad beyond words.

It did not occur to her then that she also might stay at Nathan's overnight, but that was exactly what she did. It was well into the small hours when she surfaced and the three of them ground to a halt.

'No need to go,' Nathan told her. 'There's a folding bed over there. Use that, Rhea. You're almost falling asleep on your feet—isn't she, Carrie?'

'I've got a spare toothbrush somewhere,' Carrie said, backing Nathan up, and watching as, with a few quick movements, he made a space and unfolded the bed. 'I'll get some bedclothes. It's OK, I know where they are, Nathan, love.' His hand touched hers as she passed him.

Gratefully Rhea accepted all the offers, dropping asleep almost as soon as the light was out. Carrie was there next morning. Rhea schooled herself to show no surprise, but Carrie caught her in the kitchen making the toast.

'Rhea, I have to tell you, or I'll burst!' she confided. 'Nathan said I could. He's asked me to marry him!' She half disappeared into Rhea's delighted hug. 'It won't be for a while, because he wants to clear the business of his divorce out of the way, but he's going to give me a ring. Can I see what your engagement ring's like, to help me decide what I want?'

She looked at Rhea's wedding finger, which bore only a plain gold band. What Carrie didn't know, Rhea reflected, and never would, was that that ring was there as a symbol of vengeance fulfilled.

'Leo didn't give me one, Carrie,' Rhea said simply. He didn't think I was worth the expenditure, she almost said, but kept the bitter words to herself.

'That's OK,' said Carrie brightly and tactfully, 'some couples don't bother these days. I'll just have to look in shop windows, won't I?'

'A bottle of champagne seems to be called for, Nathan,' Rhea commented with a broad smile as Nathan entered, reaching up to kiss his cheek. 'Congrats, both of you. I'm really delighted.'

'Don't tell anyone, will you?' Carrie urged. 'Not yet, not until I tell you you can. Promise?'

'I promise,' Rhea answered solemnly.

The next evening she stayed at Nathan's again. They had worked all day setting up the stalls around the hall in the town. This time Carrie went home. It was, she said, her evening on duty and Vince's night off.

The day of the craft show dawned bright and clear. Carrie called Nathan, then asked to speak to Rhea.

'Don't forget the party after the show tonight,' Carrie reminded her. 'Wearing something nice?'

'One of my own creations,' Rhea pretended to boast. 'How about you?'

'One of my handknits,' she answered with a laugh. 'Nothing like modelling your own designs to encourage people to place orders!'

Saturday crowds thronged the town's streets, and as soon as the doors opened people drifted in.

Timmy sat near the door collecting the entrance money which would go towards the cost of hiring the hall. The remainder, they had all agreed, would be divided between the exhibitors so that even those whose sales were low or non-existent would receive some payment for their efforts.

In a spare moment from the rush of customers, Rhea glanced round the hall to try and judge how the fair was going. Around Maisie Kelney's leatherwork stall three or four people lingered, while Mildred Smith seemed to be doing a fair trade in corn dollies.

To her delight, Carrie's handknits were doing so well that she mopped her brow on catching Rhea's eye. At the stall next to hers, Nathan's customers were exclaiming over his decorated pottery and, it seemed, parting willingly with their money.

Then the customers swooped on Rhea's goods again, which meant that she didn't see a couple enter, one of whom paid the entrance fee for them both. Busy answering queries about her fabric and her designs, she did not hear the woman enquiring the whereabouts of 'Rhea Dower's stall'.

It was not until the crowd had temporarily cleared again that she saw the couple approaching.

'Now, Rhea,' exclaimed Sonya, 'this is a situation where the seller can't refuse a buyer. You forgot my request to you, didn't you,' she went on over-sweetly, 'to make me a skirt like yours? So,' her eyes flitted from one item to the other, 'now I'm going to make my choice. If I buy up all your goods, you won't be able to grumble, will you?'

'Take your pick, Miss Selby,' Rhea commented indifferently. 'Just as long as you don't choose the things people have reserved and paid for.'

'Rhea!' There was rebuke in Leo's tone, while a warning flashed in his eyes.

Colouring with annoyance, she flashed right back, telling him silently, I can dispose how I like of my handiwork. When Sonya chose a skirt with a design similar to the one she had recently admired, Rhea made no demur, waiting as Sonya went on riffling through the fabrics and pulling a particularly dazzling design from the pile.

It was one of Rhea's favourites and she hated the idea of its gracing Sonya's person when made up, but her face was without expression as she accepted Sonya's cheque and wrapped the items, handing them over.

'Hi, Nathan,' said Sonya, moving to the next stall.

'Thanks for letting me know,' Rhea murmured, her wide eyes resting angrily on her husband, 'of your return. With your girlfriend in tow, as usual,' she couldn't stop herself from adding.

His smile was sarcastic and fleeting. 'I tried ringing you. No answer, *as usual.*' He echoed her words tartly.

'I—I——' Rhea just prevented the hot colour from swamping her cheeks. If she told him the truth, that she had spent two nights at Nathan's, he would put an entirely false construction on the statement. Nor could she tell him that Carrie had stayed there for one of those nights. She couldn't tell him either that Carrie and Nathan were deeply in love and were engaged to be married. 'I guess I must have been tired,' she finished weakly, pretending to be absorbed in sorting through the goods on display.

'Be honest and admit that you didn't answer the phone in case I was the caller?'

'Maybe, maybe,' she answered offhandedly as, to her relief, customers drifted round her stall, causing Leo to move on. How else could she have answered? she asked herself helplessly, but she did not miss the touch of scepticism in his eyes.

CHAPTER TEN

THE closing of the doors brought sighs of relief and, for the most part, a deep satisfaction. Sales had been high and everyone had sold something.

'See you back here tonight,' people were calling as they left the hall, stalls dismantled and disposed of, unsold goods boxed and taken home.

Rhea was surprised to find the cottage empty, then told herself to come down to earth and remember that Sonya Selby's charms were, in Leo's eyes, greater than hers. After all, she reflected cynically as she showered and brushed her hair until it crackled, Sonya had been on the the scene—Leo's scene—long before she, Rhea Hirst, had appeared on it.

She was searching for her jacket among the others on the hallstand—her nostrils picking up Leo's musky and warmly familiar scent as she foraged—when the door opened and he came in.

Finding what she was looking for at that moment, Rhea swung round, her expression full of fight, but Leo was alone. He smiled as if he had guessed her thoughts, then looked her over, clearly liking what he saw.

'Colourful and flattering. You should sew a label into your creations,' he commented, 'and set up in business as a fashion designer.'

'Joining forces with your girlfriend, I suppose you're going to add? No, thank you. If you're hungry——'

'I've eaten.'

'With Sonya.'

'With my uncle.' His hands on her hips eased her towards him. 'I do believe——' His mouth approached hers, but she struggled free.

'I am not jealous!' The words came out slowly and emphatically. But you are, a tiny voice whispered, you most certainly are...

'I don't know what time I'll be home,' she threw over her shoulder as she pulled on her jacket, then dashed out before he could insist on giving her a lift.

She was dancing with Nathan when Leo appeared in the doorway. She faltered and Nathan steadied her, asking, 'You OK?'

She nodded and concentrated on the lively steps, telling herself to pretend that Leo wasn't there, telling her heart to stop pounding so much harder just because the man she loved but who did not love her had arrived on the scene.

Dance over, she smiled at Nathan, who returned the smile briefly before allowing his eyes to wander in search of Carrie.

'She's over there,' Rhea nodded across the room, 'with Mildred and Maisie. Want to go to her?'

Reluctantly he shook his head. 'If Carrie and I are seen together too much people will start to talk, and we don't want that. Not yet, not until the legalities of my affairs have been settled. You do understand, Rhea?'

'Of course I do.'

The music started again, and Nathan's hand was coming out to take hers when another hand forestalled him, one that was stronger, more forceful, and had every right to be, in the circumstances. A hand that hammered and shaped incandescent metal, arms that wielded heavy tools, risking injury and heat-burns, pitting his strength and his will-power against even more powerful forces.

The arms she was swept into held a promise of shared delight which over the weeks had become practically irresistible. By an irony of fate, the weapon with which she had chosen to wreak vengeance on the Dowers had been turned on to her, and the hurt it was inflicting was almost too painful to endure.

Fingers tilted her face. 'Solemn thoughts, or annoyance that I took you away from Oxley?'

In spite of herself, Rhea smiled. 'Possibly to the first, definitely no to the second.'

'So tell me those thoughts.'

This time her smile defied him. 'Not on your life!'

'I could make you.' His eyes were full of meaning, hinting at past intimacies and those to come. He seemed amused at her discomfiture.

'Maybe you could,' she concurred, head on one side, 'but it wouldn't have any meaning. It would be just a means of satisfying your...our...passing...um...sensual needs, not to mention a way of demonstrating your physical domination over me. Our marriage was never meant to contain any adhesive element. Nor,' she moistened her lips which had become curiously dry under his appraisal, 'was there meant to be any intertwining of our emotions.'

'True.' His glance was hooded. 'That was quite a speech. My wife is certainly articulate.'

'I'm *not* your wife,' she returned tartly, irritated because he had tacitly agreed with all her statements.

'So what are you?' He seemed amused. 'My woman?'

'No. Sonya's that,' she riposted angrily, because he didn't dispute her allegation either by word or shake of the head.

He held her closer, forcing her to dance more intimately with him. Her head went back and she could not prevent her eyes entangling with his, her fingers digging into the casual shirt he wore, her thighs touching his, encased in denim.

Amused, he flicked the long leather 'fun' earrings she had bought from Mildred Smith's stall, touched the matching choker with fingers that lingered, making the

nerves of her skin dance at the cool, very personal
contact.

'How did the craft fair go?' he asked as their bodies
moved in perfect harmony.

'For me, very well. I've got a pile of orders, weeks of
work ahead. One day,' she grew dreamy, 'I'd like to start
a business of my own.' That would be when her marriage to him came to an end. Her eyes closed on the
thought so that he wouldn't see in them the deep distress
the thought engendered within her.

'Rhea.' He had whispered her name and her eyes fluttered open, her head tilting back.

As if her lips held a magnet his mouth came down,
and hers willingly succumbed to his possession. His kiss
made her senses swim, an exquisite ache throb deep inside
her. The kiss had no end, and its effect on her was such
that it was as though she had drunk too much intoxicating liquid, except that she hadn't touched a drop.

A buzz of conversation at the door turned into a mild
commotion, and Leo broke the kiss, turning his head,
his hold slackening. Heart sinking, Rhea guessed the
identity of the new arrival.

For the rest of the dance, Leo's mind was plainly elsewhere, his movements becoming automatic. She broke
away from him, the other dancers moving round them.

'What prompted that?' he queried, frowning.

'How can you pretend you don't know?' she retorted.
'Your girlfriend's on a telepathic line to you. Why don't
you pick up your mental phone and answer her?'

She had meant the sarcasm to jolt him so that he returned to her in mind as well as body, but, to her dismay
and disappointment, he took her statement literally.

'I'll take you at your word,' he clipped. 'If you'll
excuse me...'

'You're not going to leave me standing here?' Rhea
wailed.

An eyebrow flicked, a mocking smile flirted with his lips. 'You don't like being stood up? OK, so come with me and you'll be able to hear what we have to say to each other.' He took her hand to pull her behind him, but she snatched it free. 'It's business, pure and simple.'

'Go to her,' she choked, not believing him. 'Go to the woman you really want!' She spied Nathan alone on the edge of the circulating couples and made a beeline. 'Dance with me, Nathan,' she pleaded through quivering lips, and urged him on to the dance-floor.

Leo's contemptuous glance over the heads of the crowd made her shiver inside, but she moved with Nathan as if there were no greater pleasure than to be dancing with him. Deliberately she turned her back to her husband, but swinging round in the course of the dance, she saw him moving slowly round the floor with Sonya. He was listening intently to her words, his head inclined slightly the better to hear her. And the better, no doubt, Rhea thought angrily, to inhale her perfume and feel her warm breath on his cheek.

'Domestic quarrel?' Nathan asked with an understanding smile.

'Sort of. Take me home, Nathan,' she said, suppressing the tears that would spring, in spite of herself. 'Don't ask why.'

A glance around was sufficient for Nathan to guess the reason, and he cheerfully obeyed, first signalling to Carrie, who nodded, understanding at once.

'Thanks,' said Rhea as he drew up in the parking space at the rear of River Cottage. 'And thanks, Nathan, for helping me. I mean, for letting me invade your studio all this time, not to mention letting me stay a couple of nights. You're very good, you know, and Carrie's lucky.' She leaned across and pecked him on the cheek.

He smiled in the semi-darkness of the car. 'Am I allowed to return the compliment?' He kissed her too, on the cheek. 'Leo's a lucky man.'

She shook her head fiercely. 'He's not, Nathan. If only you knew the true situation!'

'Tell me some time.'

'Maybe. Goodnight.' She waved as he drove away.

Searching for her key, she used a small pocket torch to pick her way to the front door. As she reached it, a man came from out of the shadows behind her, and she screamed, a hand to her throat.

He took her torch from her trembling hand and flashed it upward at his own face. Stark terror was only fractionally modified by relief and recognition.

'Oh, God,' she croaked, 'did you have to behave like a would-be criminal and give me such a terrible fright?'

'A *would-be* criminal?' Jerome remarked lightly. 'I thought that, in your eyes, I was the devil in disguise where lawbreaking was concerned.'

Even when they faced each other across the living-room, Rhea could not stop herself trembling. She sank into a chair.

'You need a drink, Mrs Dower,' Jerome declared, moving towards the sideboard. 'No, don't get up.' She had made no move to do so. 'I know where the goodies are. I lived here once. What's yours? Nothing?' He helped himself, lifting the glass in an ironic toast. 'So how's my big brother treating you?' He looked her up and down. 'Can't you stop shaking? Why not? Got a guilty conscience?'

That was too much to take. '*Guilty conscience*?' she exploded, anger quelling the remaining symptoms of fright. 'For heaven's sake, you were the guilty one, Jerome, not me!'

A car drew up, scrunching to a stop. Waiting, Jerome stared apprehensively at the door.

Leo thrust into the cottage. 'What the hell did you mean, Rhea, by leaving without telling me?' Then he saw Jerome and froze. 'Good God! The embezzler returns!'

Jerome made a face, taking a drink. 'So she's told you, then?' he commented guardedly. 'How much, Rhea?'

'Enough,' was her equally guarded answer.

'You admit it?' his brother asked briskly.

'Admit what? I admit nothing. That's what my lawyer told me to say, at all times. Even to my own *dear* brother.' He raised his glass. 'To old times, Leo.' He drank.

It was, Rhea sensed, Jerome's way of reminding his brother of the days long ago that Timmy had told her about, when Leo had protected Jerome after their mother had died. And, from Leo's expression, Rhea saw that he knew it too, but whether Jerome had touched his sympathy as well as his memory she could not tell.

Looking from one to the other, she wondered how she had ever thought they were alike. Maybe they were physically, except that there was a weakness about Jerome's eyes and mouth, whereas there was strength of character and purpose in every angle and plane of Leo's face, a face she loved to touch, to kiss, a face she *loved*.

Jerome took a seat as though he belonged, which he probably did, Rhea conceded reluctantly, certainly more than she. Then he moved, putting himself beside her on the sofa. She jerked away, and he laughed unkindly.

'Still a cold fish, Rhea?' he taunted, draining his glass and disposing of it. 'Hasn't even Leo's virile heat thawed you out?' He turned to his brother. 'She went all iceberg on me, Leo, even though she wore my ring, so of course I held my horses, as they say.'

He spoke as if he had rehearsed every word, like a defendant in court who had learned his lawyer's briefing by heart.

'It's not my line to take a woman cold,' he blustered on. 'Nor did I want her running to her precious father, yelling, "He's raped me, fire him, Daddy." I thought of all that lovely money I'd forfeit by forcing myself on her. Anyway,' he looked with amusement on Rhea's aghast gaze, 'I stood her *coyness* stoically because I knew there were plenty of other women I could have fun with, without recriminations, or losing my very well-paid job, and I did.'

'Why, you——!' Unable to contain her fury, Rhea sprang at him, grasping his tie, tugging at his hair, pulling with all her might, despite his shouts for mercy.

'You rotten low-down louse!' she accused, sobbing and struggling as Leo gripped her shoulders, forcing her away and to her feet. She fought him too, until he captured her hands and grasped them behind her back.

She turned blazing eyes on him. 'I hate your brother, I hate you! I hate the Dowers, except Uncle Timmy. I don't know how I even brought myself to marry you, Leo Dower.' You *do,* a treacherous voice prompted. You loved him, that's why. You still do...

'Hey, has she got fire!' Jerome commented, his gaze frankly admiring. 'And I never knew. How does she measure up in——?'

'Don't you dare,' she cried hoarsely at Leo, desperate to free herself, 'don't you dare answer that question! If you do, I'll——' In vain, she struggled, but Leo held her easily, stilling her violent efforts until the pain of his restraining hands became unbearable. She lifted tear-stained eyes to his. 'Please, Leo, you're hurting!'

He released her at once, his face a mask.

'I'll tell you something, Jerome,' he said as she sank down in a chair, away from them both, but Leo approached her and she shrank away. He lifted her hand and indicated her wedding finger. 'This is her ring of revenge. She married me, letting me believe she was pregnant by you——'

'I told you the truth,' she broke in, 'that I wasn't——'

'She married me,' Leo went on implacably, 'to have her own back on you, on me, on the Dowers.' He moved away from her. 'She doesn't love me, but what she does love is what I give her——'

'So to speak,' Jerome interposed with a snigger, but his brother went on,

'The way my bank balance enables her to live in the way to which she was accustomed before you robbed her, or so she alleges.'

Rhea's head shot up. 'There it is again,' she accused, 'your brotherly instinct from the past to protect your little brother! *Alleged*, you said. There's so much evidence to prove he defrauded Daniel Hirst that it would fill a volume.'

Jerome began to look perturbed. Was he feeling, Rhea wondered, that the net was closing on him? His expression brightened as if he had thought of a way out.

'There are one or two things you should know about your beautiful wife, Leo, and, as your brother, I think I should warn you.'

Leo's cold eyes swung to Rhea, then back to Jerome. 'Well?'

'If you slander me,' Rhea warned grimly, 'I'll sue.'

'Where are the witnesses?' Jerome gibed. 'My sibling wouldn't testify against me. We were too close as boys.' He walked about like a lawyer in a courtroom. 'I had a drink in the Dog and Badger while I was waiting for you both to come back.'

He paused for effect, and Rhea's heart began to pound as a strange foreboding gripped her.

'The rumour's going round,' Jerome swaggered up to Rhea and away again, 'that while this lady's husband was away she slept for a couple of nights with Nathan Oxley.'

'It's not true!' Rhea cried. 'I——'

'You swear,' Leo approached, his face dark with anger, 'that this rumour's not true? You spent every night here in this cottage?'

'N-no, not every...' What was the use, she thought, of prevaricating? 'So what if I did stay at Nathan's place?'

'Which was the *real* reason why my phone calls stayed unanswered,' he gritted.

'There you are,' said Jerome triumphantly.

'Will you be quiet?' Rhea cried furiously. 'We were working flat out, Leo, to get finished before the show. I worked one night until the early hours. Nathan invited me to stay——'

'In his bed?' Leo rasped.

'No! Carrie was there too.' It could have been her trump card had she been permitted to play it, but her promise to her friends not to reveal their engagement bound her to silence.

'Sharing your room?'

'No.' I used the studio... The words tormented her tongue, but she could not speak them without letting Nathan and Carrie down.

'There you are!' exclaimed Jerome, eyes shining with triumph, and not a little spite. 'What's more,' he confronted her, hands behind his back, still playing the prosecuting lawyer, 'are you going to deny, Rhea, that when Nathan brought you home this evening you kissed him? And that he kissed you?'

'It wasn't a kiss,' she corrected, whispering now, 'it was just a peck I gave him, which he returned. I was thanking him for——'

'An entertaining couple of nights?' Leo snarled.

'For God's sake,' she shrieked, hands covering her ears, 'it's like being savaged by two vicious dogs!'

Jerome smiled unpleasantly, walking away. 'I rest my case.'

There was a long silence while Rhea sat back, eyes closed, face pale.

'You robbed her, Jerome,' Leo pronounced at last. 'You'll repay her—every penny, every cent. Do you hear?'

Jerome paled, dropping into a chair. 'I can't.'

Leo swung to him. 'You mean it's all too securely tied up?'

'No.'

'You've surely got it invested somewhere?'

'Nope.' Jerome sat forward, staring at his clasped hands. 'I spent it all, Leo, honestly. That's why I came here.' He shifted uncomfortably. 'Cash-flow problems, so to speak.'

Older brother turned on younger. 'Get out!' Rhea had never seen Leo look so angry.

'Where to, Leo?' Jerome whined. 'I thought you could put up me here for a couple of nights.' Leo's answering stare was so vitriolic that Jerome winced. He got up slowly, shoving his hands into his jacket pockets. 'Uncle Timmy won't turn me out. He's got a heart, unlike you. So long, Rhea, Leo.'

'Before he goes,' Rhea stood, facing them both, 'I want to tell you something else, Leo. Something that only Jerome and I know.'

'Rhea, for God's sake...' Jerome's voice tailed away at the determination in her eyes.

'Leo, your brother was responsible for my parents' deaths. It was his fault their plane crashed.'

'Do you deny this, Jerome?' Leo queried sharply.

Jerome shrugged, then shook his head, staring at the carpet.

'When my father flew the plane back from Scotland— the last time but one that he was to pilot it—he told Jerome he was sure a fault was developing in an engine. It was making a strange noise. Jerome promised faith-fully, at my father's request, to have it looked at and overhauled.'

'And he didn't?' Leo asked roughly.

'He didn't. He forgot, he said.'

'My God!' came hoarsely from Leo. 'Get out, Jerome,' he said at last with a dismissing movement of his head.

Jerome's feet dragged across to the door, his hand extending to pick up his travel bag. As the door slammed behind him, Leo asked harshly, 'How sweet is revenge, Rhea? Is it as cloying as syrup? Or does it taste as delectable as honey?'

'Ask yourself, Leo,' she said thickly. 'You also vowed revenge on me—for using you, as you put it. You'd make me pay, you said.' Her eyes lifted heavily to his. 'You've made me pay, Leo, dearly. Are *you* pleased? Are *you* happy now?'

He came to her that night. Unable to sleep, she stood at the window, a wrap loosely around her. She heard the door click shut behind him and all of her senses linked like forged chains to hold her responses back from leaping with expectancy and delight.

'I want you, Rhea,' he said. 'For the last time, you're going to act as my wife. Then——'

She twisted round. He stood there, arms folded, a towelling robe hanging loose, and nothing beneath it.

Desire flooded through her, threatening to swamp her, to stop her escaping. 'You can't, not deliberately, not in cold blood. I won't let you!' She tried to push past him, but he caught her, swung her round and against him.

As her body hit his, dismay fought a running battle with delight. She should be fighting him, dredging up her hatred for the Dower brothers, resisting with all her might the sensual onslaught of this man.

Reason lost out. The familiarity of his body, the musky scent of him that drew her like a magnet, overcame reason and conscious thought, allowing emotion to take control. Her love for him, for everything about him, was almost her undoing, and her resistance almost crumpled. But again her rational self fought back. She couldn't, she wouldn't let him take her knowing how much he hated her, wanting her only to complete the circle of *his* revenge, to prove once more his total domination over her.

'Stop!' she cried. 'How could you do this to me?'

He answered in deeds, not words, disrobing her in a few fluid movements. He swung her to the bed and stood over her supine figure, looking, arms folded, while her toes curled and her pulses hammered at the slow, sensual way he was regarding every part of her.

Desire for him, for his total possession, welled up uncontrollably, making her legs restless and her breaths come faster. He laughed, knowing just what he was doing to her, and the taunting sound of his laughter made her shiver with apprehension, yet *frissons* of excitement coursed through her.

He came to her then, covering her with his body, and she moaned with the pleasure of the intimate contact. He proceeded to make love to her with such controlled voluptuousness, yet such finesse, bringing her such agony and such ecstasy that all she wanted was to become one with him and never, ever, to leave him.

At last he relented, taking her with such complete possession yet holding back the ultimate pleasure for so long that she heard herself gasping his name over and over again, pleading with him to make her finally and irrevocably his.

His arms were round her when she fell asleep, her head against his chest, his legs intertwined with hers, his body her security, her sanctuary.

Waking next morning, she found herself alone. Leo must have disentangled himself from her in the night and walked away from her distastefully clinging arms.

She could tell him now how bitter was the taste of revenge. But how sweet it must have been for *him*.

He had certainly had *his* revenge. He had made her pay for using him, and pay dearly, because she had discovered to her cost that it was no longer possible to hate him, nor even to fool herself into believing she did. Through his ruthless yet passionate lovemaking, his relentless assault on her senses, her body, her emotions, he had made absolutely sure that she would love him and remember him beyond all others, for the rest of her life.

CHAPTER ELEVEN

IN THE cool light of morning, Rhea came down to earth, and the impact was shattering.

She could not stay there any longer, that was abundantly clear. She would go down and confront Leo, demand that he released her, and admit that their marriage, if it had ever been possible to call it that, was at an end.

There was no sign of him. His bed was undisturbed, and this to Rhea could mean only one thing. When he had left her bed, he had gone to the arms of Sonya Selby. There was no denying that *he* had given *her* pleasure and fulfilment, she reflected miserably, but her responses to him had plainly left much to be desired.

She rang Carrie, who answered her query like a woman somewhat distracted. 'A room, Rhea? For you? Oh, dear,' she wailed, 'we're full to bulging. I've even had to get out of my own room to accommodate a guest. All I can suggest is that you contact Nathan. He wouldn't mind at all letting you sleep on the folding bed in his studio. But, Rhea,' as if the strangeness of her friend's request had just struck her, 'for heaven's sake, why? No, forget that, I shouldn't have asked. Maybe in a couple of days we can have you here, but at the moment we're up to our eyes.'

Ask Nathan? Rhea thought, hesitating. Why ever not? she asked herself. Leo wouldn't mind. What had he said last night? 'For the last time, you're going to act as my wife.' Which meant that he had crossed her off his list of acquaintances.

'Use the folding bed again?' Nathan responded, sounding puzzled. 'Of course, but why...? No, forget that. When?'

'Is today OK? Just until Carrie and Vince have a room to spare. I'll be round as soon as I can collect my belongings. And thanks, Nathan, thanks a lot.'

As she was leaving, the telephone rang. She made to answer, held back, then lifted the mouthpiece, listening silently. If it was Leo, she would ring off.

'Leo, is that you?'

'Uncle Timmy,' Rhea answered, 'Leo isn't here.'

'Well, he's not here either, lass. I'm at the forge. He's always here before me, but not today. Know where he's gone, Rhea?'

'I—I was hoping you'd tell me that, Uncle Timmy. I've an idea where he might be found, but——'

'Hm.' Timmy sounded grim. 'Some men don't know when they're lucky.' Which could only confirm, Rhea thought unhappily, that her guess of where—to whom— Leo had gone had been correct. 'When he does come home,' Timmy went on, 'tell him Jerome's left my place. He wouldn't say where he was going either. They're a rum couple, those two brothers,' he finished scratchily. 'Tell him I need him to help me on this job, will you?'

Rhea assured him that she would, but felt bound to add that she didn't know when she would be seeing Leo again. She ended the call quickly, in case Timmy asked her to explain what she meant.

She stayed with Nathan for three nights, not one, sharing his kitchen and his bathroom, and doing her best to lose herself in her work. She had so many orders to fulfil that she knew she would have to work long and hard to get through them.

Even when Carrie and Vince offered her a room for as long as she liked, and into which she gladly moved, Rhea accompanied Nathan each day to the Dog and Badger. They made no attempt to keep it a secret that she had slept at Nathan's again, and worked in his house every day.

There had been no word from Leo. It seemed that he had returned to the forge and helped his uncle finish the project they had been working on together. Then he had gone, leaving Cuttingbeck with no word to his uncle, and certainly not to his wife, as to where he could be found should the need arise.

Rhea worked herself to a standstill, refusing to give in to the intense unhappiness that gripped her. If only, she brooded constantly, she were able to pick up her bags and walk away as easily as she had entered the village, and Leo Dower's life. But with so much work to do, so many people eagerly awaiting her products, she could not bring herself to let them down. Which meant she was tied to the place until the last order had been fulfilled.

Besides, she was beginning to suspect that something was happening to her, something that she must at all costs keep to herself. Then her suspicions were confirmed and the restraint she had imposed on her emotions, her feelings for Leo, broke down. When she confided her news to Carrie, who was chatting to her one evening in her room, she burst into tears and sobbed her heart out.

The irony of the situation was almost too much to bear. Leo had married her to protect, as he thought, his brother's child, and now she really was expecting a baby, who was indubitably his, he was—and there was no doubt in Rhea's mind—in the process of preparing to divorce her.

'Tell him,' Carrie urged, 'tell Leo about the baby.'

'And have him stay married to me out of pity? Never,' Rhea asserted, wiping her eyes. She had to tell Carrie... 'He thinks I'm having an affair with Nathan.'

Carrie looked horrified. 'You're n—— I mean... Oh, Rhea, are you?'

'How could you think that of me?' Rhea protested. 'You of all people!' Carrie said over and over again that she was sorry she'd ever asked the question. 'Of course I like Nathan. He's a good man, and I know you'll be very happy.'

'Tell Leo,' Carrie urged, 'tell him about Nathan and me.'

'But you want to keep it a secret, you said. Anyway, it wouldn't do any good. Shall I tell you the real reason Leo married me?' Rhea explained the situation that led up to Leo's proposal. 'So you see, our marriage was only ever meant to be a temporary affair. It had to end some time.'

'But with a baby coming?' Carrie exclaimed.

'If I tell him, I'll be stopping him from getting together again—that is, if he ever parted from her—with the woman he really wants in his life, Sonya Selby.'

At the Dog and Badger next day, Nathan gave the order at the bar counter while Rhea looked around for a seat. Timmy, tucked away into a corner, waved to her, and she joined him.

'How are you, lass?' he asked. 'Where have you been keeping yourself? Leo's in London. I've got a letter from him for you—it came this morning. Here.'

With a shaking hand, Rhea opened the envelope as Timmy added, 'He's attending a conference—Dower Corporation. He's the chief executive, took over from his father. But I told you, didn't I?'

Rhea nodded, then read the letter. 'Dear Rhea,' it ran, 'there are matters I wish to discuss with you. Is it possible for you to come to my hotel,' he gave the address, 'on Monday next?' The date and time were stated. 'If you cannot make this appointment, please inform my secretary at Dower Corporation's head office. Timmy will give you the address. Yours, Leo.'

Her hands, with the letter, fell to her lap. The impersonal tone, the legal proceedings to come—in other words, the first steps towards a divorce, implicit in its formal language, had knocked her sideways.

Nathan stood waiting at the bar, chatting to a friend.

'You look so pale, Rhea,' Timmy remarked worriedly, squeezing her arm. 'What's Leo said that's upset you so?'

Rhea shook her head. 'He just wants to see me, that's all. At the hotel he's staying at in London.' *That's all*? she thought. That's it, more likely, the end of something that had no real beginning.

'Will you go?' She nodded. 'Tell me, lass—don't answer if you don't want to. Do you love him?'

She had to tell this kindly man the truth. 'Uncle Timmy, I'm . . . there's going to be——'

'A *babby*?' His eyes lit up, his hand covered hers on the table. 'I can't tell you how . . . I was so sad when you told me before that there wasn't going to be any child.'

'Promise you won't tell Leo,' she pleaded urgently.

'But he must be told, lass.'

'No, no! He'd insist on our marriage going on, and it can't, not now. He doesn't trust me. He might even say it wasn't——'

'His? But it is,' Timmy broke in. 'You wouldn't be unfaithful to any man, lass. I'm years older than him and I can tell, I can judge a woman's character.'

'Thanks for believing in me, Uncle Timmy. But there's someone else in Leo's life, if not mine.'

'You don't mean Sonya? No, no, lass. He'd never . . .' But Timmy's voice tailed off uncertainly.

'Hi, Timmy,' Nathan said, setting down the drinks and the food. 'Sorry for the delay, Rhea, but they're very busy today. How are things going, Timmy? I hear Leo's gone back to London. I guess he'll return to Cuttingbeck. Can't keep away long from the forge, can he? That young man you've got to help you, is he OK?'

'Coming on nicely, Nathan,' Timmy answered. 'Shows a lot of promise.' To Rhea's relief, the conversation changed course, and she was able to re-read Leo's letter.

It was strange being back in the metropolis. The noise level hit her first, then the milling crowds, the straight, tense faces. The moors, the streams, she realised, the friendly people she had left behind had become so much part of her that, in these packed and uninterested streets, she felt lost.

The taxi dropped her at the hotel and she entered through automatic doors, hoping Leo would be there to greet her. There was no sign of him, and she wandered a little aimlessly around the foyer, pausing by the fountain, watching the spray. She was taken right back to River Cottage and the stream which wound its way past it. A voice that was so familiar it tied her thoughts into knots brought her swiftly back to her surroundings, her heart thumping loudly enough to deafen her.

Leo stood, tall and commanding, the focal point of a semi-circle of attentive people. They hung on his every word, nodding now and then, laughing as he made a final joke, dismissing them.

The man from whom they deferentially took their leave was not the man Rhea had grown to know and love. This man, immaculately dressed, his manner smoothly courteous, was a stranger. Only his hair had defied the grooming procedure the rest of him had consented to, and his eyes too... his eyes which swung towards her as if pulled by some invisible magnet.

He took in her suit, navy blue with a touch of scarlet and a blouse to match. The formal outfit had been intentional. Hadn't he phrased his letter as if this meeting were to be an interview?

As he moved, long-limbed and aloof, towards her, she was for a few seconds denied the ability to breathe. Those eyes, steely grey and piercing, that she had first seen in the semi-darkness of the forge, played over her, tearing her apart.

She wished she had never come, never left the vast silence of the moors, the village that had become part of her.

'I'm glad you made it.' His hand came out—he was actually going to shake her hand as if she were a passing acquaintance? His hand felt cool and firm, with decision and no nonsense in its brief pressure. And not a hint of warmth or friendship, let alone love.

At least, she tried to console herself, it was a way of touching him, the only way from now on in which any form of physical contact could be made. Divorce meant just that, a breaking of every bond that tied them to each other.

No, she thought, looking into his implacable face, that wasn't true, because she had something of him inside her that she could keep for ever—his child.

'I've booked a table,' he was saying. 'Will you have a drink while we make a selection from the menu?'

A drink in the circumstances was what she needed, but how could she tell him the reason for her request for fruit juice?

'Nothing alcoholic?' Eyebrows high, he shrugged.

A waiter took their order, then Leo gave her his attention.

'How's Cuttingbeck?' he asked, tracing with his finger the reflections on the glass table-top. Could he, in his mind's eye, see the village there? Empty, she wanted to answer, without you. Lonely at night, even the river seems tearful as it flows through the darkness.

'Fine,' she answered aloud.

'And your work?'

'Thriving.' Did she have to sound so falsely cheerful? 'Your uncle Timmy—yes, he's fine too, but he's—I think he's missing you.' Oh, God, she thought, how long could she keep up the pretence of cheerfulness?

'I can't see why. He's got an apprentice working for him.'

'He's your uncle, for heaven's sake! There is such a thing as family affection.' Those eyebrows rose again and the irritation in her voice took even Rhea by surprise. It was the result, she knew, of keeping such a tight rein on her emotions.

At Leo's elbow a waiter cleared his throat. 'Your table is ready, sir, madam.'

As the meal progressed, the small talk dried up. Over coffee in the lounge, he leaned back against the sofa they shared, away from her.

'Before we——' He seemed to feel the need to drain his cup, putting it down. 'Before we can get on with living our separate lives,' he resumed, 'there are matters we must discuss.'

Rhea nodded, even though she felt her insides were being put through a shredding machine.

'You told me not so long ago,' he remarked, 'that the one thing you would like to do was to start your own business.'

'I did, but, even though I said it, I knew it would be impossible. I'd need capital, which I haven't got——'

'I'd provide that capital.'

'You? Oh, you mean as a kind of settlement after the divorce?' Her voice sounded brittle even to her own ears. She had to think quickly. Any money that came her way she would need for the baby's welfare. 'Thanks,' was her cautious answer, 'but I——'

'It's money you can't turn down. I've had some research carried out, with Jerome's reluctant help, into the amount of cash he took from your father's firm, therefore from your inheritance. I intend paying that money back to you. The car he stole from you is luckily still intact and well preserved. That also will be returned to you for you to use however you wish. If it were to be sold, the cash could be added to the lump sum I intend paying you.'

Rhea was shaking her head. 'I couldn't take it from you, Leo. I'd written that money off long ago.'

He sat forward, his hands clasped. 'Will you stop acting the hypocrite?' he grated. 'From the beginning I've been aware that you married me only for what I could give you. OK, so Jerome's non-existent child was not the reason, which by elimination left only one thing, your eyes on my bank account. Now our marriage has, as they say, come to the end of its useful life, you collect. I'm freed from an unproductive relationship——'

Unproductive? Rhea thought. I'd laugh hysterically if I weren't on the brink of tears.

'And you'll be free to pursue your affair with Nathan Oxley to whatever end you had in mind.'

'Also,' she had to say it, 'you'll be able to marry Sonya Selby.'

'I have no wish to marry Sonya Selby.'

'And *I* don't want to marry Nathan Oxley!'

Eyebrows raised, Leo smiled without amusement. 'Quits. Snap. Tell me, Rhea, because I'm curious about it. Why not? No, I know the answer already. He's a struggling potter, living hand to mouth. He doesn't earn enough to keep you as I've been able to keep you.'

She had heard that pre-divorce discussions were usually acrimonious, but surely none had been as bitter as this!

She jumped to her feet. 'Thank you for the meal, but you can keep your money. I wouldn't touch a penny, a *cent* of the Dower brothers' money!'

Her footsteps took her towards the swing doors. Leo's arm linked with hers like newly forged chains and he swung her round. 'Come to my room.'

'Not on your——'

Grimly he walked her towards the door which led to the hotel's residential wing. Other guests turned idly, hoping for a scene to brighten their day. Rhea calmed her anger until Leo's key turned and she was in his room, facing him.

'I want to get one thing clear,' she declared, giving rein now to her anger. 'I did not, *did not*——'

'Calm down!' Taking her by surprise, he peeled off her jacket, throwing it aside. 'I intend this to be a civilised conversation.' He walked away, and she made for the door, but he was there before her, turning and pocketing the key.

He removed his own jacket and pushed his hands into his trouser pockets. 'Our marriage was never meant to last. Agreed?'

No, no, she wanted to shout, I don't agree. Cold reason kept her silent. This aloof, distant-eyed man was a total stranger and she wanted to shake him to bring back the man she had known, wielding a hammer, forming a red-hot piece of metal into the shape he desired.

'Agreed,' she answered levelly.

'Right. I'm ready now to free you, so that you can go your own way, marry the man you really want——'

'What man? Can't you understand?' she cried. 'There's no chance that I'll marry Nathan. Ever.' Should she tell? She had been given permission. 'He's engaged to be married—to Caroline Adley. When his own affairs have been straightened out, they'll marry.'

It was as if Leo had been turned to stone.

'Are you telling me that being married to me has caused you to lose Nathan Oxley?'

'*Lose* him? How could I, when I never *had* him? All right, so I slept at his place. That rumour, as repeated in your presence by Jerome, was right in that respect. But where it went wrong was in deducing that I slept *with* Nathan. I didn't, but Carrie did. As a result of which, they became engaged.'

'So?'

'OK, so I'll confess the rest. Then perhaps you'll let me go.' Rhea took a breath. After this, it really would be the end of everything between them. 'You may or may not appreciate that I couldn't face staying at River Cottage after you'd gone, so I tried to reserve a room at Carrie and Vincent Adley's. They were fully booked at that time, so I slept at Nathan's place for two or three nights.'

Leo looked as grim as she thought he might. Bravely she went on,

'Then I moved into Adley Guesthouse. Which brings my confessions up to date. What about you, Leo?' She looked about her. It was a better than average hotel room, well appointed and comfortable. 'When's Sonya coming to join you? Or perhaps you've told her to go shopping until you've settled matters with me——'

Like lightning he moved, and his hand over her mouth did two things—it stopped her talking and started her body throbbing in the old familiar aching way. She *had* to break free, otherwise she would break down, but he plainly had no intention of letting her go.

His hands were on her shoulders now, biting through the blouse. 'Tell me something. When I made love to you, which man were you fantasising that I was—Jerome or Oxley?'

It was too much! Rhea tore away, reaching for her jacket, pulling it on, with shaking hands smoothing her hair. 'Will you start divorce proceedings, please?' she managed in tolerably even tones.

'Oh, no. I leave that *privilege* to you.'

'But I w-wouldn't know h-how to.'

'Easy. Appoint yourself a lawyer. He'll do the rest.'

They faced each other, his eyes coated with frost, hers brimming with tears. 'Before I go,' she said hoarsely, 'I have to thank you for—for everything. Taking me in, giving me a roof while my injured foot healed. For giving me the shelter of your name when you thought I— thought I——'

She couldn't go on, because now she was, *she was*. The tears spilled over. She searched madly for a handkerchief in the depths of her bag and scrubbed her face.

'I d-didn't finish my confession,' she admitted chokily. 'Since we met, there's never been any other man be-sides—besides——'

'Who? Besides who?' Leo's eyes blazed into hers. 'Tell me, *tell me*!'

She simply had to, if she didn't want to be shaken to pieces. 'You,' she whispered. 'No one else but you.'

There was a smothered exclamation, and the powerful embrace that engulfed her felt so familiar and wonderful that she wanted to cry and laugh at the same time. The heart that she felt had been torn from her when those loving arms had turned cold and ceased to hold her had been restored to her body.

'Get this into that beautiful head of yours, Mrs Dower,' Leo decreed autocratically. 'There's not going to be a divorce, not you from me, nor I from you. Do—you—understand?' Then she was drawn into a kiss that interfered shockingly with her breathing processes, and went on and on until she gasped for mercy.

None was shown, but she didn't mind at all. Nor did she protest when she was lifted to the bed and a body that she loved beyond words joined her there.

'Oh, Leo, darling,' she whispered, 'please be careful.'

'Why?' he murmured, concentrating on caressing with his lips and tongue the burgeoning breasts that he had uncovered by unfastening her blouse.

'We—we mustn't,' she gasped, stroking the back of his head feverishly, 'hurt the baby.'

He lifted his head, eyes alight with astonishment and wonder. 'Repeat that, Rhea Dower, slowly and carefully, so that I can take it in.'

She did as he had commanded, twice more, her eyes filled again, this time with tears of happiness.

'When?' he asked, lying on his side and stroking her stomach with reverent hands which had stormed the waistband of her skirt and invaded it.

'When did it happen? Oh, Leo, I can't think with you doing that!' His laugh was a gloating growl and he went on with his onslaught on her senses. 'That—that last night, I think.' She arched beneath his possessive hands. 'Please, Leo, wait, don't...' He paused for a fraction of a second. 'That last night I thought you'd taken precautions...'

'And I thought you had.'

'I'd forgotten. You'd shown so little interest in me that way that I'm afraid I lapsed.'

He pretended to be shocked at her oversight. 'Want the truth?' She nodded. 'I had to keep away from you, otherwise I'd have been making love to you every time I saw you. As it was, I could barely keep to my own room at night.'

'After—after that last time,' she massaged his shoulders beneath his unfastened shirt, 'where did you disappear to? It wasn't—tell me it wasn't to——?'

'My God, it wasn't to Sonya's. If you must know,' even now his eyes turned grim, 'I walked across the moors until I was exhausted, then slept in a barn at Timmy's place. He never knew. Nor did Jerome, who was sleeping there. Want to know why?' He held her to him as if she were made of priceless porcelain. 'I could hardly bear the thought of you gone from my life. My conscience told me I had to let you go, to lead your own life with the man of your choice...'

'But, darling,' she whispered huskily, 'the man of my choice had walked out on me, and to me it seemed as if the world had come to an end. Especially when it was confirmed about the baby.'

'My God, we've been fools! The baby. Wait till Timmy knows! He was shattered last time when he knew there wasn't going to be another Dower making an appearance on the scene.'

'I knew that, but he does know, Leo,' she answered happily, 'and he was delighted.'

'You told him before you told me?'

Rhea tried to straighten out the frown between his brows. 'I just had to tell someone. I thought you'd be annoyed and accuse me of trying to keep you. I thought—really thought it was Sonya you wanted.'

'Now I'll tell you the truth. Once Sonya was in my life. But even before I met you, she'd gone out of it. She helps Timmy and me with the office work. She came with me on my business jaunts to do likewise.'

'And in between, she's a designer?'

'She is. I make up some of her work in metal. Which is the only reason she's there sometimes. Talking of the forge, the moment I saw you——'

'No, no, that's my line,' she broke in mischievously. 'The moment I saw *you* I fell in love with you.'

'—standing in the doorway,' Leo continued, trailing his hand down her thighs, 'I knew you were the one for me. I'd found the only woman with whom I'd want to spend the rest of my life,' he added with a long and lingering kiss.

'You fell in love with *me*?' she asked, surfacing from it at last.

'I did. Oh, yes, I most certainly did. Which, to be totally honest with you, as you've been with me, is why I married you. OK?'

'OK,' she repeated, her eyes shining. 'But suppose I'd really been expecting Jerome's child?'

'If he hadn't wanted it, I'd have adopted it as my own. Now do you see how much I loved you?'

A long time later, as they sat on a low sofa in each other's arms, Leo asked, lips to her ear, 'Tell me, how does revenge taste now?'

'Very, very sweet,' she answered, lifting her face for his kiss. 'Not like revenge at all.'

'How about—like this?' he growled, carrying her back to the bed and making love to her all over again.

...

Jennifer Taylor was born in Liverpool, England, and still lives in the North-West, several miles outside the city. Books have always been a passion of hers, so it seemed natural to choose a career in librarianship, a wise decision as the library was where she met her husband, Bill. Twenty years and two children later, they are still happily married, and she is still working in the library, with the added bonus that she has discovered how challenging and enjoyable writing romantic fiction can be!

GUILTY OF
LOVE

BY
JENNIFER TAYLOR

M I L L S & B O O N L I M I T E D
ETON HOUSE, 18-24 PARADISE ROAD
RICHMOND, SURREY TW9 1SR

First published in Great Britain in 1992 by Mills & Boon Limited

© Jennifer Taylor 1992

Australian copyright 1992 Philippine copyright 1992 This edition 1992

ISBN 0 263 77518 6

Set in Times Roman 11 on 12 pt. 06-9208-51429 C

Made and printed in Great Britain

CHAPTER ONE

'I'M SORRY, Miss Campbell, but I'm sure you can appreciate the bank's concern. Payments on the loan are already three months behind, and I'm afraid there is no way that we can allow things to continue like this. Have you any idea when you will be in a position to bring your account up to date?'

Alex glanced down at her hands, clasping them tightly in her lap so that they wouldn't tremble and betray her nervousness. Ever since the letter requesting her to make an appointment with the manager at the bank had arrived two long days before, she'd been living on a knife-edge, wondering how she would answer that simple question. Yet now that it had been asked, and Mr Simpson was waiting for an answer, she still had no clear idea what to say. If only the nest-egg Mother had left them were still intact there would have been no problem, but Kenny's antics over the past couple of years had put paid to that!

Just for a moment anger at the foolish way her brother had behaved rose hotly inside her before determinedly she pushed it from her mind. Berating Kenny would achieve nothing, as it never did. What she had to concentrate on was finding some way to persuade the bank to give her a bit of breathing-space. She'd worked too hard to get Little Gems up on its feet to sit back now and watch it stagger to its knees. She would find the money to make up the missing payments somehow . . . she would!

'Frankly, Mr Simpson, I don't see that there is that much of a problem. Oh, I know there are three payments outstanding, but in terms of hard cash it is a small amount compared to the turnover the shop is doing.' Her tone was perfect—cool, faintly amused, as though she couldn't quite understand why the bank should be making such a fuss over something so trivial; but it appeared that Mr Simpson wasn't going to fall in line quite as she'd hoped.

'Agreed, Miss Campbell, but I have your statements here for the past quarter's trading and, although as you say the shop is producing a healthy turnover, your outgoings have tended to outweigh your credits quite considerably.'

He passed a printed sheet across the desk, but Alex had no need to read the neatly totalled columns of figures. She knew to a penny how much money she'd paid out over the past few months, knew also that there was no way it could continue when she was already experiencing difficulty in paying suppliers.

Although she designed and made the more expensive items of jewellery which gave the shop its edge over competitors, it was the cheaper lines she bought in from the wholesalers which were her bread and butter. Still, now that she had finally managed to pay off Kenny's gambling debts, she should be able to plough all the profit back into the business. With Christmas and all the extra trade it brought just a couple of months away, she should be able to reverse the losses and catch up on the payments.

'You're quite right, Mr Simpson. I have had rather a lot of expenditure recently, but I assure you that won't need to continue. I know it's asking a lot, but if the bank would give me a few weeks' grace, then I am confident that I can catch up on the missing payments.'

'Well...' Mr Simpson hesitated, obviously torn between a desire to help and a need to safeguard the bank's interests, and Alex decided to give him a little push in the right direction. Leaning forwards across the desk, she gave him her most radiant smile, her blue eyes soft and luminous.

'Please, Mr Simpson. I know it has been most remiss of me to let this happen, but I'm certain that, with your... the bank's help, I can sort everything out.'

'I—er——' Obviously deeply affected by both the smile and the softly beguiling tone, he ran a finger round inside his collar, his face a trifle flushed. Alex tried hard not to gloat as she sat back in her seat. She'd learned at a very tender age that even the strongest men tended to weaken when she looked at them with that helpless little gaze. She might be a modern woman, well able to take care of herself in most situations, but what was the point in being female if one didn't make use of one's natural assets? She only had to glance in a mirror to know that with her long blonde hair curling softly round her face and her huge blue eyes she looked delicate and helpless. It was by the way that she was actually neither one of those!

Mr Simpson cleared his throat, obviously making an effort to get himself in hand. 'You really should have come to me the very minute you knew you had a problem, Miss Campbell. We could have worked something out. You must never forget that I—I mean, the bank—is here to help, my dear.'

Alex nearly choked as she swallowed the chuckle of laughter his words evoked, trying to imagine staid Mr Simpson's reaction if she had gone to him for advice... on how to pay off the thugs who were threatening to put Kenny six feet under for welshing on his gambling debts! Still, the offer had been kindly meant, and she was grateful.

'I shall remember that, Mr Simpson. Thank you. However, I do want to assure you that this won't happen again.'

'I'm sure it won't, Miss Campbell. Frankly, I was most surprised when your account was brought to my attention. You have always handled your business in an exemplary manner up to now, and it is for that reason that I shall recommend to head office that we should give you a further three months to make up the back payments.' He glanced at his desk diary. 'Let's say the end of January, shall we?'

'That would be marvellous. Thank you,' Alex said quickly, mentally totting up figures. By her reckonings she should just do it... if she didn't spend an extra penny, or even *think* about celebrating Christmas! Damn Kenny! He was old enough to know better, and this was the last time she would ever bail him out!

She left the bank, turning up the collar of her thick cherry-red coat as she hurried through the throngs of shoppers. It was market day, and Ormskirk was busy under an early October sky, but she bypassed the tempting array of goods. There would be no money over to spend on anything but necessities for the next few months, which was annoying when the shop had been doing so well of late. Now it would be at least a year before she could get it back on to a solid footing. When would Kenny ever learn to control his impulsive behaviour? He might be her twin, but sometimes she felt years older than him. Thank heavens he had managed to hang on to his job at Lang's at least. A couple of months back, when he'd had that run-in with Jordan Lang, the owner of the company, she'd thought he'd blown it; but he'd been lucky. Lang had quite uncharacteristically let him off the hook with just a severe warning. Now they would need every penny Kenny earned as well as what she could make from the shop to pay off this debt. This was definitely the last time she was going to risk everything to save his skin!

The rest of the day passed swiftly enough. There was a steady flow of customers in the shop, and Alex took two more orders for her special lines—one for the topaz scarf-clip, which had recently been featured in one of the leading fashion magazines, and one for her aquamarine waterfall earrings. Although she had made both designs several times before, each item would be slightly different when it was finished, ensuring a degree of individuality. It was the thing which made her jewellery so sought after both in the town and further afield. Every week a percentage of what she made was earmarked for one of the large London stores which were now commissioning her on a regular basis. It had taken years of hard work to get her to this point on the ladder, and there was no way she was prepared to slip down a rung or two. She would find the money to pay the bank what she owed even if it meant starving in the proverbial garret!

By the time she locked up the shop, she could feel her head humming with tension. She set the alarms, then walked through the workroom and up the stairs to the flat she shared with Kenny. Lang's was situated on the other side of town, on the outskirts of Southport, so it would be another hour or more before Kenny made it through the rush-hour traffic. Maybe she would take a couple of aspirin and lie down for a while before starting on supper. She wanted a clear head tonight to make Kenny realise exactly what he had to do to help get them out of this mess he'd created!

She awoke slowly, groaning as her cramped muscles ached in protest when she sat up. Everywhere was dark, and for a moment she felt strangely disorientated until she realised that she must have dozed off on the living-room sofa. She struggled to her feet, and switched on the light, gasping in shock as she caught sight of the figure slumped in the chair.

'Kenny! Lord above, but you gave me a fright! Why didn't you wake me when you got in? What time is it?' Rubbing the sleep from her eyes, she glanced at her watch. 'Seven o'clock! I must have been more tired than I thought. I'll go and make a start on supper because you and I have some serious talking to do tonight.'

She started for the kitchen, her footsteps slowing when she became aware of the unnatural silence in the room. She glanced around, her eyes going immediately to her brother's face, and something in his expression made her go cold in apprehension.

'What is it, Kenny? What's happened?'

He jumped at the harsh note in her voice, and just for an instant he met her eyes, before dropping his gaze back to the carpet. Alex felt the apprehension turn to fear. How many times had she seen that expression on his face when he'd got himself into some scrape or another? She'd lost count, just as she'd lost count of the number of times she'd bailed him out. But not now, please heaven, not now, when everything was so finely balanced. All it would take now was just one little push and they would be hurtling towards disaster!

On leaden legs she walked back across the room and sat down again. 'Just tell me what's happened, Kenny,' she ordered a shade more gently.

'I'm sorry, Lexie, really I am. I didn't plan it. You've got to believe me.'

'Didn't plan what?' She grasped his hands and shook him roughly. 'Listen, Kenny, you have to get a grip on yourself and tell me what you've done, otherwise I won't be able to help you.'

He laughed, a harsh, rasping sound which echoed round the room and made Alex wince. 'I don't think you can this time. I don't think anyone can!'

'Don't be so melodramatic,' she ordered sharply, feeling her stomach lurch at the absolute conviction in his voice. 'It can't be that bad. What have you done?'

'Taken the blueprints for the new engine.'

'The blueprints...? No!' She leapt to her feet, seeing the betraying, guilty colour flood Kenny's face. 'Why? Why did you do such a stupid thing?'

He shrugged, his mouth taking on a sulky line of defiance. 'I didn't plan on doing it. It just sort of happened. I was in old Morgan's office. You know him, the chief designer on the project. He's the one who got me into all that trouble a couple of months back by reporting me to Jordan Lang for talking about the project in the pub. Anyway, I was in his office collecting some data sheets when Morgan was called away. All that talk about the need for security, and that dressing down I got from Lang! That's a laugh! Morgan just walked out of that office without a thought for locking the safe. I could see the blueprints lying there and, well, I don't know. It was just an impulse to take them, I guess. I thought it would teach them all a lesson, and make them realise that anyone can make a mistake.'

'Oh, Kenny, how could you?'

Alex sank weakly down on to the chair, scarcely able to believe what she was hearing. Kenny should have learned his lesson from the last time, when Jordan Lang had hauled him over the coals and threatened him with immediate dismissal if anything else happened; and everyone in the district knew that Lang didn't make threats idly! He ran the engineering company with an iron hand, permitting no quarter to anyone who crossed him. She could understand only too well why Kenny was looking so shaken. The pity was he hadn't stopped to think about what he was doing sooner!

'I'm sorry, Lexie. I know it was a stupid thing to do, but it was just an impulse. Oh, maybe I did have some vague idea at the back of my mind about taking the plans to one of our competitors, and seeing what they'd be willing to pay for them—but that was all it was…a vague idea, even though God knows we need the money.'

'Not that much we don't! Don't you realise how serious this is? It's industrial espionage! You could go to prison for this, Kenny!'

'I know, I know. I must have been mad to even think about it. I realised how crazy it was once I'd had a chance to think things through, but it was too late by then to put the blueprints back. Morgan had left on some sort of urgent business, and his office was all locked up. I suppose in one way I was lucky he did go shooting off and never had time to notice the plans were missing.'

'But what are you going to do now?' Alex asked, trying desperately to stay calm, although it was difficult. Kenny had been in some scrapes in his time, but never anything as serious as this.

'I'll have to put the prints back somehow. If Jordan Lang finds out they're missing, then it won't just be a question of calling the police, believe me. The man's barely civilised when it comes to the well-being of his precious company! He would want his revenge to be far more personal!'

A shudder rippled through Kenny's spare frame at the thought of his formidable employer. He glanced up, a beseeching expression on his strained face. 'You've got to help me, Lexie. You're the only one I can turn to now!'

'How? Even if I agree to try, which I haven't, how can I help?'

Kenny bent down, pulled a long roll of paper from under the chair, and laid it on the coffee-table between them. Alex stared at it in silence, according it the same disgusted fascination she might have a rattlesnake, only she had the nasty feeling that this innocuous roll of paper could prove to be far more dangerous.

'It's simple, really. I've got it all worked out, and I'm sure we can do it.' Kenny adopted the soothing tone she recognised only too well, and Alex steeled herself for the punch line she knew was coming. 'All you have to do is help me put them back tonight before Lang finds out they are missing.'

No! She wanted to scream the word aloud, to shout her refusal so that there could be no misunderstanding; but it was impossible. The bond between her and Kenny was far too strong for her to ever refuse to help him.

The wind was bitter, knifing through the thick folds of the leather flying-jacket and jeans Kenny had insisted she should wear. Turning up the collar of the jacket, Alex huddled down into its fleecy warmth, feeling her stomach churning as though she were on a roller-coaster.

'Right, that should do it. The security staff should be going for their meal-break around now, leaving just one man on duty at the front door. Time to go.'

Pulling the sleeve of his jacket back down over his watch, Kenny re-started the motorbike, then shot Alex a worried look. 'Now, are you sure you know what to do?'

She nodded, not trusting herself to speak because her teeth were chattering, and hearing such indisputable evidence of her fear would make her feel worse than ever.

'Good girl. I know you can do it, Sis, and I give you my word this will be the last time I drag you into anything like this.'

He reached out and gave her trembling fingers a quick squeeze, then swung the motorbike through the gates leading to the factory, and drove steadily along the drive. Alex counted to ten, as he'd instructed her to do, then hurried after him, keeping to the shadows and praying that Kenny had been right in his assessment that anyone looking out of the windows would focus on the bright glare from the bike's headlamp and not on her. As quickly as she could she took up her position behind some bushes close to the front doors of the factory, then waved to Kenny to indicate she was ready, watching with thumping heart as he rang the bell to summon the security guard.

'Evening, Sid. Sorry to bother you, but can you let me into the office? I think I must have left my wallet behind because I can't seem to find it anywhere.'

Kenny sounded relaxed enough, but Alex could see the betraying tension in the set of his body, and held her breath. So much depended on his ability to convince the guard.

'Well, I don't know, Kenny. I'd like to help you, of course, but you know yourself how Lang has tightened up on security over the past couple of

months. I don't know if I dare risk it. He'd have
my guts for garters if he ever found out I'd gone
against his instructions. You know what he can be
like!'

There was no mistaking Sid's reluctance, and
Alex didn't know whether to be relieved or sorry.
Obviously he was just as wary of the formidable
Jordan Lang as Kenny was, and suddenly she wasn't
so certain that entering the building was the wisest
thing to do. If Jordan Lang ever found out about
it, then there wasn't even the slimmest chance that
he would view it as two wrongs making one nice,
tidy right! However, obviously Kenny didn't share
her sudden doubts.

'I understand, Sid. I never should have asked and
put you on the spot like that. Forget it. I'll manage
somehow. Pity, though; I had been going to try that
little place out in Burscough you've been telling me
about. There's this girl, you see, rather special, and
I   thought...   Never   mind.   I'm   sure   she'll
understand.'

Kenny half turned to go, his shoulders slumped
in dejection, and, if Alex hadn't known what an
accomplished actor he could be when he chose to,
she would have felt sorry for him herself. It was
little wonder that poor old Sid fell for it hook, line
and sinker!

'Hang on there, Kenny, son. I don't want to spoil
your night. I'll let you in just this once, but make
sure no one gets to hear about it. I'll get the sack
if Lang ever finds out!'

'You can rely on me, Sid. He won't find out. I
can guarantee it!'

The voices faded, and Alex slumped against the wall in a state midway between elation and despair. It seemed that part one of the Great Master Plan was up and running just as Kenny had predicted; now there was nothing standing in the way of part two... and *that* was where she came in!

Forcing herself to stay calm, she settled down to wait, blowing on her hands to warm her numbed fingers before tucking them under her arms to retain a meagre bit of warmth. The blueprints tucked inside her jacket crackled, poking uncomfortably through the soft folds of her sweater to scratch her skin, and she wriggled uncomfortably. It was hard to imagine that a few sheets of paper were worth so much that a man would go to almost any lengths to ensure their safety, but the fear she'd heard in Kenny's voice when he'd spoken of Jordan Lang had been matched by that she'd just heard in Sid's. 'Barely civilised' was how Kenny had described the man. At the time Alex had taken little notice of the remark, but now, standing hidden in the bushes outside the factory, she felt a shiver ripple down her spine which owed little to the biting cold. All she could hope was that she would never have occasion to see if that description matched!

'For heaven's sake, Lexie, stop daydreaming! Come on.'

Alex jumped when she heard her brother hiss her name in an anxious whisper. She fought her way free of the prickly den, and hurried into the building, blinking in the bright glare of the foyer lights.

'Now hurry up. Sid's checking the cloakroom for my wallet, but we haven't got long. I told him I would just run downstairs and phone you to see if you'd found it at home.' He reached across the reception desk and unhooked a key, pressing it into her trembling fingers. 'This is the key to Morgan's office. Remember what I told you: second floor, fifth door along on the right. Just leave the blueprints on the desk, and he'll think he forgot to put them away before he left, and be too embarrassed to say anything.'

'And how do I get out again? You won't be able to keep Sid upstairs much longer.' She glanced round the brightly lit foyer, her whole body shaking with an attack of nerves. She wasn't cut out for this kind of thing; she really wasn't. She was a jeweller, not some kind of cat burglar!

'There's no problem about that. After you've left the prints, go straight along the corridor, and you'll see a fire exit. It's never locked as it can only be opened from the inside. I'll meet you back by the front gate. Piece of cake, really, when you think about it!'

Obviously Kenny's confidence was returning, but Alex just glared at him. 'Piece of cake' indeed! However, now was not the time to debate the point, much as she'd like to. She ran towards the stairs, her soft-soled trainers making little sound on the marble flooring. As fast as she could she made her way up to the second level, then ran along the corridor counting doors until she arrived at the fifth. Just for a moment she hesitated, aware that until she actually unlocked that door she hadn't really committed a crime, then, with a shrug of resignation, slipped the key into the lock. There was no going back now. It was her future at stake as much as Kenny's.

The room was in darkness, and Alex waited until she had closed the door before snapping on the torch she'd brought with her. Swinging the beam around the room to get her bearings, she spotted the desk and hurried towards it, unzipping the front of her jacket to pull out the blueprints. They were very creased from being squashed inside the coat, and she tried to smooth them out, cursing softly when some of the rolls of paper slid out from the middle. Hands shaking, she bent down and un-furled the whole roll to fit the section back into place, then felt herself go cold with shock when the door opened abruptly and the light was switched on.

It was hard to say who was the most surprised, Alex or the tall, dark-haired man who'd just en-tered the room; but it wasn't hard to say who re-covered first. Alex stood up slowly, her eyes huge in her ashen face as she watched the surprise turn to something else, something which made her knees turn to water. All of a sudden she understood exactly what Kenny had meant, and she felt her heart start to hammer in a sickening heavy rhythm.

With his face all hard angles, his grey eyes glit-tering, and a strange little twist to his lips, there was nothing civilised about Jordan Lang at all!

The sharp click of the lock sounded loud as gunfire in the silence. Alex jumped then shrank back as Jordan Lang closed the door and came further into the room, stopping just a few feet away from her. Slowly he let his gaze run over her from top to toe, then smiled, a slow curving of his lips which did little to quell her mounting fear.

'So... what have we here?'

His voice was low, holding a note of quiet menace which was far more scary than any show of anger might have been, and Alex felt a cold shudder tiptoe its way down her spine.

'Cat got your tongue, then, or have you decided it might be wiser to wait and see what I intend to do before you speak?' He laughed harshly, and Alex shrank back a little further so that she could feel the coldness of the wall against her back. 'That's the hundred-dollar question, isn't it? What am I going to do now? I suppose that depends on your story. So come along; help me decide what I should do next.'

He stood and watched her, one dark brow raised in mocking enquiry, and Alex ran the tip of her tongue over her parched lips while she tried desperately to think up a reason to explain her presence in the office.

'I'm still waiting,' he prompted, almost gently, but one glance at his expression was enough to convince her that being gentle was the furthest thing from Jordan Lang's mind! She swallowed hard, forcing some moisture down her parched throat, her voice strained and raspy when she finally spoke.

'I guess it does seem odd, my being here.'

'Very odd,' he said drily, his eyes catching hers and holding them in his gaze. 'But I'm sure you must have some sort of an explanation for your visit.'

'Of course I have.' She looked away, staring down at the carpet, looking anywhere but into those cold grey eyes.

'Then don't be shy. I can hardly wait to hear it.' He folded his arms across his chest and rested a hip against the edge of the desk, his expression one of cruel mockery, which spurred her into speech.

'It isn't what you think,' she began desperately.

'No? But how can you be sure of that? I mean, I haven't said a word about what I think you're doing here, so how do you know what my views are?'

'It's quite obvious! You think I came here to-night to steal, but you're wrong... quite wrong!'

'Then I suggest you set me right, and tell my why you *are* here.' He glanced at the wafer-thin gold watch strapped to his wrist, then back at her, his grey eyes hard and uncompromising. 'It seems late to be in the office on legitimate business, but I'm prepared to give you the benefit of the doubt and listen to your story.'

He sounded almost reasonable, but one glance at the cold condemnation in his eyes told another story, and Alex felt her temper rise. He had found her guilty in his own mind without even waiting to hear any explanation she might give; but there was no way she was going to stand here and let him class her as a thief!

'I don't like how your mind works, Mr Lang! I'm no thief. I came here tonight to put... to put——' She stopped abruptly, suddenly realising what she'd been about to do. How could she tell the truth and save herself, yet implicate Kenny? She fell silent, and saw his eyes narrow thoughtfully as he studied her. She'd seen pictures of him in the local papers over the years, but none of them had prepared her for the sheer impact of the man in the flesh. Just for a moment she let her eyes linger on the broad, high cheekbones, the fine, patrician nose, the well-shaped mouth.

How old was he, thirty-something? It was hard to tell because despite the experience stamped on his face there was no trace of silver in the black hair, which was swept back from his broad brow, and no apparent softening of the muscular frame. At a little under six feet tall, he looked superbly fit, the heavy black overcoat he was wearing emphasising the width of his shoulders, the narrow trimness of waist and hips. A man in the prime of life, in fact.

The judgement flashed into her mind like summer lightning, and abruptly she brushed it aside. She was just wasting time standing here. If she couldn't talk herself out of this mess, then she would have to find some way of escaping. She glanced almost casually round the room, looking for a way out, but apart from the door she'd come in by there was no other exit. Was it possible that she could push past Lang and make a run for it? With the advantage of surprise on her side, she might just do it.

'Try it if you feel lucky, lady. It would be my pleasure to stop you, believe me!'

How had he read her mind so easily? She didn't know, but she glared at him, hating him for his perception. 'I don't know what you mean.'

'Don't you? Maybe not. After all, even *thinking* about making a run for it would be stupid, and you're far from that or you wouldn't have got in here tonight, would you, Miss...?'

He paused, obviously expecting her to offer her name, but Alex snapped her lips together like a gin-trap. There was no way she was telling him her name, no way she was telling him anything! He could forget the old name, rank and serial number routine, because this little prisoner wasn't going to utter a word, and especially not one which would link her with Kenny!

'So you prefer to remain anonymous. I wonder why? I'm sure you will have to tell me sooner or later. But let's not worry about it too much right now. It will give us something to think about over the next few days, the intriguing puzzle of your identity.'

Alex frowned, shooting him a questioning glance from under her lashes. 'I don't think our involvement will run into days.'

'Oh, I disagree. It would be a shame to part too soon. You and I are destined to get to know one another much, much better, Jane.'

'My name isn't Jane,' she snapped, feeling a *frisson* of unease dance its way down her spine at the curious statement.

'Probably not, but in the absence of any other it will have to do.' He smiled thinly, his eyes narrowed as they slid over her set face. 'Jane Doe rather suits you, I think.'

Alex sniffed her disapproval, refusing to let him see how much he'd unnerved her as she walked round the desk to confront him boldly.

'This is getting us nowhere. I want to know what you intend to do. Are you going to carry on with all this nonsense, or are you going to let me leave? There is nothing missing. You can check for yourself, of course, but I didn't come here tonight to steal.'

'Perhaps there is nothing tangible missing, nothing you can pick up and put in your pocket, but what about what's inside here?' He leaned forwards and ran a finger across her brow. Alex shivered at the cool touch of his hand against her flesh, feeling her heart jolt then start to beat in a crazy little rhythm. She drew back abruptly, fighting against the urge to touch a finger to her brow, which seemed to be burning with a cold fire. It was just nerves, that was all, just this fine nervous tension which made it seem as if that light touch still lingered, leaving an imprint on her skin; yet her voice was strangely husky when she spoke.

'I don't know what you mean.'

'It's simple. I saw you reading the blueprints when I came into the office. You had them spread out on the floor while you studied them. What were you doing, memorising the modifications we have made to the engine so that you can go back and report to whoever you're working for?'

'No one sent me here for that! Don't be ridiculous. I know nothing at all about engines, so how on earth could I memorise what's on those plans? It's all double Dutch to me!'

'Is it? But I only have your word on that, Jane, and why should I take your word for anything when so far you've not even tried to give me any sort of an explanation for why you are here? I know what I saw when I came into this room, and I saw you reading those plans!'

'I wasn't! It's the truth.' There was desperation in her voice as she tried to convince him, but it was obvious that it had no effect on his judgement.

'So vehement in your denials, Jane. It would be tempting to believe you when you're such a good actress, but I know what I saw. Our competitors will go to any lengths to find out what changes we've made to the design. Sending you here is just another example of that.'

'But I know nothing about engines. Nothing! The blueprints had fallen on to the floor, and I was just trying to roll them back together. I wasn't reading them. There would be no point when I wouldn't understand a word!'

He *had* to believe her, yet looking at him Alex knew with a feeling of cold certainty that he didn't believe a single word she'd said. She fell silent, dreading the moment when he would call the police, as he surely would soon. The shame of that, of being handed over and charged like a common criminal! She would never be able to hold her head up in town again. Tears welled into her eyes at the thought, and she brushed them away with shaking fingers, biting her lip to hold back the sobs which racked her body.

'Don't waste your time trying that routine, lady. Tears don't cut any ice with me!'

Lang's voice was as scornful as his expression as he watched the tears coursing down her cheeks, and Alex stiffened, hating him then more than she had hated anyone. How dared he accuse her of faking tears? She would rather die before she stooped to those tactics in front of him. From all she'd heard and seen of Jordan Lang, he wouldn't know the meaning of compassion.

She glared at him, wiping the glittering traces of moisture off her face. 'Don't flatter yourself. I wouldn't credit you with enough sensitivity to bother wasting my time like that.'

'I'm pleased to hear it. It should make life simpler for both of us over the next few days if you cut out the helpless little female routine. We both know you're far from that, or you wouldn't have got this far tonight!' He glanced round, his mouth tightening into an unpleasant line as his eyes stopped on the blueprints still lying on the floor. He picked them up, his long fingers running up and down the smooth paper as he rolled them into a tight tube before laying them almost lovingly on the desk, and Alex found her eyes drawn to his hands, watching the way they caressed the paper back into shape.

'Yes, take a good look, Jane, a really good one, because that's the last you or anyone else outside this building is going to get of them until the engine is unveiled next week.'

There was something in his voice, something which made the skin on the back of Alex's neck start to prickle. She looked up, meeting the cold depths of his grey eyes, which now burned with an intensity that frightened her more than anything that had happened so far. Kenny had said that Lang would go to any lengths to protect the plans, and now she knew he hadn't been wrong in his assessment.

'What a good job I came back here tonight. I hadn't been planning on it. It was just an impulse that brought me here and spoiled your evening.

Another few minutes and you'd have got what you wanted, and no one would have been any the wiser, would they? Still, that's the luck of the draw; someone wins and someone loses. Now I think I'll lock these away from any more prying eyes.'

Pulling a bunch of keys out of his pocket, he unlocked the safe and stowed the plans inside. Alex watched him, wishing she could break this thrall of fear he seemed to have cast over her, but it seemed impossible to move a muscle. What was he going to do now...what? She wished she knew, yet, equally, dreaded finding out.

'Right, that's all sorted out, so I think we'd better be on our way.'

He slid a hand under her elbow to lead her towards the door, but all of a sudden Alex came to her senses and awoke from the trance. She dug in her heels, resisting him every step of the way so that he was forced to stop.

'Let me go! What are you doing? Where are you taking me?' She was panting with fear, the questions coming in little spurts, her face ashen, her eyes huge and terrified.

'Somewhere you won't be able to cause any more trouble for a few days.' He swung her round, his fingers biting into the soft flesh of her upper arms even through the heavy jacket as he held her in front of him. 'What did you expect? That I would let you go? Is that why they sent a woman, thinking I would treat her more softly?'

He laughed, a harsh, bitter sound which made Alex struggle even harder; but to no avail. The fingers gripping her didn't loosen, allowing her no chance to break free from the punishing grasp.

Desperate to make him let her go, she kicked out, and heard him grunt in pain as her toe connected heavily with his shin; but he still held on to her, his eyes glittering with fury as he shook her until she was too breathless to struggle further.

'Cut that out if you know what's good for you! I'm not letting you go with what you've got stored in that pretty little head!'

'Then call the police and hand me over to them.'

Minutes ago the idea had been frightening, but now it seemed like a ray of hope in a darkening world, and infinitely preferable to anything he had planned for her!

'And have your friends come and bail you out? Do you think I'm stupid, Jane? Sorry to disappoint you, but there is no way that is going to happen while things are at such a delicate stage. One hint that our competitors might have seen the designs for the prototype, and we'll have investors pulling their money out. No...the police are not going to hear about your visit to the factory tonight. No one is. It's going to be our little secret, yours and mine, something for us to share.' He glanced at his watch again, his mouth curling slightly as he caught her chin and forced her head up so that he could look directly into her eyes. 'Nine-thirty, Jane. It should have been midnight, really, I expect. Isn't that the customary time for strange things to happen? But I expect you'll remember this hour just as well in years to come.'

She snatched her head back away from the strangely unsettling touch of his fingers, feeling the tension uncurling like a snake in the pit of her stomach.

'What are you talking about?' she demanded, forcing a hard note to her voice, and praying he wouldn't see the shudder working its way through her body. 'You can't frighten me by making crazy statements.'

'Can't I? Maybe not. After all, you would have to be fairly tough to take on this job. In that case, then, I don't suppose it will bother you much if I tell you that as of nine-thirty tonight you no longer exist. You, Jane, are going to disappear off the face of the earth for the next seven days, and neither your friends nor whoever sent you here tonight are going to find you!'

Alex stared at him, too shocked to find a single word to say. It had to be a joke, surely? Yet, looking into his set face, she had the horrible feeling that it was no joke. He meant it, every single, terrifying word. Somehow, some way, Jordan Lang was going to make her disappear!

CHAPTER TWO

THE silence in the room must have lasted a full minute, the longest minute of Alex's life. She licked her dry lips, her eyes huge as she stared at Jordan Lang, wondering what she could say to stop him carrying out this crazy plan.

'Look, I know you're angry, but don't you think you're being a bit ...? Let me go! Let me go, you big bully!'

All thoughts of trying to talk sense into him fled abruptly as he started to haul her towards the door. Desperately she twisted round, lashing out with her free hand, then gasped in alarm when he suddenly stopped and hauled her round to pin her against his chest.

'No! Don't do——'

She got no further, the words dammed in her throat as he bent and covered her mouth with his in a bruising kiss which stole the breath from her body. Behind her she could hear the sound of the door being opened, and she renewed her efforts to break free so that she could call for help; but with his hand clamping her head in place it was impossible.

'What the ...? Oh, sorry, Mr Lang. I ... I didn't know it was you in here, sir.'

The security guard's voice was filled with embarrassment as he realised he had broken in on what must have appeared to be a touchingly intimate moment between his employer and a lady friend, and Alex felt a surge of red-hot fury race through her as she realised that Jordan Lang must have heard the man coming along the corridor, and acted accordingly! If this was an example of how fast his mind worked, then she was going to have her work cut out catching him off guard!

The door closed again, but Lang made no attempt to remove his mouth from hers until the sound of the man's footsteps had faded. Raising his head a fraction, he smiled down into Alex's furious face with a mockery that made her want to do something desperate...and to hell with the consequences! Twisting free, she wiped a hand across her mouth to erase the taste of the kiss, her eyes filled with loathing.

'How dare you——?' she began, then stopped abruptly when he caught hold of her again and shook her roughly.

'How dare I? Haven't you got that wrong? *I* am the injured party here, and don't you forget it! It's my factory you broke into tonight, my designs which you tried to steal, my business which you have put in jeopardy, so you can cut out all the righteous indignation, and get things into true perspective! Frankly, I think you should be thanking your lucky stars, lady, that a kiss is all you've had to suffer. You wouldn't have got off half so lightly if you'd been a man!'

There was no doubting that he meant every word, and Alex shuddered as a fleeting picture of what might have happened if he'd come back and found Kenny with the plans flashed into her mind. The thought held her silent as Lang hustled her from

the room, and along the corridor to the fire-escape.
Pushing the heavy outer door open, he led her to
the top of the open steps, his fingers tightening on
her arm as she hesitated, not liking the look of the
stairway which spiralled down into the darkness.

'Get a move on. We haven't got all night to
waste.'

He urged her on, a dangerous move when she
was already so unsure. Her foot slipped on the first
frost-slick tread, and for a heart-stopping moment
she teetered on the verge of falling headlong before
he hauled her upright again.

'Forget it! Don't even think about trying any of
your little tricks. There will be no police, no am-
bulance, nothing—not even if you break every
rotten bone in your body. There is no way I am
letting you out of my sight...understand?'

Alex gasped at the unfairness of the accusation.
Muttering darkly under her breath, she marched
down the rest of the steps, then stood and glowered
at him when she reached the safety of the ground;
but he appeared totally unmoved.

'Another little puzzle, so it appears. And an
answer, of sorts.'

'What puzzle? What are you talking about now?'
She eased the collar of her jacket up round her ears,
shivering slightly as the icy wind touched coldly
against her heated skin.

'How you got into the factory. You didn't seem
to enjoy coming down the fire-escape, so I can't in
all honesty see that you found the courage to climb
in through any of the upper windows.' He shot a
speculative glance up the side of the building, then
looked back at her. 'How did you manage to get

in, then, Jane, when I pay out a small fortune on security?'

Did he really think she was going to tell him? She hadn't enjoyed coming down that fire-escape, as he'd so rightly guessed, but it hadn't shaken her *so* much that she was prepared to divulge something so crucial! She smiled sweetly at him, her voice soft and gentle as a summer's breeze. 'That's for me to know and you to find out, isn't it?'

Anger crossed his face as her words hit home, and she took a hurried step backwards, wondering if she'd been wise to push him with the blatant gibe, then knew she hadn't when he laughed, a harsh explosion of sound which made her stomach clench in apprehension.

'Do you know, I am almost starting to enjoy this, Jane? Starting to enjoy all these little puzzles you keep setting for me. First there was the question of your identity, and now the even more intriguing one of how you managed to bypass the security systems. Solving them should help pass the time nicely where we are going.'

'And where is that? I hate to be a kill-joy and spoil your fun, but don't you think this is all a bit far-fetched? How on earth do you intend to spirit me away for a whole week?' She forced herself to sound calmly confident, to swallow down the fear she could feel like a cold lump in her throat.

'I wouldn't say it was far-fetched. Not at all. But of course I have the advantage of knowing where we are going.'

'And where is that?'

He smiled, his teeth gleaming white against his tanned skin. 'Surely that's for me to know and you to find out, isn't it?' he said quietly, tossing her own words back at her. 'You wouldn't really expect me to divulge that kind of information, Jane.'

'Don't call me by that stupid name,' Alex snapped, her nerves tingling like over-stretched violin strings. It was just so much talk, that was all—a way to frighten her into telling him who had sent her to the factory. There was no way he could really spirit her away!

'Tell me what your real name is, and I'll happily use it.' He raised a questioning brow, but Alex looked away, no more prepared to tell him now than she had been earlier. Even now he was speculating on how she'd got into the factory, so how long would it be before he realised she must have had inside help? The longer she could guard the secret of her identity, the more time she would have to find a way out of this mess.

'Jane, Jane, why are you being so stubborn? You must know that I shall find out sooner or later. It's only a matter of time. But if that's the way you want to play it, then so be it. Now come along. We can't afford to waste any more time. We have a long drive ahead of us tonight.'

He took her arm and led her towards one of the rear loading yards, where she could see a car parked, its white paintwork gleaming in the yellow beams of one of the security lights. Alex dragged her feet, trying desperately to put off the moment when she must get into the car.

'Don't try anything silly, will you? I don't want to have to hurt you, but the fact that you're a woman won't stop me if you try running off. There

is too much at stake here to worry about the niceties
of civilised behaviour!'

'Civilised behaviour', indeed! He wouldn't
understand even the rudiments of it! With a
haughty sniff, Alex slid into the car, and sat staring
through the windscreen while Jordan climbed in and
started the engine. He flicked a glance sideways at
her before turning the car and heading towards the
main gates.

'Still think it was worth it, then?'

'Worth what?'

'Whatever you're being paid? Sure it's enough
to make up for all this, or are you starting to feel
sorry that you came?'

'Yes,' she snapped, turning slightly to fix him
with a hot glare. Deliberately she whipped up her
anger, using it to quell the cold shivers of fear she
could feel trickling through her body. 'Yes, I'm
sorry I came, but not for the reasons you imagine!
But don't think you'll get away with this, Jordan
Lang. This is kidnapping! You could get sent to
prison for this. It's a major crime!'

His expression never wavered from one of cold
indifference as he slid the car to a gentle halt at the
junction of the drive and the road. 'I'm sure it is.
Interesting, isn't it? Which carries the stiffer
penalty, kidnapping or industrial espionage? Seems
to me that we're well matched, Jane. We both obviously have criminal leanings.'

'Speak for yourself! I have never done anything
criminal in my life!'

'And what do you call tonight's little escapade?'
he shot back, his mouth tightening when he saw
the self-righteous expression on her face. 'You

broke into my factory tonight, and if I hadn't come
back would have made off with those plans!'

'I wasn't trying to steal them! I told you that
before. Stop trying to whitewash what you're doing
now by blaming me!'

'Who else is there to blame? Tell me, Jane. What
were you doing there tonight if you weren't trying
to steal?'

It was tempting, so tempting to put all this
nightmare behind her. For one brief moment, Alex
felt herself weakening before she came to her senses.

'I can't tell you.'

'Too damned right you can't! You can protest
all you like, but there is no way you will ever convince me that I'm wrong!'

'I don't care what you think, Jordan Lang. You
can go to hell for all I care!'

He laughed harshly, revving the engine as he
swung the car out on to the road. 'I wouldn't be
too hasty in my condemnations if I were you.
Wherever I go, you go too. For the next seven days
you and I are going to be as inseparable as lovers!'

Alex turned away, staring out of the window as
she watched the lights from the factory fading into
the distance, realising the utter futility of arguing
with him any more. He would never believe her,
not even if she told him the truth. He would think
that she had made it up, that she and Kenny had
been trying to steal the plans, not put them back.
She would say nothing more, just bide her time and,
at the first opportunity, get away from him. After
all, he couldn't watch her day and night for seven
whole days.

It sounded like the sensible thing to do but, as the car travelled on into the night, leaving the factory and Kenny further and further behind, Alex wasn't entirely convinced that being sensible would be enough...not when she was dealing with Jordan Lang!

Was this it, then? The place where he meant to hold her for the next week?

Rubbing the burning sting of exhaustion from her eyes, Alex peered through the windscreen, but there wasn't much to see apart from the sickly glow of light spilling from the cottage windows they were parked outside. Where were they? How far had they come? And, more importantly, what was going to happen now that they had arrived? She had no way of knowing, but the uncertainty if it all made her feel more afraid than ever.

'Stay here. And if you have any ideas about trying to run off, don't! You'll only regret it!'

Removing the keys from the ignition, Jordan climbed out of the car and strode towards the cottage. Alex watched him go, her eyes locked to his broad back as he knocked on the door, trying to stifle the mounting panic. She might only get this one chance, and she couldn't afford to miss it by panicking. Cautiously she unsnapped the seatbelt, then froze when he shot a quick look over his shoulder just as the door was opened, sending a flood of light spilling over the path. For a moment he didn't move, then stepped inside the house, and Alex swallowed down a half-choked sob of relief.

Flinging the car door open, she scrambled out, flinching as a cold flurry of rain pelted into her face. Steeling herself against the onslaught, she looked round to get her bearings, but it was impossible to decide which way to go when everywhere looked so darkly unfamiliar. Anxious not to waste any more valuable time, she chose a direction at random, and started forwards, then had to grab hold of the car roof when her feet slid wildly on the muddy surface.

'I thought I told you not to try anything silly, like running off.'

The voice came from behind her, and Alex gasped and spun round, then had to clutch hold of the car again as her feet lost their purchase on the ground once more. Helplessly, she watched as a dark figure loomed towards her, pressing closer to the car as Jordan Lang came and stopped in front of her— so close that she could feel the brush of his body against her own. Rain had flattened his dark hair to his skull and settled a layer of moisture over the hard planes of his face, so that he looked even more forbidding than ever, and Alex had to force herself to meet his eyes with an outward show of defiance.

'So you did, but surely you didn't expect me to follow orders, did you? That really was rather naïve of you.'

'So instead you decide to go running off into the open dressed like that?' He swept a hard look over her tight jeans and leather jacket. 'We're not in the middle of town now, sweetheart. You wouldn't last a couple of hours out on the hills in that outfit, delightful though it may be.'

'Your concern is touching,' she said, forcing a bite to her voice to hide the tremor she could feel inching its way through her body, as she felt his eyes running up the slender length of her legs in the tight jeans which were now clinging damply to every shapely curve. She moved self-consciously, then froze as her thigh brushed against the hardness of his, sending a shaft of awareness shooting through her.

'My concern isn't for you. It's for me. Frankly, I don't give a damn what happens to you, but, if you go running off, then I will be morally obliged to go after you! Now come along. Let's get a move on.'

He grasped her elbow and, after one swift abortive attempt to shake his hand off, Alex let it remain where is was rather than suffer the indignity of a tussle. She was still smarting from what he'd said and, if she was honest, still thrown off balance by that strange flash of physical awareness she'd experienced. What on earth was the matter with her? She must be more strung up by the night's events than she'd realised.

In total silence she let him lead her over the rough ground, then felt a jolt of surprise when he by-passed the cottage and carried on into the gloom of the night. If the cottage wasn't their destination, then where exactly were they going? She racked her brain, then felt her breath catch as a new and far more alarming destination sprang to mind. All of a sudden all the dreadful horror stories she'd ever read in the papers about kidnap victims being held in caves or underground passages came rushing back, and she moaned in dismay. The idea was totally uncivilised, but there again she already knew that Jordan Lang wasn't a civilised man!

Hearing the sudden whisper of sound, he shot a curious look sideways at her, his hand tightening round her arm.

'What's the matter?'

'Nothing. Why should there be anything the matter? I mean, why should any woman in her right mind be worried about being abducted in the middle of the night?'

He stopped abruptly, so abruptly that Alex cannoned into him as her feet skidded on the slippery grass.

'You've only got yourself to blame. You should have thought of the consequences before you broke into the factory tonight. Frankly, I'm not enjoying this any more than you are.'

'Aren't you? I beg to differ, Mr Lang. I'd say that you are getting quite a kick out of terrifying me like this! There's a name for people like you . . . sadist! That's exactly what you are—a sadist . . . Ohhh!'

The words dried in her throat as he swung her round in front of him, gripping her by the shoulders while he glared down into her startled face.

'Who the hell are you to be calling me names? You're nothing but a common thief, lady, and don't you forget it! If there's any name-calling to be done, then it's I who shall be doing it, do you hear?'

He set off again, dragging her with him so that Alex had to run to keep up with him; but she refused to ask him to slow down, refused to beg. She hated him to the very depths of her soul, and she would rather die first than ask him a favour!

Now that they had left the cottage behind, darkness once more enclosed them, making Alex wonder how he could see well enough to keep such a sure footing on the rough ground. It was only the punishing grip he maintained on her arm which kept her upright.

'Over there. To your right.'

With scant ceremony, Jordan hustled her along in front of him across a lumpy stretch of grass which oozed with mud. Alex scanned the darkness, but could see little through the driving rain until the dark shape of a building suddenly appeared in front of them. She stopped dead, ignoring Jordan's rough curse when he almost fell over her, her eyes locked to the building in sudden dread.

All right, so it wasn't a cave or underground passage, or any other of the places her imagination had conjured up, but, frankly, no one this side of Transylvania could call the rough-hewn building inviting. A couple of circling bats, a few blood-thirsty screams, and Dracula himself would have the ideal country retreat. But if Jordan Lang thought he could lock her up in there, then he was wrong!

She spun round, taking him by surprise as she wrenched her arm free and shoved him roughly aside. Then she was off, skidding her way across the grass towards the path. Behind her she could hear Lang's roar of anger, but she closed her mind to the sound, and concentrated on setting as much distance as she could between them. If she could only get back to the car and lock herself inside, then he would have one heck of a time getting her out again!

The jolt of some unseen restraint catching her round the knees brought her to the ground with a wind-stopping force. Alex lay still, wondering if she was dead, as a bone-crushing weight settled itself on her body, making it impossible to drag any air into her deflated lungs. Lights began to flash behind her eyes, making her head ache with their brilliance, so that it was almost a relief when everything started to go dark.

'Don't you dare pass out on me! Sit up, woman!'

The weight shifted, and she was hauled abruptly upright into a sitting position, but it was still impossible to breathe until something hit her a nasty wallop between the shoulder-blades. Her lungs whooshed open, and she coughed as she drew in great greedy gulps of the wet night air.

'Of all the crazy, irresponsible, stupid...'

The tirade ran on and on along such similar lines for several minutes and, despite herself, Alex was impressed by his repertoire of adjectives. She'd swear he never repeated himself even once! Slowly, she opened her eyes and looked at him, then felt the quite ridiculous urge to giggle. She swallowed hard, trying desperately to force it down and remember that this was not a laughing matter, but, as her vision improved and she got an even better look at Jordan Lang, it became impossible.

From head to toe he was covered in mud, his black hair plastered with it, his face spattered, his expensive overcoat sleek as a seal's under its sticky wet coating. He looked so different now from the suave picture of well-tailored elegance he'd presented in the office that Alex felt the giggle turn into a full-blown laugh.

'So you think it's funny, do you?' he ground out, his eyes gleaming in a way which made the laughter bubble and suddenly die in her throat almost as quickly as it had begun. Alex pushed her matted hair out of her eyes, and looked warily at him, her eyes huge and getting huger as she saw the dawning expression on his face—saw and correctly interpreted its meaning! With a shrill cry of alarm, she tried to scramble to her feet, but he caught her ankle and hauled her back down to the ground.

'Oh, no, you don't! You're not getting away from me again. You've had your fun, and now I think it's my turn!'

He pulled her to him and bent his head, taking her mouth in an angry kiss meant to punish. Alex twisted and turned, fighting to free her lips from the rough assault, but she was no match for his strength. He raised his hand, twisting his fingers into the damp length of her hair, pulling her head back so that she gasped in pain as the tender roots of her hair were dragged sharply. His tongue slid into her part-open mouth as he used the moment to deepen the kiss, tangling with hers, its movements deliberately provocative as he sought to force her to respond. Alex tried to avoid the hot, probing intimacy of the kiss, tried to avoid the sensuous stroking of his tongue against hers, but he was quite relentless as he held her head in place and continued kissing her until she was breathless and shaking, a fine tremor coursing through each fibre of her body.

Just for a moment, for a tiny second out of time, she succumbed to the tantalising caress, and kissed him back; then, with a low moan of anguish, she realised what she was doing. She dragged her mouth free, rubbing her hand over her lips time and again, but nothing could erase the lingering taste and feeling of heat imprinted on her skin. Tears of anger and shame sprang to her eyes, and she brushed them away, looking up at Jordan through misty lashes. He was watching her, his eyes shadowed, gleaming a flat silver as he stared intently at her; and for some strange reason Alex found she couldn't look away.

'Hey, there! Are you all right, Mr Lang? What's happened?'

The shout came from the direction of the cottage, and Alex jumped in surprise, swinging round towards it. A man was standing on the step, holding a lamp above his head as he peered out at them. He took a hesitant step forwards, and Jordan swore softly as he scrambled to his feet, pulling Alex up with him.

'Everything is fine, Owen. Nothing to worry about. You go on back inside. Leave the car until morning. There's no point in you getting a soaking.'

The man raised a hand in acknowledgement, then went in and closed the door. Alex shivered as the light was abruptly cut off, leaving her and Jordan in almost total darkness, and she wished she'd had the presence of mind to shout for help before the man had disappeared. Still, one good thing to come out of it all was that she now had a fair idea where they were, thanks to hearing Owen's lilting accent: Wales. Though her heart sank as she realised just how far they'd come.

'Come along. We've wasted enough time here.'

Jordan caught hold of her arm, and attempted to steer her back up the path, but there was no way she was going back up there again!

'No!' she shouted defiantly, pulling back like a reluctant puppy on the end of its lead.

'No? I don't think you are really in any position to refuse, do you?' His gaze dropped to her mouth, and Alex felt heat rush through her at the silent reminder of the kiss he'd forced upon her; but she refused to be beaten into compliance. There was no way he was taking her back up that hillside and locking her away in that dreadful place!

'I will *not* go back up there and let you lock me up in that... that barn!'

'Lock you up? Is that what this is all about? My God, woman, what kind of a man do you take me for?' Anger flashed across his face as he hauled her round in front of him, jerking her back when she tried to pull herself away.

'Frankly, lady, you deserve to be locked up in there for the next ten years for what you've done tonight; but for your information that wasn't what I intended to do, tempting though the idea is.'

'Then what do you intend? Why are you leaving the car here? It's hardly the sort of night for a pleasant stroll!'

'Because there is no way I can take it any further up these tracks without ruining its suspension. I keep a jeep in that barn. We'll have to use that now to get the rest of the way up the mountain.'

'Oh.'

'"Oh", indeed.' He glared down at her, his eyes narrowed as he studied her pale face, and Alex shivered at the cold anger in their depths. 'Another one, then, Jane?'

'Another what?' Her voice was low, a faint murmur of sound nearly swallowed up by the whine of the wind; but he caught it, and smiled thinly, little amusement on his face.

'Another puzzle, of course.' He laughed, a grim sound which lingered on the rough night air like something tangible. 'I wonder who it was who gave me such bad press that you believed I would happily lock you away in a deserted building? Whoever you're involved with is definitely not a member of the Jordan Lang fan club!'

Without another word he took her arm and led her back up the track, his face set into grim lines of anger. Alex stole a quick glance at his stern profile, then looked hurriedly away, wondering if there wasn't just the tiniest grain of truth in what he'd said. If Kenny hadn't implanted that idea about Jordan Lang's lack of civility into her mind, then would she really have jumped to such a hasty conclusion, and accused him of planning such a terrible deed?

She didn't know, but the idea that she might have misjudged him made her feel strangely uneasy. She *wanted* to see Jordan as the bad guy, now more than ever, because she had the feeling that to see him in any other light could be asking for more trouble than she could handle!

CHAPTER THREE

BY THE time they reached their destination, Alex was a wreck. It had taken them a good hour more of driving, an hour spent clutching hold of the edge of the seat while Jordan negotiated the jeep round a series of heart-stopping bends. In the dark, Alex had gleaned only an indistinct glimpse of how the mountain fell away into a steep drop, but that had been enough! She'd spent the rest of the journey with her eyes closed, praying that Jordan's nerves were made of sterner stuff than hers. A couple of careless inches to the left, a slight misjudgement at the next hairpin bend and... She closed her mind to what might follow, cursing Kenny to hell and back for putting her through such an ordeal!

'We're here.'

Jordan cut the engine and set the handbrake, and slowly Alex opened her eyes, breathing a quiet sigh of relief when she saw there wasn't a cliff-edge or hairpin bend in sight, just the comforting bulk of a small house, looking invitingly solid in the glow of the headlamps. For a thankful moment she let her eyes linger on the welcome sight, then looked further afield, but there were no other houses to be seen. Obviously the place was as isolated as Jordan Lang had said it would be, and a tiny cold flurry of fear started to inch its way down her spine.

'Stay here while I go and open up and get some lamps lit.'

He jumped out of the jeep and disappeared inside
the house, leaving Alex staring after him in something akin to panic. Now that they had finally arrived, the true precariousness of her situation hit
her, making her realise just how vulnerable she was
going to be, alone in the house with him. Desperate
to find some way out, she looked frantically round,
and caught sight of the keys dangling from the ignition. He was taking a chance leaving the keys
behind, wasn't he? What was to stop her from
taking the jeep and driving off?

It was a tantalising thought, and for thirty delicious seconds she savoured it greedily, wondering
if all her prayers had been answered, before coming
to her senses with a deflated bump. There was no
way she could take the jeep and drive it down that
treacherous track in the darkness. It would be sui-
cidal even to attempt it, and Jordan Lang knew it!

In a real fit of temper she jumped out of the jeep
and strode into the house, yelping as she banged
her shin painfully against some unseen object.
Hopping on one leg, she rubbed the bruised flesh,
ignoring Jordan when he came into the hall with a
lamp to see what all the commotion was about.

'I thought I told you to wait in the jeep. Can't
you ever do a thing you're told to?'

Alex ignored the sarcasm just as easily as she'd
ignored his previous, and obviously sound advice.
Gingerly she set her foot down, and shot a quick
look round but, frankly, she was in no mood to
appreciate the cosiness of the lamplit hall with its
pale grey walls and red rugs scattered across the
grey flagstoned floor.

'And what exactly do you intend to do with me now that we're here?' She flashed him a tight smile, her expression one of cool mockery which belied her true feelings, the anxiety she could still feel gnawing at the pit of her stomach. There was no way she was going to let him know how afraid she felt.

'Come along, then, Mr Lang. I'm just dying to hear what's in store for me. Is there a nice cosy little cellar somewhere, or do you intend to keep me bound and gagged for the next week?'

'What a very active imagination you have. You're wasting your time being a thief. You should be writing for television with a mind like yours.'

'I am *not* a thief!'

'Oh, spare me . . . please. I've heard your claims to virtue so many times tonight that they're starting to get boring.'

'That's because it's true. I didn't go to the factory to steal your rotten blueprints!'

'Of course you didn't. You just happened to wander in there, find your way up to the office, and there they were, lying about with a little note on them saying "Read me". Forgive me if I find it hard to believe!'

'Oh, very amusing. But I'm still waiting to hear what little treat you have in store for me.' Alex strode along the hall, and glanced into one of the downstairs rooms, then shot a quick look over her shoulder. 'I can't see any signs of racks or thumb-screws, but I'm sure a man like you won't have overlooked the necessities, not when you are obviously so adept at abducting people.'

'I wonder what sort of people you usually associate with. No, I hate to disappoint you, but there
are no racks, no thumbscrews, not even a nice damp
cellar. The best I can offer you is bed.'

'What?' Her voice rose an octave, echoing shrilly
round the hall, and she saw him wince, but she
didn't care as every single one of her fledgeling fears
sprouted wings and fluttered wildly inside her. If
he thought for one moment that she would . . . that
he could . . .

'What on earth is wrong with you now?'

He moved towards her, holding the lamp aloft
as he stared down at her white face, and Alex took
a hasty step backwards, balling her hands into fists.

'Don't you come any closer,' she warned. 'Or
I'll . . .'

'You'll what? Scream the place down? Be my
guest, but I warn you that you'd just be wasting
your breath. There's no one for miles around; no
one to hear if you stood on the roof and screamed
until you were blue in the face.' He smiled, a faint
gleam in his eyes now as he set the lamp down and
took a few more slow steps towards her. 'Getting
cold feet, are you, Jane? Suddenly realising just
what you've got yourself into?'

He reached out so swiftly that she had no chance
to avoid him as he slid a hand round the back of
her neck and pulled her to him. Cupping her chin
with his other hand, he tilted her face to stare down
into her frightened eyes. 'Does the idea of us being
here all alone bother you, Jane?'

'No! No, of course it doesn't bother me. You
can't frighten me, Jordan Lang!'

'No? Then why is your pulse racing?' He laid a long finger against the tiny pulse which was beating a frantic tattoo at the base of her neck, stroking it delicately over the soft skin. 'If it's not fear, then what is it? Desire?'

'No!' With a quick twist of her body, she broke free, and backed away from him. 'All right, so I am afraid; who wouldn't be in my position? You've brought me here to this god-forsaken spot, and how do I know what you intend to do next?'

He shrugged, but made no move to follow her, standing relaxed and seemingly at ease in the pool of light cast by the lamp. 'You don't. You're at my mercy now. I can do anything I like with you, can't I? And no one...no one will be any the wiser.'

His voice was low, even, as though he were discussing the price of shares, the weekly shopping— anything but her fate; and Alex had to hold herself rigid to stem the mounting tide of fear.

'You're mad, do you know that? Mad if you think you can get away with this.'

'And who is going to stop me? I really can't see whoever sent you to the factory tonight coming forwards and asking questions about your whereabouts!'

'You're wrong. My b——' She stopped dead, the word freezing on her lips as she suddenly realised what she'd been about to say. Jordan was watching her intently, a cold expression on his face, and in a sudden flash Alex realised that he had been deliberately goading her, hoping to rattle her so that she would let something slip. How nearly he'd succeeded!

She drew in a shaky little breath, feeling her legs trembling in reaction. 'It won't work. I won't tell you anything more than I've told you already.'

'We'll see. It's early days yet. A week's a long time, and I have the feeling that you might change your mind before that time is up.'

'Never,' she said hotly. 'Never!'

'Never is an even longer time, but I admire your loyalty even if it is sadly misplaced.' He straightened, picking up the lamp so that its rays fell directly on to his face, setting the bones into stark relief, making his features look even harsher. 'Now I think it's time for bed. Maybe things will look different to you in the morning, once you've had time to think everything through.'

He started towards the stairs, but Alex held back, still beset by her earlier fears. He glanced back at her, his eyes lingering on her pale face, the rigid tension in her slim body. 'Well, aren't you coming?'

'Look, if you think that I'm going to... to...' She couldn't bring herself to say the words aloud, colour ebbing and flowing in her face as she met his knowing gaze and saw the mocking smile which curved his lips.

'To sleep with me? Is that what you're finding so difficult to say? Ah, Jane, life is full of disappointments for you today, especially when you seem so intent on casting me as the villain. No, for your information I have no intention of carrying you off to my bed and having my wicked way with you, tempting though the idea is. I prefer my women to have less criminal tendencies than you exhibit!

'Now, if you'll follow me, I'll show you which room you can use. Oh, and just one more thing ... don't think for one minute that you can run off from here. Quite apart from the fact that the house is miles from anywhere, I have no intention of letting you out of my sight until the prototype is unveiled.' He swept a look over her, his face so hard that she quailed inwardly. 'There is too much sunk into this project to let you or anyone else ruin it. No matter what it takes, Jane, I intend to safeguard the project!'

He turned away and walked up the stairs and, after a momentary hesitation, Alex followed him. Every instinct was screaming at her to run, to get as far away from him and this house as she could, but she knew she couldn't risk attempting it at present. There was no doubt in her mind that he'd meant what he'd said, that he would do whatever necessary to protect his precious engine. But somehow, some way, she had to find a way out of here even if it meant lulling him into a false sense of security so that he would be off his guard. The one thing she couldn't do was spend the next week here with him!

Alex couldn't sleep, not with everything that had happened, and everything that was to come. Tossing back the blankets, she climbed out of bed, and crossed to the window to look out. It was still raining, a heavy driving rain which slanted across the hillside and sent huge drops scurrying down the window-pane. A faint moon had risen, and she could just make out the stark outline of the trees, their bare branches twisting under the force of the wind. It was a bleak outlook, and after a few minutes she turned away, looking round the room—

for what? Inspiration? Reassurance? Whatever it
was, she didn't find it in the small room.

With a weary sigh she walked back to the bed,
then stopped, her eyes lingering on the rumpled
covers with a hint of distaste. She didn't want to
get back into that bed and make another pretence
at sleeping, with her mind whirling in smaller and
smaller circles as she searched for a way out of this
whole mess. To hell with Jordan Lang! She was
going downstairs, and he could either like it or lump
it!

She ran down the stairs, her bare feet making no
sound on the thick carpet, then stopped at the
bottom, her eyes going longingly to the door. It
would be so easy to open that door and walk out—
the solution to all her problems. So what was
stopping her from doing it? The fact that Lang had
told her the house was isolated? For all she knew
he could have been lying, tricking her as he had so
nearly tricked her before. She would be a fool to
miss such a golden opportunity by being gullible!

She took an eager step forwards, then stopped
dead when a deep voice spoke almost directly
behind her.

'I wouldn't do that if I were you.'

Heart pounding, she spun around, her eyes huge
as she spotted him lounging in a doorway, watching
her with an expression on his face which was frankly
scary. Slowly, he slid an assessing look over her
body, then looked back at her face, his eyes flat
and devoid of feeling so that she felt chilled to the
bone.

'You disappoint me, Jane. I expected more from
you than an attempt to leave via the front door,

and in that state of undress. Unless, of course, you hoped it might distract me.' He trailed another insulting glance up the length of her legs, his lips curling in derision. 'Nice, but I think I'll pass this time, thank you.'

How dared he? Did he honestly believe that she had deliberately come downstairs dressed like this to...to distract him? She swept a glance down the bare length of her slender legs showing under the thigh-length hem of her shirt, and felt the colour rise in her cheeks as she realised for the first time exactly how revealing her outfit was.

She'd removed the wet jeans and jacket to go to bed, choosing to sleep only in the thick shirt and panties, and she had never paused to consider how she looked before rushing downstairs. Now she could feel the embarrassment curling hotly inside her as she realised what a picture she presented to the man who was watching her. She took a hasty step towards the staircase, anxious to get back to the bedroom and away from that coldly assessing scrutiny, then yelped in pain as her bare toe grazed against a sharp corner of one of the flags. Blood started to ooze from the cut, welling quickly into a small pool, dark red against the grey stone floor, and she swallowed hard, feeling suddenly queasy at the sight of it.

'Damnation, woman! Look what you're doing!' With a low growl of annoyance, Jordan stepped forwards and swept her up over his shoulder, striding towards the rear of the house along the hall before Alex had a chance to realise what was happening.

'Put me down!' she ordered, then repeated it a
shade more forcefully when he took no notice.
'Put...me...down! What do you think you're
doing?' She beat her fists against his shoulders in
a tattoo, marking time with her instructions, then
stopped abruptly when he turned his head and
glared straight into her eyes.

'Stop that now! You've caused quite enough
trouble for one night, and I have no intention of
letting you bleed all over the floor and ruin it just
to round things off!'

Well, she hadn't expected a show of concern or
even a hint of contrition that she had injured her
foot on his rotten flags, but that was carrying in-
sensitivity too far even for him! Mouthing insults
as to his pedigree under her breath, Alex was forced
to suffer the indignity of having him carry her like
some sort of lumpy package before he deposited
her none too gently on one of the kitchen chairs.

'Thank you. You are so kind,' she said sarcastically, trying to ease the shirt-tail down over her
bare thighs, yet not let him see that she was at all
conscious of her semi-nudity. 'You really have
missed your vocation. With your obvious concern
for the welfare of your fellow man, you should have
been a missionary. I can just picture you doing good
deeds, helping the injured with that particular brand
of charm you display—ow, that hurts!'

She grasped her foot, cradling it gently as she
studied the dark stain from the liquid he'd swabbed
round the cut.

'Iodine,' he said succinctly, catching hold of her
ankle to pull her foot back and take another swipe
with the iodine-soaked cotton wool. 'There's no

point in taking a chance on it becoming infected. I'm sure you're brave enough to put up with a little discomfort, with your background and training.'

'What do you mean, my background?' she snapped, rubbing a few drops of moisture out of her eyes. 'You know nothing about my background!'

'Maybe not, but I just had a vague idea that anyone who earns her living from industrial espionage would have to be tough. It isn't a job for the faint-hearted.'

'I keep telling you, I am not a spy! Why won't you listen to me?'

'Oh, I'm listening all right. It's just the believing I find difficult. Now stay there while I get a plaster to put on that cut.'

Resting her foot on the seat of one of the chairs, Jordan walked over to the cupboards, opening one to sort through the contents. Alex glowered at his broad back, her eyes shooting sparks of annoyance. Why wouldn't he even *try* to believe her? Why did he have to be so all-fired certain that she was guilty?

'I'm sure there's a box somewhere in here.' He stretched up to skim a searching hand along the top shelf, the muscles in his back rippling with the movement. He obviously kept a change of clothes at the house, because he'd discarded the suit he'd been wearing before and changed into slim-fitting denim jeans, which clung lovingly to his long legs and narrow hips. With them he wore a deep blue sweatshirt, and Alex felt her mouth go suddenly dry as it rose up when he stretched, giving tantalising glimpses of smooth brown flesh. Hurriedly she averted her gaze, then nearly jumped out of her skin when he appeared in front of her with a plaster in his hands.

'Here you are. I knew I had some somewhere.' He stripped the backing off the piece of tape and pressed it over the wound, his long fingers cool as they brushed against her bare toes. 'Right, that should do it, but you'd be well advised to get dressed before you start wandering round in here next time. It will save any further accidents.' He skimmed a look up the bare length of her legs, and Alex felt the colour flood to her face as she felt the touch of those grey eyes as if it were something tangible. She stood up abruptly, almost toppling over her chair in her haste to get away, aware that he was watching her with an intent scrutiny, which made her feel more self-conscious than ever. What on earth was the matter with her? She was acting more like some shy little schoolgirl rather than a mature woman who had experienced her fair share of male attention! Annoyed with herself, she rushed into speech.

'Thank you. I'll be more care——' She stopped abruptly as the lights went out, plunging the room into darkness.

'Damnation! The generator must have broken down. I thought it didn't look too good when I started it up before. Stay there while I get a lamp in here.'

He left the room, returning in the space of seconds with an oil lamp, and set it down on the table, fixing Alex with a hard stare as he lifted a jacket off the peg behind the door.

'You'd better stay in here while I see what I can do with it. I don't want you wandering round the place and causing more damage. Oh, and, if you have any more bright ideas about running away, then forget them, or I might just do something we'll both regret!'

Alex stiffened at the undisguised threat, hating him at that moment more than ever. 'Don't worry, I'm not a fool!'

'I'm glad to hear it.'

He walked out, closing the door quickly behind him as a blast of wind and rain flurried into the kitchen. Alex sat down again at the table, hugging her arms tightly round her body, but it did little to stem the cold chills. Jordan Lang was her enemy, and she'd been a fool to forget that even for a moment. Never again would she let herself experience that crazy flurry of attraction she'd felt before!

Where on earth was he?

Pushing the curtain aside, Alex stared out of the window, but there was still no sign of Jordan returning. He'd been gone almost an hour now, yet surely it shouldn't take so long to get the generator working again? Letting the curtain fall, she looked round the kitchen, rubbing one bare foot against the other in an attempt to warm them up. With the generator out of action the house had grown distinctly chilly, and she could feel goose-bumps rising on every exposed inch of flesh. Whether she was flouting his orders or not, she would have to go upstairs and get dressed or she would catch pneumonia.

Holding the lamp carefully in front of her, Alex made her way through the dark house, feeling easier

once she was back in the bedroom. There was
something unnerving about being in the strange
house alone, hearing all the unfamiliar sounds of
the wind whistling through the eaves. She was sorely
tempted to climb back into bed and pull the covers
over her head as she'd done as a child, but some
niggling little feeling wouldn't let her. There was
something *odd* about Jordan's staying outside such
a long time, and leaving her alone!

Dragging on her clothes, she hurried downstairs
again and opened the kitchen door to peer out into
the darkness.

'Jordan! Where are you?'

The wind caught her shouts and carried them
away, but she could hear no answering cries, and
the feeling that there was something wrong intensified. With a sigh of resignation, she stepped
outside, calling herself every kind of fool for
worrying about a man who didn't care a jot about
her; but there was no way she would be able to live
with herself if anything had happened to him.

Rounding the corner of the house, she yelped in
pain as a trailing bramble caught round her ankle,
then followed it by a gasp when she caught sight
of the figure lying on the ground. Fighting free of
the prickly barbs, she ran across the grass and fell
to her knees beside him. He was lying so completely still, his eyes closed, his dark hair sleeked
back from his forehead with rain, and Alex felt her
heart lurch with fear. Was he dead?

With trembling fingers, she reached out to touch
the side of his face, them jumped violently when
he moaned. With a fierce feeling of relief, she
pressed her hand against the pulse beating in his

neck, feeling the steady throbbing against her flesh. Heaven knew what had happened, but that really wasn't the issue right at that moment. It was far more important that she get him inside out of the storm.

He was heavy, far heavier than his lean build intimated, and, by the time Alex managed to drag him inside the house and get him on to the huge old-fashioned sofa in what was evidently the living-room, she was exhausted. Just for a moment she allowed herself the luxury of slumping against the end of the sofa, then forced herself to her feet. She might have got him inside out of the rain, but she couldn't leave him lying there in wet clothing, or he would catch his death, and that really would give her noisy conscience something to worry about!

Perspiration beaded her brow as she was forced to manhandle the full weight of his torso to get his jacket and sweatshirt off. Just for a moment her eyes lingered on the tanned width of his muscular chest with its light dusting of fine black hair, before determinedly she focused her attention lower and steeled herself to remove his sodden jeans. Slipping his shoes and socks off was easy enough, but when it came to actually unfastening the snap of the jeans she had to draw in a shaky little breath to steady her nerves. It was ridiculous to feel embarrassed when she was doing it solely for his own good, but Alex couldn't help the hot little spirals from curling through her as her fingers brushed against the hard muscles of his stomach when she pulled the metal clasp apart and slid the zipper down.

'What are you doing?'

She gasped in shock as his hand came out and caught her wrist, pressing her fingers more intimately against his body. Wide-eyed, she looked up at him, feeling her pulse skip a beat when she saw that his eyes were open and he was watching her.

'I asked what you were doing!' He spoke slowly, his lips moving with laborious concentration as though he found the effort almost too much, and instinctively she tried to soothe him.

'It's all right. Lie still; I'm just going to get your wet clothes off before you catch a chill.'

He stared at her for a long moment, obviously trying to make sense of what she was saying, his eyes hazy. Then slowly the haze began to clear, and he tried to sit up, falling back against the cushion with a groan of pain as he clutched his head.

'What the hell did you hit me with?'

Alex gasped then rushed into speech, anxious to disabuse him of that idea! 'Nothing! I mean, I didn't hit you . . . I didn't!'

'Then how did I get this lump on my head?'

He pulled her hand up to his head and pushed her fingers into the thick damp hair so that she could feel the huge lump distorting his scalp. Alex pulled away, trying to free her hand from his, but he wouldn't let her go.

'I didn't do that!' she repeated hoarsely. She struggled frantically, twisting her arm, then stilled when she saw the spasm of pain which crossed his face as she jarred his head. He closed his eyes again, his breathing short and laboured, his face turning the colour of putty under its tan.

'Are you all right? Jordan? Can you hear me? Jordan!'

There was a sharp anxiety in her voice as she leaned towards him, studying his ebbing colour, followed by intense relief when he opened his eyes again and looked at her in that familiarly mocking way.

'Such touching concern. Should I be flattered that you care so much about my welfare? Or is it more a case of you realising what you've done, and that you could have been adding manslaughter to all the other charges laid against you?'

Why, of all the nerve! After all she'd done, half killing herself dragging him in here! She should have left him out in that storm to rot! Exasperated by such pig-headed determination to see only the bad in anything she did and never the good, Alex glared at him, sorely tempted to give him a matching lump on the other side of his thick head.

'I did *not* hit you, though now I rather wish I had! You were lying unconscious on the ground when I found you.'

'And what were you doing out there? Making another attempt to escape, even after I'd warned you what I'd do to you?' He glowered at her, his grey eyes dark with anger, his mouth thinned into a mean line which made a little quiver rise in her stomach.

'No! I'd gone outside to see what was wrong. You were out there ages, and I was...' she hesitated, loath to admit her feelings to him, then carried on with a defiant toss of her head '...worried.'

'Worried? About me?' He laughed bitterly, then winced, resting his head back against the arm of the sofa. 'The only thing you were worried about,

Jane, was your own skin. What really happened? Did you creep up behind me and hit me on the head, meaning to make a run for it once I was out cold?'

'No!' She shouted the denial, but he ignored her, carrying on as though she had never spoken.

'And then what happened? Did you suddenly have second thoughts, and realise that leaving me out in that storm was tantamount to murder?'

'No! Why must you keep saying those horrible things? I didn't hit you!'

'Same as you didn't try to steal the blueprints. There are an awful lot of things you didn't do, Jane.'

There was a weary finality in his voice as he closed his eyes again, and Alex looked at him in concern, her anger suddenly forgotten. No matter how infuriating he could be, she had to remember that he was injured, though how badly she couldn't tell. He must have been unconscious for some time before she found him, so there was a strong possibility that he was suffering from concussion. What he needed was proper medical attention, and the only way to get that was by driving the jeep back down that track.

'I'm cold.'

Alex jumped when he suddenly spoke, her hand running automatically over his chest to test the coolness of his flesh with her fingers.

'Mmm, very nice, but I'm still cold.'

She snatched her hand away, feeling the colour flood into her face when she saw the glint of mockery in his grey eyes. She stood up abruptly and hurried to the door, not daring to look at him again as she murmured, 'I'll fetch a blanket for you.'

She ran up the stairs, stumbling over the top tread in the dark, wishing she'd thought to bring the lamp up out of the hall. As quickly as she could, she stripped a couple of blankets off her bed and bundled them up to take them downstairs, then paused, realising that she had to give herself time to think about what she should do. Everything had happened so fast since she'd found him lying outside, and she would do neither of them any favours by rushing headlong into the wrong course of action.

'Where the hell are you? Damn you, woman, if you're trying to run out on me, then I won't be responsible for my actions!'

Alex jumped as she heard the angry roar echoing up the stairs. Trailing the blankets, she hurried along the landing, and peered down into the dimly lit hall, gasping in dismay at the sight which met her eyes.

Jordan was standing in the open doorway, swaying perilously as he hung on to the doorframe. Even as she watched, he took an unsteady step into the hall, then staggered as his knees started to buckle. Dropping the blankets, Alex sprinted down the stairs, her blue eyes hot with anger as she looped his arm over her shoulders and half carried, half dragged him back into the room to push him back on to the sofa.

'Of all the stupid, irresponsible, foolhardy...' Now, when had she heard that before? The words dried up as she suddenly remembered where she'd heard a similar tirade, finally placing it down to when they had performed that little tussle in the mud a few hours earlier. Her mouth tightened, and she glared at him, now doubly furious both with his stupidity and with the fact that she was starting to sound like him! For her own peace of mind, if not his health, it was definitely time to end this alliance!

In angry silence she swung his legs up on to the sofa, then ran upstairs to fetch the blankets, tucking them round him with sharp, jerky little movements. Stepping back, she shot a quick glance round then marched towards the door.

'Where are you going?'

She flicked him a brief glance, one slender eyebrow raised in a mocking curve. 'I'll give you three guesses.'

'You're leaving?'

'Got it in one. Well done, Mr Lang. That blow on the head doesn't appear to have affected your reasoning at least.'

'To hell with my reasoning! You can't go and leave me here!' He half rose, trying to sit up, then groaned and fell back against the cushions. Alex steeled her heart to the pathetic picture he made lying there, the purpling bruise showing darkly against his temple, his dark hair all ruffled in a way that made her fingers itch to brush the silky strands back into place.

'I don't think you're in any position to stop me, do you?' she said, forcing a hard little note to her voice to hide the momentary softening. 'Anyway, if it's any consolation, I'm going to try and get some medical help for you, so you won't be on your own too long.'

'But I'll be alone until it arrives. Don't leave me here like this, Jane . . . please.'

He sounded so lost and helpless, his voice throbbing with something which tugged at her heart-strings, and Alex hesitated, wondering if it was wise to leave him on his own. What if he suffered a relapse? Or tried something silly like walking about again? Head injuries were tricky things, and there was no knowing what the next hour or so could bring.

Suddenly uncertain that going for help was the right thing to do, she opened her mouth to reassure him that she'd stay, then felt her temper rise in a sudden red-hot surge as she saw the expression on his handsome face. He was doing it deliberately. Quite intentionally playing on her emotions to keep her there!

'Why, you low-down, double-dealing, conniving——'

'Tut-tut, Jane, such language, and in front of an injured man as well!' He smiled suddenly, the first real smile she had ever seen him give, and just for one crazy moment she felt her heart flutter before she brought it back under control. She stormed out of the door and ran along the hall, her hand hovering on the door-lock as she heard him shout.

'I shall find you, Jane. Even if I have to move heaven and earth, I shall find you and make you pay for what you've done!'

There was no laughter in the deep voice now, no mockery, just a steely determination which made the blood rush to her head in fear. She wrenched the door open, slamming it behind her before racing over the grass to the jeep and starting the engine

with a roar. Just for a second she glanced back at
the house, then turned the vehicle in a slow circle
and headed back down the path, trying to close her
mind to those vengeful words which kept echoing
round and round in her head.

There was nothing to worry about now. Once she
had found help for Jordan Lang, then she could
put this whole unsavoury incident behind her and
get on with her life, safe in the knowledge that he
had no idea who she was or why she'd been in the
factory. There was no way he would ever find her.
She'd make certain of that!

CHAPTER FOUR

IT WAS the waiting that was the worst. No matter how positive she tried to be, Alex woke up each morning wondering if today would be the day that Jordan Lang tracked her down. It didn't seem to matter how many times Kenny reassured her that they had got away with it; there was always that niggling little doubt at the back of her mind that somehow Jordan would find her. It was ridiculous, of course, because they didn't move in the same circles, and were unlikely to come into contact again; but she couldn't prevent the feeling of impending doom which seemed to hang like a great black cloud over her head.

In an effort to dispel the feeling, she spent more and more time working, almost doubling her output of handcrafted jewellery, to the delight of the London store which had been begging her for extra supplies for months. The subsequent increase in revenue came in very useful, enabling her to make an extra payment on the loan, so maybe the black cloud had a silver lining after all.

The days crept past, slid into weeks, and finally Alex started to relax a bit. There had never been any mention made of the incident in the factory, so maybe it had all been just a storm in a teacup which wouldn't blow up into a typhoon. Jordan Lang must have realised that he had been mistaken about her, and sensibly decided to let the matter drop.

Feeling more at ease, Alex locked the shop one day and hurried upstairs to the flat, surprised to find that Kenny was already home.

'You're early. What happened, did you get sent home early for good behaviour?' She shot him a laughing glance, then felt the smile freeze on her lips when she saw the expression on his face. All of a sudden that cloud was gathering again, pressing down on her head with its full weight of impending doom. It took every scrap of strength she possessed to ask the question she didn't want to ask.

'Has something happened about the blueprints?'

Her voice was hoarse with strain, and Kenny stood up and caught her by the shoulders, his hands gripping her painfully hard.

'I'm sorry, Lexie. I never should have got you into this.'

'What's done is done, Kenny, and all the wishing in the world won't change it. Just tell me what's happened now.'

She shook him off and walked to the window, rubbing her hands up and down her arms, but nothing seemed to stem the iciness that was stealing through her body. She should have known it was all going too smoothly. Jordan Lang wasn't the kind of man who would ever turn the other cheek.

'The whole factory was buzzing when I got in this morning. Seems there has been a leak about the new design, and Lang had given orders that he wanted to interview every person who works there himself to find out who was behind it.'

Alex swung round, frowning. 'What do you mean there's been a leak now? I thought the engine was due to be unveiled weeks ago. That was the reason Jordan Lang gave for holding me in that house—so he could keep me out of circulation—and he only set a time limit of one week on that, not several!'

Kenny shook his head. 'They had to change their plans at the last moment. Seems there was a design fault—nothing major, but enough to cause concern. One or two of the larger investors weren't too happy about it, but Mr Lang managed to talk them round and reassure them. However, one of our major competitors announced yesterday that they are about to launch an engine which has so many of the features of our prototype that there's no chance it can be coincidence. There's definitely been a leak of information and, as you can imagine, Jordan Lang is out for blood!'

And whose blood was it going to be? Alex didn't need to look very far to find the answer to that! He must have put two and two together very quickly, and come up with her as the major culprit. But there had to be something they could do—not just sit here waiting until he came gunning for them. After all, if Lang was interviewing people, then it proved he still had no idea as yet who she was. With a bit of nerve and a lot of luck, then maybe she and Kenny could weather this new storm safely.

She went and sat down facing Kenny, fixing a confident expression to her face. If they were going to outwit Jordan Lang, they would have to be confident and not panic.

'I take it you haven't been interviewed yet?'

'No. Fortunately I was sent out on a job today, and missed the first round; but I won't escape tomorrow, unless I ring in sick and wait until it all blows over.'

Alex shook her head, her eyes dark with certainty. 'This won't blow over. No, you have to go in tomorrow or you'll make people suspicious.'

'But you have no idea what Lang can be like! I can't do it, Lexie. He'll make mincemeat out of me!'

'I have a very good idea what he's like! Don't forget I had the pleasure of his company for several hours.'

Kenny had the grace to look discomfited. 'Yes, I know. I'm sorry. But can't you see how hopeless it all is? He'll never believe we were putting those blueprints back. He'll pin this whole leak on us, and it'll be prison . . . if he doesn't take his own revenge first!'

There was a mounting hysteria in Kenny's voice, and Alex knew she had to stop it now. Everything was down to him now, and she wouldn't let him fall apart and ruin both their lives.

'He won't pin anything on us if you keep your head, Kenny. Jordan Lang doesn't know we are related, and there is no way he will unless you tell him. It's all down to you now, brother. Don't let me down.'

He looked up, forcing a smile. 'I'll try, Lexie. Believe me, I shall try!'

'But that isn't what I ordered! I ordered a brooch made out of those lovely Mexican fire opals you showed me.'

The indignation in the customer's voice cut short Alex's musings. Murmuring an apology, she hurried back to the workroom, and opened one of the shallow metal drawers where she stored her completed orders, and checked the details. It had been her mistake, mixing one client's surname with another's. It was the third mistake she'd made that morning, and it wasn't even lunchtime. She would have to get her head together and stop worrying about what was happening at the factory. Kenny would be all right—he'd had enough practice getting himself out of sticky situations, after all!.

While the customer wrote out a cheque, Alex slid the brooch into one of the elegant black leather boxes she used solely for her handcrafted jewellery, smoothing a finger lovingly over the gold-embossed legend, 'Alexandra', on its lid. It had taken years of hard work and effort to get to this point, but every time she sold something and packed it into one of these special boxes it made it all worthwhile.

There was a lull after the customer left, and Alex locked the display cases, and hurried through to the back to get on with some of the other orders. There was a bead curtain separating the workroom from the shop so she could easily hear if anyone came in. She set to work on yet another of the topaz scarf-clips which were still in such demand, calling out that she would only be a moment, when the shop bell tinkled, announcing the arrival of another customer. The sound of the beads rattling together as the curtain was pushed aside startled her, and she swung round, the cold rebuke at the interruption freezing unspoken on her lips.

'Surprised to see me, Jane? I don't know why. I did tell you I would find you, didn't I?'

'I...I...' She licked her dry lips, forcing her reeling senses to cope with his sudden appearance, then shook her head, wondering if she was hallucinating. But no hallucination had ever looked as dreadfully real as Jordan Lang did!

'What are you doing here?'

'What, Jane, no "how nice to see you again, Jordan", or "how have you been?" Tut-tut, not a very gracious way to greet an old friend who's gone to so much trouble to find you!'

'You're no *friend* of mine, Jordan Lang!' she snapped, stung into replying by the mockery in his voice. She stood up abruptly, holding tightly to the work-bench as her knees threatened to buckle. 'What do you want?'

'I would have thought that was obvious, especially to an intelligent businesswoman like you, Jane—or should I call you Alexandra?' He rolled the name round his tongue, as though savouring the sound of it, then smiled, and Alex felt her heart beat a little faster when she saw the expression in his eyes. 'Mmm, yes, I rather like it. I can't imagine why you were so reluctant to tell me what it was before. But then, I must confess that you will always hold a rather special place in my feelings as Jane Doe. Few women have ever left such a lasting impression on me as you did!'

He stepped further into the room, his eyes sweeping over the tools of her trade laid out on the bench before coming back to rest on her, and, despite herself, Alex shrank back from the anger in his gaze. 'Why? Tell me, why did you risk all this?

Was it just for money, or what? Damn you, woman, tell me! It's the least you owe me after all the trouble you've caused!' He moved suddenly, catching hold of her by the shoulders before she had a chance to evade his grasp. 'Why?'

'Let me go! You can't come in here and man-handle me, Jordan Lang!'

'And who's going to stop me? Your precious brother? Sorry to disappoint you, lady, but he won't be coming to your aid yet awhile. I've made certain of that!'

'What do you mean? What have you done to him?' There was a shrill note of concern in her voice. She twisted and turned, fighting to break away from the merciless grip; but he was too strong for her, as she knew already to her cost.

'Nothing . . . yet. And I shan't do anything if you and I can come to a satisfactory agreement.'

'What sort of an agreement? Damn you, Jordan, let me go!'

He smiled, scant amusement in his expression, just an icy coldness which made answering shivers trickle down her spine. 'I'm glad to hear you've decided to drop the formal title. Jordan sounds much more appropriate in view of the circumstances.'

'What circumstances? Stop trying to frighten me. Look, I know how bad it all looks, but Kenny and I had nothing at all to do with the leak of information.'

'And do you really expect me to believe that? Do you?' He shook her, not hard, not roughly, but with a restrained violence which was far more scary, hinting at the seething anger she could sense beneath the tight rein he had on his emotions. 'Your treachery has almost cost me the lot—the factory, the business, the whole damned lot! But you're going to make amends for what you've done. I'll make sure of that!'

'How?' Alex glared up at him, fear adding a depth to her own anger. He was so pig-headed, so set on believing the worst and staying blind to the truth. Fury at his unreasonable attitude made her goad him. 'And what exactly are you planning to do, Jordan? How shall you make me pay?'

She laid a nasty emphasis on his name, ignoring the way his grey eyes darkened ominously when he heard it. If he wanted her to use his given name, then she would do so, but it wouldn't stop the dozen or so more fitting ones from flying round inside her head. 'Come along now; don't be shy. What is it to be—prison? Financial ruin? I'm sure you've spent hours thinking up a fitting revenge for this crime I'm supposed to have committed.'

'Marriage.'

The word echoed round the room, softly, gently, yet with the impact of a speeding bullet. Alex stopped dead, her mouth dropping open just the barest fraction as she wondered if she'd misheard or, at least, misunderstood.

He laughed softly, the sound rippling round, filling her head with noise, her body with a feeling of unrelenting fear. 'Marriage,' he repeated quietly. He let go of her shoulders, his fingers warm and firm, sending a ripple of sensation coursing through her as he lifted her chin and snapped her mouth shut. 'You, Alexandra Campbell, are going to marry me.'

*   *   *

The coffee was hot, scalding her tongue and bringing tears to her eyes, but Alex welcomed the pain. All through the long minutes it had taken to lock the shop and lead Jordan upstairs to the flat, she'd had the feeling that she was in the middle of some horrible dream. Now the stinging pain of the coffee on her tongue brought her awake.

Her eyes lifted to the man sitting opposite, a steaming mug of coffee held in one large, well-shaped hand. While he was sitting like that, one leg crossed over the other, relaxed and doing something as mundane as drinking coffee, it was easy to be deceived into thinking he was much the same as other men: sane, rational, not given to crazy flights of fancy; but he wasn't. He had to be mad, stark raving mad, if he thought she was going to marry him!

She snorted in disgust, then felt the colour surge to her face when he looked up and met her eyes. Just for a second she held his gaze, feeling her pulse racing, then looked away, swirling the coffee from side to side in the cup. Her emotions felt like that, swinging back and forth, unable to find a level. One part of her wanted to dive right in and demand to know what he'd meant by the ridiculous statement, while the other side shied away from it with horror. Perhaps the safest way would be to lead up to finding the answer slowly.

'So, how did you find me? Did Kenny tell you?'

He shook his head, taking a long drink of the coffee before putting the cup down. 'No. I haven't seen your brother yet. I had him sent over to Yorkshire, to our other workshop, on some trumped-up excuse to get him out of the way. I didn't want him coming in here and breaking up our first meeting.'

Alex tried hard to ignore the mockingly intimate note in his deep voice, but for some silly reason her heart skipped a beat and let her down. 'Let's cut out the comedy, shall we, and just have the facts? If he didn't tell you, then how did you find me?'

'Sheer fluke, you might call it, though I prefer to see it as divine justice. I was at a friend's house last night, and she happened to be reading a magazine which featured an article about your jewellery. She made rather a point of showing it to me, in fact, possibly as a rather heavy-handed hint of what she'd like. I could hardly believe my eyes when I realised it was you. I've spent weeks trying to trace you, and there it is—a photograph plus a write-up on the Alexandra Campbell success story.' His mouth tightened, and he leaned forwards, all pretence at being relaxed forgotten.

'Is that what you planned to do with the money you got from selling the information—invest it in your business? Or was it to keep up with your brother's gambling habits?' He laughed softly when she started in surprise. 'Oh, yes, I know all about that. I've spent the night and the whole of the morning looking into your affairs, and there is nothing I don't know about the pair of you!'

'Then you must know that Kenny has stopped gambling and that he doesn't owe a penny to anyone!'

'I do know. But I also know what it cost you to pay off those debts, that the bank has been thinking seriously of foreclosing on the loan you have for this shop. The money you've been paid must have gone a long way to help you out of that!'

'No! You have it all wrong! All right, so Kenny did take the blueprints that day; but it was just a silly impulse. Once he came to his senses and realised what he'd done, he decided to put them back. That was what I was doing that night—putting them back . . . not stealing them!' He had to believe her, he just had to! But, looking at his grim face, Alex knew he didn't. She stood up, some vague idea of running from the room and away from the accusation in his eyes filling her head, but Jordan was at the door before she could take a step across the room.

'Sit down!'

She hesitated, a vein of caution responding to the harsh authority in his voice, yet warring with a desire to tell him to go to hell.

'I said sit down! I'm through wasting time like this. If you have any sense, then I suggest you sit back down and listen to what I have to say.'

Alex sank back on to the chair, gripping the arms with whitened knuckles. In silence she watched as Jordan sat down again, his eyes sweeping assessingly over the slender, elegant lines of her body, before coming to rest on the gleaming golden softness of her hair with an expression she found hard to define yet which made her feel strangely breathless.

'You are a very attractive woman, Alexandra, and you should be glad of it, because it means there just might be a solution to all this havoc you've caused.'

Alex said nothing, mainly because there was nothing she could say. She stared back at him, her eyes inky-dark against the ashen pallor of her face. Just for the moment he seemed to hesitate, as though something about her expression bothered him, but it was only a momentary lapse before he continued in that same calm, ruthless tone which flicked at her raw nerves like a whip.

'Thanks to what you and your brother have done, three of our major investors have withdrawn from the project. Without their backing the viability of the whole business is at stake. I took a gamble, you see, and sank everything into this project, and if it fails that will be it . . . the end of Lang's.'

She could understand why he was angry; given similar circumstances she would feel the same. But she still couldn't understand where she fitted in.

'I'm sorry,' she said quietly. 'I know you don't believe that I had nothing to do with the leak, but apart from that I can't see how marr . . . marr . . .' Her tongue tripped over the word, unable to breathe life and substance into such a crazy idea. However, it seemed that he had none of her reservations.

'Marriage, Alexandra. Don't be shy about saying it. The sooner you get used to the idea, the better it will be for everyone concerned—you, me, and your precious brother!'

There was such harshness in his voice that she shuddered, looking away from the mesmeric gaze of his silvery eyes as she tried to think what to do or what to say, but it was impossible while that word kept filling her mind. Marriage. To Jordan Lang. Just the thought made her heart beat wildly in a heavy throbbing rhythm, sending the blood coursing through her veins. She knew she should laugh in his face and tell him in no uncertain terms that there was no way she would marry him, but something in the depths of his eyes frightened her into silence.

'No objections? I had imagined that you would be opposed to the idea at first, but it seems I was wrong. Maybe the idea of us being joined in marriage isn't completely unappealing to you?'

He was goading her, quite deliberately and, while Alex knew it, she couldn't prevent the heated retort from rising to her lips to chase away the numbness.

'I have no objections. There is no need for any objections because the whole idea is ridiculous! There is no way I will ever marry you, Jordan Lang, not if you were the last man on earth!'

'Really? Mmm, it could be interesting trying to overcome those feelings, but unfortunately I don't have time to take you up on such a challenge. You owe me a lot for all the damage you've done, Alexandra Campbell, and I intend to see that you pay every last penny of the debt!'

'And how does marriage come into it?' She leaned forwards to glare at him across the space of a couple of inches. 'Surely resorting to threats to find yourself a wife is going a bit far, though I can understand that any woman with an ounce of sense would be reluctant to get involved with a man like you . . . Ohh!'

She cried out in alarm as he caught her hands and pulled her to him so abruptly that she fell to her knees at his feet.

'So you don't think any woman would want me?' His voice was low and filled with a note which should have warned her to reply with caution, but Alex had gone way beyond the point of caution.

'No! No woman in her right mind would want you!'

A light flared into his eyes, hot, bright, burning with an intensity she could almost feel as he swept his gaze over the flushed contours of her face. Suddenly terrified at what he was going to do, she started to struggle, but she was no match for his far superior strength, and could only watch helplessly as he held her and bent forwards until his mouth touched hers. She moaned, an anguished little cry which faded abruptly into nothing as she felt the delicate touch of his lips barely brushing hers, then the warm moistness of his tongue tracing the outline of her lips in a whisper-soft caress which made every cell in her body tingle. Expecting a brutal assault, a punishment for her temerity, she stilled, her body clenching in shock and sensation as his tongue circled her lips time after time, tracing over the soft curves, lingering to probe at the join of her lips, then moving on before she could either refuse or allow entry.

Slowly Jordan drew back, his face unreadable as he studied the red moistness of her mouth, the faint trembling she couldn't quite hide. She'd been kissed before, many times, and far more passionately, but not once had her senses been stirred as this tantalising brushing of his mouth on hers had done.

'Do you still think you're right? That no woman would ever want me?' His voice was deep, soft, stroking over her sensitised nerves like warm velvet, and she shuddered, summoning up every last scrap of control she had.

'Yes. I'm right!'

'Are you sure, Alex? One hundred per cent certain?' He raised his hand and ran a gentle finger across her mouth, tracing the outline just as his tongue had done. Alex held herself rigid, fighting to control the shudders which threatened to destroy her control at the evocative touch. Once, twice, three times he retraced the same disturbing path, then gently parted her lips to run a fingertip slowly over the soft inner flesh of her lower lip. 'I think you need convincing, that's all.'

'No! Jordan, no, I don't want...'

With a swiftness she hadn't expected he bent his head and took her mouth again, sliding his tongue between her parted lips to tangle with hers in a heady, sensual rhythm which made the blood surge in her veins. Suddenly, shockingly, she was on fire, burning up, consumed by the mastery of the kiss, the intensity of feeling he was igniting inside her. That first slow caress had been the spark, and now her emotions were alight and burning out of control.

Caught up in the kiss, Alex was unaware of the exact moment when he loosened his grip on her arms, yet achingly aware of the feel of his fingers sliding under her hair to stroke the soft skin at the nape of her neck. She could so easily have pulled away and put an end to the kiss, but there was no thought of that in her head, just as there was no thought of resisting when he pulled her into the cradle made by his wide-spread legs and pressed her closer against the hardness of his body. Her eyelids fluttered shut, and she reached up to run

her hands over the cool, silky hair at the back of
his head while she kissed him back.

The abruptness of the rejection as he pushed her
from him stunned her, so that for a moment she
couldn't understand what was happening.

'Open your eyes!'

His voice was cold and harsh, cutting through
the lingering heat of passion. Slowly, Alex opened
her eyes, feeling the colour drain from her face as
she saw the expression in his eyes.

'Are you still so sure that no woman would want
me?'

There was relentless cruelty in the question, and
Alex gasped, turning her head away, feeling sick.
How could she have been such a fool as to fall for
that and let him trick her in that despicable way?
That kiss, which had promised a glimpse of heaven,
had been founded in hell; it had been nothing to
him apart from a means of teaching her a lesson.

Cold waves of embarrassment flooded through
her, and she started to scramble to her feet; but she
should have realised that Jordan would never let
her off the hook until he had embedded it as deeply
as possible in her flesh. Catching hold of her chin
between his thumb and forefinger, he forced her to
meet his eyes.

'Be honest, Alexandra; didn't *you* want me just
now?'

There was something in his voice, something besides the harshness, and just for a moment Alex
felt her body tremble with a lingering echo of
passion before she came abruptly to her senses. She
dragged her chin away and stood up, her face cold

with contempt and a trace of pain she couldn't quite hide.

'This has gone far enough. I have neither the time nor the inclination to play any more silly games with you, Jordan. I suggest that you either tell me what you want or leave!'

'I'm not playing games. This whole thing has gone way past the point of being a game. However, I must agree that we have wasted enough time. I've already outlined the predicament the company is in, thanks to you; however, there is a chance that I can save it with more investment. And that is where you come in.'

He stood up and walked to the window, pushing the curtains aside to look out, and if Alex hadn't known better she would have said that he was weighing up his next words before continuing; but why? In his own mind, Jordan had already tried and convicted her; all that was left now was for him to pronounce sentence, and she couldn't see *that* causing him a problem! Tension hummed through her as she waited to hear what he would say, and she clenched her hands into fists, fighting to keep a grip on her control.

He swung round suddenly, the light from the window bouncing blue sparks off his night-dark hair, yet setting his face into shadow, so that Alex couldn't see his expression. But she had no need to. She knew what he thought of her. He'd made it quite plain both with words and with that devastatingly cruel kiss, yet she couldn't prevent the sudden pain which knifed through her heart at the thought of just how much he must dislike her.

Anger that she should feel that way ran through her, stiffening her spine, adding a strength to her voice. 'You know that I have no money, so what exactly are you suggesting? That I should steal someone else's secrets and sell them to pay you back?'

Jordan stiffened at her tone, taking a half-step forwards before seeming to force himself to relax. 'Smart answers aren't going to get us anywhere. I have all the money I need to see this project through to completion and put the company back on target. It is just a question of gaining access to it.'

'Then you intend to go ahead and market the engine?' There was relief in Alex's voice as she asked the question.

'Yes. Why? Are you disappointed that you have failed? You were just a shade premature, you see. We didn't discover the flaws in the design until *after* your visit to the factory, which means that our competitors don't have the benefit of knowing what further modifications we have made. It should take them some time to sort it all out, so for now we are still in the lead, and can carry on as planned.'

'Then I still don't see where I fit in. Why do you need me?'

'It's simple. When my mother died a few months ago she left me her personal fortune in trust to be handed over either when I reached the age of thirty-five, or in the event of my marrying. I shall be thirty-five in six months' time, but I can't wait that long. It's vital that I have the money now!'

'But why marry me to get it? There must be other women who would be pleased to marry you—women you know!'

'Because we both know exactly where we stand and what the marriage is for. I have neither the time nor the inclination to go through all the ritual another woman would expect before she agreed to the marriage, neither do I want a wife who would expect me to dance attendance on her. The only thing I'm interested in right now is getting the firm out of trouble!'

'And when that's done you won't need the encumbrance of a wife?' Alex asked shrewdly.

'Precisely. A divorce will be easy enough to obtain. However, I want this marriage to appear as genuine as possible while it lasts. I don't want any more of our investors pulling their money out because they've found out that Lang's back is up against the wall.'

'And how long do you envisage this "marriage" lasting?'

He shrugged. 'Six months at most. After that we could let it be known that we had decided to separate, and that's it. Divorce is common enough nowadays to cause little comment.'

He had it all worked out, all the steps written down from one to ten. Alex didn't know what disgusted her most—the thought of what he was prepared to do to get what he wanted, or the ice-coldness of his mind for coming up with such a plan. But one thing he hadn't allowed for was that she wasn't going to be a neatly numbered step in anyone's plan!

She swung round and marched to the door and opened it. 'Get out. You were crazy for coming here and expecting me to agree with such a ridiculous proposal.'

'Was I? I don't think so. I'd say you are the crazy one if you refuse and accept the alternative.'

'What alternative? Are you threatening me?'

'If you prefer to hear it stated bluntly, then yes, I am.' In a few long strides he crossed the room and closed the door, leaning against it as he studied her face. Alex tried her hardest to meet his eyes with an outward show of composure, but it was no more than a few seconds before she was forced to look away, terrified by the determination she could see in his expression.

'And if I do refuse, then what do you intend to do?'

'What any law-abiding citizen would do, of course—go to the police and have you and your brother charged with industrial espionage. I'm not absolutely certain what sentence the charge carries, but I imagine you would both be facing roughly two to five years in prison.'

'Two to five years? You can't prove anything,' she cried desperately, 'you know you can't! It will be your word against ours.'

'That's where you're wrong. I already have the sworn statement of one of the security guards that your brother was in the factory that night. He was only too eager to tell me everything he knew once I'd...pointed out to him the gravity of the situation.'

Poor Sid. He must have been terrified when Jordan had questioned him. It was little wonder he had admitted letting Kenny into the factory. But that still wasn't proof—not enough to convince a jury, surely?

'And, of course, there is the other charge to be taken into consideration.'

Alex shot him a swift glance, but it was impossible to second-guess him. 'What other charge?'

'Assault.' He ran a hand over his head, his eyes pinning hers with a steely intensity. 'Surely you haven't forgotten that bump on the head you gave me? I have medical records to prove that I suffered a mild concussion from that.'

'But I didn't hit you!' she exclaimed, horrified that he should be trying to blame the accident on her.

'That's debatable, but it makes no difference when I have a witness who will testify that you went and asked him to fetch a doctor for me after spending time up at the house, *and* that when they got there they found me semi-conscious on the settee. You remember Owen, don't you, Alexandra? I'm sure he remembers you, and can testify to your identity.'

Of course she remembered Owen. She'd stopped at his house and roused him from his bed to get him to call a doctor for Jordan that night. Now she wished she'd never bothered. She should have driven off in the jeep and let Jordan Lang rot!

'I can ruin you, Alexandra Campbell, both you and your brother. Oh, maybe there is a slim chance that you will be able to talk yourself out of any charges I bring, but can you handle the publicity, and the fact that I will make it my business to see that you suffer—that neither you nor Kenny will be able to earn a living or hold your heads up again?'

'You can't do that! You haven't that much influence.' It was more a plea for reassurance than a refutal of what he'd said, and Alex felt a shudder inch its way along her backbone as she saw the way Jordan smiled, saw the expression in the depths of his eyes.

'Haven't I? I wouldn't bank on that. Shall I get on the telephone now and call a few of your suppliers, and tell them that you are no longer a good risk? Or shall I call the bank and suggest that they should think about calling in their loan, as there is a strong possibility that you will be facing police charges soon? It wouldn't take much. Just a quiet word in the right ears and then your business will be no more than a memory.'

'You'd do that?' Her voice was a mere whisper, but he heard it. He lifted her chin with a deceptively gentle finger, and looked straight into her horrified eyes.

'Yes, I'd do it. That and more if I had to. Whatever it takes to get what I want. So tell me what it's to be. Prison and financial ruin, or marriage?'

'I . . . I can't tell you now! I need time to think,' she cried desperately.

'There is no time, that's the whole point. Thanks to what you have done, I need to start immediately if I intend to save the business. So what is it to be— yes or no?'

His fingers tightened on her chin, bruising the soft flesh, but Alex was scarcely aware of the discomfort. She closed her eyes, trying desperately to find another way out of the mess, but all she could see were the vivid pictures Jordan had painted of her future. Could she really condemn both her and Kenny to prison followed by a life of poverty? Yet she couldn't bring herself to agree.

'There must be another way, Jordan. Please!' Her eyes opened and stared straight into his, holding desperation, but there was no softening in the steely gaze, no hint of forgiveness or understanding.

'There is no other way. None! So make your choice.'

'And if I do agree, then do you promise you'll drop the charges, that you won't ruin my business, and that Kenny won't be sacked?'

He shrugged. 'Yes, of course I do. Your business will be safe, and as for your brother—well, I can hardly sack my wife's brother, can I? It would look very odd.'

'Then . . . yes!'

The word slid from her lips almost before she realised she was saying it, and she caught her breath, wishing she could call it back. Just for a moment Jordan was silent, a strange expression on his face as he studied her; then he nodded.

'Good. I'm glad you decided to see sense in the end.' He released her chin, his knuckles brushing softly across her mouth, his voice very deep and liquid. 'You never know, Alexandra, this could turn out to be quite a pleasant experience for us after all.'

Alex's face flamed as she caught his meaning, and remembered how she'd responded with such abandon to that kiss. For a tiny second sensation curled through her, heating her veins, sending the blood swirling through her in a fierce tide of longing before she forced the memories from her mind.

'Go to hell, Jordan Lang!' she said, her voice almost breaking.

He laughed, swinging the door open as he prepared to leave. 'I said it once before, and I may as well repeat it: wherever I go you go too. I guess it applies even more now than ever before. Man and wife, Alexandra. Think about it!'

He left, leaving the door open behind him. For a moment Alex stayed quite still, staring at the empty doorway, feeling her pulse racing wildly. Man and wife. Oh, she would think about it all right, would think about little else, in fact. Just the idea should have shocked her rigid, sent her running screaming into hiding. So why did she feel this crazy little spark of excitement deep inside?

CHAPTER FIVE

A CAR horn sounded in the street below, and Alex jumped, dropping the earring she'd been holding. It fell to the floor and lay in a glittering little heap on the carpet, but she made no move to pick it up. Crossing the room, she parted the curtains and looked down into the street, her heart leaping in a sickening surge as she recognised the trimly elegant lines of Jordan's car parked outside.

She dropped the curtain abruptly into place, and turned away to stare round the room with hunted eyes, but there was nothing there to offer help or comfort, nothing that could put an end to this nightmare. Even Kenny was away from home, sent to the Yorkshire factory on Jordan's specific instructions. He hadn't wanted to go, and it had taken all Alex's powers of persuasion to make him. Now she wished she hadn't. She could have done with him being here to bolster her flagging courage.

The horn sounded again, longer, louder, with a barely concealed impatience in its strident tone, and with a cold feeling of inevitability she picked up her coat and bag and left the flat, running down the stairs to let herself out through the shop.

Jordan had already got out of the car, and was walking towards the door when she appeared. He stopped and waited for her to join him on the pavement, his face devoid of any expression.

'I was beginning to think you weren't coming,' he said shortly, his eyes sweeping over her pale face.

'I wish I wasn't.' She swept past him and stood next to the car, staring along the quiet street, focusing all her attention on the darkness barely broken by the dim glow of the streetlights. A light wind was blowing, rustling the few leaves left on the trees as it shook the branches, making flickering patterns dance across the pools of light, and Alex shivered as it curled coldly round her face and neck.

'Come along. Get in, or we'll be late.'

Jordan opened the car door and held it for her while she slid inside, before striding round to the driver's side. He started the engine and set the car into gear, flicking a quick glance sideways at her before he pulled away from the kerb.

'I hope you don't intend to make any waves tonight. This evening has been arranged specifically to announce our engagement, and I won't tolerate you trying to pull any of your tricks.'

His tone was cold, the words clipped, but they left surprisingly little impression on Alex. The coldness seemed to be spreading, numbing her senses, making it impossible to feel anything but a faint surprise that this was really happening. She felt detached, alienated from everything, as though she were standing outside herself watching what was going on.

'Did you hear me?'

Rough impatience tinged Jordan's voice now as he slid the car round a tight bend then picked up speed as they left the town behind. Alex glanced sideways at him, her eyes running impersonally over his clean-cut profile, the smooth sweep of his dark hair; but she felt nothing—not anger, not attraction... nothing.

'Yes, I heard you,' she said quietly, her voice flat. 'You don't need to worry. I know what is expected of me.'

He swore softly, his hands tightening round the steering-wheel, his lips compressing. 'Then is it too much to ask that you try to show a bit more enthusiasm? This is supposed to be a wonderful occasion for both of us, but one look at you and no one is going to believe that!'

'Is that really so surprising? This wasn't my idea, remember? This was your little plan, from start to finish, so you'll have to forgive me if I appear less than "enthusiastic"!' There was a faint bite to her voice now as she felt the first stirrings of anger nibbling away at the edges of the coldness.

'It might have been my idea, but it was only necessary because of your meddling. I don't like the idea any more than you do, but I have no choice.'

'Of course you have a choice. Why are you being so blind? Why can't you open your eyes and look at the facts and see the truth?'

'Meaning?'

'Meaning that I didn't steal your information and neither did Kenny. You're just using us as scapegoats while the real culprit goes free. You would be better employed trying to find who really is responsible than in forcing me to go through with this ridiculous charade.'

He laughed bitterly. 'So we're back to that, are we? Still protesting your innocence and claiming

that you are the wronged party? Forgive me, but
I'm afraid I don't believe it any more now than I
did a few weeks ago at the house!'

'You don't want to believe it! You don't want to
look for the truth in case you have to admit you're
wrong! That's what this is all about really. The fact
that the great Jordan Lang can never be wrong!'

There was angry scorn in her voice as she spat
the accusation at him, but he appeared unmoved
as he slid her a level glance.

'I can be wrong the same as anyone can, but I'm
not wrong about this. You can say what you like,
but I will never believe that you are anything but
guilty!'

He turned back to concentrate on driving the
powerful car along the narrow road, and Alex rested
her head back against the seat and closed her eyes
in defeat. It had been a waste of time trying to convince him that he'd made a mistake. If anything,
it had only hardened his opinion of her and served
to destroy that merciful numbness which might have
helped her through the evening. Now she was back
to square one, back to feeling these cold little
tremors of fear in the pit of her stomach, which
she'd been living with ever since Jordan had come
to the shop and told her his plan. There had to be
a way to convince him that he couldn't force her
into this unwanted marriage, but so far she'd not
managed to find out how.

In total silence they drove on through the night
until Jordan slowed the car and swung in through
a pair of ornate wrought-iron gates and along a
winding driveway. Alex opened her eyes and looked
round, feeling her heart bumping painfully in her

chest as she watched the lights of the restaurant coming closer and closer.

'Have you been here before?' He slid the car into a parking space and cut the engine, turning slightly to look at her so that the lights spilling from the huge arched windows made a silvery backdrop for his darkly handsome features. Alex shook her head, glancing round the crowded car park at the expensive collection of cars, feeling sick. Now that the moment was here, when she must go into that building and be introduced as Jordan's fiancée, she felt terrified, waves of fear curling and rolling in her stomach, making her dizzy with the sheer force of them. It took every ounce of strength she possessed to stop herself leaping from the car and running screaming into the night.

'I think you should enjoy it. The Country Club is renowned for serving some of the best food in the northwest. I can vouch for that. But before we go inside there are one or two things we need to get straight.'

'What sort of things?' Alex's voice was a rough husky rasp of sound, and she felt him look at her, but she refused to meet his gaze in case it snapped that last thread of control she was clinging desperately to.

'Just a few basics which people are bound to ask about. I've made a note of everything you'll need to know. Date and time of the wedding, et cetera. It's all booked for three weeks' time. I had hoped to get it over with sooner, but unfortunately the banns had to be called, so that was the earliest that could be managed without making it look too rushed.' He slid a hand into the pocket of his suit

jacket, pulled out a folded slip of paper, and held
it out to her. Alex stared at it, her eyes dark with
a growing horror. He'd told her that the wedding
had to take place as soon as possible, but never in
her wildest imaginings had she expected this sort
of time limit!

She looked up, the refusal hovering unspoken on
her lips as she met his eyes and read the ruthless
determination in their depths.

'Don't even think about it. You made your decision the other day, and there's no way I am letting
you back out!'

'But can't you see how crazy it all is? It's the sort
of thing you read about in books, but people don't
get married for this kind of reason!'

There was a desperate plea for understanding,
but it was obvious that he was unmoved by it. He
smiled coldly, dropping the piece of paper on to
her lap.

'People get married for any number of reasons.
I would have thought you were old enough to appreciate that.'

'Maybe they do, but I don't have to be one of
them.' She drew in a ragged breath, willing herself
to stay calm and not let it deteriorate into a verbal
battle. 'Look, Jordan, I can appreciate why you
are so angry, but this isn't the way to solve your
problems. It isn't!'

'As far as I am concerned it is, and that's that!
End of the discussion.' He turned away to open the
car door, but Alex couldn't let him get away with
it that easily. She caught his arm, forcing him to
turn back and look at her.

'And what happens if I refuse to go through with the wedding? What do you propose to do then, take a shot-gun and force me up the aisle?' She laughed wildly, verging on hysteria. 'What a turn-up for the book that would be. Jordan Lang forcing a woman into marrying him!'

Jordan's face darkened, the muscles under her fingers going rigid, and Alex felt the laughter die in her throat almost as quickly as it had begun.

'I don't need anything as crude as a gun. Have you forgotten so quickly that I hold all the cards, and can play them as I choose? But if it makes you feel better about this marriage, then maybe this will help.' He pulled her to him, holding her tightly as he tipped her head back, his fingers twined in the long strands of her hair.

'Let me go!' she ordered, but he just laughed, his eyes burning with an intensity which made a hot little quiver race through her body, draining the strength from her limbs.

'You know you don't really mean that. Don't you remember the other day, how it felt when I kissed you, held you, felt your heart beating under mine as it's doing now?' He slid his hand up to lie under her breasts so that Alex could feel the rapid beating of her heart pulsing against his palm. 'Remember how you enjoyed it? If you feel so badly about this marriage, then maybe you would prefer it to become more like a real one, based on mutual attraction rather than pure convenience?'

'No! You're mad if you think I'd ever——'

She got no further, as his head swooped down and he covered her parted lips, kissing her with a heat and passion which left her breathless and trembling within the space of seconds. But she couldn't let him do this, wouldn't let him subdue her by passion as he had before with threats. When he raised his head she forced her trembling, swollen lips to repeat the denial.

'No! No...'

He took her mouth again, his tongue sliding between her parted lips, tangling with hers so that the denial was lost, only echoing in her head until that too became lost in the magic he was creating. She couldn't seem to think, just feel, as though every one of her senses had been heightened to an unbearable degree. The silky touch of his tongue sliding against hers, the taste of his lips, the rapid beating of his heart—or was it hers?—the faint, warmly fragrant smell of his skin, the rainbows of colour flashing behind her closed lids...

He drew back slowly, studying her flushed face, and Alex had the feeling that he was searching for some kind of an answer to some unspoken question, before he smiled, that old familiar taunting smile, and the impression was gone.

'See what I mean? It would be no great hardship for either of us. I may not like your moral values, but I would be a liar if I said I wasn't attracted to you.'

How she hated him! She dragged herself out of his arms, her blue eyes burning. 'Forget it! There is no way this is ever going to be anything other than a business arrangement!'

He laughed shortly, raising a hand to run it over his dark hair, and smooth it back from his forehead. 'That's fine by me. In fact, I've had a pre-nuptial agreement drawn up by my solicitor, outlining what

we can both expect from this marriage. I shall arrange for you to sign it as soon as possible. Now I
think we had better go in and meet our guests.
They'll be wondering where we are if... Oh, I
forgot. You'd better have this first.'

He reached into his pocket again and pulled out
a small leather-covered box, snapping on the interior car light before handing it to her. Alex stared
at it in silence, feeling something cold and hard
welling in the pit of her stomach, knowing that there
was no way she could open the box and examine
its contents.

'Aren't you going to open it? Let me do it, then.'

He took it back from her unresisting fingers,
easing the lid open before presenting it to her again.
'An engagement wouldn't be real without a ring. I
hope I've got the right size, but I'm sure it can be
altered. You'd better try it on and see.'

He lifted the huge solitaire diamond off its black
velvet cushion, catching hold of her cold hand to
slide it up her finger in a travesty of an engagement
being cemented. Alex stared down at it, watching
the way the huge stone caught the dim light and
bounced flashes of icy fire back. It was a magnificent stone, flawless, perfectly cut and set, and
she hated it with an intensity which surprised her.
Something of what she felt must have shown on her
face because Jordan's eyes narrowed.

'I was told it was a perfect gem,' he said harshly.
'The jeweller assured me that I would have to go
a long way to find its equal.'

Alex shrugged, feeling the solid weight of the ring
like an alien presence on her finger, unasked for

and definitely unwanted. 'He wasn't lying. It's rare to find such a perfect stone nowadays.'

'Then why do I have the distinct impression that you don't like it?'

'Do you? How strange. However, I must admit that I'm not thrilled about being responsible for such a valuable piece of jewellery. I think it would be better if you took it back. I'm sure your friends will understand if we tell them that we haven't got round to buying the ring yet.'

She started to slide the ring from her finger, but he reached over and stopped her, his fingers biting cruelly into hers.

'Damn you, woman! Who do you think you are, turning your nose up at that ring? You're nothing but a common thief, and don't ever forget that! Do what you like with the ring. Consider it a bonus if you like. Once this fiasco is all over, then maybe what you get from selling it will stop you stealing from anyone else!'

It shouldn't have hurt to hear him say those things, shouldn't have felt like a knife stabbing into her heart; but it did. Alex pulled her hand away, and opened the car door to climb out, feeling the hot wash of tears behind her lids. Uncaring if he was following, she led the way towards the restaurant entrance, wondering if she would ever grow used to hearing what Jordan thought of her. Deep down, she knew his cruelty shouldn't hurt so much but, if she was really honest with herself, she had to admit that it did. The realisation frightened her, making her face the unpalatable fact that she was far more vulnerable to him than she wanted to be.

* * *

'Tell us, Alex, just how did you and Jordan meet and fall in love so quickly? It's come like a bolt out of the blue to all his friends, I can tell you. We thought he would never find the woman who would mean more to him than his beloved business!'

A ripple of laughter ran round the table, and slowly Alex laid her spoon aside as she looked round at the expectant faces. Apart from Jordan and James Morgan, the head project designer whom she'd met once before, she knew none of the other guests chosen to share this occasion. They had all been polite and friendly since she'd been introduced to them as Jordan's fiancée, but she'd been aware from the outset that they were openly curious about her sudden appearance in his life. The question now was, how was she going to satisfy that curiosity?

Her gaze slid on to the man seated opposite her, and she felt a flicker of satisfaction when she saw the expression of unease on his face. Obviously, Jordan was experiencing some doubts of his own about how she would answer, and suddenly the urge to pay him back for how he had hurt her with his loathsome comments became too strong to ignore. She smiled sweetly at him, a coquettish tilt to her lips.

'Shall I tell them, darling?' she murmured seductively. 'Or would you prefer it to remain our little secret?'

His eyes narrowed, the hand holding the wine glass tightening convulsively round its fragile stem before he seemed to force himself to relax and smile back at her.

'Tell everyone, by all means, darling,' he replied just as softly, 'but maybe not *all* the details. Some things are just too private ever to share.'

Was she the only one to hear the underlying note of threat in his voice? Alex shot a quick look round the table, and realised that she was. She hesitated, wondering if she was asking for more trouble than she could handle by carrying on, then caught a glimpse of the smugly complacent expression on Jordan's face and knew it would be worth it just to wipe it off!

'Jordan kidnapped me.'

The effect was riveting, everything she could have hoped for, and Alex knew the sight of all the stunned faces staring at her would go a long way to make up for whatever form his retribution took.

'I'm sorry, but did you actually say that Jordan...well, that he...?' The brunette tailed off, obviously wondering if she'd suffered some sort of a brainstorm, so Alex hastened to put her mind at rest.

'Mmm, that's right. Kidnapped me,' she repeated clearly, smiling brilliantly at her attentive audience before letting her eyes drift to Jordan with a hint of a challenge in their depths. 'Isn't that right, my love?'

All heads turned towards him, and Alex rested her chin on the heel of her hand as she waited to hear how he would answer.

'Perhaps I wouldn't have put it quite like that, *sweetheart*!' There was a faint edge in his voice, but Alex ignored it, staring limpidly back at him, her eyes as huge and guileless as she could make them.

'Wouldn't you?' She gave a soft, seductive little laugh. 'But what else can you call carrying me off in the middle of the night when we'd hardly met? Come on, *darling*, don't be shy about admitting what you did in front of your friends.'

The brunette was all eyes now, obviously hanging on every word, and Alex knew as clearly as she knew her own name that the story would be all over town before very long.

'But why? I mean, why would Jordan kidnap you? It's not the sort of thing he would usually do.'

Well, it was her own fault, of course; she should have known the sort of questions she'd be inviting by telling half the story. The trouble was she'd been so intent on making Jordan sweat a little that she'd not stopped to think where it could lead to. Uncertain how to get herself out of such a sticky explanation, she glanced at him and saw that he was watching her with a mocking expression on his face. Obviously, he'd realised just how successfully she'd backed herself into a corner, and was now prepared to sit back and watch her trying to struggle out! The realisation unlocked her tongue, giving her the strength to frame an answer of sorts.

'It was all a silly mix-up, really. I'd gone to the factory one night, and Jordan found me in there. He seemed to misunderstand my reasons for being there, so decided to teach me a lesson by carrying me off to his cottage in Wales, and...well, I'm sure I can leave the rest to your imaginations!'

There was a ripple of understanding laughter round the table, and she relaxed, pleased that she'd got out of the dilemma so neatly and with so little

trouble. However, it appeared that not everyone was
satisfied by her vague explanation.

'This mix-up you mentioned; can we take it that
you managed to clear it up?'

James Morgan spoke directly to her for the first
time that evening apart from a perfunctory greeting
when they'd been introduced, and Alex forced
herself to keep her smile in place. What was it about
the man that she disliked? He had never been anything other than coolly polite to her when they'd
met previously, yet there had been something about
him then which had made her skin prickle with a
vague feeling of animosity. Now, seeing the intent
scrutiny he was subjecting her to, Alex felt it again
with a renewed force. She hesitated before
answering, wondering exactly how much he knew
about what had happened. He was the firm's top
designer, so it was possible that Jordan could have
confided in him. But if he had, then surely he would
be more concerned about glossing over the incident
than in making an issue of it?

Undecided how to handle the question, Alex remained silent, then felt a surge of relief when the
brunette spoke up again.

'Of course they must have sorted everything out!
They are engaged to be married, aren't they? And
in only three weeks' time! Oh, it's all so romantic—
love at first sight, I bet; was it, Jordan?'

She turned to Jordan, who had been following
the exchange, and Alex couldn't stop herself from
looking at him too. Just for a moment their eyes
met and held, and she felt her pulse leap and her
breath catch at the warm glow of intimacy which
flowed between them, the feeling of a secret only

they knew and shared. Time seemed to stand still, holding them cocooned in one single never-ending heartbeat, then Jordan turned away, a strange fleeting expression crossing his face as he answered the question.

'Let's just say that I was completely bowled over by Alexandra that first night, and that she has made a huge impact on my life ever since.'

Disappointment welled inside her, and she dropped her eyes to the table, picking up her wine glass to take a swallow of the pale liquid, calling herself every kind of a fool. What had she expected him to say—that he *had* fallen in love with her that first night? The whole idea was crazy, just as she was crazy to feel as though she'd just been dealt some kind of a hurtful blow! With a defiant little tilt of the glass, she drained the last of the wine, then nearly choked when Jordan spoke softly beside her.

'I'd take it easy with that, if I were you. It might loosen your tongue even more, and I think you've said quite enough for one night.'

She looked up, her eyes widening as she saw him standing next to her. She'd been so intent on her own thoughts that she hadn't been aware of him getting up and coming round the table to her. Now she flinched as he slid a hand across her shoulder, smiling at her for the benefit of several of the guests who were openly watching them.

'Dance with me, darling?' he asked smoothly, his voice a fraction louder so that it would carry round the table. 'After all, this should be a night to remember.'

It would be that all right, and, if she had her
way, Alex would have given *him* a night he would
remember for a long time to come! A host of spiky
comments hovered on the tip of her tongue, but she
got no chance to utter even one of them, as he bent
and pressed a hard kiss to her lips. A murmur of
appreciation ran round the table at the openly
loving gesture, but Alex wasn't in any position to
appreciate the easy way with which he'd subdued
her attempt at defiance. She glared at him, her blue
eyes meeting his from the distance of a mere inch
or two as he held the kiss, but he did no more than
smile faintly so that she could feel his lips curving
upwards as they pressed against hers. He drew back
slowly, reaching out to push a long strand of golden
hair behind her shoulder, his fingers lingering
against her neck in a light touch which sent a sudden
streak of fire licking along her veins. When he held
his hand out to her, she slid her fingers into his and
let him lead her on to the small dance-floor, too
shaken by that sudden flare of sensation to summon
up the strength to refuse.

They danced in silence for several minutes,
Jordan's hand resting lightly at the small of her
back as he guided her round the floor to the gentle
rhythm of a waltz. Alex could feel the light brush
of his hand even through the fabric of her dress,
could feel the heat of his palm, the strength of his
lean fingers, as though every nerve-ending had
become sensitised to an incredible degree. What was
the matter with her? Why was she acting like
some . . . some lovesick schoolgirl?

The thought shocked her so much that she
stumbled, losing the rhythm. Jordan steadied her,

pulling her closer to avoid another couple who were dancing close behind them. Just for a moment Alex let herself rest against the hard, lean strength of his body, feeling the play of muscles under her hand where it pressed against his shoulder, then drew abruptly away.

'Sorry. I seemed to get in a bit of a tangle then.'

'It doesn't matter.' He looked down into her face, studying the twin patches of colour painted along her cheekbones in stark contrast to the underlying pallor. 'Are you feeling all right? You look rather flushed.'

'Such touching concern, Jordan. It does you credit, but of course it's only right and proper that you should be concerned about your new fiancée.' Deliberately she whipped up her anger, using it as a shield against those other far more unnerving feelings she'd experienced, and heard him curse softly. He took hold of her arm, easing her between the couples dancing round the crowded floor to steer her towards a narrow glass door set into one wall. He pushed it open, pulling her through before closing it behind them and abruptly cutting off the sound of the music, the hum of voices.

Alex hesitated, then moved further into the room, looking round curiously at the lush display of vegetation. The air was very warm, filled with moisture and carrying with it the sweet aroma of damp soil as well as the perfume from the exotic blossoms.

Slowly, she followed the narrow path which wound between the beds of plants, stopping several times to examine a particularly spectacular specimen, aware that Jordan was following her. The path led to the centre of the conservatory, where there was a wide stone bench set into an arch made by the overhanging greenery, and she sat down, resting her head back against the gritty, hard surface as she watched him stop a few feet away. He drew a packet of cigarettes from his pocket and lit one, drawing deeply on it as he inhaled the smoke, his face shuttered.

'You shouldn't smoke. It's bad for you.' Her voice was low, in keeping with the quiet room, and she saw him grimace as he shot a look at the smouldering cigarette.

'I know. It's a loathsome habit, but not one I give in to very often, I'm glad to say.' He took another draw on the cigarette, then stubbed it out and dropped the remains into a stone pot which appeared to serve as an ashtray. 'However, I'm sure we have more important things to discuss than my bad habits. What did you think you were doing before, telling people that I kidnapped you? You could have caused no end of problems if they hadn't thought it was some kind of a joke.'

Alex shrugged, looking away to focus on the wide, smooth green leaves which almost touched her head, terrified that he would somehow read what she'd been feeling before in her eyes. What was the matter with her tonight? She felt as though her emotions were on a roller-coaster, swinging up in one direction before dropping down in the other. One minute she hated Jordan for what he was doing to her, the next she felt these strange little flurries of attraction when he touched her, as though she had no control over herself any more.

Suddenly, he sighed, and came across to sit next to her, stretching his long legs in front of him before running a hand almost wearily over the thick darkness of his hair. 'Look, I know this isn't easy for either of us, but you'll achieve nothing by trying to fight me. This is the only acceptable way out of this mess you've created, and I'm not going to change my mind.'

'Acceptable? To whom? Maybe it's acceptable to you, but not to me! This isn't another one of your business deals. It's marriage! You know—to have and to hold, in sickness and in health, for richer, for poorer. Perhaps it doesn't bother you making a mockery out of it, but it bothers me!'

His face hardened. 'Oh, it bothers me all right. A lot, if you want the truth. You aren't the only one to have "finer" feelings, but I'm afraid we have little choice in the matter.'

'Of course we have a choice! Even if you won't believe that I am innocent, then surely you could find some other way to raise the money you need rather than go through with this crazy plan? There must be dozens of people willing to invest in a company as profitable as Lang's.'

Jordan shook his head, his expression bitter as he stared across the dimly lit bower. 'Don't you think I've already tried everything else?' He laughed harshly, no amusement in the sound. 'A couple of months back I had investors fighting to put money into the firm. I could have had any amount of cash I wanted, and any way I chose, but that's business for you—another roll of the dice and everything can change. Now you'd be amazed how many of those would-be investors are "unavailable" when I've tried to contact them! The word's out that Lang's is going through some rough water, and no one wants to get sucked in if we go under. The only way out is by using the money Mother left me, and as far as I'm concerned the company is far more important than the rights or wrongs of this marriage!'

'Then all I can say is that you are a fool.' Alex stood up, aching inside with a strange feeling of regret she didn't understand. 'You are willing to ruin both our lives to save the firm, but if you think I shall sit back and let you do it then you can think again!'

He came to his feet in one lithe motion, gripping her by the shoulders as he held her in front of him, his face dark with anger. 'Don't make the mistake of thinking I won't do everything I threatened I would do! I'll ruin you and your precious brother if you try to renege on our agreement!'

'I don't doubt you would!' Her eyes skimmed over him, bright with contempt. 'But one thing you haven't allowed for, Jordan Lang, is the fact that you would have to release me from the agreement if I proved my innocence. Isn't that so?'

'Perhaps. But from where I'm standing there is less chance of you doing that than of you catching moonbeams.'

Alex glared at him. 'Just you wait,' she said. 'I'll prove you wrong! All I want is your word that if I manage it you will drop this whole charade, and cancel all your plans for this . . . wedding!'

He hesitated, searching her face with a scrutiny that seemed to look right into her soul, then slowly he nodded, something akin to admiration softening his face. 'All right, then, yes; I give you my word that I shall release you completely from the agreement if you succeed in convincing me.' He smiled suddenly, letting go of her shoulders to brush a fist lightly across her jaw in a mock blow. 'You pack quite a punch when you set your mind to it. It makes me almost wish that we——'

He stopped abruptly, turning away to stride along the path towards the door, his back stiff. Alex drew in a ragged breath, forcing the painful pounding of her heart to slow as she followed him. What had he been about to say—that he wished that they could have met in different circumstances? She didn't know, but in her heart she knew that was what *she* wished. Given another time and another place, then could she and Jordan have established an entirely different kind of relationship? It was a tantalising and disturbing thought.

CHAPTER SIX

THE telephone rang just as Alex was getting out of the shower. Wrapping a towel round herself, she hurried to answer it, hoping it would be Kenny. She'd spent a restless night going over everything that had happened between her and Jordan—especially those last few minutes in the conservatory—and now she welcomed the chance to talk to Kenny to set herself back on even keel. Kenny had been against the plan from the moment she had explained it to him; it had been only after she had reassured him that she could cope with a few months of marriage better than with the alternative that he had agreed to go along with it. Now she needed that reassurance handing back to her to keep her on course.

Flicking a glance at the clock as she hurried into the living-room, she smiled as she picked up the phone, certain that no one but her brother would be calling at such an early hour of the morning.

'Hello. Am I glad you rang! You're just the person I need to talk to this morning.'

There was a happy anticipation in her voice, which faded abruptly when the caller spoke.

'Well, I never expected such a greeting! Does this mean you've had a change of heart, Alex?'

The smile faded and she stood up straighter, unconsciously tucking the towel more firmly across her breasts as though shielding herself against the shock.

'What do you want, Jordan?' she asked coldly.

'Do I have to *want* something? Isn't it only natural that a man should want to speak to his fiancée?' There were a host of nuances in his voice, and Alex felt her pulse skip a beat before racing wildly to catch up with itself. She drew in a slow breath, forcing herself to remember that this was Jordan she was speaking to—the man who was willing to blackmail her to get what he wanted; but it was strangely difficult to control the flurry of awareness those seductive tones evoked.

'I...I don't have the time to start playing silly games with you. Just tell me what you want and be done with it. I'm in a hurry.'

'You seemed eager enough to talk when you answered. Who were you expecting to be calling you?'

It would be so easy to tell him, easy and simple and sensible, but, for some perverse reason she didn't fully understand, Alex chose not to take the easy path.

'That is none of your business!'

'I disagree. I think it is my business! Don't forget that we have an agreement, lady, and there is no way I intend to let you jeopardise it!'

'What do you mean?'

'Just that I hope you realise that any...relationships you had are to be terminated immediately. I don't want any hint of scandal going about that my fiancée has been seen with other men! If there is anyone in your life, then get rid of him...now!'

It was an order, plain and simple and, as such, totally unpalatable. Alex reacted to it with instinct rather than logic.

'And what happens if I refuse?'

'Then you will regret it!'

'You don't own me, Jordan Lang!' she said furiously. 'I might have agreed to this plan of yours, but it doesn't give you the right to run my life and tell me what I can and cannot do!'

'You think not? Let's just get this straight here and now; nothing, and I mean *nothing*, is going to get in the way of this marriage! You will only be storing up more trouble for yourself if you push me by behaving stupidly. You are my fiancée, and that means ending any other relationships you have. I won't tolerate you making a laughing-stock out of me! However, I didn't ring up to have an argument with you.'

'No? Well, it seems you've succeeded anyway.' There was an icy sarcasm in Alex's voice, in complete contrast to the hot waves of fury racing through her at his domineering attitude. How dared he tell her how to behave? The fact that she wasn't involved in any 'relationship', as he put it, was by the way. She'd been too busy building up the business over the past couple of years to bother with anything more than casual friendships; but it angered her that he should take such a cavalier attitude, as though she was his property!

However, he ignored her tone and carried on as though she had never spoken, infuriating her more than ever. 'I rang to ask you to meet me for lunch today. There isn't much time before the wedding, and I think it would be better if people get used to

seeing us together, to prevent too much specu-
lation. I don't want any of our investors getting
wind of the reasons why we are getting married in
such a hurry. I suggest you meet me at the factory
around one o'clock, and we'll go on from there.'

Alex snapped her lips together, her temper simmering. 'And what if it isn't convenient? I do have
a business to run, remember?'

'I'm afraid what you want is of little conse-
quence. Just meet me at one, or you will be sorry!'

'I hate you!' she said hoarsely.

'Do you?' There was a strange note in his voice
as he asked the question—not anger, which she
might have expected, nor even that cold mockery
she'd come to dislike so much—and Alex felt a little
shiver tingle its way down to her toes.

'You know I do,' she replied, trying her hardest
to put as much conviction into the words; but he
just laughed softly, a note of intimacy in the sound
which ran along her veins like a bush fire, and sent
the blood hissing hotly to her head.

'I thought you did, but I'm not so sure now that
I've seen the photograph.'

'What photograph?' she demanded. 'What are
you talking about?'

'You'll see. Just take a look at today's paper,
Alex, and ask yourself if it really is hate . . . or
something else?'

He cut the connection, leaving Alex staring
blankly at the receiver until she dropped it abruptly
on to its rest. She hurried into her bedroom, and
slipped on a robe before running downstairs to
collect the paper from behind the door. Frantically,
she flicked through the pages, then stopped dead

when she came to the society column, her eyes widening in gathering shock as she saw the photograph slap bang in the centre of the page. For one incredulous minute she stared at it, then crumpled the page and threw it on to the floor.

'No!' The cry echoed round the silence in the flat, growing fainter and fainter so that she wanted to scream it again and keep on screaming just to make herself believe that it was true; but she had the terrible feeling that it wouldn't be enough to make it convincing. Bending, she picked up the crumpled piece of paper, her hands shaking as she smoothed it out and studied the picture once again.

It had been taken last night at the restaurant, and showed her and Jordan together. Alex could remember the moment quite clearly, remember how he had pulled her close to avoid another couple dancing behind them, could remember how she had let herself lean against him for that brief moment. What she didn't remember was how she had been looking at him, but the camera had caught her expression quite clearly, and she went cold to the bottom of her heart as she saw the image of herself. She had been looking at him at that moment not with hatred in her eyes, but with the expression of a woman in love!

'Mr Lang asked me to tell you that he's been delayed at a meeting, Miss Campbell. He shouldn't be very long now. Would you like some coffee while you're waiting for him?'

Alex smiled her thanks and accepted the cup of coffee the secretary poured for her, carrying it over to an arrangement of chairs grouped round a small table near the window. Setting the cup down, she tried to relax, but it was impossible while her heart was beating so hard. What was she going to say to Jordan to explain that photograph? It was a question she had asked herself a thousand times that morning, yet she still had no idea what the answer was.

Picking up the cup, she took a tiny sip of the hot drink, then looked round the room, needing to focus her attention on something other than her own feelings. She caught the secretary's eye, and smiled self-consciously, glancing away as she set the cup back down again with a tiny clatter. It had been obvious from the moment she'd walked into the factory that everyone knew who she was and why she was there, thanks to that photograph and the accompanying article about the engagement. As she had made her way to Jordan's office, she had run the gauntlet of curious glances, the stifled murmur of comments. It seemed that everyone in the building was anxious to get a glimpse of the boss's future bride!

Her hands started to shake at the thought, and she clasped them together, willing herself to get a grip on herself. She couldn't afford to lose control now. She had to find the words to convince Jordan that what he had seen in that revealing photograph had been a mere trick of the light, nothing more, and definitely nothing as devastating as love! She *couldn't* be in love with a man who had done everything in his power to humiliate her and blackmail her!

The door opened, and she felt her heart lurch as she turned towards it, expecting to see Jordan, but

it was James Morgan who walked into the room.
He came over to her, once again subjecting her to
that intent scrutiny, and immediately Alex felt her
skin start to prickle.

'Miss Campbell, how nice to see you again so
soon. How are you today? Recovered from all the
excitement last night, I hope?'

'I'm fine, thank you, Mr Morgan,' she replied,
fixing a smile to her lips as she met his searching
gaze. 'It was a pleasant evening. I hope you enjoyed it?'

'I did indeed. I take it you have come to meet
Jordan?'

'Yes. We're having lunch together.'

'Good. I must confess we were all taken by surprise when he announced the engagement out of
the blue like that. It was all very sudden.' His eyes
narrowed, as though he was testing for a reaction,
and Alex felt a ripple of real unease work its way
through her.

'These things sometimes happen like that,' she
said non-committally, aware that the secretary was
following every word.

'They must do. Strange, though—Jordan has
always struck me as the sort of man who would
never rush into anything without a lot of due
thought.'

His tone was bland, the cool smile shaping his
thin lips firmly in place, but to Alex's hypersen-
sitive ears there seemed to be an underlying double
meaning to the observation.

'I'm sure that anyone who works closely with
Jordan would know that he would never take on a
commitment unless he was a hundred per cent

certain that it was the right thing to do.' There was a slight edge to Alex's voice, and she saw James Morgan stiffen before he made an obvious effort to relax.

'Of course. Forgive me if you thought I was implying anything else. Everyone here has good reason to appreciate his sterling qualities. Actually, that is the real reason I popped in to the office. I wondered if you would like to have a look round and meet some of the staff while you're waiting for him to get back?'

'Well, I . . .' The last thing she felt like doing was accompanying Morgan anywhere. He made her uncomfortable. Yet it was hard to think of a valid reason to refuse the offer.

'I'm sure Jordan won't mind you looking round. He can't have anything he wants to keep secret from his future wife, can he?'

There was no mistaking the challenge in Morgan's voice, and once again Alex was struck by the feeling that he knew a lot more about her situation than he should. Suddenly, and for no explicable reason, it became imperative that she should find out what he knew.

'Thank you, Mr Morgan. I would enjoy that very much.'

'Good.' He crossed the room and held the door open for her, and slowly Alex walked through it, feeling her heart thumping sickeningly fast in her chest. Call it instinct, but something told her that there was far more to this invitation than met the eyes. She would have to be on her guard!

*   *   *

'And last, but not least, my office. The design centre of the whole factory, I think one can call it, where all the plans for our new projects are hatched. Have you ever been in here before? No, of course you haven't. Why on earth did I ask such a silly question?'

Morgan laughed hollowly as he unlocked the door and let Alex precede him into the room. It had been a whistle-stop tour of the factory, as they had rushed with almost indecent haste from one department to another, and Alex had the sudden unshakeable feeling that this room and what it contained had been the real reason behind his offer to show her round.

She looked round, her mind doing a swift hop backwards in time to that moment when the light had been flicked on and Jordan had confronted her. She drew in a ragged breath, forcing the disquieting memory from her mind while she coped with what was to come. James Morgan hadn't brought her here just to admire his office—he had to have a far more deadly reason that that.

'I thought you might be interested in seeing the blueprints for the new project we're launching soon. I'm sure Jordan must have told you about the problems we've had, but hopefully we're over those hurdles now.' He closed the office door and walked over to the safe, then hesitated and glanced at his watch. 'I'd better give Jordan's office a ring to let him know where you are, in case he's looking for you.'

He made the call, then smiled blandly at Alex, his pale eyes holding a hint of something which made apprehension rise in her chest. Suddenly, in the blink of an eye, she knew that the very last thing she wanted to do was to stay here in this room with him. She took a quick step backwards, then felt her legs turn to lead when he drew a familiar roll of pale blue paper out of the safe and spread it on the desk.

'Have you seen the plans before, Miss Campbell?'

His voice was low, oily, and she shuddered in revulsion. She swallowed down the taste of bile, wondering what game he was playing by asking that taunting question. She had no idea, but she had to keep her head until she found out.

'Should I have seen them, Mr Morgan?'

'No, of course not. I just thought that someone might have shown them to you.'

'I'm afraid there would be no point, as I'm sure I would never understand them.'

'Oh, they're not difficult to understand. An intelligent person would have no problems at all. Here, let me explain them to you.'

He stood aside, obviously meaning for her to join him behind the desk, but that was the last thing she was going to do!

'No!' She forced her voice down an octave or two, fighting the urge to turn tail and run from the room. 'Please don't trouble yourself. As I said, I've no idea how to read the plans, and no real inclination to learn. So if you'll——' She broke off as the buzzer on the intercom sounded, making her jump nervously. She drew in a deep breath while she tried to regain her composure, not bothering to listen to what Morgan was saying. All she was interested in was getting out of this room and away from those plans as fast as she could.

He switched the intercom off then smiled at Alex, that cold little smile which never touched his eyes and seemed to be more a mask than a true expression of his feelings. 'You will have to excuse me for a few minutes, Miss Campbell. I'm needed on the shop floor. Make yourself comfortable. I won't be long.'

'Oh, but I'd prefer to go back to Jordan's office. I'll find my own way.'

'Nonsense. We don't want you wandering round on your own getting lost. I'll escort you back when I'm finished.'

He had gone before Alex could protest any further. She looked round, twisting the strap of her bag nervously between her fingers, hating the thought of remaining in that room until he came back; yet she couldn't just walk out and leave the blueprints lying around. They were too valuable— as she knew to her cost—to take a chance on anything happening to them. It would be better to lock them away in the safe and return the keys to Morgan later.

She hurried round the desk and started to roll them up, then looked up in relief when the door opened, thinking it was Morgan coming back already—only it wasn't him. Her heart lurched in fear when she saw the expression on Jordan's face as he saw her standing behind the desk with the blueprints in her hands.

'What the hell are you doing?'

Maybe if he had asked her nicely she would have told him, would have explained what had happened, step by careful step. But not when he adopted that accusing tone! She tossed the roll back on to the desk and faced him, colour flaring into her cheeks.

'What do you think?'

He closed the door and came further into the room, his grey eyes icy as he flicked a glance at the plans before looking back at her.

'How did you get hold of them this time?' There was a harsh bite to the words, an edge of steel that cut her to the quick, and Alex's head snapped back as though he had struck her.

'Would you believe me if I told you?'

'Damn you, woman! Don't you dare play games with me! How did you get those plans?'

There was a barely controlled violence in his voice, a tension to his body, which warned her he was on the verge of losing control. It frightened her into answering with a shade more caution.

'Mr Morgan left them on the desk when he went out of the office. I thought it would be safer if they were locked away before I left, and was just about to do it when you came in.'

'You really expect me to believe that? There is no way that James would be so careless as to leave them lying around! He's far too——' He broke off when the door opened and Morgan came into the room. The man stopped when he saw Jordan, his eyes running swiftly from one tense figure to the other, and Alex wondered if she was imagining the faint gleam of satisfaction which shone in his pale eyes.

'I'm sorry. I hope I'm not interrupting anything?'

'Of course not, James. Come in.' Obviously making an effort to control his temper, Jordan ran a hand round the back of his neck, kneading the tense muscles as he forced himself to appear relaxed. 'I just came to collect Alex, and was wondering what the plans were doing out of the safe.'

'Out of . . .? I could have sworn they were locked away when I left. Miss Campbell had asked to see them, but I'm almost certain that I hadn't got them out.'

There was a faintly puzzled expression on the older man's face as he glanced at the plans, and Alex stared at him in incredulity. What was he saying? He knew very well that he had left the plans lying around, so why was he telling all these lies? However, before she could challenge him, he picked them up and locked them carefully away. 'Good job it was Miss Campbell in here, though, wasn't it? I would have been for the high jump if it had been anyone else, but obviously our secrets are safe with her.'

Alex drew in a shaky breath, fighting against the hot surge of anger as she realised that it had been no accident. Morgan had deliberately left the blueprints out, knowing that Jordan would come to his office and find her with them! But why? What possible reason could he have for doing such a thing?

Her mind racing this way and that to solve the puzzle, she let Jordan lead her from the room, scarcely aware of what was happening until they stepped out into the car park. A cold, sleeting rain was falling, and she stopped to pull up her collar, but Jordan urged her on, seemingly oblivious to the heavy downpour which soaked them both in seconds. She glanced up at him, and something inside her seemed to shrivel up and die when she saw the expression on his face.

In total silence he led her to his car, barely giving her time to climb in before he slammed the door. It was quite obvious what he thought had been going on, and Alex knew that, no matter what, she had to convince him she hadn't been trying to steal the plans once more.

'It isn't what you think. I——'

'Why? Dammit, Alex, tell me! Why try it again? You're not stupid, but to attempt that in the middle of the day!' He swung round, his eyes burning into hers with a cold fire in their depths, and something else—something which made her stop and choose her words with care when pride demanded that she should answer just as hurtfully as he had. To see that fleeting shadow of regret on Jordan's face was something she had never expected to see.

'I didn't do anything,' she said quietly, willing him to hear the truth. 'It happened exactly as I explained. Morgan left the plans on his desk when he was called away. He was the one who insisted that I should see them, the one who took me to the office and got them out of the safe. I have no idea why he tried to make out otherwise. It was all a pack of lies.'

'Lies? Why should he want to lie to me? I've worked with the man for years, known him even longer. He was a part of Lang's when my father ran the company, so why should James start lying to me now? Why should he lie about you when he hardly knows you?'

'I don't know! I only wish I did. But it's the truth...all of it!'

'The truth? Hell, lady, you wouldn't know the truth if it got up and bit you! Your whole life is one huge pack of lies. I doubt if you even know what you're doing half the time.'

'No! You're wrong. Jordan, please! You must listen to me!' She caught hold of his hand, holding it tightly, willing him to open his mind to what she was saying. 'James Morgan was up to something today. He deliberately made it appear that I had asked to see those blueprints—but I hadn't!'

He shook her off, leaning forwards to start the engine with an angry roar. 'And you expect me to believe you after what's happened? I gave up believing in fairy stories a long time ago, Alex. But if you have any thoughts in your pretty head about taking what you know to your "friends", then forget them, or you will regret the day you ever heard of me and my company!'

'You can't threaten me like that, Jordan Lang!' she cried, willing herself to sound angry when inside she felt as though she was dying as she heard the contempt in his voice.

'I can do any damn thing I like, and don't you ever forget it. And number one on my list is bringing the wedding forwards.' He smiled, his eyes icy as they raked over her pale face. 'You should be flattered to learn I'm such an eager bridegroom. I'll arrange for a special licence this afternoon, so may I suggest that you go home now and start packing? You will be Mrs Jordan Lang within the week!'

'No! No, Jordan, you can't do this! I won't let you. I——' She stopped abruptly as he leaned over and pressed a finger lightly against her lips, damming the frantic flow of words.

'Yes, Alex,' he said softly, so softly that a shiver ran along her veins, trailing after the echo from the words. 'I'm calling all the shots now, and you will do exactly as I say or suffer the consequences!'

He drew back and set the car into gear, driving calmly out of the yard. Alex sat huddled in her seat, feeling the quaking spasm of fear racking her body as she realised she was beaten. No matter what she said or what she did, she would never make him change his mind now. But how could she face the next few months as his wife when he hated her so much?

CHAPTER SEVEN

MRS JORDAN LANG. The name sounded as unfamiliar as the weight of the gold band felt on her finger. Alex stared at her reflection, studying the pallor of her cheeks, the dull flatness of her eyes as though she was seeing the face of a stranger. That was how she felt—a stranger. No longer Alex Campbell, but for the past hour Mrs Jordan Lang. Someone entirely different.

The hotel-room door opened, and she swung round, a faint colour stinging her cheeks as her heart beat frantically; but it was only Kenny coming looking for her. He shot her an anxious glance as he closed the door on the hum of noise echoing up from the reception area, then came and sat down on a nearby chair. Alex turned back to the mirror, picking up the brush to run it through her hair again, needing something to keep her hands busy.

'Are you feeling all right? You look...' he shrugged, unable to find the right words '...well, different somehow.'

'I am different. I'm a married woman now, remember? Mrs Jordan Lang!' Her voice broke, and she bit her lip to stem the sudden tide of hysteria which threatened to crack the ice that had carried her through the morning's ceremony at the register office and the champagne reception afterwards, held downstairs in this smart hotel.

Kenny swore softly, taking the brush from her hands as he turned her to face him. 'You don't have to go through with this any further, Lexie. He's got his piece of paper to claim his inheritance. There is no need for you to go and live in his house. Tell him to go to hell!'

Alex shook her head, her eyes swimming with unshed tears. 'I can't. It was all part of the agreement, and he won't let me get away with it. He'll want his very last ounce of flesh if I know him.' She covered Kenny's fingers with hers, hating to see him looking so worried. 'It will be all right. You'll see. Just a few months, and then we can put it all——' She broke off abruptly as the door opened and Jordan came into the room. His eyes narrowed when he saw Kenny, and immediately Alex let her hand slide away from her brother's and turned back to the mirror, watching Jordan coming closer through the glass.

'Are you nearly ready? People are waiting to wave us off.'

'I...' Her throat felt parched as a desert, her tongue swollen through a sudden lack of moisture, and she swallowed hard to ease the hot, gravelly feel of it. 'I'll only be a minute now. You go back down, and I'll be there as soon as I can.'

'I'll wait for you. It will look odd if I go back on my own, without my blushing bride—won't it?' There was cold sarcasm in his voice, and Kenny rose to his feet, twin spots of colour burning in his lean cheeks.

'Just be careful what you say, Lang. Or I'll——'

'You'll what? I don't think you are in any position to threaten me, Campbell.' Jordan didn't move, his face set as he met Kenny's anger with a cool, controlled contempt which only emphasised the difference between them—the fact that Kenny was no match for him in any circumstances. Kenny must have sensed it too because fury flashed into his eyes, and hastily Alex jumped to her feet and stepped in front of him.

'Stop it,' she ordered. 'This isn't going to get us anywhere. You go back downstairs, Kenny, and I'll be there in a minute.'

For a moment she thought he was going to ignore her. 'Please,' she said softly, catching hold of his arm and shaking it gently. 'I don't want there to be any trouble. I just want to get this over and done with as soon as possible.'

Kenny glanced at her, his expression softening. 'All right. But if you need me... And you, Lang, if you ever do anything to hurt her, then you'll have me to answer to!'

He left the room, leaving a wake of tension hanging in the air. Alex picked up the brush again and sat down, watching Jordan warily in the mirror. He had seemed strangely tense these last few days, as though there was something simmering just below the surface that was bothering him. Several times she had looked up to find him watching her with an expression on his face which she hadn't understood but which had made her feel uneasy. She had tried to refuse to see him until the day of the wedding, but he had overruled her protests with a heavy-handed determination, insisting that they must be seen in public together.

Now she could sense that same tension in him again, see that strange stillness to his features, as though he was thinking about something disturbing. The need to protect Kenny from anything he might be dreaming up was suddenly strong.

'Kenny was just trying to protect me, that's all. Obviously he's worried about this whole charade.'

Jordan didn't speak for a moment, staring into space until he seemed to gather himself. 'Then he's going about it the wrong way. It's about time he learned to control that temper of his before it gets him into any further trouble.'

'What do you expect him to do? Sit back nice and calmly while I'm press-ganged into this marriage? Obviously family loyalty is something you know little about!' Her tone was sharp, cutting through the tension hovering in the air, and Jordan's face tightened at the deliberate insult. Just for a moment he held her eyes in the mirror, then turned away to walk to the window, his hands pushed into the trousers of his dark grey suit, his wide shoulders rigid.

Alex drew in a shuddering little breath, knowing she was being foolish by needling him like this. She didn't want to promote any head-on confrontations. She wanted to let these next few months pass as quietly and emotionlessly as possible, because something inside her warned her she could be opening a Pandora's box by letting emotions run riot. She put down the brush and picked up a tube of lipstick in the same pale peach colour as her calf-length dress, outlining her lips with the glossy tint.

'Has it never occurred to you that you might be doing Kenny more harm than good by always jumping in to help him out of trouble?'

Jordan's voice was low, and Alex shot him a quick glance, feeling heat run through her when she saw that he was watching her. Nervously, she put down the lipstick, running a finger across the smooth wood of the dressing-table, feigning an intent concentration in its surface as she sought to avoid his eyes.

'I don't know what you mean. He's my brother; naturally I want to help him, just as he wants to help me.'

'But at some time in his life he has to learn to help himself. You can't keep mollycoddling him, Alex! He's gone from your parents to you, letting each of you make excuses for him rather than making him face up to his responsibilities!'

Is that what had happened? Had Kenny never learned to accept responsibility because he had always been overly loved? In a sudden flash, Alex knew it was the truth. She had taken on the role her mother had always performed, protecting Kenny rather than making him stand on his own two feet. Widowed at an early age, it had been natural that Janet Campbell should pour the love she'd felt for her husband on to the son who looked so like him. When she too had died ten years later, Alex had assumed that role and continued to shield Kenny from the realities of life. Now it was as if a veil had been torn aside by Jordan's observations.

She stood up, strangely unnerved by his astuteness, which left her feeling naked and vulnerable, as though he could read parts of her she didn't want him to read. Picking up the soft cream wool coat from the back of the chair, she started to shrug it on, jumping when he came and took it from her hands and slid it up her arms. Smoothing the soft wool across her shoulders, he turned her round, catching hold of the two wings of the collar as he held her in front of him.

'Would any of this have happened if it hadn't been for Kenny, Alex?'

His voice was low, washing through her like warm wine flowing through water, and she shivered, suddenly achingly aware of the touch of his fingers against her neck, the faint scent of his skin, the warmth of his body just inches from her own. Sensation flooded through her, bringing with it the memories she'd tried so hard to erase from her mind, memories of how it had felt to be held and kissed by him. Just for a moment the temptation to feel his kiss again was so strong that she took a half-step closer to him, then realised what she was doing. Self-contempt lanced her, and she drew away, her hands shaking as she buttoned the coat before looking up at him with a forced mockery in her eyes.

'My, my, Jordan; keep on like that and I'll start thinking that you've changed your mind about me and decided I'm innocent after all! And where would that leave this sham of a marriage?'

His face closed abruptly, the light dying from his eyes, leaving them dark and shadowed. He bent down and picked up her bag, handing it to her before opening the door. Alex walked past him, her head held high, wondering if it had been her overstrung imagination playing tricks. Just for a second

there, before he had blanked it out, she could have
sworn she'd seen guilt on his face; but of course
she must have been mistaken. Jordan wasn't the
kind of man who would ever feel guilty!

Jordan's house was set at the end of a short, tree-
lined drive, a sprawling, oddly irregular building
which had been added to at various times over the
years, following the vagaries of its current owner.
Alex had been prepared to dislike the house on
sight, yet to her surprise she felt an immediate attraction to the place, finding nothing in its mellow
red brick to resemble the stark prison her imagination had conjured up!

Stopping the car in front of the house, Jordan
switched off the engine, then sat staring through
the windscreen, his face still wearing that closed
expression. He had said no more than half a dozen
words since they'd left the reception, and Alex
could feel her stomach lurching in anticipation of
what was to come. She glanced down at her hand,
unconsciously twisting the unfamiliar ring round
and round her finger, watching the way the pale
wintry sunlight reflected off its smooth golden
surface. A wedding-ring should be a token of love
and commitment, a golden promise of a future life
together; yet all this ring was, was a symbol of
Jordan's hatred for her. The thought was oddly
bitter.

'Right, then. I suppose we'd better get inside and
sort you out. There are a couple of things I need
to get cleared up this afternoon, so I can't afford
to waste any more time.'

Alex jumped when he spoke, colour ebbing and flowing in her cheeks when she glanced round and saw that he was watching her.

'I didn't realise you were going out,' she said to cover the confusion she felt, then silently cursed herself when she realised how it sounded.

He smiled, one dark brow raising slightly. 'I can always arrange to stay in if you prefer.'

Heat ran through her at the blatant suggestion in his voice, and she turned away, making a great show of gathering up her bag and the spray of orchids he'd pinned to her dress outside the register office. 'I don't care what you do,' she said snappily.

'No?'

'Of course not.' She swung the door open, then stopped when he caught her by the wrist, his long fingers locking firmly round its slender width.

' "Methinks the lady doth protest too much",' he quoted, his deep voice sending an unwanted *frisson* of heat scorching along her veins.

'Don't be ridiculous!' Alex forced a bite to the words, all too conscious of the feel of his hand on her arm. 'If you think I would welcome your company, then think again. I hate you, Jordan Lang, hate you for what you've done today, making me go through with this mockery of a marriage!'

'So you keep saying, but I can't help remembering that photograph.' He bent closer, his breath warm as it clouded on her skin. 'You didn't look as though you hated me then, Alex.'

'I . . .' Her throat closed, locking the denial deep inside. Ever since she'd seen that photograph in the paper she'd spent hours rehearsing what she would say to him if he ever mentioned it again, yet now she couldn't remember a single one of the dismissing little sentences she'd practised so carefully.

Helplessly, she watched his eyes darken as they dropped to her mouth. She knew he was going to kiss her then, knew to the depths of her soul that that was his intention, yet she couldn't seem to find the strength to stop him.

'No.' The protest was a mere token, dying on her lips as his mouth touched hers, his lips warm and gentle, so tender as they traced over hers that she felt tears spring to her eyes. Maybe if he had kissed her roughly, taken her mouth by force, she could have found it in her to fight him; but she wasn't proof against this gentlest of caresses.

'Alex.' Her name was a soft whisper of sound on his lips as he skimmed a shower of hot little kisses up the curve of her jaw to nibble delicately at the sensitive hollow behind her ear. Alex closed her eyes, letting herself drown in the exquisite sensations which made her body feel like liquid. His hand skimmed up her ribs, his fingers pausing briefly before they slid beneath the folds of her coat to curve lightly round her breast, teasing the nipple into aching tautness. Heat flooded through her, pouring along her veins, filling her whole body with a hot yearning.

'Jordan!' It was her turn now to whisper his name, her turn to skim kisses along the strong curve of his jaw, her turn to feel the shudders which rippled through him as she slid her hands over the hard muscles of his chest, feeling the crispness of hair beneath the thin silk of his shirt. He groaned softly, deep in his throat, and pulled her closer, pushing aside the soft enveloping folds of her coat

so that he could press her against him and feel the
desire-hardened nipples rubbing tantalisingly
against his chest. Then slowly he put her from him,
his hands rubbing lightly over the ends of her
shoulders as he held her in front of him.

'Do you still claim to hate me so much, then,
Alex?'

His voice was soft, but Alex flinched as though
he had shouted the question. Her eyes flew open,
and she stared up at him with horror in her eyes.
How could she have done such a thing? How could
she have forgotten who he was and why she was
here, even for a moment? Great waves of shame
ran through her, and she pulled away, opening the
car door to climb out with the stiff, jerky movements of a person in the throes of shock. Hate and
love: two opposing forces, or two sides of a single
coin? She had no idea, but there was no way she
was going to take any chances—not when this was
just day one of six long months to be spent under
Jordan's roof! She would be very careful from now
on never to toss that coin in case it landed on the
wrong side. To fall in love with Jordan would be
the biggest mistake she could ever make in a relationship already memorable for its share of
disasters!

She didn't want to go home, didn't want to go back
and spend another evening making polite conversation. On the surface, she and Jordan seemed to
be managing quite smoothly living together, but
she'd become increasingly aware of the undercur-
rents which flowed between them. Was he aware of
them too? He never gave any sign of being so, but

they had grown so strong in the past few days that he would have to be blind not to be—and it frightened her.

Three weeks hadn't dimmed the memory of how easily she had responded to him that first day at the house. When they were together, she was constantly on her guard, and the strain was starting to tell on her. If Kenny had been at home in the flat, she would have locked the shop and gone upstairs to talk to him for a couple of hours; but he had decided to carry on working at the Yorkshire depot. Alex knew it was the best thing for him; she'd already noticed a subtle change in him when they had spoken over the telephone—a hint that he was finally growing up and accepting responsibility for himself. Jordan had been right about that; he had seen what Kenny needed quite clearly. Had he been right about her too?

The thought shocked her, and abruptly she chased it from her mind, looking round the shop with haunted eyes before coming to a rapid, almost desperate decision. She wouldn't go home. She would catch a bus into Southport, and do some late-night shopping. With Christmas only weeks away, most of the stores would be open, and that was just what she needed—the hustle and bustle to take her mind off those fanciful ideas. Maybe she would make a night of it—have a meal and take in a show. It would give her a bit of much-needed breathing-space.

It was later than she'd expected when she came out of the theatre, having barely watched the comedy show which had kept the rest of the audience in fits of laughter. The warm, concealing darkness had been just the place to nurture all those disturbing thoughts she'd wanted to weed out, and she was feeling more on edge than ever. She hurried to the bus stop and checked the timetable, her heart sinking when she realised she had missed the last bus through to Rainford. What on earth should she do now? She'd spent most of her money on a few presents and the meal and the theatre ticket, leaving just enough to cover her bus fare, but definitely not enough to pay for a taxi all that way.

Anxiously she glanced round, seeking inspiration, and spotted a bus turning the corner, its illuminated display showing its destination as Ormskirk. It seemed that fate had taken a hand in the evening, giving her the perfect excuse not to go back to the house at all. She would stay the night at the flat, and ring Jordan and tell him where she was.

She was aching with tiredness by the time she got back. She let herself in and switched on the central heating, then dialled Jordan's number. The line was engaged and she replaced the receiver with a definite feeling of relief. He wouldn't be very pleased about her staying here—not when he seemed so determined to foster the impression that theirs was the perfect marriage—but it was hard luck. There was no way she was going anywhere else tonight!

Humming to herself, she went into the bedroom to collect a short towelling robe from the wardrobe, then carried it through to the bathroom, and turned on the taps, filling the bath almost to the brim. Stripping off her clothes, she sank into the steamy heat and closed her eyes. She must have dozed off, because the next thing she knew was that someone was ringing the doorbell as though he or she was using it for bellringing practice, and the water was tepid.

Anxious to put a stop to the dreadful racket, she scrambled up, cursing loudly when a wave of water washed over the side and soaked the robe she'd left lying on the floor. Muttering evilly about what she would like to do to the demented campanologist, she dragged a towel off the rack and wound it around herself before hurrying to the top of the stairs. She hesitated, suddenly a shade uncertain about the wisdom of going down and opening the door, when another strident peeling spurred her into action.

'All right! All right! What do you want ringing like that? Who is it?' There was no doubting her displeasure from the tone of her voice, but it paled into insignificance compared to the answer which came roaring back through the door.

'Who the hell do you think it is? Now open this damned door!'

She gasped, her hand going to her throat to stem the wild pounding of her pulse. 'Jordan? Is that you?'

'Of course it is!'

Hands shaking, she fumbled with the lock, then stepped hurriedly backwards when he elbowed the door open and stepped inside the hall.

'What kind of a game do you think you're playing?' There was a dangerous glitter in his eyes as he rapped the question out, and Alex stepped back another pace, suddenly wary, then flinched when her bare shoulder-blades brushed against the coldness of the wall.

'Well, answer me, then! Where the hell have you been tonight?' He skimmed a glance over her body barely covered by the skimpy folds of the damp towel, and his expression altered subtly, taking on a harsh tautness of line which made a tremble of fear run down her spine. Reaching out, he caught her by the shoulders, his fingers biting deep into her flesh as he stared almost cruelly down into her face.

'Or maybe the question should have been, "Who have you been with tonight?"'

Alex gasped, twisting away, her own temper spiralling. How dared he come in here demanding answers and throwing accusations around? Suddenly all the pain and frustration she'd been bottling up for the past horrible weeks came bubbling up, and she rounded on him in fury. 'And what's it got to do with you?' She raised a mocking brow, her head tilted defiantly as she slid an insolent glance over his rigid figure. 'Where I've been and with whom has nothing to do with *you*, Jordan Lang!'

'No?' His voice dropped to a low purr, warm, silky, yet somehow far more disturbing than the previous anger had been; but Alex refused to let it throw her off course. She'd had enough, taken all she was prepared to take from this man. He had hurt her so many times over these past weeks with his cold comments, his deliberate refusal to believe anything she told him, and now all she wanted to do was to pay him back, hurt him as he had hurt her.

'No! I shall do exactly what I want and with whom I choose, and no one, especially not you, is going to stop me!'

'And you really think I'm going to let you? You think I'm going to sit back while you run around town making a laughing-stock out of me?'

'I can't see why it matters what I do. You've got your hands on the money now, so surely our "marriage" has achieved everything it was meant to do? I don't believe that your investors would care twopence if they found our marriage was on the rocks.' She laughed bitterly, sudden tears sparkling in her eyes. 'You've got what you want, Jordan, so what are you trying to tell me now—that you're jealous of the thought of me and another man? Or is it more a case of being a dog in the manger? You don't want me, but you sure as hell don't want anyone else to have me either!'

'Oh, I wouldn't say that, Alex.' He stepped forwards, not touching her as he stared down into her face, yet she could feel the imprint of his hard body hot against her own. Desperately she fought to keep her head, fought against the hot waves of longing which were filling her and threatening her sanity.

'Then what would you say?' she challenged, glaring up at him.

He smiled thinly, his eyes sliding over her flushed face and down the bare, slender column of her neck to stop at the shadowed hollow between her breasts in a slow, assessing sweep which Alex felt to the very heart of her being. She gasped, then felt the blood rush and eddy to her head when he reached out and trailed a finger lazily over the same path, letting it lie warmly just at the top curve of her breasts covered by the towel.

'I'd say that I want you very much, Alex, and that's the trouble. So maybe the sensible thing would be to do something about it!'

CHAPTER EIGHT

THE silence was something tangible, throbbing, pulsating, carrying with it a wild excitement that made Alex's breath catch in her throat. Helplessly she closed her eyes, giving herself up to the erotic images of her and Jordan together, then forced the pictures from her mind with a cold feeling of regret.

'No! No, Jordan, it wouldn't be sensible at all! It would be asking for trouble. I won't let this marriage become anything other than one of convenience!'

'I don't think you can stop it, Alex. I think it's way too late for that.' He bent and let his mouth trail over the bare curve of her shoulder, biting gently at the soft, warm flesh in a way that made a shudder race through her body. Slowly he drew back, his eyes glittering as he caught at the ends of the towel and eased the folds apart so that it fell to her feet, leaving her standing naked before him.

'No.' Her voice was a mere whisper of sound, uttering the denial yet carrying no conviction.

'Yes, Alex . . . yes!'

He swung her up into his arms, cradling her against him as he bent and took her mouth in a fierce kiss which burned the last attempts at protest from her lips. Alex whimpered softly, pushing her fingers into the cool hair at the back of his head, pulling his mouth down to hers so that she could

146

feel the hard lines of his male lips burning against hers.

He carried her up the stairs like that—their mouths locked so that his breath flowed between her lips. Slowly he let her slide to the ground, keeping her pressed against him so that she could feel the abrasive rub of his clothing against her bare skin sensitising every tiny nerve-ending until she felt raw, on fire. His hands slid up her arms and stroked across her shoulders, his thumbs tracing delicately across her collar-bones in a rhythm which made the blood drum in her veins. Her hands came up to catch at his to stop the tormenting movement of his fingers, but he just lifted them to his mouth and ran his lips across her knuckles before setting them back at her sides. He smiled slowly, his grey eyes like satin as they slid up her body then came back to hold hers as he forged a new, devastating path down from her neck to the soft, ripe swell of her breasts.

Alex caught her breath, feeling the dizziness of heat flooding her limbs as his hands moulded gently round the lush curves, testing the weight of her breasts in his palms before sliding his fingertips just once across the tightening buds of her nipples. She cried out, her breath coming in short little spurts as sensation gripped her, her hands lifting once more to stop the tormenting touch of his fingers; but once more he set them back at her sides. Delicately his thumbs brushed across her nipples time and again until they were rigid with a desire she could feel echoed by the pulsing in the pit of her stomach. Then, when she thought she could stand the caresses not a moment longer, his hands

slid on, smoothing over her ribs and down over the
soft curves of her belly before his fingers trailed a
path into the silky curls between her thighs.

'Jordan!' His name was a cry of heaven mingled
with the hot fires of hell as his fingers found the
moist heart of her, stroking the hot flesh until her
knees started to buckle under the force of an
emotion she'd never known before.

He caught her to him, his hands sliding round
to her buttocks as he dragged her against him,
moving his hips against hers so that she could feel
the hardness of his desire pressing against her.
Taking her mouth, he kissed her hard, his tongue
dancing with hers, mirroring the intimate movement
of their bodies. When he drew back Alex moaned
in protest, her eyes flying open, wide with the fear
that he had just been playing with her again, using
her as the butt for one of his cruel lessons; but he
just shrugged off his jacket and dropped it on to
the floor, studying her flushed face and the tousled
beauty of her hair lying on her bare shoulders with
an open satisfaction which sent little thrills shuddering through her.

Running his fingertips lightly down her arms
again, he lifted her hands from her sides and laid
them against his chest. 'Now you can touch, Alex,'
he said softly, his eyes glittering as they stared
straight into hers.

Just for a moment she hesitated, suddenly
overcome by a strange shyness, until the hard
warmth of the muscles under her hands and the
steady pounding of his heart became too much of
a temptation to resist. Delicately she eased the first
button of his shirt open, then the next, her tongue

caught between her teeth as she worked her way down the row with an intent concentration that was necessary when her whole body was trembling with tension.

Her hands slid inside the folds of soft cotton and ran lightly over the warm flesh, learning the contours until her fingers found the tiny rigid nub of his male nipple. He groaned, the sound low, deep, almost of agony as she stroked a finger over the very tip of it, then began to shudder violently when she pushed his shirt aside and pressed her lips to the ultra-sensitive spot, letting her tongue slide moistly over it time after time with an exquisite delicacy.

'Alex! Oh, Alex.'

Pushing his hands into her hair, Jordan dragged her head up, and took her mouth in a kiss meant to master, yet which ended up by giving more than it took. Alex gloried in the hot, wild pressure of his lips, the moist sweep of his tongue, the faint tremble she could feel racing through his body as he crushed her against him, gloried in the power she had over him. He could make her feel things she'd never felt before with any man, but she felt no shame, no embarrassment about letting him touch her and start these fires she could feel burning deep into her soul, because he felt the same.

His heart was beating just as wildly as hers, his strong body trembling with just the same fine edge of tension, his blood racing just as hotly through his veins as hers was racing. He was not seducing her... they were seducing each other, and the knowledge filled her with a sense of wonder.

When he bent and lifted her to carry her through to the bedroom, Alex was with him heart and soul, every step of the way, no thought of resisting lingering in her head. He laid her gently on the bed, his lips skimming over the parted curve of hers in a brief kiss which seemed to promise everything. With the light filtering through the open bedroom door, he undressed and came to lie beside her, his eyes mirroring the passion she knew he could read in hers. Alex smiled almost shyly at him, running a hand up his chest to the strong line of his jaw, feeling the faint rasp of stubble against her fingertips. He turned his head and pressed a kiss to her palm, the tip of his tongue coming out to trace a delicate pattern across the warm skin before he laid her hand gently over the heavy pounding of his heart.

'Have you slept with a man before, Alex?' His voice was soft, his breath warmly sweet against her face; yet Alex felt a cold shiver run through her, carrying with it the sudden fear that he would no longer want her when he heard the answer to his question. Jordan was an experienced man, so would he want to make love with an inexperienced little virgin like her? She looked down, feeling tears smarting her eyes as all her dreams started to crumble into ashes.

'No. This will . . . this will be my first time.'

He went still, every line of his body tensing as though he had received a blow, then slowly he relaxed again, lifting her chin with a gentle finger as he stroked the tears off her face.

'Then tonight will be even more beautiful, more special, for both of us.'

A fierce, wild elation soared through her, and with a tiny cry she went into his arms, giving herself to him with all the love she could feel in her heart. Because, despite everything that had happened, Alex knew that it wasn't hate she felt for this man, but love—a wild, wonderful and powerful love!

Moonlight filtered through the window, drawing the colour out of the familiar room, yet touching it with a magical beauty in keeping with the mood. Alex opened her eyes and looked round, her hand sliding across the bed to touch Jordan; but the bed was empty, the sheets cold. She sat up, her heart beating wildly, then felt relief run through her when she saw his clothes still lying on the floor. She lay down again, letting her heartbeat steady while her mind drifted back to the beauty of their lovemaking. Jordan had promised it would be beautiful, and it had been, so beautiful that it took on a dreamlike quality, but it had been no dream. Every glorious moment had been real.

She pushed back the rumpled sheets and got up, looking round for a robe before picking Jordan's shirt up from the floor and slipping it on. Just for a moment she pressed the soft folds to her face, breathing in the scent of him, which lingered on the cloth, then smiled at her own foolishness and buttoned it up. Barefooted, she made her way through the flat, pausing in the doorway to the living-room, her eyes locked on to the tall figure standing by the window.

Dressed only in his suit-trousers, with his chest bare and his dark hair lying in heavy disarray across his forehead, he looked so vitally male that Alex felt a thrill of possession ripple in hot waves through her. This man was her husband, hers to touch, to hold, to care for... to love. It no longer seemed to matter what had brought them together; those wonderful hours in his arms, when he had kissed and caressed every inch of her body, had given her the right to call him hers, just as she was now his, in mind as well as body. Nothing else mattered.

Silently she crossed the room and slid her arms round his waist, pressing her cheek against the bare, cool skin of his back. He started violently, the hard muscles under her cheek dancing before he relaxed and covered her linked hands with his, pressing her closer against him as though he couldn't bear the thought of her moving away.

'Penny for them,' she whispered, her lips feathering kisses against his skin.

He laughed, the sound rumbling under her ear, sending delicious tremors curling down to her toes. 'I don't think they're worth a penny!'

He turned round, sliding through the circle of her arms to link his hands behind her back and stare down into her upturned face. Alex met his gaze without trying to hide what he would see in her eyes. This was no longer a battle, no longer a game to score points and outmanoeuvre one another. It had gone way beyond that now. She loved him, and she wanted him to know it even if she couldn't yet find the courage to say the words aloud.

'Alex!' Her name was a litany, a prayer, as he bent his head and kissed her so sweetly, so tenderly that she felt her heart ache with the sheer wonder of it. She kissed him back, wanting him to feel the love she had for him, wanting to let it drift inside

his heart and touch him to the very core just as it
touched her.

He drew back slowly, pressing her head into the
hollow of his shoulder, his fingers burrowed into
the heavy weight of her hair. 'How did this happen,
Alex?' There was a strange note in his voice which
she didn't understand, and didn't want to. She drew
back, seeing the harsh lines of strain etched on his
face, the heavy darkness in his eyes, and felt fear
run through her that he might be regretting what
had happened.

'Are you sorry, Jordan?' she asked quietly. 'Because I'm not . . . not a bit sorry!'

'Aren't you?' There was a need for reassurance
in the question, and she laughed softly in relief,
snuggling back into his arms to press herself against
the strong, clean line of his limbs.

'No, not a bit. Does that shock you?'

'Mmm, it does a bit.'

'Good! You deserve to be shocked out of your
composure sometimes!'

'Oh, you've done that all right, and I don't just
mean what happened between us before.' He
pressed a kiss against her forehead, his lips warm,
faintly possessive as they trailed across the smooth
skin. 'You frightened the life out of me tonight,
Alex, when you didn't come home. Where were
you?' His arms tightened fractionally, pressing her
closer to him as though trying to imprint the very
feel of her on his skin. 'Were you with another
man?'

She shook her head, feeling the slight relaxing of
the punishing grip. 'No. I was on my own. There
is no other man, Jordan.'

'Then where were you? When you didn't come home I thought you must have missed the bus, so I waited for a while, thinking you would phone. Then when I heard nothing I started to get worried. I came over to the shop and knocked on the door, but there was no sign of you, so I went back home, thinking you might have arrived and our paths hadn't crossed. It was only by chance that I decided to check the flat again before I called the police.'

'The police? I . . . well, I never thought you'd be worried.' She smiled sadly, unaware of how much of what she'd felt showed on her face. 'I knew you'd be angry that I hadn't come home, but it never occurred to me that you would be worried about me.'

He swore softly, lifting her chin to kiss her with a restrained savagery. 'Too damned right I was worried! I was almost out of my mind tonight when I couldn't find you.'

Alex gloried in the kiss, in the feeling of his lips imprinting their brand on hers. 'I'm sorry,' she whispered, running a hand gently down the side of his face. 'I just couldn't face coming back to the house tonight, so I went to Southport.'

Jordan sighed, running a hand caressingly down her back, his fingers trailing along the ridge of her spine before settling warmly in the small hollow at its base. 'Has it been so terrible, then?'

Alex shook her head. 'Not really, in the circumstances. It's just that . . .' She stopped, her face colouring delicately.

'Just what?'

'Just that there has been such an atmosphere these past few weeks. It felt as though we were living on the top of a volcano, waiting for it to explode. I couldn't face it tonight.'

'So instead you came here, and the volcano erupted just the same?' There was a wry note in his deep voice, and Alex smiled.

'Yes. I think you can definitely call it an eruption. Still, at least it's cleared the air.'

'Has it?'

'Of course it has!' She stopped abruptly, her whole body tensing on a sudden spasm of almost unbearable pain. She closed her eyes, fighting against the agony, wondering if she'd been the biggest fool in the world, and read more into what had happened tonight than he'd meant.

'What is it? Alex, answer me!' He shook her, forcing her head up as he studied her paper-white skin, but she wouldn't look at him, couldn't look at him until he'd allayed these vivid, dreadful fears.

'Do you still think I sold the information to your competitors?' Her voice was hollow, and she felt his hands clench on her shoulders so tightly that she knew she would have bruises later; but she welcomed the pain because it stopped the dizzying faintness from claiming her. Time seemed to stand still, holding them in the balance, ready to tip her from the warmth of euphoria into the cold depths of despair.

'Jordan?' Her voice was hoarse, raw with pain, and she felt him flinch as though she had struck him. Then, slowly, the biting grip on her shoulders eased, and he pulled her to him, cradling her against him, letting the warmth of his body seep into her cold flesh.

'No, Alex. I don't think you are guilty any more.'

The relief was so great that her knees buckled and she sagged in his arms, letting him take her weight. He swung her up, holding her so tightly that she could feel the heavy beating of his heart against her breast, feel the laboured draw of his breath. She opened her eyes then and looked up at him, seeing the pulsing nerve ticking along his jaw, mute testimony that she hadn't been the only one to suffer. She pressed her finger to the spot, feeling the steady tapping against her flesh, knowing that nothing in the world now had the power to hurt her. Jordan believed she was innocent!

Joy raced through her, and she turned her face to his, her eyes brimming with tears, wanting to give him something as wonderful as he had just given her. 'I lo——'

His head came down, and he took her mouth, stemming the words on her lips with a frenzied kiss that set her on fire, wanting him again just as much as she'd wanted him before.

It was only later, as she lay next to him in bed, her body languid with the aftermath of their love-making, that she wondered if there had been deliberation in the kiss. But why? Why should Jordan want to stop her telling him that she loved him?

CHAPTER NINE

IT WAS late when Alex woke up. For a few minutes she lay in bed stretching luxuriously, then she glanced at the clock and yelped in dismay when she realised how late it was. She jumped up, then paused for a second, letting her eyes linger on the rumpled pillow, which still bore the imprint of Jordan's head.

He had left a little after seven, kissing her long and hard before he'd gone home to change for a business meeting over at the Yorkshire factory. His eyes had held a hot desire as he'd lingered over the kiss, and Alex shuddered as she remembered it now, feeling the fires of passion igniting inside her again.

She had never imagined that love could feel like this—a deep, burning fire in her soul. If she'd thought of it at all, she'd imagined it to be something warm, soft, quiet, an emotion that grew slowly and gently, not this wild explosion which had rocked her off her feet. Loving Jordan promised to be just as devastating as hating him had been!

She laughed aloud at her own foolishness, and hurried to the bathroom, washing and dressing in record time before making herself toast and coffee and carrying it down to the shop. But no matter how hard she tried to concentrate on her work, her heart just wasn't in it. Finally, at a little after three o'clock, she admitted defeat, and closed up for the day. Last night the mere thought of going back to Jordan's house had scared her rigid; now she could

hardly wait to get there even though she knew he
would be late getting back. She wasn't silly enough
to think that everything had been sorted out between them. There were still so many questions that
needed answering—not least the one of exactly how
he had come to decide that she was innocent. But
that admission of his had been the turning point,
giving her hope for their future together.

In a frenzy of anticipation, she caught the bus,
sitting on the edge of her seat as it made its way to
Rainford. Traffic was heavy at that time of the day,
with the schools finishing, and they were held up
for several minutes in the village; but at last they
made it to her stop. Alex jumped off and almost
ran along the road in her eagerness to get home just
in case there had been a change of plans and Jordan
had come home early.

It came as an unpleasant shock when she saw the
car parked at the end of the drive and recognised
the driver. She hesitated, then walked the last few
yards to the door, forcing a smile to her lips as
James Morgan climbed out and followed her.

'Hello, Mr Morgan. I'm afraid you've had a
wasted journey if you're looking for Jordan. He's
gone over to the Yorkshire factory; but surely you
must already know about that? Did you come to
leave him a message?' She hunted in her bag for
the key, then felt the smile freeze on her lips when
she looked up and saw the expression on his face.

A cold chill raced through her, stealing all the
warmth from her limbs. It took every scrap of
strength she possessed to ask the question she didn't
want to ask.

'Has something happened...to Jordan?' Her
voice broke on his name, her face going ashen as

the possibility that there had been an accident suddenly occurred to her.

'Not as far as I am aware, *Mrs Lang.*'

There was a faint mocking emphasis on her name, but Alex barely noticed it as relief ran through her in hot, sweet waves, making her go limp. It was several seconds before she realised that James Morgan was still talking.

'I'm sorry. I didn't catch that, Mr Morgan.' She smiled perfunctorily at him, slipping the key into the lock to open the door, wondering if she could get away without inviting him inside.

'I said that I haven't seen him today. I haven't seen him for several weeks, to be precise.'

'You haven't? I'm sorry, I don't think I understand what you are trying to tell me.' She withdrew the key from the lock, gripping it so tightly that the brass bit into her fingers. There was something about the calculating way that he was watching her, his pale eyes glittering with a suppressed excitement, that frightened Alex, though she couldn't have explained why.

'I'm quite sure you don't. I doubt if your *husband* has told you that he sacked me, let alone the reasons why.'

'Sacked you?' The fear had intensified, chilling her with its force so that she could only stand and stare at him with a growing apprehension.

'Yes. Don't you want to know why, Mrs Lang?' There was no mistaking the mockery now, no mistaking the hatred burning in those cold, flat eyes, and Alex drew in a ragged breath, fighting the feeling of panic.

'I don't think it has anything to do with me,' she said quickly, her voice shaking. 'If Jordan has seen fit to dismiss you, then I'm sure he had his reasons.'

'How very loyal you are! I wonder if you'll still feel the same when I tell you that he dismissed me for selling information about the new project to the firm's competitors? So you see it does have a lot to do with you, doesn't it?'

'You? You were behind it ... but why? Why did you do such a thing?'

He laughed hollowly. 'Money, of course. Oh, and maybe the satisfaction I got from being able to pay Jordan back.' He stared at Alex, yet she had the feeling that he wasn't really seeing her; his thoughts were turned inwards, turning his face into an unpleasant mask of hatred.

'I've given that firm thirty-five years of my life, yet all I was due to receive when I retired was a pitiful pension and a handshake! That's it—for all the hard work I've put in, for being the brains behind most of their major projects...yet not once did old man Lang or his precious son ever acknowledge the fact and offer me a partnership!' His mouth twisted, his eyes glittering in a way that made Alex wonder if he was a little mad. However, he seemed to gather himself, running a hand over his thinning hair before continuing.

'I've been biding my time, but it wasn't until your brother came along that I realised just how easy it would be. I set him up, you see, left the plans out, knowing he would take them. He'd been waiting for a chance to get even after that dressing down he got. I made sure Jordan didn't fire him then— not when I had plans for him—but what I hadn't bargained for was your involvement. Still, in the end it turned out even better than I'd hoped.'

He laughed. 'I knew once I heard about the engagement what had happened—that Jordan thought you were behind it all. You had become the perfect scapegoat for me, and when you visited his office that day you played right into my hands. I'd needed an excuse to get hold of the modifications for my buyers, and there I had it. Perfect!'

'But it wasn't perfect! Jordan sacked you, so he must have found out that I was innocent!'

His face closed, an expression of cunning flashing into his eyes. 'I suppose he must, but no matter. I've still got enough to live comfortably on for a very long time to come.'

'But why are you telling me all this? Why did you come here today? Surely not just to let me know that Jordan thinks I'm innocent? I hate to disappoint you, Mr Morgan, but you've had a wasted journey if that's the reason. He told me himself last night that he knew now I wasn't behind any of it.'

'Did he indeed? And what else did he tell you, Mrs Lang? That he knew *before* the wedding, yet still chose to go ahead with it? Oh, I know all about his mother's will. It didn't take me long to work out that he was blackmailing you into the marriage so that he could get his hands on the money. He used you just as he and his father before him used me!'

Shock rippled through Alex, but she refused to show it, clinging on to the previous night's precious memories as a shield against what Morgan was saying. 'No! It wasn't like that! Maybe Jordan had found out I wasn't guilty before the wedding, but he must have had other reasons for going ahead with it.'

'What other reasons? You can't be foolish enough to think he's in love with you? The only thing that man loves is the business, and he would do anything to protect it. He needed that money to save the firm from bankruptcy, just as he needs the rest of it to retain control of the company.'

'The rest? What are you talking about?'

'You don't know?' Morgan laughed harshly, and Alex flinched, her whole body shaking with shock. She had to hold on, had to hold tight to those memories, which seemed to be slipping through her fingers like sand. She closed her eyes, recalling the way Jordan had held her last night, then felt the image fade like smoke on the wind when James Morgan continued.

'Jordan only received *half* of his inheritance on his marriage. He will receive the other half on the birth of his first child. I don't know what he's told you, Mrs Lang, but he most definitely didn't marry you for love! He married you to get his hands on the money... every single tainted penny!'

Time slipped past, minutes and hours drifting away, yet Alex was unaware of them passing as she sat and waited. Her bag was packed, her coat neatly folded over the back of a chair; all that was left now was this final act, and then she could put Jordan out of her life for good.

A car turned into the driveway, its headlights sweeping over the windows, momentarily blinding her; but she didn't move. She sat quite still, her eyes blank, her heart empty, her body numb now from the pain which had racked her since discovering his duplicity. She had run the whole gamut of emotions that day, tumbling down from the dizzy heights of happiness to the black depths of despair. Now all she wanted was to get this last meeting over, and be free.

The front door opened and footsteps came along the hall, slowing as he must have seen her case standing outside the living-room. Abruptly he came into the room, switching on the lamps to flood the room with light, but nothing could penetrate the darkness in her soul.

'What's going on, Alex? Why is your case outside in the hall?'

She stood up to face him then, her eyes sweeping over the familiar planes of his face and body which her fingers had touched and caressed last night, and felt the pain swamp her again. Just for a moment, she closed her eyes as she fought to control it, then forced herself to look at him again. She had to look, had to remember every single detail of this man who had taken her life and crushed it into nothing.

'Dammit, Alex, tell me what's going on!'

He came towards her, reaching out to take her into his arms, but she wouldn't let him do that now, wouldn't let him work his treacherous magic on her again!

'Don't touch me!' She spat the order at him, her blue eyes burning in the stark pallor of her face, her hands clenched at her sides. There was a roaring in her head, a drumming in her ears as the blood surged round her cold limbs; but she ignored it, her whole being centred on the man who was watching her so intently. He stepped back, folding his arms across his chest as though to stop himself from reaching for her again, his face expressionless.

'What's happened?' His voice was deep, demanding answers, answers she had every intention of giving him. When she left here, she would do so knowing that he understood exactly why.

'I had a visitor today. He was waiting for me when I came back from the shop. I wonder if you can guess who it was, Jordan?'

'I hardly think this is the time for guessing-games. Why don't you just tell me what's eating you, and be done with it?' He loosened his tie and opened the top button of his shirt as he crossed the room to pour himself a measure of whisky. He cradled the glass in his hands for a second, swirling the rich amber liquid from side to side before swallowing it in one go and setting the glass down with a sharp clatter which made her jump. 'Well, Alex?'

He raised a mocking brow, his face falling into those familiar lines she'd learned to hate. It was as though last night had never happened, as though he had never held her, kissed her, felt her come alive in his arms. Had it really meant so little to him then? Could he now dismiss it so casually, just put it down to another of life's experiences? Or had it really been a deliberate attempt to fulfil the conditions of the will, to get her pregnant with the child who would ensure his inheritance and the safety of the company? Even though she had promised herself that she wouldn't let him hurt her again, it felt as though a knife had been plunged into her heart at the thought.

'James Morgan came to see me today. He told me that you had dismissed him for selling information about the new project. Is that true?'

'Yes.' His voice was curt. He sat down in one of the armchairs, crossing one long leg over the other before glancing coolly back at her. 'What else did he have to say?'

Would it have been easier if he'd sounded upset that she'd discovered what had happened, lost his composure even for the briefest moment? Alex didn't know, but the way he was able to sit there seemingly so unperturbed twisted that knife in her heart once more. She drew in a ragged breath, forcing herself to go on, to finish this business once and for all.

'He said that you knew before the wedding that I was innocent, yet you still went ahead with your plans. Why, Jordan? Why didn't you tell me? Damn you, Jordan, what right did you have to force me to go through with that sham of a wedding when you *knew* it was him?'

'What else could I have done?' He raised a mocking brow, his lips twisting into a bitterly wry smile. 'Would you have agreed to go ahead with the wedding if I had told you, Alex?'

'No...yes...I don't know! But you promised! You promised that you would cancel the arrangements if you had proof that it wasn't me!'

'How could I cancel?' He laughed harshly. 'You know why I needed to marry, Alex, and that hadn't changed!'

'So you were prepared to go ahead with it even knowing that I was completely innocent? My God, Jordan, is there anything you wouldn't do for your precious company?' There was scorn in her voice and on the flushed curves of her cheeks. 'I pity you, do you know that? The man with everything who really has nothing. You have no real idea what is important in life. All you can think about is that damned business, and everything else can go to pot!'

He got to his feet, his eyes burning into her like molten silver as he crossed the room. 'Damn you! Who are you to make judgements about me? What do you know about how I've struggled to get ahead of competitors, how I've worked to keep this company afloat?' He caught hold of her, ignoring her frantic struggles to get free. 'Lang's isn't some little two-bit concern. It's been in my family for years. It's part of me and, yes, I would do anything to stop it from being taken from me!'

Alex stilled, her eyes shimmering with unshed tears, feeling every word like a brand on her flesh. '"Anything"? Even going as far as getting me pregnant?' She laughed when he went suddenly still, his hands bruising her flesh, hysteria rolling inside her as she realised what a fool she'd been. 'Oh, yes, James Morgan told me about that too—a very minor detail that you must have overlooked! You're good, I'll give you that. You had me fooled into thinking that it was *me* you wanted last night, but it wasn't...not really. What you wanted was a child so that you could get your hands on the rest of your inheritance. You must have been laughing your head off when I fell into your arms! Would you have ever told me what you stood to gain, or would it have remained your little secret? After all, why should you need to tell me? Once I'd fulfilled your expectations, then it would be easy enough to get rid of me!'

'Stop it!' He shook her so that her head rolled, then caught hold of her chin, forcing her face up. 'You're getting hysterical.'

'Am I? Well, fancy that. Silly of me, getting hysterical because I've just found out that I've been duped!' Her breath caught on a sob, and she looked up at him with haunted eyes, wanting even then to hear it wasn't true, and salvage just one of her shattered dreams. 'Was Morgan telling the truth, Jordan? Do you stand to inherit more money if...if you have a child?'

'Yes! Yes, it is true; but last night wasn't for that!'

'And you really expect me to believe you, after all the lies, all the deceit? If it weren't for the sake of acquiring a child, then what was it for? The novelty value of sleeping with a virgin, or just a way to satisfy your lust? Neither of them are very attractive, are they?' She tossed her hair back from her flushed face, smiling tauntingly, hurting inside so much, and wanting at that moment to hurt him back in the only way she knew she could. 'Well, hard luck, because there won't ever be a child. I shall make certain of that!'

'And what exactly do you mean by that?' There was a dangerous edge to his voice, but Alex chose to ignore it, too far beyond the bounds of caution to care.

'What do you think? No woman needs to have a child she doesn't want nowadays, and I don't want yours!'

'You'd have an abortion?' There was a strange note in his voice, but she didn't hear it, deaf to anything but her own pain and the desire to hurt.

'Yes! There will be no child from this marriage...believe me!'

'I wouldn't let you do it! Damn you, Alex, you have no idea what you're saying at the moment, but if there is to be a child then there is no way that I would let you kill it just to get back at me!'

'There is no way you will be able to stop me!' She pulled away from him, evading his hands as he tried to catch hold of her again. Sweeping up her coat from the back of the chair, she shot him an anguish-filled look, aware that her control was liable to snap at any moment. 'I'm leaving you, and I don't want to have anything more to do with you from this moment on!'

She walked towards the door, then gasped when he swung her round, his hands pinning her in front of him as he glared down into her white face.

'No! I'm not letting you leave here, not tonight or any other night. We had an agreement, and I intend to see that you stand by it!'

'Agreement? You have the gall to remind me of that after what you've done, the way you've tricked me, used me? It's over, Jordan. From now on any agreement we had is terminated!'

'No! I'll make you stay.'

'How? Surely you're not going to resort to the tactics I once accused you of planning?' She laughed into his face, feeling the bitter tears welling in her throat. 'Do you really think you can keep me locked up for the rest of my days?'

'Who said anything about locking you up?' His gaze slid to her mouth, his hands softening as he slid them up from her arms to curl around the slender column of her throat while he caressed the sensitive flesh, his fingers tracing gently, seductively round behind her ears and into the warm mass of her hair lying on the nape of her neck. 'Would I really need to lock you up, Alex? Or could I just achieve the same outcome by a much more pleasant method?'

'No! No, Jordan, I don't want——'

The words were lost as he lowered his head and took her mouth, his lips hard and bruising, forcing hers apart so that he could slide his tongue inside her mouth to run hotly round the softly sensitive contours. Alex fought him, turning her head from side to side as she tried to break the contact, but he wrapped the length of her hair round his hand and held her still. Determinedly, he deepened the kiss, running his hand down the column of her neck to slide inside the neck of her blouse and caress the soft curves of her breasts.

Alex whimpered, fighting against the sensations which were even now racing through her body, carrying with them the hot surge of memories from the night before. It would be so easy to let him kiss her, love her, make her forget what he had done; but deep in her heart she knew it would never be enough. He had tricked her, used her body, and what he could make her feel, against her, in the most cruelly destructive way possible. Even though she knew she loved him, she could never forget what he had done.

She raised her hands, catching him off guard as she pushed him roughly from her. She stood and faced him, panting slightly, her mouth red and bruised, her eyes brimming with tears.

'No! I won't let you do it again, Jordan. I've been a fool too many times, but no more. I'm leaving you, and that's it...final!'

'I can still ruin you!'

She looked at him with scorn, feeling the last of those foolish dreams shatter beyond repair. 'Do what you like, but just remember one thing: I was never guilty! You accused me of stealing that information, and refused to listen when I told you it wasn't *me*. The only thing I am guilty of is being foolish enough to let you do it!' She smiled bitterly. 'I should have called your bluff right from the beginning, told you to do your worst, because nothing could have been as bad as what you have done!'

She swung round and walked to the door, her hand trembling as she turned the handle.

'And what if there is a child, Alex?'

His voice was low yet holding a note which made her stop when all she wanted was to get away before her heart broke completely. She glanced back, her eyes lingering for one last time on his tall figure, the lean planes of his face she could have drawn from memory, and the tears she'd held in check started to slide silently down her face.

'That is something you will never know,' she whispered hoarsely. She ran from the room, hearing him shout her name, but she didn't stop, didn't even turn to look back. It was over, everything which had started in anger had ended in this dreadful anguish. She never wanted to see Jordan Lang again.

CHAPTER TEN

ALEX wasn't pregnant.

Even though she knew she should be glad not to add that to all the other problems she faced, she couldn't help the overwhelming sense of loss she felt when she discovered the fact. In her heart she knew that, although she had taunted Jordan with the claim that she would have an abortion, she would never have gone through with it. Now the fact that there would be no child was yet another wound in her aching heart.

Jordan had made no attempt to contact her in the weeks since she'd left him, but that hadn't changed how she felt about him; she wished it had. No matter how hard she tried to flip the coin again and find hate in her heart, all she felt was this love, which was slowly tearing her apart. On the surface she appeared to be handling their break-up with a cool detachment, but underneath she was hurting with a pain which went beyond words.

Even Kenny had no real idea how she felt. He had greeted the news that Alex was no longer living in Jordan's house, and that their agreement was terminated, with curiosity mingled with open relief. Alex had given him some kind of an explanation, swearing him to secrecy when it became obvious that the real reason for James Morgan's sudden disappearance from the company hadn't become public knowledge, but she hadn't been able to find the courage to tell him what had happened between

her and Jordan. That was something too personal
to share with anyone, even Kenny.

The time passed slowly. Alex filled the days by
working in the shop, then carried on way into the
early hours crafting her jewellery, hoping to tire
herself enough to sleep. But, no matter how
exhausted she was, sleep was fitful, broken by the
vivid dreams which brought her awake with tears
drying on her cheeks. She could only hope that arrangements would be made to end the marriage
soon. Maybe then she could get on with the task
of living again.

A few days before Christmas she was tidying the
display cases prior to locking up the shop for the
day. It had been a busy afternoon, with people
rushing in to buy last-minute presents, and she was
already thinking longingly of going upstairs to enjoy
some peace and quiet after all the rush. She bent
down to lock the bottom of the case, then groaned
under her breath when she heard the shop bell
tinkle, announcing yet another customer. Fixing a
polite smile to her lips, she straightened then felt
her heart flutter to a halt when she saw Jordan
standing in the doorway.

'Hello, Alex. How are you?'

His voice was just as she remembered it, just as
she heard it every night in her dreams, making her
tremble with the memories it evoked. Just for a
moment they came flooding back in a hot tide
before ruthlessly she drove them from her mind.

'What do you want?'

He stiffened at the curtness of her response, his
body going rigid, his face all stark bones and angles.
Dressed in a heavy black leather jacket and dark
trousers, he cut a sombre figure, and Alex felt

unease work its way coldly down her spine. She bent down to finish locking the case to give herself a moment's breathing-space to recover from the shock of his unexpected appearance, then stood up, gripping the edge of the counter so hard that her fingers throbbed from the pressure.

'Well, Jordan? I haven't got all evening to waste. I was just about to close up for the night so, if you have something to say, please get on with it.'

Colour ran along his cheekbones in an angry tide, and he moved closer so that Alex could smell the familiar scent of his skin mingled with the faint tang of his aftershave—a heady aroma which she remembered so well.

'You appear to be in something of a hurry. Are you going somewhere special?'

There was a faint edge to the question which she took immediate exception to. She raised a mocking brow, her head tilted at a regal angle. 'I might be, but frankly I fail to see what business it is of yours!' She smiled faintly, somewhat mollified to see the anger flicker in his eyes as the jab struck home. 'Now, I assume you do have a reason for coming here?'

He shrugged, glancing down at the display case with its glittering treasure of gold and jewels. 'I might just have come to buy something. There are one or two presents I still need to get.'

For whom? Alex bit her lip to stop the question from rushing out, feeling sickness welling in her stomach at the thought of Jordan buying presents for another woman. How was it that every time she struck out at him it ended up being such a feeble blow, one he could deflect and turn back on her? Now all those vivid dreams would be twice as awful, featuring some faceless woman who had a claim on him.

Terrified that he would sense how she was feeling, she rushed into speech. 'I've already locked everything away for the night, so I'm afraid you will have to go elsewhere to do your shopping.'

He smiled thinly, his eyes meeting hers and holding them. 'Business must be doing well if you can refuse a sale out of hand like that!' He looked into the glass case, studying the display with apparent interest. 'I rather like that ring—the emerald one. How much is it?'

She would rather starve first before she sold him some of her jewellery... to give to another woman! 'It's not for sale.'

'No? Then how about the sapphire and diamond cluster next to it?'

'Neither is that. None of them is for sale... to you!'

'I see. Well, it seems a strange way to run a business, Alex—letting your heart rule your head.'

There was a trace of knowing mockery in his voice, and she flushed. She forced herself to face him, hating the fact that he had realised just how vulnerable she was. 'I'm sure that is something you *never* have a problem with. I can't imagine you ever letting emotion take precedence over business matters!'

His face tightened, the mockery fading, leaving his eyes like shards of cold steel. 'What do you expect, Alex—that I should apologise for what happened?'

'I expect nothing from you... nothing at all! Now, if you haven't anything else to say, then I'd be glad if you'd leave.'

'Oh, I've plenty to say all right. There's a lot we need to talk about.'

'Such as? Just tell me one thing we have to——' She stopped abruptly, her face losing all its colour as she suddenly realised why he'd come. 'Aren't I stupid? I should have realised what you wanted.' Her voice was hoarse, empty, drained of all emotion—even anger—now. 'I hate to disappoint you, Jordan, but your plan failed; I'm not pregnant!'

'That isn't why I came. Dammit, Alex, can't you ever give me the benefit of the doubt?'

'The same as you gave me? You taught me well, Jordan Lang, taught me to be suspicious of even the simplest action—so you only have yourself to blame. But now that you have what you came for, I think you had better leave.'

'I'm not going anywhere until you stop all this foolishness, and listen to me.' He glanced round the empty shop, rough impatience in his voice. 'For heaven's sake lock up, and let's go up to the flat. All I ask is that you give me ten minutes of your time.'

'I haven't got ten minutes to spare for *you*. Now get out!'

'And if I refuse? What will you do then, Alex? Eject me bodily?' He slid a glance over her slender figure, then folded his arms complacently across his chest. 'Somehow I don't think you're up to a physical confrontation, but be my guest if you want to try. You never know, sweetheart, we might both enjoy it!'

Fury ripped through her at his total arrogance. He needed taking down a peg or two, and she was just the woman to do it!

'You think not?' she asked sweetly, moving slowly further along the counter until she could feel the coldness of the button beneath her searching fingers. 'I shall ask you just one last time, Jordan. Will you please leave?'

'No.'

'Then you only have yourself to blame!' She pushed the button in, jumping even though she knew what was going to happen when an ear-splitting noise rent the air.

'What the hell...?'

'The panic alarm.' She had to shout so that he could hear her over the sound, her blue eyes filled with triumph. 'It's linked in to the police station, so I suggest you leave pretty sharply if you don't want to spend the next couple of hours making a statement to them when they arrive!'

'Why you little——!' He broke off, and swung round on his heel to stride towards the door and wrench it open. Just for a moment he paused and shot a glance over his shoulder at Alex, who was standing by the counter with her hands pressed tightly over her ears, then walked out, slamming the door behind him.

Alex drew in a shaky breath, then ran round the counter and locked the door before hurrying through to the back to ring the police station and cancel the alarm call. It took her three attempts to dial the number successfully because her hands were shaking so hard. She might have won that round but, remembering that last look Jordan had given her before he'd left, she had the uncomfortable feeling that she hadn't won the whole game!

He would be back!

Even while she threw clothes into a suitcase, Alex

knew that it was a race against time. How long had
it been since he'd left? She glanced at the clock,
trying to work out how much time had elapsed, but
her brain was still too hazy with fear to cope with
even the simplest of arithmetic. All she knew was
that Jordan would be back, and that she mustn't
be here when he arrived!

With a gasp of relief she managed to close the
case, and hefted it off the bed before snatching up
her bag to check she had some money in her purse.
If she could find a taxi, she should be able to catch
the last train through to York. She would ring
Kenny from the station and tell him to collect her.

She hurried downstairs, dropping her case by her
feet while she locked up, then buttoned her coat
against the cold chill of the night air. Although it
was barely six o'clock, the sky was inky dark, heavy
clouds blotting out any traces of moonlight, and
promising another downpour of rain at any minute.
She could only hope that she would be able to pick
up a taxi before it started.

'Going somewhere?'

She swung round at the sound of his voice, her
face going paper-white as she saw him leaning
almost indolently against the wall. For one dreadful
moment she stood rooted to the spot, then suddenly came to her senses. Scrabbling frantically in
her pocket for the key, she turned to go back inside,
but she never even got the chance to put it in the
lock before Jordan was beside her, his hand
fastening firmly round her arm.

'Oh, no, you don't! You're not getting away from
me this time!'

'Let me go!' she ordered shrilly, twisting her arm,
but his fingers fastened even more firmly, his mouth

curved into a grim little smile as he watched her frantic struggles.

'No chance. You've done all the running you're going to do. Now you're coming with me.'

He picked up her case and pulled her with him as he hurried down the street almost before she had a chance to realise what was happening. She stopped dead, her eyes flashing with anger, her breath coming in short, furious spurts.

'Stop it! What do you think you're doing? Where are you taking me?'

'You'll see.'

'I don't want to "see". I'm not going anywhere with you—not tonight or any other night! Now let...me...go!'

She wrenched her arm away from him, somewhat surprised when he didn't try to stop her this time, but just stood and watched her. Her eyes narrowed thoughtfully as she wondered what kind of a game he was playing, but it was impossible to tell from the expression on his face. 'What do you want, Jordan? Why have you come back? I thought I made it perfectly plain before that you are not welcome.'

He didn't like that; Alex could tell from the flicker in the depths of his eyes, the way his jaw stiffened, but, surprisingly, he spoke quite calmly. 'Just a chance to talk to you, as I said before. That's all I'm after.'

'And, as I told *you* before, there is nothing to talk about! The only thing left to talk about is the divorce, and I don't see that will cause any major problems.' She smiled bitterly, pushing the tumble of hair back from her cheeks. 'I imagine

that was all fitted into your plan, wasn't it? All
neatly numbered?'

'I didn't come to talk about any divorce.' He
glanced round impatiently at the heavy traffic.
'Look, this isn't the place to have a conversation.
Come back to the house with me, and let's see if
we can't straighten this mess out.'

'No!' She stepped back, her face going pale at
the thought of going back to his house with him.
She couldn't bear it, couldn't bear to go there again
when that last dreadful confrontation was still so
raw in her mind. She loved him, but she wouldn't
let him hurt her again as he had hurt her before.
'It's far too late to sort anything out. The damage
has been done now, and all that is left is for us to
end this stupid sham of a marriage and go our separate ways.'

'No!' He caught her arm, pulling her back towards him, his eyes burning into hers with a silver
fire in their depths. 'It's not too late, Alex. I won't
let it be!'

The arrogance of the assertion took her breath
away. 'You won't let it be? Just who do you think
you are, Jordan Lang?' She laughed harshly, her
eyes brimming with tears, so that she didn't see how
he flinched, how every bone in his face stood out
in stark relief. 'What gives you the right to decide
other people's lives? Who said you could play God
and decide my life because it suited you? I hate
you, do you hear me? I hate you for what you've
done to me!'

Her voice broke on a sob, and she bent her head,
feeling the futility of it all wash through her, too
upset to resist when he drew her into his arms.
Cradling her shuddering body against him, Jordan

stroked her hair, and Alex was surprised to feel how his hand trembled.

'Don't, Alex,' he ordered softly, a wealth of pain in his deep voice. 'You know it isn't true. You're upset, but you don't hate me.'

'I do... I do!'

He bent and kissed her then, not fiercely as a punishment for her defiance, but so gently, so tenderly that it made her heart ache afresh for all that she had lost. Slowly he drew back, cupping her face between his hands as he brushed a shower of soft, fleeting kisses over her mouth and the damp curves of her cheeks before tilting her head up to meet his steady gaze.

'You don't hate me, Alex, although you should for what I've done to you. You love me.'

'No!' Even while her lips framed the denial her eyes betrayed her, tangling with his with a blaze of love burning in their depths that he would have had to be blind not to see. He sucked in a ragged breath, his lips rimmed with white as he struggled for control, his hands tightening convulsively against her face.

Terrified by the way she had given herself away, Alex stumbled into speech. 'No. You've got it all wrong! I don't——'

He pressed his fingers against her mouth. 'No, Alex. Don't lie to me. You love me. I knew it the other night when we made love. You would never have given yourself to me otherwise, would you?' He shook her gently, but she refused to look at him, her world and her pride lying in ruins around her feet. 'What we shared wasn't just sex. It went way beyond that for both of us, and I won't let you try and cheapen it now by lying.'

What was he trying to say? That he loved her? For one glorious moment Alex's heart lifted and soared to the heights before spinning sickeningly back to the depths. How could she ever believe anything he said after what he'd done, the way he had tricked her?

'No!' She tried to pull away, to free herself from the touch of his hands, which was ripping her heart into shreds; but he wouldn't let her go this time. 'Don't do this, Jordan,' she begged brokenly. 'Please don't do this on top of everything else.'

He swore roughly, sliding his hands down her arms to grip her wrists so hard that she winced from the pain, yet she knew he was unaware of what he was doing. 'I am trying to tell you that I love you, Alex. I know it's hard to believe. Lord knows, I've been finding it hard to come to terms with myself; but I do! All I ask is that you give me a chance to convince you that I'm telling the truth. Don't destroy both our lives because you're afraid!' He let her go so abruptly that she staggered, pushing his hands deep into the pockets of his jacket. 'Will you come with me, Alex? I can't make you. I promise I won't even try. All I ask is that you give me this one last chance, and if you don't believe me I will step out of your life for good.'

For a moment which bordered on eternity, Alex hesitated, terrified of making the wrong decision and of being hurt again as she'd been hurt before; and Jordan misread that hesitation as refusal. His face closed up and he turned quickly away, walking off down the street with his head bowed.

Alex stood and watched him go, feeling the pain rip through her once again as she realised he was walking out of her life for good.

'Don't go.'

The wind caught her whispered plea and carried
it away, swirling it up into the sky, too faint for
him to hear. He kept on walking, his long legs
setting more and more distance between them, and
suddenly Alex knew she couldn't let it end like this.
If there was even the faintest hope that he was
telling the truth, then she had to take it.

'Jordan!' She screamed his name, terrified that
he wouldn't hear her and keep on walking, but he
stopped as though he'd been struck. Slowly he
turned to face her. Alex took one small hesitant
step towards him, then another, then, with a choked
sob, ran down the street and hurled herself into his
waiting arms.

They drove in silence, a silence Alex was afraid to
break. Who was it who had said that it was better
to journey than to arrive? She couldn't remember,
yet it summed up how she was feeling so exactly.
While they were travelling along the roads like this
she could keep the hope alive that he had been
telling her the truth. She didn't think she could bear
it if she found out it had all been lies and still more
trickery at the end of the journey.

Jordan swung the car off the road, and drew to
a halt, cutting the engine to leave them in a silence
which hummed with tension generated by so many
unanswered questions. Alex drew in a shaky breath,
forcing herself to look round while she tried to
gather her composure for what was to come, and
realised that they were parked at Ashurst Beacon.
Below them, where the hill fell away, she could see
the lights of Skelmersdale like rows of glittering
jewels shining against the black velvet of the night

sky. So many people down there, so many lives running along familiar lines, yet up here the next few minutes would decide her fate. Suddenly she couldn't bear the waiting a minute longer.

'Jordan, I . . .'

'Alex . . .'

They spoke together and stopped. Slowly, Jordan reached out and pushed a long strand of hair off her face, his fingers trembling slightly as they brushed against the softness of her cheek, and that evidence of nervousness said more than any amount of words could ever have done. To know that Jordan, who had always been so assured and in control before, could shake like this, seemed to ease the tightness of fear which had gripped her ever since she'd got into the car.

She caught his hand, linking her fingers with his as she drew it on to her lap, her eyes soft and gentle as she looked back at him.

'Do you really love me, Jordan?'

'Yes, Alex, I really do. I know it's asking a lot of you to believe me after everything that's happened—but I love you.'

There was no doubting the sincerity in his voice, and Alex felt a wave of happiness race through her. But she had to contain it at least for a little while until everything had been brought out into the open and all the questions had been answered. If they were to build a future together, there could be no room in it for lies—only truth.

'Do you think you can explain everything to me?'

He nodded, lifting her hand up to his lips before letting it go and turning away to stare out through the windscreen, as though what he had to say was going to be painful. 'You have to understand, Alex, that for the whole of my life Lang's has been the most important thing in it. I was brought up on the idea that ensuring its well-being was the only thing that mattered.' He shrugged, a fleeting sadness on his face as he glanced at her. 'My parents divorced when I was twelve, and after that my father immersed himself in the business to the exclusion of everything else. Lang's was his whole life, the only comfort he had in a lonely existence. Keeping it going and ensuring that it flourished was my way of paying tribute to him. Can you understand that?'

'I think so...yes, I can. But surely your desire to keep the company safe didn't merit the drastic measures you took?'

'I'm afraid it did. There was too much sunk into this project for the company to recover if it failed. I needed that money Mother left me; let's make no bones about that!'

'But was it true about the rest of it?' Alex's face clouded, her eyes dim with pain. 'Did you sleep with me to get me pregnant so you could inherit the rest of the money?'

'No!' Jordan caught her hands, holding them firmly. 'I slept with you because I couldn't stop myself that night! I wanted you so much that I was helpless to do anything else.' He laughed wryly, bending to brush a light kiss over her mouth, leaving a trail of fire behind to linger tantalisingly on her lips. 'You had me well and truly in your clutches by then, lady, although I would have denied it if you'd asked me! I knew I was attracted to you right from the start. That's one of the reasons why I was so angry about what I thought you'd done, and went to such lengths to find you. I don't think I would have come up with this marriage plan if I hadn't been, though I was blind to that fact until it was too late!

'There was no way I could have stopped myself making love to you when I came to the flat and found you looking like something out of one of my more erotic dreams. The thought of a child and the rest of the money definitely didn't enter my head!'

'I'm glad,' Alex whispered shakily. 'You were right, of course. I would never have slept with you if I hadn't been in love with you. And later, when you told me that you knew I was innocent—well, I can't explain how I felt. I was on cloud nine all the next day, longing to see you to get everything sorted out, but instead I got home to find James Morgan waiting for me.'

He swore softly as he saw the shimmer of tears the memory evoked. 'Don't cry, sweetheart. Please. If I'd had any idea that James was going to do that, I would have stayed that day and explained what had been going on.'

'But why didn't you tell me later? Why did you let me leave believing the worst?'

He ran a hand over his hair, his face set. 'I was afraid, dammit!'

'Afraid? Of what?'

'Of being in love. I'd seen what it could do to my father. He never got over Mother's leaving him until the day he died, and frankly I was terrified to admit that what I felt for you really was that dreaded emotion called love. It's taken a lot of heartache and a whole lot of sleepless nights to make me come to my senses and realise that losing you would be a hell of a lot worse.'

'Oh, Jordan.' Alex laughed softly, loving him even more for the confession. She leaned over and brushed a kiss along his jaw, moving quickly away again when he turned to her with a naked hunger in his eyes. 'No. Not yet. Let's get this mess all cleared up first, then we have all the time in the world left for... that.'

He chuckled when she blushed. 'Is that a promise? It had better be, because I don't think I can wait much longer. Confession might be good for the soul, but it doesn't do a whole lot for the aches in my body!'

Her heart raced at the rough impatience in his voice, which belied the teasing. 'It is. But first you must tell me how you found out that James Morgan was behind all the thefts.'

He sank back in his seat with a sigh. 'Has anyone ever told you that you're a hard woman, Alex? Still, I suppose I should explain. The signs were all there, of course. The trouble was, I was convinced it was you, so I was too blind to see them clearly. It was only after I found you in the office that second time that I started to have doubts, partly because I *wanted* to believe your claims of being innocent by then. I started to keep an eye on James, and slowly things began to add up, so I back-tracked a bit and did some homework that I should have done weeks before. I discovered that the design faults in the prototype, which we'd been having so many problems with, couldn't have been the result of just bad luck. They'd been introduced deliberately by someone who had to know an awful lot about the engine, and that someone could only have been James. Once I realised that, it all fell into place, and I confronted him with what I knew. He admitted everything—selling the information, slowing

down the production by introducing the
faults...everything!'

'How awful for you after you'd trusted him.'

'I suppose it's the way of the world. He seemed
to think he had a grudge against the company and
me, so got back at us the one way he knew was
bound to hurt most.'

'What's going to happen to him now? Are you
prosecuting him?'

Jordan shook his head. 'No. The damage has
been done, so it will serve no purpose washing
Lang's dirty linen in public. I've given him an ultimatum to leave the country. I imagine that visit
to see you was his last attempt to hit back at me.'

'Will the project have to be abandoned now?'

'Thankfully, no. I've been in touch with our
competitors, and warned them that I have James's
confession on tape and will use it to blacken their
name throughout the engineering world if they
continue to work on our design.'

'Surely they wouldn't be able to market it if it
was registered to your firm?'

'Not in its entirety, but more often than not it's
the concept of a new design which is so important.
We need to get it into production before any other
competitors to gain the lead in the market.'

'So that's it...a nice tidy ending to everything.'
She smiled in pleasure, moving towards him, then
stopped when he made no attempt to take her into
his arms as she'd expected.

'Not quite everything, Alex.'

A shudder ran through her at the solemn note in
his voice. With wide eyes she watched as he pulled
an envelope out of his pocket and held it out to

her. She clasped her hands together, staring down
at the slim fold of manilla.

'What is it?'

'Open it and see.'

'No! Just tell me what it is, Jordan . . . please.'

He opened the flap and pulled out a few sheets
of thick paper, switching on the interior light as he
smoothed them out and laid them on the seat between them. 'It's a formal contract, Alex, arranging for all the money Mother left me to be paid
into a trust fund for any children we might have.'
He looked up at her, his eyes very level, holding
hers so that she couldn't look away.

'One of the reasons why I haven't come to you
sooner is because I've been working day and night
to push through a deal with a large Japanese
company who were willing to invest in Lang's. I'd
turned them down a few months ago, so it took a
bit of time to interest them again, but it was all
signed earlier on today. I shall retain the major
interest in the firm, but the capital they are in-
vesting will give them substantial voting rights. I've
made arrangements to repay the money I received
from the inheritance into the trust fund immediately. I know I used our marriage to get my hands
on it, but maybe this will partly make up for the
fact.

'As to the rest of the will, perhaps I should have
told you all the clauses but, frankly, there was never
any thought in my head about our getting close
enough to have children; so it seemed pointless.'
He grinned wickedly, his eyes teasing. 'However,
the thoughts are starting to form pretty rapidly now!
But if you stay with me, Alex, and we do have a

family at some time in the future, then at least you'll
know that it is because of love...not money.'

'But Lang's means so much to you! Are you sure
you aren't making a mistake and won't regret it?'

Jordan shook his head, tossing the papers carelessly into the back of the car before reaching for
her. 'The only thing I will regret is letting you slip
through my fingers a second time. I love you. You
are more important to me than anything else on
earth.' He lifted her face up so that he could kiss
her with a lingering passion which stirred Alex's
senses into vibrant life so that she trembled in his
arms. He drew back. 'I shall never let you go again
if you agree to stay with me, so can you stand the
thought of a life sentence?'

'So you still think I'm guilty enough to need
sentencing, do you?'

'I hope you are.' He smiled, his eyes tracing over
her flushed face with so much love in their depths
that she felt her heart shake. 'Guilty of loving me
as much as I love you?'

She moved closer to him, her lips brushing
against his as she spoke slowly. 'Oh, I am, Jordan.
Very, very guilty indeed!'

Childhood in Portsmouth meant grubby knees, flying pigtails and happiness for **Sara Wood**. Poverty drove her from typist and seaside landlady to teacher till writing gave her the freedom her Romany blood craved. Happily married, she has two handsome sons; Richard is married, calm, dependable, drives tankers, Simon is a roamer—silversmith, roofer, welder, always with beautiful girls. Sara lives in the Cornish countryside. Her writing life alternates with her passion for gardening, which allows her to be grubby again!

DARK FORCES

BY
SARA WOOD

MILLS & BOON LIMITED
ETON HOUSE, 18-24 PARADISE ROAD
RICHMOND, SURREY TW9 1SR

First published in Great Britain in 1992
by Mills & Boon Limited

© Sara Wood 1992

Australian copyright 1992
Philippine copyright 1992
This edition 1992

ISBN 0 263 77520 8

Set in Times Roman 10 on 11^{1}/$_2$ pt.
06-9208-56366 C

Made and printed in Great Britain

CHAPTER ONE

'MAWGAN! Stop the car!' Bethany leaned forwards, her cap of dark hair ruffling in the sea breeze. Her face relaxed into a pensive smile as she looked down on Portallen Bay.

'Gorgeous, isn't it?' said her brother smugly. 'Now don't you wish you'd come back sooner?'

From their vantage point on the headland, Bethany could see the sandy beach glistening in the September sun from the wash of the outgoing tide. 'How could I?' she asked quietly, her blue-grey eyes as dark as Cornish slate. 'I'd lost my nerve.' Her tongue touched her dry lips and she tasted the tang of salt. 'Heavens! I'm shaking like a leaf,' she confessed.

'I keep telling you,' he insisted. 'It's all blown over.'

'Really? They hated me so much...' Bethany's gaze drifted across the white crescent of sand to the jagged rocks where seams of rock crystal gleamed. The sun bounced off the sea, dazzling her, highlighting a beautiful ketch sailing around the headland. 'How lovely...I can't stay long,' she sighed sadly.

'I know. Just until we get the hotel back into shape. Poor Beth, it's been hard for you to return,' said Mawgan gently, squeezing her hand. 'I'm very grateful.'

'I'd do anything for you, you know that,' she said warmly, putting aside her anxiety. Mawgan needed her. 'You're all I have,' she added.

Her brother seemed about to say something, but changed his mind and fell silent. Bethany wished he'd chatter and stop her from wondering what lay ahead. It would be bad enough driving through the village in an open car and being stared at again. But there was something else that worried her more. Cavan.

Breathing deeply to calm her nerves, she inhaled the freshness of the emerald-green grass, the warmth of the sun-drenched soil, the rich smell of autumn. Bethany dragged her eyes from the humped hills rising above the deep river valley and the grazing sheep arranged artfully on their slopes, and tried to steer her mind away from her apprehensions.

'You haven't told me much about this disastrous refit you had done on the hotel,' she said briskly, being as practical as possible.

'There's a reason for that,' muttered Mawgan, starting up the car and beginning the steep plunge to the coast. 'I feel such a fool. Talk about fast-sell methods! The hotel needed modernising, and Cavan had only given me a small budget so I let this cheapjack firm go ahead. I hope you can salvage something out of the mess without much expense.'

'A bit of well-aimed drapery can hide a lot of faults,' soothed Bethany, wishing it would do the same for her. 'Are you sure I look all right?' she asked, her hands suddenly clammy with nerves. The village was in sight. She could see the stone fishermen's houses ahead, grey and severe.

'Fantastic. Like a film star,' said her brother.

'That's what I was afraid of,' she said wryly, checking her dark, glossy hair. The narrow tarmac road with grass running down the centre gave way to cobbles, and Mawgan gingerly manoeuvred his old Morris convertible at a bone-rattling crawl along the narrow street. Bethany steeled herself to withstand the intense curiosity her visit was arousing.

She knew everyone, and tried to smile in greeting. But the villagers remained unresponsive, their faces cold, unwelcoming. She felt crushed by their uninhibited stares as they inspected every inch of her from her neat, dark Sassoon bob, her huge gold earrings and necklace, the white linen suit with its tight and short sheath skirt, and the long length of slim, tanned thigh and leg, visible to anyone who peered into the well of the car.

And they did, shamelessly. As a daughter of Portallen, Bethany still belonged to them, and they assumed rights over her.

'I *knew* they'd bristle if I wore something glamorous,' she said unhappily to Mawgan.

'I wasn't having you returning cap in hand,' he said firmly. 'I'm proud of you. Chin up, we're almost home.'

He entered the lane which led to the hotel, and stopped in the courtyard. Bethany felt quite exhausted from tension. 'I don't want to do that again in a hurry,' she said shakily. 'They scrutinised me, right down to the labels on my underwear!'

'Silly! They were curious,' smiled Mawgan.

'Hostile,' she amended, worried whether she could cope. But her face relaxed into a smile as her hungry eyes examined every inch of the small medieval manor house which her father had turned into the village hotel. 'Home,' she breathed, clutching Mawgan's hand tightly. 'Home at last.'

Her brother stiffened. 'Oh, no!' he groaned. 'He said——'

Bethany followed his gaze and her face paled. In the side lane was parked a vibrant red Aston Martin. '*Cavan*!' she said in distress. Inside her, everything was jumping: her heart, her stomach, her pulses, her brain. 'What's he doing here? You said he hardly ever came here,' she reminded Mawgan, an accusing note in her voice. 'You said I wouldn't see him. You said——'

'Beth,' cut in Mawgan gently, 'he owns the hotel. He has a right to be here.'

'That's the trouble, isn't it?' she said bitterly, the resentment of years souring her voice. 'He owns it! I could just about stomach that, but he doesn't give a damn about it. I dread to think what he'll do with it eventually. I love Portallen.'

Upset and trembling, Bethany jerked down the handle of the car door. Her intended graceful exit was marred by the fact that the door was jammed. Before Mawgan could dart around to help her, a figure loomed up as if from nowhere and a strong hand wrenched the door open by sheer brute force.

'Love? You have a funny way of showing your love,' came Cavan's throaty growl.

Hiding her nervousness, Bethany slid out her long and suddenly alarmingly exposed legs to the ground, steadied herself on the spindly shoes and stood up, smoothing down her short skirt unnecessarily while she waited for the pulses in her body to stop leaping around like sprats in a net.

'Afternoon, Cavan,' she said evenly.

'Good afternoon, beautiful. Don't you have a kiss for your stepbrother?' he murmured.

His rough, gravelly voice reverberated through her body, sliding into every crevice in a warm and insistent flame. 'No, I don't,' she said firmly, reaching in the car for her bag. And still not meeting his eyes. She wasn't ready.

'Hi, Cavan,' said Mawgan with false cheerfulness, trying to prise the two from their mutual dislike. 'You look well.'

Cavan merely nodded in Mawgan's direction as if he wasn't important. Bethany held back her irritation. 'Perhaps you'd explain what you mean by saying I have a funny way of showing my love for Portallen,' she said haughtily.

He chuckled. 'Still proud, Bethany.' He blocked her way, his body as brawny as a wrestler's. Her sensory memories were instantly aroused as her nostrils were assailed by the fierce blood-heat emanating from him, mingled with the faint scent of *Pour les Hommes*—his aftershave. He'd been running, she mused. He was fired up with energy and panting slightly.

She needed time to get used to his arrival. Bethany fumbled in her bag. She brought out her compact and pretended to check her make-up.

'Yes,' he murmured softly. 'Still proud.'

'Could that be because I have a lot to be proud of?' she asked casually, snapping the compact shut. She continued to rummage in her bag and then it was closed for her by a large male hand.

'On the surface it would seem so. You're perfect,' mocked Cavan. 'Externally.'

He never lost an opportunity to hurt her, she frowned. Physical memories crowded in when he stepped closer—that body-disturbing magnetism and sexuality which was unique to Cavan flowing around her, making her throat dry up. Slowly she lifted her head. It had a long way to go. Although she was of average height, she'd almost forgotten how neck-cricking it could be to stare him out.

By the time she'd shaped her expression into haughty lines and met his wickedly crinkling ice-blue eyes with a scathing look, she'd had to cope with the sight of the daunting width of his gently heaving chest and tough-guy shoulders, giving the lie to the surprisingly conven-

tional pin-stripe navy suit which had been expertly
moulded to his strong body.

'Thank you,' she said, proud of her steady voice. 'Now
explain that gibe you made, questioning the strength of
my feelings about Portallen.'

'They seem a little...lacking in depth.' His mouth
quirked in amusement at her cold stare. 'For someone
who professes to adore the place, you sure high-tailed
it out of here fast. Let's face it, you were only eighteen
when you latched on to the first rich man who stayed
at the hotel and shot off to get married in Scotland. Long
way from Cornwall, Scotland.'

'His job was there. If you love someone, you...' She
faltered. There was a dangerous, frightening light in
Cavan's eyes suddenly, and she couldn't continue with
what she'd been about to say. Stunned by the thinly veiled
venom pouring out of him towards her, she blinked
rapidly.

'If you love someone, you will follow them anywhere,' said Cavan softly, not sparing her.

She clenched her trembling hands. 'Exactly. Dan and
I were in love,' she said tightly, frowning when he lifted
a disbelieving eyebrow.

'Oh. We're talking about Dan, are we?' murmured
Cavan.

'Haven't you got any sensitivity?' asked Bethany, dry-
mouthed. 'I'd rather we didn't discuss my late husband.
My first thought was to drive down from Aberdeen when
he died so that I could be with people I knew, in a place
I loved. And look where it got me,' she added bitterly.

'Dan died three years ago. You've been away for two,'
said Cavan remorselessly. 'Living the high life, by the
looks of you.' His scornful eyes skimmed her elegant
suit. 'When you ran from this village because of that
hate campaign, you vanished as if you'd gone from the

face of the earth. God knows where you went, but I did think you'd come back after a while, even for a brief visit to your old haunts. I suppose you prefer city life now. More hairdressers. Fashion shops. Men.'

A wry smile touched her full mouth. If he knew! The picture he was painting was far from the truth. And her banishment from Portallen had been all his fault. Her eyes flickered like sparking flint when she realised that he was taunting her with the memories deliberately.

'You're trying to upset me. And failing,' she said coldly, wondering why Mawgan didn't protest on her behalf. 'You know perfectly well why I stayed away. Those poison-pen letters were vile.'

'Yes, the gossip was malicious, Cavan. Surely you remember,' interjected Mawgan, looking puzzled. 'For God's sake, Beth had just been widowed. She came here to grieve and within a short while she was being hounded by the very people she'd known since she was a kid. She was shunned and reviled by friends. Can you imagine that, Cavan? Beth's tough, but she was damned vulnerable at that time. The gossip all but destroyed her confidence.'

Cavan shrugged. 'They gossip about me constantly.'

'But you're thick-skinned,' Bethany said curtly. 'And you aren't bothered about what people think or you wouldn't have behaved so atrociously.'

'Are you referring to my dubious employment as a thuggish bouncer in Plymouth, or as a crooked ticket-tout in the East End?' he asked sarcastically.

Bethany tried to remain calm and keep her dignity. Cavan was throwing her own words back at her, and they sounded embarrassingly spiteful. 'I mean that outrageous assault on me in Fore Street,' she said stiffly. It rankled even now.

'Oh, that.' His eyes crinkled. 'You know, we'd startled the village often enough with our rows, but that was a classic,' he recalled with satisfaction. 'Better than a cabaret, wasn't it? There's still red paint on the wall where my old Ferrari wedged your car against the butcher's shop.'

'You humiliated me!' she said tightly.

'Did I?' It seemed as if his voice became huskier than ever. 'Because I hauled you out of the driver's seat and kissed you?' He thoughtfully stroked his cheek as if remembering her answering slap, and she flushed. Cavan brought out the worst in her. She never managed to keep her emotions under control when he was around—but then he *tormented* her so. 'Is your sense of honour satisfied or shall we stand back to back, take ten paces, turn and fire?' he asked in amusement, his teeth dazzling her for a moment.

She contemplated him thoughtfully, her heart pumping hard. 'I wouldn't dream of turning my back on you,' she said quietly. 'As for my honour, you might bear it in mind that I don't like being embarrassed in public or kissed by someone whom I dislike intensely.'

Cavan took her arms in his firm, possessive grip, his face suddenly serious. 'Bethany, I was trying to persuade you not to run away——'

'You liar!' she began with soft vehemence, and then stopped herself in time. She didn't want to get into an argument with Cavan. Or to reveal her suspicions. 'Mawgan, would you help me in with my things?' she asked her brother, letting warmth flood her voice, and hoping that Cavan would take note of the contrast in her manner.

'Good God!' cried Cavan, frowning. 'You're not planning on *staying* in the hotel, are you?'

To her alarm, he'd drawn her closer, as if she belonged to him, and she desperately wanted to beat him on the chest and escape. But he would have won, then.

'You can't object to me having my old room,' she said, apparently composed. Disdainfully she tried to pluck his fingers off and failed. He was no gentleman. She frowned at his hands. Once they'd been rough from manual work. Now they were smooth and beautifully manicured.

Cavan's eyes slid to Mawgan. 'Has she any idea of what's awaiting her?' he asked, his expression forbidding.

'What do you mean?' asked Bethany warily, glancing at the building. Frowning, she saw that there was something wrong with the windows, but she couldn't work out what it was. Suddenly alarmed, she turned her head quickly back to Cavan and clutched at his lapels. 'Who's in there?' she demanded huskily. 'The Men's Committee?' He didn't answer. His eyes were brooding on her, his face growing more sensual every second, and she became even more confused and agitated. 'The Women's Institute? They want me to leave?'

'Relax,' he murmured, taking the opportunity to cover her hands with his. 'The place is deserted. The hotel guests are on a trip to Land's End that Mawgan arranged and the staff are skiving as usual.'

'That's unfair!' blustered Mawgan.

Cavan gave a snort of exasperation, and Bethany dragged her hands away. 'No, it's not,' he said curtly. 'The hotel is as deserted as the *Mary Celeste* and there isn't even anyone on Reception. What kind of a business is that?' He fixed Mawgan with a hard, uncompromising stare. 'You gather that I've been inside,' he said through his teeth.

'Oh, hell!' groaned Mawgan, rolling his eyes up, and Bethany looked from one to the other, sensing trouble.

'That describes it adequately, I think,' agreed Cavan harshly. 'I repeat: has Bethany any idea of what you've done?'

Mawgan flushed and looked uncomfortable. 'Well...I told her that I got a firm to do the re-fit last February before the summer season began——'

'While you pushed off on a painting holiday,' scowled Cavan. 'I don't know why I left the arrangements to you. I must have been seized by temporary madness.'

Mawgan flushed. 'It's a mistake I'm putting right. In fact, if you hadn't turned up today, you would never have known the re-fit was a disaster,' he muttered. 'That's why Beth's here—to see what she can do to improve things. After next week the hotel will be empty and we'll make the place look OK again. Dammit, Cavan, what do you care? You haven't come to see what I've been doing for almost a year.'

'There's been nothing to bring me here,' said Cavan quietly. He turned to the bewildered Bethany. 'If you want to, you can stay with me——'

Her chin lifted. 'Is that what this is about? Good grief, Cavan, before I took up your offer it would have to be wall-to-wall breeze blocks and cold steel carpets in there.'

'Close,' said Cavan laconically. 'Well, there's a pair of oyster satin sheets waiting for you if you need them. I had the impression that you were on edge. The villagers might be stand-offish for a while and I thought you might need a bolt-hole—as you did before when you ran off into the blue yonder. This time I'm offering to make room for you——'

'Oh, sharing,' she said with light sarcasm, 'the Cavan Trevelyan multi-storey harem. No, thanks.'

'Your tongue hasn't got any blunter,' frowned Cavan. 'I meant that my yacht is at your disposal. With or without me.'

'Your yacht?' Following the curt angling of his head, she turned to look at the glorious ketch on the shimmering blue sea. She cocked an eyebrow at Cavan. 'That's yours? I saw it sail in . . . So who drove the flashy red Aston Martin?' she asked calmly. 'One of your ticket-touts?'

'Your hostility is showing,' murmured Cavan, sounding pleased. 'I drove the car.'

'And I sailed the boat,' husked a honey-warm voice from somewhere directly behind him.

Cavan stepped aside, mercifully releasing Bethany, who grew wide-eyed at the pocket-sized vision in front of her. Mawgan was equally pole-axed, judging by his village-yokel stare.

'I think you know Tania,' drawled Cavan. 'Tania Blake.'

Tania held out a tiny hand glinting with diamonds. 'Hello, Beth. Long time since we were in that ghastly school uniform, isn't it?'

'Tania?' Bethany could hardly believe the transformation. From a dumpy village girl, Tania had become a gorgeous woman. She was dressed in a casual jogging suit, but it was Italian and pure silk, in a rich green which matched her eyes and also the emeralds that sparkled ostentatiously in her ears amid a tumble of artful blonde waves. Someone was footing an expensive clothes bill, by the looks of it, mused Bethany. Tania had always said she'd land a millionaire. Her stomach muscles clenched in a sudden spasm. Cavan must be that man, she thought bleakly.

'My, my! What a thick skin you've got, Beth! I'm amazed you're here, after what the villagers said about you,' said Tania spitefully, smiling when Bethany blanched.

Cavan reached out with his big fist, opened his palm and gently pressed it against Tania's neat rose-bud mouth. Tania's lashes fluttered at him appealingly. 'Shut it,' he said amiably, with a slight tightness in his jaw.

'You don't have to worry about me,' insisted Bethany bravely, determined to protect herself. 'I don't care what anyone thinks any more. I have no feelings left about the matter. I'm here purely for Mawgan's sake, nothing else——'

'I'm sorry you don't care, Bethany,' said Cavan in a soft growl, removing his hand from Tania's mouth. 'I always did think you suppressed your feelings too much at the time of Dan's death instead of letting them fly.'

'Was that why you deliberately made me cry?' she asked huskily, remembering his cruelty.

'Oh, you remember that,' he said softly, his eyes darkening. 'You were like a zombie. I had to really work hard on you before you would burst into tears.'

'And you enjoyed every minute,' muttered Bethany in resentment.

'He did say at the time that you weren't acting normally,' put in Mawgan awkwardly. 'He said you needed something to jerk you out of your shock.'

'He did that all right,' she said flatly.

'I suppose,' husked Tania with deceptive sympathy, 'it didn't help having half a million pounds landing in your lap.'

Cavan's brooding eyes flickered briefly at Tania and then returned to the white-faced Bethany. Seagulls screamed and wheeled overhead, and she wanted to give vent to her own feelings by screaming too. The staggering sum of compensation paid out so quickly on Dan's accidental death on the oil rig had brought her nothing but misery.

'Still living off the money?' queried Cavan. His piercing stare bored a path of glittering ice into Bethany's soul, and she flinched noticeably. Her reaction made a contemptuous smile touch his lips. 'You are. Dammit, Bethany, you're wasting your talents,' he said, when she didn't deny his assumption that she was a lady of leisure.

'What I do is my business. I'm twenty-six, not twelve. You can't try to run my life for me any more.'

Bethany felt too unsettled by his intrusive questions to tell him the truth. In actual fact, she'd given away every penny of the compensation. Her whole outfit was three years old, but he wasn't to know that because its lines were classic and everlasting. She had no intention of letting him find out that she had been living hand to mouth, unable to find design work, standing behind the ticket counter of a local theme park all summer. She was Cornish, and proud.

'Beth's going to use her talents,' reminded Mawgan, 'on the hotel.'

'She'll need them,' remarked Cavan cynically. 'You've damn near ruined it.'

Bethany's mouth compressed when she saw Mawgan's hurt expression. 'I want to judge for myself,' she said curtly. 'Let me go. I'm not one of your bar-room girls, Cavan Trevelyan!'

'So you acknowledge my name at last,' he observed grimly, his big face filling her vision. 'I remember when a teacher called me Trevelyan you whirled on your lace-up brogues so fast that your socks fell down and your plaits stung your face, and you yelled out to all and sundry that I had not a drop of Trevelyan blood in my veins and had no right to use the name.'

Tania giggled merrily, and Bethany blushed with shame. What a welcome she'd given him! She'd been wrong. But then, she'd been only twelve, and horrified that her father should have married the big, hearty Rosie, who had filled the house with loud laughter. Bethany had been jealous that her position had been usurped in her father's heart and because Rosie had cheerfully taken over running the house. But Bethany had also taken her cue from the disapproving women of the village.

Rosie had been a barmaid from Plymouth, older than her father and with an illegitimate son—and such a son! There were wildfire rumours about him. No one had ever liked the fierce, surly sixteen-year-old Cavan who had stood up to every taunt and bullying attack and had given back better than he'd got. But Rosie's warm and jolly personality had soon melted opposition and had packed the bar at the Inn to overflowing.

'It was only natural that I was disturbed and upset,' defended Bethany.

Cavan nodded. 'That goes for me too. Coming here was a culture shock for me, after city life, city sophistication. Still, like you, I got out fast. You always said I needed a bigger stage where I could strut. Big, brash, common and showy, that's me, isn't it?' he mocked.

She looked at him doubtfully. Somehow he didn't fit that description she'd flung at him during one of their endless quarrels. He was more groomed, more quietly sure of himself, and she felt he was even controlling one or two emotions—though she was certain that the wild and violent spark still lay simmering inside. Tough guys didn't change their penchant for fisticuffs and confrontation overnight.

'You said it,' she smiled coolly. 'Excuse me.' She turned towards the hotel and realised the old stone mullion windows had been double-glazed. She frowned.

'So you're going in?' asked Cavan quietly, noticing her hesitation. 'Tania, go and check on the Longchamp situation.'

'But——' pouted Tania.

'*Now!*' he barked.

Tania jumped and slid sulkily into Cavan's car, picking up a handset.

'She's well trained,' observed Bethany with distaste.

'Best secretary I ever had,' said Cavan with a bland smile.

The penny dropped. Bethany remembered that Tania had excelled at business studies. Judging by Cavan's enigmatic expression and Tania's air of possession, she also excelled in pleasing her boss in other ways. An uncharacteristic jealousy knifed through her with a startling thoroughness. Annoyed, she marched past Cavan and into the Inn. Two steps inside what had once been a slate-flagged hall, she stopped dead.

'You see what I mean,' panted Mawgan, coming up behind her and sounding as if he'd run with her case from the car. 'The décor isn't really suitable——'

'Not suitable——!' Words failed her.

'Come and have a drink.' Cavan's body pressed against hers and virtually forced her to move in the direction of the empty bar. The partition wall seemed to have disappeared. Numbly she let herself be propelled forwards, too dismayed to protest. 'Mawgan, get her a Cinzano, quick. I'll have a brandy.'

'At this hour? Lord! It's three o'clock——!' began Mawgan.

'Do it!' snapped Cavan sharply. Like Tania, Mawgan jumped to obey him. 'Can't you see your sister's overwhelmed at the extent of the alterations?' he growled.

'I hadn't realised they'd made such huge changes,' said Bethany slowly. 'It's not my home any longer.'

The cosy, intimate atmosphere of the old beamed lobby, bar and restaurant had disappeared. Instead, a huge open space had been created, which glittered with chrome and glass. It would have been fine for a London wine-bar, but was totally inappropriate for Portallen. The character had been utterly lost. Her eyes widened at the uniformly dull modern prints on the walls.

'Mawgan!' she said in dismay. 'Where are your lovely paintings?'

'They didn't look right.' Mawgan sullenly poured himself a glass of cider. He came over and slid into the scarlet banquette beside Cavan. 'Look, I was tricked. I somehow signed a form giving them a free hand, and they unloaded some fittings that no one wanted. It was a mistake, and I'm putting it right.'

'Damn right you are,' growled Cavan. 'And it had better be at no cost to me. No wonder the takings are down. Not much call for yuppy pubs in Cornwall.'

'What else is different?' asked Bethany gently, seeing Mawgan was being put on the spot. 'The garden? The bedrooms?'

'You *are* out of touch, Bethany, aren't you?' muttered Cavan, glaring at Mawgan accusingly. 'And so was I. I should have come down here before, but... Tell us about the bedrooms, Mawgan,' he said grimly.

Her brother shifted in his seat. 'The bedrooms have been modernised in the same way, I'm afraid. Chrome and glass.'

'The four-poster beds?' asked Bethany anxiously.

'Stored in the attic. I was going to get them down, but then I didn't know what to do about the colour scheme. The brocade hangings didn't match the new check carpets,' he said helplessly. 'But the garden's unchanged, if a bit run down. I haven't had time——'

'The garden is a total shambles,' interrupted Cavan contemptuously. 'Like everything you do here. *Hell*, Mawgan! I'd throw you out of the damn window if it wasn't double-glazed and impossible to open!'

Mawgan leapt to his feet. 'It's your fault! You said I had to smarten the place up and I had to do it on the cheap. You kept issuing directives about making more profit and constantly criticising the way things were going! You *bombarded* me with memos and complaints. People don't have money to burn any more! You know that in the current economic——'

'Oh, don't excuse your inefficiency by blaming the lack of spending power on the populace in general,' snapped Cavan. 'You're a hopeless manager, that's the fact of the matter. Your staff pilfer from the till, and you sign the overtime chits without even checking them. Your stock-taking is non-existent and I imagine half of Portallen has smuggled drink out and is boozing away at home at my expense.'

'Don't you dare to insult my brother!' seethed Bethany. 'He's admitted to a mistake anyone could make. He couldn't do anything about it till the guests had departed, and he's done his best with little help from you, it appears, if you didn't even know what was going on in your own hotel.'

'Hotel?' Cavan's lip curled. 'I've had more complaints about the running of this so-called hotel than I've had from any of my East End pubs. Tell me, what do the locals think of the way you've changed their pub? What do the fishermen do, now you've removed the small Stable Bar?'

'A few still come in,' Mawgan said awkwardly.

'My mother would turn in her grave! Dammit, man, apart from being a local service and a meeting place, this pub survives in the winter by its local trade. Lose that, and...' Cavan shook his head in exasperation. 'You should have consulted me. It's my damn building!'

'Apparently you've never shown interest before,' Bethany pointed out stiffly.

'Well, all that is going to change,' Cavan said, giving
her a challenging stare. 'I'm going to be around a lot
more now.'

Her hand flew to her mouth, and she saw his preda-
tor's eyes go there, and the slow, sultry parting of his
sensual lips. A quiver ran through her, as sharp and deep
as if she'd been harpooned. Cavan's sexuality seared
across the table at her, rendering her mute.

'I...I think I've got a few things to do,' said Mawgan,
eyeing them both. 'Excuse me.'

Bethany thought there was the shadow of a smile on
Cavan's lips, and she wanted to leave too, but her legs
were leaden. She'd come here specifically to help
Mawgan, knowing it would be an awkward situation because of the malicious stories which had been spread
about her in the past. She'd even steeled herself to the
probability that she'd see Cavan once or twice. But she
hadn't bargained on this.

'You don't need to stay in Portallen,' she said huskily,
longing to moisten her dry mouth but knowing he'd find
that infinitely provocative. All his girlfriends had declared in awe that he was incredibly over-sexed. 'I am
perfectly capable of restoring the character of the hotel
at the minimum cost to you.'

He didn't reply at first, but studied her minutely, inch
by inch, and she had to force herself to act normally
under the disconcerting pressure of his gaze. Then he
nodded. 'I know that.'

His eyes had reached her shapely breasts, firm against
the fabric of her jacket. Without seeing any need to
hurry, he let his gaze slide over her waist and—aided
and abetted by the glass-topped table—to her slender
stockinged thighs, visible beneath the fashionably short
skirt.

'Looking for signs of my alleged dissolute life?' she asked haughtily, trying to divert his attention from her legs.

'Surprisingly, the effects are not showing yet. In fact, you look as if you've spent the last two years sitting in a beauty parlour,' commented Cavan sardonically.

She made her eyes crawl contemptuously up the kind of chest that any navvy would display with pride. 'And you look as if you've been heaving bricks and building one,' she retorted defensively.

He laughed shortly and leaned forwards, his strongly featured face a little too close to hers for comfort. 'Life good for you, is it? Money in the bank, no reason to work, men fawning all over you?' he murmured.

His hand lifted, and she waited with tense anticipation as his forefinger slowly uncurled and lightly stroked her cheek. Some of her blusher came off on to his finger and he smiled into her eyes. Bethany trembled involuntarily. And saw his eyes narrowing.

'Life is a ball,' she lied, thinking how deceptive appearances could be and floundering for some form of normal conversation. 'How's the underworld these days?'

'Ticking along,' he said nonchalantly. 'Like Captain Hook's crocodile in *Peter Pan*. Remember the crocodile who swallowed a clock? It ticked so loudly that everyone could run to safety. That's me. I give everyone a chance to escape a savaging from me. Just one chance,' he added with soft menace.

'I suppose you're expecting me to ask what happens when people have had that one chance,' she said, trying to sound indifferent to his answer even though her nerves were on edge.

'Clever girl,' he said approvingly with devastating patronage. 'Obviously I eat them for breakfast.'

Bethany met his relentless gaze boldly, only just managing to remain composed. 'I must remember to remove my earrings so you don't get too much roughage, then,' she said drily.

Cavan gave her one of his dazzling smiles. She picked up her Cinzano, using the gesture as an excuse to drop her lashes and avoid his eyes. He was as hard as nails and as ruthless as any pirate on the high seas, and he had some nasty treat in store for her, she was certain. There was a definite air of smugness about the set of his mouth.

'I've missed you, Bethany,' said Cavan quietly.

Totally disarmed by the unexpectedness of his remark, she hurriedly placed her drink on the table before he had a chance to notice the way she was shaking. To her alarm, her hand was covered by his. Her big Celtic-blue eyes lifted. He seemed serious. What was he trying to do to her?

She waited for the punchline, the joke, the ridicule. A long, tense silence stretched between them and she found herself incapable of breaking it or of avoiding the extraordinary pull of his unnervingly softened blue eyes—soft as the silken water in Portallen Harbour, as deep, as treacherous, she thought wildly.

Her fingers were gripped tightly and raised to his lips, and he never stopped looking at her while he did this, not even when he curled her hand over and kissed the palm, sending tiny shivers through her body. She still ached for him, then. The knowledge filled her with misery. He had a terrible and inexplicable hold over her. If he should ever become aware of it, he'd do just what he'd said—eat her for breakfast.

'Bethany, there's something I must say to you,' husked Cavan, his breath on her face making her shiver.

'Darling! Sorry to butt in, but Johnny's on the phone from the Dorchester.' Tania was bending close to Cavan, her hand possessively on his broad shoulder, her blonde curls softly sweeping his jaw. A waft of expensive perfume drifted over to Bethany.

Cavan's mouth quirked and he gently placed Bethany's hand back on the table. 'Your timing is appalling, Tania,' he drawled, still holding Bethany's eyes. 'You may be a good secretary and an even better sailor, but you have no appreciation of a tense and highly charged atmosphere.'

'Oh, you're wrong, I do,' demurred Tania. 'That's why I phoned Johnny in the first place and why I interrupted.'

'You——!' Cavan chuckled at Tania's pert smile. 'My saviour,' he said fondly to her, giving her bottom a very familiar and insolently chauvinistic slap. She wriggled and giggled, her eyes flirting with his. 'Excuse me, Bethany. We'll talk later about your brother's job—and how I see your role.'

Her eyes widened. 'Is that what you were going to say just now?' she blurted out.

'Of course. What were you expecting?' he murmured, rising from the seat, mocking her with his dark, steady gaze.

'Almost anything, knowing you… Wait a minute! His job? My role? What do you mean——?' Bethany half rose in agitation, but he gave her a mysterious smile and she was left facing the triumphant Tania.

'He'll explain,' said Tania in an offhand manner. 'He has plans for you.'

'Plans? Oh, no. I won't let that man manipulate me,' declared Bethany with determination. 'I have my own plans, and he doesn't come anywhere in them.'

'Is that so? I thought for a minute you were contemplating a merger,' said Tania coldly.

'With Cavan? You can't have forgotten,' frowned Bethany, 'that we've been at daggers drawn since he stormed into my life at the age of sixteen and proceeded to turn this house upside-down! It was like having a flame-thrower in the house! No, thanks. I'd rather merge with a ticking crocodile.'

Tania frowned, not having had the benefit of Cavan's earlier remark. 'His arrival certainly sparked us all,' she agreed. 'It was dull before he came. He's so *passionate*. Portallen came alive, didn't it?' she sighed wistfully.

'Yes, I suppose it did,' Bethany said with reluctance. Cavan had been rough and ready, spoiling for a fight, but had brought with him a breath of fresh air and vitality which had made the sleepy village fizz. For a moment, Bethany saw the old Tania; teased by the boys because she was overweight and mooning hopelessly over the dynamic, exciting and hot-headed Cavan. 'We were friends, then, you and I,' she said quietly.

'You dumped me when the boys started hanging around you,' Tania remarked with a sullen expression.

'Oh, Tania!' Bethany said, hurt. 'That's not true! You left me with them——'

'Because I was in the way,' snapped Tania. 'The boys made that clear enough with their hurtful comments. But now I'm equipped to get what I want, and, in case you haven't realised, what I want is Cavan. Leave him alone, Beth. Stop flashing those endless legs of yours at him and giving him those long, sultry looks.' Her small face grew sharp and a little desperate. 'I've worked hard to hook him and I don't want some flash millionairess distracting him by waving wads of bank notes around. He's not for sale or even for hire.'

'Is that what you think? You don't know Cavan very well,' retorted Bethany, feeling a brief, unreasoning dislike for her old schoolfriend. She ought to feel sorry for her, because Tania apparently imagined she could 'land' the slippery East End charmer. 'Cavan has always been available to the highest bidder. Money is his only God, his only love. It sends him into ecstasies. He left here to make his fortune, and he's achieved that ambition. He'd sell his mother if she was on the market—and take a discount for cash.'

Disconcerted by the extraordinary bitterness of her words, she swept out to the kitchen in search of Mawgan, leaving Tania gripping the side of the banquette in suppressed rage.

Bethany paused in the corridor, gathering her composure. It was becoming a little frayed at the ends. Once again, she was in danger of being destroyed by Cavan. She closed her eyes briefly, vowing to herself that he wouldn't succeed.

The situation might seem like a normal clash between a stepbrother and his stepsister on the surface, but she knew better. The scurrilous poison-pen letters had almost wrecked her confidence and had driven her from the home and the brother she loved. And it had been Cavan who had written them.

CHAPTER TWO

BETHANY clenched her fists. Yes, Cavan had begun the smear campaign. Who else had actively disliked her and had known so much about her? The truth had been twisted quite expertly, by someone who had hated and resented her, making it easy for the recipients of the letters to believe the dreadful stories.

Slowly the rumours had spread: she'd left Portallen as a teenager because she was pregnant; she'd married Dan purely for his money; in Aberdeen she'd 'entertained' oil-riggers on leave while Dan was on shift duty. The letters had accused her of being a merry widow and sleeping with half the males in Portallen because she had an insatiable sexual appetite. If her light was on all night, there were knowing looks in the morning when she appeared, drained, exhausted. If she spoke to a male hotel guest, she was making an assignation. If she went for a walk, women followed her in case she was meeting their husbands or boyfriends. Men freely made lewd propositions to her.

Sometimes she had wanted to take a midnight stroll to think about her future without Dan. She'd been unable to, fearful of whom she might meet, or what the gossip would be the next day. So she became a prisoner in her own house, despised by people she'd thought of as friends. And Cavan had been responsible.

The sheer vindictiveness had been hard to take. Her doctor had explained that rumour-mongering wasn't unusual when an inhabitant of a tightly knit community suddenly became wealthy. He said she'd stepped out of their world and returned a stranger, that their hostility was bound up in the fact that she'd rejected them by leaving. He'd recommended a new start somewhere far away.

For a long while now she'd been convinced that it had been Cavan who manipulated the stories, who had turned the village against her. They'd squabbled from the very first. He'd disliked her so much that he'd avoided her as much as possible. Their rows had become a standing joke. Yet it was from the time she'd announced her intention to marry Dan that he'd become unbearable, as if he had resented her for marrying into money instead of working for it like him.

Bethany tipped her head back and wondered what Cavan had in store for her this time. And suddenly she felt a fierce, stubborn determination that he wouldn't succeed in driving her from her childhood home until she was good and ready to go under her own terms. She'd survive. She always had. It would be a matter of existing, not living, but then she'd forgotten what it was like to be really happy.

At least she was with Mawgan, at least she was in Portallen. A little more optimistic, she pushed open the door to the kitchen. She smiled. Mawgan *had* made an excuse to leave her with Cavan; he didn't have any jobs to do at all—he was sitting hunched over a cup of tea and a plate of pasties.

'Hi, Beth. Are you mad at me for ruining our home?'

Smiling, she shook her head, letting her anger with Cavan and Tania evaporate, and automatically went over to the hob to light the gas beneath the kettle. Mercifully the kitchen was the same: the old wood-burning Aga, low beams, huge stone butler's sink and the enormous pine table in the middle of the room. She sat down, suddenly tired.

'You'd better put me properly in the picture,' she said quietly. 'I need to know what money I have to play around with.'

'Not much,' answered Mawgan ruefully. 'I haven't saved a lot from the salary Cavan pays me. Canvases and oils are so expensive nowadays. Have you any cash to spare?'

'Not a penny,' sighed Bethany. She'd bought a cottage on Bodmin from the proceeds of the sale of her effects in Aberdeen, and there had been little left to live on. 'All the compensation went towards the Inshore Lifeboat. No one knows about that, do they?' she asked anxiously.

'No. Why didn't you let me tell them? It might have altered their opinion of you.' Mawgan bit into his pasty and chewed for a moment. 'They never dreamed the donation came from you. They thought it was Cavan.'

'Him? He wouldn't give his hard-fought money away,' she said tartly. 'No one must know it was my compensation money. The villagers would be mortified. *You* wouldn't accept any of it, and you're my brother.'

'It was good of you, Beth, but I couldn't go through art college on a dead man's money,' said Mawgan quietly.

'I know what you mean. I never liked the idea of being given cash in exchange for Dan's life,' she admitted. 'But... I wish you'd approached me sooner for help. I could have done the re-fit myself in February, at cost-price.'

'Six months ago you weren't ready to come back,' Mawgan pointed out. 'I had only to mention Portallen and you went as white as chalk and dropped things. I'll have to borrow the money somehow, though God knows where from.'

'Cavan?' she suggested reluctantly. 'It's his hotel. He might cough up, now that he's seen it needs doing.'

Mawgan looked up hopefully. 'He didn't sound too keen earlier. But a loan... Would you ask him? He'd do it for you.'

'You're joking! Only if he thought he'd get something in return,' she said ruefully. Mawgan seemed upset, and she touched his hand in concern. 'What's the matter? There's something else worrying you, isn't there?'

He grunted. 'I think Cavan's come down here to throw me out.'

'What? Sack you? But it's your home! We were brought up here!' she cried in horror. 'He can't do that to you. Five generations of Trevelyans have lived in this building! Oh, Mawgan, he'll sell it to some property developer for a fat profit! That man has got no soul, no decency, no sense of honour!' she seethed. 'He's like a basking shark, cruising around for someone to savage!'

Mawgan shifted awkwardly in his seat. 'He's not that bad. I did make a mess of things. My mind was on painting. I've been working on a series of canvases... I can't excuse my vagueness. He's going to give me an ultimatum, I know.'

'Damn right I am!' They both whirled at Cavan's tight, clipped voice. 'No soul, no decency, no sense of honour, eh?' Bethany flushed, but defied him with a look. Her brother was in trouble, and Cavan was causing it. 'The basking *shark*,' continued Cavan angrily, 'is currently gnashing his teeth and looking for some rotten piece of carrion to tear into bite-sized chunks—and I think I've found my pound of flesh,' he bit, looking directly at her.

'How dare you?' she said, her voice low with rage. 'If anything's rotten around here, it's you.'

'You know nothing about me. Not how I work, what I've done, what I do now,' he rasped. 'You make assumptions all the time. You're blind to what's in front of your nose, Bethany Trevelyan, and I'm going to open

your eyes good and wide.' He reached down and hauled
her to her feet, giving her a sharp shake, and when
Mawgan moved forwards in outraged protest he turned
his back on him, effectively preventing Mawgan from
coming to her rescue. 'You bitch,' he muttered, for her
ears only. 'Wait till I've finished with you. You'll wish
you'd never fluttered those two-coat-mascara eyelashes
at me.'

'Cavan!' cried Mawgan urgently. 'This wasn't what
we——'

'Shut up!' ordered Cavan as Mawgan tried vainly to
shoulder his way in.

'Let me go,' Bethany gasped. 'I don't know what
you're talking about. And if you think you can threaten
me and interfere in my life——'

'Why not? You interfered in mine,' said Cavan curtly,
suddenly letting her drop unceremoniously to the chair.

She rubbed her faintly bruised bottom resentfully,
glaring at him from under her brows. 'Me?' she asked
in amazement.

'Every minute of every day,' he breathed, his chest
rising up and down rapidly. Bethany looked at him in
alarm. For some reason he was building up into one of
his spectacular rages. 'From the moment I stepped into
this house with my mother, you tried to make my life
hell, you selfish, unwelcoming little——'

'That's enough!' rapped Mawgan. 'You're going too
far. You always did. Admit it; you did throw your weight
about a bit at first. Bethany was only trying to stop you
bossing us around.'

'No,' he denied quietly, his eyes riveted on the white-
lipped Bethany. 'She has always wanted to be the centre
of attention. She resented my mother and resented me.
Selfish little girl! Well, she got what she wanted, didn't
she? With a vengeance. She became the centre of at-

tention all right.' He tipped up Bethany's chin with a rough, hurting finger and thumb which bit into her soft flesh. 'And you didn't like it, did you? The gawping Press, the gossip, the foul accusations, the resentment——'

'Oh, you bastard,' she whispered shakily. 'You evil, cruel, heartless bastard!'

His eyes closed momentarily as if in pain. 'That's me,' he said bitterly. 'And you made me one, pushing my patience to its limit as you did just now. You, a twelve-year-old girl, had the power to hit all my raw nerves bang on target by telling me I didn't belong and never would, constantly pointing out my ignorance of country ways, lighting my short fuse. You, at eighteen, teased and tormented all the young men in the village till their tongues were hanging out——'

'That's not true!' she gasped.

'You never dated any of them, and they asked often enough,' Cavan went on relentlessly. 'You pranced around in skin-tight T-shirts and brief shorts and that incredible scrap of a blue bikini——'

'What? They were hand-me-downs from the jumble sale,' she cried indignantly, flushing at the scornful curl of his lip. 'I deny that I knew I was being provocative——'

'Oh, come off it, Bethany!' sneered Cavan. 'I *told* you to cover up. I warned you that you couldn't go clambering about on the rocks and sunbathing on the beach half-naked without raising the blood-pressure of every male in sight. You knew well enough.'

Her lashes swept down to cover her guilty eyes. Yes. When he'd told her that, she'd become intensely aware of the potency of her body. Desperately infatuated with the handsome Cavan, she had deliberately wandered about in what she'd hoped were alluring and womanly clothes, hoping he would fall for her and stop tormenting her by flirting with every other female in the village. Instead, he'd become even more bad-tempered than before.

'I didn't tease the boys,' she insisted. 'I didn't mean to, anyway,' she amended.

'You were a lot of things from the age of sixteen to eighteen, Bethany, but you weren't innocent,' scorned Cavan. 'Oh, you knew what you were doing, all right, practising your come-hither glances on the boys—and on me, whenever I appeared. And then, dammit, as soon as you'd perfected them, you jumped into the lap of the first man with money who had the misfortune to stay here and be dazzled by your seductive body. If I'm a bastard, it's because of you and the cynical impression I formed of women from your calculating, cold-blooded example.'

'That's ridiculous——' she cried.

'And when you came back to the village after Dan died it was the same,' he continued unsparingly. 'The men flocked around you like seagulls behind a plough. You arrived with a tarnished reputation and certainly left with one.' His hand slid down to her throat, hovering there, and to her alarm she saw a murderous glint in his cold eyes. 'But now I've had experience of many, many women, and know exactly how to deal with you,' he said in a tone of soft menace.

His threat hung in the air. Bethany stared into his merciless and malevolent eyes, and felt the crackling hostility which leapt backwards and forwards between them. She let out a harsh, croaking sound of protest.

'Cavan, I think you'd better get out of here,' grated Mawgan, his voice quivering with anger. 'And let go of Bethany before I offer you a knuckle sandwich with the compliments of the management.'

'I will leave when I want to and not before. I *own* Portallen,' snapped Cavan, nevertheless releasing his hold on Bethany. Her eyes blazed and kindled an answering fire in his. 'You hate that, don't you?' he said, taunting her. 'You loathe the fact that mother inherited the hotel when your father died, and that after her death it came to me.'

'Of course I hate it,' she said proudly. 'Because you don't deserve it, because you don't feel the same way about it. It's Mawgan's by rights. You were only our stepbrother and you had no time for the hotel, the village or the villagers. Your heart was always in the city, with the bright lights and gaudy women.'

Cavan smiled coldly. 'My heart? What heart?' he mocked. Bethany set her chin stubbornly, and he gave it an insolent tweak then turned to Mawgan. 'OK. Enough of this. Sit down, Mawgan. I've got something to tell the pair of you.'

'Oh, lord!' groaned Mawgan. 'I know what's coming. You're going to give me the sack.'

'Got it in one,' said Cavan bluntly.

'Cavan, you can't. You have a moral obligation to let us both live here if we want to,' asserted Bethany in desperation, seeing how pale Mawgan looked. She wouldn't let Cavan hurt her brother. She'd stuck up for Mawgan all her life, and would defend her family home with the same ferocity if necessary.

Cavan gave a derisive laugh. 'Moral? Me?' He shook his head emphatically. 'Morality doesn't enter into it. I've come to a decision and I never change my mind. I'm offering you both a choice. One chance each, Bethany.'

'A chance? Then he can stay on as manager?' she asked hopefully.

Turning to her brother, Cavan smiled with deceptive innocence. 'You think a lot of this place, don't you, Mawgan? How keen are you to keep it in the Trevelyan family?'

'Don't answer that!' shot Bethany. 'He'll use whatever you say to some crooked purpose.'

Cavan ignored her. 'Mawgan, you make a rotten manager. I kept you on because of your ties here. Out of the goodness of my heart.' He ignored, too, Bethany's snort of disbelief. 'This might be paradise to you, but to me it's a business on a profit-and-loss sheet. I can't let this place go to rack and ruin, and I can't stand inefficiency of any kind.'

'I've tried——' began Mawgan.

'That's not good enough. I want achievers, not triers. It's a matter of authority,' interrupted Cavan brutally. 'And you haven't got it. I want you out.' He paused, his hard eyes boring into Mawgan's. 'You have a week's notice,' he said curtly.

'A week? You can't do that!' cried Bethany, springing immediately to her startled brother's defence.

'How would you stop me?' murmured Cavan, turning smoky blue eyes on her. 'Bargain with the devil?'

She paused, her instincts telling her to back away. He wanted something from her, she was convinced of that. Yet Mawgan's livelihood was on the line.

'If need be,' she said coldly, her hands trembling with apprehension.

'Good. Exactly what I was hoping,' he declared with barely suppressed triumph, and Bethany's heart sank. 'Mawgan, leave us. Your sister and I have something to discuss.'

'Like hell I will! With you in this mood? No way. Besides, you said I had a choice——'

'The choice depends on Bethany,' said Cavan smugly, as if he had just landed a prize fish.

'Cavan, when we talked, you said——' began Mawgan.

'I said, when we spoke on the telephone, that it was time your sister faced the realities of normal life, and that I knew how to force her to do so,' growled Cavan.

Bethany's eyes darted backwards and forwards to Mawgan and Cavan. 'Oh, Mawgan,' she groaned, 'what have you done?'

'It was all he said,' cried her brother in distress. 'He never told me he was coming here, or that it meant I'd get the sack or...'

He paused, and Bethany tried to interpret the look which passed between the two men. It was as if Cavan was signalling to Mawgan. 'What is going on?' she asked suspiciously.

'I'm warning him,' said Cavan implacably. 'The more he says, the harder it will be for us all.'

'For you to force me to face life?' she scorned. 'My God, Cavan! You've got a nerve!'

'You can't jet-set around forever,' said Cavan grimly.

Bethany and Mawgan stared at him, and she remembered that no one knew she was virtually broke and had been living like a recluse for the last two years—and for the whole summer, walking three miles to work, sitting alone in a small wooden hut all day and walking back again. So much for the glamorous life he imagined she was leading. The thought that the great Cavan Trevelyan had some misinformation cheered her up and gave her strength.

'It's OK, I can handle him,' she said to her brother. 'He's no problem—not compared with a whole village hurling abuse at me.'

However, when the disgruntled Mawgan reluctantly left, Bethany turned to the impatiently waiting Cavan with a leaden heart. He wanted to hurt her. If he did but know, he could do so easily with one callous, brutal kiss. Her knees buckled and she folded them under her as she collapsed with as much grace as she could into the deep armchair by the Aga.

'Oh, the legs approach,' mocked Cavan in derision. 'Who was it who said you had yards of them, up to your armpits?'

'You,' said Bethany with commendable calm.

He grinned. 'So I did. How well they'll look, draped over a big, cosy sofa. Any visiting guests will love them.' His head tipped on one side as he surveyed her from head to toe.

His smouldering gaze was worrying. A heavy sensuality filled the air, projected with such a compelling force that it made her body tingle. Bethany felt the panic building up inside her, spiralling tightly, urgent to escape. 'What are you talking about?' she asked with great indifference.

'You're a class act. You and your legs would fit in perfectly here—once it's been done up properly.' He half lowered his heavy eyelids, his eyes mesmeric beneath them.

Bethany swallowed and tried to keep her mind on what he was saying. 'I'm not having anything to do with any guests. If you think I'd make a good waitress or a receptionist, you're mistaken. Are you being funny?' she asked frostily.

'No.' He came over and crouched in front of her, intimidatingly close, a habit of his which she found irritating in the extreme. 'I want to put Mawgan through art college,' he said, watching carefully for her reaction. He wasn't disappointed.

Bethany's eyes had widened in amazement at the bombshell. 'You? Why?' she gasped.

'Because he's a square peg in a round hole here and because he's very talented. Raw, untaught, but talented. We've both grown up with his paintings. I know how well they compare with professional work.' His eyes mocked her stunned face.

'There must be a profit in it for you somewhere,' she said caustically.

'You're right,' he acknowledged. 'It would be an investment, you understand. I have every intention of taking a percentage of his future earnings. He'd be my protégé. You know, Bethany, I never understood why you didn't cough up some of your compensation for him, so that he could do what he's always wanted to do.'

'It's really none of your business, but we discussed it,' she said, her voice neutral. 'He refused the money. Partly pride, partly because he couldn't bear to see anyone else running Portallen. I did try to persuade him. He was adamant.'

'Well, as sure as hell he's not going to run the hotel any more, so he might as well go to college,' he said laconically. 'I could even find him markets in my pubs and some of the hotels I know. There are countless bare walls around, waiting for paintings as good as his.'

'And?' prompted Bethany cynically, knowing that wasn't all. Mawgan would agree. He'd sell his soul to be able to paint all day. Cavan would get his ten per cent and she... She gulped.

Cavan laughed softly, one big hand resting on her knee. 'For a woman with a limited education, you're very quick on the uptake,' he commented insultingly. 'You can read my mind like a book, can't you?'

'There aren't many pages and the words are simple,' she said tartly. He gave her a suspiciously innocent grin, and the hand crept upwards. 'Slide that any higher and I'll slap your face,' warned Bethany. 'No man touches me.' Cavan removed his hand as if it had touched fire. 'Get to the point,' she muttered.

'Even before I saw the bodged re-fit, I'd decided that it was time the Portallen Inn was revamped and pushed up-market for the luxury trade. You know the kind of thing I mean: choice of bath oils, quality fittings, subtle furnishings in keeping with the age of the place——'

'It's thirteenth century. Do you mean trestle-tables, roast boar's head and straw on the floor?' she asked flippantly, furious with herself for wishing that his hand had stayed on her thigh. Where it had been, the skin was cold.

She suddenly felt desolate and lonely. And painfully aware of the gnawing ache in her body. Cavan mixed up all her emotions. Too often she became shrewish, bitter and shallow—all because she wanted him and always had, adored him and always had, was bewildered and resentful about her uncontrollable need. You ought to be able to hate someone without tossing about every night wanting them too, she thought crossly.

Cavan evidently didn't find her remark amusing. He was scowling at her, his heavy brows drawn together, his lips tight and disapproving.

'Careful. The shark is a notoriously bad-tempered beast,' he reminded her grimly. 'I take a certain amount of backchat and then I retaliate. Don't push your luck, Bethany. There isn't time for clever remarks. I want this place ready to open for the Christmas trade.'

She laughed in his face. 'Good heavens! Even you will never get anyone to turn Portallen into an up-market country hotel in that time!'

'Oh, yes, I will,' he said quietly. 'You.'

Bethany looked at Cavan with growing horror as she realised he was deadly serious. 'Not me!' she breathed.

'The kettle's been boiling for some time,' he murmured. 'Shall we have tea?' Calmly, under her startled gaze, he filled the pot and placed two mugs on the table.

She stared at them numbly. 'I came here to help Mawgan,' she said slowly, her brain refusing to function.

'And so you shall,' soothed Cavan, sitting opposite her and spooning in an unseemly amount of sugar. 'My way.'

'No! If Mawgan's going to college, there's no reason for me to stay at all,' she said hastily, resisting his blatant manipulation of them both. 'I certainly don't want to do any work for you.'

'Oh, dear. No co-operation from you, no art college,' said Cavan blandly.

She stared at him helplessly. '*Why?*'

His eyes mocked her confusion. 'Before I answer, hear the prize you get for completing the renovations in time,' he told her in his resonant voice.

'Prize?' She frowned irritably.

'Yes. It's not a bad one. A bribe. You get Portallen.'

Bethany blinked. There must be a catch. He'd never hand it over just like that. 'I don't believe you! Why——?'

'Work for me, finish the contract, and the hotel will revert to your family,' he said quietly as if he meant every word.

Bethany's mind was whirling at the implications of the deal. It made sense in the kind of contorted logic Cavan used. After all, he was a confirmed bachelor, playing the field happily from all accounts. He'd have no family to leave his fortune to, and in any case he didn't care anything about Portallen, so he was perfectly prepared to dangle one insignificant hotel in front of her eyes as a bribe. Her mouth became grim. He was obsessed with getting his own way.

'That would mean that I'd have to stay here till Christmas,' she said doubtfully.

'Are you afraid?' he queried. 'Didn't you just say you cared nothing for the villagers and their sharp tongues?'

Hung by her own lies. They'd been brave lies, flung in Cavan's face, the words torn from her by her own pride and his ever-present threat to dominate and crush her. She shrugged helplessly.

'I can't stay that long,' she said in a low voice. 'I have my own cottage on Bodmin——' Her eyes flew up to his in dismay that she'd revealed what she and Mawgan had kept from everyone.

'*Bodmin*? You? Good God!' he marvelled in a lazy drawl. 'I'd never have believed it! I'd imagined you hitting the nightclubs and fashion shops somewhere in Paris or Rome, since you were nowhere to be found in London.'

Bethany tensed. 'Why do you say that? Did you try to find me?' she demanded.

'Oh, Bethany Lowena Trevelyan, I've been trawling the city streets looking for you for ages,' he said huskily, a mocking look in his eloquent eyes.

The distance between them seemed to shrink, and the room closed in around them, the low ceiling pressing in on her. It was as if she and Cavan swam in a warm golden glow, suspended in mid-air... Bethany gritted her teeth and cursed her wild imagination. It was only the sunshine pouring in through the lattice window and the warmth generated by the Aga. And her own crazy dreams.

'What for?' she asked flatly.

'To revamp the hotel, of course; what else could I have in mind?'

He was lying. That soft growl was purring with sexual innuendo. She was afraid he'd force her to do more than work for him. He'd use any kind of threat—perhaps say he was going to withdraw financial support from Mawgan if she wasn't nice to him. He wanted her submission. He'd made that plain long ago. She bit her lip.

'I wouldn't know,' she lied. 'Something nasty. I don't have much experience of men like you.'

He smiled as if that were a compliment. 'There aren't many of us around,' he sympathised. 'Anyway, I've had the idea for a long time. I knew Portallen was losing money, and that Mawgan hadn't the temperament to be a good manager.'

'There are hundreds of people who could do the renovations.'

'I know. I wanted you.'

She winced at the quick pain that shot through her ribs. Those were the very words she'd longed for him to say, all these years, from the moment she first set eyes on him and he'd thrown her burgeoning teenage emotions into disarray.

'Why?' she asked guardedly.

'God, Bethany, I wish you wouldn't pout like that. It's an open invitation, and makes men want to kiss you,' frowned Cavan. 'Come on, you know me. I want you to do it because I want to control you, and this will offer me the means.'

'C-c-control?' she spluttered, beside herself with fury.

'Of course. You see,' he said, ignoring her gasp of amazement at his nerve, 'you're the only person I've ever met whom I haven't been able to dominate. It's like...like never quite mastering one's backhand in tennis. Irritating. Something unfinished, you understand.'

'Tennis? If I had a racket in my hands you'd discover how good my backhand is,' she grated. 'You're power-mad! You'll never control me, never!'

He shrugged his broad shoulders as if conceding the point. 'Well, I thought I'd try. I must say,' he laughed, 'I never thought you lived in Cornwall still! I'd concentrated on searching Knightsbridge and the restaurants where celebrities hang out. Mawgan refused to give me your address. When I didn't find you, I imagined you'd fled abroad.'

'I don't want to leave Cornwall again. You seem to have gone to a lot of bother to get someone to decorate a hotel,' she observed.

'Not someone. You. I told you. I hadn't finished with you,' he smiled. 'So I had to find you some other way.'

She froze and then let her eyes flick up to his. Somehow she knew that her presence here wasn't the result of a decision between Mawgan and herself or even a casual telephone call between the two men. Cavan's expression was unreadable, but she'd seen a glint of amusement and self-satisfaction sweep across his face when she'd looked up and caught him watching her.

She licked her lips and bridled at Cavan's speculative glance. He was earthier, hungrier and more dangerous than she remembered, his whole body charged with sexual tension. His lips softened to a sultry line beneath her panic-stricken gaze and a wash of warm sensuality filled her with a weakening languor.

Bethany fought up to the surface, refusing to let his carnal desire swamp her senses. And then she realised what he'd done. 'You are the most unscrupulous, vile and unprincipled man I've ever met,' she said in a hard tone, her eyes a dark granite. 'You deliberately put the screws on Mawgan, didn't you, pressuring him, knowing he'd buckle?'

'Yes,' he confirmed easily.

'Oh!' she gasped. 'You don't even mind admitting it! Don't you care about his feelings? I wouldn't put it past you to have personally arranged for that crooked firm to make a mess of doing up the hotel.'

'I hadn't thought of that,' said Cavan in admiration.

'I can't believe that you have the gall to admit forcing Mawgan into a corner,' she muttered. 'What do you think it's done for his self-esteem?'

'How else was I to lay my hands on you?' he asked mildly. 'It won't have done him any lasting damage, and it's only brought things to a head. He knows perfectly well he's not cut out to be a manager, and you know that too. I would have sacked him anyway and booted him in the direction of art college. I knew that eventually Mawgan would have to lean on you, as he's always done ever since he was a kid, and that I'd finally flush you from cover.'

'You swine! You made my brother half demented with worry just so that you could put me in a position of subservience to you. You are really quite beneath contempt!' she seethed.

'No. Practical,' he corrected. 'Don't forget that I was born in the East End and then spent half my formative years in a pub in Plymouth while my mother earned enough to keep us both. Life rather leaps up at you in places like that and grabs you by the throat. It's sink or swim. The sharks or you. You grow up fast. I became a shark myself. If I want something, I go for it—none of your genteel shilly-shallying around.' He eyed her speculatively. 'Well?'

'You honestly are serious? You want me to do a complete turnkey job between now and Christmas?' she asked numbly, still shell-shocked.

'A what?'

Bethany heaved a sigh. 'Turnkey. It means the decorator is responsible for every single item in the renovation of a property, even down to the books in the bookcase, the wine in the fridge and the tea in the tea-caddy.'

'How does it work?' asked Cavan, his eyes narrowed with interest.

She shrugged. 'The client leaves a large cheque and the house key and comes back several months later with an even larger cheque in settlement. They turn the key in the lock, walk in and begin living without even having to shop for groceries, a sewing kit or a teddy-bear.'

He grinned. 'I'll buy that. Yes. A turnkey; that will suit me fine. Though there are some things I want a say in which I'd prefer not to leave to you. Like the wine we'll stock.' He beamed at her appalled face. 'We'll have fun thrashing out what you'll do and what I'll do.'

'*We*? You and me together? Oh, no, that's not on, Cavan!' Quickly she realised she was betraying her fear of him, and sought an excuse. 'I'd be no good, you see. Better you should find someone else. I've lost most of my contacts——'

'Find them. Or the deal about Mawgan is off,' he said ruthlessly.

She closed her eyes. 'You're not being reasonable——'

'Me, reasonable? When was I ever?' he asked cynically. 'You must agree, I'm consistent. It can be done, Bethany, if you have the will and the incentive. You could start soon. I can find you the craftsmen when you want them. They'll work like hell for me because I'll put them on good piece rates. You only have to provide the ideas and the stylish eye, they'll interpret whatever you want.'

'It's impossible!' frowned Bethany.

Cavan heaved a deep sigh. 'Then I must sell to the highest bidder, and you lose Portallen through your own selfish fault.'

'That's blatant blackmail!' she complained. 'Look, you must see that I can't do it. I won't——'

'I fail to see why. Wouldn't you like to see Portallen looking beautiful and thriving again?' murmured Cavan seductively. 'Money no object? The garden restored, herbs and fresh vegetables for the kitchen, the herbaceous borders restocked, a few palm trees, a swimming-pool maybe? Antiques in every room, well-burnished brass on the walls——?'

'Don't,' she said miserably. He had her beaten, and he knew it. He was going to gloat next.

But he took her gently by the shoulders and made her look at him. 'I don't like to see Portallen run-down any more than you do,' he said quietly. 'Neither does Mawgan. Nor would your father, if he was alive. Do this turnkey job and make Portallen a place to be proud of. You might even enjoy it. Mawgan will be in his element in art college, and you'll be able to return to this cottage of yours on Bodmin at Christmas. Why Bodmin, for God's sake?' he asked with a frown.

'That's my business,' she said stiffly, trying to resist the temptation to put her head against his oddly comforting shoulder and howl.

'There can't be much call for interior designers out on the moors, or for gorgeous clothes like those,' he mused. 'So you must have been quite isolated and...' He went quiet. Bethany waited miserably for him to get tired of waiting for her response. 'Did you want to run away from it all?' he asked in a voice so full of compassion that Bethany had to screw up all her muscles against his tender, lulling tones. 'I hadn't honestly realised until this moment that the whole thing had affected you so badly.'

His hand began to stroke the nape of her neck, and she stiffened. 'I tried not to show that I was upset,' she muttered.

'You succeeded. We thought you were as hard as nails. You were hurt, then.'

His eyes had become sympathetic and the languorous touch of his fingers was unbearable. She'd reveal how pleasurable his caress was in a moment if he didn't stop. Desperately Bethany thought of a way out.

'Yes,' she said throatily, 'I was hurt. Mainly because of Dan. Because of his death.'

He released her immediately, as she'd known he would, his pride stung that she'd married Dan when she should have been gasping at his feet like the rest of the women in Cornwall, whether he wanted them or not.

He moved to look out of the window at the incoming tide, an angry-looking back to her. 'Look at the advantages,' he said curtly, returning to his persuasion. 'If I sack Mawgan and offer him this chance, he'll be forced to take the plunge into the art world and stop dithering on the edge. He'd be launched on a glittering career. You'd be doing a job you enjoy then returning to a life of leisured luxury and——'

'You said Portallen would revert to us,' she reminded him quickly, 'but you carefully omitted to say *when*. Another thing: do I get paid for my services?'

'Board and lodging. Nothing more. You're worth a cool half-million. You don't need money.' A smile crept to the corners of his mouth. 'You can get me, too, if you play your cards right.'

A small twinge of alarm prickled her nerves. 'That's it?' she asked coldly. 'The right to sleep and eat in what ought to be my own home and the offer of a night or two with a voracious shark?'

'Finish by Christmas to my satisfaction and you get a half-share in Portallen,' he said abruptly over his shoulder. 'That's what I meant about it reverting to a Trevelyan. I should have said *half* reverting.'

Bethany lifted her head slowly, terribly disappointed. 'Not all of it,' she said dully.

'Be thankful for small mercies. You'd have to do a bit more than flash a roll of wallpaper around to win all of it,' he grinned.

'Then I'll have to make do with half,' she retorted. 'I'll have that in writing, too.'

'Done.'

'My God! You mean that!' Her mind raced and her heart began to thud with excitement. Mawgan could have that half-share and he could have a home here forever if he wanted. And when he married, then his children would inherit. Portallen would belong to the Trevelyans again. A smile spread over her face.

'In case you're wondering,' murmured Cavan, 'I'm making this once-only offer of a half-share because I think it's the only way to get you to move that idle backside of yours and do the job properly.'

'No one's ever complained about my work before,' she challenged.

'No. I've heard. Where you learned to do it, I don't know. You brought home some good artwork from school, but you weren't as talented as Mawgan. Did Dan pay for you to attend a course or something?' he asked curiously.

'Or something,' she agreed, her eyes wistful as she remembered. Cavan shifted impatiently, and she started guiltily.

'I want to know,' he said curtly. 'If I'm employing you I have a right to know your qualifications. So tell me.'

'I'm not qualified. But I have a good deal of experience.'

'How?'

'Accident, really. Dan was out on the oil rigs for weeks on end, and I got a bit bored,' she explained. 'I'd done up our home in Aberdeen and had helped a few friends with their decorating schemes. I found I had an instinctive flair for it. When Dan was sent to the Mexican Gulf, I took up interior decorating in a big way, preparing homes for whoever was flown out there by the company.'

'Pity you gave it up,' commented Cavan. 'Do you honestly *like* doing nothing all day other than counting your money?'

Bethany sighed. 'I don't know how much you intend to put in an appearance while I'm working at Portallen,' she said, 'but I'm making my own condition—that you don't mention Dan, his accident, and the compensation I received on his death. And, where possible, that you avoid passing fatuous remarks about the way I was hounded out of this village by gossip and innuendo. It's bad enough being here, Cavan,' she added, fixing him with a glare, 'without having you rub salt into the wound. OK?'

He nodded his agreement. 'I take it that means "yes". You won't regret the decision,' he said softly.

'I'm sure I won't, provided you keep your hands and your oyster satin sheets away from me.'

'I'll say this for you, Bethany,' he murmured, his voice betraying his admiration, 'you've got guts. And loyalty to your brother. You always did fuss over him like a replacement mother. But you must remember that he's a man now and you must let him make his own mistakes.'

'I don't need you to tell me that,' she said coldly. 'Just keep out of my hair.' Her eyes became cynical. 'I suppose Mawgan will see you as his benefactor.'

'I doubt it,' grinned Cavan, his eyes dancing wickedly. 'I intend to leave him in no doubt as to my opinion of him as a manager. I don't want to run the risk of him refusing my offer under the delusion that if he sacrificed his chance to paint he'd save you from a fate worse than death.'

'Tania won't be too pleased,' mused Bethany.

Cavan's grin broadened. 'Staked her claim, has she?' he enquired. When she ignored him, he glanced at his watch. 'Well, I suppose I must acquaint Mawgan with the facts of life and then, speaking of the facts of life, I ought to return to the yacht. Tania will probably have prepared a cordon-bleu supper for us.'

'She sounds a catch,' observed Bethany, trying to keep a casual smile on her face. And failing.

'She is,' smirked Cavan. 'A good all-rounder.' Bethany wondered if that included bed. Probably, she decided unhappily. Cavan wasn't the sort of man to kiss at the bedroom door, and Tania wasn't the sort of woman to let him, either. 'Trouble is,' he continued, 'she's so obviously out to land a millionaire this side of ninety that I can hear her tick coming a mile off.'

Bethany let out a laugh of delight before she recovered herself, ashamed that she'd laughed at her old friend. Cavan was looking at her in a strange, brooding way. 'What——' Her voice gave up, strangled into a croak by the dryness of her throat. He was walking towards her, and it was clear from his eyes, his sensual mouth, the animal prowl, what he intended to do. A parting gesture. Goodbye. A means of showing that he was now in control and dominating her.

She rose and backed against a wall, her palms flattened against it. He had come closer, his nostrils flaring, his eyes hypnotic. Anticipation set her on edge, her helplessness increasing with the drugging sensuality of his expression.

Gently Cavan took her head between the palms of his hands and gazed into her eyes, which had become the colour of soft Cornish rain. He leaned against her, the strength and vitality of his body almost overpowering her. Deliberately he shifted so that her body rubbed against his. He let out a low, throaty grunt, and she bit back her own sinful sigh which surged up.

Cavan's hot eyes were covered by his lowered lids as his long black lashes swept his cheeks and his head angled to kiss her.

'No!' she gasped.

'Why not?' he murmured huskily.

'Because you're bad news! Because I—I——'

His mouth was fuller and infinitely desirable. Bethany shrank against the wall, feeling the heavy thud of her heart echoing through her body. A wild desire arose inside her, the need to grab Cavan fiercely and draw his dark head down hard so that their kiss should blot out the world, the past, the future, and serve only as a rough, raw satisfaction for her eternal, remorseless hunger. Her body quivered with the effort of remaining cool and reluctant.

All she could do was plead with her eyes, for her protest emerged as small, plaintive noises in her throat which sounded alarmingly like urging demands of frustrated passion.

'Bethany,' he whispered. His breath flowed over her parted lips like a gentle sea breeze.

She hastily licked her mouth and tasted salt. His lips were irresistible and only a fraction away. She remembered the last time he'd kissed her, in full view of everyone in Fore Street—roughly, violently, flinging her from him in contempt. 'I don't want your damn blood money,' he'd roared, 'just your physical subjugation. Crawl, damn you, crawl!'

Bethany let out a groan of despair and turned her head to one side. Cavan must have thought it was a hoarse cry of need, for his mouth descended remorselessly on her throat, searching out the sweet hollow where her pulse hammered against her skin at the erotic touch of his lips, his probing tongue and his grazing, tormenting teeth.

'Cavan——' she husked in distress. She wanted him. She wanted to surrender.

'We'll take our time,' he murmured against her shoulder.

Bethany's eyes opened in alarm at the sensation of his lips moistly caressing her flesh. Her shoulder was bare. 'Time?' she cried harshly, trying to shrug her jacket back on. How had he managed to undo the buttons without her knowing? Oh, lord! she groaned inwardly. He was like a practised pickpocket whose hands could stray anywhere they chose with impunity. '*Time*?' she repeated in growing rage. 'You haven't lost much time in trying to strip me!'

'Mmm?' His head lifted, desire spilling from his eyes and making her legs infuriatingly weak. 'It just...sort of happened,' he explained, with a disarming grin. 'Gorgeous shoulders. Warm satin.'

Bethany raised her hand, and he stepped back quickly and stayed warily a short distance away from her, laughing. 'Don't you try that again!' she glowered.

'Can't promise,' he said, walking to the door as if she'd not really affected him at all. Bethany spluttered, muddled by the conflicting rage and longing which battled inside her treacherous body. 'I thought you said this turnkey business included everything?' he added insolently.

He'd slammed the door behind him, laughing merrily, before she had a chance to throw the teapot she'd picked up. Incensed, she banged it down and spent the next few minutes trying to clean tea from her expensive suit.

'Cavan Trevelyan,' she muttered grimly, sponging herself down, and wishing she could sponge away her need for him, 'you'll regret manhandling me as if I'm one of your popsies!'

CHAPTER THREE

TWENTY minutes later, Bethany had changed into her bathing costume, intending to cool herself down with a swim. She pulled on a pair of old cotton jeans and a loose T-shirt, slinging a towel around her neck, and strode briskly across the beach. Picking her way over the rocks and rock pools, she headed for Wrecker's Bay, the tiny cove tucked in the headland where there was a smart new coastguard station. As usual, the beach was deserted. She sat on her favourite flat rock and stared out to sea, stilling down her mind.

Cavan would be telling Mawgan now of the arrangement. Her face softened. She couldn't let Mawgan down. Of course she had to agree to Cavan's ultimatum. A few months here was no big deal. Bethany wrestled with her conscience and smiled wryly at her eagerness to convince herself that she could stay at Portallen, become involved with Cavan again—and not get hurt.

He'd always ended up hurting her. Even after her triumph in the end-of-term school play, when she'd spotted him at the back of the village hall, and had acted her heart out as the most convincing Juliet the drama teacher had ever known, Cavan had ruined her pleasure.

While everyone was congratulating her and she was smiling gently, wishing she could tell them that she had drawn her emotions from her own feelings, she'd been aware of Cavan's scornful eyes on her.

'What did you think of my performance, Cavan?' she'd finally blurted out, desperate for his admiration.

He had given her one cold look before turning on his heel. 'As a teenage seductress? *Alarmingly* practised,' he'd flung over his shoulder.

She had flushed scarlet, and the boys around her had sniggered knowingly.

Bethany lay back on the rock and closed her eyes, letting the late afternoon sun warm her body while she listened to the gentle wash of the waves. Her hand trailed idly in the clear water of a small rock pool as she tried to face her feelings honestly. Did she want Cavan because he was so completely unattainable? After all, he didn't like her, and merely saw her as a body he coveted, nothing more. Pure unfulfilled lust. Was it her vanity that kept urging her to try to captivate him?

She thought that perhaps Cavan had been right—that there were some people who just *had* to master everything and everyone they came across. He was definitely one of those people; maybe she was, too.

It was ironic. He kept making a play for her despite his unconcealed contempt, because she was apparently indifferent to him. His masculine pride was offended by her evasion. She secretly longed for Cavan—maybe for the same reason. She grinned ruefully. She was being incredibly juvenile, and ought to scurry off to Bodmin at once. And yet . . .

She found herself beaming, blissfully content now that she was back in Portallen. Unnerving though it would be, working with Cavan, it might be a good discipline professionally. She *had* lost touch with the design world, and had also lost much of her self-confidence. Doing this job might give her the assurance to summon up the nerve to work in London, and later, perhaps, to set up her own business.

There was another benefit. By owning half of Portallen, she'd have an excuse to come here now and again, rationing herself, of course, to the occasions when Cavan wasn't around.

One of her fingers came into contact with a sea anemone, which gently captured the finger, sucking it in with its tentacles. Afraid of damaging it, she waited till it had discovered it didn't want to devour her and let her go. Shaking her wet hand and sitting up, she began to plan.

Cavan wouldn't stay for long; he didn't like the country life. He'd left Portallen for London the moment he'd saved up enough for the train fare, shortly before his seventeenth birthday. Reassured by that thought, she lay back again, imagining brief holiday visits when Mawgan returned on weekends, full of his activities at the art college...

'If you're doing sit-ups, that's only two in the last five minutes.'

Bethany kept her eyes resolutely closed on hearing Cavan's voice. 'I came here to get away from you,' she retorted with a slight frown.

'Failed again,' he said cheerfully.

She heard a rustle and then felt his body close to hers. Every inch of her tingled. It was as if he'd flicked on a powerful generator inside her, she thought resentfully, and lit up all her lights.

'Please, Cavan,' she said in a reasonable tone. 'I need personal space. I've been used to isolation. It's been a long time since I lived with anyone——'

'Really? No man on the moors with you?' he enquired smoothly. 'Not even a toy boy, perhaps?'

'No. Don't you mellow with age? You must be thirty now. Time you curbed your belligerence,' she rebuked. A warm, firm finger traced the line between her brows, and she quivered.

'I was only asking a question. I am your stepbrother. I'm interested in what's been happening to you over the past two years,' he said quietly.

'I've had no relationships,' she said flatly. 'I've lived a very private life.'

'You turned in on yourself.' It was a statement, not a question, and she didn't confirm it, feeling a little disconcerted by the unusually thoughtful-sounding Cavan. She was dying to open her eyes and see his expression. 'I'm not surprised; you must have been a fish out of water up there. You don't belong on the open moorland. You looked happy, lying on the rock,' he observed perceptively. 'There's something here that holds you, isn't there? It holds me too.'

Bethany peeked through her lashes. He was staring at the distant horizon, a look of intense longing on his face that made her throat catch. He'd changed into jeans and a white open-neck shirt which made the most of his mountain-range chest and what looked like a Caribbean tan, judging by his deep-gold throat and forearms. She sat up and wilted under the glorious smile he gave her. It was like being gently sucked in by the sea anemone.

'Once upon a time Portallen *was* perfect,' she mused, a little irritated with herself because she wanted to reach out and touch him. And be captured. But then, she'd only be spat out again after a brief, exploratory period. 'Mawgan and I had an idyllic childhood.'

'And then I came along,' he said softly. 'The fairy-tale turned into a different kind of story. The minute our eyes met, straight away a tempest blew up.'

Her face sobered. 'You made my life hell——'

Cavan's sharp inhalation interrupted her. 'Mutual,' he said with a low savagery. 'I could hardly breathe in that house without your eyes on me. If Mother hadn't been so much in love... Bethany, you do know how happy your father was with my mother, don't you?'

'Yes,' she said reluctantly. 'He was nuts about her. But you ruined it all by arguing with him constantly——'

Cavan shrugged. 'I'd never had a father. I'd been my own man for years. I was sixteen and street-wise, Beth! It was hard being told what to do and what not to do. Your father was used to Mawgan's quiet obedience, not an adolescent stepson who prowled around where and when he liked.'

'All those girls!' recalled Bethany with faint distaste. Girls from the village, from Polperro, Looe, Liskeard and Plymouth, then London—she'd been able to trace Cavan's wanderings by where the girls came from.

A blissful look came over Cavan's face, and Bethany felt the humiliating pangs of jealousy. 'It was wonderful! I was in and out of love more often than a kid's fingers in a bag of chips,' he said with a low, husky laugh.

Bethany's breathing shortened, her breasts rising and falling quickly. It distressed her to remember those girls—all ages, sizes, but all beautiful and all madly in love with Cavan.

'Father was worried sick about your morals and whether you'd get any of the girls into trouble,' she said stiffly—and then wanted to take the priggish words back.

Cavan smiled. 'No, he wasn't. Not for long. He had no need—I assured him of that. I never risked hurting them.' His eyebrows lifted. 'You don't look as if you believe me.'

'No. I heard a different story from them,' she said, remembering the tears, the pleas for her intercession, the hints that Cavan had taken what he wanted and ditched them.

'Ah, but Bethany, you know how gossip distorts the truth, how lies can be spread,' he pointed out gently. 'Women can be very proud. Try not to believe everything you hear about me.'

'If I believed half, I'd be wary of you.'

'Ditto.'

Bethany bristled. 'What do you mean by that?'

'Your father was much more concerned about you than he was about me.'

She turned her head slowly to meet his serious eyes. 'Whatever for?' she asked in surprise.

'Anyone could see you were a hothouse flower in a bed of dandelions,' he smiled ruefully. 'We all knew you'd spread your wings one day. We——' Cavan avoided her eyes, as if changing his mind about what he'd intended to say, and he glanced up to scowl at the cloud which was obscuring the sun. 'He was very upset when you left home to marry Dan. You were very young.'

'You don't know what I was like at the age of eighteen,' she retorted. 'You were working in the nightclub in the West End.' And, judging by the joy in his face when she'd seen him shortly before she decided to marry Dan, he'd been perfectly happy there, living the sophisticated life of the big city. She'd felt very provincial beside him in his smart suit and with his smart talk. Particularly she'd felt humiliated by a rather patronising woman he'd brought down to stay. Some hotel receptionist.

Portallen had lost him and so had she. The familiar haunts cruelly reminded her of that loss. In addition, Rosie and her father had innocently hurt her with their public displays of warm, tender affection because she knew she'd never feel such passion for anyone other than the callous Cavan. That was when Bethany had impulsively agreed to marry the persistent Dan, who had promised her his love and an escape from the house which held such painful memories.

'I knew you, nevertheless,' he said, his eyes piercingly blue. 'Every inch.' Bethany's breath was suddenly trapped in her lungs. The back of her neck tightened at the way his eyes were roaming over her body. 'I'd know your body and your voice and your perfume in a room of a hundred people. I knew then that you weren't ready for marriage.' He gave her a speculative look. 'Perhaps you are now.'

She gathered her wits together. 'You couldn't be more wrong. Men are a turn-off for me,' she said pointedly.

'Oh? When did your tastes change so drastically?' he countered. Bethany gave him a withering stare and half rose, but he pulled her down again. 'Dan?' he suggested in a hard tone. 'You've convinced yourself that you're pining?'

'You don't pull your punches, do you?' she muttered.

He grunted. 'I want to know. I'm not much good at pussyfooting around.'

Bethany's mouth twisted into a wry smile. He'd always plunged straight for the jugular, and she'd always lunged straight back in defence. 'Look,' she said, trying to be reasonable, 'what happened to me was extremely painful and traumatic. I'm still getting over it. I'll *never* put it behind me.'

'You must,' he frowned.

'Why? After all, *you* can't even forget or forgive my attempts to put down an arrogant, overbearing, bullying stepbrother. Why should I forget the man I was married to and the nightmare events after his death?'

'Because you're alive!' he growled, gripping her arm fiercely. 'Alive and young and beautiful. And aching for the things that no man has yet given you.'

Bethany's jaw dropped open. 'Aching? My God, Cavan! Words fail me! Just because you think of nothing else, you needn't imagine sex is on everyone else's minds.'

'You think I'm talking about sex?' he asked huskily.

She flung her head back in exasperation, her body taut and proud. 'What else do you ever think about?' she scathed. Cavan's lashes fluttered a fraction. 'In your narrow and limited imagination you have pictured me, rich and lonely, sitting alone on Bodmin moor, and have smugly come to the conclusion that I need a man! Really! Of all the chauvinistic——'

'It's you who are obsessed with sex,' he said shortly. 'You were deliberately provocative as a teenager. Even now every movement of your body is designed to enslave any man who happens to be around.' Bethany saw that there was a glittering light in his eyes, one which warned her that his desire to master her physically was very strong. 'I have to admit, I'm tempted. Every time you move, every time you speak,' he murmured.

She quivered throughout her responsive body. 'Don't pester me, Cavan,' she complained in a low voice.

'You never loved Dan,' he continued relentlessly. 'You were just running away from life.'

'It was hardly running away. I travelled the world,' she insisted.

'You don't have to go further than your front door to live deeply,' said Cavan huskily. 'And when you returned to Portallen, after Dan died, I knew by merely glancing at you that you were untouched inside. Own up, Bethany,' he demanded roughly. 'Wild passion wasn't a feature of your marriage.'

She kept her mouth firmly shut, ignoring him. Because he was right. She and Dan had enjoyed being together, but it had all been on the surface. They were apart for long periods and when he was on leave they seemed to be forever having parties. There was no deep relationship. How could there be?

'Have you no consideration for my feelings? I asked you not to talk about Dan,' she said eventually in a shaky whisper.

'I know. But I feel that until you come to terms with the truth of those feelings you'll never be free of the past. You're pretending to yourself you loved him to salve your conscience for accepting all that money.'

Bethany drew in a harsh, ragged breath and jumped up. 'You think you can play me on a line till I'm exhausted. You think you can hook me, chalk me up on your achievement board and throw me back in the sea!' she cried, her huge sea-storm eyes betraying her distress. 'Well, you're wrong. I've learnt the hard way to be tough inside. Life's smashed me down but I'm coming back up, and I won't let you destroy my confidence. I'll work for you because I have to, because I want Portallen. But that's *it*.'

He stood, his body blocking out the late afternoon sun. '*Now* you've woken up. You're going to live again. Thank God! I thought you'd lost your fire.' His eyes brooded on her. 'You know there's something unfinished between us,' he said huskily.

His face was shadowed, but it seemed to Bethany that his eyes carried a blazing message of need. Her mind fought; her body began to surrender. There was a melting note in his voice which was infinitely seductive, and she felt the magnetism between them pulling her inexorably towards him.

'No, Cavan,' she mumbled almost incoherently. She concentrated on holding herself erect, preventing her body from swaying towards him as it wanted to.

'Bethany,' he whispered, 'we want each other. You can't deny that. It's a primitive urge that has nothing to do with common sense. This heat, this ... burning, the extraordinary excitement that's generated between us——'

She had clenched her teeth, refusing to acknowledge that he'd put her own feelings into words. And so she lied to him. 'Primitive?' she echoed, faint scorn in her voice. 'Heat? Oh, come on, Cavan! You've been watching too many bad films.'

He shrugged. 'I just said what I felt. I was never much good with the flowery words,' he said, all defenceless innocence.

Despite herself, Bethany's heart jerked. 'You were never much good, period,' she said defensively.

His eyes suddenly lost their helpless look and became unnervingly sultry. 'Wrong. I was always very good,' he said in a husky voice. 'And still am. You'll find that out soon, or——'

'Or your name's not really Trevelyan?' she finished for him defiantly.

Cavan roared with outright laughter. 'I like it! I adore you, Bethany,' he murmured. 'You fight me, you kick and struggle, you make me laugh. Life's never boring when you're around.'

The tension had been broken. And Bethany felt a contrary disappointment and a sense of loss. 'Wish I could say the same for you,' she said crossly, turning her back on him.

It had been a mistake. She sensed his arms coming around her. In a flash she had deftly slipped out of them and was up off the rock and running, caution and cowardice overcoming her pride. He looked too sure of his strength to hold her a prisoner in those powerful arms of his, and too darn set on bending her to his will for her to take any chances. Better to lose her dignity, she thought breathlessly, as she pounded over the sand with a laughing Cavan in hot pursuit, than to have her mouth and body ravaged by his roaming lips and hands.

'You...tease...me...Bethany...Trevelyan,' he yelled, 'and you'll...regret it!'

She whirled, and he stopped some yards away, grinning at her. 'This isn't a tease! I was running away from you! It isn't a "come-on",' she protested vehemently.

Bethany realised that she couldn't get around the headland because the tide was almost up over the rocks. And Cavan barred the way back to the main beach. All that was left was a choice of clambering up the sheer cliff, or escaping via the sea. Waves were lapping at her feet, even now. Uncertainly, she turned to face him, watching him warily, both of them up to their ankles in the white surf.

'Old films... bit like *From Here to Eternity*, isn't it?' he said triumphantly, his teeth flashing in his dark face like a predatory shark's.

Worrying about any possible connection between the steamy love-scene in the surf in that film and Cavan's intentions, Bethany folded her arms across her chest in defence and focused her attention pointedly on the perfect white teeth.

'More like *Jaws II*,' she retorted, trying to deflate him.

His dark eyebrow crooked high. 'Do you think so? Didn't the shark win in that film?' he enquired, wide-eyed and disarming.

'Oh, leave me alone!' she said in desperation.

His eyes narrowed. He studied her closely for a while, and then nodded slowly. 'All right. I will—for now. It's early days yet, and we have all the time in the world.'

'Until Christmas,' she reminded him quickly.

He smiled, and she felt a beat of fear in her throat. 'I don't need that long. I'll catch you when you least expect it. Don't be misled into thinking that I've given up. I never do that. I've wanted you for as long as I can remember. Until I have you, I'll never know whether you've been worth the wait or are merely a totally illogical craving.' He began to walk away and then spun on his heel to face her again, looking rougher and tougher than she'd ever known. 'Anticipation is sweet,' he growled, 'but I believe that making love to you will be sweeter.'

'You'll never know,' she said, alarmed to hear how husky her voice had become from panic at his threat. Her lips parted softly and she looked at him warily from under her lashes.

'You bitch! You are teasing me! A real man-tormentor, aren't you?' He paused, his chest heaving. '*Alarmingly* practised,' he grated.

He strode towards her, and she found to her dismay that she couldn't move. There was such anger in his face that she was terrified. He yanked her into his hard, unyielding body and kissed her brutally, his mouth forcing down on hers, his arms crushing the breath from her. And then he had pushed her contemptuously away and had abandoned her, with the waves breaking over her ankles, undermining the sand beneath her feet so that she rocked unsteadily.

Bethany felt a moan wrench from deep within her chest. The kiss had made him even angrier; she could tell that from the set of his high shoulders as he walked across the beach. For her, the kiss had taken away some of her explosive energy, but not enough of it.

She waited till he'd become a small, distant figure on the stone jetty on the other side of the bay and then she strode back above the high-tide level. Methodically she began to remove her clothes. In her old blue bathing costume, she ran down to the sea. It was freezing, but she needed to exhaust herself physically. She needed the cold shock to clear her mind and to chill down her reluctantly awoken body.

Stony-faced, she waded through the coldly slapping waves, her feet like ice. With a sudden lunge, she dived in and came up breathless with the cold. Her eyes lifted, drawn helplessly to the figure on the jetty. Cavan was apparently watching her and gesturing for her to come out of the sea.

Of course she defied him—she couldn't have him dictating to her. She'd have a quick swim to show Cavan that she wasn't going to leap to his bidding whenever he snapped his fingers, but she wouldn't stay in for long. Recklessly she struck out for the open sea, quickly finding all her old swimming skills returning, and suddenly she felt as if she'd been born in the water. Exhilarated by the discovery, she abandoned her mind to the rhythm of the fast crawl.

And then she felt an agonising pain in her calf and she disappeared beneath the water in a flurry of flailing arms and legs. Her head surfaced briefly.

'*Cavan*!' she screamed. She raised an arm in a desperate signal before the cramp paralysed her again and she sank like a stone, the dark water no longer friendly and welcoming but terrifying. Cavan, she thought. *Cavan*.

Had he been watching? Or...?

Her head was bursting. She clenched her teeth and kicked strongly so that she shot to the surface. She floundered for a while, trying to stay afloat despite the vicious pain in her calf. She could see the grey bulk of the Portallen Inn, the uninhabited jetty. Cavan had gone. Despair racked her.

'Cavan!' she sobbed hopelessly.

'Hold on! For God's sake, Beth, hold on! Keep shouting; I can hardly see you.'

His voice had come thinly over the waves, above the sound of an outboard engine. She yelled, dipped below the surface and swallowed sea-water. Suddenly a huge, welcome hand grabbed her shoulder in a grip of steel. Half fainting with fear, she caught a brief glimpse of Cavan's dark, alarmed face leaning from a boat, before she slipped from his grasp and the agonising cramp doubled her up, rolling her in a tangled ball beneath the waves again.

He must have dived in immediately because his body cannoned into hers, drawing her upwards, and she joyously abandoned herself to him, wrapping her arms around his neck and curling her legs around his waist.

'Beth! *Beth*! Open your eyes! God...!'

She choked. Felt his hands unravelling her arms and legs and turning her around.

'Grab the boat!' he cried in her ear.

Bethany felt the hard wood slam into her ribs as he thrust her upwards out of the water. 'I can't!' she gasped.

'You damn well can!' he roared, giving her an almighty shove.

She tumbled into the boat, hitting her head on the seat and lying in stunned relief, aware that the boat was rocking violently as Cavan clambered in too. And then she was in his arms, the water falling from his clothes in a silver shower. She didn't protest. This wasn't the moment. All she cared about was that she was alive and he was holding her and he couldn't see her expression so she could enjoy every second.

She shivered, and he clasped her closer till she could feel the thunderous beat of his heart from his recent exertion. 'My God, Bethany,' he cried hoarsely, huge gasps of breath tearing his body, 'I thought I'd never see you again!'

'What?' she mumbled in confusion. She must have misheard what he'd said. There was a roaring in her ears. She pushed him away slightly and passed her hand over her head. Her fingers felt sticky.

'You're hurt,' he said gently. Delicate fingers felt her brow, and then she thought she felt his lips there. 'We've got to get you back,' he told her reluctantly, his eyes melting into hers.

'Yes,' she whispered. Her hands flattened in wonder and pleasure against his torso. Beneath his saturated shirt, she could feel the outline of every strongly defined muscle. 'You are soaked to the skin,' she said stupidly.

'And you.'

His husky voice made her look up, and then she followed his gaze to her own breasts, their shape beneath the wet costume leaving nothing at all to the imagination. She blushed, still shaken, still blissfully relieved that she was alive. Suddenly she felt that anything was possible. Even discovering that Cavan had emotions somewhere beneath that tough-guy exterior. The brief moments of danger had put everything into proportion. She cuddled into him, utterly thankful.

'Oh, Cavan!' she sighed, before she could stop herself.

'Hell!' he growled.

His mouth covered hers, warm as the sun, sweet as honey and as potent as barrel cider. Before she could catch her breath, he kissed her again and her arms seemed to float up to link in his wet black hair. Then he slid her slowly to the bottom of the boat, covering her with his body as if to keep it warm, and she revelled in every exquisite second of the movement, allowing herself to go along with his pretence.

'Are you all right?' he murmured softly.

'I am now. I was frightened,' she croaked, excusing herself for not pushing him away.

'Shh. I'm here now. You're safe.' His mouth roamed
over her jawline while his hands involuntarily ran up to
her breasts. When they touched each firm peak, she inhaled sharply at the shock which ran through her and
which deepened the terrible ache in her loins. He
frowned. 'I didn't mean to touch you... Oh, Bethany!'
he groaned.

With difficulty, she fought her way out of the deep
water she seemed to have got herself in. Confused, she
tried to understand why he should be so shaken by
touching her breasts and by her give-away reaction.
Astonishingly, she did feel safe with him—why, she had
no idea.

'Frightened,' she mumbled. 'I had cramp...oh!' Her
rambling was interrupted by the spear of pleasure
coursing through her, created by Cavan's delicate fingers
caressing her hardening nipples. Despite her intentions,
her head had tipped back at the glorious sensation and
her eyes had closed. All she could hear was Cavan's heavy
breathing, all she could smell was the sea-water on his
body.

'I ought to be getting you to shore,' he said huskily.

'Yes. Oh! Please...don't...Cavan!' she jerked out,
protesting half-heartedly. She was now fully aware of
what she *should* be saying and doing, and was wishing
fervently that she didn't have to deny herself what she
wanted so very much.

Cavan's fingers were driving her crazy, his tender kisses
and gentle murmurings arousing her senses. He drew
back a little and his bemused eyes searched hers. With
a smile, he bent and kissed her full on the mouth, his
tongue lightly stroking her upper lip.

'Enough,' he growled throatily. He raised himself,
looking puzzled. 'God! What am I thinking of? I'm
sorry. I lost my head. We can't stay out here. You'll get

pneumonia. Bethany, I know you're a superb swimmer. You had cramp, you say? Has it gone or shall I massage your leg?'

'It's gone.' Her wet-lashed eyes were fixed on him, and she saw his expression become cautious. He held out his hand, and there was an impassivity about his features suddenly as if he wanted to hide his thoughts.

'You'd better sit up and cuddle into me,' he said gruffly.

Without another word, he hauled her up and drew her to the stern of the dinghy, where he tucked her into him and started the outboard engine. Crushed against his chest, she wondered what had stopped him from taking advantage of her. It wouldn't have been *that* difficult, she thought ruefully. Perhaps he was cold. His hand lightly stroked the bump on her forehead and she began to wonder if Cavan was quite as heartless as he made out.

'Throw yer line, boy.'

Bethany lifted her head from its warm shelter, and saw to her dismay that several fishermen were waiting on the jetty steps. They pulled in the dinghy and Cavan lifted her in his arms, his face inscrutable. Jory Pengelly's face appeared in her line of vision, and she felt the heavy weight of his fishy-smelling cable-knit sweater being wrapped around her.

'All right, boy?' asked Jory, when Cavan stumbled slightly on the slippery step.

'Shaky,' he admitted in his gravelly voice. 'I thought she was a goner.'

'You saved my life,' whispered Bethany, staring up at him.

Tiny drops of water pattered down on her face from Cavan's black hair. He looked rather vulnerable when his eyes met hers, and then they slid away and he increased his pace, striding towards the hotel ahead of the fascinated men, his gaze firmly ahead.

'I know. I have plans for it,' he said to her softly. 'I'm damned if I'm letting such a gorgeous body feed the fishes. I want my share first.'

She slumped limply in his arms, her wistful dreams dashed. For a moment, in her stupid, dazed condition, she'd thought he had been genuinely concerned for her.

'Put me down!' she mumbled miserably. 'Put me *down!*' Surprised, he stopped and set her on her feet, steadying her when she swayed. 'I'm caught between the devil and the deep blue sea,' she husked. 'What a choice I have!' Stumbling blindly, hearing the astonished murmur of the men behind her, she made her way into the hall and collapsed on the floor.

The door slammed, rattling the windows as Cavan stormed in. 'You stupid, impetuous, stubborn... Oh, Bethany! You deserve a thrashing!' said Cavan in exasperation, his soaking-wet socks coming into view. His hands reached down and slipped them off so that he was barefoot, and then he had picked her up again and was carrying her upstairs to her room.

'You put me down!' she ordered, her lips trembling.

He ignored her. 'Going out there for a swim! It was freezing,' he muttered. 'You still behave like a stubborn kid sometimes, don't you? I suppose you saw me beckoning you to come in, and decided to show me who was boss. Sometimes you make me so mad that I really want to teach you a lesson!'

Without any gentleness, he threw her on the bed, where she bounced. Before she could scramble away, warned to make the attempt by his threatening expression, he had yanked away the warm sweater and his hands were pulling on the straps of her bathing costume.

'No!' she cried, her eyes enormous.

To her utter humiliation, he ripped it down expertly as if he'd been stripping women all his life. She tensed her muscles in fear, but he kept his glittering eyes fixed relentlessly on hers. 'Are you expecting rape?' he seethed.

Her hands covered her body as she struggled to speak. 'Don't,' she breathed in terror.

'God!' he ground out through his teeth. Brutally he rolled her in the duvet. Half hidden, her startled face peeped out at him in astonishment. 'You've got a low opinion of me, haven't you? Don't you dare move. I'll bring a plaster for your head and some soup for your stomach and then I'll go and give myself a massive slug of whisky for my reward,' he said savagely.

She watched him stride to the door, feeling miserable and contrite because she'd misjudged him. He was angry because he'd had to rescue her and had got his clothes wet, with little thanks at the end.

'Cavan!' she croaked. 'Wait! I thought...I thought...'

He stopped, his back to her. 'I know what you thought, Bethany,' he muttered grimly. 'I had no idea you held me in such contempt.'

'I—I am grateful,' she managed, her heart pounding. 'If it weren't for you, I might be dead.'

'Yes. Possibly. Therefore you owe me a debt of gratitude,' he said. His head jerked around and he scowled at her. 'And now I know where I stand in your estimation, I'll make damn sure I collect,' he said with soft menace. 'But not until you're fully aware of what I'm doing.' Bethany swallowed. 'Oh, God!' he whispered, and strode quickly through the doorway.

She cuddled into the duvet, feeling her chilled body slowly returning to normal. Which was more than she could say of her turbulent emotions.

CHAPTER FOUR

MAWGAN, at least, was blissfully, radiantly happy. He spent the next few days sorting everything he'd need in case he did manage to get a place in art college that year. Bethany sat on the quayside one evening, enjoying the sunset and thinking of her rescue. Cavan had been gentle with her, she mused. With a woman he could trust, he'd be very caring.

'None the worse fer wear, then?'

She turned her head slightly and smiled hopefully at Jory. It was the first time anyone in the village had voluntarily spoken to her. 'I'm fine, thanks to Cavan.'

'Aye. Good man, that.'

Her mouth dropped open in amazement. They disliked him, surely! 'He was very brave,' she said uncertainly.

'No,' scoffed Jory. 'It weren't nothin' to Cavan. Saw him pick two kids off a lilo near Tallen Point last year in worse seas than that.' Jory scrutinised her carefully. 'Goin' home soon?' he asked slyly.

'I am home, Jory,' she answered evenly, meeting his hostile eyes with a start. 'I'm staying for a while,' she added defiantly.

'Yeah. Tania said.' He looked over to a group of his friends some yards away. To Bethany they looked faintly threatening, the way they were staring at her with hard, cold expressions on their faces. 'Don't take a hint, do you, girl?'

Her pulses quickened and she tried not to look scared. 'I hadn't noticed one,' she replied pleasantly.

'You're not welcome here,' said Jory impassively.

'What do you——?' She stopped in mid-sentence and heaved a sigh of angry frustration. Jory had stalked off, evidently telling his mates what he'd said because they kept looking back and laughing. It hadn't ended, then. It was just beginning. She wondered how long she'd be able to stand it.

'Beth!'

She hastily rearranged her face and managed a smile when Mawgan came running down to see her, his face lit up with excitement. 'What's happened?' she asked affectionately.

'Cavan phoned! He's got me an interview at the art college for tomorrow,' cried Mawgan, his eyes shining. 'How, I don't know—I would have thought they were full, but there's one place free. Anyway, you know Cavan; he doesn't let anything stand in his way when he sets his mind on something.'

'That's true,' she agreed with a wry laugh. 'I'm thrilled,' she said, giving him a hug and putting aside her anxiety about Jory's attitude. 'One place. What luck,' she said slowly, wondering if that was a coincidence.

'If I'm accepted, I can start at the end of next week, since there aren't any more visitors coming here,' continued Mawgan enthusiastically. 'And he's found me a flat near the college through some contacts. He doesn't let the dust settle when he gets started. Isn't Cavan amazing?'

That, thought Bethany, was no coincidence. Cavan had planned the whole thing some time ago, she was certain. 'Don't forget that he'll own a bit of you,' she pointed out, reluctant to dampen Mawgan's excitement but even more reluctant to acknowledge that Cavan was amazing. 'He *is* going to take a percentage of your future earnings.'

'It's not much return for his money. He deserves a reasonable return for his investment. It'll cost him thousands. I'm determined not to let him down. I'm going to be a success for all our sakes, believe me.'

'I know you will,' said Bethany warmly. It was ironic. Stubborn Cornish pride had made Mawgan refuse her offer of the compensation money. But now Cavan had succeeded where she'd failed. By tying the allowance to a strictly business deal, Cavan had ensured that Mawgan kept his self-respect. He'd motivated Mawgan, too, knowing her brother would consider it a matter of honour to work hard and justify the financial investment.

Cavan knew her brother better than she did. She chewed her lip, considering the implications. Far from being blunt and direct, Cavan was showing a clever and rather devious mind. But then, any man who rose from being a bell-boy to running a multi-million pound ticket agency couldn't exactly be a slouch. He had a sharp mind, and it would be stupid of her to underestimate his ability to manipulate situations and people to his advantage. She must be on her guard all the time.

'Beth?' Mawgan was giving her arm a shake. 'You're not listening!' he said, hurt.

'Sorry,' she smiled in apology. 'I was thinking of what lies ahead.' She shivered, feeling Cavan's tentacles closing in around her. He was getting his own way too frequently. 'I'm going in. It's getting cold.'

As she ran up the stairs, she thought angrily that this time she'd make sure Cavan didn't get everything he wanted. He could relieve his appetite with Tania. Her mouth turned down at the idea and she stopped short with a silent groan. Jealousy again, and quite illogical of her.

Showering hastily and dressing in a thin cream wool dress for the cooler evening, Bethany slipped downstairs and found Mawgan rushing about in the kitchen like a demented thing, preparing supper.

'Chef's off sick,' he said tersely. 'Phoned in ten minutes ago.'

'I'll help.' Bethany had intended to borrow his car and find a quiet pub somewhere to spend the evening, but hadn't the heart to leave him in the midst of such chaos. She grabbed an apron and commandeered the grill-pan.

'You'll be all right when I go, won't you?' asked Mawgan, prodding the broccoli. 'Cavan will be here now and then.'

She decided not to tell him about Jory. 'Mmm.' She tried to be non-committal. She didn't want Mawgan worrying.

'I know you two will get on,' he said earnestly. 'All that arguing—it's only a front. You've got the wrong idea about each other, you know. He isn't some Neanderthal tribesman, trying to drag you into his cave.'

'Then he shouldn't keep trying to do his impression of one,' she frowned. 'I thought you'd always loathed him?'

'No, Beth.' Mawgan swung her around and held her shoulders. 'You did. You were my mother, my sister, my friend. You flared up like a torch whenever he was around, and I adored you so I backed you up. We didn't give him much of a welcome. Look at it from his point of view; he was like a fish out of water. Remember how he learnt to sail?'

She grinned. 'Don't we all! Cavan fell in so many times you said he'd get webbed feet.' Her grin faded. Exhausted, wet and laughed at by the local boys, Cavan had persevered through the day till darkness fell. And eventually he had mastered the art of dinghy-sailing so

well that he became more skilled than anyone. Nothing
beat him. Not ever. Her face became very thoughtful.

'He's a tough nut,' smiled Mawgan. 'You've got to
admire his guts. Give him a chance, for my sake.'

'He pulled me out of the sea, and of course I'll always
be grateful. But it doesn't mean I have to like him.'

Mawgan shrugged and went to turn over the roast po-
tatoes. His eyes slid over to his sister's pensive face. 'He
rang from the yacht. Tania was doing some exotic dinner.
Lobster and profiteroles,' he said. 'Candle-light. Very
romantic, with Tania in some slinky number. Hasn't she
altered? I could hardly believe my eyes. Fancy having
her as a secretary!' he laughed. 'What do you think of
her?' he asked idly.

'I think they're perfect for each other,' she said ferociously, spearing the chops and turning them over.

'It's a cosy arrangement,' mused Mawgan. 'She's really
landed on her feet. Flying all round the world together...
Thrown together like that, they must be quite
close——'

Bethany banged the grill-pan back, her face stormy.
'I wouldn't know and I wouldn't *care*,' she said, quickly
interrupting him. She didn't like the images he was con-
juring up. Cavan kissing Tania. Tania's fluttery lashes...
'What else can I do for you?' she asked sharply.

Mawgan smiled. 'Not much,' he said, holding back a
grin. 'I think I have the situation sussed.'

Bethany luxuriated in bed. It was Sunday, and all the
visitors had left. Mawgan had gone too, his car laden
with his possessions, an ecstatic smile on his face.
Tomorrow she'd start work, so this would be her last
lazy day. Contentedly, she plumped up her pillows and
reached for a magazine.

Her hand froze in mid-air. The door-handle of her room was turning. Bethany clutched a pillow defensively. She was alone in the house. No one was within earshot.

'Who's there?' she called sharply, her voice shaking slightly. 'Mawgan?'

The door swung open to reveal . . . nothing. Bethany stared at the empty corridor, her head cocked to one side in a listening attitude, her breath shallow and high in her throat. Then she blinked. Around the side of the door appeared a fishing-line, on the end of which dangled a child's inflatable shark.

Her relief was intense. 'Cavan! I know that's you— no one else would be so stupidly childish. What are you playing at? Come out! Are you trying to scare me?'

'Peace offering.' The shark jiggled appealingly, its toothy smile and huge eyes suddenly making her want to laugh.

'*Peace* offering?' she repeated in surprise. A sou'wester hat was thrown into the room followed by an enormous bunch of parsley, a lemon and finally a spade. A spade?

Despite herself, Bethany began to giggle uncontrollably, laughing so much at the ridiculous objects that she was clutching herself weakly and lying back on the pillows when Cavan finally peeked around the doorway.

'Can I come in and do penance?' he enquired hopefully.

'To the door only.' Still grinning, Bethany took the precaution of sliding beneath the duvet a little even if he didn't look in the least bit threatening.

He beamed, ignoring her request and coming in to stand humbly at the bottom of her bed. She managed to wipe her eyes and made a brave attempt at composing herself. '*Parsley*?' she queried. 'Shouldn't it be flowers?'

'Oh. Clumsy me,' he said disarmingly, pushing a hand through his tumbled hair. 'I suppose "say it with parsley" doesn't have the same glamour,' he apologised. 'But, being a practical and unromantic man, I thought roses wouldn't go with fish.'

He was far too appealing for his own good. 'They don't. Neither does the spade,' she said drily, dying to know the connection and wondering ruefully how many women he'd *laughed* into bed.

'We need the spade. To bury the hatchet,' he explained. Bethany sternly suppressed another giggle, but her mouth twitched, giving her away. 'It's nice to hear you laugh,' Cavan said contentedly. 'It's been a long time, Bethany.'

Her amusement faded abruptly, and she thought for a moment 'It has,' she agreed in wonder. 'Ages.' She refrained from telling him when. The last time she'd been totally helpless with laughter was when Cavan had played the Ugly Sister in the village pantomime, sporting a pair of yellow wellies and a hairy chest above an enormous bosom which kept slipping and being ostentatiously adjusted, with a wicked wink from his amazing false eyelashes. She found that she was smiling at the memory, and sighed.

Cavan had been watching her. 'Am I forgiven?' he asked quietly.

'It depends what for.'

'Coming on strong on the beach,' he said bluntly. 'I realise that was probably why you went for a swim. You needed to release your anger with me. I'm sorry. I didn't want to put you in danger like that. To tell the truth, I was rather wound up.'

'And now?' she asked uncertainly, wondering if the romantic dinner with Tania had unwound him. 'You made a threat before you left. Do you intend to carry it out?'

'You come straight to the point, don't you?' he said ruefully.

'Well, I think I'd better let you know that if you try anything on I'll report you for harassment,' she warned him. 'I'd be working for you so I'd be legally entitled to protest. You must see that I won't get much work done if I'm spending half my time dodging your great groping paws.'

'I know,' he said amiably, giving in with surprising alacrity. 'And I want everything finished... It'll have to be Ticking Tania, won't it?'

Bethany met his laughing eyes and her mouth curled up in delight at the nickname before she managed to control its waywardness and look prim again. But Cavan was laughing his wicked laugh, and his wrecker's eyes were flashing merrily at her, and she became convulsed with giggles once more.

'You are quite the most infuriating man I've ever met,' she protested eventually.

'Aren't I just?' His eyes glowed and he sat down on the bed. Immediately alert for danger, Bethany resisted the urge to shrink back, and gave him a challenging stare instead. He leaned forwards, his mouth soft, and she wanted to touch it. 'I'll tell you this, Bethany,' he said huskily. 'You're going to love every second of the next half-hour.' He let his tongue slick over his lips and his gaze roamed slowly over the length of her body, which was outlined beneath the thin summer duvet.

She snatched up the bedside lamp and waved it threateningly. 'That does it!' she said crossly, disappointed in him. 'You promised——'

'Don't you want the breakfast I've cooked?' he asked with hurt innocence. 'Local home-cured bacon, local

eggs, field mushrooms from the headland and your own
tomatoes?'

She became aware of the glorious smell coming from
downstairs, and replaced the lamp very carefully, giving
herself time to let her annoyance subside. He'd been
teasing her as usual. Like an annoying older brother,
endlessly teasing his sister. Irritated, she surveyed him
from under her eyebrows, wondering if that was how he
saw her, and if that was why he tormented her so
relentlessly.

'One of these days, Cavan, you'll get your come-
uppance,' she promised wryly. 'I'll get the better of you,
see if I don't!'

'Sounds fun,' he grinned. 'I love masterful women.'

'No, you don't. You hate them. You ache to crush
them and assert your masculinity.' Bethany tore her eyes
away from his and sought for normality. 'Breakfast,'
she said briskly. 'I'm starving.'

'Chew on Jaws here till you can make it downstairs,'
he suggested, getting up and tossing her the toy shark.
She caught it and eyed him with reluctant amusement.
'Two minutes, and breakfast will be on the table, ready
or not,' he said smugly.

'Two——!' Compressing her mouth, she grabbed her
nail scissors from the bedside table and stabbed Jaws.
The toy shark deflated with a sad sighing sound.

'I think that's significant,' grinned Cavan. 'Or it will
be, when I've worked it out.'

'I'm pretending it's you and I've punctured your ego,'
she explained drily.

He winced and left with a cheerful whistle piercing
the air. He thumped down the stairs two at a time.
Bethany ran into the bathroom, dragging off her nightie
and clambering into her underwear, a pair of jeans and
a cotton shirt. Inside two minutes she was dashing into

the kitchen, her cap of dark, glossy hair bouncing, her face bright pink from a quick dousing with ice-cold water.

'What kept you?' he asked laconically, picking up his fork. She ignored him and tucked into her breakfast. 'You have one hell of an appetite,' he remarked softly. 'It matches mine. Sorry! Pax!' he cried, holding up his hands in apology at her fierce glare. 'It's habit, I'm afraid. Put me in front of a beautiful woman——'

'You can cut out the flattery. I'm in my scruff, without make-up, and I probably have egg on my chin,' she said in a matter-of-fact tone.

'You have,' he sighed, reaching forwards with his forefinger and gently dabbing at the corner of her mouth. The gesture was unnervingly sensual. 'Somehow the egg decoration makes no difference. You're a *woman*.' She gave him her most withering look, offended by being lumped in with the mass-market appeal. 'The lines on your forehead have gone,' he observed.

'What?' She forked up a piece of bacon and held her fork suspended in mid-air while she tried to work out what he was getting at.

'You've relaxed,' he murmured.

'That sounds rather unwise,' she said drily. 'If I had any sense, I'd still have all the barricades up.'

His mouth quirked appealingly at one corner, but his eyes were thoughtful. 'The war should never have started. It certainly shouldn't continue. I was worried about you, Beth. You were so uptight when you arrived here a few days ago——'

'It was hardly surprising,' she said, munching on a piece of crisp bacon. He'd cooked it to perfection, just how she liked it. Perhaps he'd remembered. 'I'd left the village in a cloud of exhaust fumes and a state of hysterics,' she added, trying to make light of it all. 'I never thought I could look the butcher in the face again after you'd bent me back in that ridiculous Hollywood pose and kissed me outside his shop.'

Cavan didn't smile at her deliberately flippant description of their stormy parting. 'I was trying to make you see sense,' he said in a low voice.

'Sense?' she frowned. 'That's hardly fair—you're the one who'd lost his senses. Surely it wasn't stupid of me to say I wanted to buy you out. I wanted to buy the hotel from you, to make it mine and Mawgan's again, and you refused——'

'I told you,' he said shortly, 'I didn't want your money.'

'Dan's money,' she corrected.

'All right,' he muttered. 'Have it your own way. However, if you'd asked me to *give* Portallen to you because you were homeless and it had once belonged to your father, I would have done. But no, you had to insult me by flashing around the money you'd acquired because your husband had a fatal accident at work,' he growled.

She flinched at his cruel bluntness. 'You wouldn't have given me Portallen,' she said, tipping up her chin defensively. 'You never give anything away free!'

'Once I did, more's the pity. Something very precious to me,' he said quietly. 'But you never knew about that and never will. Bethany, I did feel sorry for you and the way the villagers had treated you. I would have let you have the Inn. But you would have had to beg me first. That's what I wanted from you—some acknowledgement that——'

'Oh, Cavan! Your obsession with dominating me is never far from the surface, is it?' she broke in sadly. She paused and plunged on, 'You'd even go so far as to arrange a hate campaign to drive me into your clutches.'

Cavan stiffened, his eyes a fierce blue in his tanned face. 'Me? Arrange... Is that what you believe?' he asked softly, his body totally still.

Her hands trembled but she persevered. She had to say it. 'I've thought about it for a long time. There was no one else with the motivation or the devious kind of mind to want to do such a thing. You wrote those poison-pen letters.'

She bit her lip at the unnerving way his jaw clenched and her eyes were drawn to his fork, quivering in mid-air, shaking with pure rage in his bone-crushing fist.

When he spoke, however, it was in a tightly controlled voice with no emotion in it whatever. 'I never thought you mistrusted and hated me to that extent,' he said in a harsh whisper.

'I've always mistrusted you,' she retorted shakily.

'And you think I wrote the letters.'

'Yes, I do,' she whispered.

His inscrutable eyes examined hers. 'I'm the worst person you can think of.' She was silent. 'Mawgan was wrong, then. He said we'd get on together.'

'He was wrong,' she agreed, keeping her voice even.

He put down his fork very carefully and leaned back in his chair. 'I tell you this, Bethany,' he said in a tone utterly devoid of all expression, 'I did not have anything at all to do with those letters, or with the gossip. I swear that on my mother's grave. You can believe me or not, as you choose, but that's the truth.'

He meant that. No one could doubt the honesty in his eyes. Bethany bit her lip. 'I—I was wrong. I was sure... I—I'm sorry,' she said, distressed by the hard glitter in his eyes. 'You're rightly angry with me,' she added, hanging her head guiltily. 'I just couldn't think of anyone else who wanted to see me wriggle, who resented the easy way I'd acquired a lot of money. You had to work so hard——'

'So you fled to Bodmin.' He seemed to have dismissed the matter because he continued eating as if he didn't care what she said. 'Have you been happy there?'

She hesitated. There was nothing to be gained in lying. 'No. I'm only happy here,' she answered honestly.

'Then why stay somewhere you hate? You could go anywhere in the world.'

'I wanted to be near enough to Mawgan so he could visit me. I couldn't live here because of the hostility and because I wouldn't have been able to avoid you.'

He was lifting his cup when she said that, and Bethany saw that it didn't shake even a fraction. So he'd known that she had hated him enough to deny herself her own home, her own brother. Ached for him, hated him, they were the same violent feelings, which she longed to discard for a more normal relationship with a less unpredictable man. But she was bound hand and foot, body and soul to Cavan. For her own sanity she had to keep clear of him.

'Go on.'

'I wish you'd go back to London,' she said woodenly. 'It would make my life easier. I'm sure I could gradually persuade the villagers that I'm not a selfish jet-setter. It would be possible for me to live here, then. Where I belong.'

'Your life would be easier,' he agreed non-committally, 'but less interesting. Tell me honestly. Did you love Dan, really love him?' he asked suddenly, startling her.

'I told you,' she said stiffly. 'That's off limits.'

'You've answered,' he said enigmatically.

'No, I haven't! Oh, darn you! I don't know why you keep making me lose my temper! Let's keep our relationship to a polite working one, shall we?'

'If that's what you want,' he said, his eyes watching her over the rim of his cup.

'I don't want any other kind.'

'So you keep on telling me,' he murmured softly. Then he seemed to abandon the conversation, and pushed his chair back. 'Very well. We'll try. I'm going to a farm sale this morning. Want to come? You might see some useful items for the Inn. You can tie a rope around my hands if you like.'

She smiled. 'Once I might have said that I'd rather it was your neck,' she said wryly, risking a joke at her own expense. Cavan's eyes smiled back at hers. 'OK,' she agreed. 'We might as well make a start.'

'That's what I was thinking.'

Bethany frowned at Cavan, but he looked perfectly innocent. As she helped him put away the breakfast things and stack the dishwasher, it occurred to her that he'd never been innocent in his life. Her body tensed and her mind sharpened in preparation for the next few hours. He'd called a truce, but she couldn't trust him.

Disconcertingly, she noticed that adrenalin was making her feel full of energy and rather exhilarated, as if something in her found it exciting that she and Cavan were working together. Even more alarming was the fact that he, too, was fired with exuberance. Her awareness of him was intensified, and she saw that his face was alive with a vital energy, his whole body taut and poised like a high-tension wire.

And in that state he was dangerously attractive.

They borrowed a Land Rover and drove up the river valley through unspoilt woodland. Cavan didn't spoil her pleasure by teasing her or making sarcastic remarks.

They talked about Mawgan, and Bethany relaxed completely, thrilled that her brother would have the opportunity to realise his considerable potential at last.

'We'll split forces,' Cavan said when they arrived at the farm. 'Meet you by the hot-dog stand in half an hour. That'll give us time to compare notes.'

Bethany was a little disappointed. She'd looked forward to walking around with him. When they came nearer to the cluster of buildings she realised how run-down the farm had become. 'It's an "All Up" auction by the looks of it,' she said, not liking what she saw.

''Fraid so. He must be deeply in debt for all these personal items to be included in the sale,' commented Cavan. 'See you in a while.' He strode off across the farmyard, looking surprisingly at home among the deer-stalker hats, the home-knitted jumpers and the rash of Barbour jackets.

She was back by the hot-dog van in twenty minutes, deeply distressed. She'd met the farmer's wife, who had been white-faced and upset from watching strangers foraging through her possessions.

'Cavan!' she yelled, when she saw his dark head above the jostling people near the tool shed. She hurried over, anxious to leave.

'Beth? You've been quick. I haven't finished yet.'

His familiar face and body looked immensely comforting to her eyes. Her impulse to throw herself in his arms appalled her. She was upset, but that was no reason for her to look to him for consolation.

'I didn't see anything we could use. It was a waste of time,' she told him tersely.

'Just come on a final tour around with me and then we'll go,' he said, tucking her arm in his. 'They're about to start on selling the first lot in a few minutes.'

With extreme reluctance, she let herself be dragged around the sheds and stores packed with boxes of crockery, lampshades, farm equipment, garden tools... Bethany watched the sharp-eyed dealers and avaricious-looking women picking over what represented a few generations of a farming family's life. Miserably she wondered if this was what had happened when she had let an agent sell all of Dan's things and hers—everything they'd shared together.

'I want to go now,' she mumbled.

Cavan turned her around to face him. 'Look at me, Bethany,' he said in a low tone. She flicked sullen eyes up at him and then lowered her lids to hide the feelings which were churning away inside her. 'You look dreadful. Is something the matter? Tell me!' he ordered.

She could tell from the way he spoke and the way he'd planted his legs apart—in fact, the whole set of his body—that he wouldn't rest till she'd answered. 'It's awful. It's like vultures picking over a carcass,' she said with a small shudder as she looked around.

She heard the auctioneer's voice in the dilapidated barn ringing out. 'Two-pound bid? Don't do anythin' rash, me dears.'

'This is one of the harsh realities of life,' said Cavan quietly.

'Yes, but,' she explained huskily, 'it seems incredibly sad. The farm here has died on its feet and the farmer is selling everything he ever owned. Did you see his wife? She shouldn't be here. She shouldn't be watching people poking around her things.'

'I know. I used the auctioneer's car-phone to order a taxi for her, and shoved her into it,' said Cavan. 'I felt terribly sorry for her. It's an awful situation.'

'That was nice of you,' said Bethany impulsively.

Her hand was caught by his. 'That's the first time you've ever said anything remotely pleasant to me,' Cavan told her in astonishment. 'I hope it won't be the last.'

'Lot two. Come on, now, pound to start, pound to start . . .'

Bethany tore her eyes away from his, confused. 'That bid is for the box of wellington boots,' she said hurriedly. She caught sight of a woman laughing at the farmer's taste in paperbacks, and bristled. 'Look, Cavan!' she cried indignantly. 'The nerve of it!'

'I agree,' he said, his brows drawn together heavily. 'I must say,' he mused, reaching to test the weight of a log-splitter, 'if I owned these tools I wouldn't want to sell them. There's a lifetime's collection here. Must have been his pride and joy.'

'You do understand, then,' she said, surprised at his sensitivity. 'Let's go. I can't stand it, Cavan. It makes me feel sick. It's like invading his privacy. Take me away.'

Her sad eyes lifted to his warily. There was a guarded expression on his face.

'Fifty pence a door ain't bad, me 'andsome . . .'

Bethany was agonising over her misdirected emotions. Her distress was magnified because she felt more sorrow for the farmer and his family than she had at selling her things in Aberdeen. Maybe she'd been in shock. Or perhaps it was because it was a part of her life that had never touched her emotions at all.

'It can't be easy, losing your family home,' Cavan said.

She started, her mind switching immediately to the prospect of losing Portallen. 'I couldn't bear this to happen to my home, to the Inn, Cavan,' she admitted huskily.

'I realise that. I once thought you didn't care about it, but now I know different. Look, Beth, this sale has upset you and I wish it hadn't. But perhaps it's no bad thing. Fix this in your mind; remember it all. Because there are going to be times in the next few months when you will want to go back on our arrangement and when your instincts will tell you to run away again—and that you must never do.'

His hands slid to her shoulders and he forced her to keep looking at him when she tried to avoid his glittering eyes.

'Why do you think that I'll want to leave?' she asked, her voice cracking. 'What—what are you planning for me?'

'I'm looking ahead, knowing how we behave together. We're going to argue and make up, we'll want to throttle each other and we'll also desperately want to make love——'

'*No!*' she ground out in quick denial.

'I'm being honest, Bethany. I'm preparing you,' he said ruthlessly. 'Be absolutely clear on this; if you haven't the guts to carry out the renovation of the Portallen Inn, I will put it on the market faster than you can hurl insults at me, because I'll have no reason to keep it or the memories it has for me.'

'You hate it?' she asked, wide-eyed.

'You'll find out what I feel over the next few months, I hope,' he said, his mouth crooking wryly at one corner. 'What happens to the hotel is up to you. Until now, whether you've lived there or not, you've always known it's been there, with a room for you if you've wanted. With Mawgan out of the way——'

'You planned that?' she breathed.

'Every step of the way,' he agreed, his eyes remorseless. 'I wanted this arrangement to be between us and no one else.'

'That sounds like revenge,' she said huskily.

'Does it? It's not meant to. I wanted the coast clear so we could have a free run of the house. I don't want anything to interfere with my intention to make you work for me.' He paused. 'This sale has brought the situation sharply into focus. Portallen represents your childhood memories. I *own* those memories, Bethany, more than you realise. Go back on our deal, and, as God is my witness, I'll sell everything: your mother's curtains, the linen, the tablecloths she embroidered, the lampshades she made. Your father's home-made shelves and the books he left to me, the Toby Jugs he collected——'

'Stop!' she whispered, her face as white as a sheet. Tears filled her eyes. 'Oh, Cavan, for God's sake, stop!' A tear ran down her cheek. She sped across the cracked concrete yard to the field where the cars were parked, and waited blindly by the Land Rover.

The hotel was full of memories. Dim ones of her mother, happy, loving ones of her father and Mawgan. Turbulent ones of Cavan, thundering through the house like a line-squall. Her eyes closed. Finding him asleep one morning, after he'd stayed out all night, his lashes thick and appealing on his sleep-warm cheeks. Seeing him sitting in the kitchen mending a cormorant's broken wing, his forehead creased in concentration. His voice, his vitality, his hunger for life.

All that she'd lose if he carried out his threat.

Cavan came up after a while and helped her in, then drove off without a word, tension in every line of his body.

She didn't care. The way she felt, she never wanted to speak to him again. Hurting her was becoming a way of life to him. He was incredibly cruel. She stiffened as Cavan applied the brakes and drew the Land Rover to a halt near the desolate, ivy-clad ruins of an old engine-house where copper had once been mined.

'Calmer now? We have to talk,' he said expressionlessly.

She slid a quick glance to his hard profile. He was going to lecture her. 'No,' was all she could manage.

Cavan let out a sigh of exasperation. 'I can't stand this, Bethany,' he muttered.

'Then release me!' she cried passionately.

He flinched. 'I can't.'

'Why? You don't even like me! Do we have to have this cat and mouse game just to satisfy your vanity? Do you have to keep blackmailing me?' she continued wildly.

'I didn't know you'd be so affected by the farm sale,' he grated.

She grew wary, knowing she dared not tell him the whole truth. 'Perhaps I should tell you just where your blundering schemes have taken you. The auction upset me because I'd sold all of Dan's things in the same way,' she cried unhappily, wanting to hurt him as he'd hurt her. 'Every single thing in the house. Our furniture, our bed and bedding——' Cavan winced and she gritted her teeth and carried on '—his clothes, his effects, the records we'd played together——'

'All right, Bethany! Please; this is not helping either of us!' he cried, his face haggard. 'You don't need to go on. Oh, God!' he groaned. 'I had no idea, I didn't know——'

'No. You were too hell-bent on making your damn point, weren't you?' she said bitterly. He was silent, every muscle in his body flexed and tense. 'You bastard. And you wonder why I don't trust you, why I regard you with contempt. Take me home,' she finished wearily.

'Bodmin?' he asked hoarsely.

'Portallen.' She noticed that he didn't make any sarcastic remark about it not really being her home.

'I'm sorry. I'm truly sorry. I ask you to forgive me for being so crass and blundering in on your feelings.'

She was startled. He'd never apologised so humbly in the whole of his life, and it sounded as if the apology had been wrenched out of him. 'The damage has been done,' she said flatly, and suddenly she felt her eyes fill with tears.

'Yes, and I wish it hadn't.' He turned in the seat to face her. 'Oh, Beth,' he said gently. 'Please don't cry.'

The tears ran down her cheeks. 'I'm so tired of struggling to keep my neck above water,' she sobbed. 'If only things would go smoothly for once——'

'They will,' he promised, dabbing at her eyes tenderly with his handkerchief. 'Poor Beth. No one's ever looked after you, have they? You were so young when your mother died and you took charge of your brother. Always the tower of strength, hiding your own needs. You wouldn't even ask Rosie for advice, would you?'

'I did once,' she muttered, flushing a little. 'She told me to go and get what I wanted.'

He roared with laughter. 'Sounds like Ma,' he chuckled. 'Nothing subtle about her, was there?' he added fondly. 'Bright red hair, eyelashes you could fan your face with and a heart as big as the Albert Hall. I wept when she died, Beth,' he said huskily.

Her eyes widened. 'Oh, Cavan!' she exclaimed unhappily, seeing his bleak face. A few more tears fell for him. 'I'm so sorry. I was in Mexico when I heard.' She reached out a friendly hand to his.

He gave her a gentle smile. 'We had one hell of a Wake. Went on for days. I miss her very much. Do you know, she'd given me the same advice that she gave to you? That's why I had left Portallen in the first place, knowing I'd never make my fortune there. I gave myself five years to get what I wanted, but...' he shrugged and looked away '...I got the timing wrong,' he breathed. 'For the first time in my life, I was too late.'

'At twenty-two?' she asked in surprise. 'Cavan, you were doing well then. And it wasn't long before you made your first million. We were all very proud.'

'You never said,' he pointed out. 'You kept your feelings and your thoughts to yourself. Beth, I think it's time you shared your problems with someone and leaned on a strong shoulder.'

It sounded wonderful. He was right; she'd never been free of responsibility, had never fooled around like the other kids, but had snatched brief moments of leisure and made hurried visits to the beach in the hope that Cavan would admire her.

'I'm just over-sensitive at the moment,' she confessed, sniffing. 'Coming back and finding the villagers still unfriendly was a bit of a shock. Mawgan said the trouble had blown over.'

'I can help there. Let me ease that particular situation,' he suggested. 'And please, turn to me for help. You have never let me help you before, but I'm asking you to stop trying to deal with all your difficulties on your own. My shoulders are broad; lean on them. Why be so prickly where I'm concerned? Give me the benefit of the doubt for a change.'

She could hardly tell him that she erected unnecessary barriers to stop herself from leaping over them and throwing herself into his arms. 'Don't tease me,' she said miserably.

'Beth.' He put a brotherly arm around her shoulder and took over the business of drying her tears. 'I'll be gentle with you if you'll be gentle with me.'

She managed a small smile. Her eyes slanted up to his and met only openness. 'I suppose we ought to be friends,' she said. 'Break the habit of a lifetime...'

He laughed and gave her a squeeze. 'We'll put up a united front and then the villagers will be totally disarmed,' he said comfortingly. 'Once they're eating out of your hands, you'll find life a hell of a lot easier.'

He dropped a kiss on her nose and then, after a brief pause when she sat without moving, he kissed her lips gently. For a fleeting second, Bethany thought the kiss was deepening, but to her mingled disappointment and relief he drew away and started up the Land Rover. It was hard when he was foul to her. It was worse when he was nice.

Far from being settled, her emotions were turbulent as a stormy sea. Staring out at the tumbled stones of the giant engine-house and its tall chimney smothered in choking ivy, she mused that her life seemed to be desolate and in empty, silent ruins, too, with no future. Cavan had shown her a glimpse of a tender, caring man. That had made her own feelings for him more powerful. And she was unhappier than ever. She had neither the home nor the man she wanted.

CHAPTER FIVE

THEY drove through the village, and Cavan stopped by the butcher's shop, saying he had an order to collect. Knowing he had to return the Land Rover, Bethany said she'd walk back to the hotel. At the bottom of the street was a group of fishermen, their dark Celtic faces watching her sullenly. Her steps faltered but she kept going.

'Mornin', Beth. Not married Cavan yet, then?'

She came to a halt a few feet from them, disconcerted by the spiteful tone of Rowan's voice. Married? she thought, a pang piercing her heart. 'I'm not looking for self-torture, Rowan,' she said in a low tone.

The men laughed in delight. 'Still fightin', then?' asked Rowan. 'And come back for more! What about they kisses, eh?'

She blushed, knowing he referred to the day of her departure. The violent, intensely sexual kiss was engraved on her memory and was uncomfortably unforgettable.

'I've returned to do something for Mawgan,' she said with quiet dignity.

Every man there scowled at her. 'Arr. We was saying; Beth could do somethin' fer the village,' growled Ewen. 'All they millions of pounds wasted on a woman's back. New storm-gate's needed, you know.'

She looked at them in dismay. 'I—I can't——'

'Can't? Won't, more like it,' accused Rowan roughly.

'You'll get your gate, Ewen,' said Cavan's firm voice behind her.

Like the men, Bethany heard the slicing steel in his words. They tipped their caps respectfully, and she felt her body relax with relief. Her legs were trembling. Ewen sniffed again. 'Could get it quicker if Beth weren't so selfish 'n mean——'

She drew in her breath sharply, and Cavan's hand descended heavily on Ewen's shoulder. Bethany couldn't make out whether it was a friendly gesture or one of warning. 'Bethany's trying to sort out her life,' explained Cavan in a confidential voice. 'She needs us. Don't you, darling?'

Bethany's eyes widened at the deeply affectionate way he said that. Before she could gather her wits and deny that there was any affection between them, Ewen eyed her speculatively.

'So you did come back fer more!' he said in his lilting Cornish brogue, as she dazedly shook his hand. 'You two always was larkin' around. She your'n, boy?'

Cavan looked bashful. 'Come on, now,' he grinned, shifting his feet. 'Give a guy a break.'

Bethany was open-mouthed at his deceit. And his skill. Ewen was briefly disarmed, a faint smile appearing on his face. Then it vanished. 'Village don't like her,' he said flatly.

'Isn't my judgement good enough for you?' asked Cavan quietly. The men shifted awkwardly. 'Come on, man, the past is past. We've all matured since that tittle-tattle. Beth is working for me. She's helping Mawgan and me to undo the damage that cowboy firm did. You're always mizzening in your beer mug that it was about time Portallen got its character back, aren't you?'

Bethany saw that the men were laughing with Cavan at the discomfited Ewen, and that Cavan had enough goodwill to get away with the gentle ribbing.

'I'll give you mizzen,' chuckled Ewen. 'You'll be miz-zenin' when I've beaten you at darts!'

'Best of nine,' challenged Cavan, his eyes dancing. 'Oh, before we go,' he added, 'I'm relying on you all to help Bethany for me if she has any serious problems. I'll be glad of your support. I don't want any hold-ups. You know how impatient I am,' he grinned.

'Womenfolk tells us so,' chuckled Rowan. 'Mebbe us'd help.'

'Thanks,' smiled Cavan. 'She might need it. You can see how things are. She's a little dazed. I've rather swept her off her feet.' He glanced with fond concern at her stunned face.

Bethany found her voice. 'I don't——'

'It's OK, darling. They know me. They understand.' Cavan curved a possessive arm around her shoulder.

'No, it's——'

'Hush.' Her voice was muffled by Cavan's mouth. She heard the men chuckling, and Cavan began to kiss her more thoroughly, his arms imprisoning her. When the men's footsteps had died away, he released her. 'You must go with the tide, not against it,' he said softly. 'Couldn't you see that the men would begin to accept you if they thought you and I were friends?'

'Friends, maybe. That's ludicrous enough, but do we have to act like lovers too?' she asked huskily, her mouth burning and hungry.

'It's what they've expected since we first collided,' he smiled.

Bethany found it hard to tear her eyes away from his tempting mouth, and that irritated her beyond belief. One kiss and she was his. She wanted to grind her teeth in rage. 'I can't think why!' she snapped. 'That's the most illogical statement you've ever made!'

He heaved a great sigh. 'I could see how upset you were,' he explained. 'I was thinking on my feet and trying to get you out of a tight spot. They still resent your money. Bethany, I know you don't like this but it's a temporary solution. It won't hurt you to be linked with me. They've been nudging and winking about your rescue and how you've come to live in the hotel. Word will get around that you and I are an "item", and the village will gradually accept you to their bosom——'

'Because I'm your girlfriend?' she asked in astonishment. 'What have you done? Brainwashed them all? I know you'd never be able to buy them outright.'

'They've discovered a few of my better qualities,' he said laconically. 'I haven't been around much but we've learnt a lot about each other over the last six or seven years. Look, Bethany, I'm doing this for another reason. If you're working here for the next few months and you need help when I'm not around, then where will you turn?'

'I hadn't thought. The workmen on the hotel?' she suggested.

'Supposing you need help outside working hours? No. You must be able to call on the villagers. You of all people know how everyone pulls together in a crisis. You could have trouble one day, whether it's a burst water-main or a storm, or a fire...' His dark eyes brooded on her. 'If I'm on the other side of the world, I want to know that——' His voice stopped short. 'That the Inn won't be destroyed because no one will come to your aid,' he finished curtly.

'Protecting your interests,' she said cynically.

'Yes.' His eyes gleamed and he seemed amused for a moment. 'There could hardly be any other reason, could there?'

Bethany frowned, picturing the scene he'd painted. 'You're right,' she acknowledged with reluctance. 'I don't want anything to happen to Portallen either. But I'd rather it was because I was accepted for myself, rather than as your appendage!'

He smiled apologetically. 'You can clear things up later. Give them time to get used to you first. Sorry about the kiss. I had to shut you up somehow. It seemed better than gagging you with my hand. That *would* have been suspicious.'

'I suppose so,' she muttered. 'But I wish you weren't so free with your lips. They seem to be glued to mine at the slightest opportunity.'

Cavan's hand curved around the back of her neck. 'Well, that's your fault for having such infinitely kissable lips,' he said lightly.

'Try exercising a little self-control,' she retorted waspishly.

Back home in the kitchen, Bethany made herself a sandwich while Cavan watched, his hands thrust deep into his pockets. 'I think, since there's a deadline looming, we might as well start discussing the renovation,' he said casually.

'I'd like that,' she replied with enthusiasm. It would mean that his mind—and possibly his hands and mouth—would be occupied.

They argued, of course, but productively. Bethany was a little disconcerted to discover how much she was privately enjoying the cut and thrust of the session. Cavan was a quick thinker, picking up the threads of her suggestions fast, and when she struggled to describe an effect she was aiming for he skilfully drew enough information from her to clarify the idea and commit it to paper.

Bethany's excitement increased. If she could carry out everything they had discussed, Portallen would look wonderful, and she couldn't wait to start. Cavan didn't think small.

Her eyes glowed as she looked at Cavan, arguing about the placing of a fire escape so that it would be unobtrusive. His body seemed fired with energy as he leaned across the table, his big hands gesticulating and his face... Her heart lurched crazily.

Dynamic, compelling, he was irresistible. That expressive curve of his mouth, the gleaming white teeth as he made a joke, the softening of his eloquent eyes as she laughed; all these added up to a man so vitally alive that his life-force was almost tangible. And whose sexual chemistry electrified her.

'I'm hungry,' she said suddenly, breaking into his persuasive argument.

'Me too.' He made no effort to rise, but sat very still, and the long, slow look which passed between them created an unbearable tension.

'I'll put something in the microwave,' she said, getting up blindly and grabbing the first thing she could find in the freezer.

'My goodness, you are woolly-minded. If you don't mind,' said Cavan softly, taking the packet from her hand, 'I'll give the spinach a miss. It might suit Popeye but I like variety. Could I have one of those pasta dishes instead?'

She flushed and fumbled in the freezer for something more suitable. Fortunately he was still so intent on discussing the renovation that he forgot to tease her about her confusion—or perhaps he hadn't realised what had caused it. In any case, she was more than glad to continue talking over supper.

After eating, by mutual consent they pushed the dishes to one side and carried on.

'I thought, now we've solved most of the major problems of alteration and the re-arrangement of rooms, that we'd have a brain-storming session,' Cavan suggested. 'How about listing everything we can think of that a luxury hotel should have?'

'Keeping it in the country-house style,' she reminded him. She was pleased about that. It would seem almost as if the Portallen Inn was her home.

'Sure. Let's take it as read that we'd have antique furniture, good furnishings and china. What small touches do we add?'

'Oyster satin sheets?' she asked innocently.

He grinned and wagged his finger at her. 'I'll never live that down, will I? Who let out my guilty secret?'

'The hotel receptionist,' she said cynically. 'The one you brought down to stay.'

'Oh, yes. I didn't know you two had chatted. She was incredibly jealous of you.'

'Me? I was eighteen! She was mature, smart, worldly wise and very beautiful.'

'And very perceptive,' he added enigmatically. 'Let's get on with the luxury items—oyster satin sheets being taken for granted,' he said with a wicked look at her.

'A library of local books and information,' she offered enthusiastically. 'And a range of glossy magazines,' she added wistfully. It had been years since she'd been able to buy any.

'Padded hangers,' he added, writing the ideas down. 'Women like those. Hairdriers. Shoe-cleaning service.'

'Plants. Palm trees. Blue or green striped awnings.'

'Home-grown food, discreet service, two large basins in each en suite bathroom, big vanity units with those enormous, well-lit mirrors——'

She nodded approvingly. Just what she'd like. He certainly had the finger on female pulses, she thought wryly. 'It must look cosy and welcoming. I wish we had a fire in the hall. How about a grand piano, country flowers freshly picked from the garden, lots of rugs——?'

Cavan reached out his hand to cover hers. 'Hold on a moment.' He scribbled furiously and then removed his hand when he'd caught up with their ideas. 'And a conservatory where we—they—could eat breakfast, pure linen on the beds—oh, and women love having dozens of fluffy towels around.'

Bethany made no comment, though his intimate knowledge of women's likes was beginning to irk her. 'This is going to cost a fortune. You haven't once said you can't afford any of this. Will it ever pay?' She looked up, and thought he'd been smirking at her remark, but he met her eyes quite calmly.

'It'll be worth every penny,' he said blandly. 'How about fast-filling baths for the man in a hurry?'

'Deep ones, cast iron,' she said dreamily, 'each one provided with a yellow plastic duck.'

Cavan laughed. 'Whatever you say,' he grinned. 'If you like it, we'll have it. Tomorrow I'm going to get some plans drawn up by an architect. In the meantime you can start searching for colour schemes on the themes you suggested earlier. I want to see all the material and wallpaper you choose, remember. OK. That's enough for now,' he said, shutting his folder.

'Oh!' she cried, disappointed.

'Enjoyed it?' he queried softly.

'Enormously. I always enjoy my work,' she answered quickly, hoping he hadn't got the wrong idea. But it would have taken a fool not to notice how well they'd sparked ideas off each other, and Cavan was no fool.

'But this is for your old home; you must feel differently about it,' he probed.

'Since the circumstances are that I can't properly live here, then doing it up sympathetically—and having a hand in the conversion—is at least a second best,' she answered stiffly.

'You could live here permanently if you wanted to,' murmured Cavan, a strange light glittering in his eyes. 'With no ties unless you want them,' he said in his gravelly voice.

Pain etched lines on her face. Something in his tone told her that there would be ties, enough to rope her down so that she was totally under his control. Oh, yes, she thought, she wanted so badly to live in the new, restored hotel.

Unintentionally, she and Cavan had been planning her dream home.

'That's not fair,' she said shakily. 'You're only saying that to raise my hopes, and then you'll announce some kind of condition or say that you're going to live here yourself.'

The skin on his face seemed taut. 'If I did say I intended to live here——'

'Oh, you wouldn't!' she cried in disappointment. 'There's only one staff bedroom. You said I'd own half of the hotel, and I thought that bedroom was for me or Mawgan.' She groaned. 'God, you're cruel! You've got me hooked and you're constantly letting out the line and reeling it in, aren't you? You show me how lovely it will be here and torment me by putting it in my mind that I could make it my home.'

'You'd like that?' he asked softly.

Her mouth twisted bitterly. 'Of course I'd like that! What are you trying to do to me? Rip your damn hook through my body? If you're intending to live here...'

She flicked up her eyes at him and gave him a shrewd look. 'You're not suggesting we share the same bedroom?' she asked tightly.

'It's a single,' he pointed out. 'It would be a bit cramped.'

She let out an annoyed breath. 'Everything was going so well, and you've ruined it with your innuendo. Yes, I know we have to work together tomorrow. That's why I'm not throwing things at you,' she said irritably. 'I need a breath of fresh air. Excuse me.' When she got to her feet, she realised how stiff she was from sitting for so long. 'I'm going for a walk.'

'It's dark.'

'There's a hunter's moon. Anyway, I know this area blindfold.'

'Nevertheless,' he said quietly, reaching out to help her into her jacket, 'I'm coming.'

She shrugged. 'Short of murder, which has occasionally crossed my mind, I can't stop you,' she conceded with studied indifference.

Striding unhappily ahead of him, she heard him collect something from his car and then hurry up the cliff path after her. When she reached the top of the cliff, she looked down on the white surf crashing on the black rocks, and lifted her face to the cool night breeze. Her head tipped back to gaze at the stars in the intense black sky, each tiny twinkling light patterning the sky like silver glitter.

And her love for Portallen and for Cavan mingled, her desolation at having neither of them making her want to open her mouth and rage at the fates. To live in Portallen with him. That would be her eternal fantasy. She stopped dead. She loved Cavan. Her hand shook as it went to her brow. She loved him—desperately, deeply. It was no longer an obsession, a kind of angry reaction, or even some carnal need. She wanted to spend the rest of her life with him, to seek out all that was tender and loving within him, to share...

'Hold this a minute, will you?' muttered Cavan, sounding preoccupied.

'Mmm?' She looked down in surprise at the wooden reel he'd thrust into her hand. 'What on earth are you doing?' she cried, seeing that he was solemnly unravelling a long-tailed kite.

'I'm unravelling a long-tailed kite,' he said.

'It's dark!' she protested with a half-laugh.

'There's a hunter's moon and the kite knows this place blindfold,' he said drily. 'Right. Let the string out a bit so I can go ahead.'

'I don't believe I'm doing this!' muttered Bethany. 'Flying a kite in the middle of the night!'

'Let it go a little,' called Cavan, ignoring her and intent on the matter in hand.

She could see his big familiar face and his hands holding up the bright yellow kite. Her hands felt the tug as the wind jiggled impatiently at the kite, eager to take it and drag it away. Cautiously she let out the line, and the kite soared into the sky.

'More!' urged Cavan, hurrying up to her, his eyes on the kite. But there was something strange in his voice, a fierce urgency and an undercurrent of excitement, and her heart opened to him, the joy filling her body.

The kite was fighting to be free, the strength of the wind surprising. She could feel the small gusts which grabbed the kite greedily and, needing some outlet for her soaring emotions, she began to run the line out faster till it was at full stretch, taut, fiercely dragging at her hands.

'I can't hold it!' she cried in excitement.

Cavan's hands clamped over hers. He stood behind her, shielding her body from the wind, tucking her into him and letting her feel the struggle between kite and wind. It was almost as powerful as the one going on inside her. She leaned into him a little and his arms tightened imperceptibly, and she was happy.

Bethany felt like a child again. She laughed at the way the wind sought to take the kite from them, a surge of triumph going through her as they succeeded in harnessing its power. Their faces were upturned to that small yellow shape high in the sky with its fluttering tail, glorying in the force which they were battling with, the fierce, relentless force of nature.

And Cavan showed her how to make the kite dip and swoop, to dance in the sky as if it were alive. They were both laughing, the wind catching her throat and filling her body with a sparkle as potent as champagne.

'Let's run,' suggested Cavan, elation lighting his face.

Without waiting for her agreement, he grabbed her hand and pulled her along. Knowing the smooth lie of the grass, she ran fearlessly, barely managing to keep up with him. Now and again they looked back together to see the kite obediently rushing through the air behind them. Almost at the edge of the grass, just before the sheep fence, they came to a halt, panting and laughing.

Bethany was crushed in Cavan's arms, her head roughly tipped back, and then she felt the warmth of Cavan's face against her cheek as he hugged her. She pushed against his body, but there wasn't an inch of movement.

'Cavan——'

The wonderful softness of his lips met hers in a long, endless kiss, and she was so exhilarated and happy that she sank into his arms more deeply, feeling liberated and free up there on the cliff, with the kite hovering above them.

It was almost as if they were on another planet, she thought dazedly, as his kiss grew more insistent.

'God! I could stand here all night,' he whispered. His mouth passionately devoured her face, her throat, her neck, filling her with the changing sensations as she felt his lips, moist tongue and gently savaging teeth roaming over her skin.

'This has gone far enough. I don't think we ought——' Bethany gasped and let out a small moan. 'Please don't,' she whispered in alarm, as Cavan's hand slid under her shirt. But she leaned into him, shuddering at the touch of his fingers, which were sliding inexorably up each rib. And then they stopped. Her eyes flicked open to plead with his, though she didn't know if she was begging him to stop or demanding that he should reach out and touch her throbbing breast.

'You are so beautiful,' he murmured softly. 'More beautiful and desirable than any woman I've ever known—or ever will know.'

Bethany swallowed. 'I—I——' she croaked. In dismay, she moistened her lips.

With a sexy growl, Cavan dipped his head and took her tongue between his lips, drawing it into his mouth. It was such an erotic sensation that Bethany's whole body weakened, and she would have slid to the ground if he hadn't supported her. Gently he took the kite from her trembling hand and tucked it securely in his belt, his eyes never leaving hers for a second, holding her a willing prisoner.

She lifted her arms and brought them around his neck, arching her back so that they were body to body, thigh to thigh. Hardly knowing what she was doing, she drew his dark head down to her waiting mouth and kissed him sweetly on the lips, then let her hot, urgent mouth explore his face.

'Go on, go on,' he urged huskily, his hands caressing her back. Then they were smoothing over her buttocks in a rhythmic movement that was driving her crazy.

It was as if she was drunk on the magic of the night, intoxicated by the taste, the smell, the sound of Cavan and Portallen. Without a thought for the consequences, she abandoned herself to his arms, his lips, his seductive voice and exciting touch, letting him push off her jacket and impatiently fumbling with the zip on his till he pushed her hands away and removed it himself, his hands shaking as much as hers had.

They were a few inches apart, staring at one another, panting slightly, and Bethany wanted him with a pain that was tearing her apart, filling her body with a thudding, pounding heat.

'I'm setting the kite free,' said Cavan softly, releasing the reel from his belt and holding it in his hand.

Bethany's eyes widened. 'Why?' she whispered.

'It's begging to be free,' he said huskily, his gaze dark and savage with passion. 'It can't tell me in words but I know from its every movement that it wants to soar as far as it can go. It's been controlled for too long.'

Her breath caught in her throat as he opened his hand and for a few seconds the reel remained almost motionless as if it didn't know it was free. Then the wind tugged at the kite and she looked up as it was jerked away from Cavan's hand. For a moment the kite lurched in all directions and then it began to rise, higher and higher, up to the stars.

And then she couldn't see it any more.

She was trembling. Cavan reached out for her hand. She took it, and he picked up their coats and they walked back to the Inn. Their silence was one of expectancy, the tension electric between them. Cavan's arm encircled her and she felt his warm body beside hers, their hips moving together in an increasingly arousing rhythm. Gradually, to her sorrow, common sense began to prevail upon her madness.

When they entered the hallway, Bethany drew her hand from Cavan's. 'Goodnight,' she said as evenly as she could.

'Bethany——' he began in a sensual growl.

'No,' she whispered. 'Goodnight.'

'It was fun.'

'Mmm.' She didn't trust herself to speak.

He stared down at her, his face without expression. After a few interminable seconds he dropped his eyes. 'Goodnight,' he said courteously.

Bethany climbed the stairs numbly. With every step she took, she yearned to whirl around and to invite him with a smile to follow her. Doggedly she plodded on, such a tremendous force compelling her head to turn and look at him that she had to grind her teeth in the effort to resist it.

'I'll be on the yacht if you want me,' he called hoarsely.

Bethany froze, his words knifing through her. 'Is Tania there?' she grated, before she could stop herself.

'I do hope so,' replied Cavan fervently.

Only barely suppressing a strangled cry of rage and frustration, Bethany stumbled up the stairs. The front door slammed soon after, and in a short while she heard the sound of the boat taking him to the waiting Tania. She dragged off her clothes, took the traditional cold shower, thumped her pillow a few times in temper and lay awake for most of the night listening to the complaints of her body.

She dared not let go. She dared not trust him with the strings of her fragile emotions. He was a rover—always

had been, always would be. Her heart lurched. She loved
a man who was so hungry for sex that he'd never wait
for her. And she was too proud to share.

Blearily the next morning she mooched around till a
jug full of coffee had revived her. She wanted to stare
out at the bay where the yacht bobbed on its mooring
as if she'd be able to see into the cabin and know whether
Tania had once again triumphed. But she kept her eyes
averted.

Finding this more difficult than she expected, she decided to go out. She slipped into an elegant outfit and
rang for a taxi to take her to the station and on to Exeter.
She returned with an armful of swatches and spent the
rest of the day frantically cross-matching patterns and
colours, slowly building up an art-board.

Cavan didn't return. Obviously, she thought sourly,
Tania was keeping him busy and he was expending some
of that boundless sexual energy. She found it hard to
sleep that night as well.

Five days had passed and still there was no sign of
Cavan. She had almost bitten Mawgan's head off in disappointment when he had telephoned, and she felt horrified and overwhelmingly guilty that she'd offended her
brother. She began to jump every time she heard an outboard engine. She found herself hovering by the windows
that looked out to sea. She kept falling asleep at odd
moments during the day, because she prowled around
at night playing loud music to block out the insistent
memories of Cavan's hands, his mouth, his voice . . .

She whirled when she heard the back door open, and
ran helter-skelter from the sitting-room into the kitchen.
'Oh. You,' she said rudely to Tania, filled with despair
that she'd hoped it was Cavan.

'You look terrible,' said Tania, inordinately pleased.

Bethany bridled, because she'd thought she was looking rather good. She'd dressed in a couture suit in a soft green, since she'd just returned from Truro that afternoon, having found a superb warehouse there which sold four-poster beds. 'You don't like my Valentino outfit?' she asked haughtily.

'I meant those bags under your eyes,' said Tania uncharitably. 'Where's Cavan?'

Bethany blinked. 'What? I don't know. I haven't seen him for... oh, I suppose it must be a few days now,' she said with nonchalance. She knew how long it had been— right down to the hour—but she wasn't intending to let Tania know that.

Tania frowned. 'You haven't?' she squawked. 'I was sure he was with you! I've not seen him all week! He always lets me know where he is in case there's an emergency. And I've got one. A gang of businessmen stranded... Are you *sure* you haven't got him tied up on the bed or something?' she asked suspiciously.

Bethany gave her a scathing look. 'Don't be ridiculous! What would I want to do that for?'

'I can't imagine you'd keep him here any other way.'

Coldly, Bethany stared at Tania. That was a declaration of war, if she ever heard one. 'Go and see if you don't believe me,' she snapped. And then she realised what Tania was saying and that the woman's face was frightened. Bethany's hands suddenly dropped lifelessly to her sides and she stared at Tania aghast. 'Wait a minute!' she cried in alarm. 'He left me on Sunday evening saying he was going off to the yacht. I heard the boat...' Her voice trailed away as she waited hopefully for Tania to confirm that he'd arrived safely that night.

Her hopes were quickly dashed. 'He never turned up,' quavered Tania. 'I waited up for him, too.'

'Oh, my God!' whispered Bethany. 'It was dark. He could have misjudged the tide——'

'Don't be silly,' scorned Tania. 'Cavan can handle any boat anywhere.'

'In that case,' said Bethany, her voice shaking, 'where is he?'

The two women looked at each other, wide-eyed. Bethany saw tears forming in Tania's eyes, and reached out a sympathetic hand. It was roughly shaken away.

'If anything's happened to him, it'll be your fault!' yelled Tania. 'I'm phoning the coastguard.'

Bethany reached the telephone first. 'Wait till I've tried all the numbers he left by the phone,' she frowned, trying to keep a clear head. 'He could be in a number of places. You know how unpredictable he is and how he does things on impulse. You can't call out the coastguard unless you're certain someone's lost at sea.'

She didn't add that after five days' delay it would be too late, anyway. Her heart was thudding and her fingers were so limp and trembling that she could hardly dial the numbers. She drew a blank at the first four. The last one, a number for central London, rang and rang. A lump formed in her throat. She'd have to ring the coastguard, the police... She tried desperately to stay in control and not think of the possibilities. The phone was still in her lowered hand when she noticed that the ringing tone had stopped. With a sharp gasp, she lifted the receiver to her ear.

'Mmm?'

'Cavan?' she squeaked in a high-pitched, disbelieving voice.

'Who the hell's that?' he growled.

'Oh, *Cavan*!' she cried in joyous relief, while Tania wiped away her tears and waited impatiently to know what was happening. 'Oh, I thought you might be drowned! Where have you been? Do you know what trouble you've caused? You said you were going back to the yacht, and Tania said you hadn't turned up and she hadn't seen you for ages, and when I said that I hadn't either——'

'Good grief, Bethany,' he interrupted in lazy amusement, 'you sound as if you've been waiting for me at home like an anxious wife. I hadn't realised I had to report my *every movement* to you. But since I do, here goes... I'm just getting out of bed,' he said, sounding suddenly very husky. 'I'm totally nude. I'm stretching. Now I'm——'

'Cavan!' she snapped, her pleasure rapidly vanishing. 'I don't give a damn what you've been up to or who you've been up to it with. I mean with whom... Oh, *hell*!' she yelled, at his deep laugh. 'You inconsiderate swine! Why don't you go back to bed and do your stretching with whoever you've been snuggling up to?'

'Grammar!' he reproved gleefully. 'You should have said, "With whomever you've been——"'

Bethany slammed the receiver down and glared at it.

'He's alive, I take it,' said Tania drily.

'Don't say anything,' she growled at Tania. 'Don't you dare utter a word.'

'My, my!' murmured Tania, taking no notice. 'Cavan said you still had one hell of a temper on you, and he was right. He sure sets you off, doesn't he? No wonder he grumbles about you so much.'

'I don't know what you're so pleased about,' snapped Bethany, furious with herself for being so childishly cross. 'Cavan's been making whoopee with some female in his London flat. I got him out of bed,' she said tightly. 'At four in the afternoon!' Tania's face fell, and she looked as if she was going to cry again. 'Oh, let's have some tea,' sighed Bethany, her sympathy getting the

better of her anger. She reached out and touched Tania's
arm. 'You really ought to know that no one will ever tie
Cavan down,' she said gently. 'He's the original free
spirit.'

Tania glared. 'I'm going to give myself a facial,' she
said grumpily. 'Ready for when he comes back. He's too
good to give up on.'

Sadly Bethany watched Tania go, and then lost herself
in work. By the time she heard Cavan calling from the
hall some five hours later, she had calmed down and was
in control of herself once more.

A beautiful bouquet of red roses was placed by her
colour-board. 'I thought this wasn't the moment for
parsley,' he murmured.

She pushed the roses out of her way and carried on
working. 'Put them in the bin,' she suggested coldly.

'I couldn't do that,' protested Cavan.

'Flowers won't make me like you. I don't want them.'

'You're not getting them,' he said mildly. 'They're for
Tania!'

Bethany clenched her teeth. She could have kicked
herself. Now she'd never know if he'd said that just to
be difficult! 'Don't interrupt me,' she said, looking as
busy as she could. 'I'm concentrating.'

Cavan poured himself a whisky and sat beside her,
watching her matching colours and discarding patterns.
'That's nice,' he remarked absently, reaching out for
Bethany's favourite material. It was Venetian and cost
a small fortune a metre, but she was determined to have
it for the main bedroom suite, and would economise
elsewhere.

She slapped his hand away. 'Don't move it,' she said
curtly. 'I'm seeing if the blue goes with it.'

'Try the champagne,' he suggested. 'Would you like
a ticket to the Longchamp races?'

The champagne brocade looked wonderful. 'What for? Did you say Longchamp?' She looked at him suspiciously and blinked in surprise. He was immaculately dressed in a dark business suit, but he looked as if he hadn't shaved for some time, the dark shadow on his jaw unnervingly sexy.

Apparently he'd seen her eyes on his jaw because his hand smoothed it ruefully. 'Sorry about the beard,' he said. He waved his feet at her. 'And the odd socks. I got dressed in a hurry. Longchamp is my next big "do". I have five hundred tickets for the flat race,' he explained. 'I've just done a Tina Turner concert in Hollywood——'

'Oh, yes?' She clipped the brocade to the Venetian sample and hunted for the right gimp to edge the chair she wanted to cover in the fabric.

'God, I'm jet-lagged!' he complained, kicking off his shoes. 'I shouldn't be drinking this.' He stared gloomily at the whisky. 'I'd hoped to get some sleep,' he scowled, 'but I was woken up by some hysterical woman ranting on.'

Bethany studied his face carefully. He did look tired, his whole body slumped, the vitality temporarily depleted. She realised he had probably been jetting around the world after all. 'You could have phoned,' she told him stiffly.

'I had the impression you didn't want to know where I was or what I was doing,' he said soberly.

'I didn't. Tania was worried. You ought surely to keep in touch with your secretary,' she mumbled.

'I'm training her up to handle crises on her own. If she always knew where I was, she'd turn to me for help. Besides, I loathe accounting for my whereabouts to women. I go where I have to, if I have to, when I have to.'

'We were only worried because the boat was gone. Naturally we thought you might have d-d-d...' She couldn't say it. A lump had come to her throat.

'Drowned? Died?' he suggested baldly. Bethany flinched at the physical pain inside her, and Cavan's voice gentled. 'When I left you last Sunday I met some of the fishermen in the bay,' he explained. 'They'd had a bad catch and had given up for the night. We all decided we were fed up and fancied painting Looe red, and we motored up the coast there. The Mackerel Club ran out of beer so we only managed a pink undercoat on the town before everyone went home.' He yawned and gave a rueful grunt. 'I was wide awake and in need of action——'

'You needn't go on,' Bethany said hastily, her imagination working overtime.

He passed a tired hand over his drained face. 'I don't always reach for a woman when I want entertaining,' he said in a soft rebuke. Bethany felt the heat flushing up to her face. It was the word *always* that infuriated her. 'I caught up on my work in London,' he explained wearily. 'Then I went on to Hollywood.'

She bit her lip. 'And I woke you. I'm sorry,' she said in a low voice.

Cavan let out a deep sigh. 'That's OK,' he mumbled, closing his eyes and stretching out his legs luxuriously. 'Oh, God! It's wonderful to be back home. It's all very well being a ticket baron, but Mr Fixit gets tired of rushing around the world ensuring that his clients are satisfied. Talking of satisfaction, that reminds me. Hang on. I'd better ring Tania.'

Bethany let her lashes hide her eyes. Cavan ruffled her hair and strode out. It was over half an hour before he came back, and she was half eaten by jealousy.

'Would you like something to eat?' she asked brightly, trying to make amends.

'My stomach isn't sure what time it is,' he groaned. 'I've crossed so many time zones I'm not even sure of the date. I have to go,' he said reluctantly. 'Tania wants me back.'

'Oh. Perhaps we can discuss my schemes tomorrow some time, when you've recovered,' she said stiffly.

'Mmm.' Cavan rocked on his feet.

She looked at him in alarm. 'I don't like you taking the boat out when you're so tired——'

'Oh, hell!' he frowned, passing a hand over his forehead. 'I forgot. I left the boat at Looe. Damn! I'm too tired to go hacking around borrowing one from a local. Tania will have to lump it. Do you mind if I crash out in the spare bedroom?'

'N-n-no. I'd better ring her, though, and let her know,' she said doubtfully.

'Do that. She's bothered about a client. Tell her she'll have to organise the tickets for the party of stranded businessmen herself. Alitalia owe me a favour, so she can use my name.' He swayed in the doorway.

'I'll fetch some blankets and pillows from the airing cupboard after I've rung Tania,' she said briskly.

Cavan plodded slowly up the stairs. Tania wasn't pleased, but Bethany just gave her the message and rang off in the midst of Tania's protest. Picking up an armful of blankets and topping the pile with a couple of pillows, she went to the spare bedroom.

A gentle smile lit her face. Cavan was face down on the bed, fast asleep, sprawled out as if he'd fallen there. Bethany quietly placed the bedding on the floor and went over to the bed, wondering whether she could remove his shoes without waking him. Gingerly she gripped the soft leather heel of one shoe and slid it off, then the other. Cavan stirred, rolling on to his back.

Bethany's heart somersaulted at his vulnerable, sleep-softened face. His lashes were thick and black, like smudgy crescents on his cheeks, the imperial nose jutting into the air above his slightly parted lips. One arm was flung over his head. His breathing was steady and deep, lifting his ribcage in a regular rhythm. In his sleep he frowned and moved his head as if his tie was constricting his throat.

How she loved him, she thought gently. Her fingers tenderly eased the knot of his silk tie, and she bent over, holding her breath as she attempted to push his top shirt button through the buttonhole. Her tongue slid between her lips in concentration.

'Bethany.'

Her lashes flicked upwards warily, but Cavan was muttering in his sleep. Probably having nightmares, she thought with a wry smile. And then she found herself lying on top of him, trapped by his arm, which he'd brought down over her, the soft skin of her cheek rasped by his beard.

'Cavan!' she whispered, wriggling.

'Mmm,' he grunted, smiling in his sleep and turning over on his side with her wrapped securely in his arms.

Bethany rolled her eyes to the ceiling, wondering what to do. She could wake him—again—but he looked so incredibly contented that she didn't have the heart to do that. She could stay there, or try to prise herself out inch by inch. She went for the latter. He held on to her like a limpet to a rock. It was like a scene in a farce or an old Doris Day movie. Whatever she did, he drew her back to him. If he hadn't been so obviously exhausted and sleeping the sleep of the dead, she would have been highly suspicious.

Exhausted after lack of sleep herself, and from struggling to get free from Cavan's possessive arms, she took a breather for a few minutes. And promptly fell fast asleep.

CHAPTER SIX

'WELL, this is nice,' murmured Cavan's voice in Bethany's ear.

Drowsily she registered that he was awake and his bristly chin was rubbing against her jaw. Struggling to consciousness, she drew away from his whispering breath, opening her eyes, which seemed to have been shut.

And discovered that the sun was streaming through the window and it was now morning.

'Oh, no!' she groaned in dismay.

'Do you always sleep with your tights on?' he asked with interest. 'No,' he husked, his voice betraying his pleasure, 'correct that. Stockings.'

'Cavan!' Bethany tried in vain to remove his inquisitive hand from her thigh. Her tight skirt had wriggled right up in the night, exposing the whole length of her long, shapely legs. 'Get your hands off me!' she gasped, wondering what she'd done with her shoes.

'Gorgeous,' he growled. 'I love stockings.' His hand admired them thoroughly while Bethany moaned and complained bitterly. 'Oh, those legs of yours!' he groaned. 'I don't think you ought to writhe around like that,' he breathed jerkily, his eyes heavy with need. 'I'm always *very* sensitive in the mornings.'

His hand slipped to the soft warmth of her thighs between her legs, and Bethany's eyes became huge. 'Please, Cavan!' she croaked.

'All in good time.' He smiled, his mouth drowsy with sleep and sensuality. 'Let me enjoy your body first,' he said huskily, his fingers creeping unnervingly upwards with a slow, inexorable movement.

Bethany jerked in alarm. 'I meant——!' She thought better of speech. Her voice was telling him that his touch was arousing her. Desperate to escape before she was seduced by him, Bethany made a sudden move and rolled off the bed on to the floor. She was on all fours, in the act of rising to her feet, when Cavan landed beside her.

'You're very resourceful,' he grinned, removing her discarded shoe from behind his ear.

'And you're very energetic for a man who's suffering from jet lag,' she retorted shakily, estimating the distance to the door.

He leaned back on one elbow, surveying her. 'I recover quickly. My stamina is legendary.'

She gulped. 'I fell asleep,' she said lamely.

'You seem a little confused,' he soothed.

'I think I'll go and get some breakfast,' she mumbled, half crouching.

'How long are you going to keep running away from me, Bethany?' he asked quietly.

'I'm not running away! I'm trying to avoid you,' she snapped back.

'Same thing,' he laughed. Cavan began to slide his jacket off, and Bethany sidled to the door warily. 'Run, Bethany,' he said in a low growl. 'Run as you always do. You won't confront problems head on, will you?' he taunted. 'You turn tail and take the easy way out.'

'I'm glad that you've accurately diagnosed yourself as a problem,' she said coldly, incensed that he should think she was a coward. 'And you can't claim that I'm running away if I'm staying here and working for you, despite the fact that I find you very irritating.'

'No,' he admitted, 'and you did curl up with me last night. Forgive me for asking, but I can't remember much after I drove down here from London. I can't even remember going up to bed. I hope I didn't miss anything. Did we do anything interesting?'

She looked at him scathingly. 'If we had, you'd know about it,' she said, tossing her head and stalking out to the sound of his rich chuckle.

Bethany went to her bedroom and had a long soak in the bath, ignoring the sounds and smells in the house that indicated Cavan had shaved, showered and dressed, and was now cooking breakfast again for them both. For a macho man, she mused, he was quite handy around the house. Too handy. He never lost an opportunity to touch her, awake or asleep.

As for running away... Her mouth firmed. That was one thing she wouldn't do again. Whatever he did, whatever he threw at her, she'd stick this out and finish the renovation, if only for her own pride's sake. And to see the hotel restored, of course, she thought warmly. She jerked herself out of her reverie and her eyes flashed. Cavan thought he was irresistible and that she'd end up as yet another of his conquests. She'd prove otherwise.

Over the next two weeks, neither of them had much time for anything apart from work. The arrangements seemed endless, but Bethany had a growing suspicion that Cavan was throwing himself into the work as a release for his sexual energies. She welcomed that, their relationship becoming brisk and efficient and utterly impersonal. Bethany the woman didn't seem to exist for him.

She heard his step on the path outside, her ears attuned to his movements. 'I'll put the kettle on,' she said, when he came into the kitchen. Coffee on arrival had become a ritual. Bethany frowned, thinking they had established several rituals together, almost as if they were man and wife.

'I met the postman outside,' said Cavan, waving a large envelope. 'Ah. The architect's plans,' he observed casually, dropping them on to the kitchen table.

Bethany pounced eagerly on them. 'He's taken his time,' she grumbled, examining them carefully. 'Now that's odd!' she declared. 'There isn't a reception area!'

'Er—no.' Cavan came to sit next to her, his face close to hers as he examined the drawings. He smelt fresh and was glowing from his morning shower and the short trip across the bay from his yacht. 'I overruled your instructions there. Too formal.'

'Hmm,' she said doubtfully, but not arguing the point—though the doorkeys had to go somewhere. 'Something else...'

'Y-e-s?' drawled Cavan cautiously.

She flicked him a quick glance. He seemed tense, and she wondered why he was so much on edge. 'I still think we could get more than four bedrooms on the first floor. The bridal suite doesn't really need two settees. Cavan!' she cried in exasperation. 'He's put in a jacuzzi! Was that your idea?'

'They'll get bored with the bed,' he argued. 'I thought we should offer them some alternatives. That's why there's a large area in front of the fire for one of those thick, deep-pile rugs so that——'

'I get the picture,' she said drily. 'You've gone over the top, though. You could put another bedroom in easily if you followed my suggestions. And where,' she queried, searching inside the large manila envelope, 'are the plans for the top floor?'

'Oh, dear. It looks as if he's forgotten them,' said Cavan innocently.

She studied him coolly. 'What are you planning up there?' she asked, her suspicions deepening. 'A brothel for jaded businessmen?'

'You have wonderful ideas,' he said fondly, gazing into her eyes. 'One would almost think you knew exactly how to please a man.'

'Some men are easy to work out. They like anything that satisfies their base lusts,' she retorted caustically. 'Don't try to distract me. I want to see those plans, Cavan. I need to know if you've changed any of the bedroom arrangements otherwise I can't plan the detailed schemes properly.'

'I can't tell you,' he said. 'You're not——'

'Softened up by a night in your arms?' she suggested coldly.

'Trust me——'

'You must be mad. I may be gullible sometimes but I'm not entirely off my head. Those plans had better arrive soon.'

'I'll get on to the architect about them. I can't think how he left them out. Look, let's forget them for the moment. I think I'd like you to concentrate on everything else and leave the top floor till you're sure you can do it up in the time. I'd rather have four bedrooms and all the downstairs ready for Christmas than nothing at all.'

He smiled at her winningly, and she gave him a broad, false smile back and surreptitiously moved her body further away. He had that light in his eyes again and she wasn't taking any risks.

'You're the boss,' she said stiffly.

His laugh sounded a little hollow to her as if it was forced. 'I'll get the plans faxed. Oh, before I forget, are you doing anything special today?' he asked, covering her hand with his.

By now, Bethany knew better than to tussle with him. So she let the hand stay there and gritted her teeth against

the way it stroked her skin gently, pretending his touch
did nothing to her.

'Depends what you mean by special. The landscape
gardeners are coming to begin the pool and level the
lawn, I have to keep an eye on the men building the
conservatory and I have that chap from the quarry
coming with samples of slate for the hall floor,' she said
with calm efficiency. 'Other than that, I'm not doing
much. Why?'

'I want to help set up the village hall for the harvest
festival,' he told her surprisingly. 'While I do that, would
you keep an eye out for a large vehicle delivering a medieval staircase and two carved stone fireplaces? I expect
you'll hear it bashing down the village street well in advance of its arrival. If it ever gets down,' he added. 'I
told them the width of the street, and they promised the
lorry would fit. Just.'

'It's not for us, I hope. I didn't order them,' Bethany
frowned.

'No. I did—from the architectural salvage people in
Bristol. Saw them last week. The staircase and smaller
fireplace will be perfect for the hall, and the larger fireplace is to go in the drawing-room. Log fires are very
welcoming, aren't they?'

Bethany gave him a sour look. 'You're going over my
head again,' she said said tightly. 'You probably haven't
measured to see if anything will fit, and I doubt what
you've bought will be in keeping. I've a good mind to
tell the driver to turn right around when he arrives.'

Cavan's finger touched her lips to silence her protests.
'Give the poor devil a cup of tea first, and have a peek
under the tarpaulins. If you don't like what you see the
staircase and fireplaces can go straight back,' he murmured. He leaned forwards and dropped a light kiss on

her mouth. 'That's for pouting,' he husked. 'I told you not to. Don't mind, do you?'

'Yes,' she said flatly. 'But that won't stop you from annoying me, so I might as well save my breath.' She wiped her mouth deliberately with her handkerchief and persisted with her objection. 'I wish you'd consulted me about the staircase. How much did it cost? A decent one fetches thousands. You'll never get your money back, you know.'

'Thousands? It could have fallen off the back of a lorry, or been stolen from a country house by my gangster friends,' he suggested.

'If I thought you were serious, I'd call the police to investigate,' she said shortly. 'But I know you're only winding me up. I don't want you throwing your money around like this,' she rebuked.

'Do you care if I go bankrupt?' he mocked.

'Not a lot. What does worry me is that you'll sell your half of the building when you discover you can't make any profit running this hotel.'

'Saved by the bell,' muttered Cavan, at the sound of the front door-chimes. 'Good grief! The lorry is early. Come and see.'

Bethany joined him outside, her eyes widening at the sight of the enormous delivery van. 'Where's it going to go?' she asked uncertainly. 'The stuff can't be brought in here and fitted until the slate floor is down——'

'I thought of that,' he said smugly. 'I've bought the disused seine sheds where they used to hang the pilchard nets. Brought a smile to Jory's face!' he grinned. 'Look, I think I'd better lend them a hand,' he said, hurrying to help the gang of men unload the sections of the staircase.

Ever ready with an answer, she thought sourly, running back to answer the telephone. She hastily arranged for the men to plumb in the new en-suite bathroom units, and then became embroiled in a discussion with the gardeners. It was almost two hours before Bethany was able to join Cavan and view the fireplace in all its glory. To her delight, it was a skilfully carved and highly polished oak masterpiece, and it was absolutely perfect for the hall because it would restore its manorial appearance immediately.

'Oh, Cavan!' she breathed, standing in the big doorway of the seine shed. 'It's incredibly beautiful!'

'I'm glad you like it,' he said in pleasure. 'I took a gamble that you would. You wanted a fire in the hall, and now you've got one. There's some panelling to go with it. Linenfold. Yes, it cost me a year's income,' he said impatiently. 'But I had to have it. You must admit it will look fantastic.'

He hugged her in evident glee, and Bethany couldn't help but agree. She wanted to dance about in excitement too. 'I can't wait to see it in place,' she said breathlessly, turning shining eyes on Cavan. 'You're idiotic and impulsive, wildly extravagant and quite crazy, but I love——'

'Me?' he asked, a mocking gleam in his eyes. He sighed when she flinched, but her face immediately lit up again when she looked back at the staircase in all its beauty. 'Bethany...will you do something for me in return?' He chuckled at her wary glance. 'Nothing illegal or immoral!' he grinned. 'Come with me to the harvest festival tonight. I think you ought to start integrating with the villagers a bit. They'll wonder why you avoid them.'

'Tell them it's because I can't bring myself to pretend I'm your girlfriend,' she said lightly. Pretending would be too hard.

'You must make bonds with them,' he insisted. 'Come with me. I can't do much in a crowd of people, can I?'

'No. I don't want to do anything social with you. You'll only use the opportunity to paw me.'

Surprised at the way he flinched, Bethany drew away from him and wandered over to the fireplaces, tracing the stonework carving with her hands. Cavan had remarkable taste—and a bottomless pocket, it seemed. Portallen was being returned to its former glory, and she was part of that transformation. It gave her a happy glow.

'Your old friends will be there,' he coaxed. 'I think you should show your face and let everyone get used to the fact that you'll be here for a while. I can help you, Bethany. Stick with me and I'll get them on your side again. But you have to break the ice. Why not do it under my protection?'

'I don't know.' She hesitated. 'You'll make the most of our supposed relationship and I'll be unable to relax all evening.'

'Until they accept you, you won't be able to ditch me,' he reasoned. 'You're only delaying that. If I didn't know you better,' he murmured, 'I'd think you were keeping up the pretence of our close relationship deliberately, because you rather like the idea of being my girlfriend.'

'Now that is silly,' she said, slight breathlessness in her voice. She cleared her throat. He was right; it would be a good opportunity for her to make a start on establishing her friendships again. She had missed chatting to the people she'd grown up with. 'All right,' she agreed quietly, feeling slightly nervous already. But she'd vowed not to run away from anything—other than Cavan's grabbing hands. 'For my own sake I'll come.'

'Good. I really must go and help them up at the hall. Before I do, there's one thing I ought to warn you about,' said Cavan casually, covering up the staircase and the fireplaces with tarpaulins. 'If anyone asks what's going on down here, just remember that, for the present, we're getting rid of the chrome and glass decoration. It's true, of course. Just don't mention anything about turning Portallen into an exclusive hotel. There could be opposition to that.'

'Are you telling me that they don't know you're upgrading the Inn—and it would be an unpopular move?' Bethany's eyes narrowed.

'Well, there are all kinds of rumours as usual, of course,' he said dismissively. 'Though I get the feeling that everyone would like to see the place restored.'

'They won't be very comfortable drinking in a smart bar,' she said doubtfully. 'Fishy jumpers and sea boots don't exactly look right in exclusive hotels. I'm not sure you're doing the right thing.'

'It's right, surely, to bring the building back to manor-house status. And keep this under your hat, but a local brewery is intending to make an offer on Smugglers' Cottage. It's rambling enough for an atmospheric local, and has been derelict for years. I've suggested a suitable landlord, too. So play it cagey.'

'You've got it all worked out, haven't you? Now tell me why it has to be such a secret,' she said sharply, sensing a fiddle. Perhaps this was why he hadn't let her see all the plans and why he'd been shifty about one or two other points. Like the fact he was looking for one long manorial table instead of a series of smaller ones for the restaurant. They'd argued about that for a long time. 'Is this something to do with income tax?'

'Nothing at all,' he assured her. 'It's merely that I never reveal all my plans to anyone. Natural caution.'

'Well...won't the villagers know what's going on? Won't they have seen the request for planning permission in the local papers anyway?'

'Oh, I doubt it,' he said with a disarming smile. 'The truth is that I don't want gossip. You know villagers. Their mouths are as wide as an open-cast mine.'

'I, of all people, know that. You're working some racket,' she accused, her voice hard. 'What is it, Cavan? I demand to know!'

'We have to keep this quiet till I can fix things with the planning department,' he explained with a huge wink. 'They turned me down flat last time I applied.'

She stared, appalled. '*What*?' she cried. 'Are you saying I could do all this work and the whole thing will fall through because you haven't got planning permission yet?'

He strolled to the door, his hands comfortably in his pockets. 'Oh, no,' he said cheerfully. 'I said I'll fix it. Throw around a few free tickets for——'

Her face was a picture. 'You can't!' she cried in horror. 'This isn't that kind of place! What you're suggesting is bribery and corruption!'

'Yes,' he agreed amiably. 'Do you want Portallen done up or not?' He slid quickly out of the door.

For a moment Bethany was rooted to the spot in disbelief. Then, collecting herself together, she ran out, but he had disappeared. Bethany leaned against the seine-house wall, aware that he must have begun to run the moment he stepped outside so that she wouldn't catch up with him. But she'd tackle him that night.

She was furious with him. She didn't want to be involved in anything underhand. Cavan might resort to backhanders as a matter of course, but she could only work for him if everything was above board. All that they'd worked for could be in jeopardy. If Cavan didn't get permission, the Planning Department could legally request that the hotel be restored to its original condition—glass, chrome, open-plan rooms and so on. And that she couldn't bear.

The rest of the day flew by. Bethany had only a brief time to eat and tidy up before she heard Cavan arriving, and she wasn't even half ready.

'Bethany? Leaving in five minutes!' he called up to her.

'Then you'll go alone!' she yelled back, and was disconcerted by the laughter which greeted her reply. It sounded as if he'd brought reinforcements, she thought, hearing the sound of voices and the chink of glasses. Irritably she realised she'd have to wait a little longer to tackle him about the intended bribery of the Planning Department.

In her soft apricot shirt and easy skirt, she ran down the stairs some minutes later. Cavan was in the midst of a crowd of villagers—most of them their old schoolfriends. A momentary frown of annoyance creased her forehead and then she walked forwards with a smile of greeting on her face to hide her nervousness. She gave Cavan a look which indicated that she'd get him later, and he grinned wickedly.

'Here she is!' he said, stating the obvious. 'You look wonderful, Bethany. My favourite outfit.'

He'd never seen it before, she was thinking, and then she was being pressed against his clean white shirt front in a breath-taking hug. She looked up at him with mockery in her eyes. 'Full marks for opportunism,' she said drily.

His kiss took her unawares, and he seemed equally surprised that she didn't push him away. Unwilling to miss his chance, apparently, Cavan became more deeply engrossed in the kiss till a few awkward coughs from the onlookers reminded them both where they were and she emerged dishevelled and confused. Cavan looked triumphant.

'Darling!' He put his arm affectionately around her shoulders, his fingers biting in when she tried to ease herself away from his distracting nearness.

'I reckon we'd better wish you luck,' said Jack Hoskin, his voice lifting at the end of every sentence in the Cornish way. 'You'll need it.' He raised his glass to Cavan, rather obviously excluding Bethany.

'Your happiness, Cavan. Cheers!' All were holding up their glasses now. Except a scowling Tania in the background.

Bethany wondered if she'd wandered into the wrong room.

'They know, darling,' said Cavan with a ruefully apologetic smile.

'Know what, darling?' she asked sweetly, her lashes fluttering ridiculously. He wanted an act, he'd get it, she thought grimly.

He chuckled and bent on the pretext of kissing her ear. Instead he whispered into it. 'I'm afraid they think we're engaged. Can't think how. Don't disillusion them. Play up to it. Darling. Jilt me later.'

She gasped with shock, and there were some sniggers.

'Keep your lewd mutterings for tonight, Cavan!' said Jack. 'You're embarrassing the women here. Hope you've thought hard about this,' he added, looking doubtfully at Bethany as if he disapproved heartily.

'Oh, I have,' smiled Cavan. 'You know I love a challenge. Never happier when there's a rogue fish to land, a bucking yacht without a keel to bring under control, perhaps a wayward animal to master——'

'You're taking advantage of the situation,' muttered Bethany, infuriated by the sly comparisons.

'Later, darling,' he promised her huskily in a stage whisper, as if she'd been murmuring sweet nothings in his ear. He chuckled indulgently and raised his voice so everyone could hear his words. 'We're going to have to get married soon, by the looks of it, or the first of our kids will be illegitimate! It'll be nice to have a Trevelyan family in Portallen again, won't it, darling?'

Bethany felt faint. The cruelty of the situation was hurting her terribly, making her stomach churn. She smiled around brightly, and only Cavan's steadying arm, now firmly around her waist, kept her from crumpling to the floor. That and perhaps the red mist of fury which was sustaining her.

'Children?' she croaked, uncomfortable beneath the faintly hostile stares.

'Our kids,' said Cavan huskily, making Bethany splutter. He patted her heartily on the back. 'Gently, darling,' he said in concern. 'We must watch that cough of yours. I'll give you a Vick rub later.'

'You—you——!'

His fingers squeezed the muscle in her shoulder, relieving her of speech. 'I think it's the plaster dust,' he explained. 'Things are a bit chaotic. There's so much to do in the house.'

'Tell us all about it while we walk up to the hall,' said Jack curiously. 'We're all interested in knowing what you're going to do. Will you change much?'

'Well, there'll have to be a playroom, kids' bedrooms and a nanny's room on the top floor if we're to accommodate our family,' grinned Cavan, propelling the pole-axed Bethany to the door.

'Won't have much room for guests,' mused Jack.

Cavan shrugged. 'The first floor is huge,' he said innocently.

Bethany's mouth had opened in amazement at his quick mind, and she was reluctantly impressed by his brilliant improvisation. He was definitely inspirational at thinking on his feet, and it was an ability she must watch. However, by the time she'd finished with him that night, she thought grimly, he wouldn't be standing on his feet at all. In fact, he wouldn't even know which way up he was.

'Our plans for having children are a very long time in the future. I have no intention of giving up work,' she began.

'That's why we're having an office behind the drawing-room, with two desks facing one another so we can spend the day together,' said Cavan, smiling down on her.

'Isn't that heavenly?' she cried, with saccharine insincerity. His smile broadened at her simpering look. She'd decided that something as twee as two facing desks deserved a suitably vapid response. 'You rat!' she whispered.

'Shark,' he reminded her softly, then spoke to Jack. 'We'll have computer links with my offices around the world, of course. Good, eh? We have our cake and eat it. Portallen, a stimulating business life and...' He gave a husky growl, making everyone laugh, and his sharp white teeth flashed in amusement.

'I'm taking up shark fishing,' Bethany said tartly, flashing her teeth back at him.

'I'll make sure you catch one,' he murmured.

Jack nodded, his manner to Bethany thawing a little. 'Take him up on that, girl,' he urged. 'Cavan's not a bad fisherman for a foreigner.' His voice grew warm. 'And I have to say this; no Portallen fisherman who sets out to sea will ever forget your generosity, nor will his family.'

'Is this something I've missed?' asked Bethany curiously, when she caught Cavan making frantic signals at Jack.

'Dammit, Jack——' he protested.

'You're getting no apologies. It's about time the secret was out of the bag, me 'andsome!' Jack stopped Bethany and pointed to the new coastguard hut. 'There's been a few changes here since you left. First, couple of years back, we had an anonymous donation to buy an Inshore Lifeboat,' he explained.

Bethany stiffened warily, knowing he was referring to her own contribution, and wondering if Cavan had claimed that he'd made the donation. 'Jack, perhaps if you know something about that, you ought to keep it quiet,' she said with a frown.

'I don't hold with that,' said Jack stolidly. 'Not with secrets. Tania's Dad got saved from certain drowning off The Ranneys because the lifeboat was right on hand. She'd have liked to thank whoever donated it, wouldn't you, Tan?'

'Yes. I would.' Tania's face was gentle, and Bethany remembered how much she idolised her father.

It was wonderful, Bethany mused, that her compensation money had been of real use. She felt a warm glow through her body. 'I didn't know, Tania,' she said, putting a hand on her old friend's arm. 'I'm very glad he was saved. I was fond of your father.'

Tania frowned and moved away, to Bethany's disappointment. She had hoped that she could start to mend their relationship.

'Anyway, there's more,' continued Jack. 'Cavan heard the breakwater had been destroyed by the gale, and he paid for it to be rebuilt. After that, the government closed the coastguard down——'

'Closed?' Bethany's eyes rounded. 'But it's still there, modernised and——'

'That was Cavan,' said Jack proudly. 'You got a gem there. You'd better deserve him or you'll have the village to answer to. He got it done privately and I was the only one who knew. Proper job, new building and equipment, monthly salary for someone to man the station,' he revealed while Cavan shifted impatiently. 'I got the job. I'd been out of work for a year. Cavan can't do no wrong, far as I'm concerned, and sooner the village knows the whole truth the better, to my mind.'

'I'm stunned,' said Bethany honestly, and so, it seemed, was everyone else. They began to chatter and show their appreciation of Cavan's generous gesture. She began to smile ruefully to herself. Cavan had used his money for the public good...or... Her mind raced and she reluctantly considered the alternative. Was it a carefully calculated backhander from him to ensure that no one in the village raised any objection to his development of the Inn?

'I can see your brain working,' murmured Cavan.

'I hope you're suitably worried, then,' she said sweetly, 'I'm planning something spectacular for you as a reward for being so smart.' She drew away from his grasp and walked to the village hall on her own while the others crowded around Cavan to discuss Jack's revelation.

Standing in the old hall, which looked smaller than it used to, she felt a warm glow purely because she was beside Cavan. The friendship and welcome shown to him rubbed off on her, and she enjoyed the harvest festival more than any she could remember. The hall was a glorious sight, filled with banks of vegetables, bread baked in the shape of wheatsheaves, home-made preserves and armfuls of country flowers.

After the simple service, and with the rafters still ringing with the vigorous sound of the fishermen's choir and their rendering of 'Harvest Home', Bethany left on Cavan's arm, a lucky corn dolly for the Inn held tightly in one hand. Smiling faces beamed in his direction, men slapped him on the back. Word had got around about his generosity. It worried her that he was so popular. If she jilted him now, everyone would take his side. Cavan was more admired than ever. It would be impossible to leave him without earning the undying hatred of everyone in Portallen. She'd have to wait till the euphoria died down a little, or she'd never succeed in breaking down the barriers.

'How about a nightcap?' Cavan called to everyone in earshot.

Bethany was deafened by the enthusiastic response. 'Aren't you overdoing the generous Mine Host bit?' she muttered to him. She was finding it quite a strain, coping with his affectionate glances, and the thought of a few more hours of being caressed by his hands, his eyes, his voice, was too unnerving to contemplate.

'Careful, Bethany. You're supposed to adore me.'

'Oh, is that it? You want to show everyone how deeply affectionate we are! If you think——'

'Smile. Don't turn nasty on me in front of all these people, or you'll find it hell to work here for the next few months.' His ruthless eyes met hers mockingly as they set off down the cobbled street.

She took a deep breath. 'I think I know this scenario. This is where I plaster myself all over you and make goo-goo eyes at you, is it?' she asked through her inane smile.

'Please yourself,' he said amiably, helping her to keep her balance on the big, uneven cobbles. 'Me, I'm going to milk this situation for all I'm worth.'

'Since you're worth nothing, you won't get much out of it, then,' she retorted sourly.

'Let's see, shall we?' he retorted smugly. In the darkness of the street, he bent his head and kissed her, his eyes dancing wickedly as she glared at him and kept her mouth hard beneath his forceful lips. 'Respond, damn you!' he muttered.

'I won't——' Too late, she realised he'd intended her to speak. It meant he could slide his tongue into her mouth, and she was having to steel all her nerves against the erotic sensation as he explored her mouth with a slow, lingering pleasure.

'Fair,' he said, lifting his head, with the others now tactfully far ahead of them. 'But I'll have to give you plenty of lessons. You hardly aroused me at all.'

'That was my intention, you swine!' she whispered.

'Oh, dear. You do keep getting your animals muddled up,' he said fondly, releasing her but keeping a firm grip on her wrist.

'Roll on Christmas,' she grated furiously when he hurried her down the street to catch up the others.

'Nights before a roaring fire, opening Christmas stockings, wearing paper hats and pulling crackers?' he hazarded.

Her lips compressed at the brief stab of knife-blades in her heart at the cosy scene. 'Yes,' she said grimly. 'With me in Bodmin and you somewhere—anywhere—else.'

'You'll get your wish,' he said quietly. 'I'm going to Brittany tomorrow, then Paris, then Hawaii.' He assessed her reaction with calculating eyes.

For a few seconds, her overwhelming disappointment showed, and then she had covered it up with a bright smile, quite perplexed by the sadness that had descended on her. She didn't want him to go. The place would be like a ghost village without him.

'How long for?' she faltered.

'Want me back quickly?' he asked huskily.

Bethany flushed. Yes, she said fervently to herself. 'No!'

'You don't sound too sure.'

'I am, I am,' she answered irritably, incapable of preventing her mouth from drooping and betraying her innermost longings.

Amusement softened his cynical features and his eyes laughed openly at her. 'I think we'll turn this into a night to remember,' he murmured. 'Tania!'

Tania sullenly turned around to look at Cavan, the big gold buttons on her scarlet blouse glinting under the streetlamp. 'What?'

'Party?' smiled Cavan engagingly.

Tania lit up and she ran to Cavan, taking his arm. 'Party, everyone!' she called to the others.

With whoops of delight, they all poured into the bar, keeping Jack and Cavan constantly busy serving drinks 'on the house'. Towards Bethany there was a strained politeness. No one really trusted her, and they didn't seem ready yet to abandon their long-held beliefs that she was 'fast' and definitely undesirable to have around. She felt very much the outsider, and remembered wryly that once Cavan had been an outsider. Now she knew how he'd felt, thrown into the deep end, introduced to a new family, new surroundings, a new way of life.

He'd coped. So would she. Bethany smiled at one of her old schoolfriends and received a faint smile in return. She could have hugged the girl for giving her hope. It might take her a while, but she'd eventually get accepted again—of that she was certain.

'We're dancing.'

Bethany looked up at hearing Cavan's arrogant order, and saw the warning light in his eyes. Chairs were being pushed back and a romantic ballad was being relayed from the music-centre behind the bar. She shrugged, knowing she couldn't avoid close contact with him, and slid into Cavan's encircling arms. No—melted into them, she thought hazily, bemused by the music and warm glow of happiness which kept surfacing.

Perhaps it was because he was gazing down at her so lovingly in his award-winning act of a man infatuated with his fiancée. Or because he was leaving soon and she wanted to make the most of this evening. Perhaps it was because his personal approval was easing the hostility she'd come to expect and it was a joy to feel the first few grudging acknowledgements that she existed and wasn't a two-headed monster.

'Our engagement is having some results.'

'What?' she asked Cavan, a little disconcerted. She'd been thinking how lovely it was to be held securely by him.

He chuckled deeply, the sound resonant in her own body. 'You're not getting such wary glances from the women, now they think you're tied up with me. I suppose they imagine you've got your hands full and won't play around with their men. Let's convince them a little more, hmm?'

Silent in his embrace, Bethany allowed him to draw her close and hold her against his heart. Her body shaped to his as if it had been formed especially for him. Cavan growled in his throat but he did nothing more than hold her and let their bodies sway to the rhythm. It was enough for Bethany. More than enough.

Someone turned the lights down. In the semi-darkness, she found herself wishing the pretence could go on for a long time. It meant she could touch and be touched

without Cavan's cynical smile of triumph coming between them.

'Beth,' he murmured.

She quivered. He had adjusted his body imperceptibly
and his hand had clamped on her lower back and pushed
her hips hard towards him. Until then she hadn't known
she'd been keeping a distance between her hips and his.
Now she did. Her face flamed when she felt the hardness
of his arousal against her.

'I want to sit this one out,' she breathed, the cruel,
spiralling need hurtling through her body with a ruthless
and dizzying speed.

His wicked eyebrow lifted in amusement. 'You can't
leave me on the dance-floor in this state,' he said in a
deep growl. His lips nuzzled her earlobe. 'They'll wonder
what you've been promising me.'

He thought of nothing but sexual pleasure. With an
effort she kept her temper and her head. He was building
up a huge backlog of situations which needed a suitable
vengeance, she thought angrily. 'You're not doing this
for me at all, are you?' she said miserably. 'You're
hoping I'll enjoy being your girlfriend so much that I'll
let you whisk me off to your bed.'

'That's very true,' he admitted huskily. His hand slid
to rub gently at the nape of her neck. 'I can hardly deny
what you're doing to me, Bethany.'

'To what extent have you set all this up?' she asked,
hoping she sounded indulgent. To put him off the scent,
she arched more firmly against him, and was rewarded
by his shuddering gasp. So she did have some power over
him, then, she thought in wonder.

'Oh, Beth, I want you!' he whispered. 'I have to have
you!'

His mouth descended to hers, bruising in its predatory
hunger. She let her hands twine around his neck, gripping

his hair tightly as he savaged her mouth. For a few seconds she responded, yielding to the unbearable urge to surrender. And then she pulled back.

'People,' she mumbled, running her tongue over her swollen mouth. 'Too public... Cavan, you arranged everything to get me here, to bring me to this moment, didn't you?' she asked again, her heart thudding as she waited for his answer.

'I must confess I did,' he said in a low tone.

Bethany barely managed not to tear him limb from limb. 'How far back?' she asked huskily, stroking the back of his neck.

'When I started putting the pressure on Mawgan. Almost everything that came after that was planned. I wanted you so much,' he said helplessly.

Want, she thought bleakly. She was only an ache in his body, that unfulfilled conquest, an unmastered woman. The fish that got away. She clenched her jaw. She was planning her own arrangements for his come-uppance. And it would mean sailing so close to the wind that she might end up drowning. She'd hit him in his vanity.

'I'm impressed,' she said softly, her hand stroking his big chest.

'You're not going to hurl abuse at me?' he asked shakily, his voice very husky.

She slid her hand beneath his jacket, caressing his body. Cavan's breath sounded heavy and uneven in her ear. She might not be able to reach him any other way, but she could reach him through his overweening ego, she thought resentfully.

'It's rather a compliment,' she sighed, laying her cheek against his. His heartbeat juddered unevenly, matching hers, and she fought for control, knowing she had to stay clear-headed.

'I had to do something to get you,' he smiled.

She shook with rage and turned it into a sensual wriggle. It electrified Cavan. His hands were everywhere in the half-darkness, the drugging rhythm of his surreptitious fingers crawling inexorably to her breast, softly throbbing beneath the fabric of her shirt.

He took her face between his hands, kissing her forehead, her nose and her lips so tenderly that she wanted inexplicably to cry. Her eyes darkened and she felt a crazed wanting surge up inside her to threaten her composure.

She told herself severely that he'd set her up—and Mawgan. The relentless pressure on her brother, getting her back to Portallen, wheedling his way into the villagers' good books, blackmailing her to stay by using her old home as a lure, and 'accidentally' ensuring that people thought they were engaged.

All because he had to have her. He was unswerving in his pursuit. Consumed with lechery. Pitiless in his drive to be the boss. He'd sworn to 'have her' as if she were some prize to be wrenched from a trophy stand. She took a deep breath. He didn't even consider that he might hurt her in the process.

'You want me?' she husked.

'You know I do.'

There was something savage about his answer, and Bethany felt afraid. Her eyes widened as she became alert to what she was intending to do; to lead him on and then—at the crucial moment—reject him. Her hand explored the muscles of his chest. Forcing a small, flirtatious smile, she allowed her fingers to drift to his biceps. His latent strength daunted her.

In a blinding flash she realised that she'd been kidding herself. Even if she did manage to withstand his remorseless seduction, he'd never let her escape. There was a tension in his body which was almost menacing, a barely controlled violence that would erupt and engulf her if she attempted to thwart him. Cavan wasn't a boy to be turned down. He was a grown man who always got what he wanted.

And he looked as sure as hell that he'd get it tonight.

Bethany was terrified at what she'd done. She couldn't go through with it. Cavan held her close, and they barely moved to the music, swaying dreamily like some of the other loving couples to the sensual music. But her mind was whirling as she attempted to find a way out.

She could faint—but why? She could have a row with him, but people would probably side with him, not her. What it needed was a public and overwhelmingly powerful reason for her to be angry with him. But what? She needed time and space and peace to think, without Cavan's distracting presence. She must extricate herself from Cavan's trap before she was emotionally destroyed.

'Cavan,' she husked, 'I need to powder my nose.'

'You're not running away, are you?' he asked quietly.

'No. I swear on my honour that I'll be back in a few moments,' she said shakily.

'Darling. You're as keyed up as I am,' he murmured, letting his finger trace her soft, trembling mouth. She gasped, and he pushed her away. 'Go, but hurry back,' he said hoarsely. 'I'll see if I can persuade these people here that they're all playing gooseberry.'

'Cavan!' came Tania's sharp voice. 'I need to speak to you!'

Bethany paused, wondering why Tania looked so white, and sensing that her old friend was on the edge of her temper.

'Not here,' said Cavan curtly, 'and not now.'

'Yes, now!' hissed Tania. 'I won't stand by and see you make a fool of yourself. Are you blind? Don't you see what's in front of your eyes?' Her hands ran lightly down her soft blouse, almost as if by accident, drawing Cavan's attention to her generous breasts.

Distressed, Bethany realised that Tania had not given up her ambition to hook Cavan. He stood stock still, sweeping Tania with a slow look. Bethany saw how she bloomed beneath his glance, her lips pouting seductively, her breath shortening so that her chest heaved and strained the large gold buttons fastening the lacy blouse.

'Tania,' he began, his eyes apparently reluctant to leave Tania's sexy body. She wriggled seductively, and Cavan obviously was incapable of resisting the invitation. 'OK,' he said, capitulating with unseemly haste. 'Now. Outside. Five minutes. Bethany——'

'I think I'll turn in now,' she cut in in a chilly voice. 'Say goodnight to everyone for me. Goodnight, Cavan.' Quickly, before he realised what she was doing, she leaned forwards and pecked him on the cheek, moving hastily out of his reach again.

'Is that it?' he asked quietly. 'A cool goodnight? Will your bedroom door be locked against me?'

She reeled at his nerve. 'Definitely,' she answered, her eyes blank.

'I'm not waiting, Bethany,' he frowned. 'Not any longer. I've done all the waiting I intend to do.'

Grimly he took Tania's arm and pushed her outside, leaving Bethany with all the wind taken out of her sails. There was a terrible sick feeling in her stomach. By rejecting him, she'd driven him directly into Tania's willing arms. He was a passionate male with basic needs who'd hoped for an end to the physical hunger he'd been unwillingly suffering. He'd had enough of the starvation diet—he needed sex, now, tonight. And if Bethany wasn't going to provide that, he was determined to let her know that there were plenty of women who would. Tania happened to be around.

Five minutes. Bethany knew he'd be making his pitch, flirting, propositioning, perhaps kissing Tania. He had every right to, of course. He was fancy-free, since their engagement was a farce. She winced at the thought.

Instead of going straight upstairs as she'd planned, Bethany stayed on the fringe of the party, miserably sipping a drink at the bar. She dared not admit that she was waiting for Cavan to return—and that she half dreaded how he might look. Satisfied? Smug? Dishevelled . . . ?

For the tenth time she checked her watch. They'd been gone for twenty minutes, and suddenly she could take her self-torture no longer. She slipped up the stairs, her legs trembling, and sat down on the bed. She'd known the kind of man he was. This should have come as no surprise. Yet being confronted so cruelly with the truth was still a shock. Somewhere inside she'd believed Cavan to be decent and sincere, to have more depth and tenderness than any man she'd ever met. It was a devastating blow to discover that she'd been wrong.

Bethany groaned. She got up and went over to the window, opening it to take a deep breath of air before she went downstairs again. There was a knock on the door.

'It's locked!' she yelled.

'It's me!' called Tania. 'Someone on the phone for you. Cavan's phone, in the car.'

'Oh!' Bethany jumped up. 'Who would—is it Mawgan?' As she opened the door, she heard the sound of feet on the stairs and caught a brief glimpse of Tania disappearing into the bar again.

With a puzzled frown, Bethany ran down to the car and flung open the driver's door, leaning in to reach for the handset. When she picked it up, however, the caller had rung off. Disconsolately she replaced the receiver and, as she did so, her hand came to rest briefly on something hard on the driver's seat. Her fingers closed around the object and she knew immediately what it was.

The whole of her body stilled down as if it had been chilled in ice. Slowly her fingers uncurled to reveal one of the gold buttons from Tania's blouse. Attached to the button was a piece of material as if it had been... Her eyes glazed. As if it had been impatiently ripped off by someone in a hurry. At that moment, as if to underline more thoroughly what had happened, Bethany became aware of a lingering perfume filling the inside of the car. Tania's perfume.

Her head lifted and she stared unseeingly into space. Cavan had gone further than she'd thought, faster than she'd imagined. She'd wanted a reason to jilt him in public; now she had it. And she wished she hadn't.

CHAPTER SEVEN

BETHANY felt as if someone had thrust her into an icebox, she was so cold, frozen into immobility. Then something snapped in her brain and she ran to the jetty, flinging the button away from her into the sea as if it burnt a hole in her hand. Stumbling across the courtyard, she rushed blindly, hysterically into the bar.

Everyone looked up in surprise when the door slammed open and Bethany stood, dishevelled and scarlet-faced, her enormous eyes accusing Cavan. The faces became a blur, the whispers fell to silence. The focus of her whole attention was on his cheating eyes.

She took a deep, shuddering breath. 'You—you—*bastard*!' she croaked. 'You lying, cheating, two-timing——'

His eyes pierced into her. 'What——? What are you playing at, Bethany?' he growled menacingly, tensing his body for a fight.

'Evidence!' she cried miserably. 'Of your deceit, your lies! Oh, Cavan! How could you? I thought——' She broke off, unable to continue, only dimly aware of the muttering around her. They faced one another, a white line around Cavan's mouth and hot ice in his eyes. Whereas she was distraught, as any woman who had found firm evidence of someone else in the life of the man she loved would be. She looked around for Tania. She wasn't there.

'What evidence?' he asked flatly. 'What are you trying to do, Bethany? You're making it up——'

'No!' she cried wildly. 'Do you think I'd be reacting like this if I were?'

'God! You might,' he answered, so low that she could hardly hear him, 'if you were trying to find an excuse to jilt me.'

Her face was pale, the trembling of her lips and hands the only visible signs of movement about her. Ironically, she knew that if she had tried to deceive him she would have failed. Cavan was so sharp-witted that any false, invented accusation would have been laughed away. But he could see—*anyone* could see—that she was not acting, that she was genuinely shocked.

Why, she didn't know. She'd been aware of Tania from the start. It was seeing something tangible of his promiscuity that upset her. 'Oh, Cavan,' she said brokenly, letting all her sadness spill out, 'you've hurt me. I thought—I—oh-h!' She burst into tears.

'Hold it!' roared Cavan, his eyes blazing in his white face. 'Get out, everyone,' he said through his teeth, trying to control himself. 'I want to be alone with Bethany.'

'Don't leave me!' she pleaded to the group.

'As God is my witness,' snarled Cavan, 'if you won't leave I'll make you, one by one!'

'Now look here, boy——' began Jack.

'Don't "boy" me!' growled Cavan. 'Bethany has staged this. I don't know how and I don't know why. One of her jokes, probably. But you all know what there is between us, and you damn well owe it to us both to let me sort it out.'

Bethany grabbed hold of a chair and dragged it to her, sitting down, her legs giving way. Embarrassed, people began to leave, a deadly silence over the room. All she could think of was that Cavan had been making love to a woman in his car as if he were an adolescent boy who couldn't wait till a more discreet time and place presented itself. The last person left, and she was alone with Cavan.

She put her head in her hands and then found herself jerked to her feet. Her eyes lifted up to meet Cavan's in fear. She could smell the blistering anger pouring from him. His eyes were as cold and hard as hot sapphires, the hostility leaping between them.

'What is this evidence?' he asked, his face savage.

Her vocal chords wouldn't work. She croaked something, and he shook her impatiently. 'S-something belonging to another woman that I found on the s-s-seat of your car,' she pushed out through parched lips.

His mouth tightened. He swept her up bodily into his rough arms, a savage expression on his face, and began to stride to the stairs, anger carrying him forwards while she struggled ineffectually, almost incapable of breathing because of the way he was ruthlessly imprisoning her in his hard, unyielding, unloving arms.

'No, you didn't, Bethany. I'm going to get the truth out of you,' he threatened grimly, 'if I have to shake every syllable out of those lying lips.'

Frantically Bethany wriggled in his grip. 'You won't hurt me,' she rasped, trying to convince herself.

'Won't I?'

Her apprehensive eyes saw the sharpening of the bones of his face. Cavan was ferociously angry. Panic robbed her of the ability to move, to plead for sense to prevail, to beg him to stop and listen to her explanation. He carried her to her bedroom and hurled her on to the bed. This was a Cavan she had never seen, had always suspected lay beneath the surface, but had subconsciously dreaded knowing. A man whose only intention was revenge for the public shattering of his pride.

'I...' Desperately she sought to lubricate her arid throat, her lips shaping words which never emerged.

'You bitch,' he said in a soft, harsh growl. 'How dare
you try to destroy my reputation? I suppose this was the
spectacular reward you'd been planning for me. You even
warned me it was coming. You thought that making some
false accusation would let you off the hook, didn't you?'
he breathed. 'If I wasn't so damn sure that I haven't
made love to a woman in that *particular* car,' he said
with an emphasis that made her jerk with anguish, 'you
might have got away with it. As it is, you've hit the
penalty clause.' He surveyed her cynically and began to
ease off his tie.

Bethany's eyes grew enormous. 'Pen-pen——' She
scrambled up the bed at the look in his eyes. 'No, no,
no!' she choked, finding her voice at last. 'You won't!
You can't! You daren't!' Cavan flicked his top shirt
button undone then eased the links from his cuffs and
threw them carelessly across the room. 'It's not what
you think!' She knelt up to plead with him, but Cavan
continued to undo the buttons of his shirt with slow and
menacingly deliberate movements.

'Isn't it?' he asked harshly. 'You gave a very convincing performance down there.' Her eyes swept downwards in shame, but her chin was clamped between his
bruising finger and thumb and jerked sharply up. 'Now
you're going to give another kind of performance,' he
seethed.

She quailed at the ruthless glitter in his eyes. 'No!
You've no right to be angry! You're the one who's in
the wrong; you and Tania . . .' She swallowed at the look
on his face.

'Tania? You think——' His breath hissed out in exasperation. 'I went out to talk to her——'

'In your car!' she flung.

'Sure. Tan said she was cold.'

'I'm not surprised, if you'd ripped her blouse open.'
Appalled at her words, torn from her by violent jealousy,

Bethany hung her head in shame. Cavan forced her to behave in an uncivilised manner, she thought resentfully.

'That's going to be your story, is it?' he asked grimly. 'You're actually going to implicate one of your oldest friends without caring what the consequences might be for her?'

'I'm telling the truth and you know it——'

'If you haven't been putting on a show and pretending I've outraged your honour, then why are you upset?' he frowned. 'What do you care if I make love to another woman?'

'I—I...' Bethany desperately tried to think of a reason.

'There's no answer to that, is there?' he said, his eyes glittering. 'Because my reading of the situation was correct in the first place. You calculated the best way to humiliate me.'

'No!' she cried, panic making her incapable of thinking straight. 'When I went to your car to answer the phone, I saw I needn't have bothered. The evidence had been there all the time.'

'The phone? Is that what you've just thought of as an excuse to be in my car? Sorry,' he said coldly. 'It won't wash. I know you're lying. And if there's anything I hate more than a cold-hearted, calculating bitch it's one who lies to me and tries to shame me in front of my friends. Tania aside, what do you think you've done to my pride, to my character? I've had a good name in this village.' He clenched his jaw. 'You've tried to ruin that.'

'You can't keep this up,' she breathed. 'You know you're guilty! I know you are! You're trying to keep your so-called "good name" at my expense because I'm the one who has been gossiped about and you think you can make the mud stick again.'

'I've heard enough,' muttered Cavan. 'You have an answer every time. Lies, lies, lies. I can't tell you how angry I am, and how disappointed that you should stoop to such a low trick. I'm going to do what I should have done a long time ago, and in doing so I'll prove to you that I couldn't possibly have made love to a woman half an hour previously.'

Bethany groaned. Her nerves were skittering around chaotically. Cavan's body seemed to fill the whole room, looming menacingly in front of her, his broad shoulders emphasised in silhouette. His face was in shadow and he seemed frighteningly primitive in his rage.

'If you assault me——' she husked. The shirt dropped to the floor. His hand went to his belt, and Bethany drew in a sharp breath which shuddered right through her. '*No!*' she breathed.

He had no mercy, no gentleness now. The man who'd flown the kite and fooled around had vanished. This was the raw, hurting Cavan, who never let anyone get away with a slight, who fought back, measure for measure, blow for blow, whenever he was attacked.

'I'm not going to assault you,' he muttered, his hand on the zip of his trousers.

She averted her head. 'Rape?' she whispered.

Cavan's nostrils had scrolled scornfully, but he said nothing. Yet to Bethany his eyes had been eloquence enough, telling her of his hate and of his determination to see her crushed. 'Crawl, damn you, crawl!' he'd raged at her that time they'd quarrelled so publicly. Her teeth drove into her lower lip. Here in her own bedroom she was defenceless.

Out of the corner of her eye she was aware that he was half naked, the blurred, tanned image ruthlessly impressing itself on her fevered brain.

'Look at me,' ordered Cavan.

She shook her head mutely and tipped her head back in despair. 'Have pity on me!' she whispered.

'You've gone too far,' he rasped. 'Before I leave for my trip I have to seal this intolerable, painful, inescapable bond between us. If I don't, God knows what you'll do, where you'll go.'

Her ankles were grabbed, and with a scream she found herself drawn out full length on to the bed. Cavan lowered his body on to hers, and she shrank into the mattress at the intensity of the heat burning through her, right through her clothes. He lifted her arms over her head and studied her face.

'There is no bond. You'll have to force me,' she grated. 'You won't have the satisfaction of surrender.'

'Oh, yes, I will,' he said arrogantly. He kissed her sullen mouth, and she wrenched her head away, but it didn't matter to him that she was trying to avoid his touch. 'But I don't think I'll get anywhere by forcing you. There are better ways,' he said with a softly sensual threat. 'More enjoyable. Ones which will give me physical and mental satisfaction. To hear you begging, to know you're ready to *crawl* . . .' His mouth searched warmly over her neck.

Bethany kept herself rigid, suffering in silence. When his hands reached up to undo the buttons of her shirt, she struggled to stop him, but he was remorseless, his fingers roughly and skilfully laying her body open to his hungry eyes.

'Please don't shame me,' she whispered.

'You're beautiful,' he breathed, resolutely ignoring her. He kissed the skin below her collarbone with a delicate brushing of his lips that made her quiver through and through. She smelt the warmth of his hair, felt it across her mouth, the glossy strands clean and fresh. Gradually Cavan's barely controlled anger subsided completely and desire took over. His kisses became more seductive and caressing, and she found it harder and harder with every second to stand the touch of his lips and the grazing sensation of his teeth over her shoulders.

He was too practised a lover, too well-versed in women's likes and dislikes for her to loathe what he was doing, and that filled her with despair. He *wouldn't* succeed in making love to her; that would be her ultimate defeat.

'*I hate you*!' she whispered with a sudden ferocity.

'Fine,' he said harshly. 'Any reaction is better than none. So go ahead. Hate me.'

More ruthlessly, his mouth covered hers, surrounding her parted lips, and the warm moistness of his tongue sent a tremor through her receptive body.

'Oh, Cavan, you don't know what you're doing,' she moaned.

'I do,' he growled. 'I'm rolling back the years. I should have done this before you married and changed the course of our lives.' His eyes glowed and his voice dropped to a low, husky growl. 'If I'd made love to you then, my obsession with possessing you would, perhaps, be over. You might not despise me so much as you do now. So let's pretend. You're eighteen and crazy about boys. You're teasing me, flirting, hungry for a man's touch.'

Bethany closed her eyes and felt a light kiss on each lid. Imagining they could turn the clock back was cruel. 'You can't—ohh!' she groaned in sheer carnal pleasure.

He had tantalisingly allowed his fingers to trail down her arms and then had lifted himself slightly so that he could see and touch her breasts. They sprang into life, anticipating his touch with a deep, throbbing need. She made no attempt to stop him. She couldn't. The sensation was too intense and too welcome. So, with triumph on his face, he brought her breasts to such a hard fullness that she could hardly hold down her need to wriggle and

relieve the spasms in her womb created by his hands and
his mouth curving around her swelling, voluptuous flesh.

'Warm. Sweet to taste, to touch, in my mouth, beneath my hands...'

'I'll sue you for all you've got,' she husked in a last
desperate attempt to hold back. 'Assault. Rape——'

'No chance. You'll be willing,' he repeated. He licked
his lips. They parted. They enclosed one throbbing
nipple, and she gasped in sheer delight at the tiny quivers
of heat which coursed into her loins and filled her body
with weak lassitude.

This wasn't rape. It was wonderful seduction, everything she'd dreamed of, and she could no longer resist.
Cavan growled huskily in his throat, nursing at her
breast, his eyes closed in rapture. Barely knowing what
she was doing, she took his head in her hands and gently
moved him to her other starving breast, and she settled
into the mattress with a sigh at the sweet tugging sensation as he obediently suckled there.

'Cavan,' she mumbled, half in despair, half dreamily.
Her hand lightly stroked his dark hair. And then it stilled.
He was caressing her hip, and within her body there was
a feeling like hot red wine, her head as dizzy as if she'd
drunk a whole flagon.

'I didn't make love to Tania. Can't you tell that?' he
murmured. She didn't want to answer—or to tell him
that she was beginning to believe what he was saying.
'You're gorgeous,' he husked. 'Soft, silken, probably
wickedly expensive, but what the hell.'

'No, I——'

She found that her protesting mouth was claimed
again, but this time more fiercely, and he groaned softly
as she clung to him, straining up to feel the strength of
his powerful body. Her skin was humming, tingling, beneath the onslaught of his exploring lips.

'The shadow of your throat,' he murmured, kissing the hollow tenderly. 'The curve beneath your breast...'

Bethany jerked spasmodically as his tongue left a moist path there. She heard a rustling and reached down to clutch frantically at her skirt, her eyes frightened. It had been so long since she'd made love. Too long.

'Oh, no, Cavan,' she pleaded hoarsely.

'But you are beautiful,' he crooned, covering her body with kisses. 'Every inch, every curve and valley.' His voice ended in a croak as he surveyed her lying there beneath him. 'Sweetheart,' he whispered thickly, 'I've waited so long for this. I even left Portallen because of you.'

'What?' She frowned uncomprehendingly. She shuddered. Cavan was stroking her hip lightly, rolling his fingers over her flat stomach, and she gritted her teeth, trying to push his hands away.

'You were driving me crazy even then,' he whispered, kissing her sweetly. 'You matured far too early. It was disturbing, having you around in the same house, wandering about in your underwear with that fabulous body already like a woman's. I had to get out, or find myself in gaol! Oh, Bethany,' he groaned, his weight pressing hard down on her.

Her head spun. He'd wanted her. With a groan, she lifted her arms to his neck and dragged his head down so that she could kiss him hard and rid herself of some of her terrible need.

'Bethany,' he muttered, 'it's ironic it should end like this. I went to London to make a fortune so that I could come back and impress you, perhaps dazzle you into bed.'

Her mouth paused in its demands. He'd wanted her that much? They could have been lovers, perhaps for months, a year... Her fingers found his shoulders and she pushed. Cavan drew back and looked down on her. 'You really wanted me?' she asked shakily.

His blue eyes pierced into her. 'When I came to claim you, I was too late,' he said flatly. 'Dan had you.'

She flinched. Tears filled her eyes. Her head turned helplessly to one side, and then she felt Cavan's weight leave her. Listlessly she heard sounds which told her he was dressing hurriedly.

And then there was a long silence. Miserably she looked around and saw he was sitting on the end of the bed, his back to her. He couldn't leave her now, she thought with an inner moan. How could he? She was unbearably aroused.

'You're cruel,' she whispered wretchedly.

'Because just in time I remember your late husband and find it hard to trespass on his property?' he asked harshly.

'I think I'd better tell you about Dan,' she breathed, fumbling for her shirt and drawing it on.

'Thanks,' he said curtly, 'but I'd rather not know.' His hand banged down on the bed. 'Yes, dammit, I would! It might take away this ache, this violent need I have to make love to you! It might make me sane again and let me get on with my life!' He twisted around, scowling at her flushed, love-softened face. 'God!' he groaned. 'Do you think I could be interested in Tania when my mind is totally taken up with you?'

'Oh, Cavan!' she said brokenly. 'You...' She bit her lip. He'd said nothing about loving her. Only need. Male pride, male desire.

'You made me what I am. Successful. You were scornful of me, and that got me right where my pride lives. I worked night and day to prove to you that I could make it on my own, that a Cockney kid was as good as you proud Celts in Cornwall. I was going to show you the flat I'd bought, take you around the West End. And you robbed me of that pleasure when you calmly announced that you were getting married!'

'I didn't know I'd hurt you so deeply,' she mumbled. 'We all admired you——'

'And no one ever told me, ever showed it,' he said tightly. 'There was a grudging respect from the men here, perhaps, but a reserve, too, and they were so darned sure I was going to take their girls and women that I was never accepted as a friend. I was closer to you than anyone. We touched, even if it was in anger half the time. And then you left.'

'Dan and I——' The words stuck in her throat. Cavan had needed her, and she hadn't seen that. Her eyes filled with tears because she couldn't tell Cavan what she felt about him, and to hell with the anguish it would cause her when he'd had enough of her.

'OK,' he said, his face harrowed. 'It's too painful for you. I get the message.' He stood up, and Bethany saw to her astonishment that he was shaking. Angrily he grabbed the back of a chair and scowled at the ground. 'I'd rather not have anything to do with Portallen any more. I'll leave. Goodbye.'

'Oh, Cavan,' she moaned miserably.

'Do you want to know why I fixed it so we could appear to be engaged?' he asked curtly. 'Because I wanted to create the situation where we became lovers in private as well as public. I apologise that I misjudged your feelings. I honestly didn't think you had been in love with Dan. I didn't know you missed him so desperately.'

Cavan spun on his heel and walked from the room. Her mind seemed to be frozen. She heard him stumble along the corridor, heard the front door bang, heard him walking across the courtyard.

And then she realised she couldn't let him leave forever without telling him the truth about herself and Dan. There had been misunderstandings in the past because people had kept back their true feelings—the villagers who had been in awe of Cavan's physical prowess and grit and had never thought to tell him, her father who had loved Cavan and had desperately tried to keep his youthful exuberance in check, Rosie who had loved everyone and never thought to tell her own son that she loved him specially. Those misunderstandings had made Cavan wary of love, and she didn't want him never to experience its pain and its pleasures.

No more lies. No more pretences. Bethany felt her heart wrench with the poignancy of it all. If she had been given the chance to admire Cavan's flat and his achievements, they might have mellowed towards one another. He might not have become so passionately determined to dominate her sexually.

She gave a long moan and leapt up, dressing hastily and flying out of the house. Still shoeless, she stood on the cold stone step outside and frantically searched the darkness.

'Cavan! Cavan! Where are you?' she yelled.

She listened, but could only hear the roar of the sea on the shore. Heedless of her last pair of stockings, she raced down to the harbour, hoping to stop him before he reached the dinghy and returned to his yacht.

Breathless, hopeful, she flew along the sand. 'Cavan, Cavan, please *be there*, oh, Cavan!'

Something dark by the water stirred, and then she saw the blur of a shirt front. Sobbing, she flung herself at the figure, huddling in the welcoming arms, mumbling her relief in a muffled voice into the soft cloth of his jacket.

He thrust her from him. 'What are you saying? What are you *saying*, Bethany?' he demanded fiercely.

'Oh, Cavan!' she laughed hysterically. 'You have to know about me! I don't want you to go without knowing! I was very fond of Dan and we had some good times together but——'

He froze, but it was the stillness of expectancy. 'But?' he prompted gently when she hesitated.

Her face lifted to his. 'I feel so guilty,' she confessed. 'I wasn't everything I could have been to him. He adored me, but he knew that I had married him as second best. I didn't *know* that then because I was in a muddle about life and I had no idea what love really is—that it's hopeless and wonderful and warm as summer sea, and you don't care what happens to you so long as the person you love is happy.' She smiled dreamily. 'And you need him so much it's terrifying and you can't live without him . . . and life is miserable when you're not around and I can't bear to think of you going——'

A hard, ruthless mouth had possessed hers. She sank contentedly into the kiss, and was disappointed when it ended, knowing it must be their last. Her mouth had reached out to his, demanding more, but he had eased back from her, his eyes amused. She tensed and waited for his parting mockery because she'd wanted him to go on kissing her.

'I think you've given away a piece of unintended information. You said "life is miserable when *you're* not around". You "can't bear to think of *you* going". Does that mean me?' asked Cavan cautiously.

Her eyes widened in dismay. 'I said that? Did I?'

'Freudian slip,' he said huskily. 'Or I hope so.' His hand stroked her hot cheek. 'You were talking about love as if you really knew what it meant. Bethany,' he murmured, 'your heart is thudding so violently it's going to leap from your body. And I'm reading your eyes and discovering your secret. I was right. My instincts told me you cared for me, my brain said you didn't. You do, don't you?'

She avoided his eyes. 'I—I——'

He kissed her tenderly, and she tried not to enjoy it but her lips began to savour his hungrily and their passion deepened. 'You do care for me,' he said. She didn't answer, and he continued with the kiss. 'I'll go on doing this,' he told her huskily, 'till you answer truthfully.'

Her body tingled. Their mouths were welded together and the flames cruelly ate into her, destroying her resistance. His mouth lifted from hers, but his tongue flickered out, lightly running over the high arch of her lips, and she flung her head back in a helpless gesture.

'Tell me,' he insisted. His hands smoothed over her hips. She was finding it hard to breathe and her eyes were too drowsy to keep open.

'Tormenting...' she mumbled.

'Tell me.'

'All right!' she moaned. He immediately stayed his unfair assault. 'What's the use of denying it?' she said hopelessly. 'I fell head over heels for you when you first arrived. It was infatuation then. I fought it like mad. But...' She shrugged.

'Dear God!' he muttered. 'If Dan was second best, why on earth didn't you wait instead of rushing off to marry him?'

Bethany smiled faintly. 'What was the point? Whenever I tried to flirt with you, you scowled and walked off. I knew you would never settle in our little village, or look twice at an ordinary girl like me. You were so thrilled with your smart life in London. The receptionist,' she added ruefully, 'was equally thrilled with *you*.'

'Sweetheart, ever since I started shaving, women have been claiming all kinds of things where I'm concerned,' he said gently. 'I brought her down to Portallen because she said she wanted a job in a small country hotel to get over a boyfriend. It wasn't till we arrived that I realised she'd hoped I'd help physically to wipe away a few memories for her. I didn't make love to her. I was too wrapped up in my passion for you, and resisting it like hell. You were young and too close to home to play around with.'

'You hid your desire well,' she said ruefully.

He smiled. 'I had to. I knew what fire there was in you. I wanted to make my way in the world, and didn't want to get tied up with emotional entanglements before I'd made my fortune. So I convinced myself I was a rover, and fell in love twice a week like clockwork.'

He bent his head and kissed her, and they clung to one another for what seemed like an eternity. 'I think I ought to go home,' she breathed in his ear.

'No,' he growled. A quiver shook his body, and her eyes widened that he should want her so much. He hesitated. 'You must believe me when I tell you that Tania and I aren't lovers,' he said soberly, 'any more than that receptionist was.'

'I believe you,' she told him. 'I trust you.'

Before she knew what was happening, he had drawn her down to the hard, flat sand, kissing her with an urgency that left her breathless. Her body, already pushed to its limits, began to surrender, and her mind was weakened by her confession, which had swept away the barriers she'd built up against Cavan.

There, on the beach, with the sea roaring in her ears a few feet away, Cavan gently removed her clothes and then his, laying them beneath her willing body. The air was cold but she was filled with a madness, a hungry heat in her body that had been burning for so long that it desperately needed the long, slow plunge into the unknown depths with Cavan.

The world swirled around her, his hands and lips like silken water running over her body. They twined together, aching, longing, loving, the darkness of the night and the pounding of the surging tide on the rocks near by serving as a cloak of privacy.

His tenderness was shattering. Gently, persistently, he aroused her till she cried for release, and when it came it was in a long, shuddering sequence of ecstasy that drove her to the limits of pleasure till her ears thundered with it and the whole of her existence seemed to be focused in that one place.

'I love you,' she whispered. 'I love you.'

'Beth.' Cavan's voice came from a long way off, rich and deep and very, very satisfied.

'Mmm.' She couldn't move. Didn't want to. He loved her and she loved him and they'd just sealed that bond.

'I know this isn't romantic, but my feet are getting wet, sweetheart.'

'Mmm.' Then she gasped. A trickle of water had run along her naked thighs. Her eyes opened, and she saw Cavan propping himself up over her, his eyes laughing at her.

'Is this *Jaws II* or *From Here to Eternity*?' he murmured, as the tide lifted her body and gently pushed it up the beach.

She began to scramble up, laughing, her face flushed with shame at her total abandonment. 'I hope it's the latter,' she cried, shivering. 'Oh, my clothes!'

Cavan quickly caught them up, but it was too late. They were soaked. 'My plans didn't get this far,' he said helplessly. Bethany shivered again, and he opened his arms to her and he cuddled her, rubbing her back to keep her warm. 'My darling,' he murmured. 'I'll remember this for the rest of my life.'

She felt a pain in her heart. That sounded as if he was going to take the memory away with him—and not see her again. He'd got what he'd wanted. She tried to be matter-of-fact. 'This is so embarrassing! What are we going to do?' she whispered, peering around. 'Supposing anyone sees us on the way back? I'm freezing,

Cavan, think of something!' She saw the light in his eyes, and slapped his chest reprovingly. 'Greedy,' she reproved.

'Perhaps a little further up the beach?' he suggested huskily.

'Oh, lord,' she mumbled, trying not to enjoy his roaming hands. Her body arched into his. 'We *were* going home,' she reminded him.

'I found it impossible to wait,' he confessed. Water swirled around their ankles. 'We could slip around the beach to the dinghy and sneak out to the yacht,' he suggested. 'Unless Tania's taken the dinghy and is there already, in which case we'd have to borrow another boat to take us out.'

'I don't go in for threesomes,' she said tartly.

'Sweetheart, she's got her own cabin, thank God. We could use the double. Well, come on, Beth, it's all I can think of. Yes or no?'

'I can't...' She bit her lip. It would be wonderful to lie in the same bed as Cavan, but... 'Cavan, I can't... I think I'll put on my wet things and make a dash for it,' she mumbled. 'The idea of being in the same bed as you while Tania sleeps next door is too much.' With great difficulty she shook out her wet things and began to wriggle into them.

'I wasn't expecting to sleep,' admitted Cavan. 'Still, I tend to agree. You respond so very *noisily*.' Laughing at her blushes, he slipped on his jacket and, with a look of distaste on his face, yanked on his trousers, bundling the rest of their clothes into his shirt. 'Come on,' he chuckled. 'This is quite an adventure, sneaking home half naked! I feel like a teenager!'

'I think I'd rather not know what you got up to as a young man,' she said drily.

'I'll show you what I learnt when we get back,' he promised.

'I thought——'

'What did you think?' he asked gently. 'That I'd take you and leave you? That I'd taste paradise and turn my back on it? I'm not that disciplined, Bethany. Come here. I'll show you what I intend to do.'

They spent a blissful night together, making love, loving. Cavan was tender, passionate, fiery, impatient... Bethany could hardly believe that she could have felt so incredibly happy and utterly content, and she began to hope that the relationship would last.

Ignoring her protests in the morning that the workmen were arriving, he coaxed her into the bath, where he gently soaped her body, and then his hands became more urgent, his voice huskier and he had hauled her out on to the carpet, his fierce need for her melting her resistance. After, they lay dazedly in one another's arms till he finally rose and dried her.

'I'm crazy about you, Bethany,' he muttered into her thigh.

'I think I have proof of that,' she smiled contentedly. Her whole body sang and tingled. If this was the extent of Cavan's ability to love a woman, it was more than enough for her. She felt warm and very much adored. Bethany heaved a long sigh. 'I can hear noises in the kitchen. I suppose the workmen are having their tea before they start work.'

'Sweetheart,' laughed Cavan, leaving the bathroom to find his clothes, 'that's coffee they'll be making. It's gone eleven o'clock.'

'Oh!' She sat up quickly and ran in to the bedroom to dress as well. 'What will they think?' she cried, aghast.

'Look 'em in the eye and defy them to snigger,' Cavan advised drily. 'Though they'll have a job, if you go down with your jumper on inside out.'

She blushed at her fumbling, inept attempt at dressing. 'I seem to be all fingers and thumbs.'

He kissed them. 'And I can still feel their pressure all over my body,' he husked.

'Please, Cavan,' she said shyly.

'You are embarrassed, aren't you?' he remarked gently. 'Come on. Hide behind me.'

Bethany felt the eyes of the men must be boring into her when they entered the kitchen. But, before she could lift her head and answer their greetings, Cavan had stiffened in front of her. When he shifted slightly to one side, she saw that Tania was sitting at the kitchen table, a hard expression on her face.

'Well! You two look as if you've kissed and made up,' she said nastily.

'We have. Glad you realise that,' answered Cavan, not in the least put out.

Bethany accepted a mug of coffee from one of the men, her face rosy red. Tania looked sensational in a long white skinny-rib jumper and white wool tights, no skirt, but with high red boots. The workmen were mesmerised by her. Cavan, extraordinarily, didn't seem to notice anything unusual about Tania at all. He was busy raiding the fridge for bacon and eggs.

'You're very tolerant,' Tania said to Bethany. 'I'm damned if I'd forgive him for——'

'This is not the place to discuss what happened,' broke in Cavan. 'Besides, its no one's business but ours, so keep your dainty little nose out, Tania.'

Her dainty little nose wrinkled insolently. 'Darling,' she cooed to Cavan, 'in the excitement of the chase and the thrill of a successful kill, I think you've forgotten something. A teensy little trip you and I are supposed to be making together.'

'Oh, hell,' he frowned. 'The Brittany-Paris trip. You're right. I had.'

Bethany let Tania's implied taunts about Cavan's conquest go over her head. She was too disappointed that he was leaving to worry about Tania's bitchiness. 'I'd forgotten you were going away,' she said in dismay.

He glanced at his watch. 'I'll have to take breakfast on the run. I'd totally forgotten too, sweetheart. I ought to have left a couple of hours ago.'

'Can't Tania go on her own?' suggested Bethany, suddenly possessive. 'We've only just——' She stopped with a flurry of blushes colouring her face, aware that everyone was listening, fascinated.

'I can't get out of it. There has to be two of us,' he said with regret. Cavan took her hand and kissed her fingertips. 'It's too big an operation for me to miss it. I'd ask you to come, but I'm afraid——'

'Three's a crowd,' husked Tania, giggling.

'Don't be stupid,' scathed Cavan, kissing Bethany's cold lips. 'Darling, she's joking. This is business. Trust me. You have to, I'm afraid. Get used to this because I'll often go on these ticket "do"s. Our reunion alone with be worth it. Smile.'

She smiled. Falteringly. He was coming back to her, then. 'When will I see you again?' she asked, her face very wistful.

'Before you can get those curtains up in the drawing-room,' he assured her. 'In four days, five at the most.'

'There's Hawaii next,' drawled Tania. 'A week in the tropical paradise——'

'You can do that,' frowned Cavan.

'No, I can't, darling,' she said smugly. 'I'm on holiday. Remember?'

'Damn!'

'Could I go with you?' asked Bethany hesitantly.

Cavan took her in his arms. 'Time your coffee-break was over?' he suggested to the workmen. They took the hint. Cavan tenderly kissed Bethany. 'I can't let you come. Every second of every day is mapped out. It'll be awful. Totally exhausting. I'll be back in twelve days'

time, then,' he said regretfully. 'I might not be very good
company to begin with. I won't have had any sleep for
two or three days.'

'*Naughty*,' murmured Tania.

'Find something to do in the coal cellar, will you?'
suggested Cavan irritably. 'I want to say goodbye to
Bethany, and the way I'm going to say it is not for your
eyes or ears.'

'Don't be long,' said Tania, sounding spiteful. 'You'll
need all your strength for this trip with me.'

She flung out of the room before Cavan could catch
her with his outstretched arm. Heaving a sigh, he kissed
Bethany again. 'I think that woman's got to go,' he muttered. 'She's too jealous of you.'

'Is she a good secretary, really?' asked Bethany
unhappily.

'Terrific. I could shift her job sideways,' he mused.
'Give her responsibility, say... in Toronto. Hey! I'm
wasting kissing time!'

Bethany surrendered to his passionate embrace. But
in the back of her mind was a small, nagging doubt.
When she waved him goodbye and watched him leave
in the dinghy, she saw how close Tania stood by him,
and that small, nagging doubt niggled in her mind, telling
her that Cavan was highly sexed and Tania wanted him,
and that anything could happen between a man and a
woman at night on a boat.

CHAPTER EIGHT

HOWEVER, despite Bethany's worries, Cavan rang her every night, sounding adoring and loving. Hearing his voice was wonderful, and left her in a state of blissful happiness afterwards. Mawgan was delighted with her news, and teased her relentlessly. Cavan began to ring her during the day, too, and she gently rebuked him for wasting his money, but he only laughed and teased her, saying he was checking up on her in case she had slipped off with the electrician somewhere.

Then the calls stopped. She tried not to mind, to remember that he didn't belong to her in any way and was a free agent. It was hard, and for three days she worried—partly for Cavan, partly for herself. After all, he'd said that he had wanted to make love to her because it would relieve his obsession. Perhaps he'd got over her now, and he and Tania were laughing at her willingness to surrender herself to his demands.

Sitting in the kitchen, half-heartedly listening to the radio with its warnings of southerly gales one morning, she thought that it was sad that the house was becoming more beautiful every day as she was growing unhappier. Bethany glared at the postcard on the dresser which had been sent by Tania. From Hawaii.

'See your planning application's in,' commented the tiler, working around the sink unit.

She reached for the local paper he'd indicated eagerly. 'Did you say planning application? At last,' she said, turning to the page. 'Oh, yes. Here it is.' Her eyes widened as she read it. 'What? Application to convert

173

hotel at Portallen Bay to a private residence? Private?'
Bethany sat back in the chair in astonishment. *Private*?

Grimly she reached for the phone and dialled
Mawgan's number, grateful that the tiler had politely
left the room. Mawgan was amazed at her news.

'God, Beth, he's not trying to sell Portallen after all
the work you've done, is he?' Mawgan exclaimed.

'I don't understand,' she said dully, a terrible fear
shaping in her mind. 'Mawgan, you don't think he deliberately...that he... Oh, God!' she wailed.

'What is it?' cried her brother urgently.

'It's occurred to me that he only m-made love to me
to keep me quiet, so that I'd go on renovating this place
without charging him a penny.'

'I don't see why he should be so foul.'

'He said once I'd ruined his life,' she said in a flat
tone. 'I did think at one time he'd written those poison-
pen letters, remember. I could have been right. If so, he
must hate me. This would be an amusing revenge,
wouldn't it? I put my heart and soul into the Portallen
Inn and he sells it at top-of-the-market rates. It would
be a very neat kick in the teeth. He knows how much I
love it.'

'But you said he'd rung you daily,' objected Mawgan,
'and been very affectionate.'

Her eyes closed in misery. 'How can I believe anything he says now? He deceived me about the Inn for
ages. No wonder he wouldn't let me see the plans, or
the proposed application,' she rasped. 'He'd decided on
this from the start, I'm sure. There's something else,
Mawgan. I didn't tell you, but Tania's sent me a postcard
from Hawaii, and they both pretended she wasn't going
to be with him.'

'Is that the problem? Don't worry,' he said comfortingly. 'I expect he needed her to do some work for him.'

'I do worry!' cried Bethany. 'She says they're having parties all night and that she's exhausting poor darling Cavan. She says he has a gorgeous tan and——' her voice shook slightly '—and that his white bit is startling,' she finished in a harsh voice.

'She's only trying her damnedest to make you jealous——'

'And succeeding,' muttered Bethany. 'That kind of information would shake any girl's confidence. I don't trust Tania. She'd do anything, say anything, I'm afraid, to get him. She said as much to me. Oh, Mawgan, she could have run to him with some story about me——'

'Boss is back.' The tiler's grinning face appeared in the doorway.

'I must ring off,' cried Bethany, her heart pounding. 'Cavan's here.'

'See, I told you,' laughed Mawgan. 'Brace yourself for a reconciliation scene.'

'Silly,' she smiled, her lips still trembling.

But she was nervous. When she reached the front door, there was no car to be seen, and she was about to go back and ask the tiler what he'd meant when she saw the yacht, bobbing in the choppy bay. Her heart stilled and became peaceful. She'd been wrong to suspect him. He'd come back to her. She leaned against the stone wall, waiting for the dinghy to come ashore, the strong wind whipping her hair into tangles.

After five minutes had passed, she felt cold so she slipped inside to put on a warm jacket, and then, on an impulse, she ran down to the quay.

'Jory, take me to Cavan's yacht, would you?' she cried urgently.

'OK. Don't be long out there,' he said, watching the scudding clouds. 'He'll need to run for shelter soon. We're too exposed here for him to stay anchored in the bay.'

Bethany nodded. A strange feeling welled up inside her and she pushed it aside. He'd be battening down hatches and preparing to leave, she told herself. That's why he didn't leap into the dinghy and make for shore. He was intending to shelter in the safety of Plymouth harbour and ring her from the yacht or take a taxi to Portallen for their reunion.

Her sense of foreboding increased as she approached the yacht. No one was on deck and there were no signs of life. She called but there was no reply. With difficulty, because of the windy conditions and the rising swell, Jory helped her on to the ladder and she clambered on board.

'Go back,' she called to him, shouting above the wind. 'I'll go out to sea with Cavan when he leaves the bay. It'll save time.' The boat lurched, and she grabbed the rail then scrambled over to the hatch. When she climbed down the steps into the big cabin she saw the remains of a meal, an empty bottle of wine on a cushion, two glasses in the sink, two plates, two...

'Cavan?' she called nervously. To her horror, Bethany heard a sound, a woman's voice. Her body became motionless while she listened, wondering what to do. If she didn't face up to this, she thought, she'd never know the truth.

The polished mahogany door opened to reveal Tania, in a flimsy baby-doll nightie. 'Beth!' cried Tania in genuine surprise. Mockingly she leaned against the bulkhead, a sultry expression on her face. 'I don't think you ought to go in there,' she said, indicating the cabin behind her. She smoothed her hands down her curvaceous body. 'Better be ignorant of what's been going on.'

'Cavan's in there?' whispered Bethany. 'Is that his cabin?'

Tania shrugged. 'His, ours, it's all the same.'

Bethany couldn't bring herself to go in. 'Where's the single cabin, then?' she asked tightly.

'Behind you.'

Spinning on her heel, Bethany pushed open the smaller door. The cabin contained a single bunk which was made up neatly. No one had slept in it that night. That was evidence enough for her. 'How long has this been going on?' she asked in a hard tone, stemming her longing to cry. 'You and him?'

'Since I started working for him and he took me on his knee in his office,' said Tania jauntily.

Bethany dropped her eyes, feeling sick. 'The classic boss and secretary situation! He won't get away with this,' she grated.

Suddenly she pushed past Tania into the room. Cavan lay on his stomach, his face to one side, cradled against the satin pillow. He was fast asleep—as heavily asleep as the day he'd crashed out in her bedroom. The upper part of his body was glistening with sweat as if he and Tania had been making passionate love. Tania came in behind Bethany, chuckling.

'Seen enough? He's quite dead to the world, poor darling. Handsome devil, isn't he? Sexy and rich as well. What more could a girl want?'

Bethany's contemptuous eyes blazed down on Cavan, the infamous oyster-coloured sheets rumpled in shimmering folds over his obviously naked hips. 'Cavan!' she said sharply.

'Don't wake him!' Tania's hand curled around Bethany's arm, but Bethany shook the red talons off with a violent gesture.

Cavan stirred and opened bleary eyes. 'My head!' he groaned, closing his eyes again. Tania ran over to sit on the bed and stroked his brow with a wet towel which was on a small table. A stab of anguish scorched through

Bethany's body. 'Mmm. More of that,' muttered Cavan in appreciation. 'What a night.'

'You miserable two-timing, conceited, badly bred gutter-snipe!' seethed Bethany.

'Whaat?' Cavan rolled over, and pushed himself up on his elbows. 'Beth...Bethany?' His eyes looked glazed as if he could hardly see her. He passed a shaking hand through his tousled hair, and she noticed that his voice was slurred.

'Drink is no excuse for what you've done,' she said sharply. 'Thanks, Tania. I'm grateful. I suppose if it hadn't been you, it would have been some other woman.'

'What—what's she saying?' frowned Cavan.

Tania smiled and dabbed at his forehead with the towel. 'Never mind, darling,' she crooned, stroking his back with her other hand. 'She's found out about us so we might as well own up.'

'I don't know how I could have been so blind,' said Bethany with quiet rage. 'You tricked me, I know. Lied like a trooper to get what you wanted. Well, you're welcome to each other. One of you is a man-eater, the other a common shark. And like all sharks you have to keep swimming in all the seas of the world to stay afloat, taking what you can, where you can with total disregard for the destruction that's left behind.' She tossed her dark head. 'Take Portallen,' she cried. 'Do whatever you want with it. I wash my hands of the place!'

He seemed stunned. 'Darling, give me a moment...I can't—you——'

'Don't you "darling" me! I'm walking out of Portallen, never to return. I leave you to pick up the pieces. Find yourself another fool to do all the hard work on that hotel free of charge.'

Cavan struggled to sit up, and every fumbling movement he made sliced into her with an agonising pain. He'd made love to Tania in the car and made love

to *her* on the beach. He certainly had stamina. He'd lived
it up in Hawaii, made passionate love to Tania after an
alcoholic evening, and now he was suffering the consequences. She despised him, and was disgusted by the
way he'd sated his lust with such crude thoroughness.

'You can't leave Portallen. You love it!' husked Cavan.

'I do!' she said angrily. 'That's the pity of it! But I'd
rather go than finish the work and see it looking as I've
always dreamed it would——'

'No, Beth, you mustn't go, you mustn't leave the job
half done,' mumbled Cavan almost incoherently.

'You drunken swine! I can't live on thin air,' she
snapped.

'You've got money,' said Tania sourly. 'You've got
enough to buy yourself any man you want.'

'Me? That's a laugh! I haven't got a penny,' retorted
Bethany recklessly. Her eyes glittered like striking flints.
'Who do you think bought the lifeboat?'

Tania flinched, her fingers lifting from where she'd
been stroking Cavan's broad, naked shoulders. 'You?'

'Yes,' said Bethany, grim-faced. 'Every penny I had
went into it.'

'Oh, no! You gave all your...' Tania gave a mirthless
laugh. 'I don't believe you.'

'I can produce the receipt,' said Bethany coldly.

'You have no money?' frowned Cavan, holding his
head as if it ached.

'None. I'm broke.'

Tania gave a low moan. 'Bethany! You—oh, my God!
All this time I've been——' She bit her lip hard, her eyes
troubled. 'You spent every penny of your compensation?' she asked.

'For the lifeboat,' said Bethany quietly.

'No, no! It saved my father,' cried Tania. 'Without
it, he'd be dead.' Her mouth quivered and then she let
out a wail. 'Oh, Beth!' To Bethany's astonishment, Tania

ran to her and flung her arms around her, sobbing hysterically. 'I'm sorry, I'm so very sorry,' she cried. 'I didn't know you'd done that. I wouldn't have hurt you if I'd known. But you had everything: money, boys, looks, and Cavan.' Tania dropped her arms from around Bethany's waist and pulled away. 'I have something to tell you. Something awful and it's tearing my insides out. I wrote those poison-pen letters. I'm sorry. I know you'll never forgive me, but I was so desperately unhappy when you came back to Portallen looking so beautiful and——'

'You bitch, Tania! Get off this boat,' hissed Cavan, shakily wrapping a sheet around his waist, 'before I tear you limb from limb.'

Tania took one look at the malevolent glare on Cavan's face, the broad, powerful shoulders, the menacing way he was forcing his exhausted body from the bed, and scrambled back into the living quarters. 'I'm going, I'm going,' she moaned, climbing into a set of oilskins. She ran up the steps on to the deck, crying all the time.

Bethany couldn't move at all. Her mind whirled. It had been Tania, her old friend and confidante. Now everything fitted into place. She heard the outboard engine start up, and glanced at Cavan sympathetically. He'd made love to a spiteful, vicious and yet unhappy and unfulfilled woman who'd stopped at nothing to get him in her clutches.

Cavan had fallen back to the bed, breathing heavily, apparently still too dazed and drunk to stay upright for long. 'I feel terrible,' he muttered. 'Please find some ice.'

'I'll make some black coffee,' she said coldly. If he was to get his boat away before the gale struck with full force, he needed to be sober first. Her heart sank. Tania had taken the dinghy. She was stuck with Cavan.

She managed to brew the coffee with some difficulty. By the way the boat lurched and wallowed, it seemed the wind had increased in strength. When she got back to the cabin with a pot of coffee, she found that Cavan had dressed and was hanging on to the bulkhead, looking rather pale. The sweat still shone on his skin.

'Check on the weather,' he rasped through cracked lips.

Giving him a puzzled look, she slid the coffee-jug and his mug into the stabilising stand. He was terribly ill-looking. 'Drink all that,' she said sternly.

She heard rain begin to beat down on deck, and grabbed some oilskins. On deck, she could see the swell had increased—a sure sign of bad weather out to sea. The gale warning on the radio earlier had mentioned force eight to nine. Jory had been right; they couldn't stay in the harbour. No one wanted to be on a lee shore with weather like that approaching. They'd be safer if they stood off, or beat it to Plymouth.

Hastily she tumbled down the steps into the cabin. 'Hang on,' she told Cavan. 'It's going to be a bumpy ride. We're motoring out to sea.'

'Right,' he said hoarsely. 'I'll come up.'

'I have painful proof of your legendary stamina,' she snapped sarcastically, 'but you don't look as if you could handle a cuddly kitten let alone a yacht in a strong wind.'

But he joined her nevertheless, as she turned the nose of the boat into the wind and forged out to sea. Glancing quickly over her shoulder, she searched the bay to see if Tania was safe, and saw to her relief that the orange oilskinned figure was being helped ashore by Jory.

'Is Tania all right?' asked Cavan, concentrating on keeping his balance.

Bethany's mouth compressed into a hard line. 'She's a survivor,' she said crossly.

A sheet of rain, as fierce as hail, tipped from the leaden sky. Bethany could hardly see anything. Cavan switched on the radar and came up behind her, holding the bucking wheel with her. It was a nightmare journey. She forgot everything but the need to get through the gale and into Plymouth Sound. At last the bulk of the breakwater came into sight and then Drake's Island. They hove to, and stood shaking for a while, cold, wet, exhausted.

Without speaking, they went below, shed their oilskins and drank mugs of hot soup, then Bethany went to the single cabin and shut the door, flinging herself on the bed and sleeping fitfully.

The rocking of the boat grew less violent, and she eventually rose and went into the living quarters. To her alarm, Cavan was sprawled on the floor as if he'd been there all the time, his body saturated in sweat.

'What's the matter?' she asked anxiously when his eyes opened blearily.

'I'm sick. Food poisoning. Was getting over it,' he whispered, leaning his head back weakly. 'Pills.'

She ran into the cabin and found them, watching him while he swallowed one. His eyes closed. He fell asleep.

Bethany dragged him into the bedroom, inch by heavy inch. Unable to lift him on to the bed, she hauled all the blankets out of the locker and covered him up, then wet the towel to mop his brow. She paused. Tania had been doing that. Cavan had been ill even then.

Dismissing pity, she cooled his head and chest down and then tucked him up. And left him. He'd been Tania's lover. He should have stuck to one woman, not shared himself out. What had he said? Something about the need to master her because he'd never be satisfied if he didn't, like never managing to master backhand in tennis. Angrily she dumped the wine in the bin and began to clear up. It took a long time. Tania hadn't touched anything, and there were the remains of several meals lying around.

'Beth?'

It was a couple of hours later. Cavan had slept like a log, his heavy breathing vibrating through the boat. She'd been deliberately re-living his seduction so that she didn't weaken when he woke and tried to coax her to forgive him.

She turned. 'You look better,' she said evenly.

'I needed that sleep. The pill helped. I was taken ill in Hawaii,' he explained.

'I'm sure Tania was able to look after you. Was that why she abandoned her holiday, to look after you?' she asked with feigned interest.

Cavan gave her an odd look and began to pace up and down. 'It's like trying to dam the sea,' he muttered to himself. 'You build what you imagine to be something impregnable, and then all your efforts are wasted when a tiny little wave seeps in and undermines the foundations.'

'I don't see Tania Blake as a tiny little wave,' she said tartly.

'No,' he agreed morosely. 'She's as destructive as a tidal wave. Beth, I swear that we didn't make love——'

'Sorry, Cavan,' she said coolly. 'I'm past that kind of stupidity. I found her button in the car with a piece of material attached to it——'

'Then she tore it off herself,' he growled. 'Because I certainly didn't.'

'You were gone long enough,' Bethany said without emotion.

'I was trying to persuade her to lay off. I told her I wasn't interested——'

'I'm not stupid, Cavan! You lied when you said she wasn't going to Hawaii with you——'

'She turned up,' he protested irritably.

'Don't bother to make excuses. It's not worth the effort. I caught you both in bed together. It would take a woman of incredible denseness not to cotton on to the fact that you and she have been having an affair. Now I know for how long. Since she perched on your knee while you dictated to her,' she said bitterly, her calm manner vanishing.

'Don't be ridiculous. The only time she sat on my knee I pushed her off and she crashed to the floor,' he said grimly. 'How do you know she was in Hawaii?' he frowned.

'Postcard,' Bethany said succinctly, trying to control her anger. 'So don't flannel. She gave almost a detailed diary of your activities together.'

He groaned. 'I'll throttle the life out of her!' he muttered.

Bethany's eyes were the colour of the storm clouds outside. 'I don't take kindly to being two-timed. I despise you,' she scorned. 'All the time you were chatting to me on the phone and telling me you loved me, you were hot from Tania's arms, weren't you? My God! I'm going to make sure that you never set foot in Portallen again. I'll ruin your reputation——'

'Do that and I'll sue you for slander,' he frowned. 'I can prove I didn't have time to make love to her in Hawaii. Either my business partners or my clients were with me all the time. And they all know that I fell ill with severe food poisoning. I spent two days in the local hospital and then was invalided out on a stretcher. I have witnesses.'

'But you managed to have a romantic dinner for two on the yacht and then crawl into bed together after arriving in Portallen Bay,' she cried, unable to prevent herself from accusing him. 'I saw the wine, the plates— and I saw you both virtually naked in bed.'

'I remember nothing of a meal,' he said quietly. 'Tania must have eaten, I suppose. She never clears up after herself—it's usually me, but this time I was too ill and heavily sedated. Look, I don't even know how I got on to the boat. Tania must have organised everything for her own ends—my transfer to Plymouth airport, and I suppose on to the boat, though I didn't know where I was when you walked in on us. I was *ill*, Bethany!' he cried in exasperation. 'You must have seen.'

'I—I don't know...' She remembered the sweat on his body, his dazed look, and felt a little uncertain. 'I thought you were hung over.'

'You won't believe me, will you?' he asked in despair.

'You never tell me the truth,' she said unhappily. Her head lifted in defiance. 'Now wriggle out of the fact that you've changed your mind about Portallen! You intend it to be a house, don't you? A private house. That explains the design you approved, the alterations you insisted on. The single table. The——' she drew in her breath sharply '—the children's rooms on the top floor,' she grated. 'You bastard. You're going to sell it to some wealthy family. You never, ever intended it to be a hotel, did you?'

'No. Never,' he said bitterly. His eyes met hers and they were so full of pain that she felt an arrow shaft through her. 'Hadn't you realised?' he said wearily, seeing she didn't understand, and slumping to sit on the bed. 'It was to be your house.'

'Mine?' she scorned. 'Oh, that's clever——'

'Yes, I thought so,' he admitted. 'It was all done for you. I carefully found out your opinion on furniture, fittings, your likes, your dislikes, so that I could prepare it and make it absolutely what you wanted. It was for us,' he said moodily. 'What an arrogant, optimistic bastard I was! It was meant to be our future home. For you and me.'

Stunned, Bethany could only watch as he downed the rest of his tea. 'You and me? *Our* home?' she repeated stupidly.

'I have deceived you,' he conceded. 'But only for that end. I confess that I manipulated every situation. I made sure we got "engaged" so that we'd be thrown together. I wanted you to fall in love with me, and then I was going to present you with the house. Hoping, of course, that we'd marry and live in it together. But you won't believe me, you won't trust me and there's nothing I can do about that.'

'The nursery suite,' she repeated dully. 'That sweet little chair, the rocking horse——'

'God, Beth!' he groaned. 'Don't torture me! Isn't it enough that none of my dreams will come true? That I'll have to leave everything I've lovingly prepared for us and never see Portallen again, that I will never be able to touch, to see, to hold the woman I've wanted all my life? To see our children playing upstairs, learning to sail . . . ? You've defeated me, Beth. I thought I could dominate you, override your objections to me, make you love me. It seems I can't.'

Bethany was still confused. What he was saying didn't tie up with his behaviour. 'I can't quite grasp what you're saying. Tania——'

'If she's got any sense, she'll be on her way to the airport. I told her she'd have to go to Toronto when she turned up in Hawaii and began to bat her eyelashes at me. I said I couldn't have a secretary who didn't give one hundred per cent of her working time to work. I've arranged it so that she's dumped on a friend of mine who's sixty-eight and happily married. She's lethal, Bethany. I'm beginning to realise how lethal.'

Suddenly, something occurred to Bethany. 'Cavan,' she said urgently, 'it was Tania who told me there was a call on your car-phone, the night of the harvest festival. That's when I found the button on the driver's seat.'

'Tania,' he breathed harshly. His eyes kindled. 'I won't throttle her. I'll bury her alive!' he said savagely.

Bethany's fingers touched his chest to stay his temper. 'No,' she said quietly. 'I know what it's like to be denied the man you're deeply in love with. She will be very unhappy. She deserves nothing else.'

'Oh, she'll soon be happy when she finds a Canadian millionaire,' Cavan said grimly. 'Any rich man between puberty and death will suit her. She's very shallow.' He inhaled harshly. 'Do you want me to get you ashore?' he asked with simulated indifference.

A slow beautiful smile broke over Bethany's face. She was beginning to register what Cavan had said, turning it over in her mind. He'd gone to an incredible amount of effort to create the home she desired. She looked at him with tenderness. 'You bought that expensive fireplace for us?' she asked in awe.

He scowled. 'Stupid, wasn't it?' he said with a self-mocking laugh. 'I was thrilled when you said you liked it.'

'The top floor. That was going to be for our children's bedrooms, a playroom and a nursery suite?' she asked breathlessly.

'Someone will buy it,' he said gruffly, turning his back on her.

She sat on the bed beside him and put her hand on his arm. 'Cavan,' she said gently. 'You say you've wanted me all your life and that you've wanted me to love you. But there's something you haven't told me yet. Something important.'

He kept his head low and averted, and she could only see his clenched jaw and the slight sheen on his face where the fever still lay within him. 'That I love you?' he asked hoarsely. 'That you are everything in life to me and without you I have no meaning and no purpose? Is that what you want to hear? Do you want to exact all your revenge on me, Bethany, because I fixed my love on you years ago and never wavered? All right,' he cried, facing her belligerently, 'so I love you! But how can you ever trust me?'

She smiled gently at him, and his hot despair melted away to be replaced by a growing realisation that she was looking at him with loving eyes. He'd gone to an enormous amount of trouble to please her. 'Cavan Trevelyan,' she murmured, reaching up to touch his chiselled mouth, 'for a street-wise ticket-tout, you're amazingly stupid.'

'I—I can hardly believe… You mean you're not angry? Oh, Beth, I do love you, passionately, so much that I'm afraid of hurting you,' he said fervently.

'I love you, Cavan,' she said softly.

He grinned in sudden, blinding delight, his eyes searching hers in amazement. 'You love me. You love me! We can live in Portallen? Fill the nursery with our children——?'

'Steady. I'm having a career first,' she said firmly. 'We have to use those twin-facing desks for a while, don't we?'

'You'll marry me?' he asked, still bemused. 'A jumped-up ticket-tout?'

'How else can I get tickets for the centre court at Wimbledon every year?' she laughed. Life was suddenly wonderful. Maybe she had a little way to go before she won over the villagers, but, with Cavan's help, she'd make it.

He growled sexily in his throat. 'I think,' murmured Cavan, drawing her down to the bed, his eyes adoring her, 'that I'm at last going to be able to perfect my backhand.' He kissed her and stroked her face. 'And my forehand.' He touched her parted lips and kissed her neck. His hand slid down to her thigh. 'And my serve,' he whispered.

Bethany's eyes began to close with desire. 'I have the feeling that this is going to be a very long match,' she husked as her body arched into his.

Cavan shuddered, his mouth devouring hers passionately while the boat rocked gently in the sheltering harbour, the gale blowing itself out down the coast. 'With only one score. Love all,' he breathed.

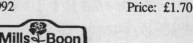

CELEBRATING THE BRITISH COUNTRYSIDE SURVEY 1992

Packaging 4 full length Romances together in one volume, with a special theme is a new idea for us, and we would be very interested to hear what you think about it.

Please spare a few minutes to tell us your views about the 4 Romances all featuring the British Countryside and WE WILL SEND YOU A FREE BOOK AS OUR THANK YOU.

Don't forget to fill in your name and address, so that we know where to send your FREE book!

Please tick the appropriate box to indicate your answer ☑

1 From where did you obtain your Countryside book?

Mills & Boon Reader Service	☐	W.H. Smith, John Menzies, Other Newsagents	☐
Boots, Woolworth, Departmental Stores	☐	Supermarket	☐
Received as a Gift	☐	Other: _____	

2 If you bought the book for yourself, why did you decide to buy it?

Attractive cover design	☐	The 'Countryside' theme	☐
Good value for money	☐	Like the authors included	☐

Liked the back cover descriptions of featured Romances ☐

Other: _____

3 Did you enjoy reading this collection of stories which featured the British Countryside as a setting?

Very Much	☐	Quite a lot	☐
Not very Much	☐	Not at all	☐

4 How do you feel about 4 full length stories in a single volume, compared to our usual gift packs of 4 books?

_____

_____

5 Are there any other settings or themes you think would work well in a collection of stories like this?

_____

6 Do you have any other comments to make about the Countryside book?

_____

7 How many Mills & Boon Romances do you usually read in a month?

One or less a month	☐	Five to Ten a month	☐
Two to Four a month	☐	More than Ten a month	☐

8 Which of the following do you usually read?

		Duet	☐
Mills & Boon: Romances	☐	Masquerade	☐
Best Seller	☐	**Silhouette**: Sensation	☐
Medical Romance	☐	Special Edition	☐
Temptation	☐	Desire	☐

9 What age group are you?

16-24	☐	35-44	☐	55-64	☐
25-34	☐	45-54	☐	65+	☐

10 Are you a Reader Service subscriber?   Yes ☐   No ☐

If yes, your subscription number is _____

THANK YOU FOR YOUR HELP | NO STAMP NEEDED |

For your FREE book please send your completed forms to:
Mills & Boon Reader Service, FREEPOST, P.O. Box 236, Croydon, CR9 9EL

Ms/Mrs/ Miss/Mr: _____ CB

Address: _____

_____

_____ Postcode _____

You may be mailed with offers from other
reputable companies as a result of this
application. Please tick box if you would
prefer not to receive such offers ☐

ASSOCIATION OF MAIL ORDER PUBLISHERS

mps
MAILING
PREFERENCE
SERVICE